The Man from the Welfare

First published 2025

Published under licence by Brown Dog Books and
The Self-Publishing Partnership Ltd, 10b Greenway Farm,
Bath Rd, Wick, nr. Bath BS30 5RL, UK

www.selfpublishingpartnership.co.uk

ISBN printed book: 978-1-83952-885-9

Cover design by Andrew Prescott based on an original illustration by Jack Norris
Internal design by Richard Powell

Printed and bound in the UK

This book is printed on FSC® certified paper

MIX
Paper | Supporting responsible forestry
FSC® C013604

The Man from the Welfare

Bob Quant

BROWN DOG BOOKS

Contents

Acknowledgments

I was offered interest, help and advice from all sorts of friends and acquaintances for which I was generally grateful. However, the help I received from 'the Quant Clan' was a major factor in my completing the book.

My grandson Jack, a designer, designed the book cover illustration.

My granddaughter Katie, at university, selected the photos for the back cover.

My eldest daughter Sarah, a company director, kept my use of the laptop up to scratch and arranged the publishing.

My middle daughter Becky, a teacher, spent many hours editing the text.

My youngest daughter Louise, a nurse, checked my medical information.

And of course, my wife of 58 years, Tricia, gave me constant support and understanding and an endless supply of black Americanos.

Preface

I left school a couple of months before my seventeenth birthday (1960) with a handful of GCEs and no idea what I wanted to do for work. University was never an option, I wanted to earn money and quickly.

It was a time of full employment and several of my school friends decided they wanted a white-collar job and the local council was seen as an easy choice. I went along for the ride, passed the very simple interview and was allocated a post as a clerk with Bristol Mental Health Department. My friends thought it was an appropriate choice and fell about laughing at my expense.

In fact, it turned out to be the first small step towards my lifetime career in social work, which has suited me just fine.

The mental health headquarters was based in a rambling old Victorian building, Marlborough House, on the same site as both a junior and an adult training centre for the mentally handicapped. I was in regular contact with a whole host of clients who attended the training centres. Whilst at Marlborough House I was also in daily contact with a bizarre mixture of people called mental welfare officers. I took every opportunity to learn about their role and read virtually every client file over the lunch hours spent eating my sandwiches with my feet up on my desk.

There was an awful lot of dross and repetition to be waded through, but the reports of one particular social worker, Mary McNaught, always held my attention.

Her ability to describe individuals in a sensitive, intuitive and often amusing way really made me feel that I knew them. At the time I can remember thinking that such prose was wasted in some dusty old files and should be presented in the form of a book.

That was the germ of idea, was to remain with me but dormant for many years as I got on with my life.

Within six months of starting work I was promoted to the post of trainee social worker and in fact it was not until I finally gave up paid employment at the age of seventy-five that I decided to give the idea sometime of its own. This story is the result, I hope you like it.

Chapter 1

(Autumn 1964). The Pioneers.

The tops of the high rise flats appeared through the drizzle as he approached the brow of the hill. Scruffy little fields divided by a mixture of materials including old tyres and ancient bed parts were to the left and right, empty of animals except for a sad looking horse head down trying to get food from the mud bath he lived in. The battered old Cortina always started to struggle at this point as if it could sense Ben Newman's reluctance to enter the Highfield estate. He was only 25 years old but it felt as though his future was destined to be more of the same, not altogether a happy thought. He had enough insight to know his mood was always affected by the need to get to work on time, as team leader of his small social work outpost he had to try and set an example. But in the early morning before 10 am he always felt sluggish and low spirited. He was not a morning person and never had been. He waited for and got the usual reaction to this stage of the journey to work, a sharp pain in the guts rising to nausea in his throat. A prolonged belch eased the pressure and raised a smirk of self-satisfaction, 'well up to standards' he thought to himself.

The engine picked up as the car topped the hill and life on the Highfield estate spread out before him. Several blocks of high rise flats, all named after local 'big wigs' grouped each side of the road forming a sort of gateway to the estate to be followed by row upon row of almost identical red boxes extending as far as the eye could see. The Highfield estate in all its glory! Much of Ben's job as a social worker on the estate was to do with 'new town neurosis' which was a posh name for his bread and butter. The year was 1964 and the estate was the councils answer to the severe housing shortage of the 1950s. Life on the estate inflicted a fair amount of pain on its residents and on the imported support workers alike.

None of the professional workers, the doctors, health visitors, teachers or social workers who worked on the estate would have given a second thought to living there. At the end of the day they were all only too pleased to get in their cars and head off; it was hell enough to have to work there. Admittedly there were a couple of vicars, one Catholic and one C of E, who had their vicarages attached to the only two churches on the estate, but they rarely lasted longer than a year or two before heading off for pastures new or a nervous breakdown. Finally, there was the calming presence of Police Constable Roger Richards, who lived with his family on the estate occupying one half of a pair of semidetached houses with his neighbouring property being built as a police station complete with detention rooms. It was now the tail end of 1964 and Ben by some miracle had lasted almost four years, but he knew this was a direct result of his innate lethargy rather than any affection for the place. *God I really hate this estate*, he thought as he pulled into the car park next to his single-storey, L-shaped prefabricated office. He automatically scanned the premises for any fresh sign of damage and for once the site appeared to have passed a night without suffering some new act of vandalism. Perhaps 'they' had run out of fresh ideas for destruction, but the pools of water all over the car park reminded him that it had poured down in the night and any ideas of attack would have been put off for another day. He fitted the crook lock and double-checked that all the car doors were locked. It was only two years old and it really was a heap, but it was his heap and he intended to hang on to it despite the odds. The old Cortina, bought very cheaply at the local car auction, had over 100,000 miles on the clock and bore all the dents and dings of a hard life. Most of his colleagues took out a car loan from the council to buy much more salubrious vehicles but car loans had to be repaid and with his wife Sandy, his two sons Jack and Nick and a mortgage to support it remained no more than a pipe dream. He hurried across to the front door, collar up against the wind and the rain that was now lashing down; another day on the Highfield Estate with all the potential to give him another day of misery.

As always Alice had beaten him to it and he could hear her shrill singing coming from the small kitchen at the far end of the corridor.

'Morning,' he shouted, and quickly ducked into his office in an attempt to avoid any chance of a prolonged discussion. For the hundredth time he told himself that he really should get the office key back from Alice. She was, after all, a client and should have no right to free access to the office as there was loads of confidential client information about the place. Then he reminded himself as usual that Alice could barely read and of the length of their relationship and as always put off recovering the key for another day. He could hear her approaching with his morning tea and barely had time to light his first cigarette of the day before she appeared in the doorway. Between coughs he looked up at her and even with tears in his eyes one glance was enough to tell him that she was high.

Alice Pearson would have looked strange even to a casual observer but then to be truthful she always did. Her tall, matchstick-thin body was habitually draped in innumerable layers of drab clothes that almost covered her from head to toe and never seemed to alter in quantity whatever the season. Her feet were housed in ankle boots of considerable vintage and the gap between boots and skirt was bridged by dark brown socks which looked as if they might be more at home on a boy scout. The whole outfit was topped off by a navy balaclava which covered all but a small circle of elfin face and it was this area that gave away her current condition. She was wearing makeup! Not the subtle stuff worn by most women, not even the exaggerated daubing favoured by beauticians in high street stores. No, this was a stark red gash at her mouth, enormous black circles around her eyes and huge splashes of rouge on her cheeks. The overall effect was reminiscent of a demented clown but it didn't make Ben laugh.

He reached for his tea and pointed to the chair at the side of his desk. This was a scenario that they had been through many times before and both knew their parts instinctively Alice was a spinster who had spent more than half of her fifty years at the local mental institution St Benedict's. She had suffered from an early age with a schizophrenic condition that had caused her to go completely mad from time to time. From her youth onwards she had spent less and less time at home with her family until she had finally lost all contact with them and the hospital had become her full-time home. At her best she was a dowdy old lady who wouldn't say boo to a goose. When ill she became unrecognisable and the voices in her head took her over, causing her to become paranoid, hostile and out of control.

Undoubtedly in years gone by she would have spent her whole adult life under heavy sedation, shuffling her life away on some back ward somewhere. Improvements in medications had meant her condition could now be controlled and changes in attitudes had given her a chance on the outside. When the day had arrived for her to move to her 'nice little flat' Alice had been terrified and had hidden under her hospital bed. It had taken considerable persuasion and some little force to get her to Highfield. She had found her way back to the hospital by seven the next morning and the weaning process had been prolonged. She still felt the need to visit the institution from time to time as if to check it was still there for her if required. She had been Ben's first long-term hospital patient to be housed on the estate almost four years ago and he had put a lot of effort into making it a success as there had been considerable hostility from all sorts of quarters about the programme of rehabilitating long-term psychiatric patients. Alice had had no idea how to cope with day-to-day living, as for years all decisions had been made for her, but together they managed. She had been impossibly lonely and had no capacity to make friends. She had quickly filled her flat with an assortment of stray animals that prospered and bred with amazing rapidity and regularity. In no time at all the place deteriorated to a disgusting level as their mess contaminated every room. Even Alice realised that the situation could not be allowed to go on but it was beyond her to sort it out. Ben and the RSPCA stepped in and Alice was now left sharing with a neutered tomcat called Benny. Ben and the other staff in the office were her only friends and like some pet animal she spent her days nearby making herself useful by making tea, tidying up or just being at everyone's beck and call. She made few demands other than to be there and to be talked to from time to time. She had somehow acquired a spare key to the office and now saw it as her duty to have a cup of tea ready whenever anyone came into the office and to keep the place clean and tidy. She had gradually made herself indispensable and was generally quite content within her replacement institution.

One look at the 'war paint' was a clear indication that Alice had not been taking her medication. Ben dug his keys out of his trouser pocket, unlocked his desk drawer and reached for the bottle of pills hidden under a miscellaneous pile of papers. The fault, as always, was Ben's not Alice's, as she only stopped taking her medication when she was feeling neglected by him. He knew only too well that he had been avoiding their usual early morning chat of late but the problem was that the subject of their discussions rarely varied from the functioning of Alice's bowels and their various intricacies. She was obsessed with her bowel movements or their lack of movement and the sample of her diarrhoea that she brought in for him to see the previous week had really made him sick to his stomach. Alice took the proffered tablets without a murmur and they both knew that they would be resuming their little chats the following day.

Normally the day followed a familiar pattern, with the time before coffee being taken up with opening the post, phone calls and dictating to Mrs Freeman, the now full-time shorthand typist cum receptionist cum general administrator. She had started almost from day one with Ben initially on a half-time basis, which just recently become a full-time post. She was a very close friend and ally to Ben and the formal use of their surnames to each other in no way reflected the closeness of their relationship. It worked well for both of them, Ben benefited from having a very loyal colleague and Mrs Freeman had an employer who was sympathetic to her problem. Her husband, Steve Freeman, had been in middle management in the Housing Department until deteriorating health with multiple sclerosis meant he had to take early retirement a couple of years before. The passage of his condition tended to fluctuate alarmingly ever since. Ben had tried to visit him a couple of times but it was obvious that Steve was very reluctant to let anyone see him and the level of his loss. When times became more difficult Ben was able to be flexible about Mrs Freeman's hours and he never felt that she took advantage. At first they had had a lot of talk about the future but as it became clear that Steve was on borrowed time they were both inclined to bury their heads and stick to dealing with the problems of Highfield. Ben had already prepared his welfare services colleague about the potential need for respite care and possibly full nursing care, but for the time being that was all he could do.

It was rare for any of the clients to call at the office in the morning but they did get the odd caller; frequently very odd! Today was a bit different, as Ben had planned an early visit to a new client referred the previous day by Dr Eddoll, who now worked in a joint practice with Dr Smyth at the recently opened health centre. The doctor had said it was urgent and as he was never one to make a fuss unnecessarily Ben gulped down the last of his tea, stubbed out his second cigarette of the day and glanced out of the window. Mrs Freeman had just got off the bus at the stop across the road and was hurrying in the direction of the office. Happy that she would be there to pick up on Alice's condition, Ben slipped out of the fire door at the rear of the premises and cut down the lane towards the centre of the estate.

The Highfield Estate was aptly named, having been built on the exposed south side of the beginnings of a lengthy range of hills. It was planned primarily as a massive council housing estate, mainly to rehouse people from the inner-city slum properties, many of which had been very badly damaged during the heavy bombing in the war. The ground was scrubby and poor, which must have made for one very happy farmer when the Exworth District Council had served him with the compulsory purchase order. Long straight rows of very similar red brick houses grew up with an apparent fertility which had never been equalled by the crops of the former owner. The first few desperate families moved into their new homes well before the roads were laid or the services properly connected. It had happened during the prolonged period of intense cold in the winter of 1960 and it was this single factor that had made the migration possible. The sea of mud which had engulfed the area where roads would eventually be laid had frozen to form a passable rutted track for the conglomeration of furniture vans, borrowed lorries and the occasional handcart which were used to move in the possessions of the pioneers. Ben had arrived in the first week and considered himself to count amongst the pioneers. He had been based in a single-storey wooden building, little more than a tatty hut that had previously seen service as a site office. It was located next to a row of portable lavatories used by the workmen which never seemed to have been emptied. Fortunately he had quickly developed a stinking cold that had left him incapable of registering the constant stench from next door.

As Ben progressed through the estate at a march he thought over his early days on Highfield. It had all looked very different then. It had been his first job after qualifying and it had been a temporary post with the fancy title of 'Resettlement Officer'. God, he had been green. He had not for a second questioned why he had got the job and it was too late by the time he discovered that he had been the only applicant following three separate advertisements. The job had quickly become a nightmare, with him constantly performing the role of buffer between the residents and the authorities, the residents and the builders and not infrequently between the residents and the residents. After twelve months of chasing his tail it was of some considerable relief to him to have his post absorbed into the Health Department.

He now functioned under the rather bizarre title of Mental Welfare Officer /Team Leader. Ben had thought it an appropriate title at the time as he felt pretty mental after his baptism of fire, but had no idea about which team he was meant to be leading. The new role brought with it a pay rise, much to Sandy, his wife's relief as she struggled to manage on his salary. It also meant a move from the builder's hut to a more elaborate prefabricated office that had been occupied by the planners of the estate. It was intended as a temporary move but needless to say he was still working from the same building four years on. Initially he had shared the building with staff from the planning office but they had finally moved out a couple of months before leaving part of the building unoccupied. No information had been forthcoming about its future use and Ben had decided to keep his head down in the hope that it would be forgotten about and allow him to spread his little empire at some point in the future. It had all the disadvantages of a temporary prefabricated building but at least it wasn't next door to a workman's lavatory!

The wind whipped relentlessly around Ben's legs and landed unerringly on the thin part at the seat of his trousers. Having a 'numb bum' seemed to be a permanent state for Ben these days and he cursed once again his wife's night school class where she had been shown how to convert shirt tails into replacement collars and cuffs. The top half of him might look less scruffy but one's lower half was no place to feel a draft. He had enough insight to realise that Sandy only attended night school in an attempt to get him home at a reasonable hour at least once a week so that he could spend some time with the kids, Jack aged five and Nick four. However, he pushed this knowledge and the guilt that went with it into the recesses of his mind and preferred to blame the poor pay he received as a social worker for his cold bum and misshapen collar.

He entered Peasedale Avenue and sorted out the house he wanted by finding one with a number and then counting in twos as he progressed along the row. Number 28 was fronted by a dense overgrown privet hedge, which was dented probably by the passage of numerous dogs and children in too much of a hurry to use the gateway provided. The gate was absent and the path was cracked, weed covered and liberally decorated with dog turds of varying age. It led to a scarred front door which had once been the standard pillar box red of all the front doors in Peasedale Avenue, but it now bore a variety of other markings, few of which one would want to identify. Ben navigated the path, with all its potential pitfalls, with practised ease and knocked on the door in defiance of the notice pinned there 'DO NOT KNOCK NIGHT WORKER SLEEPING'.

He shuffled his feet in an attempt to avoid the worse ravages of the wind that was a constant feature of life on the Highfield Estate. He glanced around the garden, which was about par for the course; unmown grass attempting to camouflage bits of bike and other assorted debris which constituted toys to kids around here. The only attempt to influence nature was a single row of plastic daffodils, some decapitated some not, that bordered the path. The daffodils were instantly recognisable to Ben, who had been brought up by a mother who was a compulsive collector of bric-a-brac, garden gnomes and inevitably plastic flowers. These were undoubtedly the give a ways of a free gift campaign run by Daz soap powder a few months before. The sheer quantity of them on display suggested that the householder had to be a compulsive washer but the more likely explanation was that they had nicked them from the nearest Tesco.

The wind was really getting to him now and he reached forward to bang the knocker with renewed vigour. The force of his repeated knocking would have woken the dead let alone a sleeping night worker. Finally, the door was flung wide, not by an irate night worker but by a small sallow faced little girl of about eight years. She had large brown eyes and the saddest of expressions and would have proved very lucrative on an appeal by the NSPCC. She rubbed her nose on the back of her hand, looked Ben up and down and then shouted over her shoulder in a voice loud enough for the whole street to hear. 'Mum it's the man from the welfare.'

So much for confidentiality, thought Ben as he followed her into the gloomy interior. The stale stench that engulfed him had in no way been influenced by excessive use of Daz. Those daffodils were nicked!

Chapter 2

Katie

The interview had followed familiar lines and Ben had to concentrate really hard to stop his mind from wandering. One look at Ruth Andrews was enough to confirm Dr Eddoll's diagnosis of depression. She was slumped on an old sofa dressed in a frayed, soiled housecoat with the butt of a cigarette in the corner of her mouth from which a trail of smoke flowed up over her face and spread amongst her hair. She looked a mess, obviously unwashed and her hair was lank and greasy from a long night without sleep. It was clear that she was past caring and she made no reaction to Ben seeing her in such a state.

Early thirties, thought Ben, but not well preserved; everything had dropped and spread and would keep on going if she didn't make an effort soon. It was clear, however, that Katie, the wide-eyed kid who had opened the door, was determined that her mum would be making an effort. It quickly emerged that Katie had taken control and that she was not prepared to let her mother sink any further into the black hole of depression. Ben avoided asking why she was not at school as he realised that this eight-year-old was all that stood between Mrs Andrews taking a trip to the local psychiatric hospital. Katie put her arm around her mum's shoulders, lowered her face to her mum's and spoke to her in a strangely maternal manner.

'Mum, you know the doctor asked him to call, you must talk to him, Mum, you really must.' Her voice was a mixture of command and imploring but the little sob and sniff at the end showed just how much she cared.

'My name is Ben Newman, I am a social worker on the estate and I have come to try and help you. I really would like to try and help if you would like me to.' The response was slow in coming but Ben maintained the silence, sat and waited for her. Slowly, very slowly her eyes met his and he held her glance but remained silent. A tear crept from her right eye then another and another. Her nose ran and her shoulders shook as she sobbed with increased intensity. Then she wailed; an awful guttural sound from deep within. Ben reached for her hand and Katie cuddled her as a mother would a distressed child. Slowly Ruth calmed down and the story began to come out in a disjointed and incoherent way. The pieces were all there, Ben just had to put them together like an imaginary jigsaw.

It was to her GP's credit that she was not already 'popping the Valium'. In reality the sort of problems she had could not be helped by tablets: her problem was her life. As the second of a family of six children with an alcoholic mother and a consumptive father she was a skivvy well before she left school. Pregnant at eighteen, married at nineteen followed by two more kids in quick succession had led her to the Highfield Estate, which had to be better than the one-bedroom basement flat they had previously rented down by the docks. Two miscarriages, dangerously high blood pressure and severe morning sickness had resulted in sterilisation on medical grounds. This had the desired effect of preventing further pregnancies and the associated excessive vomiting but also the unfortunate side effect of causing her to fall out of favour with the Roman Catholic priest at the church she had regularly attended since a small child. She had been told that she had committed a mortal sin by being sterilised and should no longer attend the church. Her religion had been the mainstay in her life and without the support of her church she felt rootless and alone.

She had become convinced that sex had no further significance to her, in fact it was a self-indulgence which should be avoided. Life for Mr Andrews must have been pretty joyless – three school-age children to maintain, a tired and frigid wife and employment as a low-wage earner on the night shift at the local shoe factory.

However, the sign on the front door was two weeks out of date as Mr Andrews had moved out to take up residence with a blonde single parent living just four doors away. This sort of happening was common on the estate and would pass almost without comment outside of the Andrews' home. The Housing Department policy of Exworth District Council was to offer single parents housing on the Highfield Estate or nothing. This resulted in a high incidence of young single mothers making the estate a happy hunting ground for many a would-be stud. It had a sort of knock-on effect like an elaborate game of musical beds and one such change usually resulted in a whole chain of similar happenings. Unfortunately, in all such games someone seemed to have to miss out and, in this case, it was Mrs Andrews, and she was devastated. She presented as a beaten woman with nothing to fight back with and with no inclination to even try.

She eventually stopped talking and Ben left her to compose herself as he headed to the kitchen with Katie to put the kettle on for the inevitable tea. It was a shambles with dirty crockery, some sporting a growth of mould, but Katie took command and found the makings as Ben ran some cups under the tap. He chatted away to Katie as calmly as he could and tried to reassure that her mum would soon be better. Over tea, which was weak, warm and sweet, he listened again as Mrs Andrews repeated over and over how she felt about her husband, the church, her marriage, the kids and the church again. Gradually she began to show signs of coming to a halt and was at the sink making a token gesture of tackling the mountain of dirty dishes that had collected there as Ben moved to leave. Katie was beside her, grubby wiping-up cloth in hand, determined that her mum would be back to normal as soon as possible. Ben had arranged to visit again in two days and he left the house drained of the required energy to avoid the various pitfalls that decorated the path.

Chapter 3

The Haven

Ben turned left along Peasedale Avenue and at the end of the road cut across the triangle of rough grass which opened on to the main grass square of Highfield. This had the dual advantage of getting his shoes clean and also gave him a better chance of getting to his destination on the far side of the square before the doughnuts were all gone. Ben's expanding waistline demonstrated his fondness for sugary things but as he regularly explained, most carefully to anyone who would listen, he needed plenty of sugar to replace the nervous energy his job used up. Today was undoubtedly a two or even three doughnut day, he determined.

The quickest way to the rank of shops which serviced the estate was diagonally across the square, as was made quite obvious by the muddy path worn into the grass, but he skirted around the edge. He did this to avoid getting in the way of the kick-around which was underway in the middle of the grass. A group of youths were kicking into a goal mouth made up of a conveniently placed signpost prohibiting the playing of all ball games and a rather beaten-up old parking cone. At one time Ben would not have been able to resist the urge to get involved in the action. Even as a youngster he had had more enthusiasm than skill and it was only now at the ripe old age of twenty-six that he was beginning to develop skill. Not football skill, but the skill of avoiding situations where he was guaranteed to end up looking stupid. As often happens at such times fate took a hand and a mishit shot sped the ball towards him. He trapped the ball with ease, did a dazzling dribble, a feint to the left, a swerve to the right and then let fly with a firm shot on goal. His well-worn size nine Italian slip-on scored at the base of the far post; the ball meanwhile sliced off to the right to land with a resounding thud on a passing dustcart and then rebounded with amazing precision back amongst the youths.

The jeers turned to cheers and then to laughter all in quick succession and a blonde head appeared at the window of the dustcart. 'Nice one, Mr Newman.' It was Nobby Phillips, one of last year's crop of special school leavers who Ben had helped to get a job on the bins. With a feeble attempt at nonchalance Ben briefly acknowledged the audience, rescued his shoe from the goal mouth and tucked it under his arm as he limped off the field of play. Head down he narrowly resisted the urge to break into a run.

Still panting from his exertions Ben entered the small rank of shops which were typical of those found on many such estates. They were mainly family run and most of the owners lived above them. Unfortunately they were the constant target for the young, who spent their evenings on the streets bored and seeking excitement. The original décor had been liberally added to by the 'spray can artists' and grotesque and incomplete displays of extraordinary genitalia were crisscrossed with such pearls of wisdom as 'Highfield pukes', 'kill all pigs' and 'Rockers rule mods are shit'. The street was full of litter and even with the bustle of shoppers there was a general air of decay. The post office, newsagents and off licence had all been particular targets over the years. Their reinforced glass windows and doors all bore the cracks and scars of determined attack and they had all had metal shutters added to protect them when closed. In the centre of the rank was the haven where Ben was heading.

It was quite unlike any of the other shops and its steamy glass windows bore no graffiti, cracks or bars. It simply had the words 'Joe's bistro' painted in large black letters in an arc across each of the windows. To even the most casual observer such immunity from vandals would suggest that the café was run by one hell of a big man. And in reality, it was, but not big as in muscles, height or physical strength, this big was a much subtler commodity. In fact, Joe was only five feet tall in his stocking feet and his lean wiry frame made him look like a candidate for feeding up. He was a man of few words but when he spoke people listened. He had an easy smile and one might easily expect him to be a lady's man, but that was far from the truth.

The café was a series of three rooms which extended for the full depth of the building. The first and largest of the rooms contained the counter and a series of cubicles running down the length of the room.

The second room was almost completely filled by two long tables with stacking chairs on each side of them. The wall was covered by a large notice board on which were business cards ranging from posh embossed ones down to bits torn off of old cigarette packets all offering a range of services offered by regular customers. The third room was protected by a closed door marked 'PRIVATE' and only the privileged few ever saw the inside. Joe made no attempt to provide entertainment. There were no fruit machines or pin ball machines, certainly no juke box and not even a daily paper other than ones left by earlier customers. The atmosphere was thick with steam, tobacco smoke and a pungent all-prevailing smell of frying bacon and coffee. It was the sort of atmosphere that you could almost cut with a knife but there was no doubt about the popularity of the place as was clearly apparent from the variety of vehicles that were parked on the nearby streets. Every sort of workman, gasman, milkman, insurance man, dustman, postman, in fact 'every butcher, baker and candlestick maker', who serviced the estate made at least one visit to Joe's most days. All except Sunday; Sundays Joe closed. If they had all turned up at once the place would have burst at the seams, but over the years a pattern had developed and they all knew their time to call. The tradesmen always aimed for the middle room and the nonstop chat and back chat of the bare room was a way of life to them. Each new dirty joke, bit of gossip or strange experience was quickly shared and embellished as it was repeated over and over again throughout the day. A fly on the wall would have reported that men can out-gossip women any day. Many a woman on the estate who had a brief encounter in the morning found herself attracting very strange looks and comments before the day was out. Without doubt the centre of the estate's jungle drums was located in Joe's middle room. Apart from the tradesmen there were numerous other characters on the estate who were loyal supporters of Joe's. The basis for this special relationship between Joe and the estate had its roots in the very beginnings of the estate.

Joe had been one of the pioneers; he arrived in a battered van armed with a Calor gas cooker and a willingness to serve tea and hot dogs at all hours of the day. In the chaos of the early weeks and months many a resident was grateful to Joe for warm cheap food. Joe occupied the first shop to be completed, in fact the reason it was completed first was because it was for Joe and the workmen building the estate quickly reaped the benefits of their labours. Joe's reputation for good food and straightforward dealing grew and by the time the estate was finished Joe's place had become an institution. The secret of his success was not just the speed in which he produced good, simple food but more his general acceptance of people. Everyone was treated the same and everyone was welcomed and as a consequence Joe's place was generally accepted by young and old alike. Ben was privileged to know much more about Joe than anyone else on the estate. The fact that he wouldn't dream of sharing the knowledge with anyone had never been raised, but Joe knew and Ben received other privileges because of it, the most important being his right to use the third room in the café, the one marked 'Private'.

The story behind their special relationship was unusual and the main character in it spent each day behind the counter of the café. Mavis suffered from Down's syndrome. Her round moon-like face, her slanted eyes and her constant simple smile made it obvious to even the most casual observer. Her movements were heavy and clumsy and her speech was guttural and at times difficult to understand. Mavis was Joe's daughter and arrived with him in his van as a child of fourteen.

The confidential report from the authorities in Glasgow had been circulated to all the health departments in the country and about six months later a copy of the report had percolated through to Ben. The description left no doubt in Ben's mind. Joe's real name was actually something long and complicated in Polish, ending in ski. The authorities told a story of a girl with Down's syndrome being cared for by her father alone following the death of his wife. He had chosen to keep her at home with him and her non-attendance at the local training centre was followed by a series of threats and eventual court action. The decision of the court had been residential special school for Mavis, but Joe and Mavis had reacted simply but effectively; they had disappeared.

Ben was not noted for an unorthodox reaction to problems and his discovery of Joe's true identity caused him to agonise for days. Clearly the expectation of his employers would be to advise the authorities in Glasgow of the arrival of Joe and Mavis in Highfield. But Ben knew only too well the importance of Joe to Highfield and everything he had seen of Mavis convinced him that she was totally content with her life with

Joe. He carefully folded the report, sealed it in an envelope and put it in an old biscuit tin, which was left over from Christmas. The tin was then locked in his desk drawer. He later got to thinking of the tin as his memory box and over the months he had added other bits and pieces which were important to him at the time.

Finally, after much deliberation he decided to confront Joe with the problem and that evening after work he had gone into the café at closing time and asked him for a private word. Joe took the news with dignity, poured out a couple of teas and led Ben through the café to the back room for the first time. The remains of a log fire burned in the grate and an old comfortable three-piece was drawn up around the fire. The other three walls of the room were covered in an assortment of boxes and deep freezers. The room doubled as a stock room.

Mavis already occupied one of the armchairs and was busy 'reading' the evening newspaper. Ben noticed it was upside down. She had a couple of cats sharing her chair and showed no surprise that Ben was there. Joe built up the fire, pointed Ben to the settee and took the other armchair himself. He filled Ben in without emotion as if he had a prepared speech which had been waiting for an audience. He had come to this country as a teenager with his mother from Poland a couple of years before war had been declared. His mother had seen the way things were going for their country and proved to be correct as her every other relative had died in the horrors of Warsaw. His mother had at first worked in the kitchen of a café in Glasgow and after a couple of years had taken over the business and had nursed the former owner until his death as part of the takeover agreement. Joe had grown up working alongside her and had been well satisfied by the arrangement. Whilst still in his teens he met and married a Scottish lass and they in turn took over from his mother and together built up a flourishing business. A planned and much wanted child came quite quickly and the shock of her being handicapped had had the effect of bringing them even closer together. They had decided to have no more children but to concentrate all their efforts on Mavis. Life had been really good for the family and Joe began to show some distress for the first time as he reached this stage of the story. He paused, took a long swig of his tea, paused again just looking at Mavis, then continued with his emotions back under control. Mrs Joe had become ill, suddenly and without warning and had died of breast cancer within a month. Joe had been devastated, Mavis apparently less so, but they had clung together with renewed force.

Ben and Joe had struck a bargain that evening and they had kept to it ever since. Ben was to be allowed to supervise Mavis as he would any other mentally handicapped person on the estate. If at any time he felt her best interests were not being met Joe had to agree to any alteration that Ben put forward; in return Ben had agreed to say nothing to the authorities. Neither Joe nor Ben had ever regretted the decision and Mavis was now nearly eighteen and almost beyond the reach of the authorities. From trust had grown friendship and Ben and Joe were now firm friends.

Ben pushed open the door and breathed in the warmth. He gave a wave to Joe through the door to the kitchen and collected a cup of tea, a doughnut and a huge grin and grunted greeting from Mavis. The fire burned brightly in the backroom and Ben thought to himself, not for the first time, that he felt more at home here than almost anywhere; perhaps even more than with Sandy and the boys.

Chapter 4

The Team

Being Monday, Ben was always slow to get going and in any case he always tended to loiter too long at Joe's. The combination of the settee and the fire made him reluctant to return to the grey chill that was September at Highfield. Mavis, as always, made a fuss of him and topped his mug up at regular intervals. Meanwhile he read through his notes of the visit to Ruth and Katie Andrews and considered the possible alternative ways ahead. It was far too early for any definite plans but he suspected that Ruth's problems with her church might be one possible way of helping her to cope with the realities of her life. It was about an hour after he had first entered the café that Mavis reappeared at the door with the determined statement that she had come to sing to him. Her version of 'Rock Around the Clock' bore little or no relationship to the original but what it lacked in quality it made up for in quantity for it went on and on. After several fruitless attempts to bring her to a halt he was left with no alternative but to head for the door. As he passed the counter he caught Joe's eye and noticed his too straight face. Joe had used Mavis to winkle him out and to send him back about his business. 'Cheers, Joe, you sod,' mouthed Ben with a grin.

As he made his way back to the office he thought over the recent changes that had taken place. Just over a month ago, quite out of the blue, he had received a telephone call from one of the bosses at headquarters. It was simply to advise that he was going to have a social worker from another area transferred to his team as of the following week. Her name was Phyllis Jenkins 'call me Phil' and she was an experienced worker with the mentally handicapped but was now employed as a mental welfare officer. That was the only information offered and Ben was given no choice in the matter, it was a fait accompli. Phil duly arrived the following week and presented as a formidable lady. She was a large lady in her mid-forties with an unfortunate face and a strong tendency to wear men's clothes. She seemed to be surprisingly relaxed about her transfer to Highfield but made it quite clear that it had to be her way or no way. Ben could see problems ahead but as usual decided to avoid direct confrontation if possible and wait and see how things panned out. He knew she would be gone to lunch by the time he got back, which was just as well as she was always impossible company in the mornings. Ben had learnt that he was more relaxed in her company once she had topped up her alcohol level at midday, then she could be quite a laugh. She made no secret about being lesbian and it emerged that this, along with her strong feminist views, had caused problems with some of the staff at her previous office which probably had resulted in her transfer to Highfield. Her being lesbian was of no consequence to Ben or Mrs Freeman and Alice remained blissfully unaware. On balance Ben was not unhappy with his new colleague. She had brought with her a stack of files of mentally handicapped people living on the estate and the surrounding area and he was in the process of reading through them, a couple each day, to extend his knowledge of the people on his patch and their needs. From reading the files it appeared that Phil had a very professional and caring attitude to her work and would be a useful if not straightforward first addition to his team. In time it would become clear that Phil was not fully comfortable with her role as a mental welfare officer and whenever possible chose to focus on the needs of the mentally handicapped rather than the mentally ill. Just a couple of days later Ben found a message on his desk for him to ring the big chief at head office and he felt sure that there was bad news coming. In fact the news was far from bad as he was told that the department was recruiting a new type of worker called a social work assistant and he would be able to recruit one to join his team. This was heady stuff for Ben, who had never been in the position of recruiting staff before. He realised that anyone appointed would not have a professional qualification so he was determined to have someone who was mature and who had a good experience of people and life in general. He planned to talk to both Phil and Mrs Freeman about his ideas of a suitable candidate and he hoped that they would both be in agreement with his ideas for the new member of the team. He was keen to increase the size of his team and wasted no time in talking to the personnel department at headquarters and arranging for a job advert to appear in the local newspaper. He had bought an evening paper every night for ten nights and last Friday's paper had his advert giving his name for the person to contact for further information. He had never had his name in the paper before so the advert had been cut out ready to go in his memory box in due course. Meanwhile he wondered if he would be inundated with applicants and walked back to the office planning how he might he might handle the rush.

As he crossed the car park Alice was at the door which in itself was unusual. She was shaking from head to foot and her eyes were darting back and forth. Her mouth opened and closed as if she was desperate to say something but the only sound was of her sobbing breaths. Ben's immediate reaction was to feel a sense of foreboding. It looked as if Alice had really gone over the top again after being 'well' for so many years. She grasped his hand desperately and cowered against him with real terror. He attempted to lead her back into the office but she wouldn't be budged and after a couple of abortive efforts he moved her towards his car; ideas of driving her straight to St Benedict's began to form in his mind. This time she moved easily with him and he eased her into the passenger seat without too much difficulty. All the while she kept throwing darting glances towards the office entrance as if expecting some horror to appear at any moment. Ben sat beside her in the car and held her hand, all the time talking in soft gentle tones as one would to a frightened child. Alice visibly relaxed and after locking her car door seemed much more like her old self. The extreme makeup was still present but the terror seemed to be receding, and Ben realised that her tablets were still in his desk drawer. He carefully explained what he was going to do and with some difficulty broke away from Alice's clutches. She uttered her first words of the encounter, demanding that he should lock her in the car, which he did before heading back into the office to fetch her medication. A huge Black man was sat at Ben's desk and he leapt to his feet as Ben entered his office. Ben nearly fainted on the spot and then realisation hit him. It was his turn to have a nursing student and he had forgotten all about him in the rush to get out early that morning.

Apologies and greetings over, Ben had time to work out what had happened. Alice was high and had begun to show symptoms of her schizophrenic condition. When she was ill her main symptoms had been a paranoid delusion that she was being persecuted by a foreign power and the arrival of the student without warning had been enough to send her into a real panic. At the best of times Alice didn't like Black people and she regularly blamed much of her bowel problems on the Black men who worked for the water board, and that was when she was well! Ben quickly filled the guy in on what was happening, grabbed Alice's tablets and beat a hasty retreat back to the car where he was welcomed by Alice with uncontrolled enthusiasm.

Alice was in no mood for explanations and he quickly gave up on attempting any. He strapped her in as firmly as possible and set off for her flat. Once there Alice was like a demented jack in the box. Just as she appeared to be settled in her armchair she would pop up again in a fresh state of agitation. Yet again Ben made the inevitable tea and gave her a dose of medication, but by the time he finally got her settled it was well into the afternoon. She had by this time consumed several cups of tea, two more tablets and at least three days rations of Ben's cigarettes. The agitation seemed to have passed, to be replaced with thinly disguised attention seeking. Ben felt able to make a gradual exit, all the time giving repeated reassurances that he would visit the next day. They had agreed that she would stay home for the rest of the week as she was after all entitled to annual leave just like the rest of them. Without doubt this solution would take up much more of his time than her coming into the office, but he couldn't risk her coming face to face with 'the Black man', Dave Wilkins, whilst she was unwell. Hopefully by the end of the week the tablets would be back in control and in any case the student would be completing his stay on Friday. Alice followed him out to the front door and by the time his car turned the corner she had reached her gate. He pretended not to notice and kept on going, his mind turning to the more immediate situation of his student.

Each of the psychiatric nurses at St Margaret's, one of the local psychiatric hospitals, spent a week of their final year of training with one of the mental welfare officers and Ben's turn came around every couple of months. It was all a bit of a lottery who you got and the list of names sent out at the beginning of the year gave no clue as to the age, sex, race or ability of the person who eventually turned up. Some of his colleagues told horrendous tales of weird students, but by and large Ben had been favourably impressed. There had even been one lass from Bermuda who had put him off his stroke for the whole week of her placement. She had been lovely and Sandy, Ben's wife, had reaped the benefit of his fantasies with surprised delight. By comparison Dave had to be a disappointment.

Phil had returned from lunch and all the signs were that she had had more 'lunch' than usual. Her face was flushed and her manner was laid back almost to the level of collapse. She was slumped in her chair and her feet were up on the open top drawer of her desk displaying a wide expanse of legs fortunately veiled in thick black tights. She was holding forth on her favourite topic of women's rights and had just reached the point of men seeing women as nothing more than sex objects. Fat chance, thought Ben, taking a fleeting glance into the depth of her classic old spinster's stance. He skilfully avoided a second look, after all he had had no lunch, he reminded himself and it would take a brave man to explore those depths on an empty stomach. He noticed that the student did not share his fortitude; he looked like a trapped animal and was positively squirming. It was quite obvious that he was in dire need of rescue. Taking advantage of Phil's relaxed state, Ben adopted a bold frontal approach and marched straight up to the student and whisked him away whilst Phil was still in full flow. He managed to get them into his office and the door shut before she had fully realised what was happening. No doubt there would be a price to pay, but the look of relief on Dave's face made it all worthwhile.

The banging of drawers and general clatter from next door confirmed that Phil was far from happy. Ben and Dave hit it off straight away and spent the rest of the afternoon in relaxed conversation about working with the mentally ill. Ben carefully filled Dave in on the problem earlier in the day with Alice's reaction to him. Dave accepted the situation without surprise and it was clear that his colour and size had attracted strange reactions before and he understood that he could initially be seen as hostile. However, he had a warm smile, a soft voice and a ready wit, all of which Ben thought would quickly allay such feelings. Unfortunately, Alice's reaction had been immediate and she had not given him a chance to use his undoubted charm.

Dave was already familiar with one aspect of Ben's role as a mental welfare officer and he knew that it was the responsibility of some social workers with special training to arrange the admission to hospital, often as a voluntary patient but not infrequently on a compulsory basis when the patient was unable or unwilling to accept admission to a psychiatric hospital. On occasion the patient was admitted in a very angry and aggressive mood and the disruption caused to the peace on the ward naturally led to resentment on the part of nursing staff. In fact, Dave had been on the receiving end of such admissions on several occasions and had very mixed feelings about them. Dave was mature enough to realise that these were tricky situations to handle but nevertheless felt at times they could have been handled much better.

Ben had to agree as he was only too aware of the difficulties he had encountered and the mistakes he had made, but he pointed out there was a lot more to his job other than simply forcing people into hospital. He explained that Alice was just one of almost a hundred chronically mentally ill and or mentally handicapped people living on the estate. Most of them would always need a bit of support if they were to survive in the community without causing too many waves for themselves and their neighbours. They were nearly all identified by the rest of the community as 'oddballs' but by and large were tolerated reasonably well. In addition there was the constant steady stream of 'ordinary folks' who needed help and support to overcome an acute depression, neurotic or psychotic illness. This sort of illness was often associated with life events such as divorce, death or childbirth and most people were able to be treated at home or if they needed hospital treatment accepted this as voluntary patients. Nevertheless, their problems were often serious and complex and affected all aspects of their life and that of their families. This frequently involved a lot of time and effort before they were able to continue to live an independent life back in the community.

Ben arranged to meet Dave the following day at about 9.30 am, which would leave him enough time to attend to Alice first. The plan was to introduce him to a few of the more 'interesting' clients on the patch, many of whom had spent lengthy periods of their lives in hospital. It promised to be an interesting and informative day and he hoped that Dave would not have the same effect on all his other clients as he had had on Alice, otherwise St Margaret's would soon be bursting at the seams. Still, as Dave was returning to work there on the following Monday there might be quite a fast turnaround of patients! Ben sorted out several files for David to read and left him whilst he attended to his other work of the day.

Chapter 5

A Good Week

It was a Tuesday morning much like any other and yet there was something different about this morning and Ben couldn't quite put his finger on what it was. He was setting off as ever in his car for work and as usual it was raining. The sky was overcast and appeared full of rain and the wind was huffing and puffing, pushing all the litter around. The dustbin men had already been on their rounds and the residue of their efforts provided ample supplies for the wind to enjoy. The cut and thrust of the traffic was as bad as ever and the people he passed looked as miserable as ever. Yet Ben felt a strange sense of wellbeing and found himself breaking into song as he drove along his all too familiar route to Highfield. At first he had not even realised that he was singing out loud and it was not until he spotted the horrified look on the face of the driver in the adjacent car at the traffic lights that he became conscious of his elated state. He decided that it felt good and continued to sing with increased volume. Maybe he was no Sinatra but who cared. The driver of the neighbouring car did for one and he roared off with a rude gesture and a racing start as soon as the lights changed to amber. Ben waited for the green and pulled away steadily. Even the car seemed affected by the moment with man and machine in rare harmony. The long drag up the hill to the Highfield Estate was approached with apparent ease by the car and even failed to get the usual explosive reaction from Ben's digestive system.

He looked around as he surmounted the hill and not for the first time spotted the dejected figure of the old horse eking out an existence in one of the scrubby fields by the side of the road. On impulse he stopped and reached for his work bag to remove the apple Sandy had put in his lunch box. He had always had a soft spot for horses ever since the years of his early teens when he had spent every Saturday helping out in a rundown stable near his aunt and uncle's home in the country. He would spend the morning mucking out the stables in return for a free ride out with the afternoon group. He loved it and almost always rode a favourite old chestnut called Boxer, but after two or three years his relatives had moved up north and that was the end of his riding.

Ben went over to the old iron bedstead that served as a gate to the field and called out, 'Come on, Boxer.' The old horse responded with curiosity and ambled towards him. It had an old sack tied around its body but this did little for him as it was soaking wet and he had a covering of mud on his legs and under belly. But it responded when it saw the apple Ben was holding out for him and came right over. As it ate the apple Ben patted its neck and smoothed its forehead, both of which seemed to be appreciated. He noted that there was an old bath of reasonably clean water and a small pile of rather muddy hay just inside the gate. It wasn't much but it did show that someone was trying to care for the animal. It certainly wasn't Boxer, but it was a horse in need and Ben determined to stop on a regular basis and introduce the odd treat to Boxer Mark Two's life. By this time Ben was pretty soaked himself and he hurried back to the car. Damp he might be, but his spirit remained undampened. He sat for a while and contemplated his current mood.

He reflected that the previous evening had been something of a surprise. For a start he had arrived home in good time and for a second, he had been in good humour. Tea had been a pleasant family occasion and he had found himself listening with interest as the boys told of the events of their day. Sandy had warmed to the occasion and the evening had progressed through an exuberant game of snakes and ladders to the family enjoying a repeat showing of 'Steptoe and Son' on the box. The kids had been infected by the atmosphere and had gone to bed with only token resistance. Ben had made the coffee and later Sandy rewarded him with an urgency and enthusiasm which made words superfluous.

Now as the car drove along the familiar route to Highfield he tried to work out why he felt so much better than normal. He could think of only one conclusion and that was that he was looking forward to spending the rest of the week with Dave. Of course, he had known for ages that he was bored with his day-to-day activities, the clients were fine but in truth Mrs Freeman, Phil and Alice had very little to offer by way of stimulation. They were just like him, each wrapped up with themselves, a familiar and uncomplicated group of individuals all doing their own thing in their own way. It was much the same at home. The kids were growing up and showing the beginnings of growing away and Sandy immersed herself in the day-to-day demands of bringing up two rapidly growing children on a limited budget with an often absent husband. They both contributed to bringing up the family but not as a pair, and often with little or no discussion.

He remembered their time at university together. They had lived with a group of friends in a shared house. It had been great and they were soon sharing everything as they became a recognised 'item'. It had been tremendous and they had enjoyed it all in a state of fun, laughter, work, sex, more fun and a lot more sex. They obtained their degrees at the same time, Sandy achieving a first and Ben only barely scraping a second. There was no doubt who had the brains but Sandy had already been pregnant and they saved like mad to get set up before the baby arrived. They had managed to acquire their small two-bedroom terraced house, but this was only made possible with the generous help of a deposit from Sandy's parents. Jack was quickly followed by Nick. The kids were great but the place was bursting at the seams and there had never been enough money for any of life's little luxuries. Undoubtedly the annual event would have continued indefinitely as neither of them was strong enough to take responsibility for birth control on any regular basis. Sandy couldn't cope with the pill – it simply messed her about too much – and all the other methods involved commitment. Sandy was becoming increasingly cold and Ben became increasingly conscious of 'making advances', whereas before things had just happened. Sandy mainly didn't want to know and Ben reluctantly decided that the only solution was for him to have a vasectomy. It had caused him agonies of fearful anticipation but surprisingly little discomfort in reality. Sandy had been largely indifferent and had not reacted to the new freedom with anything approaching enthusiasm. The months since the operation had been pretty joyless for them both, which made last night so much more surprising. Ben found it impossible to equate the bright, attractive and attentive playmate of his university days with the shadowy figure who ran his home and shared his bed. Nowadays her mind seemed to be in neutral whilst she devoured an endless supply of mush from one Mills and

Boon after another. Yet he reminded himself in detail of their lovemaking of the previous night and he felt his senses react to the memory and had to force himself to concentrate on his driving. He changed down for the final hill to Highfield and his mind changed gear too as he moved his thoughts to the day ahead.

He had planned to use today to introduce Dave to the realities of community care for the mentally ill and the mentally handicapped. He ran through a list in his mind of the various people that they would visit. They were an odd collection of individuals who had collectively spent many years in mental hospitals. Their histories were very different and yet they were roughly the same age and there were other similarities. Ben knew they were almost exclusively the lucky ones who had had someone left in the community who had been prepared to have them back once the worst of their symptoms had passed. Once out they mainly clung on to their freedom with dogged resistance, a surfeit of medication and a watching brief from Ben. There could be no doubt that he was fond of them all despite their idiosyncrasies and unusual habits. In some ways he saw their survival as his primary task and measured his success by them remaining out of hospital. As ever, before making any visits with students on placement Ben planned to make a tour of his patch showing how the town had developed over the years. He usually started off at the most northern part of his patch, the Cuttings. This was the largely working-class area made up of road after road of terraced housing built mainly at the end of Victorian times to house the workers in the various industries which had sprung up along the banks of the canal which split the town in two. There were some obvious gaps in the rows of houses caused by the bombing in the war and these were now mainly filled with either small blocks of flats or compact three-bedroom housing. This area was particularly well known to Ben as it had been where he had lived for all his married life. The next band of housing was the district of Ensley made up of larger homes complete with gardens and many with garages or space for a car. These were mainly occupied by middle-class white-collar workers and Ben was able to tell Dave that there was very little demand for his services from this area of housing. The town then opened up to a large area of scrub land that came on to a prefab estate on the right called the Landings and various industrial sites on the left, including a collection of scrapyards dominated by one huge area enclosed in vivid green painted corrugated iron sheeting. The single word 'Scaddings' was painted along the length of the fence in large black capitals. The tops of numerous pillars of stacked wrecked cars rose up into the skyline. The hill then progressed until it passed the tower blocks before entering the Highfield Estate with its apparently endless red brick boxes which went off into the distance. This was Ben's normal pattern when he had a student and it usually ended up with a visit to Joe's for the inevitable coffee and doughnuts. However, on this occasion he varied the pattern and he was not too proud of himself for doing so.

In truth he was not at all sure what Joe's customers would make of Dave for he had rarely seen a Black customer at Joe's and he was aware that there were already some there who resented the privileges Ben enjoyed, and taking Dave there might just rock the boat. So, he decided to reverse the journey and end up at his home where he had primed Sandy to receive a visitor.

It all went well and Sandy received Dave warmly and laid on a great lunch of pork chops, chips and peas followed by apple pie and custard, which was well received and one of Ben's favourites. Sandy and Dave chatted away like two old friends and Dave was soon showing her photos from his wallet of his wife and kids, who were still back home in Jamaica. Ben found himself becoming a bit jealous at the ease of their relationship, so retired to the kitchen to make the tea and do the washing up. Sandy made no comment but he saw her smile to herself and he guessed she had been pleased at his reaction.

After lunch Ben and Dave set off to visit the Farthing family, who were one of the pioneer families on the estate and a family that Ben knew about in considerable detail.

Chapter 6

Four Farthings

Whenever Ben had a student placed with him he made a point of taking them to meet the Farthing family. Ben called on them regularly as part of his normal supportive work and he had to admit to himself that they were particularly interesting to him. He knew more about the Farthings than any other of his clients and they had moved on to the Highfield Estate within days of Ben starting to work there. He had just about moved into his ex-workmen cabin office when a large special delivery parcel arrived. It was a tea chest almost full of a variety of files with a covering note from a social worker on the north of the city which simply read 'they are coming your way very soon, over to you, it's all in the files'. As yet Ben didn't even have a filing cabinet to put the files in so he put them all in date order and stored them in the boot of his car for safety. With time on his hands and bitterly cold outside he started the mammoth task of reading all about the Farthings. In no time at all he was hooked. The story emerged bit by bit just like a novel. There were obvious times here and there when the Farthings went off the radar but it was quite easy to fill in the gaps. The first file was Frederick Farthing, born in 1923 in a small mining community in South Wales. He was the youngest of six boys and seemed to have been the runt of the litter. His school attendance was problematical; he could neither read nor write and when he did attend school he preferred to act the fool rather than work and no amount of the strap changed his behaviour in any way. He was a petty thief within school and soon extended his activities into local shops, the local chapel and neighbour's houses. At this stage he acquired the nickname of Foxie because he was not to be trusted and was always on the lookout for easy prey. He was not at all offended by the name Foxie and he adopted the name as his own and refused to answer to any other. He had several court appearances which seemed to have little effect on him other than to make him decide to change his modus operandi and he moved on to become the local poacher. School became a thing of the past at the age of twelve and he wandered the local woods and rivers building up a sizeable cliental for the odd rabbit, trout or pheasant that he acquired. The 1930s were hard times for most people and Foxie's efforts were generally well received. However, in time demand began to outstretch supply and the moaning of 'regular customers' at the local pub soon got back to the ears of the local constable. He bided his time whilst Foxie plotted to increase supply by returning to his thieving ways. He broke into the explosives store at the local quarry and stole four sticks of explosives. This was discovered by the quarry foreman the very next day and the constable was notified. He knew his stuff and realised that this was not a big criminal act, reasoning that they would have stolen everything from the store. He put the moaning at the pub with the need for Foxie to increase his activities together and on the next fine night settled down by the local Laird's fishing lake to wait. He didn't have to wait long and just after midnight there was a loud explosion from the lake. Foxie was still busy fishing out dead and dying fish when his collar was felt. It was all downhill for him from there as the police discovered the other three sticks of explosive under his bed, which had they exploded would have wiped out his family and those of his neighbours.

Foxie was remanded in custody for medical reports and found to be of subnormal intelligence. To add to his problems the chairman of the magistrate's court was a local landowner who had had his share of problems with poachers. In his court address he labelled Foxie as a dangerous bomber. This was picked up by the local press and even made several of the national press. All the press cuttings were on Foxie's file and Ben removed one to go in his memory box; after all it is not every day you have 'a bomber' as a client. Foxie was committed to the large institution for the mentally handicapped in Cardiff. His story on file came to an abrupt end at this point and the only additions for the next few years were the usual annual medical check-ups. The last entry on the file was just one word: 'absconded'. In Ben's mind eye Foxie took the form of the crafty Fox in the Beatrice Potter stories his mother had repeatedly read to him as a child.

He had built up a comfortable fug of cigarette smoke and heat from the electric fire and he poured himself another mug of tea before settling down with the second file, which was older and fatter than Foxie's. Elsie Morgan, now Foxie's wife's story could only be described as tragic and she had been dealt tough breaks all her life. Her mother had been a prostitute on the docks at Cardiff and her father had never been part of her life. She had been exposed to unpleasantness on all sides from an early age. Her mother Gloria had been brought up in poverty in a slum dwelling which was overcrowded and where tuberculosis was endemic. Elsie had been born in 1922 into a family where most of the male members had died in the Great War. By the time she was six her grandfather had died of consumption and her mother was surviving by being a prostitute to the various seamen who moored up and unloaded at the docks. Ben could only imagine what sort of life this was for Elsie, who later told him of a life of being locked in the toilet whilst her mother entertained her customers. She realised eventually that this was her mother's way of keeping her out of harm's way but at the time she felt she was being punished for something and she didn't know what. By the age of eight Elsie could see that her mother was in failing health and she was having to resort to a rougher trade for less and less money. Gloria and Elsie were taken into the workhouse in 1932 where her mother subsequently died. Elsie, now an orphan, had been moved to a large children's home run by nuns. The rules were strict and Elsie went more and more into herself, keeping her head down to ensure she didn't suffer the wrath of the nuns. Love was almost non-existent and Elsie later told Ben that if it hadn't been for one particular nun called Sister Margarita she thought that she might just have curled up and died. Sister Margarita used to give her a hug and said to her over and over again 'penny for your thoughts' in an attempt to get her to talk. Finally, Elsie started to respond but concentrated her efforts on learning about domestic work, sewing and laundry work. She learnt about money and could read a little but her education remained at a very basic level. At fourteen she was moved to be a residential domestic worker at a large country estate on the fringes of Cardiff. She was alone again and didn't know what would happen to her next. What happened was to dictate the rest of her life.

Within six months Elsie was pregnant and the lady of the house took control. She was sure that her only son was the father of the child and in order to avoid any scandal she persuaded Elsie to accept one hundred pounds to say nothing and she even took her to a post office and put the money in a post office book in Elsie's name. To Elsie such a sum was a fortune and she sewed the savings book into a secret pocket in her vest for safety. There was a further twist in the story when the master of the family also gave her fifty pounds, unbeknown to his wife, as he had also been 'mucking me about', as Elsie told Ben the tale later. Elsie was rapidly moved out to a Catholic mother and baby home, where she remained once again with generally uncaring nuns before going into labour and being rushed to hospital. Elsie was alone and terrified and then worn out by a thirty-hour labour, but she produced a beautiful little girl who she promptly called Penny. Elsie later explained to Ben that she had been determined to call the baby Penny because of what Sister Margarita had said to her so many times: 'penny for your thoughts'. Elsie had sobbed as she explained to him later about her thoughts at the time. 'She was mine all mine and was in my thoughts all day and night. Then they took her away and placed her for adoption.'

Elsie was distraught and fell to pieces, so much so the authorities committed her to the same institution as Foxie in Cardiff. In order to do so they used the grounds of her being a moral imbecile, which was a classification which had been introduced into legislation in 1913. That category was removed from the legislation over fifty years later in the more enlightened 1959 Mental Health Act. Exactly as on Foxie's file the reporting was just about her annual medicals and a record of illness and such like. She was described as a quiet self-contained girl who caused no problems and after a couple of years her status was changed to that of a voluntary patient. This was what Elsie had been waiting for and she began to hatch a plan for her future and it was only made possible by the post office book she still kept hidden away. However, there was still one more twist in the tale, Elsie got pregnant again and the soldier she had secretly been seeing didn't want to know. Now she was in real danger of being recommitted so a plan B had to come into operation. She approached Foxie and offered him the chance of getting out of the institution. She had learnt that if they both managed to get out and then got married the law did not allow them to be readmitted unless they committed further offences. This was a unique opportunity for Foxie, who could see no other way of getting out in the foreseeable future. She told him of the pregnancy and Foxie had seemed delighted at the idea of a ready-made family. The plan was made and Elsie walked out the following week with just her few clothes and belongings, including the essential secret savings book.

Two days later Foxie slipped away during the night and managed to get a couple of lifts before meeting up with Elsie in Chepstow the following day as arranged. They were in London within hours and went straight from the railway station to the local registry office and arranged for an urgent wedding. They lay low for the three weeks before the ceremony in a series of cheap bed and breakfasts, terrified that they would be caught. The time spent waiting was helpful in setting the 'rules of engagement' and Elsie emerged as the leader and Foxie as the faithful follower. It all went off without a hitch with a passing shopper and a road sweeper hauled into the registry office to act as witnesses. They were married and over twenty years later remained married and about to move into a brand-new three-bedroom house in Highfield. It must have seemed like winning the pools to the Farthings.

Ben had read enough for one day and had plenty to think about so headed off to Joe's for a well-deserved coffee and doughnut. Ben couldn't spend long at Joe's as it was a Tuesday and he was under strict instructions from Sandy to be home on time. Tuesday was Sandy's night school dress making class and she usually went out for a drink with friends from the class afterwards. So Ben was in charge of the boys for the evening and they had it worked out well in advance. First children television, then a swift trip in the car to the local fish and chip shop for sausage and chips and a large bottle of lemonade. This was consumed on their laps in front of the television with the boys staying up thirty minutes after their bedtime to watch 'Z Cars'. They then went to bed with minimum resistance whilst Ben cleared up the evidence before Sandy returned home. She was well aware of what went on but sensibly made no comment. The Newman home was always a nice place to be on a Tuesday.

On this particular occasion once he had cleared up he treated himself to a beer from the fridge and settled down to watch a bit more television. However, he found his mind wandering back to the Farthings and he switched off the television and went to his car parked as usual right outside his front door and recovered the remaining files. By the time

Sandy came home the dining table was liberally covered by papers, which Ben was trying to put together in a chronological order.

It had quickly become clear that the Farthings had lived a nomadic lifestyle never staying more than a few months in any one place. When Elsie gave birth for the second time she had twins, a boy and a girl, and they had taken up residence in a chalet near Bournemouth which was let as a holiday home during the summer. The hospital had alerted the local health visitor of the birth and the family history came to light and the Farthings acquired the label of 'a problem family' which had attracted attention from a whole series of the authorities ever since as they regularly moved around. Ben was therefore to be just the latest of a long list of workers who had tried to work with the Farthings who carried on doing their own thing in their own way. If the relationship between them and the authorities became too heavy they simply moved on, only to come to the attention of authority workers elsewhere. It appeared that the paperwork usually took months to catch up and Ben was in a unique position having their history arrive before they did. The twins were called Penny, the same as Elsie's earlier child, and Ernest, and were very slow developers. By the time they were four they had both been assessed to be of subnormal intelligence and formally classified as uneducable.

Therefore they could not be accepted into the normal education system and were referred to the mental health service for admission into a junior training centre. When they moved on it was never very long before the relevant local authority caught up with them and places found for day care for the twins. Their development was erratic to say the least, with Ernest growing tall and wide and becoming a gentle giant, far outgrowing Foxie. Unfortunately, he never learnt to speak properly and attempted to communicate in a heavy guttural sounding voice that was at times almost impossible to understand. Other children avoided him as he appeared to be frightening and dangerous when in reality he was a pussy cat. Penny was also large but in a fat and extremely flabby way. She talked clearly but tended to be in a world of her own, which revolved around her massive doll collection and eating, which she did at every opportunity. The family had moved to the Exworth area from somewhere up north just before the twins reached their sixteenth birthday. They were offered places at an adult training centre but the offer had been declined. Foxie worked as a totter but whilst most rag and bone men had a horse to help them with their work, Foxie had Ernest, who spent his days pulling a hand cart which Foxie managed to fill with scrap most days. They became a familiar sight on the road to Highfield most days as they carried their spoils to Scadding's scrapyard to be sold. Penny meanwhile played with her dolls and ate. By her late teens she was huge, really grotesque and never seemed to leave her home where her mother waited on her hand and foot. She had then become aware of the new phenomenon of the Barbie doll and she abandoned all her other dolls to fixate on Barbie. She collected them avidly and identified with them so strongly that she was constantly trying to be like a Barbie doll herself.

She spent hours making herself up with cheap Woolworths makeup. She had acquired a long blond wig which she wore from morning to night and dressed in layers of gaudy clothes that would have been better used in a children's dressing up box. She became an eighteen-stone weird person who would have been funny if she had not been so sad. Elsie Farthing helped to support the family by doing office cleaning in the evenings in a couple of commercial premises on the far side of the Cuttings. Ernest and Foxie took on the responsibility of looking after the ever-demanding Penny whilst Elsie worked. In this way the Farthing family had struggled on until they were finally evicted from their basement flat and rehoused to their three-bedroom house in Highfield. Now they were on their way to Ben's domain, which seemed like an interesting challenge, but he hadn't realised how much of a challenge it would prove.

The day of the move was about as bad as it gets. The temperature was well below freezing, which made the lack of proper roads an inconvenience, but the small, oddly constructed group could still make slow progress over the frozen and rutted mud. There was a heavy fall of sleet that quickly soaked everything, including Ben's Cortina, which he was sat in at the entrance to the estate awaiting the anticipated arrival of the Farthings. It seemed like hours before he could see any movement on the road below but he kept the engine running and the heater on so he was much better set up than the pathetic group who very slowly came past him. It was headed by a giant young man pulling a fully loaded hand cart. It was full to overflowing and topped off by a double mattress with a very fat lady who seemed to be dressed from head to toe in highly coloured clothes of mixed origin. Immediately behind was an older lady carrying a homemade cage of about six hens which had little in the way of feathers and looked more dead than alive. To the rear came a diminutive man pushing an old delivery bike loaded with all sorts of things tied on to it with string. Ben's heart went out to them and he didn't know whether to laugh or break out into spontaneous applause, but as they had got this far against all odds he decided to let them go the last few hundred yards and drove off to get them all a meal of fish and chips from the chippie in the Cuttings. He stopped at home on the way and made a flask of hot tea, then went on to the chip shop and back to Highfield as quickly as possible. The Farthings were in their new home by the time Ben arrived and most of their belongings were piled in a heap in the living room. He introduced himself as the resettlement officer and the Farthings seemed unsurprised by a visit from the authorities. However, they were surprised when he produced the food and drink and an impromptu picnic took place with considerable enthusiasm on the living room floor.

Meanwhile, Ben took the opportunity to run his eyes over their belongings and as he had anticipated they had very inadequate resources. It was clear that the urgent priority was beds as they had none, just three very grubby mattresses, which were now soaking wet from their journey. They also had no cooker and were therefore dependent upon the fire grate for cooking and hot water. Once they had finished eating Foxie very efficiently got a fire going using wood and coal, which was in the basket of his shop bike. They all steamed off for a while whilst Elsie and Foxie talked with obvious delight about their new home. A bathroom with indoor toilet seemed to be beyond their wildest dreams and three bedrooms an unheard of luxury. Ernest grunted his approval at regular intervals but Penny's only contribution was to suddenly announce that she was an old bike and to giggle hysterically. It was clear to Ben that he was the only one to be aware of the unfortunate connotation of the remark but he could see that her name being Penny Farthing meant she was factually correct and held his council. After walking around the house together and showing them how things worked he left them to it, agreeing to come back the following day to help them get settled in.

The following day Ben made a phone call to the Welfare Services Department, which he knew had a furniture store of second-hand furniture which had been started in war time for people who had to be rehoused when they were bombed out. Now some twenty years later it was largely defunct as National Assistance was now able to help in exceptional circumstances. After going round the houses several times he was finally put on to an admin officer who had been involved in the store, and what was even better he still had the key to the basement where the furniture was stored. He was very honest about it and said no one had been down there for years and it was probably all rubbish, but if Ben wanted to take a chance he was game. Ben made the appointment for that afternoon. A reluctant Ernest was left to supervise Penny and it was quite clear that he would have much preferred to be out between the shafts of his hand cart rather than pandering to the needs of his spoilt sister. Elsie wisely insisted in accompanying Ben and Foxie on the furniture-seeking trip as she was well aware of Foxie's attraction to rubbish and she wanted to ensure that their new home was kept special. Ben had made them aware that the second-hand furniture store was no longer functioning and that it might be a wasted trip.

The approach to the store was not encouraging and involved going into a dark and dingy basement in the bowels of city hall. The door creaked open with an ominous screech and the huge room they entered was full to the gunnels with piled up brown furniture, over-stuffed three-piece suites and bed frames stacked in front of a mound of mattresses covered in a huge blue plastic tarpaulin. Foxie was in heaven, Elsie seemed quietly pleased and Ben very surprised. Clearly much of the stuff had been saved from council places which had closed down, and though not modern everything was still very serviceable. Ben and Elsie had to work hard to control Foxie, who would clearly have liked to get his hands on the lot, but after much discussion they collected together a healthy pile of things to grace their home. Firstly they sorted out three bed frames, two doubles for themselves and for Penny and a single for Ernest. Elsie pointed out that it was the first time that Ernest had had anything more than a mattress on the floor or at times just two chairs pushed together. The mattresses were quickly chosen and were surprisingly clean and dry. Two wardrobes, three chests of drawers, a dining room table and four chairs and a patterned three-piece suite were all added to the pile that was stacked in the corridor just outside the basement door. Everyone including the council officer seemed well pleased and arrangements were made for the furniture to be collected over the next few days. Foxie and Ernest were going to be busy.

Ben left it about a week to give the Farthings the chance to settle in. Meanwhile he had spoken to the National Assistance Office to enquire about a special one-off payment for the family to help them get established. At first he was met with a blank refusal but didn't back down and insisted on speaking with a manager. After a lot of argument it became clear to the person on the end of the phone that Ben was determined and was not going to go away, and he was put through to a manager. This was a whole different ball game and the guy listened patiently as he explained about the Farthings, their background, how they made a living and then played his ace card, pointing out that they claimed no benefits of any sort. A one-off payment of fifty pounds was agreed on the requirement that Ben supervised the spending of the money. This he readily agreed to do.

When he made a follow-up visit he was amazed what the family had achieved. Every room was furnished and looked spotless and every window sill, mantlepiece and flat surface was adorned with all sorts of china ornaments, patterned crockery and plaster figures. On closer inspection it was immediately apparent that they were all broken or chipped in some way and were obviously Foxie's gleanings from his totting over the years. Nevertheless, the overall effect, enhanced as it was by a good wood fire in the grate, was most effective and Elsie delighted in showing him over the house and he was impressed how good the old furniture looked. As he had anticipated, Penny's room was the most comfortable and Penny, dressed in shocking pink baby doll pyjamas, sat in the middle of her bed playing with her dolls. Her only contribution to the conversation was yet another obviously well-used statement, 'Four Farthings make a good Penny and that's me,' this was followed by a silly high-pitched laugh and she returned to her dolls. Foxie and Ernest were out working and Ben was able to explain to Elsie about the grant and asked her what were her most pressing needs. After careful thought she said she was still having to cook on the fire and she would love a proper cooker. If that wasn't possible she would like some lino for the living room floor. Ben said he would see what he could sort out and after a trip to the local auction house the following week a tidy electric cooker and a good size piece of lino were purchased and arrangements made for the hand cart to be put to good use. Elsie was over the moon and insisted on cooking a sponge cake for him, which he shared out in the office, declared good and the leftovers going home with Alice to be enjoyed on another day.

Ben's visits tailed off as the Farthings went about their lives as before, except there was no more moving on. Foxie and Ernest were often spotted by Ben going about their business and he usually tried to have a brief word. It was clear that the pickings on the estate were good for Foxie with building work going on for months all over the estate. Oddments of cable, scrap metal and anything else left lying around were fair game to Foxie and the builders soon learnt to lock up anything they didn't want to disappear. As the months went on Foxie and Ernest had to go further afield in search of scrap and he saw them infrequently and usually from a distance. He did notice that Foxie looked unwell but put it down to the extra miles he had to travel each day. The Farthings had proved that they were survivors and he left them to contact him if they needed help.

Dave and Ben spent the rest of the week visiting clients who Ben knew would be of interest to Dave and they enjoyed sharing experiences of their work. Ben was particularly interested when Dave spoke of the work they were doing at St Margaret's and what he knew about how the hospital had changed over the past twenty years. Dave was enthusiastic and passionate about ways in which the quality of life for the patients was slowly improving. He had made an effort to learn what it had been like in the past by taking every opportunity to ask questions of those older nurses he worked with who had been there throughout the war and since. He said from what he had learnt it was clear that the life of an inpatient in even the recent past was pure hell. The asylums had been a dumping ground for people who were eccentric, mentally ill or just incapable and once in few people ever left. The hospital conditions were generally appalling with dormitory after dormitory of beds so close that you could walk from bed to bed without stepping on the floor. Privacy was non-existent, nobody had personal clothing or toiletries and it was a case of survival of the strongest. There were no organised therapies and the primary activities for most of the patients were endlessly wandering the corridors and masturbation. Improved drug treatments and particularly the introduction of phenothiazines in the early fifties brought about hope for the first time for many long-term patients with schizophrenia. Attitudes amongst staff in psychiatric hospitals had to change as the whole ethos moved from being an asylum where people were contained to a place where people were treated with the intention of returning them back into the community. Not all staff welcomed the change as they had become used to treating the patients without any regard for them as individuals.

There were many tales about the changes required but one story that Dave had heard about really hit home with Ben when he was told about it. It involved a patient called Jimmy who had spent over twenty years on a back ward at the local hospital. He suffered with catatonic schizophrenia which meant he had no voluntary movement and was mute. With the introduction of the new drugs there was a remarkable almost instant change in his condition and he spoke for the first time in over twenty years. This apparent miracle was saddened by what he chose to say first. 'The charge nurse Bill Evans eats my porridge every morning instead of giving it to me.' Just imagine what it must have been like for Jimmy when this happened to him every day and he had no means of protesting. It is to be hoped that Bill Evans got the sack at the very least but given the body in control at the time it probably passed with a verbal warning if that.

Times had changed and people like Dave were now the patient's helpers. His enthusiasm for his job really delighted Ben and he encouraged him to talk about his job and the current life within St Margaret's. It quickly became clear that Dave was particularly impressed with the head consultant psychiatrist Professor Michael MacFarlane, who had been in post now for some ten years and spent all his time and energy trying to improve life for the mentally ill.

Ben had met him several times when out on admissions from the community but these were emergency situations and had to be assessed and acted upon quickly and efficiently so there had been no time for any informal chat. However, Ben had noted that considering his rather exalted status he was very down to earth and always considerate to the client and their family.

However, Ben's first meeting with the professor had been to say the least unfortunate. He had been forced to give a rather difficult client a lift to the day hospital when his hospital transport had failed to turn up. The client was in a fairly disturbed state and Ben had been distracted whilst parking in the crowded hospital car park. As he pulled up he was aware that his car had made contact with a parked car to his left. Of course it had to be a new top of the range Mercedes which was now sporting a six-inch scratch on its shiny rear bumper. Ben delivered the client and then reported the incident to the receptionist. Her horrified look struck doom to his heart as she told him it was the professor's car which he had had for less than a week. He had no choice but to bite the bullet and asked to speak to him. The phone conversation was short and to the point and he was told to stay where he was. A rather red-faced professor appeared as if by magic and they went outside together to view the damage. The professor rubbed his hand lovingly over the damaged surface and asked what Ben was doing parking there. Ben explained who he was and about his mission and waited for the worst to happen. In fact all the professor had said was, 'I am busy right now so I will get back to you.'

He never did and had never mentioned it since when their paths had crossed. Ben had assumed that he had seen the state of his old Cortina and had realised that money was short. 'That's just like the man,' was Dave's reaction, 'he's not one to hold a grudge and understands an honest mistake.' Dave went on at length. 'He is passionate about the future of the long-term patients he inherited when he took up post and admits quite openly that there was a lot wrong with the way they were treated. He had to fight for resources, change practices and get the existing staff to modify their attitudes. The revolutionary 1959 Mental Health Act helped by being a catalyst for change by stressing the need to move the focus of care from the hospital to the community.'

Dave went on to share with Ben the details of a treatment programme set up by the professor that he had been involved with for about two years. 'The main problem for enabling long-term patients to return to the community wasn't their mental health conditions, which were largely under control, but that they were all without exception institutionalised.'

The professor and his staff had selected a group of twenty patients and had moved them into a small unit away from the main hospital building and over a period of several months had begun to help them learn the skills to survive in the community. They had a selected group of staff, including Dave, who worked alongside the group members preparing their own meals, doing their own cleaning and their own washing and ironing. They were each provided with their own individual bedroom complete with storage for their clothes and belongings. As time went on a small workshop was set up and they were encouraged to 'go to work' five days a week and they earned money for the work they did. The work was simple repetitive tasks like putting ballpoint pens together, making carrier bags or packing hospital dressings, but they had to compete on the open market as it was all sub-contract work.

The money they earned allowed them to make a contribution towards their food and board and they were left with enough to spend on personal wants and for many to start a savings account. A regular meeting of the group took place each Friday evening and became quite lively at times when widely diverse issues were open for discussion. This needed a bit of control from staff from time to time and another difficult area was the taking of prescribed medication. Obviously if they left the hospital they would have to be able to cope with this, but meanwhile the nearest this could be dealt with responsibly was to leave individuals to ask for their medication just before meal times. This often required reminding by staff but was one of the useful ways of deciding who was ready to move on. There remained just eight of the original group of twenty still residing in the hospital and the professor was currently trying to arrange two small hostels in the community where two groups of four could live as minimal support groups.

Ben let Dave come to a natural stop and told him he already knew a bit about the project as two of the recipients, Bert Abrahams and Victor Smith, were now living in Highfield and he was keeping a friendly eye on them. Dave was really interested and full of questions about how they were getting on so Ben told him that they could try to visit so he could see for himself. Dave readily agreed for him to try and arrange an evening visit later in the week when they should be home from work. Both Bert and Victor had left the hospital after almost twenty years of 'incarceration' and set up home together in a two-bedroom maisonette in Highfield eighteen months before and Ben had worked with them ever since.

They both worked at Remploy, a special workshop set up by the government for disabled people many of them war veterans. Ben had helped in negotiating their trial placements although there had been some resistance from the workshop management as all the other workers were physically rather than mentally disabled. He was able to stress that they were fully mobile, which could be useful in a workshop of physically handicapped workers and so it had proved. Bert had even been promoted to a foreman, which was evidence that things were going well. Ben rang the manager and asked to speak to one of them and Bert came to the phone. He seemed delighted about having a visit from Dave, who was clearly seen as an old friend and a date was made for Thursday evening at 7 pm.

Ben decided to use the earlier part of Thursday evening to introduce Dave to two very special friends where he knew they would be sure of a warm welcome.

Chapter 7

The Plans of Mice and Men

Wednesday was every bit as wintry as the day before, except there was also a dusting of snow which had drifted a bit during the night. However, this was not enough to affect the driving conditions or Ben's mood and once again he broke into spontaneous song all the way before stopping to deliver a couple of carrots to Boxer Mark Two, who was already at the gate in anticipation on him stopping by.

The old horse chewed the carrots up in a matter of seconds and then began to push his nose into Ben's pockets in the hope of further goodies. As it happened he was in luck and Ben pulled out the remains of a packet of polo mints, which were well received by the horse. Ben sat back in the car to complete his journey with good mood intact and his head full of plans for the day ahead. The rain was coming down in torrents as he pulled into the car park, and head down he rushed for the door. Unusually it was firmly locked and he briefly wondered where Alice was as she always seemed to manage to get in before him. Then he remembered she was on 'home leave' for the week and that he was committed to fitting in a visit to her at some point today. The locked door was not a real problem but did involve a trip back to the car where he always kept a spare set of keys in the glove box. As he returned from the car he glanced into the bike shed and was about to enter the office when he noticed something very white sticking out of the pile of black rubbish sacks stacked in the rear of the shed awaiting collection. He froze in horror as he moved back to the shed and the something white that had caught his eye was confirmed as a pair of pale white legs, complete with traditional school black shoes. He feared the worst as he reached forward and lifted off a couple of the bags and exposed Katie Andrews curled up and apparently asleep.

He gently shook her awake. He felt her hands and she was freezing cold and her little face looked pinched and drawn. Large tears started to flow down her cheeks and Ben just picked her up and held her to him. Her whole body jerked in convulsive sobs and it was impossible to know if it was from cold, fear or relief. He carried her quickly into the office when he recognised the now familiar sound of Dave arriving on the incongruous little pink Vespa that he had borrowed from one of the other nurses as transport whilst on his placement at Highfield. Under any other circumstance Ben would have been unable to resist making a rude comment but on this occasion he simply signalled Dave to follow him in and ducked in through the office front door.

The office was almost as chilly as outside because Alice was not there to turn up the heating. He headed straight for the kitchen and carefully put Katie down in the big old armchair which would normally have been occupied by Alice. He then went straight over to the cooker and turned on all the rings and the oven at full blast to get instant heat into the room. He knelt before Katie and rubbed her arms and legs back into life and her tears were reduced to intermittent sniffs as she got herself back under control. A phone rang in persistent demand from the front office and he delayed answering it for several moments but it didn't stop.

'Won't be long, love,' he said and smiled down at her as he clambered to his feet and headed to the phone. She managed a tiny smile in reply and Ben felt a lump come up in his throat at her sheer guts. He passed Dave in the corridor and briefly told him what was happening and pushed him gently in the direction of the kitchen. The message on the phone was simple and direct. Phil would not be in as she had a migraine. Ben felt less than sympathetic as he knew it was her turn to cover the north of the county for mental health emergencies and that made it three times in the past few months that he had had to cover for her at the last moment. His plans for visiting clients with Dave for the rest of the day seemed doomed.

Meanwhile, Dave had worked his magic on Katie and she was up on her feet alongside him preparing three mugs of tea. Ben adjusted the cooker and switched on the proper heating before sitting down at the kitchen table and waited for Katie to explain. She kept her back firmly towards him as she said in a wobbly voice, 'Our mum's worse. You'll have to come.'

He responded immediately, reassuring her that he would visit within the hour and then waited to hear the rest. The story tumbled out in no particular order and Katie's desperation to get it all across was only too apparent. Her dad had returned the previous evening and the effect on her mum had been immediate. Within minutes she was putting his favourite meal of eggs, bacon and chips in front of him on the dining table whilst she started to tidy around properly for the first time in ages. Katie had gone on to bed without being told, happy to see her parents together and the other kids had gone about their business just like they always did. Katie had been woken up by an almighty row going on downstairs and had crept out on to the landing as her parents screamed dreadful things at each other. There was the sound of blows and her mother's screeches turned to wails. Her father burst from the living room and Katie only just got back under the bed clothes as he came rushing up the stairs. She had heard him throwing things into a bag before pounding back down the stairs and straight out of the front door. Her mother had spent a long time at the door shouting obscenities after him and at the neighbours, who by this time were watching the free show from around their bedroom curtains. As an encore her mum had then spent ages throwing his remaining possessions out of the bedroom window to litter the front garden like some bizarre jumble sale. For the rest of the night Mrs Andrews could be heard wandering around and around in the house, shouting and apparently breaking anything that came to hand. Katie had curled up in a ball and quietly wept, too afraid to confront her mum in her present state. The house finally went quiet well after twelve and Katie fell into a troubled sleep. She awoke up very early and crept downstairs and attempted to clear up the wreckage as best she could. Her brother and sister simply got themselves some toast and dripping and set off for school as usual, leaving Katie to see to her mum. She made a cup of tea and took it upstairs to her mum but simply could not wake her up. Katie was terrified by this time and had run straight around to tell Ben only to find the office locked and unoccupied. She settled down in the only shelter available amongst the rubbish sacks in the bike shed and had fallen asleep with exhaustion.

By this time all sorts of panic bells were going off in Ben's head and he said, 'Look after Dave for me will you, Katie? I am sure he would like another cup of tea. I'll just pop round and see your mum, won't be long.'

He filled Dave in on the way down the corridor and hurried off to his car. Within a matter of moments he was pulling up outside the house and picking his way through the debris that littered the front garden. He was relieved to see that Katie in her rush had left the front door wide open and he took the stairs two at a time before hesitating for a moment outside the closed bedroom door. He knocked gently, and taking a deep breath went in. There was a troubled heap of bedclothes on the bed and the rest of the room was chaos. The top of Ruth's head could be identified amongst the tangled bedclothes and he spoke her name in a quiet voice in an attempt not to frighten her. There was no sign of movement and he continued to talk to her as he cleared the clothes from around her face. She was pale and damp but the sound of her breathing was quite obvious as Ben let out a sigh of relief. She was alive. He shook her gently and then with greater force and she responded with a grunt. He persisted and her eyes slowly opened as she dragged herself back from unconsciousness. Ben helped her to sit up in bed and knelt beside her and put his arm around her shoulders. She looked pathetic, years older, and there were vivid red wheals on her face and heavy black bruising on her arms. Her body sagged within the stained and crumpled underclothes that she had not bothered to remove from the night before. However, despite all the physical signs for concern there was one very big change in her that caused Ben to feel a lot more positive about Ruth and her family. Her lethargy had disappeared to be replaced by deep anger. She began to pound the bedclothes with her fists and to string together an impressive list of swear words to describe her husband. Ben got back on his feet and took a step back as Ruth let rip. She was angry beyond angry and swung herself up on her feet, pushed past Ben and thrust her bruised arms into the sleeves of a dressing gown that she recovered from behind her bedroom door. She sat back on the bed and began to brush her hair with unnecessary force. 'That bastard came back, you know,' and off she went on a vivid description of what had taken place.

He had suddenly appeared at the front door at his usual time for finishing work at the shoe factory. They had both fallen into their old routines without comment. He had washed at the sink, disregarding the piles of dirty crocks which had accumulated there since his departure and had sat down at the table, pulling his paper from his jacket pocket.

As he sat and read and smoked his pipe Ruth had hurried to prepare a meal for him. He had received it and eaten it in silence and Ruth had been too nervous to break the spell. 'I fed the bugger, that's what gets me, not a penny piece from him for weeks and I fed the bugger then he announces that he has only come back for his things!' Ruth spat out the words with real venom. She went on to describe the events that followed with great waves of emotion that caused her to shake, shout, cry and curse in quick succession. However, Ben became more relaxed with each new reaction as he felt sure that she was at no immediate risk as her depression had tumbled over into aggression and all the aggression was directed towards her husband and 'his cheap blonde whore', not on herself.

Ben left a somewhat calmer Ruth making a token effort to sort out the kitchen whilst he went to reassure Katie and to get her off to school. God, he thought, Mr Andrews and his new woman had better keep their heads down as there is nothing like a woman scorned to create mayhem. Needless to say, Dave and Katie were already firm friends and were immersed in some game when he arrived back at the office. The giggles and hoots from Katie seemed a million miles away from the terrified child of barely an hour before. She simply nodded her acceptance when Ben told her that mum was okay and then insisted that it should be Dave who returned her to school. They went off hand in hand looking an odd couple but chatting nineteen to the dozen. Ben stood in the doorway and watched them go and it was clear that Katie was insisting that they had to avoid walking on any cracks in the pavement. This was easy for her with her short legs but Dave at six foot four was struggling to conform. He was up on his toes and had all the appearances of a demented ballet dancer. Ben smiled to himself as he remembered walking home from school himself doing the crack avoidance game. He then returned to his office and rang Mr Hamilton, the head of the local junior school to update him on the Katie situation. Mr Hamilton as usual was very receptive and grateful to be updated. 'Katie is a super kid, bright and caring. Let me know if we can be of any help.'

Ben noted his words and the germ of an idea formed in his mind. But that was for later, he still had Alice to visit. He sat at his desk and made a few notes of the morning's happenings to use as the basis for a further more detailed report that he would dictate to Mrs Freeman later. He felt his mood begin to sink and the usual sense of liverishness began to creep over him. He would normally head for Joe's back room, the fire and a strong cup of coffee as his tried and tested method of dealing with such feelings but circumstances didn't allow. He could hear Mrs Freeman at her desk next door and the steady clatter of her typewriter slowly eased his tension and he headed for the kitchen to make a cuppa for himself and Mrs Freeman. They would all be more than pleased to see Alice back after the weekend. Ben felt guilty that he had not yet visited Alice as he had promised and whilst they shared their drinks he filled Mrs Freeman in on the happenings of the morning. He explained that he was having to cover for Phil, but as he really had to make a quick visit on Alice would she mind holding the fort? As always she reacted calmly, her only concern being that he would be back in time for her to go off at midday. She had to get her husband's lunch and as always her priority was that her husband should not be put out and she had no regard for herself. Ben gave her a quick hug of thanks, which surprised them both, and he left in a rush of embarrassment.

Alice wasn't at her door waiting for him as he had anticipated she would be and she didn't reply when he rang the bell. For the third time that day Ben feared the worst but rang the bell again for several seconds, again with no reply. He bent down to look through the letter box and was faced with the vision of Alice coming along the hall adjusting her knickers and then the numerous layers on top. He had caught her in the loo. She opened the door totally unconcerned and with all the appearances of being back to her 'normal self'. Ben was so relieved that he had to control himself from throwing his arms around her. Dangerous stuff this euphoria, if he didn't watch it he could find himself in all sorts of bother. Alice was super, quite her old self and quickly into a long diatribe about her bowels, but fortunately without specimens on this occasion. He sat back and let her get on with it, thinking to himself that the sooner she was back at the office the better. As the conversation eased he tried tentatively to explain about Dave and why he was in the office, but Alice was having none of it so he didn't press the point. She appeared to be enjoying her break and was planning a bus trip into town the next day to start her Christmas shopping. Ben had noticed her taking more than a passing interest in his feet recently; more socks for Christmas.

After the inevitable cup of tea and unavoidable refill plus a rather burned fairy cake he managed to slip away, having wrapped the cake in his hankie behind Alice's back to be disposed of later. He headed off to the office as fast as he could, anxious to catch up with Dave to fill him in on the day's developments but also desperate to use the loo from the number of teas he had drunk that morning.

Chapter 8

Happy Landings

As he arrived back in the office he was greeted by the sound of girlish laughter from the general office and carefully looked around the door. He took a double take for there was Mrs Freeman not sat as her desk as usual but actually sat on her desk swinging her legs unconsciously. Her back was towards the door and she was in deep conversation with Dave. Three things struck him in quick succession, he had never heard Mrs Freeman giggle before, he had never realised that she had great legs and Dave must be some sort of miracle worker. He quietly backed off and came in again making enough noise to ensure he was heard. By the time he popped his head around the office door a somewhat flustered Mrs Freeman was sat at her desk and things appeared back to normal. She quickly reported that there had been no emergency calls, grabbed her coat and handbag and announced that she was off to get her husband Steve's lunch. After she had left Dave said, 'Vivian has sure got it tough but her husband is a lucky man, as she is devoted to him.' Ben nodded his agreement and went off to use the toilet. He thought to himself how strange it was that Dave called her Vivian after just a couple of days whilst he still called her Mrs Freeman after as many years. Still, why change what works for them was his considered conclusion.

Ben went back into the office and changed the subject by asking Dave how he had got on taking Katie to school. He reported that she had been a joy but had insisted that he should take her right into her classroom. Their appearance in the middle of a maths lesson caused quite a reaction and Katie as ever assumed control and announced with thanks that he could go now. He was met in the corridor by the head, Mr Hamilton, who had been very receptive and had given Dave a bit of a tour of the school which left Dave impressed by its colourful walls and general sense of calm. 'Not a bit like the smelly and dilapidated old building that was my school back in Jamaica. I left when I was twelve.' They sat on each side of Ben's desk and Ben explained that their planned visits for the rest of the day had to go by the board because he had to cover the emergency standby duties that should have been done by Phil.

This reminded him that he hadn't advised the necessary authorities of the change of duty officer for the overnight period. He quickly rang the headquarters switch board, the central police station switch board and ambulance control, which were the contact points for the emergency service and gave them the change of duty officer and his telephone number. He would normally have used the time spent in the office to catch up on administration and report writing but made the easy decision to spend the time chatting to Dave about their respective roles. Dave seemed completely content to stay in the office and chat but said that he had an errand to run first and was soon beetling out of the car park on his pink transport. Ben used the time to make a list of possible visits for the next day. He tried to select a variety of situations where people were coping with real problems with only minimal support from the welfare services.

There was Frank and Rosie Sullivan, a couple living on the top floor of one of the twelve-storey blocks of high-rise flats which were a popular solution for planners at the time. He added Leslie's name to the list, who was a multi-handicapped teenager who lived with his parents and was mainly cared for by his mother. He thought that a brief visit to Ruth Andrews would be OK and would give Dave the chance to fill out the picture of Katie and her mum. Then after careful consideration added Freda Davies to the list, who was an elderly lady with a long history of repeated admissions. With the planned evening visit to Bert and Victor it seemed like a full and interesting day's work and all the visits were ones he would have made in the near future as part of his normal support work. He quickly gathered together the files for Dave to read just as he heard the buzz of 'the pink peril' returning. The special scent of fish and chips came in with Dave and they sat down each side of Ben's desk, paper packages in front of them and enjoyed Dave's treat all washed down by a large bottle of cola.

Ben pointed to the small pile of files he had collected together and told Dave that was his homework ready for the following day. They chatted amicably as they ate and Ben introduced the subject of the friends they would be visiting at tea time tomorrow. 'The two Marys are quite something and have meant a lot to me since I came here to work right from day one.' He explained how Mary Harris, the local health visitor had called in to see him in on his first day in post when he was feeling so depressed in his smelly old builder's shed. She had summed up just how wretched he felt in a flash and immediately invited him to come to tea at the prefab that she shared with Mary Winstone, who everyone called Jessie for some reason or other. He had gone to tea the next day and very many days since and considered Mary and Jessie to be very dear friends.

'The whole estate of prefabs that they live on is really quite unique and has retained a special something that is difficult to precisely define.' He went on to explain that the prefabs were set out in a geometric grid pattern consisting of a pair of long straight roads with a central island of grass running between them. The roads were both for a single lane of one-way traffic, one for going into the estate then at the far end turning around in a semicircle to exit the estate back at the beginning. The main roads were lined with prefabs and at regular intervals, going off to the left and right, were cul-de-sacs each consisting of eight prefabs. At approximately eight prefabs to an acre the fifty-acre site provided well over three hundred homes each set in its own neat rectangle of garden. The estate had been built in a hurry at the end of the Second World War as a way of providing emergency housing mainly for survivors of the bombing of the Cuttings. This was the area of back-to-back housing which had been home for generations of dockers who spent their working life loading and unloading the steady stream of barges that serviced the warehouses that lined the cut. This man-made waterway divided the city and had contributed greatly to its prosperity for well over a century. With the onset of war, three of the largest warehouses had been commandeered and converted into a factory for the production of aircraft engines. As a direct consequence the area had become a prime target for Hitler's bombers. The factory itself had seemed to have a charmed life but the surrounding houses had suffered heavily as a result of the enemy's determination to have mastery of the skies.

Ben could see he had Dave hooked and at least partially for effect paused to finish the last of the Coke, clear up the fish and chip papers and open the window for a while. He sat back down and was just about to carry on when the phone rang. It was a reply to his job advert for a social work assistant, which he remembered was in that night's paper and for a further two nights. Someone is keen, he thought, but fortunately he had done his preparation with Pete Evans, the personnel officer at headquarters and had the file to hand. The conversation went back and forth and Ben ended it by taking the applicant's details down in the file ready for Mrs Freeman to send them an application form, having pointed out that the closing date was in a fortnight.

Dave had started on the files but quickly put them down and sat back to hear more of the prefabs. Ben went on to fill in the background of the development. He explained that the prefabs had been built on the northern quarter of a wartime airfield that had been laid on flat scrubland adjoining what was later to become the Highfield Estate. Ironically the airfield had made way for the very people who had been made homeless by war planes. A bizarre quirk of fate but nonetheless tragic when one considered the number of people who had died, or been injured and all the people made homeless in the process. The prefabs had been planned as a temporary solution to an urgent problem and were intended to last about five years at the most. Twenty years on they were still there, as were many of the original tenants. Jessie and her father had been amongst the first to move in and it had been Jessie who had sat down with Ben on a particularly wet day months ago and filled him in on the history of the estate.

Like almost all council developments it was originally intended to be named after some important bigwig of the time, usually a local politician who wanted his or her name recorded for posterity. On this occasion the name nominated had been that of the Lord Mayor Councillor Lansdown and the name proposed was the Lansdown Estate. However, after some correspondence to the local press from people offering a number of other suggestions some bright spark came up with the idea of naming it the Landings in reference to the wartime airfield it was replacing. The proposal received popular agreement and to his credit the lord mayor, who had lost a son in the war, readily agreed. For once the council used its imagination and named the whole estate after wartime aircraft. The main street through the estate was named The Runway. Each of the cul-de-sacs was given the name of a British wartime aircraft such as Spitfire Close,

Blenheim Place, Hastings Ave, Typhoon Terrace and Wellington Way. The former airfield control tower, which had remained largely intact at the far end of The Runway, had been incorporated in the development of a three-storey block of elderly person accommodation, utilising the observation room as a sitting room cum meeting room. The meeting room at Tower House became an important place for a whole range of social activities on the estate and was used at least once a day by groups of all ages.

Unusually for old people dwellings the whole complex at Tower House was humming with life and there was always a waiting list of old age pensioners anxious to move in. With so many of the original tenants of the estate coming from the war-damaged cuttings area it resulted in a community whose shared hardship had reinforced an already existing community spirit. It was no surprise that the residents often referred to the estate with the nickname 'happy landings'. Young families who had been used to dark, often damp terraced houses and outside lavatories quickly adjusted to detached weatherproof homes with all mod cons and a garden for the kids and vegetables to grow in. The population was now twenty years older and there were few small children, quite a few widows and one or two widowers.

The telephone broke into the conversation once again and was quickly followed by two other calls all seeking more information about the social work assistant post. Ben duly did the chat and recorded their details promising to have job application forms in the post that day. 'I had better get Mrs Freeman going on these as I could be called out at any time, won't be long.'

With Mrs Freeman doing the necessary, Ben re-joined Dave and spent the rest of the afternoon going through the files of their planned visits for the following day. The afternoon passed pleasantly with no further calls about the job or emergency calls, causing Ben to have to swing into action. He left early to ensure he was at home in time to take any telephone messages about mental health cover. He left Dave chatting to Mrs Freeman and hoped they would enjoy the chat; judging by his observations earlier he felt it would do Vivian's spirits no harm at all.

Chapter 9

The Following Day

The day was dull but dry and the journey into work passed without Ben needing to concentrate too much. As had become his habit he stopped en route to say hello to Boxer Mark Two, who was waiting at the gate of his field in expectation of breakfast. Ben didn't let him down and two apples and two carrots were quickly dispatched. This was beginning to get expensive but it was obvious that they both enjoyed their daily meeting and Ben vaguely wondered if he ought to visit at weekends as well, but rejected it as a step too far. He was the first at the office and put the kettle on and started to open the post. Phil arrived next, which was unusual as she normally didn't surface much before ten and she not surprisingly appeared very shame faced. It had been a busy night covering her emergency duty and Ben was feeling drained but as usual where Phil was concerned he decided to avoid confrontation. He did, however, make a point of asking her how her migraine was and she looked suitably embarrassed.

The night duty had been completely without incident until midnight and he was in bed asleep when he received a phone call from the central police station custody suite, which resulted in him spending the best part of an hour locked in a police cell with an obviously very disturbed man probably high on drugs. The station sergeant, who knew Ben from previous cases, filled him in on the story so far. An unknown man with no identification on him had been picked up outside the bus station apparently out of his mind ranting and raving and appearing to be in danger of throwing himself under incoming buses. He had been brought in by the local beat bobby as needing a place of safety under section 136 of the 1959 Mental Health Act. This was the police power to remove someone from a public place when they appeared to be suffering from a mental disorder to a place of safety, which was usually a police station awaiting a psychiatric assessment.

The station sergeant at first had thought he was probably yet another drunk to add to the others he already had locked up in the cells. There had been a local derby football match earlier in the evening and Exworth Athletic had lost heavily. Consequently the cells were occupied with noisy supporters who had been drowning their sorrows and causing minor incidents in the town. The sergeant explained that he was now sure that this guy was no drunk and for that matter no football supporter. 'But see for yourself. He is a real one-off.'

He led Ben along the grim row of Victorian cells to the very last one and let him into the cell to make his assessment of the man's condition pointing to the call bell push by the door for him to press once he had finished. There was the usual overpowering smell of disinfectant that always seemed to be present in the cells. The cell itself was about eight-foot square with a concrete slab for a bed covered by a thin mattress and a toilet basin made of steel and devoid of a loo seat. The client, so far only known as John Doe, was a short middle-aged man, well dressed but rather dishevelled who didn't stay still for a moment. There was no smell of alcohol and his speech was rapid with a posh accent but the words that came out of his mouth were pure rubbish. Ben attempted to get his attention but John Doe was having none of it and at first appeared to be unaware of Ben's presence. From time to time he would stop the stream of meaningless rubbish and appear to be listening to voices in his head. It was clear that he was suffering with auditory hallucinations and would be very vulnerable if allowed back on to the street. The assessment took less than ten minutes and Ben was pretty sure that John was suffering with either acute schizophrenia or a drug-induced psychosis; either way he would need a period of observation in hospital. Satisfied that he knew how to proceed he pressed the bell but nothing happened. After several attempts he realised that someone must have disconnected it, which he knew was common practice when prisoners made a pest of themselves by repeatedly pressing the bell. Unfortunately the sergeant must have been unaware of this and went on about his business thinking that Ben was being very thorough. No amount of banging on the door brought any reaction and Ben spent a good three quarters of an hour moving around the cell closely followed by the client talking a constant bizarre mixture of fantasies and fears. The sergeant finally came to check that all was okay and a relieved Ben was released to proceed with arranging the client's emergency admission to hospital. The sergeant was most apologetic but they knew each other well and quickly agreed to put it down to experience and to keep their mouths shut about it, as it could have resulted in a formal enquiry and possibly disciplinary action. It was 4 am by the time Ben got home and a very sleepy Sandy asked if he was all right and he told her of his misadventure as he undressed. She seemed to find it funny and he slipped into bed and cuddled into her body, anxious to absorb her warmth. Nothing else was said and they slipped into a comforting sleep. Ben did not mention the incident of the lock-in at the office but he knew that he would always have a bond with the station sergeant that might well prove useful in the future.

Mrs Freeman and Dave arrived at the office at the same time and just for a moment Ben wondered if Mrs Freeman had come to work on the back of the pink peril, but quickly rejected the thought as a flight of fancy. Tea was served by Phil for almost the first time ever and life at the Highfield mental health office got down to business. The post was sorted through and Mrs Freeman assured Ben that she would cope with any job enquires and they agreed to meet up just before lunch hour. By 10 am Ben and Dave were in the car on their way to the first visit to see one of his senior citizens, Freda Davies. Up until six months ago he had considered her to be one of his more successful cases. Freda had spent many years in various hospitals suffering with paranoid schizophrenia which took the form of acute periods of religious mania during which she became hostile and violent as the voices took her over. The introduction of Chlorpromazine in the 1950s had been a major step forward for people like Freda and after most of her adult life being spent on backwards under sedation she could now be considered for a life back in the community. She was lucky in that as a young woman she had married and had a daughter, Heather. Her husband had long since given up on her but fortunately for her Heather remained faithful to her despite spending many months in care herself whilst her mother was in hospital. Heather was now a single parent and had a small boy, Peter. Life was not easy for her as she was determined to make her own way in life and worked several part-time jobs, which she fitted around Peter's needs. She offered Freda a home and in doing so added many more complications to her own life. Freda was stabilised on Largactal and the gremlins were pushed under cover, causing her to appear much more 'normal'. But unfortunately the treatment came with side effects and she felt drowsy, anxious and generally rather switched off. To add to the complications after several weeks of feeling well mentally but poorly physically she always decided to stop taking the medication. The inevitable would happen and she had regularly had to be readmitted under section during some sort of violent manic outburst. At this time the family were living in a well-established council estate on the extreme north of Exworth and Freda's regular psychotic episodes had resulted in her becoming known locally as 'the mad woman'. This also meant that Heather and Peter had to live with that label, which wasn't easy, but Heather remained faithful to her mother and applied for a transfer to Highfield whilst it was still being built in order to make a fresh start.

Freda was in hospital when the family moved to Highfield and Heather had called into the office to see if she could get any help with her mum. Ben had listened to her problem, which he had come across with other clients, and together Heather and Ben hatched a plan for coping with the problem and stopping the severity of Freda's relapses. Basically, Heather would keep an eye on Freda's medication and would let Ben know if there was any sign of her stopping taking it. He would then increase his visits to Freda and try and persuade her to continue taking it. If this failed he would step in and try to arrange for her to have a brief period of voluntary care at St Margaret's to have her medication stabilised. This had worked well and together Heather and Ben had managed to keep Freda reasonably stable with only a couple of brief voluntary admissions without any obvious outward indications to arouse any neighbour's suspicions about Freda's sanity. After the best part of a year it was fair to say that Ben was pretty pleased with how Heather and he were managing her condition. Unfortunately as the old saying goes 'pride comes before a fall' and he became overconfident.

Heather had rung up late on a Friday and Ben had put off visiting Freda until the following Monday. When he did visit he found Freda to be very agitated and more uncooperative than ever before. He attempted to calm her down by offering to make a cup of tea whilst she got her things together ready for the inevitable short hospital stay. This did not have the desired effect and Freda just bounced about the house packing and unpacking her small suitcase over and over again. Ben remained calm and talked to her in a quiet and caring way and it was at this juncture that he made his fatal error. 'Take your time, Freda, we are in no rush, I won't get cross.'

The words were barely out of his mouth when Freda erupted. 'Cross, Jesus Christ, the crucifixion,' and she raced for the back door, knocking Ben flying in doing so.

By the time he had recovered and made it to the back-garden Freda had disappeared, apparently having climbed over a five-foot fence. Very athletic for an old woman in her sixties but he knew that mania could be a considerable driving force. The next couple of hours were spent with Ben searching the surrounding area with no success and he had been forced to leave a note for Heather, explaining what had happened. He heard no more before the office closed and advised the local police station and the on-call mental welfare officer of the fact that Freda was at large and likely to be quite manic.

Next morning there was bad news and good news. The bad news was that she had been found by a policeman during the night in the graveyard of the church just a few yards from where she had formally lived. How she had got there was unknown but it was likely that she had walked the ten or so miles to the church. She had been found stretched out on a grave talking in a loud voice to the stone angel on the headstone. She had been beyond reason and had been taken to the central police station before being sectioned to St Margaret's by the duty mental welfare officer. The good news was all this had taken place miles away from her home in Highfield and she had not been identified as the local mad woman by her current neighbours.

Ben knew he had contributed to the crisis by delaying his visit and by using the word cross to a client with religious mania. He wouldn't make those mistakes again. Dave listened to Ben's tale sympathetically and recognised how easy it was to be overconfident when dealing with people with mental illness. Ben had visited Freda in hospital a week or so later and she was much like her 'normal' old self. He had bumped into Dr Rani, the prof's senior registrar, whilst he was there and they had a brief chat in Dr Rani's consulting room. They had met on numerous occasions whilst doing joint assessment visits in the community and it was fair to say that they shared a sense of humour boarding on the ridiculous. However, Dr Rani was in a serious mood and wanted to discuss Freda and how they might be able to avoid her pattern of readmissions. He told Ben that he was taking part in a national programme trialling a new form of Chlorpromazine medication called Modecate. It was the equivalent of Largactal but was given by injection once a month, which broke down slowly in the body and made daily tablet taking unnecessary. Dr Rani thought that Freda would be a very suitable person to trial this breakthrough but she would need to be seen once a month at the day hospital to receive her injection. Could Ben arrange this?

It was left that he would discuss the plan with Heather and that Dr Rani would suggest the treatment to Freda. It all fell into place and after her first injection Elsie returned home to Heather and Peter. Nearly six months had elapsed since and even though there were still some side effects of the medication Elsie remained well and there had been no need for further admissions to hospital. Dave was keen to meet Freda and to gently ask her how she felt about the treatment as he could see that it was a real breakthrough. After the statutory cup of tea Ben and Dave took their leave from Freda and Ben reminded her that he would pick her up the following week to take her for her next treatment. In the car he pointed out that in two weeks' time Freda would be reaching the longest period she had spent in the community since he had been working with her. Modecate seemed to be a real answer to her problems. Dave was very enthusiastic about the effectiveness of the treatment and the positive way it could help to cut down on the readmission rate for many of their chronic patients. 'I am sure the prof and Dr Rani must be delighted and I will enjoy mentioning our visit when I next get a chance to chat to them.'

Their next visit was quite different and seemed to have a profound effect on Dave, who was left wondering how some people could tolerate their lives. Ben explained that he had a few multi-handicapped children on his caseload, a fact that had haunted him through Sandy's last pregnancy. He had seen repeatedly how this tragedy affected families and he had prayed that this would not be their misfortune as he knew it could happen to anyone. However, there was only one Leslie Groves on his caseload and he had real admiration for the determination that the Groves and Mrs Groves in particular brought to doing what they believed to be right in caring for him. Leslie was in his teens, over five feet tall but with the mental and physical development of a small baby. He could not talk or walk, was doubly incontinent and had to be spoon fed. He could not focus and appeared to have no recognition of anyone or anything. Experts over the years had all recommended his admission to a special hospital or at the least special day care unit but all such recommendations had been firmly declined. They were in an almost unique situation for Highfield residents as they were owner-occupiers, having bought their detached cottage years ago from the farmer who had subsequently had his land compulsorily purchased by the Exworth Council. Over the years they had spent a small fortune on adapting the house to meet Leslie's needs. Mrs Groves devoted each and every day to his care and had no social life of any sort. The only time she went out of the house was to do the family shopping once her husband came home from work. When Ben had inherited the family on to his caseload he quickly became aware that the physical strength needed to lift Leslie and to meet his needs was really beginning to tell on Mrs Groves, as he was now as tall as her and a dead weight. She lived in fear of Leslie developing bed sores and explained that she set an alarm to go off every three hours day and night so that she could turn him regularly. This meant that she had not had a proper night's sleep for years.

On her behalf Ben had obtained a ripple mattress with a constant flow of moving air for Leslie's bed on permanent loan from the local general hospital, which enabled her to abandon the alarm once she had tested that the ripple mattress worked. However, old habits die hard and it had been months before she started to sleep better. Apart from this small relief Ben was at a loss to find more ways of helping the family. He had arranged for them to have a complimentary ticket to take Leslie to use the Spastic Society's heated indoor swimming pool, which was equipped with hoists to get him in and out of the water. They reported that he appeared to enjoy it. Unfortunately the effort needed to take him made it a rare outing and Ben felt his efforts did little to improve their lot.

At various times he had offered to arrange respite care for Leslie but until four months ago this had always been declined. However, last May the family had been invited to a family wedding in Edinburgh and as this was Mrs Groves' sister and only sibling she desperately wanted to attend, but it would be impossible for Leslie to make the journey. During one of Ben's regular visits she had told him about the invitation and he had once again suggested a couple days of respite care at a specialist residential unit in town. After much discussion she agreed to let him take her to meet the staff and see the unit one evening. She had been impressed and met a couple of other young people with similar problems to Leslie, who seemed content, clean and were obviously handled with genuine affection by the care staff. After much soul searching the placement was made for the last weekend in May and Mr and Mrs Groves went away together for the first time in well over ten years. Ben had bumped into Mr Groves in the street one evening a short while after the trip and he had been given a massive hug and he had been almost overwhelmed with thanks. 'For the first time for years we have things in the future to look forward to and my wife and I can see a future for Leslie when we have gone.'

The visit today was to sort out some dates for Leslie to have respite care to allow the Groves to have a holiday. The visit went well but Dave was unusually quiet until he was back in the car. He let out a long sigh and said that he had never met anyone who was so determined and brave. 'You did well to bring her around to accepting help. She must have really built up trust in you.'

Ben just grunted shyly and drove on to their next planned visit, grateful as ever for his own family and their good fortune.

Chapter 10

The Rest of the Day

A couple of other visits went without incident. One was a no reply, which was part and parcel of routine visits which had not been organised in advance. The other was to a man, Mr Alec Simpson, who had suffered such serious anxiety over many years that the consultant in charge of his care about ten years before had finally arranged for him to have a leucotomy. The operation was extreme and involved cutting into his brain and removing a particular part and it was the only time that either Ben or Dave had met someone who had had it done. In some ways it had been successful as it had dealt with his extreme anxiety problem, but unfortunately it had left him as little more than a 'zombie', with no visible sign of emotion and generally with no interest in communicating with the rest of his world.

Ben saw his role as trying to offer the client's wife some support. She had suffered with her husband's problems for years and it was primarily her Christian beliefs that kept her going. From time to time she needed to let out her frustrations and Ben was content to listen and to offer support. This was one of those occasions and Ben retired to the kitchen with her to allow her let off steam. Meanwhile, Dave sat with her husband as he in turn sat in front of the television with the sound off and making no attempt to communicate. When they got back to the car Ben was not surprised to hear from Dave that all his efforts to talk with Mr Simpson went without any reaction and he wondered which was worse, the extreme anxiety or the state Mr Simpson had been left in.

'Thank god we have some reasonable drug solutions nowadays. Some of the old treatments were cruel in the extreme.' On impulse Ben pulled into the car park of the White Hart as he felt that they both needed cheering up. A pie and a pint might just do the job was Ben's inspirational thought, and Dave just smiled and nodded his approval.

About an hour later and somewhat recovered, Ben returned to the office to check with Mrs Freeman on the current state of play. He was presented with a list of four telephone numbers of people who were enquiring about the job of social work assistant. He sat down at his desk and rang them all back whilst Dave made coffee to help cover any smell of beer that might be lingering on their breath prior to their afternoon visits. Ben noticed that Dave had taken his coffee into Mrs Freeman's room and he soon heard laughter coming from that direction. Within minutes, three further application forms were on their way, the fourth had been clearly in need of psychiatric help and had been sensitively put off by Ben. The list of potential applicants had now reached twelve and there were still several days to go to the closing date. It looked promising.

The first visit was to Chelsea House, one of the high-rise blocks at the entrance to the estate. It involved a trip to the twelfth floor but fortunately the lift was working. He reminded Dave that they were going to see Frank and Rosie Sullivan, who had moved on to the estate some eighteen months before. Ben had been aware of the couple briefly when they had lived just up the road from him in the Cuttings. They had worked as caretakers at Ashley Park, the local primary school where Ben's boy Jack had started two years ago. School gate gossip told a tale of a lovely couple whose world in the past few months was rapidly falling apart as a result of Mrs Sullivan's mental health situation. The parents were generally very sympathetic but she was clearly suffering from dementia and her behaviour had started to frighten the children. The outcome was inevitable and it came as no surprise to learn that the Sullivans had taken early retirement during the summer school holidays. Retirement meant them having to move out of the small detached house overlooking the school playing field, as it went with the caretaker's job and was needed for the replacement caretaker and his family. The Exworth Housing Committee offered the Sullivans the top floor flat in Chelsea House, a high-rise block with a view of nothing except endless sky and then contacted Ben for him to follow up.

He prepared Dave for a nightmare scenario as the lift shuddered to a halt and the doors opened on to a dim passageway with a lone door set in the far wall. The doorbell was answered by a wild haired woman in her early sixties dressed in a floral sack like dress liberally covered in cigarette ash. Her words of welcome were all too familiar to Ben: 'Got a fag?' In fact, they were the only words she ever seemed to utter these days and she did so over and over again. There was a slight clanking noise as Mr Sullivan joined the group at the door and Dave remembered that he wore a calliper on his right leg, presumably to correct an old illness or injury. Ben had assumed that Frank had probably suffered from polio in his youth as he had seen similar use of callipers for that condition, but this had never been confirmed to him. Frank eased Rosie to one side and invited them into the living room, which was light and airy but simply furnished, and there was an all-prevailing smell of smoking despite all the top windows being open. He got Rosie settled in an armchair and as if by magic produced a cigarette, which he lit before passing it her.

Dave was mesmerised by the speed in which she devoured it, as it seemed to burn down an inch with every inhalation. Ben had seen it all before and knew the quiet brought about by her smoking was for a limited period of time depending on the time it took her to consume it. Frank used cigarettes as a way of coping with Rosie's care and the cost involved used up a significant part of their pensions. He remained devoted to her and never seemed over-burdened by her. As an added complication he had to cope with her other long-term condition, that of her being diabetic. Her own ability to manage her sugar by doing regular urine tests followed by injections of an appropriate amount of insulin with a very long needle every morning and night had long ago ceased. Frank now managed the regime but it must have caused him considerable concerns and no little practical difficulties trying to get Rosie's cooperation.

The only real practical help Ben had been able to arrange was to persuade a local care home to offer one day a week respite day care to Rosie. The staff there were brilliant and ensured that she had a bath, had her hair done and her nails trimmed each week. Frank drove her there every Friday morning equipped with the essential two full packs of twenty cigarettes and her diabetic paraphernalia returning promptly at 5 pm to take her home. It wasn't much but it allowed Frank to do the weekly shopping, and when finances permitted to have a lunchtime pint and the chance to have a reasonable chat with the guys at the pub. All too soon Rosie was back in business and the 'got a fag' monologue was directed to them each in turn. This was Frank's lot day in and day out and if ever wedding vows were tested to the limit his were, and he paid the price day after day.

In the lift down Dave commented that human misery seemed to be prevalent on the Highfield Estate and Ben had to remind him that for every person living with a major problem there were hundreds just getting on with their lives. 'From time to time I get depressed with the misery, but in this job you keep on trying to take small steps forward. It doesn't always work but you keep on trying and there are often little victories that help me carry on. They are only little victories but they are the best you can hope for as there sure are no miracles!'

The next visit was a surprise for Dave as Ben had arranged a visit to Ruth Andrews and had planned it carefully for them to arrive just after school had closed for the day. The first thing Ben noticed was that the garden was almost all clear of Mr Andrew's belongings and he imagined that he had probably crept around after dark to rescue his stuff. Amusingly, he had missed an off-white pair of underpants that now gently waved in the breeze from the top of the overgrown privet hedge. Dave's comment was, 'Well I guess that must be his flag of surrender.' This caused Ben to have to quickly stifle a laugh as the front door was opened by Ruth. She had clearly made an effort in anticipation of their visit and appeared clean and tidy with her hair brushed and was even wearing a little makeup. She welcomed Dave warmly and as they were about to go into the house a loud shriek came from behind them. Katie had arrived home and couldn't contain her excitement at seeing Dave.

She dived on him and gave him a huge hug of welcome before grabbing his hand and dragging him off to the kitchen to play hostess. That worked well for Ben, who was able to spend time with Ruth sussing out how she was. There was every indication that she was on the mend and a quick glance around the room helped to reinforce that she was functioning more ably. He decided to pursue his idea to try and put Ruth back in touch with her faith. He had made provisional enquires about the current Roman Catholic minister on the estate and had been delighted to hear that he was young, open minded and more interested in meeting the needs of the people rather than those of the papacy. Ruth was clearly ambivalent about his suggestion but after a lot of discussion Ben came away with her permission to talk to the priest on her behalf and to discuss it further afterwards. He was delighted as he was all too aware that Ruth had always relied upon the support of her church when she was struggling and it was pretty certain that her life would often be difficult.

Meanwhile he could hear Katie chatting and giggling with Dave and Ruth smiled and said how good it was to hear Katie happy and acting like a little girl for a change. Katie had brought home jam tarts she had made at school that day and she insisted that they should all have one with yet another cup of tea. They left the Andrews to make their way to the rendezvous with Mary and Jessie at the Landings. Dave was clutching the last of the jam tarts wrapped in a tissue, which Katie had slipped to him as they left. Ben noticed that Dave's mood had lifted and it was obvious that he had a soft spot for Katie. Not for the first time he wondered how he would cope if it was his wife and kids who were all the way over in Jamaica. At that moment he decided to discuss with Sandy the possibility of inviting Dave to spend Christmas with them. Clearly one shouldn't be alone at Christmas and he felt sure Sandy and the boys would enjoy Dave's company.

As they turned off the main road from Highfield on to The Runway Ben found the lay-by outside the two coaches that made up Jessie's shop already occupied by the regular hourly double-decker which serviced the Highfield Estate. From experience he knew that Jessie would be busy dealing with the mini rush for papers, cigarettes, sweets and the occasional tea or coffee to take away. He drove past slowly and did a circuit of the Landings, pointing out the special features linking the area to the wartime airfield it had superseded. He was delighted by the interest that Dave showed and by the time he completed the circuit the bus had pulled away and he was able to replace it in the lay-by. Jessie was busy tidying up after the bus customers and after shaking Dave's hand told Ben to give him the grand tour.

'I am expecting Mary home anytime soon so come on through to the lounge when you are ready for tea and some of my lemon drizzle cake freshly baked today.'

Ben enjoyed everything about this unique shop and the people who lived here. Dave quickly caught the magic of the place. The two coaches were parked in their prefab's front garden side by side and linked by a wooden bridge through what had formally been their emergency exits. The first coach was decked out as a small general store with the main counter just inside the door being used for preparing teas and coffees and the newspapers, cigarettes and sweets required by her regular bus customers. Jessie seemed to spend most of the day sat on a high stool behind the counter ready to welcome all customers and to collect the monies due in an old wooden till. Both sides of the coach were lined with shelves containing a surprisingly large variety of household goods and fresh vegetables together with an old-fashioned set of scales and a pen for people to write the weight of what they had bagged up on the paper bags provided. The system clearly depended upon the honesty of the customers and could have been disastrous anywhere other than the Landings, but here it seemed to work just fine. Crossing over the bridge was a whole new experience. The first section of the second coach was taken up with a couple of fridges containing bread, milk, cold meats, bacon, sausages, black pudding, cheeses and eggs all packaged in small individual lots designed to meet the needs of the single people or couples who made up the majority of the householders at the Landings. Most of them still used meat safes and had no fridge at home, so small quantities were the order of the day. The next section was made up of two bookcases full of second-hand books. Those on the left mainly romance or Catherine Cookson type books, and on the right a mixture of thrillers, travel books and small sections for gardening and cooking.

This was the Landings' free lending library and a system of honesty borrowing was in operation and worked so well that more books were returned than had been borrowed. At the end of this coach was a collection of old coach seats set in a rectangle with a table in the middle. The table had several piles of magazines on it. Judging by their rather worn condition, *People's Friend*, *Woman's Own*, *Reader's Digest* and the all-time favourite titbits were the most popular. On the wall behind the seats on each side were two large notice boards with Community Corner in large letters at the top of each. One held various notices about future local events and the other held a few postcards offering things for sale, details of local services and one rather sad picture of a missing cat with the offer of a reward if found. To finish off this local gathering point were three shelves running the width of the coach with an odd collection of bric-a-brac for sale with a sign saying, 'make a donation, all monies collected to go towards the grand party to celebrate the twenty-fifth anniversary of the Battle of Britain on Saturday 18th September 1965.'

Dave just pointed at the honesty box awaiting donations and laughed. 'This place really is a one-off. That sign would be seen as an open invitation to nick the lot anywhere else.' They wandered out of the coaches and joined Jessie in the prefab. They noticed a large hand bell had been left in the doorway of the coaches for any customers to ring for attention. Mary had arrived home and could be heard making tea in the kitchen. Ben stood by Jessie, who was relaxing in a comfortable armchair and said, 'Before we top up our bladders I really must use your loo, as we have got through quite a few cups of tea this afternoon.'

Jessie pointed down a corridor which ran the length of the prefab and just said, 'Last door on the right. Help yourself.'

This was the first time that Ben had ventured so far into their prefab and out of curiosity he looked to left and right as he passed along the hallway. The first room on the left was the kitchen and he saw the back of Mary as she was slicing up a cake. The first room on the right was a bedroom and through the gap of a partially opened door he glimpsed a double bed and two single wardrobes. He guessed the second room on the left would also be a bedroom and was surprised to see that it was full floor to ceiling with supplies for the shop. The second door on the right was indeed the bathroom and he was just lifting the seat when realisation hit him there was only one functioning bedroom, which meant Jessie and Mary were partners in every sense of the word.

He was amazed that he had never guessed before but the idea had never entered his head. He knew they were very good friends but he had never seen any sort of overt familiarity pass between them. He thought it over as he washed his hands and decided that he was really happy for them. After all, everyone should have a little love in their lives. He quite understood why they chose to keep it private and at once determined that he would never share the knowledge with anyone, not even Sandy. When he returned to the lounge he could see that Dave was using his charm to good effect. Jessie was in full flow telling him how before the war her dad had owned a corner shop in the Cuttings but it had been destroyed during an air raid. Ever resourceful, he had bought two old coaches and used them to continue to provide a mobile shop service to the streets around the Cuttings. He had always allowed a certain amount of credit with essential purchases 'going on the book' in times of hardship for his regular customers. She assured Dave that the families had invariably repaid him when money became available. Many families were able to cope through troubled times because of her father's consideration.

By the time Jessie and her dad had moved to the Landings he was already in failing health and the coaches had been parked up in their garden and had never been moved since. However, their new neighbours were largely from his former customers and they had long memories. As a consequence, Jessie began to run a shop in the coaches in her front garden and the customers still came to this day. She went on to explain that Mary Harris, in her capacity as a health visitor, had started to visit regularly to help her care for her father, and as his condition deteriorated had stayed there overnight. After he died some couple of months later they had decided that she should give up her flat and move in with Jessie permanently. Now nearly fifteen years later this was the home they shared.

The ladies had got Ben and Dave settled in comfortable armchairs and were plying them with copious amounts of tea and a generous selection of three different types of cake. Ben was content to sit back and relax, leaving Dave to entertain the ladies in his usual confident manner. The photos of his wife, Carmilla, and his two daughters, Elsa and Gloria, were soon out of his wallet, much to the delight of Mary and Jessie. They were full of questions about his life back in Jamaica and were keen to know if the family were hoping to settle in England. The bell clanged at regular intervals and Jessie was always quick to respond. Ben noticed that Mary made a point of updating her on any salient facts she had missed whilst away serving customers. With his newly found knowledge about their relationship it became quite apparent that they were very harmonious.

The time slipped away and a casual glance at his watch gave him a start as they were already late for their evening visit. With hugs all round they hurried to the car and set off for the final visit of a very full day.

Dave surprised Ben by saying, 'You know that shop kind of reminds me of many of the shops in Jamaica. They pop up in shacks and old vans all over the place. Most of them are illegal and make their money by selling booze, and the authorities work hard to close them down. However, as soon as one is closed another pops up in its place. It is simply a way of life. I can't imagine the authorities over here allowing that to happen.'

Ben didn't reply but was not so sure, as he had always suspected that Jessie's shop had just happened and fortunately no official had ever been stupid enough to get involved. Just as well as he was sure that any attempt to close Jessie down would undoubtedly cause a local revolt.

Bert and Victor were at their garden gate eagerly awaiting their visitors. They shook Ben's hand politely as was normal when he visited but their welcome of Dave could only be described as ecstatic. They were ushered inside and immediately shown over the maisonette that the two of them shared. It was very clean and tidy with everything in its place. The furniture was clearly mainly second hand but polished within an inch of its life. There were few pictures or ornaments but a single group photo had been framed and stood on top of their elderly massive black and white television. Dave spotted the photo at once and picked it up for a closer look.

'Well I know this lot,' he said with a laugh. 'It's all the lads.' The three of them then stood in a tight little group identifying each of the lads by name. Ben listened with interest but had nothing to contribute as he realised that this was a group photograph of the patients and staff making up the prof's project. The rest of the guided tour passed quickly with both Dave and Ben praising Victor and Bert for the way they had built up their home. They seemed to glow under the praise and it was clear that Dave's approval in particular meant a lot to them.

They ended up sat in front of an electric fire with tea being served on a coffee table in front of them. They shyly produced a large plate of tinned salmon sandwiches with the crusts cut off followed by another plate full of chocolate éclairs. Ben guessed that visitors were rare and was very impressed that they had made so much of an effort. They couldn't have got it more right as far as he was concerned, as both the offerings were very much to his taste. Once again he sat back and let the conversation flow over him. It was all about people who he didn't know but quickly realised that this group of men were like family to Bert and Victor. He began to form the beginnings of an idea which he would discuss with Dave later.

Meanwhile, he relaxed and decided that today had been a pretty good one. Dave and the two of them had a lot of catching up to do and the conversation flowed back and forth without a break and Ben let his mind wander and could feel his eyes getting heavy in the warmth from the fire. Suddenly a topic of conversation came up that brought him to with a jerk. The guys were telling Dave how they relied on Joe's for their breakfast before going to work each day and that combined with a lunch in the canteen at work made up the bulk of their catering.

'You have never lived if you haven't tasted Joe's fry up,' was their joint opinion and Dave looked questioningly at Ben. Ben had already regretted his decision not to introduce Dave to Joe's at the start of the week and but fortunately responded with uncharacteristic speed. He reassured Dave that he had left a visit to Joe's as a special treat to round off the week.

'I agree with the lads Joe's is a real haven on Highfield, as you will find out tomorrow.' The conversation moved on and Ben returned to his siesta, conscious that a potentially difficult situation had been avoided by the skin of his teeth.

On the way back to the office to recover the 'pink peril' for Dave he shared the idea that had been running through his mind regarding Victor and Bert. 'Having listened to the three of you talking today it is obvious that the group of men at St Margaret's are very important to Victor and Bert. I suspect that they look upon them as family and I know for a fact that neither of them have any contact with actual relatives of their own. I bet they would love to be invited back to the hospital to spend Christmas with their friends. What do you think?' Ben enquired.

The two of them mulled it over as they drove back to the office and ended up agreeing that it would be a good idea and may actually help to encourage the remaining patients that it was possible to return to live in the community. The plan was hatched with Dave agreeing to prepare the idea with the other nursing staff in the unit, leaving Ben to bite the bullet and to discuss the idea with the prof. It was a pretty tired Ben who arrived home to Sandy. The boys were already in bed and he went up to read them the next chapter of the Biggles book that they were currently having as a bedtime story. The boys settled down and he went back downstairs and flopped out on the sofa, with Sandy joining him along with two mugs of hot chocolate. She was keen to learn how his day with Dave had gone and he filled her in but left out his discovery about Jessie and Mary. It seemed quite natural to raise his suggestion to invite Dave to spend Christmas with them and was pleased with her immediate agreement to the plan. It was left that Ben would make the offer the following day prior to Dave's placement finishing. They were both tired and didn't bother with television and soon went to bed, where they cuddled and drifted off to sleep quite content together.

Chapter 11

A Busy October

One man's misfortune sometimes results in another man's good fortune, and that had been the case three or four months ago, but in that instance it had been women not men involved. The Newman household had started off as usual with Ben in a rush to get off to work and the boys dawdling through their breakfast and Sandy trying to hurry them along. After dropping the boys off at school Sandy had stopped for a chat with a couple of other mothers before heading for home for a much-deserved coffee. Unfortunately, the boys and Ben had been heavy handed with the milk on their cereals and the bottle was now empty and would not be replaced until the milkman arrived at his usual time in the afternoon.

Sandy decided to pop down to the corner shop at the end of their road which primarily sold tobacco, sweets and papers but also carried a small stock of provisions. Sandy knew the shop well and called in regularly for odds and ends she was running out of before her big shop at Tesco on a Friday. The shop had been there for years and had originally been run by an elderly couple who had been firmly stuck in the Victorian age. Not that Sandy had ever known them as they had died years ago, but the formal photograph which still hung in the shop to this day left one in no doubt of their vintage. Mr Driscoll sported a winged collar, waistcoat and bowler and his wife a full-length dress, a sizeable hat and gloves and they had the shop in the background with a shop bike leaning against the window.

For many years the shop had now been run by the diminutive figure of their daughter Olive Driscoll. She was an octogenarian spinster who spent her days sitting behind the counter apparently happy with her lot according to her usual demeanour. The shop and an aged spaniel called Henry were her whole life, which most people thought was sad but she was well liked and known by all and sundry as Ma Driscoll. She was rarely seen away from her shop, except in the evening when she took Henry out for a walk and to let him spend time sniffing around on one of the local bombsites, returning home once he had done his business. When Sandy pushed open the door of the shop she was greeted by the usual ring of the shop bell but Ma Driscoll was not at her post. Sandy had waited for a moment before hearing moans coming from behind the counter and when she peered over she spotted Ma Driscoll flat out on the floor.

She lifted the flap to the counter and hurried around to see if she could help. Ma was able to say that she had had a giddy turn and had slipped off her stool. She wasn't in any pain but simply didn't have the strength to get up. Sandy lifted Ma up with surprising ease as there was nothing to her and Sandy wondered if she ever ate properly. With the support of Sandy's arm they made their way into the back room and Ma was soon stretched out on a sofa with a blanket over her and Henry at her side. Sandy put the kettle on and went back into the shop in response to a ring of the shop bell. Sandy spent the rest of the morning alternating between caring for Ma and minding the shop and eventually Ma fell into a sound sleep.

When she awoke she had a good old chat with Sandy and confessed that at times the shop was too much for her and the time had come to get some help. The upshot was that Ma had offered Sandy a part-time job with flexible hours and at acceptable wages. It was just what they both needed and Sandy's general mood started to improve from that day and all because she had run out of milk.

Ben was sensible enough to encourage Sandy, even though it meant that he had to take on the task of taking the boys to school before going on to work himself. It was a small price to pay for having something like the old Sandy back, and the extra money coming in was a real help.

Today had started with Sandy getting up at 6.30 am as usual, but unusually bringing cups of tea up to the bedroom for them to share. She sat on the bed looking crumpled but very attractive and they chatted amicably about the day ahead. Ben was aware that Sandy no longer seemed bored and was relishing the ever-increasing responsibility that Ma Driscoll at the corner shop was allowing her to have. She was slowly bringing the shop into the 1960s and Ma was shrewd enough to know that

Sandy's intervention was reflected in increased profits at the end of the week. She had been sensitive to Ma's feelings and had been careful not to rush changes, but her latest development of the introduction of a freezer for ice cream and loose frozen food had proved a money spinner. Sandy chatted away happily and Ben had to point out that she was running late to get to the shop. Her normal pattern was to arrive at the shop in time to load up the two paper boys who delivered papers in the local area. Ma always prepared their separate bags, as this was where her experience of the various wishes of her customers was second nature to her. However, in recent months she had still been in her dressing gown when Sandy took over and was keen to have her shower and breakfast. Sandy rushed off for her own shower returning with damp hair and completely naked.

Ben watched her getting dressed and enjoyed every moment, but resisted getting involved in any horse play because she was running late. Once she had gone he thought about their relationship in recent months, which was much improved as she was no longer bored out of her mind. Her job was making a real difference and he decided that he needed to give some thought to how he could make an effort to keep things on the up. He had accepted that he would sort the boys out in the mornings and it usually fitted in well with his own need to get to work on time. For some reason today, which had started so nicely, was not helped by the boys, who seemed to be taking an age getting their act together. The last straw was Jack announcing that he had football practice in the afternoon and couldn't find his football boots. The hunt took far too long until they were finally located covered in dried mud at the back of the cupboard under the stairs. Ben had a mad mind flash of himself as a border collie nipping at the heels of a couple of feckless sheep trying to get them moving into a pen, which in his case was the car.

By the time this was achieved they were already late, which meant a queue of cars at the school gates, which made him even more late. His usual relaxed drive to work was done at top speed and poor old Boxer Mark Two was almost force fed with his apple and a couple of carrots. Ben was back in the car and about to pull away when he was passed by an enormous old army lorry loaded down with scrap metal of all descriptions. He was greeted by a loud double blast on a cow horn and a friendly wave from someone he didn't recognise. He had no time to give it any real thought, put his foot down and dashed off to Highfield. When he pulled into the car park he was met by Dave sitting on his parked 'pink peril' and Mrs Freeman just getting off her bus. He apologised for his late arrival, picked up the post from the mat and passed it to Mrs Freeman to be recorded in the post book as normal. Dave required no instruction and headed to the kitchen to turn up the central heating and put the kettle on.

There were three more completed application forms for the social work assistant position in the post, which Ben simply added to the file. He had decided to get all the completed forms collected together for him to read over at home at the same time once the closing date had passed. Meanwhile, he asked Mrs Freeman to set up a date for her, Phil and himself to talk over what sort of person they should try to recruit. He was conscious that they were a very small team and that there was no room for personality clashes, but he did have some clear preference for the type of person he would like. However, that was for another day as this was Dave's last day with them and he wanted to ensure that it finished on a high. He planned to make three routine visits to a variety of clients and also to try to call again on Agnes Morgan, the person who was out yesterday. She was an elderly widow living alone who was inclined to be confused and get lost and find herself unable to remember her way home.

He left Dave chatting to Phil, who was usually pretty grumpy this early in the day but thought that Dave was quite capable of working his magic. So it proved and they were chatting amicably when he went to dictate the previous day's reports to Mrs Freeman. Ben explained to Mrs Freeman about Dave asking to visit Joe's and told her they would be calling in there for lunch and would be back in the afternoon. The visits went well, including the missed lady from the previous day who had been in Exworth visiting Tesco to get her weekly shop. She had got there and back without incident, which seemed to show she was at her best at present.

The door to Joe's opened to welcome them with the usual smell of coffee and bacon and a general hubbub of several people all talking at once. It seemed to Ben that the volume dropped suddenly as they entered and he guessed that Joe noticed it too as he came out of the kitchen and made a point of shaking Dave's hand in welcome. However, any reduction of noise lasted no more than a second or two as several people called out to Dave by name. He was obviously well known. To say the least Ben was puzzled and Dave quickly explained that these were old football friends. It turned out that St Margaret's had a football team and played in a local league on the recreation ground. The team had originally been made up of staff from the hospital, but this had long since changed with players coming from all over the place. They ordered the all-day breakfast and large mugs of tea and joined a group of men on the long central table when they squeezed up to make room for them.

The first comment made was a direct question to Dave from one of the group, 'So how is our hero then?' which came accompanied by a hearty slap on the back. The guy saw that Ben was again confused and went on to explain that Dave was the bucket man for the St Margaret's team and was well known on the local football scene, often dealing with minor injuries for both the home and the away teams. A month ago one of the away team collided with another player and collapsed in a heap. Most people thought he was unconscious and called for the smelling salts. Dave rushed to help and realised the man couldn't breathe because he had swallowed his tongue. He quickly put his finger in the man's mouth and hooked the tongue free, leaving him gasping for breath but otherwise unharmed. It was generally agreed that Dave had saved the man's life but he tried to play it down.

Ben was amazed that Dave had made no mention of the incident during the week they had spent together and felt very guilty that he had ever thought Dave would not be accepted by the men at Joe's. They finished their meal and the banter flowed freely with Dave very much one of the gang. Ben went back to Mavis to get two more drinks and Joe once again came out of the kitchen to speak to him. 'Hayley was looking for you and I think he has a bit of a problem he wants to share with you. He is usually in about this time just before he starts the second post.' Ben knew Joe was talking about the local Highfield postman, who had worked on the estate since day one and was well known to Ben. He had only recently been rechristened as Hayley following an unfortunate incident at Joe's and had previously always been known as Whistling Willie.

Bill Mills was a compulsive whistler as he went about Highfield on his rounds. He never seemed to stop whistling and could be heard on his way long before he became visible. One needed to concentrate on the whistling in order to identify what tune was being interpreted and it was rarely possible to pick out any particular one, but what the performance generally lacked in quality was made up for with volume. He always started his deliveries at some unearthly hour when most other people were still in bed and the first post was always awaiting Ben's arrival at the office. The reaction of people to his whistling was mixed and some people complained that it woke them up when others said it was better than any alarm clock. Ben knew Bill really well as he often met him at the office when he was delivering the second post. With the absence of public toilets Bill occasionally needed to use their toilet, and in bad weather could sometimes be found with Alice in the kitchen drying out and warming up.

This was always a high spot of Alice's day. Ben had a lot of respect for him and considered him to be a very kind and sensitive man who kept his eyes open for any problems amongst the more vulnerable residents of Highfield. The incident at Joe's had happened about three months before. Ben hadn't been there at the time but he had heard the story so many times from all sorts of people that he felt he might as well have been. There was one other main character involved who was also a regular customer and something of a ringleader at the long table at Joe's. This was Fred Baker, who had a most appropriate surname for someone who was the bread delivery man on the estate. However, he was commonly known as Beefy Baker, related to his physique. Now in his late forties Beefy had been a body builder in his youth and was something of a local celebrity, having been the runner up in a couple of Mr Wales body building competitions in the early 1950s. At one time there had been a framed paper cutting of Beefy showing off his muscles pinned for all to admire on the café notice board. It had been there for quite a while when some bright spark decided to draw a bra on it. Almost inevitably the same person decided to run a book on how long it would take for Beefy to notice and at a shilling a time a healthy purse had built up. It was probably a good thing that Joe decided to remove the picture when he spotted the addition and insisted that the money went into the charity box for guide dogs for the blind, which sat on the counter.

Beefy was known for his sense of humour but he was rightly proud of his muscles and he could have proved more than a little upset if he had felt he was being belittled. He was still happy to flash his six-pack at every opportunity and it was rumoured that quite a few of his lady customers had been granted a viewing. However, Beefy wasn't one to flash and tell and preferred to talk about the Charles Atlas's course of body building which he had followed throughout his adult life and to point out that he still carried the top of the range Bullworker exerciser in his van every day for the odd session of exercises whenever the mood took him. Ben had to smile about this as he knew that Charles Atlas was a trade name and that the original Charles Atlas was now an old man in his seventies and nothing like the image portrayed in the adverts still being shown in comics, magazines and newspapers. Ben had read all about it in an old copy of *Reader's Digest* when he was last waiting to see the dentist, but he had never sought to undermine Beefy's total confidence in the exercise system. The results spoke for themselves and it had certainly worked for him and no one would ever think about kicking sand in his face.

The incident at Joe's happened when Bill (alias Whistling Willie) had stood up from the table to get another cup of coffee. The room was relatively quiet when Bill suddenly let out an enormous involuntary fart much to his complete embarrassment and the delight of his audience. The room responded with loud applause and cheering and that would have been that if Beefy hadn't responded with one of his quick-witted comments.

'Well, Bill Mills, I think that after that you should be renamed Hayley just like your namesake.'

The comment was lost on every one and there was only a polite but puzzled half laugh in response. Beefy didn't let it go and went on, 'Come on, you lot, use your brains, Hayley Mills is the famous actress and she was the star of that recent film *Whistle Down the Wind*. You must have seen the film. Well our Bill has got the surname, the whistle and the wind so he should be rechristened Hayley.'

The reaction was slow but built up quickly as everyone was impressed by the speed of Beefy's mind to get so quickly to such an obscure conclusion. Bill was doomed to be called Hayley from that moment on and Ben had been amazed how often he heard the story from people over the next few days. He made a point of continuing to call Bill by his proper name as he always had, and Bill seemed to appreciate it, but for the rest of the estate he was forever Hayley.

Just as Ben collected more tea for Dave and himself from Mavis, Bill appeared through the door. Ben quickly ordered a tea for him and they sat down in an empty cubical opposite to the counter, leaving Mavis to play waitress to Dave, which she managed with only minimal spillage and a big smile. After the usual small talk Bill dived straight in to share his concern for one of his customers. Mr Davis was a man in his early 60s who had lived with his wife in a maisonette on the estate for a couple of years. He was a quiet spoken man, always smartly dressed, and ready to pass the time of day. But the past few weeks had brought about a marked change in his wellbeing following the sudden and unexpected death of his wife. His unkempt appearance of scruffy clothes and long uncut lank hair and a marked loss in weight resulted in the appearance of a shuffling old man unable and uninterested in going on.

'I am really frightened that he could end up being suicidal and I feel helpless to know what to do about it. Can you step in to help?'

Ben listened to the story as Bill elaborated on the situation as he saw it, saying there had also been a rapid deterioration in the appearance of the home with curtains remaining closed at all times and the garden completely unattended. 'I have also noticed an increase of mail, which has all the appearances of being final demands for service bills. I think Mr Davies has lost the plot and simply is not the man I have known for ages.'

Ben had every confidence in what Bill was saying and respected him for his compassion and concern for his customer. After talking it over for a while he agreed to follow up on Bill's concern by speaking to Mr Davis's GP and made a note of Mr Davis's full name and address.

When Ben returned to his place at the table the conversation was all about the men's selections for their pools that week. Dave was really involved in the discussion, which was of no real interest to Ben as he had never done the pools in his life. So he let it all flow over him and he thought through what he would do with Dave for the rest of the last day of his placement. There were several issues that needed to be followed up on but in view of the level of Bill's concern he decided that as a priority they should drop in on the health centre on the way back to the office and try and identify who was Desmond Davis's GP.

It was well after two when they eventually left Joe's and there was a mass exit at the same time as all the workmen went off about their business. The health centre was situated on the far side of the green and they were there in a matter of moments. The place was buzzing with mothers and toddlers and there was also an afternoon general practice session about to start, resulting in every seat in the waiting room appearing to be occupied by a senior citizen.

However, Ben was lucky to catch the eye of Mary Harris, who came over to say hello to Dave. He explained why they had called in and Mary quickly went to the records card index and identified Mr Davis's GP as Dr Eddoll, which suited Ben just fine. He arranged with the receptionist that he would call in to see the doctor when the surgery was due to finish at five o'clock. Within a matter of minutes they were back in the office and Mrs Freeman was updating Ben on the day's developments. It was now well into the afternoon and Dave confided in Ben that he had an early start at the hospital the following day. They mutually agreed that there was nothing more to be gained by cramming in further visits so they sat down together and ran through their activities of the week. Ben brought up the subject of Dave spending Christmas with him and his family and he seemed both surprised and delighted by the suggestion, but there was a problem as Dave had already agreed to provide a whole day cover on the ward for Christmas Day. He had done this for the last couple of years to allow colleagues with children to spend Christmas at home with their families. 'It means I keep busy and don't miss my own family so much.'

After a brief discussion it was agreed that Dave would join them for Boxing Day, which he already knew he had off. The pink peril and Dave set off at about 4.30 pm, leaving the team sad to see him go but happier than when he had arrived just five days before. The office showed signs of needing Alice's attention and hopefully she would be back on Monday to resume her unofficial duties. Ben linked up with Dr Eddoll, who knew Desmond Davies from the normal coughs and colds but had not seen him for months and was unaware of any mental health history. It was agreed that Ben and Dr Eddoll would make a joint home visit after morning surgery on Monday.

Chapter 12

Back to Normal

Alice arrived at his office door before he had even had a chance to sit down. The cup of tea was put in front of him and she sat down, clearly planning to make up for lost time. Ben was pleased to see her and particularly so as there was no sign of the 'clown' make up. She had definitely been taking her medication during her absence from the office. After the upheaval the previous week, when Alice had been so upset by Dave's presence, he felt duty bound to let her update him on the state of her bowels. Alice took full advantage and gave him a day-by-day account of her bowel movements over the past week. They got to this morning's efforts and Ben bought the subject to a close by assuring her that they had all missed her and that the office was in urgent need of a good clean and tidy up. Alice liked nothing more than being needed and went off straight away to put the office back in order.

Ben still had a couple of hours before his joint visit to Desmond Davis with Dr Eddoll and took the opportunity to get together with Mrs Freeman and Phil to discuss the recruitment of the new position in the team of a social work assistant. He explained to the others that he was looking for a mature person who had some experience of working with people and of life in general and they gave their general agreement. Ben suggested that the new recruit would start with a small caseload of established clients just to give his or her role some real interest but would generally assist Phil and himself with their day-to-day clients. The applications had been delivered to the office from Pete Evans, the personnel officer, that morning for Ben to read through and select a shortlist. He explained to the others that he intended to read through the fourteen application forms received at home that night and would select the ones to follow up for references. His plan was to hold the interviews in the Highfield office with Pete Evans, which would give the others the chance to meet the applicants and show them over the office.

After morning coffee Ben set off to meet up with Dr Eddoll at his surgery and they went off on the visit to Desmond Davis in the doctor's rather flash Riley, which had every modern comfort including the luxury of heated seats. Mr Davis's house looked sad and unkempt and the garden neglected and unloved. The doorbell didn't work and it took repeated knockings before Mr Davis came to the door. Dr Eddoll took the lead as he already knew Mr Davis, who simply turned around and walked down his hallway back into his kitchen, leaving the front door open for them to follow him in. The smell was not very pleasant and there were dirty dishes and unfinished food on all the surfaces. Mr Davis was beyond concern and slumped down into an old armchair and promptly burst into tears.

He could barely speak but managed to get the message across that he was completely lost and everything was out of control and beyond him. Dr Eddoll was at his caring best and pulled up a chair next to him and slowly helped him to get back under control. 'The whole place is a mess, go and see for yourself,' he said, pointing to the room next door. 'Hilda would have hated to see it like this, she was always so house proud.' His sobs broke out afresh and Ben left the doctor to continue with his support and went into the living room as Mr Davis had suggested. It was a revelation and showed just how bad things had become for Mr Davis since his wife's death.

The living room was like something out of a Dickens novel, just like Miss Havisham's room in *Great Expectations*. It had all the appearances of being frozen at a point of time. Someone had been in the middle of redecorating and the walls had been stripped and the woodwork half painted. All the materials for doing the work were still there on the dining room table. The tin of paint was still open, the paint brushes left uncleaned and gone hard and there was a pile of rolls of wallpaper spread out on the table, some having fallen on the floor and rolled about. Everything was covered in a layer of dust and the whole room appeared to have been abandoned. The confusion was added to by a mound of unopened post, which on examination included a lot of letters which were clearly unpaid bills. Ben realised that they would have to be sorted as a priority if Mr Davis wasn't to end up being cut off from his services.

Ben could hear Mr Davis talking to Dr Eddoll and felt it wise to let them talk together for a while. Meanwhile, he sorted through the accumulated post, extracting those letters which appeared to be important from the junk mail. By the time he returned to the kitchen Dr Eddoll was able to fill him in on the background to Mr Davis finding himself in his depressed condition. His life in the past twelve months had been a nightmare for him. He had been made redundant when the firm he had been with since leaving school went into receivership. Aged sixty-two, the chance of him finding work had proved to be nil despite making numerous job applications. His mortgage had proved beyond his income as he had taken it out quite late in life, having sold his previous house to pay off his only son's gambling debts. Unfortunately, his son continued to gamble and after running up a whole new set of debts had simply disappeared and Mr Davis and his wife had heard nothing of him for months. Their home had been repossessed and they found themselves rehoused on the Highfield Estate, where they knew nobody but they had each other and were determined to make the best of it. Then the final tragedy struck. Mrs Davis had a chesty cold which she couldn't shake off and she developed pneumonia. This quickly turned into sepsis and she was rushed into hospital via casualty, but nothing could be done and she died during the night.

Mr Davis was alone and it was all too much for him and his life stopped as he steadily fell apart. By today he was incapable of making any decisions and would have gone along with anything that Dr Eddoll's suggested. After a phone call to the duty consultant Ben helped Mr Davis to pack a bag, secure the house and drove him to St Margaret's. Ben thought that Mr Davis's life had probably been saved by the simple fact that his postman cared. He considered that the world sometimes seemed a tough old place.

That evening Ben went to bed early and read through the application forms and reduced the fourteen down to four for follow up. The four he selected were quite a diverse group but all had a couple of things in common, namely they were all in their thirties or forties and all had some previous experience of working with people. The added bonus as far as their usefulness in the team was that they were all drivers with their own transport, which would prove invaluable considering the limited public transport available in Highfield. The following day he called into the personnel department to run through the applications with Pete Evans. They talked them through and Pete largely agreed with Ben's selections, but suggested the addition of one other applicant who had previously worked as a social worker with a national voluntary organisation. It was agreed that Pete would organise the following up of references and that the interviews would be conducted by Ben and Pete in the office at Highfield in three weeks' time.

Chapter 13

Many Happy Returns

The weekend was unusually mild for the time of year and the Newman household relaxed as a family. Sandy had to work Saturday morning but finished up at midday and Ben and the boys all enjoyed a lie in before getting up to prepare a 'surprise lunch' for Sandy. The kitchen looked like a bomb had dropped when she arrived home but she was full of praise for the eggy bread and baked beans they had prepared. Ben reflected that Sandy was much easier to live with in recent months and determined to do everything in his power to keep her happy. Her birthday was coming up in November, which had always been something of a non-event as it came so near to Christmas. He usually gave her money, which she invariably spent on clothes to top up her wardrobe, but this year it was going to be different; he had a plan.

The germ of the idea had started all the way back in January when 'Top of the Pops' had first appeared on the television every Wednesday evening at 6.30 pm. It was an immediate 'must watch' for the whole family and they cuddled up each week after tea on the sofa armed with either sweets or packets of crisps. They each had their favourite artists. Ben favoured the Rolling Stones, Sandy preferred the Beatles from day one and the boys enjoyed the mad antics of Freddie and the Dreamers. However, much like the rest of the country, the family soon declared the Beatles as their number one choice. This was just as well as they had dominated the hit parade over the past year and even had their album *A Hard Day's Night* at number one of the album charts for an amazing twenty-one week run. Ben became a huge fan of John, Sandy favoured Paul and the boys thought Ringo on his drums was the cat's whiskers. The BBC soon changed the time of the programme to 7.30 pm, which made it even more popular with the boys as it ran past their normal bedtime. The Newman institution of watching 'Top of the Pops' was firmly established and the later time just contributed to the sense of naughtiness and fun.

Ben's own interest in pop music had, to say the least, been a bit hit and miss in his teens although he had often listened to Radio Luxemburg in bed late at night. On balance he much preferred the comedy programmes on the light programme and serials like 'The Day of the Triffids' and 'The Hitchhikers Guide to the Galaxy'. He had been introduced to American pop music and pop concerts by Andy, a close friend from university. In fact they had both gone to the same grammar school but were in different streams and barely knew each other whilst at school. From memory Ben had recalled Andy Beaufort as a bit of a posh geek whose gabardine blazer and large tortoiseshell glasses stood him out from the flannel blazers and national health spectacles worn by the majority. It was therefore a bit of a shock when Andy turned up at Bristol University to live in the same halls as Ben, and in fact the neighbouring room on the first day of the university year. The shock didn't end there as Andy had reinvented himself during the summer holidays by modelling himself on his idol Buddy Holly. He had taken to wearing a tight dark suit with drainpipe trousers, thick black rimmed glasses, and had his hair piled in a Brylcreem-created quiff finished off with the beginnings of a DA at the back.

Ben thought it did look a bit like a duck's ass but the overall effect was pretty impressive. He and Andy hit it off from day one and although they were doing different courses spent a lot of time in each other's company. Ben learnt that Andy's dad was something big in the city and worked in London for most of the week. He was generous to Andy with his money but rarely with his time. Andy always had money in his pocket, unlike Ben, who struggled to make ends meet and this resulted in Andy paying for most of their activities which Ben gratefully, quickly got used to and it became the acceptable norm. Andy had a huge record collection and was happy to share it with Ben and their other housemates. He was an avid reader of all pop music magazines and loved knowing obscure facts about the artists, which he delighted in sharing with Ben. Thus Ben came to know that Elvis thought Roy Orbison was the greatest singer in the world, that Chuck Berry couldn't read or write and loads of other irrelevant facts. Their joint interests brought about Ben's introduction to pop concerts and paid for by the generosity of Andy's allowance they saw a lot of famous singers; most noticeably the likes of Little Richard, Chuck Berry and Gerry Lee Lewis, all of whom performed concerts at the Colston Hall in Bristol. The concerts had been completely beyond anything Ben had ever experienced.

The audiences were almost exclusively male and seemed to be largely made up of Teddy boys all dressed in the traditional 'uniform' of colourful draped coats, drainpipe trousers, boot lace ties and brothel creeper shoes. There was never any sign of the sort of trouble often associated with Teddy boys and the audience sang along with all the songs and appeared to know all the words. The atmosphere was electric and the cacophony of sound reverberated around the theatre. Ben and Andy loved it and went back to their halls in a state of excitement to listen to records of the songs they had heard live at the concerts long into the night. These activities tailed off as Ben's course proceeded but had been briefly resurrected several years later on 27 May 1963 when Andy rang up and invited Ben along to a Roy Orbison concert at the Capitol Theatre in Cardiff.

In the second year at university in Bristol, Ben and Andy moved into a shared house in Clifton quite near the university with a mixed group of students and Sandy, also from Exworth, was amongst the group. It was perhaps predictable that Ben and Sandy would pair up, but unlike most such pairings, which were not uncommon, they remained as a couple which inevitably effected Ben's relationship with Andy. Sex proved a bigger draw than pop and his interest waned, but Andy and Ben remained on good terms. Sandy introduced several of her girlfriends to Andy but none of the relationships went anywhere. At the end of their university courses Ben and Sandy returned to Exworth but Andy joined his father's firm in London. Ben and Andy wrote to each other for a while but this moved on to be a long letter each way at Christmas. Last year's letter from Andy was a real surprise as he told them that he had come out as gay and had been living with a partner called Brian for six months and had never been happier. Ben wrote back immediately to congratulate Andy and to invite him and Brian to visit at any time. Sandy and Ben agreed that they were truly pleased but were surprised at their own naivety, as neither of them had ever considered that Andy might be gay, but it did explain why none of Sandy's friends had ever made progress.

Apart from the annual exchange of letters Ben and Andy did not meet up again until just over a year ago when quite out of the blue Ben got the phone call from Andy inviting him to attend the Roy Orbison concert in Cardiff. Ben was only too pleased to accept the invitation as he had always wanted to see live the guy who Elvis had described as the best singer in the world. Andy arranged to drive down and pick him up and said he would drive him home afterwards before going on to his parent's home in Exworth for a fleeting visit. However, things had moved on from their university days and the biggest change of all was in Andy.

Ben and Sandy barely recognised him. All traces of Buddy Holly were long gone to be replaced by a stylish haircut, a smart executive suit, and a Rolex watch and handmade shoes. He arrived in a Mercedes convertible with a personalised number plate but he still seemed as friendly as ever and pleased to see them and to meet the boys. Despite his obvious success in London it emerged that there was one big problem in his life and that was that his parents could not accept his sexuality and refused to meet with Brian.

'We are devoted and it means I see very little of my parents. That's no change where my dad is concerned but Mum and Dad have now divorced and I feel very guilty that mum is on her own and I really don't see enough of her. Still, I am going to stay with her for a day or two after the concert and I hope I can bring her around to meeting Brian and getting to know him.'

The concert was nothing like their past experience of concerts by the American greats. Roy Orbison could sing but lacked stage presence and made no effort to have any rapport with the audience, and as a consequence the atmosphere in the concert was lukewarm. Fortunately, the evening was saved by the joint top of the bill, which was none other than the Beatles. Andy explained that at the start of the tour the Beatles had been the support group but with all their phenomenal success they had been redefined as joint top billing with Roy Orbison. Ben thought that might explain why Roy Orbison seemed to be just going through the motions.

The moment the Beatles came on to stage the concert hall burst into life and just for a moment Andy and Ben were back to their former days, bouncing about and singing along with the music. Their evening was complete when the Beatles finished their set with the classic Little Richard hit 'Long Tall Sally'. They parted on good terms back at Ben's house but Andy drove straight off to his mum's saying that she would be wondering where he was. Ben suspected that they were unlikely to meet again, but then life moves on and they were definitely going in different directions. Sandy was very jealous when he told her about the Beatles and the germ of an idea for her birthday was formed.

In the following August, Ben had been looking through the local paper whilst enjoying a break in the back room at Joe's when he spotted an advert for a future concert at the Colston Hall on 10th November just three days before Sandy's birthday and the opportunity to bring about his plan came to him in a flash. He raced back to the office and rang the booking office at the Colston Hall, and was fortunate to be able to purchase two tickets which had just been returned because of a family emergency. He couldn't believe his luck and sat for quite a while thinking through how this good fortune could be turned into something very special for Sandy and himself. They both knew Bristol really well and had regularly walked down Park Street to the city centre to meet up with friends in the pubs and jazz clubs. They now lived some 150 miles away from Bristol and would have to use the old Cortina for transport. It would obviously be better to stay in Bristol overnight but they would need somewhere to park, which was notoriously difficult in the city centre area. Then Ben remembered the swanky Royal Hotel at the foot of Park Street which had an underground car park and was within a hundred yards of the Colston Hall. They had often fantasised about staying there each time they had passed it when at university and it was obviously a pipe dream then, but why not now? Of course it would cost an arm and a leg but he had already saved a little money towards the treat by cutting right back with his smoking and he decided that now was as good a time as any to become a non-smoker.

The hotel booking was made and confirmed, including an underground parking place and the all-important concert tickets were delivered to him at his office. That just left a babysitter to be arranged for Jack and Nick and unfortunately the concert was on a Tuesday with school for the boys the following day. This meant that he had to involve Sandy in this part of the planning as she was the one with all the potential contacts for babysitters. So he simply told her that they were going away for the night to celebrate her birthday, but flatly refused to give her any other details. Sandy was full of questions and got quite cross when he refused to give her any answers. Still it was arranged that Becky aged fifteen from two doors along would move in with the boys for the night. Her mother, Angela, would be around to keep an eye on the situation and would take the boys to school on the Wednesday. Becky was delighted to earn extra pocket money and the boys were thrilled to have her sleeping over. Becky had babysat the boys before and the boys knew it would be fun and a late bedtime.

On the day Ben and Sandy set off at midday and three hours later pulled into Bristol with Sandy still guessing all sorts of possible destinations and happenings. However, she was totally surprised when Ben turned the car into the Royal's car park. She was dumbfounded when he proceeded to sign them in as guests and their room turned out to be as special as they had always imagined.

The evening meal was booked for 6 pm so they had a couple of hours to enjoy returning to the afternoon bed activities that had been such a major part of their student days. Dressed in their smartest gear and feeling rather conspicuous they went down to the dining hall and enjoyed a leisurely three-course meal. Ben then suggested a walk around the centre to visit some old haunts. They wandered past the Wimpy Bar next to the Hippodrome Theatre, which had been one of their favourite eating places in the past any time that they had been in funds. Then strolled along towards the jazz club situated at the top of Colston Street but were confronted by a sea of people. As they approached the Colston Hall Sandy spotted a poster advertising the Beatle's concert and stopped dead in her tracks. 'You haven't, have you, you have, you lovely man,' she said and kissed Ben with a passion that brought cheers from the crowd around them. At that moment Ben knew he had scored a major success, and so it proved. The concert was just brilliant, not that you could hear much of the music for the constant screaming of the many girls in the audience. Sandy just loved it and even let out a few screams of her own when Paul shook his head violently in time to the beat. The evening was rounded off by them sharing a Wimpy and fries and two frothy coffees on the way back to the hotel. Not that they were hungry, but it just seemed like the right thing to do. They had a full English breakfast in the morning before the trip home, involving a slight detour to pass their old shared house, which they agreed looked every bit as run down as it did in their day but was still special as it was their first shared home.

When the boys came home, they were full of their evening with Becky and showed no interest in what their parents had been up to whilst away. However, that all changed when the family sat down together to enjoy 'Top of the Pops' at 7.30 pm. As usual the programme featured the Beatles and Sandy just mentioned, very casually, that they had seen them live the previous evening. The boys were well impressed and even more so when she showed them the programme with the message written on the front, 'To Sandy, love from Paul xx'. The boys pranced around the room chanting 'Mum's got a boyfriend.' They didn't for one moment notice how near the writing was to their dad's usual scrawl. As a final treat Sandy produced the poster of Ringo on his drums, which she had bought for the boys at the concert. As soon as 'Top of the Pops' had finished the boys rushed up to their bedroom armed with Sellotape, arguing about the best location for the poster.

Chapter 14

The Day of the Interviews

Sandy's birthday successfully completed, Ben had to settle down to a busy few weeks at work in the run up to Christmas. The day of the interviews for the new post of social work assistant had finally arrived and he was feeling a bit apprehensive as it was the first time he had been in the situation of recruiting anybody to join his team. Up to now his small team had just sort of happened, and he realised that he was lucky that they all muddled along reasonably well. He did not want to rock the boat, but was determined that the new appointment would be a positive addition to the team. The references were all in and didn't really add much as they all seemed to be positive and none raised any obvious controversial issues. Pete confirmed that in his experience this was usually the case as the names of the referees had been submitted by the applicants and it was unlikely that they would suggest anybody with something negative to say.

Ben had prepared for the interviews and had planned with Pete in general terms who would ask what. He had cleaned his shoes to an unusual shine, Sandy had pressed his trousers and he was wearing his best shirt as yet still retaining its original collar and tail as it remained unaltered by Sandy's night school training. The outfit was completed by his old school tie, which had remained unworn for the best part of a decade, and a sports jacket Sandy had acquired for him from a charity shop. The jacket almost fitted him perfectly and along with a careful shave that morning and a recent haircut he looked at himself in the mirror and found himself saying what he had heard his father say out loud to himself in the mirror almost every day when he was a boy: 'Bigger men have I seen but smarter never!'

He was as ready as he was ever going to be but his guts still played up as he drove up the hill to Highfield. The rain was pouring down and he drove straight past Boxer Mark Two, who was waiting at the gate to his field. Not risking messing up his interview preparations on the muddy roadside verge, he shouted out sorry and promised double helpings the following day but the old horse showed no signs of hearing.

There were three men and two women to be interviewed, starting at ten o'clock and programmed for one each hour, with a break of an hour for lunch. Ben intended to introduce Pete to the joys of a big breakfast at Joe's at lunchtime but would not be sharing the right of passage to the inner sanctum, which was a privilege not to be shared. The interviews would be taking place in Ben's office, which was just about big enough to accommodate three people. The interviewees would wait in the general office, which would give Mrs Freeman and Phil the chance to meet them and form initial impressions.

The first applicant was Tony Cross, who was the one Pete had chosen to be included from the pile of application forms. On first sight he seemed a good choice. He was early thirties, unmarried, casually dressed but clean and tidy and had a relaxed and responsive manner. He had worked in a variety of day care and residential units for the mentally handicapped and had also done some work with homeless and vagrant people. The interview progressed in a relaxed and un-confrontational manner and Ben found himself warming to Tony Cross and was scoring him highly on the point scoring system that Pete had suggested they should use. However, as the interview was coming to an end Pete asked Tony if he had any questions and he asked about sponsorship by the county for Professional Training Courses. He explained that he had been offered a place for the course in Exeter starting the following September and was seeking financial support. Pete responded by explaining that the county had quite a number of unqualified staff needing sponsorship and that the current plans could take five or more years to complete. The atmosphere in the interview changed dramatically and Tony Cross quickly became aggressive, stating that they had been wasting his time and they could stick their job and at that point walked out, slamming the door to Ben's office violently and then the front door to the building, which seemed to shake under the impact. Ben crossed through the favourable score on his score sheet!

Things went from bad to worse as the next candidate was a no show. Pete reassured Ben that this was not uncommon and within a few moments Alice brought them in a cup of coffee and some of her special jam tarts. Ben noticed Pete's jam tart was carefully put away in his handkerchief and he remembered the effect Alice's appearance could have on the un-initiated. He ate two without any qualms. The spare hour was spent just chatting and they both learnt a lot more about each other's lives, which were surprisingly similar and the basis of an ongoing friendship was forming. Two down and three to go. Blanche Donaldson the twelve o'clock was waiting for them in the general office and one look at Mrs Freeman's face spoke legions. She appeared stunned and when Ben saw Blanche he could quite understand. She was a good six feet tall and wide with it and was dressed completely in leathers. The ensemble was completed by heavy knee-length boots and she had a black motor cycle helmet under her arm, which sported a large white skull and crossbones. When she followed him into his office she seemed to take up all the available space and when she spoke for the first time it was with such a strong northern accent that it was a struggle to understand a word of what she was saying. But whatever she had to say there was plenty of it as she proceeded to take over the interview by going into a long diatribe about herself.

She was in her thirties, never married but lived with her current partner and her three children from different old relationships. She appeared to be immensely proud of this achievement. Ben attempted to regain control of the interview by taking her through her application form, focusing particularly on her work history and her current position. For many years she had worked in the prison service and more recently was working in a probation hostel. She quickly assured Ben and Pete that she was a tough lady and took no shit from anyone and that she had dealt with a lot of mad people in her time. She confided that her system with them was to be tough and found that as a consequence they never caused her any problem. Ben really believed it as she was one of the most intimidating people he had ever had the misfortune to meet and any client would have been terrified. The interview struggled on for a few more minutes, during which Blanche proceeded to roll herself a thin cigarette, which she lit before offering her tobacco pouch around. The offer was declined and the interview eventually came to an end and she clumped her way out.

Both Ben and Pete were exhausted and Ben had a quick word with Mrs Freeman before leading Pete out of the fire door and across the green to Joe's. Pete was impressed with everything about Joe's and declared his envy of Ben for having such a welcoming place on his patch. 'Of course we have a canteen at work but it is a miserable sort of place that serves up school dinner type food and surrounded by long-faced colleagues who tend to eat and leave with little or no chatting. Nothing like this place with its proper food, good coffee and loads of chat and joking. I love it, you lucky sod.'

Ben laughed and went on to apologise for the wasted morning. Pete was unconcerned and told him that it often took several batches of interviews before getting the right candidate. 'I don't mind at all as it gets me out of the office where I am usually bored stiff with the same old bureaucratic nonsense that is my job.' He went on to explain that it had been his father who had suggested that he should work for the local authority when he left school at sixteen. After all it was 'a job for life', unlike his father experience of being made redundant no less than three times and 'the council gave good pensions'.

'Christ I was only a kid and here was my dad talking about pensions still I had no better ideas and went along with it. At first it went well and once I was courting I became very ambitious and surprised myself how quickly I progressed through the ranks. The money was good enough to get a mortgage and I now have a nice home, a lovely wife and two gorgeous daughters but I am bored out of my skull at work and have nothing else to aspire to, just waiting for dead men's shoes and they are not much older than me.'

Ben sympathised and the conversation went back and forth between them in a comfortable fashion, and the time to return came around all too quickly. Ben decided that the day had not been a complete waste of time as he now felt he had a 'mate' at headquarters.

Three down only two to go, Ben was not feeling optimistic. The two o'clock candidate was waiting for them when they returned to the office. He was in deep conversation with Mrs Freeman, who seemed relieved to see them back. 'This is Mr Colin Peterson, who arrived in good time for his interview and we have been chatting for almost an hour, but I must get on now as there is a lot to do; so over to you.'

Ben and Pete introduced themselves and shook hands with Mr Peterson which proved to be a rather limp and damp experience. He was in his mid-thirties, short and sort of barrel shaped but was smartly dressed in a suit and tie and highly polished shoes. Ben smiled to himself that he was not the only one who had polished his shoes for the occasion. His round face was quite florid and the small veins around his nose suggested that he enjoyed a drink. This may well have been the case as Ben had noticed a strong smell of peppermint when they had shaken hands. The whole image of Mr Peterson was topped off by a Bobby Charlton wrap over which he checked regularly throughout the interview. As usual Ben started the interview by asking him to tell them a bit about himself.

His background was unusual, as he said he was an ex-Baptist minister and had spent five years 'doing missionary work abroad'. When Ben enquired further it emerged that the five years had been spent teaching English in a school in Italy but he then claimed that he had had to return to this country to look after his elderly parents. Ben didn't pursue this subject as he could already see that Mr Peterson was rather fragile and would crumble under any more insightful questions. His strong suspicion was that Mr Peterson had had some sort of breakdown and had returned home to the sanctuary of his parent's home. So he just let him talk for a while and he rambled on about having had several temporary jobs recently but nothing that met his needs to serve. When Ben asked about any experience he may have had of mental illness there was a lengthy pause before he said that he had known people who suffered with it. He then claimed to have done some work with the Samaritans, but when Ben flipped to the references in his file of papers there was nothing from the ministry nor the Samaritans, which he thought probably spoke volumes. Throughout the interview Mr Peterson's conversation was liberally scattered with 'Praise the Lord and God bless' which quickly got on Ben's nerves, and he guessed the clients would soon find it wearing. The interview came to an eventual finish with another limp handshake and a couple of 'God blesses' which Mr Peterson could be heard repeating to Mrs Freeman on the way out.

Four down, none of any use, and just one left to see, Ben's disappointment deepened after all these were meant to be the best selected from all the applications received. Pete remained unconcerned and Ben suspected that he was anticipating another trip out of headquarters and a second lunch time at Joe's. When Ben went to the general office to collect the final applicant no one had yet arrived and it was just two minutes before three. He was beginning to think it was another no show when the sound of hurried footsteps could be heard in the corridor and a diminutive, dishevelled figure appeared in the door way. This really was a sight to behold: a short blond-haired lady dressed smartly with a short skirt not at the Mary Quant level but only a little longer. The skirt was unfortunate as it displayed a pair of grubby knees partially covered by stockings laddered beyond saving. Her face had a long streak of dirt smeared across the bridge of her nose and running down her left cheek on to her chin. The whole effect was finished off with a beehive hair style, which was obviously designed to give her height, but now had a strong lopsided lean to the left. Her obvious state of distress was exemplified by the shake in her voice as she said, 'I hope I am not too late, I am Susan Fraser. I left home in good time but I got a puncture right out in the sticks and had to change the wheel. The old one was on really tight and it took me ages.'

Mrs Freeman was the first to react and she eased Mrs Fraser into the office and pushed Ben out, telling him to go and get a cup of tea and leave her to sort things out. Ben explained to Pete what was happening and took the opportunity to check through Mrs Fraser's application form. It showed that she lived in the village of Little Poppy Field some twelve miles or so from Highfield and out in the country. Ben knew it quite well as it was on the old road to the coast, which he had travelled along many times as a child on route to their annual holiday location of Bude. However, he had not been through the village for years as a dual carriageway bypass designed to ease road congestion had circumnavigated the village altogether, leaving it a peaceful backwater. He sat back in his chair and sipped the hot tea that Alice had been only too pleased to provide. He felt sure he had seen Mrs Fraser somewhere before but he couldn't think where it had been, then it suddenly came to him and he laughed out loud. Pete wanted to know what he found so funny and he explained that Mrs Fraser reminded him of the new member of the Carry-On team who was appearing in the most recent Carry On film *Carry on Spying*. Barbara Windsor had been an immediate hit, playing the part of a saucy young girl who had a problem keeping her clothes on. Both Pete and Ben immediately became more optimistic about their final applicant, who had already impressed by being able to change a wheel.

The image that appeared at the doorway a few minutes later was a marked improvement. Her hair was piled on top of her head in an attractive neat bundle, her face had lost it dirty smudges, which had been replaced by just a touch of makeup and her laddered stockings had been consigned to the bin. The only visual evidence of her traumatic journey was her bare legs now sporting a plaster on her right knee and the fact that her bright red nail varnish was suffering a chip or two. Ben welcomed her and immediately asked where she had learnt to change wheels and was rewarded with a wry smile and just the hint of a giggle. She told them that she had seen her husband do it once and she had simply done what he had done and it worked, but added that it was a lot harder than it had looked when he had done it. They congratulated her on her resourcefulness and invited her to sit down if she was happy to continue with the interview.

She sat down and tugged her skirt down in an attempt to cover her bare knees and Ben thought to himself that she was no Barbara Windsor, who would undoubtedly have seen the advantage in flashing a little leg. As before with the other candidates Ben asked Susan to tell them a bit about herself and she visibly relaxed as she filled in her details. She was forty-two and married to John Fraser, who owned a couple of butcher and wet fish shops, one in Little Poppy Field and the other on the high street in the centre of Exworth. When they had first got married they had put all their savings into the small shop in Little Poppy Field, which had been empty for several years. They had lived above the shop and had worked really hard to set it up. They had concentrated on locally sourced produce wherever possible and over time had built up a good little business. Village life suited them well and their two boys, born less than a year apart, had gone to the small local school and enjoyed a carefree childhood. They had gone on to the Exworth Grammar School and were now both at Leeds University, one reading law and the other architecture.

As the boys were growing up both Susan and her husband had put a lot of time and energy into building up the business and about five years ago had opened their larger shop on the Exworth high street. It had been very successful and they expanded it to include a delicatessen. Unfortunately, about three years ago, running the two shops had proved to be a step too far for John and he had suffered a mild heart attack. The medics had suggested that he should cut back on his workload and he was started on medication. After a family conference it was agreed that they should put a manager into the Exworth shop and leave John free to run the Little Poppy Field shop, which proved to be a good solution. A side effect of this was that Susan didn't need to assist with the business apart from doing occasional paperwork and she found herself with time on her hands.

She took over the running of the local Brownie pack and helped with the delivery of meals by the WVS but with the boys now away at university she felt able to consider a full-time job of her own, hence her application and the interview. By this time Susan was fully recovered and presented as a mature, caring woman who was happy to respond to questions with no apparent hidden agenda. Ben asked about her experience of working with mentally ill or handicapped people and she admitted that it was limited. She said that she had had a girl with Down's syndrome in her Brownie pack for over two years and described her as a delight. She also delivered meals to several clients with dementia and she said she really wished she could spend more time with them as they were obviously vulnerable, but her time was limited by the number of meals she had to deliver. Ben explained about the members of the team and the roles they performed and stressed that she would be expected to work with clients and their families in their own homes with only limited supervision. Susan did not seem at all phased by this and said that she would be happy to help the team in any way. She asked various questions about the scale of demand and the area covered as well as practical questions about salary and expenses. Pete took on the replies and Ben sat back and observed the discussion.

Susan was obviously the best candidate they had seen and seemed competent and full of energy. He had warmed to her from the start and was pretty sure he had found his new staff member, but decided to sound out Mrs Freeman and Phil before making a final decision. So he brought the interview to a close and told Susan Fraser he would be in touch shortly and she thanked them for their time and stopped on the way out to thank Mrs Freeman for her help. Pete's opening comment was straightforward and he simply said that she would 'do nicely'. That sentiment was echoed by Mrs Freeman and Phil and the decision was made with Pete agreeing to make a formal written offer once Ben had rung Susan to confirm that she wanted the job. A starting date of the first week in January was agreed and Susan was delighted to accept when he rang her later that evening. Ben then dictated short letters to the other candidates, thanking them for their interest and advising them they were unsuccessful on this occasion.

Chapter 15

Busy Times

With the new staff member sorted Ben hoped to get back to more routine matters and the new week started much as normal. After dropping the boys off at school he set off for the office in a relaxed way, choosing to spend a few minutes more than usual with Boxer Mark Two. He felt a bit guilty that he had not given him any treats for three days so he gave him the full works today of an apple, a couple of carrots and nearly a whole packet of polo mints. Boxer Mark Two seemed to be appreciative and just stood there and allowed Ben to fondle him on the nose and neck. Ben was whispering sweet nothings to him when the big lorry he had seen before pulled up and the driver jumped down. He was a middle-aged, big, heavily built man who was a bit overweight but not someone you would want to argue with. However, he had a jolly face and smiled warmly as he stuck his hand out to be shaken.

'Hello, I know who you are, you're the welfare man, and Jessie and Mary have told me all about you. I am Robbie Scadding and it is my yard just down the road, you can't miss it. I am really pleased with the way you have been spending time with old Solomon here, he hasn't had much of a life.'

He went on to explain that the horse belonged to one of his long-standing regular customers. Reggie Brooks, who was an old-fashioned rag and bone man. Robbie went on to explain that at one time there had been half a dozen horse and carts plying their trade in and around Exworth but Reggie and Solomon were the last. Solomon had lived the past 15 years in Reggie's garage and had been out each day pulling a cart as Reggie had gone totting all around the area. But the horse had become too old to work now and the ever-increasing traffic meant that Reggie had replaced him with a second-hand electric milk float. It looked like Solomon was doomed for the knackers yard but no one wanted that to happen so he ended up in Robbie's scrubby field whilst they tried to sort out a better solution. 'You won't be seeing him much more as we have located a place for him to retire to at a charity called Horse World in Whitchurch near Bristol.'

Ben and Robbie parted on good terms and Robbie made a final comment. 'Keep your eye on this field though as I have big plans for it.' He tapped the side of his nose knowingly and laughed to himself as he clambered back into his lorry. With a short fanfare on his cow horns he pulled away, leaving Ben in a cloud of dust. Ben was left none the wiser about his plans for the field but was pleased that Boxer Mark Two was heading for better things and would end his days being properly fed and cared for with other horses for company.

On arriving at the office Ben sat down at his desk to drink the tea promptly delivered by Alice and to plan his visits for the week. At any one time he had six or eight clients that he was working with intensely, where the work involved trying to effect some significant change in the client's circumstances or understanding. This usually required lengthy interviews and frequent visits. In addition, Ben supervised well over thirty clients and their families who had long-term problems with either mentally handicapped or mentally ill members but were mainly able to contain the problems involved without too much intervention from Ben. In addition, there were always new clients who were suffering with an acute mental illness, which often involved an admission to a psychiatric hospital and follow up in the community. He usually tried to put a day or two aside each week to visit some of the more straightforward clients on a sort of rotational system, but his plans were frequently upset by some emergency or additional call on his time. He made a short list of four or five clients due a visit and also planned to call in to see Desmond Davis, the man who had been referred to him by Whistling Willy, alias Hayley. However, he didn't even get out of the front door before he was called back by Mrs Freeman as he was wanted on the telephone. She whispered to him that it was 'Councillor Rudge, and he has asked for you by name.'

Ben's heart sank. Councillor Rudge was the local Labour man and was notorious for being a pompous and aggressive man who delighted in making critical comments about local authority staff, particularly in the local press. He took a deep breath and prepared himself for an onslaught. He was surprised by the almost reasonable tone of Councillor Rudge's opening gambit and knew immediately that the man wanted a favour and so it proved. He advised Ben that he was the chairman of the Ensley rotary and they had a meeting in a couple of days' time. They always had a meal followed by a talk and this week's talk was planned to be by a man who had swum the channel three times but he had dropped out at the last minute with a heavy cold. 'I would like you to take his place.'

Ben tried to buy some time to think of a good excuse and said rather stupidly that he knew nothing about swimming the Channel. In fact he couldn't swim. Councillor Rudge was no fool and quickly advised him that it was a golden opportunity to do some useful PR for the department. Ben reluctantly agreed to give a talk on community mental health services and wrote down the details of time and place. He had done such talks several times over the past couple of years but it was usually to various women's groups who frequently either nodded off or were otherwise engaged with their knitting. The sound of clicking knitting needles was often the usual accompaniment to his talks but he knew that this would be very different as the rotary was made up of influential businessmen and women in the area whose primary aim was to do charity work. He would have to be on top form and he returned to his office to read through and update his notes. The routine visits would have to wait for another day.

Once he felt he was up to speed for his talk to rotary he decided to grab an early lunch at Joe's before heading across the town to St Margaret's to visit Desmond Davis. He had spoken to the charge nurse on male admissions a couple of times in the past two weeks and the reports of Mr Davis's progress were encouraging so Ben felt the time was right to help Mr Davis begin to get back in control of his life. He located Mr Davis in the lounge sat reading a newspaper and the signs of improvement were obvious. He was tidily dressed in pullover and slacks and was even wearing a tie unlike the other patients dotted around the room. He recognised Ben immediately and jumped up to shake his hand. 'Good to see you and my most grateful thanks for getting me in here. I think you could have saved my life.'

Ben and Desmond were quickly on first-name terms and soon had their heads together to sort out what needed doing. Desmond agreed that a priority would be to sort out the pile of correspondence and unpaid bills that remained unopened on his kitchen table at home. It was agreed that Ben would collect them along with a few other things that Desmond needed and they would get together the following day. Ben was given a front door key to Desmond's home and was also asked to bring in his cheque book from the bureau and a small stash of cash, which was hidden in a milk jug in the kitchen cupboard. When he got back to the office he found Phil sitting with Mrs Freeman catching up on dictating her reports.

He had had a bad experience a year or so before when a client's relative had claimed to head office that he had stolen from an elderly lady client, whom he had found collapsed behind her front door when he had visited her routinely. She was in a dreadful state and had been on the floor for a lengthy period of time and was hypothermic. He had rung for an ambulance and she had been admitted to the general hospital where she died a few days later. Headquarters had invited the complainant in for a meeting and Ben had been summoned to attend. It turned out to be a ridiculous nonsense with the relative claiming she could not find a skirt she had purchased for her aunt's birthday present amongst her belongings when she went to clear the house. A phone call to the hospital confirmed that the skirt and the rest of her clothes had been heavily soiled from her time on the floor and had been confined to the hospital incinerator. Ben had not receive an apology from the relative, who walked out without further comment. Headquarters cleared him of any accusation but he knew that mud tends to stick and he was less than happy. As a consequence Ben introduced a rule for the team that if anyone was dealing with a client's property when they weren't there they must always have a second person present and all dealings had to be fully recorded and signed by both members of staff involved. Phil accepted that her involvement was needed and once she had finished her dictation they went off to Desmond's together.

Chapter 16

A Very Special Client

The journey into the office passed without Ben really being very aware of it. Everything was the same as it had been many times before, drizzling rain, stop-start traffic and the usual rumble from his guts. Solomon, alias Boxer Mark Two, was on duty at the makeshift gate to his scrubby field and was rewarded with a bag of carrots that Ben had bought at Jessie's shop en route to the office. He had taken the opportunity to talk to Jessie about his meeting Robbie Scadding a couple of days before and Jessie had broken into a warm smile.

"He is a real rough diamond but one of the best. We were in the same class all through school and he was always into some mischief or other." It was clear that Jessie had a lot more to tell but the arrival outside of the bus to the Exworth bus station brought the usual rush of customers and she sent him on his way with the promise of more next time they got together. Ben was pleased to note that the horse had fresh water and hay and that the filthy old covering of soaking wet sacking had been replaced by an ancient green waterproof tarpaulin. As ever the carrots were well received and after a brief chat Ben left him to his lonely existence.

Over cups of coffee Phil and Ben spent a couple of hours running through the list of clients on their caseloads trying to build up a small caseload for Susan Fraser to work with when she started after Christmas. The clients selected were a mixed bunch, but all people with long-term problems and a good relationship with the department. Ben had also decided to introduce Susan to one of his more complex clients that he had worked with intensively over the past year or so. He was able to rationalise the choice as he felt that the particular client would benefit from having a woman working with her and Susan's bubbly personality could prove to be a bonus, but it was not an easy choice as he had invested a lot of time and energy into helping Hanca Parsons.

Hanca had never been classified as mentally ill and she was certainly not mentally handicapped, but from anyone's viewpoint she was clearly an eccentric, a strictly one-off. She had been brought to Ben's attention about a year ago when he was summoned to an emergency meeting with the District Housing Subcommittee at headquarters. He had never met the chairman of the committee, Alderman Herbert Anstey, before but knew him by reputation as he was rarely out of the local newspaper. He was certainly a local bigwig with the reputation of being tough and good at getting his own way. He owned an engineering metal turning company that was amongst the biggest employers in the area and had also been the chairman of the local football club Exworth Town for well over thirty years.

The subcommittee was made up of four councillors who quickly emerged as totally subservient to Herbert Anstey, whatever his wish might be. The only other person in the meeting was Oliver Manning the Highfield Housing manager who was an old friend of Ben's from his early days as resettlement officer. Instinctively they sat together, which was just as well as they were the objects for all that followed. Herbert took the central seat, which Ben noticed was just that bit higher than all the other seats, and took control of the whole meeting. He explained that he had a personal interest in the situation to be discussed and that his involvement went back more than twenty years. He went on to explain that for many years he had been the chairman of the Exworth semi-professional football club which for most of the years had languished around mid-table of one or other of the divisions of the Southern League.

He went on to describe how the football manager at the time had recruited a local teenager called Terry Parsons, who was a raw but natural talent. He quickly displayed remarkable football skills and by the time he was seventeen he was a regular in the team and a prolific goal scorer. During the next three years Terry scored over a hundred goals and at the age of nineteen was made captain of the team. Under Terry's leadership the team prospered like never before or since and after a couple of promotions the team was hovering near the top of their division with the prospect of promotion to the dizzy highs of the football league proper. Scouts from the major clubs in the country started to pursue Terry with all sorts of incentives to join their clubs. Vast sums were offered to the club to get his signature but Herbert rejected them all out of hand and he and Terry continued to press on with their ambition to get their small club into the football league. Terry knew that personal fame was there for the taking but for the time being was content to be a large fish in a small pond. War changed everything as it did for so many, and Terry and most of the team signed up to fight and the football team ceased to exist during the war years.

Herbert Anstey's speech became emotional at this juncture and it was easy to suspect that he almost saw Terry as the son he had never had. Herbert had kept informed as far as possible about Terry and the other ex-player's lives via family and friends and learnt that several of them had been killed or were missing. Then the news came through that Terry had been captured by the enemy and was believed to be a prisoner at a camp somewhere in Germany. That was the last Herbert heard of Terry until several months after the war had ended, but what he heard then made him all the more proud of Terry. After fighting for almost three years all across Europe he had finally been captured after being shot in the chest. His recovery was slow and painful with only limited medical help available and most people would have sat back and waited for the war to end. But not Terry, who made several attempts to escape and finally succeeded in 1944 from his camp in Germany. He disguised himself as a German soldier and along with a friend they simply walked out of the main door when the garrison was being changed. By this time the guards were a ragtag bunch whose morale was at a low level and they were far from alert. Both Terry and his compatriot were still fit and were able to run thirty kilometres through the night before their absence was noticed the next morning. Sleeping by day and running by night they managed to get into Poland in the first four nights, well on the way to their target, Switzerland.

By this time they were very tired from lack of sleep and very hungry, having to try and make their limited food last as long as possible. On the fifth night tragedy struck when they were manoeuvring their way through dense woodland. Terry's foot went down into an animal hole and there was an ominous crack; he had broken his ankle. The pain was instant and intense, which meant all hopes of further escape were over. Terry collapsed on the floor in a pile of fir tree needles and his friend helped him to get as comfortable as possible. Don, his fellow escapee, filled Terry's water bottle for him from a nearby stream and encouraged by Terry went on with the attempted escape, leaving Terry to await his fate. Waves of pain shot through his leg but he was exhausted and wrapping his great coat around him like the blanket it originally had been he fell into an uneasy sleep.

Someone was splashing water on his face when he next came to and he opened his eyes with a start thinking his escape was over. What he saw was a young woman dressed in drab clothes from head to toe looking down on him with concern. Fortunately, he had long since discarded his disguise as a German soldier and the offending articles were now safely buried many miles away. The girl spoke to him in hesitant German but he couldn't understand and she followed up in a more fluent language which he didn't recognise. He later discovered it to be Polish, which proved to be the girl's natural language. Her third attempt at communication was in schoolgirl French, of which Terry had some simple grasp, and he was able to tell her that he was English and pointed to his broken ankle. She appeared to understand the situation and even looked a little relieved. She attempted to help him up but his scream of agony alerted her to the severity of his injury. She eased him back on to the ground and made him as comfortable as possible before moving away after gesturing that she would be back. As time passed Terry slipped in and out of consciousness and when he finally came around it was already getting dark but he could hear the sound of something heavy coming towards him. The girl suddenly appeared before him but this time she was wearing a sort of harness that was attached to a wooden sledge. Somehow between the two of them they managed to get Terry on to the sledge, where she tied him very firmly.

The journey that followed was a nightmare for them both with the girl dragging the sledge behind her inch by inch and foot by foot all the while with Terry doing his best not to scream in agony as they bumped over the rough forest floor. By the time they came to a halt they were both exhausted with barely enough energy to get Terry off the sledge and into what appeared to be a natural cave, set into a hillock, which was almost invisible amongst the undergrowth and creeping ivy. Terry was soon stretched out on a simple bed and when he looked around him he had never seen anywhere like it in his life. He later learnt that the girl was a Jewish woman called Hanca Kowalska and this had been her hideaway from the Germans for almost two years. Her parents had lived near Warsaw but when the Germans began to arrest Jewish people and transport them to concentration camps she just happened to be staying on her aunt and uncle's farm, where she had stayed regularly each year since a small girl. It wasn't much of a farm and her relatives barely scraped a living but Hanna had always loved it there.

Her aunt had taught her how to cook and to make nourishing meals using lots of herbs and fruits gleaned from the countryside. Her uncle had enjoyed hunting and fishing, which usually involved poaching on the larger farms around them, and had always stored all his nets, traps and other gear in this cave out of the way of prying eyes. When the Germans arrived at the farm Hanna had managed to slip into the forest where she hid as her aunt and uncle were thrown into a lorry and driven away. It was now dark and she lit a small fire at the rear of the cave to boil water for a hot drink and to heat up a large cooking pot of some sort of stew. It was a very basic meal but it was wolfed down by Terry, who hadn't really eaten for days.

The pair of them had then spent many months living a secluded life in their secret den. Hanca went out each day looking for food and ingredients for her aunt's cooking recipes, which helped her to provide edible meals most days. Her attempts at hunting using her uncle's traps proved largely unsuccessful but she became quite good at fishing their nearby stream. Meat was a rare treat and depended upon her finding some roadkill on the road running along the far side of the forest. It was a risky business as the road had a lot of German military traffic. But she was very careful and the roadkill, whatever animal it might be, made a welcome addition to their cooking pot. The inedible scraps of meat or fish weren't wasted as they were used as bait in the crayfish pots which were sunk in the nearby steams. There was plenty of dead wood to be gathered but they only lit their small fire at the back of their cave at night when there was little risk of their smoke being seen.

A pattern of day-to-day life developed with the high spot of each day being a warm meal, a chat by the embers of their fire and then to cuddle down together in the small bed for the night. They were both content to see the war out in each other's company. As time went on Terry and Hanca grew close, very close and the only real problem was the lack of medical treatment for Terry's broken ankle. Hanca did the best she could by putting the leg in a splint, having first manipulated the broken bones back to their original position. It time the bones knitted back together but it resulted in the ankle being misshapen and with limited flexibility.

Terry was eventually able to walk but only with a marked limp. His football career was over. He would never make it to the heady heights of the football league which had been his destiny.

Somehow they survived in their forest hideaway and Terry was able to take on the role of wood gatherer whilst Hanca concentrated on keeping them fed and watered. It was surprising how well they ate with their favourite meal being the occasional crayfish caught in baited net boxes in their local stream. When boiled they went pink just like lobster and they swore they were every bit as good. Terry's wood gathering trips usually involved a few minutes watching the nearby road from the safety of a concealed den in a thick cluster of bushes. The road was frequently busy with heavy German transport, but as the weeks and months went by the pattern changed and there began to be a movement of transport in the opposite direction. Many of the vehicles showed signs of damage and most had exhausted looking soldiers hanging on all over them. The tide of war was changing and Hanna and Terry did a spontaneous little dance of joy when Terry reported the development back at their base. They were finally able to leave the forest six weeks later and they joined the host of refugees on the road heading to their various futures somewhere. The first thing they planned to do was to find a priest and get married, which they achieved within days. Terry could now head for home and his wife Hanca would be able to accompany him.

Herbert's lengthy monologue began to falter at this point and he was fortunate to be rescued by the arrival of a tea trolley with a chirpy elderly lady dispensing tea and coffee and a plate of custard cream biscuits. No one attempted to fill the silence as they all enjoyed the rather lukewarm coffee and slightly stale biscuits. Meanwhile, Herbert was able to regain his composure and in a more controlled voice continued with his story. He explained that the war had been over for several weeks when he had bumped into Terry in the street. He barely recognised him and was appalled that the emaciated figure in front of him was none other than Terry, who had been a young vigorous man when he had left the football club that both loved to fight for his country. Herbert had insisted on taking him out for a meal, which was followed by several pints at a local pub, which loosened tongues and enabled Herbert to learn of the events in Terry's life over the past few years. He discovered that Terry and his recent bride were staying with his parents in their local authority sheltered housing flat and were having to sleep on the floor in the living room. However, this had come to the notice of the housing authority and they had been told to leave by the end of the week just four days away.

Herbert, the chairman of the housing subcommittee and a man of action, had gone into overdrive and Mr and Mrs Terry Parsons had been rehoused in a ground-floor council flat within a mile of the football ground with hours to spare. Admittedly they still had to sleep on the floor over the weekend but with Herbert's help they were soon kitted out with most of the essentials from the welfare department's furniture store. Herbert ensured that they had enough to live on by giving Terry a job as a store man at his engineering works and within weeks he persuaded Terry to take on the coaching of the reformed Exworth Town Football Club. From time to time he met Hanca but she rarely left their home and seemed quite content to pass her time providing Terry with good food, a warm and comfortable home and genuine love and companionship.

During the time they had spent in the forest they had developed an odd mixture of a language of their own and Hanca's knowledge of English remained limited to short phrases with little or no use of grammar. But there was no doubt that they were devoted and you only had to see them together to realise they had a rare form of happiness. The job went well and the football club did okay but never again looked to have any chance of football league status. Herbert and Terry attended every match together and Herbert always drove them to away matches. Things went on like that for over ten years and the two men were the best of friends and often had a pint or two together after a match. Herbert went quiet for a few moments and it was evident that there was a dramatic statement to be made. It came out all of a rush.

'He was walking home from the late shift at work and a drunk driver knocked into him and he was killed instantly. The driver didn't stop but there was a witness and he was arrested within a couple of hours and ended up in prison.'

Herbert went on to explain that Hanca appeared to cope with her loss better than might have been expected, but as time went on she became more withdrawn and quite paranoid. He did what he could to ensure she had enough to manage on but she began to become a bit hostile when he visited and his contact with her had gradually petered out over time and he now only visited at Christmas time with a hamper.

'I have nothing but compassion for the poor woman who has ended up in a strange country with no friends and family, and if that wasn't enough the local kids have decided that she is a witch. They seem to delight in causing her aggravation and are constantly knocking at her door, shouting through her letterbox and even smearing faeces across her door and windows. This has all had the effect of Hanca reacting by shouting back at them, which was the worst possible thing as the little horrors tormented her even more. The final act happened just last weekend on firework night when they decided it would be funny to let off a rocket through her letterbox. There was a draft-proof curtain behind the door which was set alight and Hanna was trapped in her bedroom until she was rescued, more dead than alive, by the fire brigade. She is now in intensive care at the general and it is touch and go at present.'

The room went quiet as Herbert let the rest of us have enough time to realise the severity of what we were being introduced to. Herbert went on to explain that he considered Hanca to be a hero who had undoubtedly risked her own life to save Terry's when he was lying in a forest in a hostile country unable to move independently. She had shared the little she had and endured many months living in fear of discovery. She then came with him to a foreign land where she knew nobody and could barely speak the language. After several good years together she was then suddenly widowed and chose to be isolated and to bother no one, only to be burned out of her own home and ending up fighting for her life as a result of the way she was perceived by the neighbouring youth.

'I can't stand by and do nothing as the total injustice of the situation cannot and will not be tolerated. I want you, Ben, to link up with Hanca and try to help her decide what would be best for her. Meanwhile, I want you, Oliver, to go through all the vacant housing stock and then get together with Ben and Hanca and find her something suitable for her needs. It won't be easy but I have every faith in the pair of you being able to sort it out. I will of course be available at all times to ensure that there is no unnecessary bureaucratic nonsense put in your way. Any questions?'

Neither Oliver nor Ben could think of anything to ask and Herbert closed the meeting. In the pub across the road the pair of them recovered with a pint and then just looked at each other and broke out into laughter, which almost became hysterical. The sheer control influenced by their lords and masters had never been more apparent so they did the only thing open to them, they made their plan of action.

It was agreed that Oliver would spend the next couple of weeks drawing together details of everything that was available and Ben would use the time getting to know Hanca and where she might ideally like to live. This involved Ben in a daily visit to Hanca who was really poorly and initially rejecting of his approach. But with perseverance and as her health slowly improved she began to think about her future and to see that he was there to try and help her to find a place to live. She talked a lot about the time she had spent with Terry in the forest all those years ago and it was clear that that was where she had been happiest, despite the hardships. Now all she wanted was to be away from people and with a garden where she could grow food and perhaps keep a few animals. It was a tall order and Ben couldn't imagine such a council place existing in Exworth, but he promised to try and find somewhere that might meet her needs. When he met with Oliver a few days later he was greeted with a tall stack of files of over twenty available properties. However, when he explained that Hanca had become increasingly reclusive since Terry's death and now the destruction of the home that they had shared meant she was afraid to live in close proximity to other people. Oliver and Ben went through the details of the available properties, which were almost exclusively either high-rise flats or maisonettes and were quickly rejected. In almost no time at all they were left with only one possibility and that was very much a long shot. It wasn't even a proper home but had once been a barn when the land it was on had been part of the farm that was now the Highfield Estate. It was situated on the farthest fringes of the Highfield Estate and had been converted to a secure store for all the fixtures and fittings needed by the builders when they were building the estate. It had been locked up and abandoned when the work was finished and the long-term plans for it had always been to convert it into a home.

However, its isolated location and the cost of conversion had always meant the project was put off for another day. Both Oliver and Ben felt it might have possibilities and stopped only to collect a camera and a set of keys from Oliver's office before climbing into Ben's car to go and make a recce of the site. From the road the approach to the building was up a series of overgrown zigzag concrete steps, turning first to the right then to the left and then right again before coming to a sturdy single-storey stone building. It appeared to be of sound construction with a recent weatherproof slate roof and surprisingly almost all the windows seemed to be undamaged. It was set into a hollow in the hillside with scrubby land all around it and the hill continued up behind it for over a hundred feet. All the land had been taken over by bracken and brambles which now surrounded the building, making access difficult and painful, but they persevered and arrived at the door of the property, which was made of reinforced steel secured by a massive padlock. There were iron framed windows running along the front of the building which were covered by iron bars in turn covered by heavy metal mesh.

Inside the property was a series of four rooms each leading off a corridor running the length of the building and each was filled with the abandoned rubbish left by the builders when they vacated the building. It looked sad and unloved and the smell coming from the ancient toilet did nothing to improve the ambiance, but they felt it could have real potential for Hanca. Oliver busied himself by taking a whole reel of film of the internal and external parts of the building whilst Ben wandered up the hill to the boundary hedge. When he reached the top of the garden he turned around in a circle, taking in the views in every direction and realised that he couldn't see another property in any direction. If Hanca wanted isolation this place had it in spades!

They returned to the car and discussed what they needed to do. They agreed that before Ben discussed the property with Hanca it was essential to find out whether the council would agree to make the place habitable. That was a decision way beyond Oliver's power and they agreed that an early meeting with Herbert Anstey was the only way forward. Three days later they found themselves back in Herbert's office and this time he was listening rather than talking. Ben told him about the outcome of his meetings with Hanca so far and explained that she had been so damaged by her life experiences that her primary wish was to achieve an isolated lifestyle. Oliver explained that all the available housing fell far short of her need for privacy. Then he produced the photos of the abandoned builder's store and explained it had always been the plan to eventually convert it into a home. Herbert picked up the photos and looked at them carefully and commented that the building appeared to be dry and weatherproof.

'What needs to be done to get this place straight within weeks ready for her to move in to?'

Oliver answered with a frankness which was unusual of an officer to a councillor. 'It will need a new kitchen, bathroom and central heating and of course decorating throughout, but what it needs most is someone with enough clout to make it happen.'

Herbert went quiet for a moment then laughed out loud. 'Clout is my speciality, so let's do it.'

That was the decision made with Ben charged with getting Hanca's agreement, and once obtained Oliver would then see about getting the work done as soon as possible.

Hanca had needed very little persuading after she had pored over the photos and did not seem at all put off by the state of the building or the amount of work required to make the garden productive. The fact that there were no immediate neighbours seemed to swing it for her. Her health seemed to have improved each time Ben visited and she was soon moved from intensive care unit to an ordinary ward. The work on the property seemed to rush ahead with a speed never before seen on a council project and Herbert's regular visits to the site kept things moving at a pace. The bars and grills were removed from the windows but the solid iron door remained at Hanca's insistence as she was confident that no one would ever be able to burn that door down. Three weeks later she was well enough to be sent for convalescent care to Cerne Abbas in Bournemouth for a couple of weeks to aid her recovery.

Ben collected her from the ward and took her to Bournemouth in his faithful old Cortina, which meant that they spent several hours in each other's company. Initially Hanca was nervous about going but when she saw the lovely old house set in expansive gardens she seemed to accept the move relatively confidently. Their relationship had come on a long way and over a fish and chip lunch partway down she had become more communicative. She told Ben that she had been saving up her widow's pension whilst she was in hospital and she was looking forward to spending it. When he asked her what she was going to buy her answer was typical Hanca, and she said her priority was a machete to tackle the brambles as soon as possible and an axe to help her collect firewood. They agreed that they would call in at a hardware shop on the way back from Cerne Abbas in two weeks' time so that she would be able to get straight on with clearing the garden.

After lunch they set off to complete the journey in companionable quiet until the silence was suddenly broken by Hanca bursting out in laughter. Ben realised that this was the first time he had ever heard Hanna laugh and he pulled into a convenient lay-by to see what it was all about. She shyly pointed out of the window to a huge figure carved into the hillside which with its huge appendages left no doubt it was a male figure. Ben remembered reading about the centuries old Cerne Abbas giant which was almost 200 feet tall and explained to Hanna that it was of historical interest. She even made a joke saying it was enough to scare the public.

With just two days of Hanca's planned return home Ben went to see how the project was coming on and was amazed. It was decorated throughout and the kitchen and bathroom were completed and ready to go and there was a good-sized wood burner in the living room. What was even more surprising was that all Hanca's furniture had already been moved in. Ben later learnt that Herbert had arranged for the Exworth footballers to spend a couple of training sessions moving all her belongings. He told Ben that lumping stuff up the steps to the property helped them to get fit and he had rewarded them with beer and a barbeque in the garden when they had finished.

When Ben collected Hanna from Cerne Abbas the improvement in her was obvious for all to see. She was as brown as a berry and she had had her hair permed and her nails varnished. She was smiling and chatty and eager to make the promised visit to the hardware shop. So by the time they got to her new home she had purchased not only a brand-new machete and axe but also a heavy duty saw and an expensive pair of secateurs. Ben guessed that her new feminine look would not be lasting long. When she got to the house she was overwhelmed by it all and couldn't stop wandering from room to room, touching everything and clapping repeatedly. She ended up in tears and completely out of character threw her arms around Ben and kissed him on the cheek.

In the months that followed he had kept in touch with Hanca regularly and introduced her to the idea of catching the bus to Jessie's shop each week for essential supplies. There was always an hour wait at Jessie's before the bus returned and this developed to a regular cup of tea and chat between them, which in turn got Ben a regular report on how she was doing. He had recently shared with Jessie that he was going to largely hand over the department's contact with Hanca to Susie when she started and she had agreed that there were benefits in doing so. 'She could do with a woman's touch, but don't pull out entirely as Hanca sees you as a special friend.'

As always Ben valued Jessie's opinion.

Chapter 17

Christmas Planning

With just over three weeks to go to Christmas Day, Ben would normally be panicking. In the past he had usually left arrangements until the last minute and then found everything doubly difficult as shops began to run out of things that were considered to be essential to the Christmas festivities. But this year it was different in many ways. For a start there was a break in the tradition that Sandy, Ben and the boys spent Christmas Eve, Christmas Day and Boxing Day at Sandy's parents' home in their five-bedroom house in the posh district of Ashcombe on the fringes of Exworth. They had always been joined there by Sandy's sister Deborah and her husband, Brian, and their two small daughters. The house was always full to bursting and although they all got on reasonably well at a distance by the time three days had elapsed they were all more than ready to get back home. Ben in particular felt on edge as he had never been forgiven for getting Sandy pregnant and ruining her chance of a fruitful career. This had been introduced into conversations by her parents on a regular basis and last year Ben had decided to tell them in no uncertain terms just how keen Sandy had been on their bedroom activities when they had shared a home at university.

However, the issue never came up last Christmas holiday and the moment had passed, which he thought was probably just as well. His main failing last year had been his lack of interest in rugby. Brian and Sandy's dad, Roger, talked about it endlessly and when Ben tried to introduce football into the conversation it was quickly disregarded. But this year it was going to be different and Ben welcomed the change. Earlier in the year Sandy's father retired and moved with his wife to live in Lyme Regis where they had holidayed each year throughout their married life. The five-bedroom house had been exchanged for a small three-bedroom bungalow with panoramic sea views; fine for them but too small for family gatherings.

Ben and Sandy were thrown back on their own resources and once they got used to the idea were delighted. In many ways they were starting from scratch as they had never decorated the house, put up a Christmas tree or cooked a Christmas dinner. But they were both excited about it all and had lots of discussions and made a lot of plans together, which was a rare happening. The boys seemed very keen on the idea of staying at home for Christmas and Ben suspected that they had always found having to be well-behaved for the three days over Christmas at their grandparent's house an effort difficult to maintain. The boys had one more week of school before the end of term, which involved such excitements as a school disco where lots of boys and girls ran around and made little or no attempt to dance, and the annual nativity play in which the boys were both cast as sheep. Sandy had been working hard on the boys' costumes, which were made up from an old sheepskin coat from Sandy's hippy days turned inside out and topped off with cardboard masks in the shape of sheep's heads. The overall effect was pretty good, as Ben made a point of saying to Sandy when they attended the nativity together and were able to see other parent's efforts.

Ben found himself immensely proud of his two sons as they paraded on stage. It appeared that there was a natural progression from an animal, to an inn keeper, to an angel, to a wise man or shepherd with the ultimate target after five years in primary school being the heady heights of Joseph or Mary. Inevitably all sorts of things went wrong, much to the delight of everybody; the worst being that somebody had forgotten to put a baby in the manger and when Mary reached for the baby all she had was a handful of blanket. A red-faced teacher clambered on stage, passed a baby doll to Mary, gave a little curtsey and exited quickly left. The hall erupted with laughter and the festivities proceeded without a further major hiccup. Ben and the family all stopped for tea or juice and biscuits in the school canteen with loads of kids running around very excited before walking home together with a definite skip in their step. This Christmas was definitely going to be different, with Sandy planning to cook a 'proper Christmas dinner' for the first time in her life. She was both nervous and excited and had delegated the preparation of the vegetables to Ben and the boys whilst she concentrated on the turkey, stuffing and sausages.

Ben had drawn the short straw, as it was his turn to provide the mental health cover for the county on Christmas Day. It meant that he was unable to have a drink and was stuck at home with the phone on hand ready to receive any emergency calls from the police, ambulance service or any medical person. The telephone had been paid for by the county and installed when Ben had been made team leader and was a mixed blessing. Their house was the first in the street to have a phone, which seemed to reinforce the neighbours' idea that he was rich. After all there were only two other neighbours with cars and now he was the first to have a telephone. His phone had quickly been seen as a local resource and much better than the nearest public phone box outside the chip shop four streets away. A steady stream of people started to knock at their door at all hours to ask to use the phone. This was a real pain as their home had no hallway and the phone was in the living room by the side of the television. Sandy didn't put up with it for very long before she acquired a money box and attached a sign to it 'Minimum charge a shilling'. As the cost of using a public phone box was four pence this had the desired effect of radically reducing the callers. Sandy mentally labelled the contents of the box 'Christmas money' and they enjoyed emptying the box as a family and the proceeds were given to Jack and Nick so they could go Christmas shopping.

Money was less of a problem this year as Ben had had a pay rise. In addition Sandy was also earning for the first time in their married life. It was not a fortune but it gave Sandy a much desired bit of independence. She was much brighter and full of chat and their relationship was definitely on the up. Ben was determined to make this a special Christmas for the whole family and had bought Sandy's Christmas present weeks ago, making a previously unheard of trip to town and to Marks and Spencer on Exworth High Street. His first stop was to the beauty department where after smelling a whole string of perfume testers he settled on Yves Saint Laurent 'Kouros' which the assistant assured him was very special. It ought to be, he thought, at nearly £40 for a small bottle, but he had saved up £50 to spend on Sandy so he girded up his loins and headed up to the underwear department. Now he really was on dangerous ground as he had once before bought underwear for Sandy but it had not been well received and had never seen the light of day.

He had been away on a training course in Wales at the time and was wandering around the shops killing time before the next lecture. He had passed an Anne Summers shop and being in a strange town where he would not be recognised let his curiosity get the better of him. Most of the stuff was beyond his imagination but there had been a special offer on a stack of bra and pant sets and on the spur of the moment he had bought a very gaudy set with lace. When he handed the gift over Sandy's face had said it all and the underwear had rapidly disappeared; Ben was in the dog house. As it happened he had found the Ann Summers underwear at the back of Sandy's bedside drawer when he had been checking on her bra size in anticipation of his Christmas shopping trip. He left it undisturbed.

This time he selected a pretty blue set with tiny white bows in the centre of both. He knew blue was Sandy's favourite colour so he felt pretty safe and was pleased when the shop assistant offered to wrap it up for him. Job done he went back to the office and locked it in his desk drawer away from prying eyes at home where the boys were always keen to locate secret hiding places. The previous weekend the whole family had gone into town to finalise Christmas gifts, get a real tree for the first time ever and on the spur of the moment they also bought several packets of paper chain strips for them to stick together to festoon their living room. The shopping trip was rounded off with fish and chips at Harry Ramsden, much to the delight of the boys as it was one of their favourite treats. When Sandy and Ben were chatting over the day together as they got ready for bed Sandy confided that he could expect handkerchiefs from Jack for Christmas with him having taken advice from her. Ben retorted 'snap' as he had suggested the same for her when Jack had asked his advice and they ended up giggling together like a couple of school kids. It appeared that Nick had chosen to shop alone and had announced that he was going to get something for them all to share. Sandy saw him smuggle a Fry's selection box up to his bedroom and wondered how much of it would survive until Christmas Day. A good day got even better before they went to sleep.

As well as planning for Christmas at home Ben had been busy at work. Every autumn the Lord Mayor of Exworth got together with several of the charitable organisations to raise money for those in need in the community at Christmas. All sorts of fundraising events went on, including 'a shopper's loose change line' which went up and down the pavement of the high street each coin end to end. It was mainly made up of coppers but over the month of December it really added up and together with other monies raised it meant that there was several thousand pounds available for enhancing people's Christmas. As local authority social workers Ben and Phil were able to apply for vouchers from the proceeds for food, clothes and toys, all of which could be exchanged at the Co-op in town. They got together and drew up a shortlist of their clients who met the criteria. They completed the required application forms and submitted them in good time. Amongst those they selected were Ruth Andrew's family and the Farthing family.

Some months before, Ben saw Ernest out with the cart by himself and he had asked where Foxie was. With some difficulty Ernest managed to tell Ben that his dad was in bed unwell. Ben had been a bit surprised but thought no more of it at the time. However, when he had not seen Foxie out and about for weeks he decided to make a visit. The Farthing family were struggling with Foxie suffering with terminal lung cancer. A lifetime of ducking and diving in all weathers and smoking rolled-up cigarettes largely made from other people's discarded dog ends had finally caught up with him. He had struggled on for as long as he could but was now bed bound and not long for this world.

When Ben visited he was shocked to see how Foxie had deteriorated. Never a big man, he was now reduced to little more than a shrunken little person propped up on a heap of pillows struggling for breath. When he saw Ben he started to cry and begged that he should be allowed to stay at home rather than going into the hospice that his GP had suggested. Ben sat with him and held his hand until Foxie slipped into a shallow sleep. Elsie confirmed that she wanted to keep Foxie at home and had stopped work so that she was there full time. Ernest did what he could to help with shopping and house work and still went out totting with the handcart but had none of his father's innate skill at finding scrap of any value. Their problems were intensified by Elsie's loss of earnings and she had started to make inroads into her small amount of savings in the same old post office account. Penny was less than useful and continued to live in her make-belief world surrounded by her vast collection of dolls.

Ben had come up with a possible solution to their financial problems when he spotted an advert in the council's in house magazine for a road sweeper for the Highfield Estate. He immediately rang the council cleansing department and gave the man in charge, Sam Paterson, a call and arranged to go in to see him. They had met before when Ben had taken the special school leaver Nobby Clark along for an interview for a job on the bins. Fortunately he had proved a success and Mr Paterson's only comments were 'a bit cheeky but works hard and keeps good time'. On the back of that success Ben gave an honest rundown on Ernest and his strengths, also his limitations. He stressed that for all his mental limitations he was as strong as an ox and a really hard worker. By good fortune Sam Paterson had a cousin who was mentally handicapped so was genuinely sympathetic. Ben finished his approach off by offering to allow the road sweeper's cart to be kept by the bins in the office car park overnight. This would have the advantage that Ben could keep an eye on Ernest's comings and goings and the cleansing department would save money as they would no longer need to deliver and collect the cart by lorry each day. The deal was struck with a handshake and it was agreed that Ernest would be able to start a trial period in the following week.

When Ben delivered the news Ernest was clearly delighted and Elsie broke down in tears as it was the first time any of them had had 'a proper job'. The news together with the vouchers meant that Foxie's last Christmas would be as good as possible given the circumstances. Ben felt it was job well done and went over to the local health centre to try and have a chat to his friend Mary Harris the local health visitor who lived nearby on the Landings. She was up to her eyes with a baby clinic but quickly agreed to take a tea break and to listen to Ben's concerns. Within minutes she had grasped the nature of the problem and agreed to call in on Foxie and Elsie on her way home at the end of the clinic. Ben later learnt that she had called in to help them every morning and night seven days a week right up to Foxie's inevitable death a little while after Christmas. What a woman!

Chapter 18

Religious Revival

One of the other recipients of vouchers organised by Ben was Ruth Andrews, and her situation unlike Foxie's was on the way up. Ben had visited Ruth regularly over recent weeks and there had been ups and downs, but judging by the state of the home and Ruth's personal appearance the overall trend was up. He had kept in contact with Katie's headmaster, Mark Hamilton, who reported that she was much less anxious and making good progress academically. He also reported with a laugh that Katie's street credit with the other kids had soared when she had turned up at the school with Dave the student. Having a 'minder' who was huge and Black made her unique and she had been frequently heard to boast about her special friend.

Ben had worked hard at building up Ruth's confidence and was pleased to note that the sign on the door knocker had been removed. Ruth seemed to have accepted her single parent status and to have grown in stature. He considered that it might be the right time to move the situation forward and raised the proposition with Ruth that she should try to renew her contact with the Roman Catholic Church. Ruth was very unsure, feeling she might be exposing herself and the children to another rejection. However, after a lot of discussion she gave him permission to discuss her situation with the minister of St Jude's the local Catholic church on the Highfield Estate. Ben had made some informal enquires about the current minister and had been reassured that he was reported to be young, approachable and modern in his attitude. In fact, he was reported to be a man for the people not the papacy. Nevertheless, Ben was nervous about making the approach as he had been brought up C of E and had only a limited knowledge of Catholicism based on attending a couple of Catholic funerals and having had a boyhood friend who was Catholic. The funerals seemed full of pageantry but lacking in much human emotion. The churches seemed over ornate with numerous statues of Christ and the Virgin Mary surrounded by a mass of burning candles letting off evil smells in competition with the incense being spread around the church.

His friend from his teens had been a rogue, constantly up to some mischief and the scourge of any young girl he happened to fancy. He seemed to be lacking in any conscience and had explained to Ben on numerous occasions that if things got too heavy he just went to confessional, said a few Hail Marys and then could start off where he left off. It was fair to say that Ben had a pretty jaundiced view of the Catholic Church, after all there was no such let-out if you were C of E. However, he was committed to trying to help Ruth and made a telephone call to the local church, spoke to the minister and made an appointment for the following day. On the telephone the minister had introduced himself in a strong Irish accent as Patrick MacGinty. The name seemed familiar to Ben but he was pretty sure they had never met. So it was with some trepidation that he walked up the gravel path to the two storied red brick building that had obviously been built at the same time as the rest of the estate. A wide flight of eight steps with a ramp on one side led to massive solid double doors and they swung open with a surprisingly light push.

The doors opened into a wide porch that was almost completely filled with pushchairs all pushed together in no sort of order. The sound of screaming kids was not the reception that he had been expecting but as he pressed on through another set of doors he was met by a host of little children, some riding on little tricycles, others fighting over the control of sought-after toys and amongst it all some toddlers just sleeping on a pile of beanbags apparently unconcerned about the din echoing around the room. In the far corner there was a group of young mums, most with a mug of tea in one hand and a fag in the other, chatting happily and seemingly blissfully unaware of what the toddlers were up to. A large older lady separated herself from the group and came straight over to Ben with a severe look on her face. Clearly men were not welcomed here but Ben got his word in first and explained that he had an appointment with the vicar. He was directed to a lift in the corner and was happy to escape so lightly.

The lift went to the first floor and directly into the main church, which proved to be nothing like the Roman Catholic churches he had seen previously. It was a single rectangular room with a small simple altar at one end and a cosy looking confessional box in a corner. The seating was ordinary stacking chairs set in a circle around the room and the only idolatry was a statue of the Virgin Mary, with several tiers of candles in front of it all waiting to be lit. The minister appeared from a side door and again was nothing like Ben had anticipated. He was a tall man, about Ben's age, casually dressed and had hair down to his shoulders and a small gold crucifix earring in his right ear. His smile was welcoming and his handshake firm and his opening words were, 'Hi, Ben, welcome, and before you ask I don't have a goat.'

Ben was confused for a moment then remembered that his name was Patrick MacGinty and tied this into the popular Val Doonican song about Paddy McGinty who bought himself a goat. As an opening to a conversation Ben thought that it was right up there and they left the church through the side door, which opened into Patrick's small flat. Over a glass of beer Patrick explained that the church had been jointly funded by the council and the Catholic Church so the downstairs was a toddlers' group during the week and the upstairs a church on Sundays and Saint days. He confided that the congregation was quite small and that he would be very pleased to get additional church members. Ben filled him in on the background to Ruth being rejected by her former minister and Patrick reacted with genuine anger.

'The church has come a long way in recent years but I am afraid that it still has a long way to go. I can assure you that Ruth and her family will be more than welcome to join our church community.' There was no doubting his sincerity and between them they planned to make a joint visit to see if she would be prepared to give it a try. Ben left feeling that he had made another valuable contact with someone trying to give Highfield some heart.

Chapter 19

Unusual Happenings

Despite Ben being nervous, the talk the following day to the rotary meeting went well. The audience seemed really interested and the super three-course meal complete with wine which preceded the talk had the effect of putting everyone in a receptive mood. Ben explained how the area of Exworth was divided into separate patches, each with a small team of social workers working with people in the community with neurosis or psychosis and also with people with mental handicaps. He explained about the different conditions and what treatments were now available. In answer to a question from the floor he went into the problem of depression in greater detail, explaining that it was generally considered to break down into two sorts, namely exogenous depression and endogenous depression.

In order to explain the difference between them Ben used the example that he always tended to use to explain exogenous depression, namely Wellington of the Perishers comic strip featured daily in the *Daily Mirror*. He looked around the room and there were nods from all quarters to show that they were familiar with it. He went on to briefly explain that his father had worked on the railway and returned each day with a copy of the paper. He told the gathering how as a young teenager he had begun to look at the paper each day after he came home from school and always turned to the comic strips first mainly to see what misadventures Jane had got herself in. This drew a laugh from the audience and he continued by explaining that he had also noticed that from time to time the character of Wellington was wandering around with his own dark personal cloud over his head for no apparent reason. 'That is how I see exogenous depression, it's from within and beyond one's understanding or control. It is often referred to as the Black Dog, as it was a black mood which follows the sufferer around wherever they go and whatever they do. This can be very difficult to treat and there is a strong possibility of suicidal thoughts or actions, which can often result in admission to a psychiatric hospital. Endogenous depression is easier to understand and is usually triggered by one or a series of life events happening in close proximity. Death of a loved one, divorce, redundancy, stress at home or work, severe debt or gambling problems can all result in this sort of depression. People can only tolerate so much and when it gets too much they just cease to function.'

Ben went on to outline some details of the recent client Desmond Davis, who had ended up in the 'Miss Havisham' type of situation. He obviously did not give enough information so that Desmond could be identified but the story was enough to strike a chord with some of the audience and a couple of men came up to him at the end of the talk and asked to have a meeting with him. Ben assumed they had a problem they wished to discuss and he arranged to see them in the office the following day.

The next day was a rare dry one, windy and cold but really quite pleasant for December. Sandy had the day off and decided that she would walk the boys to school that morning, meaning that Ben was free to set off for work earlier than usual. On impulse he decided to call in on Jessie on route to stock up with carrots and apples for Boxer Mark Two. His arrival at the shop coincided with Jessie having just made fresh coffee, which smelt divine and he needed very little persuading to stop for a cup. They moved to the seats at the rear of the coach and Ben opened the conversation by asking Jessie for more information about Robbie Scadding. Jessie let out a little laugh and a warm smile ran across her mouth which made it abundantly clear that Robbie was viewed with favour.

'As I told you I have known both Robbie and his wife, Patricia, since we started primary school together. Robbie was mischievous from day one and spent a lot of time being sent out to stand in the corridor or at the headmistress's office. He was a big lad for his age but never bullied anyone and his main aim in life seemed to be to make people laugh. He was far from studious and spent all his time out of school helping his dad with his rag and bone business. Patricia was always top of the class and her pretty good looks meant she was never short of friends. In fact Robbie and Patricia were poles apart and their paths rarely crossed despite being in the same class. Then puberty happened and the whole scene changed. Patricia developed a trim little figure and Robbie tried all sorts to get her attention but she played hard to get, and that was the situation when Robbie left school at fourteen to work full time with his dad. Fate took a hand about five years later when Robbie went to help an old lady who had collapsed in the street. She had banged her head and was bleeding heavily but Robbie didn't hesitate, he simply picked her up bodily and put her into the passenger seat of his van and drove her to the casualty department of the general hospital. There he sat holding her hand and supporting her through the tests and patching up performed by the staff. Three hours later she was declared fit enough to go home and he was in the process by getting her back in the van when a young woman came over and put her arms around the old lady and called her gran. Both Robbie and Patricia, the young woman, recognised each other at once and from this chance meeting their relationship blossomed and flourished and they are now happily married and still very much in love. Patricia has been the making of Robbie and encouraged him to work hard and treat people fairly. His reputation grew steadily and his business has flourished ever since and they are now an important part of the local community.'

Ben would have liked to have asked more but the bus had just drawn up outside and Jessie was on her feet ready to serve her customers. He went back to his car and on to supply the horse with his daily treats.

The appointment with the two Rotarians had been set for eleven, which gave Ben time for a lengthy session with Mrs Freeman to sort out the post and catch up with his dictation to get his files up to date. The two men arrived promptly at eleven but appeared rather different to their appearance at the rotary meeting when they had been dressed in dark suits and identical club ties. Today they were dressed in sport coats and flannels and their shirts were open at the neck. They looked like what they proved to be, normal working-class guys. They introduced themselves as Albert Watts and Samuel Watts who could easily be assumed to be brothers but in reality were first cousins.

Albert emerged as the natural leader and succinctly told Ben what they were calling about and it was not what he had anticipated. He explained that the two of them had been partners in a small building firm for over forty years up until the middle of the previous year when a larger local company had made an offer for their firm that was too good to turn down. At the time it had seemed to be an opportunity to retire early and to take things easy and so it had turned out to be, but a year on they found that they had time on their hands and were frankly bored. However, part of the takeover agreement had been that they would not open another business for at least ten years and by then they would both be well over formal retirement age. They both briefly got jobs with another company but they were used to being their own bosses and they didn't like cutting corners on jobs, which had been their instruction once too often and they resigned.

'We talked it over and decided the best way we could use our time and our skills was doing voluntary work but we had no idea how to go about it. Then we heard your talk and particularly noted your example of the chap with depression who had simply stopped halfway through decorating his new home. We thought we could help him to finish the job and at the same time offer him friendship at a time when he feels so alone. What do you think, is it a good idea, could it help him?'

Ben was quiet for a few moments letting the offer sink in. It was not what he had been expecting and seemed to be a most generous suggestion and even if Desmond Davis turned it down he was sure that there were other clients who could benefit from their help. He thanked Albert and Sam for their approach and agreed that it seemed a fine idea. It was left that Ben would discuss the offer with the patient and then talk to the two men again.

Ben visited Desmond the following week and with his agreement took Sam and Albert to meet him a couple of days later. Several weeks later the work was completed, Desmond had been discharged, the Rotarians had a new member and Ben had gained access to a useful little team of volunteers he could call on for help if the need arose.

Chapter 20

Christmas Is Coming

In the week before Christmas, the Christmas spirit had begun to creep into the office at Highfield. Alice had been busy collecting holly and ivy and other greenery to decorate the place and had even attempted to put up a variety of coloured shaped balloons. Unfortunately, she hadn't learnt the art of tying them off securely and they had almost all deflated to end up looking like a lot of coloured condoms hanging around the place. The kitchen walls were hung with Christmas cards received by the staff from grateful clients and one or two professional colleagues. Ben had provided Mrs Freeman with a supply of cards and stamps and she ensured that everyone who sent a card got one from the Highfield office by return of post.

By far the favourite card received had been popped through the door a week or two before. It was obviously homemade and featured a colourful Christmas tree with sequins stuck on it for baubles. Ben didn't need to open it to learn who had made it as the 'fairy' on the top of the tree had a Black face and wore trousers. In Katie's eyes Dave the student had reached celestial heights and Ben put it in his pocket to show Dave when he joined the family at Christmas. Ben had planned for a gentle wind down at work with the promise of five days off to look forward to after he had done his twenty-four hours on call over Christmas Day. But his plans had to be put on hold when he received a call from 'the management' inviting him as team leader to the departmental Christmas gathering on Christmas Eve, which was held each year in the conference room at headquarters. The invitation was made in such a way as to be an instruction rather than a request for his company. He realised that there was no way of getting out of it, even if a glass of mulled wine and mince pies with a lot of people he didn't know held very little appeal. So it was fair to say he was pretty miserable by the time he got home but he was met by a very happy Sandy, who thrust a colourful card under his nose the moment he arrived. It was from Dave's wife Camilla, thanking them for sharing their Christmas with Dave. She had enclosed a chatty letter and photos of her two daughters and Sandy was already in the middle of writing a reciprocal letter and sorting out a couple of photos of the boys where they looked reasonably angelic. Ben showed Sandy the card he had received from Katie, which made her laugh and she immediately included all about it in her letter. He suspected that this was going to be the beginning of a pen friendship that would be enjoyed by both Camilla and Sandy. He read through Camilla's letter and was pleased to learn that Camilla and the girls hoped to join up with Dave as soon as he was qualified and had found somewhere for them to live.

The day of the Christmas party, or Christmas purgatory as Ben had taken to calling it, came around all too quickly. The early part of the morning was taken up with them all gathering in the kitchen to exchange presents and share hot chocolate and the inevitable mince pies. Ben received socks as usual from Alice and said they were just what he needed, much to Alice's delight. Phil presented him with a rather nice pen and pencil set with his name embossed on the side and he promised to try to not lose it, as he was notorious for never having a pen. Mrs Freeman as usual gave him a big box of homemade sausage rolls which she knew would be well received by Sandy and the boys. Having had help from Sandy all the ladies had received colourful scarves from Ben, which they all promptly put around their necks. They were all quite different but Sandy seemed to have cleverly matched them up well; Ben didn't hesitate to take the credit.

He made sure he had all the forms and information that he would need for his period on call on Christmas Day and then hung around the office as long as possible until Mrs Freeman pushed him out to the car park and virtually insisted he get on with it. 'Fine friend you are,' were his parting words, but he managed to say it with a smile and Mrs Freeman just laughed.

The headquarters car park was bursting at the seams and he had to drive around twice before squeezing the Cortina into a space vacated by a motorbike and sidecar. He had never been in the conference room at headquarters but the hubbub of talking punctuated by the odd burst of laughter led him straight to it. The place was packed with little clusters of people all over the place working hard at having a good time on the firm's time. Ben's natural inclination was to grab a glass of wine and a mince pie and to find a quiet corner to hide in. At the far side of the room he spotted a free window seat and head down made it his target. The only person he recognised en route was Pete Evans, the personnel officer, who had recently done the interviews with him for the new post of social work assistant. He shook Ben's hand warmly and whispered, 'I would rather be at Joe's.'

Ben laughed and pressed on to his target haven hopefully out of the way of the clatter of the rest of the room. He sat down in the window and did his best to be invisible which worked really well for a while. Then a short, smartly dressed curvy lady a bit older than Ben but with a nice smiley face came up and sat down next to him.

'Room for a little one?' she asked and he found himself welcoming the interruption. Pam Townsend introduced herself and quickly admitted that she hated this sort of gathering and that from the looks of him she strongly suspected that Ben felt much the same. The conversation between them flowed easily with them both telling the other about their roles in the department and their home circumstances. Ben talked about his family and Pam seemed genuinely interested. She explained that she was unmarried and was the youngest of four brothers and sisters, but the only one still living at home with her mother, who had been a widow for ten years and was now quite frail. She told him about her nieces and nephews, who were clearly 'the apples of her eye' and perhaps helped by several glasses of wine they found themselves chatting away like a couple of old friends. Pam went on to tell him that she worked as a secretary in the secretary pool on a part-time basis but also had a little empire of her own. She suggested that Ben might like to see where she did most of her work and he jumped at the chance of a change of scenery away from the crowded room. They slipped out of a rear door of the conference room and wandered along a long corridor with Pam identifying what normally went on behind the various doors to the left and right as they passed.

They finally stopped outside a locked door on the right and Pam produced a key from a chain around her neck to unlock it. Ben had no idea what to expect but it certainly wasn't what appeared as they entered which turned out to be a huge windowless cupboard with floor to ceiling shelving on all sides. Pamela switched on the light and closed the door behind them and he was confronted with stationary of every sort stacked up in orderly fashion on every shelf.

'All the various departments get their stationery including all their specialist legal forms from this room and it is my job to keep a track of it all and to ensure we don't run out of anything.' Ben was impressed at the organisation involved and said so, and as if on impulse Pamela turned to face him and moved in closer to him and smiled a funny sort of smile. Ben acted instinctively and his right hand went unerringly to her left breast, which was soft, warm and comforting. Her reaction was equally spontaneous, a throaty giggle, and she reached up and kissed him gently on the lips. The moment was complete and who knows where it might have led had they not been suddenly interrupted. The two of them sprang apart as they heard someone coming down the corridor opening and closing doors as they came and whoever it was was heading in their direction at a rate of knots. Pam quickly switched out the light and Ben grabbed the door handle and held it as firmly as he could. The footsteps drew nearer and suddenly he felt a hard-downward pressure on the door handle, which he managed to resist. The steps moved away and the two of them hugged and struggled to contain their urge to laugh.

'I bet that was Creepy up to his old tricks. I'll tell you all about him but for now we had better make our separate ways back before we are missed. You go first, but I suggest you stop off at the gents three doors down on the left just in case Creepy sees you and wonders where you have been. I'll lock up and come back via the ladies.' She squeezed Ben's hand and looked around the door to check the corridor was all clear before pushing him on his way. He made his way back to the conference room without incident and collected two more glasses of wine before making his way back to their convenient window seat. Pam was already there and was also holding two glasses of wine, which meant they were set up for the afternoon.

'So tell me about Creepy. Who is he and what's his game?' Ben asked in a low voice and Pam pointed out a short man with thinning red hair over the far side of the room hovering beside a small group of people in deep conversation. Even from across the room it was obvious that he was listening to their conversation surreptitiously.

'That's him, Gordan Wood, alias Creepy as he is known behind his back, and that's what he does, always trying to get information about people that he can pass on to his immediate boss Eric Sully. They are a really odd couple but Sully is a terrible bully and Creepy is his pet informer. They have both been at headquarters for years and don't seem to realise that everyone is well aware of their liaison. At first there had been a suggestion going around that they were a couple of queers but that was soon scotched as they are both married with families. However, what emerged was that they were both members of the same Freemason Lodge and attended meetings together on the first Monday of each month. They never talked about it but it is painfully obvious as they both came to work in their best suits on the days of the meetings and they both go off carrying identical little leather cases to carry their regalia. They really are disliked by everyone and they are a nasty combination. Sully is very self-opinionated and very vain and never passes a window or mirror without admiring his reflection, but he is also fiercely ambitious and has clawed his way up the ladder stepping on anyone who got in his way. But he is now very frustrated because all the more senior posts above him are occupied by people with a medical qualification and his only medical experience was as a Red Cross ambulance driver for a few months at the end of the war. You could have felt sorry for him if he wasn't such a pig, but as it is he is tolerated because he has to be but apart from Wood doesn't have a friend in the department. Creepy is just a despicable little man who seems to think he is god's gift to women and seems to be constantly in your space uttering some double entendre or other. He is always touching and the women all hate him and see him as some sort of poisoned dwarf with piggy pink eyes and receding red hair, but he needs watching as he delights in causing grief. If you can avoid the two of them then do, Ben, as they are really bad news.' Ben and Pam continued to chat amicably and amused themselves by observing Creepy's movements around the room.

From time to time various councillors made an appearance and Pam was able to identify most of them. They tended to have brief conversations with the hierarchy who were clustered by the entrance before finishing their statutory glass of plonk and going on their way. Ben suddenly felt

Pamela stiffen beside him and he looked across to see who had come in. 'It's Councillor Rudge, this could be fun.'

Of course Ben recognised him instantly from the rotary meeting he had talked at just a few days before. It was evident from the reaction he received that he was far from popular and several of the groups closed ranks and presented their backs to him. Unfortunately, he spotted Ben in his alcove and came directly over and with a hearty shake of his hand expressed in a loud voice for all to hear that he had been delighted with Ben's talk. 'A first-class job, very professional and pitched just right.'

Ben was conscious that all eyes were upon him and would have liked the ground to open up beneath him, but managed to say something in reply. He noticed that Pamela had moved as far away as she could without making it too obvious, and after a few moments Councillor Rudge walked straight out with his pride intact. Ben was aware that people all over the room were looking at him with curiosity and to avoid any direct eye contact turned around and looked out of the window. A few minutes later Pam moved back to him and reported that the room appeared to have moved on as several other councillors had come into the room and were chatting to different groups of staff. It was apparent that they were more popular than Councillor Rudge as they were soon surrounded by staff keen to get their attention.

Ben and Pam withdrew to their window seat and were back in comfortable chatting mode when once again they were approached by an unexpected person. None less than Alderman Herbert Anstey, chairman of the housing committee, came up to Ben and once again he found himself being greeted warmly. He felt as it he had wandered into a Brian Rix farce and wondered what was going to happen next. Alderman Anstey told him that he had just delivered his usual Christmas hamper to Hanca Parsons and he had been thrilled with the improvement in her.

'You and Oliver Manning really got your acts together when you rehoused Hanca, she seems very happy and she told me that you have been a real help. Well done, you can be really proud of the work you are doing and I will be letting your bosses know how grateful I am.'

Ben managed to mumble his thanks and Herbert Anstey moved on around the room. So much for keeping my head down, he thought, as once again all eyes seemed to be on him. After a while Pamela re-joined him and commented with a grin, 'Superman strikes again but watch your back, Creepy is taking more than a passing interest in you.'

Within minutes the farce that was happening to Ben had one more act to play and this one was beyond belief. It took the form of the arrival of a tall, elegant man in the doorway and Pamela whispered to him, 'This could be interesting, just watch all the cretins' reaction now, that's the big chief, the medical officer of health, Doctor Alex Wynne-Jones.' His presence was impressive and immediate as the senior staff moved towards him *en masse*. Ben had heard of him and seen pictures of him in the press and his importance was expressed by everything about him. He wore a designer three-piece suit with a gold double Albert across his chest tucked into the side pockets of his waist coat. His shoes were highly polished and handmade and this was all enhanced by his grey flecked hair and strong jaw line, and he still had the physique of an athlete from the days he had been an international rugby union player for Scotland.

He entered the room and made a few cursory handshakes and brief comments but his eyes were sweeping the room the whole time and he suddenly spotted who he was looking for. Fortunately, as far as Ben was concerned, he headed diametrically away from him and came to a stop in front of Pete Evans, the personnel officer. After a brief conversation watched by the whole room Pete nodded and pointed straight at Ben, who felt Pam move swiftly away. He felt utterly confused and just like an animal trapped in a car's headlights, there was no escape. He couldn't for the life of him think what he had done wrong but it was obviously something serious to have come to the attention of the top man.

Dr Wynne-Jones came straight up to him and surprisingly sat down next to Ben on the seat recently vacated by Pamela. 'I understand that you are Benjamin Newman and I would like a word. I am Dr Wynne-Jones, the medical officer of health, and your name came up at a recent planning meeting I had with Prof Macfarlane looking at ways in which we can develop a closer relationship between the community mental health services and the hospital based services. The prof suggested that it would be helpful to have a community based social worker as part of his team when he holds his psychiatric outpatient clinics at the general hospital each Friday afternoon and he specifically asked if you could be asked to do it. I think it could be helpful, but it's up to you. Is it something you would be interested in doing?'

It took a few seconds for Ben to become clear about what was being suggested, but he was then able to say that he was very flattered to have been asked and would of course be delighted to work more closely with the prof.

'That is fixed then, give the prof's secretary a ring in the new year and she will let you know the details. Well done then, my boy, it is good to know that my staff are appreciated.'

He then got to his feet and made his way to the door, leaving Ben dumfounded. The eyes of the whole room seemed to follow the MOH as he walked across the room and out of the door before turning their attention back to Ben. There was a burst of conversation from all over the room and Pam sidled up to him and whispered, 'Look out, Creepy, is on the move in this direction.'

With a hurried goodbye to Pam, Ben slid out of the rear door and made a swift exit to his car. He sat there for several minutes, his head spinning trying to make sense of what had happened. He thanked his lucky stars that he didn't have to work in the mad house that was headquarters and gratefully turned the key and headed off for the security of Highfield. He drove faster than usual but then remembered that he had had several glasses of wine and that the local police were having a seasonal campaign against drinking and driving. He slowed to a more leisurely pace just in time as he approached the hill into Highfield and saw a police car parked up in the lane at the far end of Scadding's yard, ready to chase the unwary. It was with relief that he arrived outside Joe's and settled down in the back room with a strong coffee and an 'all-day breakfast'. He needed to get his head in order and the warm fire, comfortable sofa and good food and drink had the desired effect of helping him to have a doze.

About an hour later he was fit enough to get back to the office to tidy up anything outstanding before the holiday break. Mrs Freeman had taken several messages from colleagues across the county about things which might blow over Christmas, mainly about people on leave from hospital who were spending the holidays with their families. The combination of lengthy days in each other's company mixed with excessive alcohol could often result in an urgent return to hospital. There were several telephone numbers for Ben to ring but one leapt out at him and he headed down the corridor to his office and closed the door. Pam was just checking he was OK but also told him that Creepy had caught up with her and was full of questions about what the various dignitaries had talked to him about.

'I just played dumb but Creepy was clearly unhappy and had ended their conversation by saying that Ben needed watching and that he would be the one to sort him out. He had gone on to say that he would have to make a visit to the Highfield office to see what was going on. I will keep my eyes and ears open but be prepared, as he has got you in his sights.'

Ben thanked her warmly for her support and for being the best bit of his day and they rang off wishing each other a happy Christmas. When he got home Sandy was full of questions about the office party and he filled her in on all the happenings, omitting any mention of his new interest in stationery cupboards.

Chapter 21

The Christmas Break

The boys had gone to bed reluctantly, both declaring their intention to stay awake to catch Father Christmas when he arrived with their presents. They could be heard talking and wandering about until well after 10 pm and both Sandy and Ben went up to them several times before things finally went quiet. They enjoyed an evening of better than average television and a cuddle in front of the Parkray but resisted having any alcoholic drink until another day as Ben was on call from midnight. The pillow cases of Christmas presents were safely delivered to the bottom of the boy's beds without disturbing them and on the stroke of midnight they mutually agreed to exchange Christmas presents, after all it was now Christmas Day and with Ben on call they might not have another opportunity.

Sandy seemed really impressed with Ben's choice of perfume and the nod of approval when she opened the underwear was in direct contrast to her reaction to the Ann Summers gift of a couple of years before. Ben tried hard to disguise his disappointment with Sandy's gift to him, which was a bottle of port that he was sure he would enjoy on high days and holidays, but he felt it lacked imagination. Sandy picked up on his reaction and quickly reassured him there was more to follow and her rather smug smile got his imagination working overtime but she would say no more.

The boys inevitably came charging into their bedroom at some unearthly hour, lugging their pillowcases of presents along, which quickly became a heap of toys, a few bits of clothes that were given only a cursory glance and a mess of ripped paper. Sandy was prepared with paper and pen to record who gave what to whom in anticipation of the thank you notes the boys would have to write later in the week. Ben reluctantly got up from his cosy bed and went downstairs to make hot chocolate all round. After the bedroom picnic of hot chocolate and toast and peanut butter the boys were persuaded to play downstairs whilst Sandy and Ben enjoyed a peaceful cuddle. They talked about the plans for the day and Sandy remembered that Dave had rung the previous day to wish them a merry Christmas and to apologise that he wouldn't be able to get to them until after six on Boxing Day as he had a previous engagement. Sandy had reassured him that they would be quite happy to delay dinner until the evening and confessed to Ben that she was anxious about cooking the full works Christmas dinner and was grateful of having the whole day to prepare.

Her plans for today's lunch couldn't be more simple: sausage and chips all round, which would have appalled her mother and Ben was sworn to secrecy. As if it was planned the telephone rang soon after eight and with an oath Ben grabbed Sandy's pad and picked up the phone, ready to record details. However, it was only Sandy's mum ringing to speak to the boys and to remind them to listen to the queen's speech, as this was considered to be an essential part of Christmas by her parents. After a brief comment or two Ben gratefully handed the phone over to Sandy, who he could hear in reply to a question reassure her mum that Christmas lunch was all in hand. Ben waved a finger at her pretending to chastise her before heading to the bathroom for a shower ready to face the demands of the day. The boys were full of it and didn't really settle to play with any of their new toys for more than a few minutes. Finally, Sandy decided to take them to the park to let off a bit of steam and Ben declared that he would have the lunch ready for them by twelve as they were always hungry after a session in the park.

He was sure that he would be mentioning that he had cooked Christmas lunch all by his self when he wanted to wind Sandy up in the future. He had just started to peel the potatoes for the chips when there was a deep throaty roar of a vehicle pulling up outside his front door. The sound of the engine ticking over was music to his ears and he dropped everything to go and see the source of the special noise and he wasn't disappointed. There was a young man in full leathers parking up what was Ben's idea of the dream machine right outside his house. He recognised the bike immediately as it was the one he had coveted ever since he first saw one as a small boy. It was an original Vincent Black Shadow 998cc and it was immaculate to look at and sounded tuned to perfection. Ben was not surprised to see several of his neighbours drawn to their front doors to see the spectacle that had drawn up.

The rider cut the engine and kicked the bike on to its stand before dismounting and removing his helmet. He was taller than Ben and had shoulder-length hair and seemed to be in his late teens. He smiled warmly and announced that he had come to deliver Ben's Christmas present and Ben nearly collapsed on the spot. However, before he could say a word and thereby make a complete fool of himself the rider put his hand into his leather jacket and pulled out a parcel wrapped in newspaper. Just at that moment Jack and Nick came running down the road closely followed by Sandy, who went straight up to the young man and gave him a hug.

'Thanks for coming, Tony, your timing is spot on and I have managed to keep the secret. Ben has no idea why you are here.' She turned to Ben and said, 'This is Tony and he is a sort of 1960s Father Christmas who has come to deliver your Christmas present from me.'

Tony laughed and said, 'Ho Ho Ho.'

Ben just didn't know what was going on but judging by the bike it was going to be something special. 'Give Tony your car keys and leave him to it. Come in and have a cup of tea, Tony, when you are ready.'

Ben found himself meekly passing his keys over before going indoors to put the kettle on. Meanwhile the boys were allowed to sit on the motorbike, much to their delight. In a matter of a few moments Tony joined Sandy and Ben in the kitchen along with the boys, who could hardly contain themselves with the knowledge about the secret that they now shared. Ben for his part could not contain his curiosity any longer and asked Sandy direct what was going on. So they sat around the kitchen table, partially occupied by a saucepan of peeled spuds, drinking tea and devouring Christmas chocolate biscuits, which Sandy had produced from some secret hiding place. She explained that Tony was a regular customer at Ma Driscoll's where he bought the French cigarettes that he favoured and which Ma got in especially for him. Sandy had got chatting to him and had learnt that he could often get second-hand car parts for local people. Sandy had given that some thought and had asked him if he could get a replacement radio for Ben's Cortina, as the existing one had never worked properly. She knew that it simply would not stay on station and she had made Ben promise not to use it when he was driving as he had had a couple of near scrapes when trying to adjust it as he drove along.

Tony piped in at this point. 'I have got you the correct radio for your motor and have tuned it in to the light programme, as Sandy told me that that is your favourite channel, come and see for yourself.' It looked identical and Ben was truly delighted, but he was also worried as he knew some people stole bits and pieces to order.

'How did you manage that then, Tony? It can't have been easy.'

Tony just laughed and said, 'My surname is Scadding, you may have heard of us, and we have loads and loads of radios and all sorts of other parts which we have removed from scrap cars before we crush them.'

All suddenly became clear and Ben said, 'Yes of course I have heard of Scaddings, I pass your yard every day and I know Robbie, your dad!'

Before he left Tony made the Christmas for the boys by giving each of the boys a ride on the back of his bike up and down the road, making sure that they in turn wore the spare crash helmet which he removed from the pannier on his bike. Ben couldn't let himself ask but Tony knew and gave him a somewhat longer and faster ride to Highfield and back, which left him breathless but happy. As they waved Tony off Ben hugged his wife and said she couldn't have given him a better present.

'It's an inspired gift, which means I can listen to the news on the way to work. Up to now I have had to depend upon catching up on things by reading the newspapers left in the café at Joe's each day, and they are always at least a day out of date. In fact, I would quite like to try the radio out right now but that will just have to wait.'

As it happened Ben didn't have to wait very long as he had just finished his sausage and chips when he was called out to the central police station. One of their beat bobbies had found an elderly man without any topcoat wandering in the high street. He had presented as very confused and cold and didn't remember what his name was or where he lived, so the constable had taken him to the station for his own safety. By the time Ben arrived at the police station the station sergeant had managed to get the name Russell Pascoe from a name in the old man's purse, but still had no more information than that. Ben thought he recognised the name and was fairly confident he would recognise the man when he went to meet him in the staff canteen, but he quickly realised he had never met him before.

The old man seemed reasonably fit and well having just consumed a good English breakfast and several cups of tea, but he still seemed very confused. Ben sat and chatted to him and used a ploy he had used before with confused old people by asking him about what he had done in the war. Russell had no difficulty giving him chapter and verse and gradually Ben brought him around to the present day and was able to learn that he lived on the Landings Estate, but he couldn't recall his street or house number. Ben got on the telephone to Jessie and Mary and they knew immediately who Russell Pascoe was as he called into their shop frequently and always did his 'big shop' there on a Friday.

'I bet he called in today being a Friday but had forgotten it was Christmas Day. We went to church this morning for the Christmas Day mass so weren't there for him. Poor lamb, I bet he just wandered off and got lost, he's a lovely man so bring him around to us and he can share our lunch.'

The sergeant seemed well impressed with the speed in which the problem had been resolved and Ben helped Russell into the Cortina. The sergeant's parting words were that he wished all his problems could be sorted out so simply; from the shouting and banging in the holding cells as they passed Ben doubted it. When they arrived at the Landings Jessie and Mary fussed over Russell like a couple of old hens and he lapped it up. His Christmas was about to get a whole lot better. Meanwhile, Ben mentioned to Mary that the name Russell Pascoe was vaguely familiar to him but he couldn't think why. Mary looked at him for a moment or two then asked him what he knew about capital punishment. It seemed a weird question and then the penny dropped and the memories came flooding back from a visit he had made to Bristol about a year ago when he had attended a regional meeting of the Society of Mental Welfare Officers.

The meeting had been pretty dull and on impulse he had decided to make a duty call to the elderly persons home where his grandmother on his mum's side was resident. He had been close to her as a child but it was the first time he had visited her since her admission and it wasn't a good experience. She didn't know him. Her room was on the top floor of a large house in Bishopston, which despite spending his student days in Bristol was not a part of the city with which he was familiar. He did his best to make conversation and at one stage wandered over to her window, which had a panoramic view across the city and a huge red brick building surrounded by a very high red brick wall dominated the view. His gran remained mute and after several attempts at conversation Ben gave her a peck on the cheek and a single tear ran down her face. On the way out he stopped to have a chat with a carer who confirmed that Gran was slipping away and they were just keeping her as comfortable as possible. He thanked her for her kindness and as a way of leaving on a more cheerful note asked about the large red building he has seen from the window. It turned out to be Horfield Prison, which was not the nicest of views to have in your dotage.

Curiosity got the better of him and he headed in the direction of the prison for a closer look before he made his way home. The road ran alongside the wall of the prison and then passed a paved area leading up to the enormous gates, which totally blocked any view of the internal area of the prison. On this particular day there was a circle of dark-clothed people with heads bowed standing silently apparently on some sort of vigil. By this time Ben was sufficiently nosey to pull the car up and to ask a passer-by what was going on and his reply had been that they were the anti-hanging brigade who had been there day and night for three days protesting because there was to be a hanging at the prison at 8 am the following day. Ben hadn't realised that people were hanged in Bristol but was aware that there was an increasing movement to abolish capital punishment. He stopped at a local newsagents and bought a copy of the evening post, then went into a small café next door to have a cuppa and to read all about the planned hanging.

The name of the prisoner was Russell Pascoe, which Ben had thought seemed far too posh a name to be that of a convicted murderer, and the name had stuck in the recess of his mind. At the time he had done a bit of reading about capital punishment and he had been left wondering if it was ever justified in a modern society. He had concluded that fortunately times and attitudes were constantly changing, not always for the best but generally he thought in the right direction.

He was given a glass of sherry by Jessie to celebrate Christmas, which he drank with what he hoped was apparent pleasure, but in reality sherry was not something he enjoyed. He was able to decline a top-up on the grounds he was on call and gave them both a peck on their cheeks before escaping to the safety of his car. As he set off for home he clicked on his new radio and was rewarded by the Christmas version of 'I'm sorry I'll read that again' which always made him laugh and raised his spirits as the radio behaved perfectly and stayed on station all the way home.

There had been no further calls by the time he arrived home and apart from a couple of calls from family the telephone remained silent throughout the night. It had been a very light day on call and ended on a special high when Sandy came to bed in the new underwear he had bought for her. It came off beautifully and the Newman household settled down for a peaceful and contented night's sleep.

Chapter 22

The Rest of the Holiday

The following day, Boxing Day morning, the boys and Ben all slept in but Sandy was up with the lark planning her first attempt at a full Christmas dinner. She had forgotten to mention to Ben that she had invited Ma Driscoll to join them for dinner as she would have been on her own and she had seemed to be delighted at the invitation. That meant that Sandy was cooking for six so there was a lot to do. She took Ben up a cup of tea and broke the news to him about Ma coming and he reacted better than she had expected, saying that he agreed that she shouldn't be alone all over Christmas. Never slow to miss an opportunity, Sandy then said she could do with help preparing all the vegetables and Ben rose to the bait and rolled out of bed to have a shower. Thirty minutes later he was busy at the kitchen table peeling potatoes, sprouts, parsnips and carrots when the telephone rang and it was Dave.

He explained that he would be with them at about eleven but would have to be out most of the afternoon as he was due to be bucket man with St Margaret's football team who would be playing Rutterhams United, an annual fixture that was always keenly fought and could be bloody. 'Would you like to come along, Ben, to watch?'

It sounded like an interesting suggestion so he said he would check with Sandy and decide later in the morning. Dead on eleven Ben heard the high-pitched buzz of the pink peril pulling up outside and he got up from the kitchen table and went to let Dave in. He glanced up and down the street and was not surprised that the buzz of the bike had not drawn any interest from the neighbours unlike the roar of the Vincent Black Shadow of the previous day. Dave was his normal cheery self and was soon on the floor with the boys playing with their new toys. Ben returned to his labours at the kitchen table and took the opportunity to raise the possibility of going to the football match more in hope than certainty. To his surprise Sandy thought it a good idea as Ma Driscoll was coming around in the afternoon to give her some moral support and perhaps advice with the challenge that was preparing Christmas dinner.

Vegetables all done, Ben made some coffee and joined Dave on the sofa in front of the fire. Dave admired the tree and the decorations and seemed a bit overwhelmed by Katie's Christmas card when Ben showed it to him. 'Quite on honour,' he said, 'but it looks a bit painful where the top of the tree has ended up.' Ben recovered the card to go in his memory box later and Dave recovered his composure with a laugh and went on to tell Ben all about Christmas Day back in the hospital.

Bert and Victor had joined the group just after ten, having walked all the way to the hospital because no buses seemed to be running. They were made very welcomed by the group and particularly so after they produced a pack of rolling tobacco and a packet of papers for everyone in the gang as a Christmas gift. This was always welcomed, even by the non-smokers who now had collateral to trade for things more to their taste. Lunch had been the full works, prepared in the main kitchen but served up in the group's own dining room by none other than Father Christmas. It was the first time anyone had ever seen an Indian Father Christmas but the bottles of beer he produced from his sack guaranteed his welcome. Dave had confirmed with Dr Rani in advance that the beer was non-alcoholic so it would not clash with the men's routine medication.

Despite the lack of alcohol the frivolity which followed would have suggested it was high proof stuff, which just went to prove the power of a placebo. During the afternoon members of the local branch of Toc H arrived to give a film show in the main dining hall, which was opened for the whole hospital. The group attended en bloc and the whole hall gave the prof and his family a great round of applause and cheers when they came in and took the seats reserved for them on the front row. The show was a double bill of films from the fifties,

namely *Genevieve* and *Doctor in the House* and they had proved to be well chosen as they were both merry romps easily enjoyed by the mixed audience. Everyone's favourite, Kenneth Moore, appeared in both and he was well supported by great casts of popular artists of the time. There was a break in the middle to change films and the prof and his wife did their stuff by handing out ice creams all round. There was an outburst of comments when James Robertson Justice appeared as Sir Lancelott Spratt, the head consultant in doctor in the house, with someone calling out, 'Oh look he is just like the prof,' quickly followed by someone else shouting, 'Oh no he's not like the prof he reminds me of our ice cream man.' 000

The prof stood up and made a bow. Once the film show was over and Toc H had been warmly applauded for their entertainment the patients all returned to their various wards for a high tea, again prepared by the central kitchen. The evening stretched ahead and the day could have gone flat but the charge nurse had prepared an unlikely surprise which rapidly became a high spot of the day. Charge nurse Abbott's wife Cynthia was a member of her church's Mothers' Union and amongst their activities was a hand bell ringing group of which she was a member. She had managed to get ten of the members to come to the unit in the evening to perform a short concert for the group. So the men were suddenly confronted by a group of ten or so mainly middle-aged ladies all dressed in pale blue tops who all looked a bit nervous and not knowing what to expect.

They set up their music stands and with two bells each played several carols; by the time they got to 'Silent Night' the men had started to sing along and it all became quite moving. But the best was still to come as each of the ladies linked up with one of the men and an impromptu bell ringing lesson took place. It was chaotic and the 'music' produced sheer rubbish, but it was good fun and the two groups laughed together in a relaxed way which couldn't have been predicted. The guys served up tea and small apple tarts they had made themselves the previous day and they all chatted together like old friends. Dave thought everyone would remember the evening with pleasure and you never know, it could even become an annual event. 'So all in all it was a great Christmas, Bert and Victor's returning to the group for a day or two was just like what families do at Christmas and helped me a bit as I was missing Camilla and the girls.'

Sandy rustled up a scratch lunch of bacon, egg and fried bread for the men and the boys then shooed them out of the kitchen so she could have the place to herself to get on with the preparations for dinner. Dave filled Ben in on the details for the afternoon football and strongly advised him to wrap up warm and to bring a pair of sturdy boots as the place was always a bit of a mud bath from over use. Ben dug out his old student duffle coat and an equally old pair of walking boots from under the stairs.

They were both leftovers from a brief involvement that he and Sandy had had with the university hill walking group; it hadn't lasted long as they had soon found a better form of weekend exercise which didn't even involve the need to leave the room they shared.

The boys were beginning to niggle at each other and turned to Ben and Dave to provide entertainment. As ever Dave was up to the task and produced two shiny yo-yos, one blue and the other red, from his jacket pocket. The next few minutes were taken up with the men showing off their prowess, doing tricks from their youth such as basic throws, 'walking the dog' and over the top. When the boys finally got hold of them they discovered that it was far from easy but they soon managed to simply get them to go up and down. Ben and Dave readied themselves to go off but before setting out Dave recovered the yo-yos from the boys and pressed small buttons on the side of each. 'Try them now,' he said and passed them back. To the delight of the boys the yo-yos now flashed with multi-covered lights and made a loud whizzing noise each time they went up and down. As Ben and Dave closed the front door behind them Sandy closed the kitchen door firmly as the whizzing had quickly got on her nerves. As they pulled away in the Cortina they could see the diminutive figure of Ma coming along the street. She was dressed up in her best bib and tucker but the overall effect was rather spoilt by the two massive bags she wore crossed across her chest. They were the ones normally used by the paperboys who delivered the daily papers, but today they appeared to have turned Ma into a sort of pack mule. She managed a little wave as they passed and Ben could only guess at what treats were within the bags.

Dave had been spot on when he said it would be muddy. It was a quagmire and if it hadn't been for the goal posts and corner flags it would have been almost impossible to tell where the pitch was. There were no changing rooms, just a short row of portable toilets along the side of a rough car park. Most of the players turned up with their kit under their top clothes and proceeded to do an impromptu strip tease by the side of their cars, chucking their clothes anyhow back into their car boots. They appeared to Ben to be rather a motley group mainly made up of men in their forties, most going bald and sporting beer bellies. In contrast there were a few rather weedy looking teenagers who seemed more than a little apprehensive about the challenge ahead of them.

The team colours were blue and white striped jerseys with a broad mixture of shorts and socks. Dave sent them off on a gentle run around the field to loosen up having first insisted that all fags were put out. Whilst they were off he explained to Ben that each team contributed to the cost of an independent referee but had to each produce someone to act as linesmen. 'We might have a problem there but we shall see.' At that juncture an old coach turned into the car park and the opposition, already dressed in their red kit, poured out. They gathered together in a group, a few lighting up the inevitable cigarettes, and proceeded to barrack the St Margaret's players as they trotted back.

From what Ben could see there wasn't much difference in the make-up of the two teams but when he counted heads he realised that St Margaret's were one man short. At this point Dave drew him to one side and started by telling him that as he had suspected he had a problem as they were a man short. For one dreadful moment Ben thought he was going to be asked to play and was already trying to think up an excuse when Dave continued, 'Alfie Watkins, the team captain, has brought his fourteen-year-old son Simon along to act as linesman. He has previously talked about him several times as being able to play a bit and if you would take over as linesman I am prepared to give the lad a game.'

Without giving it a second thought Ben agreed even though he had only a limited understanding of what the role involved, but reasoned that if a fourteen-year-old was up for it why not him? Simon was clearly delighted to be playing and was already pulling on a spare jersey several sizes too big for him. This made him looking more of a callow youth than ever and Ben wondered if he would be a lamb to the slaughter. Meanwhile, armed with two flags Ben took up his place on what remained of the touch line and glanced across at his opposite number on the other side of the field. He was amused to see that he appeared to be quite elderly, at least in his sixties, but best of all he had a large plaster cast on his leg and walked with a stick. The referee had arrived by now and was well known by both sides as a strict disciplinarian, as well as being super fit himself so well able to keep up with the play.

The match got under way and mainly took place around the halfway line. The players had difficulty in keeping on their feet and it quickly became evident that most of them had eaten and drunk well the previous day. The ball got heavier and heavier and the field became a sea of mud. Ben realised that he was given very little regard by the referee, who largely overruled or disregarded any part either linesman attempted to contribute. Dave was kept pretty busy attending to the walking wounded whose cuts and bruises largely occurred following minor tussles well off the ball. The breakthrough came just before half time when the opposition's centre forward spotted the St Margaret's goalkeeper well off his line and made a hopeful punt on goal. The goalkeeper fell flat on his face in his rush to get back and had the ignominy of watching the ball bounce once and then roll ever more slowly through the mud and into the goal.

One nil at half time and a pep talk from Dave as he handed out half oranges to all the team including Ben before thoughtfully passing one to the referee, who was standing nearby looking at his watch. By this time the other linesman could hardly move as his plaster cast was weighed down with moisture and mud. Ben had every sympathy for him as he too was suffering, having developed blisters on both feet from wearing boots with rock-hard leather from years of neglect. The second half started spectacularly when Alfie Watkins made a run down the wing and knocked a high cross, which was met firmly by son Simon and flew into the goal. Simon ended up flat on his back with several of the team flinging themselves in a heap on top of him. It was a somewhat battered Simon who regained his feet and he largely disappeared from the play for the rest of the half, but the game had one more twist for him. With just a few minutes to play he received the ball on the halfway line and went on a run, beating several of the opposition before avoiding a fierce lunge from the goal keeper, who he rounded for a sweet tap in. That was it. St Margaret's had won the battle and the hero of the day was a fourteen-year-old boy who had scored a winning goal that he would remember for the rest of his life. The referee promptly blew for time, five minutes early by Ben's watch, and Simon was clapped off the field by both teams and even the ref joined in.

Dave was a happy man and took pity on Ben and his damaged feet and decided to take over the driving on the way home. He quickly changed from his boots into his shoes and pulled his trousers out of where he had tucked them into his socks before helping Ben into the passenger seat. He then very caringly removed Ben's boots to expose socks stained with blood in several places. When they arrived home Ben limped into the house in his blood-stained socks and the family all came to meet him, worried about his condition. Dave took control and soon had Ben settled in an armchair with his feet, still in his socks, soaking in a bowl of warm salty water. Within ten minutes the socks had been eased off, the feet carefully dried and a pattern of plasters covered the worst of the blisters. Meanwhile Ma was in the kitchen making coffee and the adults all sat around to share their afternoon's experiences. The boys returned to a corner of the room where they were surrounded by a stack of comics including a lot of *Dandys, Beanos, Toppers* and *Beezers* and even a few *Eagles*. This was obviously the contents of the paper sacks which the men had seen Ma carrying earlier and they had kept the boys quiet and content throughout the afternoon. Sandy explained to Ben later on that any unsold papers or comics were normally returned to the suppliers for a refund and she would have to check that Ma was doing it regularly, as it could add up to quite a lot of money.

Once Ben and Dave had filled the others in on the story of the match the ladies retired to the kitchen to continue with the dinner and the men settled back to catch up with the activities of Dan Dare the *Eagle* hero of their youth. They had soon nodded off, leaving the comics to slip on to the floor. A delicious smell of roast chicken seemed to fill the house and both Dave and Ben woke up feeling starving and ready to enjoy a feast. Sandy had surpassed herself and everything was just perfect and nobody could have guessed that this was her maiden attempt at preparing a Christmas dinner.

The only thing rejected by the boys was the sprouts, but that was nothing new and everyone else thought that they were cooked just right and it was clear plates all round. The Christmas pudding that followed had been bought from the Co-op but it had been enhanced by a liberal amount of brandy, which Ben set alight to the amazement of the boys. It came with homemade custard prepared by Ma, who blushed when the boys asked for second helpings. No one was in any rush to move and Ben produced the bottle of port that Sandy had given to him for Christmas and the adults all had a sherry glass full and the boys had 'special red wine', alias Ribena. The conversation flowed easily and eventually Ben made coffee, which he served to the ladies in the lounge whilst the men set about clearing the table and doing the washing up. Jack and Nick did a token amount of wiping up before their pile of comics drew them away. Sandy and Ma chatted away and could be heard comparing notes on the queen's speech of the previous day and it was quite clear that they were both confirmed royalists. The adults all sat around the Parkray in the living room, which was putting out a comfortable warmth. The conversation got around to comparing what their memories were of their childhood Christmases. All remembered it as a very special time when there were treats but sometimes disappointments when the hoped-for gift failed to materialise. Ma was the last one to describe her memories and the biggest difference for her had been the importance of attending church several times over the Christmas period and the cold both indoors and out.

'My parents were very Victorian and although I knew they loved me there was little time given to indulge me and as an only child I was often lonely. However, I was recently clearing out a wardrobe in my parent's old bedroom and I came across something that brought back lovely memories. Hang on a minute and I will show you.'

Ma reached down behind the sofa and pulled out one of the paper sacks that Ben had seen her carrying earlier. She produced an odd-shaped parcel tied up with string and put it on the floor in front of her. She explained that this was something she had prepared at home for the boys to open. The comics were immediately abandoned and they scrambled over to see what was happening. 'Before we do anything I want to explain that this parcel represents the twelve days of Christmas from Christmas Day to the Epiphany, when it is traditional to take down the decorations. Before we go any further I want to check that you all know the song about the twelve days of Christmas that begins with "on the first day of Christmas my true love sent to me a partridge in a pair tree".'

The boys looked blank but the others were surprised by how much of the song they could remember, but predictably it ended up with Ma singing the last few verses as a solo in a surprisingly sweet little voice.

'Well done but could be better, and I want the boys to learn the song over the next few days and I will be checking. That's just what my mum said to me when I was a small girl. So the boys can open one layer of paper each day for twelve days and they should find a small reward in every layer. They can open two today, one for Christmas Day and one for today Boxing Day.'

The boys were intrigued and always anxious to receive rewards so readily agreed to the conditions outlined by Ma. Sandy carefully untied the string and the boys peeled off the paper to produce two sherbet dabs and an envelope. The boys went straight for the sherbet dabs, which was one of their all-time favourites and left Sandy to open the envelope and pull out a large piece of wooden jigsaw.

She turned it over in her hand and let out a cry of delight. It was an exquisite hand drawn and coloured picture of a partridge in a pear tree. Sandy exclaimed that it was simply beautiful and Ma clapped her hands with glee. 'It was my mum's when she was a girl and she passed it on to me many years ago, but it has just been stuck away in a wardrobe so I thought it was time I passed it on for someone else to enjoy.'

'Well I love it and will make sure it is looked after, thank you, it is a lovely idea.'

The second layer was then opened with Sandy taking charge of the envelope containing the jigsaw piece of two turtle doves and the boys claimed the opal fruits. The next ten days would have something for the family to look forward to and enjoy each day. The evening continued with a couple of silly games, which everyone joined in with and relaxed quite naturally into childish behaviour, which the boys just loved. By eight o'clock Ma was ready to go home, explaining that she would still have to take Henry out for his evening walk, and Dave insisted on accompanying her home as it was already very dark outside. With hugs and thanks all round they eventually set off and Ben and Sandy took the opportunity to give the boys a quick bath and settled them down in bed.

Dave returned a bit later and explained that he had gone with Ma on Harry's walk and she hadn't stopped telling him what a treat the day had been for her. 'Talking of treats I have a little one for you two,' he said, and produced from his bag a bottle of Jamaican rum and a beautiful illustrated book called *The Real Jamaica*.

'Carmen sent it over for you, Sandy, and she has marked up bits and pieces in it which are part of our lives over there. She thought it might help you when she talks about things in future letters. As for the rum, it is the real stuff, forty proof and will blow your socks off, Ben, when we start on it later.'

Sandy got the message and after making up a bed for Dave on the sofa said she was tired and would enjoy starting on the book in bed. The men were starting to pour as she made her way upstairs.

Chapter 23

Another Year

Ben dragged himself back into consciousness as he heard the familiar buzz of the pink peril pulling away from outside of the house. He peered at the alarm clock, which was showing 6.30 and he let out a groan which caused Sandy to turn over away from him, apparently still in a deep comfortable sleep. Ben's head thumped, his mouth was bone dry and tasted foul and his bladder was seeking urgent action. He dragged himself to the toilet and recalled times at university when he had suffered similar hangovers and once again swore that he would never get drunk again. That damned rum was lethal and despite Dave warning him on several occasions he had matched Dave glass for glass. The day of reckoning had come and he crawled back into bed filled with admiration for Dave, who had been able to turn out for work as usual. No doubt the freezing cold drive on the scooter would help him wake up but Ben preferred to close his eyes and come to slowly.

The day started late and the boys were warned to leave Ben to suffer alone with Sandy providing the Alka-seltzer and black coffee at regular intervals. He got up at four and was feeling well enough to eat a light tea of cold chicken and pickles but the leftover Christmas pudding went untouched. All the while the empty rum bottle was still sitting on the sideboard seemingly taunting him about his discomfort. Sandy made no attempt to remove it and was clearly far from happy with him.

The following morning the postman delivered the first of the usual bills but also a belated Christmas card from his old university friend Andy in London. Ben had sent the usual letter updating him about life in the Newman home and had been a bit disappointed not to have had a letter in return. The card had a lengthy message inside and on the back cover telling him of Andy's promotion within his finance company and how he was now involved in a lot of international travel. On the personal front he was still living with Brian and they were looking to buy a home together.

The good news was that Andy's mum had met Brian and liked him and seemed to have accepted that she would not be having grandchildren. His dad, however, continued to refuse to discuss anything to do with Brian. He had recently remarried himself to his secretary, who was not much older that Andy, and there was now only minimal contact between them. Ben was glad that Andy had some joy in his life but realised that their contact was likely to cease in the foreseeable future as their lives were growing poles apart.

The rest of the holiday passed without incident with him spending a lot of time with the boys and Sandy working almost full days at the shop. In previous years the family had always called in on Ben's parents on the way home from spending Christmas with Sandy's family. Their visits had never lasted very long as the atmosphere had never been very welcoming as Ben and his dad had seemed to have little to say to each other. This year Ben decided to take the boys to see his parents during the day and Sandy had made sure that the boys had written thank you letters to take with them. They were short and based on a crib sheet that Sandy had prepared for them to copy, but what they lacked in words was made up for with an abundance of kisses of various sizes.

Ben's parents lived in a small semidetached house on the opposite side of the canal overlooking the railway shunting yard which serviced the various industries that operated in the heart of Exworth. The trip there involved a short bus ride but as it was a dry day Ben had decided they could walk there and bus back and that should have the effect of using up some of the boys' excessive energy. Gran Newman seemed genuinely pleased to see them and insisted that they should stay for lunch. She was pleased that the boys were wearing the jumpers she had made them for Christmas and which Sandy had cleverly insisted they should wear. Ben's dad was as usual 'down the allotment' and Ben would usually have left him in peace as he had always seemed to have preferred his own company. But the boys had been there before and had enjoyed the chance of running free with all sorts of interesting places to explore so Ben capitulated and they walked the couple of hundred yards to the allotments overlooking the railway. The gate swung open with the boys clinging on for the ride and Ben managed to get them past the two huge mounds by the side of the gate, one of soot and the other of farmyard manure, without incident. His dad heard them coming and managed a wave of greeting. He was sat on an ancient bag of compost that had been shaped to fit his backside over many months of regular use and he had his back against his shed and his pipe in his hand. He looked the picture of contentment and Ben felt guilty to be disturbing him. However, he seemed pleased to see the boys and asked them all about their Christmas before arming them each with a bean stick from the pile leaning against the shed and sending them off to explore with the instruction, 'Keep to the grass paths that divide the plots and no messing in any sheds.'

From their elevated position in front of his shed Ben and his dad could keep an eye on the boys, who ran off happily with their newfound freedom. Meanwhile his dad ducked back into the shed and produced a folding chair for Ben to sit on. He set it down next to his perch and chucked a few bits of wood into the old oil drum full of holes that had been smouldering and which now responded by breaking into flames. They sat there in silence for a while, neither knowing what to say until a passenger train crossed in front of them. Then his dad said out of the blue, 'That's the eleven thirty-five to London on time for once.'

The silence was resumed but was punctuated regularly by him identifying each train that passed before them. Ben was impressed by his dad's knowledge and asked him why he was so familiar with the train timetables. 'I ought to know my stuff after thirty years on the railway. If you look over to the distant left you will see a bit of flat land on the side of the tracks. That, believe it or not, is what is left of Blandford Street Station after that old bugger Dr Beeching got his hands on it. I worked there for the best part of twenty years with two old mates, Arnold Farmer the signalman cum acting station master and Old Alfie the porter and general helper. It was a super little station, very busy with both passenger and goods services and we kept it beautiful with lovely flower beds and everything spic and span. Arnold had a greenhouse at his home and took loads of geranium cuttings every year so the beds were a mass of red in summer. We clubbed together to buy a couple of sacks of daffodil bulbs, which made a wonderful show in spring. Everyone admired it and we even won the best-kept station award a couple of times. Alfie always made sure there was a good fire in the waiting room on cold mornings and most of our passengers were regulars who often found time for a word or two. Things became more difficult as the old steam trains were gradually phased out, which meant that Alfie could no longer scrounge a bucket of coal from the train drivers when they stopped there. But we managed to salvage enough scrap wood to carry on with the fires and the waiting room was always warm for our tea and lunch breaks. Then that old bugger Beeching wiped it all out with a stroke of his pen. I spent the best part of my working life there and loved every minute of it and after all that time I was made redundant and here I am watching the trains go by.'

Ben had never heard his father swear before and he had never heard him talk with such feeling or for so long. He felt more compassion for his dad than ever before and sat back, content to hear his father rattle on about his life on the railway. His dad produced a flask and they shared hot sweet tea and a special few moments like very few others in their lives.

'Alfie passed away last year. He was only seventy but the station had been his whole life, however, Arnold is still going strong, in fact, that is his allotment three plots over, the one with the flag pole. We get together here on the allotments most days for our sandwiches and a chinwag and make a point of hoisting a Union Jack on high days and holidays and always at half-mast on the anniversary of the station closure. Some of the older train drivers spot the flag and give us a blast on their claxons as they pass, we love it when that happens. In particular we love it most when the flag is at half-mast as they then let out a prolonged blast as if to indicate that they mourn the passing of Blandford Street Station too. Still, my philosophy is what can't be changed has to be endured.'

Ben felt that that summed his dad up perfectly but made no comment as the boys suddenly reappeared, breathless, grubby and hungry. Ben left his dad with the words, 'I will come over to see you again soon,' and to his surprise realised that he meant it. His dad smiled and repeated the wave as they headed back up to the gate where the boys had the reverse swing as the gate slammed shut then headed off for egg and chips with Gran Newman.

The rest of the holiday went pretty well and Sandy made a point of bringing the family all together around the kitchen table each evening to open the next layer of Ma's Christmas gift. Each layer produced more favourite sweets for the boys. Flying saucers were followed by penny whoppers, sweet cigarettes by liquorice strings and Milky Ways by hundreds and thousands. Not knowing what was coming thrilled the boys and Sandy was equally thrilled by each piece of puzzle as it appeared. The two turtle doves piece was followed by three French hens then four calling birds and so on. Each piece was quickly secured by Sandy to be safely squirrelled away in some secret place ready for a future project. The holiday seemed to fly by and all too soon it was the fourth of January and time for the boys to return to school and for Ben to make his way to Highfield. He was sorry in one way but also found that he was looking forward to returning to work and the challenge of a new year of happenings. That was a strange feeling. Was he beginning to like his job?

Chapter 24

No Time to Be Bored

The day did not start well despite Sandy having made all the necessary preparations the night before. It should have been straightforward. The boys' clean clothes were all laid out ready, their school bags packed and their lunch boxes made up and in the fridge. But they were both reluctant to get up and get going. Breakfast was a nightmare as Nick managed to drop the full bottle of milk, which smashed on the floor leaving milk and broken glass everywhere. When Ben started to clear up the mess he succeeded in cutting his hand on the broken glass and dripped a trail of blood as he tried to locate the plasters only to find the box was empty. He finally set off with a piece of kitchen roll, stuck down with Sellotape, wrapped around his hand.

The boys were grumpy as they had missed out on their cereal and the toast replacement breakfast was bordering on burnt. The traffic up to the school was slow and ponderous and Ben was already very late as he headed up the hill to Highfield. Nevertheless he stopped the car at Boxer Mark Two's field and was encouraged by the sight of the old horse wandering across to greet him. It was nice to have been missed and to see that the horse looked in reasonable fettle. There was a good mound of hay and the bath of water looked clean and fresh, moreover Boxer Mark Two had been cleaned up and recently groomed. Ben gave him the extra apples and carrots he had brought to make up for his neglect of the past week. After a few pats on his neck, several strokes of his face and their usual one-sided chat Ben returned to his car and in improved spirits headed for the office. He wasn't to know that that was to be one of the last times he was to see the old horse. As he turned into the office car park he was confronted by papers all over place and it was pretty obvious that the local vandals had had a field day breaking open all the waste bags which were awaiting collection and throwing the contents everywhere. Alice was already on the job along with Ernest who was helping her, and so was the tidy little figure of Susan Fraser, who had just started her new job and had got stuck straight in. Ben felt a bit guilty that he had not been there to welcome her but was more worried that there might be something confidential amongst the loose papers. He realised that they were not always good at shredding their wastepaper and reminded himself to talk about it at the next team meeting. 'Well done, team, great job please try and get every last bit then come in for a warm and I will make you all coffee.'

He ducked into the office and was immediately aware of an unusual smell. He was well used to the musty smell which normally pervaded the prefabricated office after it had been closed up for a weekend or holiday period but this was quite different. It usually took the combined action of opening a few windows and Alice getting active with her spray polish to improve things but this smell was perfumed and uniquely pleasant. He looked into the reception area and immediately spotted a pot of pink hyacinths in full bloom, mystery over. As he progressed down the corridor to the kitchen to put on the kettle he glanced into each office as he passed and each had a similar pot of flowers in a variety of colours. His room had blue hyacinths, which just happened to be his favourite colour, and he guessed that Mrs Freeman had had a hand in it. After filling the kettle and lighting the gas he went back to the general office to thank Mrs Freeman for the flowers. She replied, 'Nothing to do with me, all I did was put them around, they are all Susie's work. She thought they would brighten the place up a bit and I think it is a lovely idea. She'll explain how it came about. Meanwhile, she saw Alice and Ernest struggling to clear the car park and got straight into helping whilst I held the fort here. Phil hasn't turned up yet and you had been delayed. By the way, Mary your friend from the health centre would like a word and I said I would get you to ring her back.'

Coffee all round was the order of the day, which Ben made much to the surprise of Alice, who didn't seem at all sure whether to be pleased or upset at him doing her job. Ben thanked Susie for the flowers and she explained that they were really from her husband, John. 'He orders fifty pots of hyacinths each Christmas time from a friend's market garden which he then uses to decorate the shop. He generally gives them away over the holiday period to favoured customers but there are always some left over and he was happy for me to bring them into work.'

Alice announced that she would be taking hers home to share with Benny her cat and Ben donated his to Ernest for him to give to his mum. He enquired about Foxie and Ernest just shook his head, his eyes filling with tears and he hurried off to collect his cart and head off to keep the streets of Highfield clean. Ernest was replaced in the kitchen by Phil arriving for work and she joined them in the kitchen to reheat the kettle for a cup of coffee. She welcomed Susie warmly and said just the right thing by admiring the flowers and commenting on how good the place smelt. Ben gave Susie a whistle-stop tour of the offices before delivering her back to the desk she would be occupying in the room she would be sharing with Phil. He had previously suggested to Phil that it would be a good idea for Susie to spend her first week learning the ropes from her and Phil had seemed pleased with the suggestion. He left them to it and went off to catch up with his phone calls. He started with Mary at the health centre who filled him in on the Farthing family situation. Foxie was still alive but it was only a matter of time as he was not really eating and spent most of his time asleep.

Elsie seemed to be just about coping and to be resigned to Foxie's inevitable death in the near future. However, she was desperately worried about what would happen next as she had no money for a funeral. Her precious post office book was almost empty and the whole family were dependent upon the money that Ernest got as a street cleaner. In the back of his mind Ben knew that the council could, in exceptional cases, make provision for a 'pauper's funeral' but he had never had to use it. So he agreed with Mary that he would make enquires and get back to her before visiting Foxie and Elsie. He rang headquarters and got through to the switchboard, whose operator was on the ball and put him straight through to the responsible officer. Andrew Unwin was obviously from either Devon or Cornwall and had a pronounced accent, which took some getting used to. His manner was relaxed and interested and he explained that this was a part of the service which was rarely called upon and was only a small part of his responsibilities.

'Give me a chance to look up the regulations and paperwork and then call into the office and we will look at it together. I realise it is urgent so why not come in at lunch time tomorrow and we will have a chat over lunch in the canteen? Mind you, the food is nowhere near as good as in Highfield, if what Pete Evans told me about is anything to go by, but we will be able to find a corner to chat it through away from the damned telephone.'

Joe's reputation was obviously spreading and Ben thought that Andrew Unwin had to be one of the good guys if he was a friend of Pete Evans. The time was set for 12.30 the following day. The next call was to the prof's secretary, Mrs Hemsworth, to arrange about joining the prof's team at the psychiatric clinic at the general hospital. She was a formidable lady who saw her role as protecting the prof from unwanted approaches, but she had been expecting Ben's call and efficiently filled him in on the relevant information. 'Get there a bit early,' she suggested, 'then the prof can run through things with you.' Ben's week was beginning to fill up, so he thought it was as well that Phil was looking after Susie, but it was just about to get even busier.

He had heard on the news in the car on the way in that the unions were planning random power cuts across the country. They had been attempting to arrange a wage increase for their members across the board and the strikes were their way of trying to move the negotiations forward. Ben hadn't taken a lot of notice and simply listened to the rest of the news contented that the radio stayed on station for the whole journey. His ears pricked up as it was announced that the government planned to abolish the death penalty and replace it with life imprisonment. It was for a trial period of five years but had come a year too late for people such as Russell Pascoe, and Ben reflected on the decision. After witnessing the vigil outside Horfield Prison he had borrowed a couple of books from the library and had read up on the subject. He had been struck by the number of cases where the wrong person had been hanged and decided that life imprisonment could at least be reversed whilst hanging was definitely permanent. On balance he felt that the government had made the right decision as far as he was concerned.

The next incoming call was from Alderman Herbert Anstey and as ever he was organising a subcommittee meeting 'to deal with the emergency'. Ben was careful not to ask what emergency and held his council as Councillor Anstey ploughed on. It emerged that he was concerned about the threats of power cuts but Ben still couldn't work out what it had to do with him. He quickly decided it was safer to go along with the councillor's plans and agreed to be at the local housing office the following day at 4 pm. As soon as he put the phone down he rang his contact in the local Housing Department, Oliver Manning, to find out if he knew the nature of the emergency. Oliver knew all about the meeting and was most helpful and explained that the problem was all about the high-rise block Chelsea House. Ben knew it well because it was where Frank and Rosie Sullivan lived on the top floor and he listened with interest as Oliver filled him in.

The problem was all about a fire that had happened at the house over the Christmas holiday. It had apparently started in one of the large waste bins that contained the rubbish sent down the waste shoots from all of the flats. The bin in question had been pushed up against the cage of the emergency generator that serviced the flats and it had been severely damaged. The fire brigade had been able to prevent the fire spreading to the flats but in doing so the water and foam that they used had further damaged the generator beyond repair. They thought that the fire had been deliberate and had put it down to bored kids' idea of fun. The matter was now in the hands of the insurance company and PC Roger Richards, the resident Highfield Bobbie who was sounding out contacts to try and identify the culprits. 'As you know, Ben, the whole place is dependent on electricity for everything and power cuts would make life in the flats impossible. The emergency generators are there for just such an emergency but Chelsea House would be left without heating, lighting, water and sewage systems and lifts. It would just be impossible and there is no way of knowing when the generator will be replaced. So Councillor Anstey wants some contingency plans put it place and I must say that I agree with him; so come along armed with any information you may have about any particularly vulnerable tenants.' Ben thanked Oliver for the information and put the phone down and went to chat to Phil and Mrs Freeman. They gave it their full attention and went through their card index system looking for any contact they may have had with anyone with a Chelsea House address.

After an hour or so the sum result was just three tenants known to them. In addition to the Sullivans there was a mother and daughter on the ground floor and an ex-psychiatric client on the third floor, but he had now recovered and was living independently. Agnes Knowles was an elderly widow who lived with her mentally handicapped daughter Peggy and they were well known to Phil. She advised that there were two other children, both married and living locally, who should be able to help out short term in an emergency.

The following day Ben duly turned up at headquarters for his meeting with Andrew Unwin, who came as something of a surprise. For a start he was well over six feet tall and had broad shoulders and a weightlifter's physique. His hair was long and very ginger and he sported a full ginger beard. Anyone less like a civil servant would be hard to imagine and Ben's surprise must have been obvious by the expression on his face. Andrew was clearly used to this reaction and burst out laughing and explained that he was a bit of a fraud as he was really a frustrated semi-professional player with Exeter Rugby Club but it paid little more than expenses.

'I am in my thirties so won't be playing much longer but I still love it and want to go on playing as long as possible. Exeter is a great little team and has ambitions to grow into the top league and I have had some great years with good mates. Meanwhile, my job with the council pays the bills, is far from stressful and the regular hours mean that I can fit in training three times a week.'

Ben tried to imagine what it must be like to be tackled by this amiable giant but decided it didn't bear thinking about. He told Andrew all about the Farthing family, explaining that they had all been classified as mentally handicapped over the years but had managed to survive without depending on National Assistance, but their current situation was desperate as Foxie had not been fit enough to earn any money from totting for at least six months. Ernest's earnings as a road sweeper had to cover everything including rent, but by skimping and saving they had managed to stay debt free. Andrew listened sympathetically and recognised that Ben was committed to trying to help the Farthings. He produced an application form for Ben to help Elsie complete and said he thought it should go through okay. He went on to tell him to let him have the completed form back as soon as possible and he would personally take it to the council chairman for ratification. 'Now let's have lunch. My treat as long as you promise to take me to Joe's for an all-day breakfast next time I am out your way.' Ben agreed without hesitation as he could quite see why Pete Evens liked this guy.

The lunch of cottage pie and vegetables was passable and reminiscent of school dinners. The conversation ebbed and flowed and Andrew took the opportunity to explain the extent of the provisions within a 'pauper funeral'.

'There's no frills, just the hearse, no second car, it's always the first cremation of the day at 8 am, no music just a few prayers and the ashes can be collected the next day in an ordinary little cardboard box from the crematorium office. I have had to attend two such funerals in the past as part of my job and they were very sad and dismal affairs. They were both vagrants found dead on the street and no one else attended. The crematorium staff scattered their ashes in the garden of remembrance where I guess they did some good for the roses. Just to add to the misery it poured with rain on both occasions.'

Lunch over they parted company and Ben started for the exit but stopped in his tracks as he spotted an old friend across the room. Pam Townsend, his 'stationery cupboard friend' was sat by herself reading a book and eating her sandwiches; he changed direction and headed straight for her. He came up from behind her and she didn't look up from her book until he whispered in her ear 'room for a little one'. She let out a laugh and her face immediately registered a look of real pleasure. They shared a hand squeeze and Ben joined her at her table. The chat that followed was the usual stuff, she told him that her mum had been poorly but was on the mend but that their Christmas had been quiet. 'But I discovered a new author who I hadn't read before and that helped.' She passed the book she had been reading to Ben who saw it was called *Nerve* by Dick Francis.

'It's a thriller all about horse racing and ever since I was a small child I have always been keen on horses but never had the chance to try horse riding. I love thrillers and read them all the time. The author is that famous jockey who almost won the Grand National on the queen mother's horse Devon Loch, but it collapsed on the run in to the winning post when it was well ahead. He has retired from riding now and this is his second novel and they are really gripping.'

Ben smiled and told Pam about his teenage riding experience and his special horse Boxer. He went on to tell her about Solomon, alias Boxer Mark Two, and she seemed fascinated by the idea of him stopping each day to befriend an old horse. The conversation went quiet for a while and Pam suddenly looked very serious.

'I am sorry to have to warn you but Creepy is still on your case. He has asked me a couple of times about what I overheard when you were at the Christmas gathering and I have each time said that I heard nothing, but he's clearly not happy and I guess it is only a matter of time before he arrives at your office. I will keep my eyes and ears open and will let you know if I hear anything, but be on your guard. He really is a little shit.'

A bit more general chat, a parting squeeze and a promise to link up again at the next office shindig and they went off in separate directions. Ben decided he should take the warning seriously and make sure he had his house in order.

Ben also made sure that he was on time for the meeting with Councillor Anstey and once again sat next to Oliver as the rest of the places around the table filled up around them. The people attending were largely the same ones who had attended the meeting about rehousing Hanca Parsons back in October. There was, however, one additional person who was sitting next to Councillor Anstey. He was in his early forties, tanned and looking very fit with smart crew cut dark brown hair flecked with grey. He could have been a film actor but his fireman's uniform, complete with officer's pips, left no doubt about his job. Councillor Anstey, in his usual slightly higher seat, called the meeting to order and introduced Leading Fireman Humphries to the meeting. As usual Councillor Anstey led from the front and made it quite clear that he wanted a contingency plan in place for the tenants of Chelsea House should there be a power cut.

'We must ensure they are safe and be able to show we have acted responsibly, meanwhile, I will be putting my weight behind getting the generator replaced as a matter of urgency. I understand that there are eighteen flats there and that several are occupied by vulnerable people. I want them all seen and a plan produced for each and every one.' Not for the first time Ben was impressed by the man's drive and energy it was easy to see why he was so successful in business. The meeting did not last long and resulted in Ben, Oliver and Paul Humphries being set the task of producing the report. As before, Ben and Oliver accompanied by Paul retired to the pub for a much-needed pint having been well and truly steamrollered by the dynamic Councillor Anstey. Paul had been taken by surprise by the way the councillor had assumed that he was in a position to commandeer resources when he had a problem, but admitted that the fire service could probably be helpful with this particular problem. Oliver and Ben sympathised with Paul's feelings but both confirmed that Councillor Anstey wasn't a political animal but did have a real desire to help his constituents.

Between them they divided the flats up for follow up and agreed to get together in a week's time to try and agree a provisional emergency plan for each of the tenants of Chelsea House. Ben focused on the flats of the three clients already known to him and also agreed to visit several other elderly tenants who were living alone and possibly vulnerable. He made a start the following day and took Susie along with him to help record details of possible need if the power cuts happened. This gave him the chance of seeing Susie's abilities at dealing with people and he was generally impressed with the way she involved people without alarming them. She was particularly sensitive with Rosie Sullivan and made a real effort at involving her in conversation. She wasn't particularly successful but she did enable Ben to have a one-to-one with Frank for longer than at his usual visits. He found Frank more breathless than before and looking unwell, and he admitted to Ben that he was suffering some chest pains but had not been able to see a doctor as of yet. Before Ben left he got Frank's agreement for him to speak to his GP, who was Dr Eddoll's partner, Dr Smyth.

On the Thursday Ben managed to get in to see Dr Smyth, who he didn't know very well and who seemed to lack the warmth and concern that Dr Eddoll always presented. Nevertheless, the doctor had had some previous contact with Rosie Sullivan and rather reluctantly agreed to make a home visit in the next day or two. Ben figured that was the best he was going to get and left saying that he would call in to the surgery again the following Monday for an update. Ben visited the other flats along with Susie and helpfully there was someone in at home at all of them. He left the call to Agnes and Peggy Knowles on the ground floor to the last as they were already well known to Phil, who would be able to fill in most of the information needed.

Meanwhile, he asked Susie to pop back up to Frank and Rosie to advise them of Dr Smyth's anticipated visit. 'I have one more visit to make so if you make your own way back to the office I will link up with you later.'

After his visit to the Knowles, Ben headed straight to Joe's for a much-needed coffee, which was a treat he didn't want to share. Tomorrow looked like a full day with the visit to Foxie and Elsie in the morning and his first session at Prof's outpatients in the afternoon. To be truthful he was a bit anxious about what would be expected of him at the clinic so he used the peacefulness of Joe's back room to try and get his head around it.

He was pretty sure that he would be expected to gather up a social history for any new clients to present to the prof and Dr Rani before they saw the patients. With this in mind he drew up a rough form listing what he thought might be relevant and then hurried back to the office to get Mrs Freeman typing up several tidy copies ready for the following day. On the Friday Ben's journey to work included a brief stop with the old horse who was waiting at the gate in anticipation. Instead of going straight to the office he went on to call in briefly at the health centre to update Mary on the possibility of arranging a 'pauper's funeral'. Mary confirmed that she was now going in to see to Foxie morning and night seven days a week and that he was slowly slipping away.

'I have dealt with this situation several times before and I would doubt if it will go on much more than a few days. Dr Eddoll calls in regularly and has prescribed morphine to ensure that Foxie is in no pain. Elsie is just about holding it together and will be relieved that Foxie can have a proper funeral. Ernest spends most evenings just sat by Foxie's bed holding his hand and giving him sips of water. Meanwhile, Penny is on another planet and still expects to be waited on hand and foot by her mother. I can't see her ever changing.'

Ben thanked Mary for all the help she was giving to the Farthings and said he would call in to do the funeral form with Elsie later in the morning. When he got into the office he cleared the post with Mrs Freeman and then asked Susie to complete a list of the details of the tenants they had seen at Chelsea House ready for the meeting with Paul and Oliver the following week. The visit to Elsie went as he had anticipated: she was tearful and appeared worn out and when Ben went in to see Foxie he could quite see why. It was almost as if there was nothing left, just a sad little heap almost lost in the bedclothes. He appeared to be unconscious and Ben did not stay in his room more than a few moments. Elsie was relieved about the funeral and seemed to understand the form when he went through it with her and signed it with a shaky signature.

'I still can't help feeling I am letting Foxie down. Over the years we have had some tough times and he has always done his best for us, going out in all winds and weathers. He is going to die and there will be nothing left to show he was ever here. If I could I would buy a headstone for him but even if I could afford one where would I put it?'

Ben attempted to reassure Elsie by saying she had been a good wife and was showing how much she cared for Foxie by her care of him during this last difficult period of his life. He left the sad household and went straight to headquarters to drop the completed form into Andrew Unwin, who agreed to process it as quickly as possible. The general hospital was only a few blocks away so Ben found a convenient parking space nearby and decided to walk to the hospital to clear his head. After grabbing a sandwich and coffee in the hospital canteen he took the lift to the outpatient department on the third floor, paused and took a few deep breaths before stepping forward to take on a new challenge. He had never had cause to come to the outpatient department before, his previous visits to this part of the hospital having been to casualty with the boys.

A year or two ago Jack had managed to break his arm by falling out of the apple tree in the back garden and when Nick was a toddler he had pulled a hot cup of tea over himself. Both incidents had now faded into the past but at the time had been very traumatic. The outpatients department consisted of a large rectangular room with three banks of seats facing in different directions. By the side of the two lifts was a sizeable counter covered in stacks of files and behind them was stood a rather large middle-aged lady who was busy sorting the files into some sort of order. Looking around the room Ben could see numerous doors, most of which had a board up identifying the occupant and their speciality. This afternoon in addition to the psychiatric clinic there were gynaecology and dermatology clinics for the receptionist to sort the files out for appropriately. There was no other sign of life so he stopped in front of the receptionist's desk and waited for her to see him. This took a few seconds but she suddenly let out a small squeal and smiled at him warmly and said, 'Sorry, I didn't see you come in. Can I help you?'

Ben explained who he was and why he was there and Wendy – learnt from the name badge on her ample right boob – directed him to the prof's office. The prof and Dr Raj Rani were sharing a drink from a large flask, which was now on the window ledge, and the prof welcomed Ben by serving him with a cup of milky coffee and the invite to sit down and join in the review of clients due that afternoon. The prof explained that the patients they expected to see that afternoon were the usual mixture of follow-up appointments and the rest new referrals, of which there were six during the afternoon's clinic.

'I would like you to see all the new referrals first, Ben, and get a social history from them for you to present to either Raj or myself dependent upon how we have previously allocated them. As soon as you have finished come straight into one of our offices once the electric "WAIT" sign outside the door is turned off. We always have a lot of people to see and your help should speed things along. Are you okay with that?'

Ben said that that was what he had anticipated doing and showed them the forms that he had prepared to use. They seemed pleased and the prof's comment was, 'Good lad, well let's get going.' Once back in reception Ben spotted his name on the next door along, which helped with his confidence as it made him feel an accepted part of the team. The room was kitted out as a medical examination room but did also have a desk and a couple of chairs so would serve his purpose well. The afternoon went without a hitch, even if it was a bit hectic and the prof had a few words with him at the end of the clinic.

'That seemed to go well and I think your form will be very useful. I think it should go on the patient's file for future use and I would welcome a section on the end of the form for you to make any observations you may have. It is always useful to have views from a different perspective and you must of course sign the form with your title of psychiatric social worker.'

As he walked back to his car Ben felt like he was walking on air and he couldn't wait to get home to tell Sandy all about it. It is always good to be valued and particularly by someone you respect.

Chapter 25

It Is All Happening

After a weekend of almost constant rain with the boys stuck indoors and bored Ben was relieved to drop them off at school. The rain had reduced to a drizzle with just a hint of sleet but not enough to stop him from making a stop en route to see Boxer Mark Two. The field was empty and the bath of water had been removed. On impulse Ben turned the old Cortina around and soon pulled up outside Scadding's yard. He decided to park outside just in case someone mistook his car for a scrapper with it ending up as part of the dead car mountain. The first thing he saw as he entered the yard was a massive Alsatian dog, which started barking frantically and seemed anxious to eat him alive. Fortunately, it was restrained on a strong chain and a voice from under a car on a ramp nearby yelled at it to shut up, which it reluctantly did. Ben recognised the voice as being Tony Scadding of car radio fame and saw that he was busy disembowelling an old Vauxhall prior to sending it on one last journey to the crusher. Tony climbed out from under the car and showed Ben a pair of filthy and oily hands, indicating he could only mime shaking hands. Ben quickly told him the car radio was working fine and that it made his journey to and from work a much more pleasant experience.

'Do you want to talk to dad?' asked Tony and he pointed to two massive containers, one on top of the other, which were partway down the yard. 'He is in the top cabin which he uses as an office. Go on up the stairs at the side, he'll be pleased to see you.'

The door to the office was closed and Ben duly knocked and was promptly called to go in. The heat from the room hit him like a blow. Clearly Robbie liked his comfort. There was a large desk just inside the door that was covered in paper being efficiently shuffled by an attractive middle-aged blond lady dressed casually but with style. Robbie was stretched out on an ancient settee reading a newspaper and clutching a mug of something hot and steaming. He leapt to his feet and hurried over to welcome Ben warmly. He immediately made the introductions.

'This is my wife Patsie, who keeps me in line and the business running, and this is Ben Newman, the welfare man I told you about.'

Patricia smiled at Ben and offered him a hot chocolate, which he gratefully accepted and he then joined Robbie back on the settee. 'I can guess why you have come, you are wondering about Solomon. Well I am pleased to say he has gone to his new home in Whitchurch. I took him there in my lorry over the weekend with Reggie Brooks his owner, and it really is a great place. There are plenty of stables for cold nights and the fields there are lush with grass. There are a lot of other old or rescued horses there so it is quite an improvement for Solomon, but I can't thank you enough for the care you showed him over the past few weeks.' Patricia brought the hot chocolate over and sat down with them, content to join in the conversation. It was Patricia who was the first to ask Ben about Foxie and she seemed genuinely upset to learn that he was almost at the end of his life.

'I have got to know him and Ernest quite well over the past few years and I really admired them. They turned out day after day, sometimes earning only a few shillings for a day's efforts but they never gave up. Life must have been a real struggle for that family but they never looked for charity, even though Robbie always made sure they got top dollar for their scrap. If there is anything we can do to help please let us know, we Totters have to stick together.'

During the conversation Ben mentioned Elsie's anxiety that she had no way of providing Foxie with some form of permanent memorial and was surprised by Robbie's immediate response. 'Let me give it some thought and I will talk it over with Tony, as he is a great ideas man. I feel sure he will come up with something and he can turn his hand to anything.'

Ben was delighted to have the offer of help and went on to say how pleased he was with the job Tony had done on his car radio.

'Then there is that fantastic motorbike of his. I have always admired Vincents and his is a real beauty.'

Robbie beamed with pleasure and said, 'What you don't know is that it was my first bike and I used to show off with it terribly until the day I overdid it and smashed into a wall and ended up in hospital and wrote the bike off. It was stuck in the back of a shed for years until Tony, who was about fourteen years old at the time, asked if he could have a go at fixing it up. I didn't think he had a hope in hell of getting it going so I let him have his head. It took him over two years to do it but he did it all by himself even down to paying for replacement parts out of the money he earned keeping the yard tidy at weekends. Patsy and I were truly amazed by the result; the bike is like brand new and now worth a small fortune. Right there and then I decided to start a new project with Tony as my business partner and Solomon's old field is to be the location so watch that space.'

Neither of them would give any further clue and Ben left having been told to pop in anytime as he would be very welcomed. Tony was in the driving seat of a mobile crane and was swinging the dismembered Vauxhall on to the top of a growing pile of scrap cars waiting to be crushed. A sizeable pile of car parts remained by the ramp ready to be added to the spare parts stored in the lower container. Tony gave him a wave and the Alsatian let out a few barks, but you could tell it was only a token gesture and it made no move towards Ben, who gave it a wide berth anyway. As he drove on to the office he was pleased that he had called in on the Scaddings and he could quite see why Jessie had a soft spot for the rough diamond that was Robbie. It felt like he had made a new friend.

The office was running smoothly when he arrived and Mrs Freeman had opened and recorded the post and it was in a folder awaiting his attention. As he sat down to read it through, Alice appeared with a cup of tea and he was pleased to note she seemed well, and for once made no comment about her bowel movements. The post was the usual boring stuff from headquarters and consisted of various memos of no real interest to him or the workings of his team. He passed the whole lot back to Mrs Freeman for her to file away appropriately and asked her to modify the form they had designed for Prof's clinic and to get a supply run off for future use. This involved her having to produce a stencil which could go on the ancient duplicator that had been left behind by the planners when they had vacated the office next door. The machine was a beast, temperamental and prone to breaking down, but it could save hours of work when the need for something in volume arose. Inevitably

Mrs Freeman would end up covered in ink and far from her usual placid self. The only person who enjoyed working with the beast was Alice, who never seemed to tire of turning the handle and producing sheet after sheet of printed matter. Ben made the request and backed off rapidly to the sanctuary of his office.

A few minutes later Susie popped her head around the door and came in clutching a sheaf of papers. She was her usual chirpy self, full of smiles and presented Ben with the papers. 'Here's all the info on the tenants we visited at Chelsea House ready for your meeting later today. I think we only need to worry about the Sullivans on the top floor as the other two known to us are well covered by family nearby.'

Ben thanked Susie for her work and asked how she had got on in her first week on the job.

'I loved and enjoyed going around with Phil, who helped me to understand what we have to do to help these people with their situations. I went for a drink with Phil after work last Thursday and we linked up in the pub with her partner, Lizzie, who is a poppet and we never stopped laughing.'

One up to you, girl, thought Ben, who had not as yet met Phil's partner, but it was good to know that Susie was not at all phased by Phil's sexual proclivities. Ben went on to tell Susie that he was hoping to visit several of his more complex situations later in the week and that he would like to take Susie with him so he could introduce her and possibly involve her in the future. He gave her a list of four clients that he had selected so that she could read through the files prior to their visits. Susie went off full of enthusiasm just as the phone started to ring. He picked it up and was greeted by Oliver, who had rung to confirm that Paul would be joining them in Oliver's office in the Housing Department at three to prepare for their meeting with Councillor Anstey at four.

Ben and Paul arrived together in the car park, Ben in the old Cortina and Paul outshining him in an immaculate full-size red fire engine. Paul opened up a hatch on the back of the appliance to show Ben a selection of emergency heaters and lights that would be available if the power cuts went on for any length of time. When they got together in Oliver's office Paul took the lead and said that he had decided to use this problem as a training exercise for his crew. He had set them the task of designing a plan for evacuating a high-rise block in the case of a fire when the lifts would not be in operation.

'As you know there are several such blocks on our patch and most of them have some vulnerable people or young families living in them so there is always a risk attached. In fact I think it would be a good plan for us to have an annual review of tenants from your department, Oliver, so we have a good idea of occupants.'

Oliver agreed to put this in hand and passed around a list of Chelsea House tenants floor by floor. The task of going through it was relatively straightforward as most of the tenants were able bodied and would be able to manage to get out by the stairs if the power was off. Of those most had friends or relatives who they could stay with and the rest would be able to find their way to any emergency centre in a convenient hall or school, which could be set up at the time. There remained only four flats which were cause for special concern. They were made up of the Sullivans, the Knowles, and an infirm single lady, Louise Eglestone, who was fiercely independent but, in a wheelchair, which would make the stairs an impossibility. The final cause for concern was Bert Tranter, who lived on the eleventh floor. He had been totally blind his whole life so the loss of lighting would not affect him directly, but in recent years he had developed Parkinson's disease and his uncontrolled shaking made eleven flights of stairs an impossibly dangerous hazard. The major problem for Bert in the event of a power cut would be the loss of the lifts. Without them he would be unable to exercise his guide dog Rex at least twice a day on the green surrounding the flats, which he still managed to do each day via the lift. It took little imagination to visualise the problems that would soon arise for Bert and Rex in the event of cuts.

It was agreed between them that Ben and Paul would visit the four flats and come up with an individual plan for each and Oliver would write to the other tenants advising them to stock up on torches and about the availability of emergency centres, which would be set up at the time.

The meeting with Councillor Anstey went surprisingly well and on this occasion he simply sat back and listened to the three of them talk him through their research and their proposals for action. He then demonstrated the business acumen that had made him such a successful businessman by drawing the meeting to a close with none of the usual waffle common in dealings with committees and members. 'It sounds like a good plan, gentlemen, well done. I agree with the idea of an annual review of tenants in high-rise blocks and will raise that at the next housing committee meeting with the intention of extending it across Exworth. Meanwhile, I am on the case of the replacement generator and it should be with us in the next month or two but it has to be made especially and delivered from Germany where they are manufactured. As for the problem with the dog, I am sure I can get one of my footballers who lives on the estate to help out if you find you need help. He has a young family and always looking for ways of making a few bob extra, I would be quite happy to cover the cost. Well, gentlemen, I am happy to leave it to you. I declare the meeting closed.' Ben decided they could do with a few more like Councillor Anstey on the council and arranged to do the joint visits with Paul on the Thursday coming.

Ben didn't go back to the office as it was already well past four-thirty and he decided to have an early finish, much to the delight of Sandy who had spent most of the day at the shop as Ma Driscoll had had a bit of 'a funny turn' and had been mainly resting on the sofa in her living room with Henry curled up beside her. The boys were watching children's television and barely acknowledged his arrival, but Sandy was scratching her head over what to do for tea as the larder was pretty empty. Ben sat her down and made her a cup of tea before heading to the chip shop, first checking he had enough cash for fish and chips all round. The smile Sandy gave him made the sacrifice of his 'pocket money' worthwhile and could perhaps signify a reward later. Good result, problem resolved and the possibility of being on a promise.

The tea went down well and when they had finished Sandy produced the much-depleted Christmas parcel that Ma had given them on Boxing Day. It was the twelfth and final day, which was twelve drummers drumming, and the boys hastily unwrapped the last of the paper to discover a bumper lucky bag for each of them, which had been generously enhanced by Ma with a selection of favourite sweets. As always Sandy claimed the final envelope containing the piece of jigsaw before hurrying upstairs to put it away and to get ready for her night school class. Ben made a fresh brew for himself and set about clearing the kitchen before joining the boys in front of the television and sampling a couple of Ma's sweets.

The following day he found that he automatically slowed the car as he approached Boxer Mark Two's field but put his foot down as he remembered there were no more meetings with the old horse. As he neared the estate he spotted a movement on the grass land to the left but it was only the large stray dog that had been hanging around the estate in recent weeks. In the past there had been quite a big problem with loose dogs running around the estate causing general mayhem and frightening a lot of people. The situation had come to a head when they had linked up to form a couple of dog packs which had met head to head in the shopping precinct and decided to have a ferocious battle. The shoppers were terrified and rightly so as a young mother had her push chair knocked over in the fracas and her young toddler was thrown out right amongst the scrapping dogs.

The young mum bravely recovered the little boy before any more damage was done to him but in doing so received several bites herself before the dogs were chased off by some passing bin men. The incident caused a major reaction from people who witnessed it and several of them reported their concern to PC Roger Richards, who undertook to sort it out. It was clear that most of the dogs were pets that were simply turned out to wander by day and returned to their homes when they were hungry. It was fairly easy for PC Richards to identify where some of the dogs belonged by chatting to Hayley the postman and Beefy the bread man as between them they called at almost every house on the estate. They knew, often from bitter experience, which house had a dog and were able to describe in some detail which dog lived where.

Most days PC Richards could be seen walking around the estate stopping to have a word here and there but making his presence felt in a quiet and unobtrusive way. However, for the assignment of the dogs he went for maximum publicity and drove around the estate in his panda car parking deliberately outside each of the houses he wanted to visit. The message to each householder was the same that if their dog was found wandering unsupervised again PC Richards would be back demanding to see the dog's licence. Failure to produce it would result in the dog being put down and the owner facing a heavy fine from the magistrate's court. By this time few people bothered with paying the annual charge for a dog licence and it wouldn't be many years before the licence was discontinued. The word went around the estate like lightning and the problem of packs of dogs running loose was resolved almost overnight.

The current stray had turned up with a group of travellers who just before Christmas had briefly parked their caravans and transits on the central green of the estate. They didn't stay long as there was no interest from any one in Highfield in having their driveways tarred, Foxie and Ernest had had the pickings of available scrap and PC Richards made his presence felt regularly throughout each day. They left as quickly as they arrived, leaving behind a stack of rubbish for the council to clear and tethered to the 'no ball games signpost' an enormous dog who looked part lurcher and something else which might have been husky. It was only a matter of minutes before the dog had bitten through his rope and he had wandered the estate ever since. Several people had bravely attempted to approach it but it seemed terrified of people and always limped off as quickly as it could. Ben felt compassion for the animal as it looked in a sorry state, appearing to be underweight with a long mud-covered matted coat and an obvious injury to one of its front legs. For no apparent reason he suddenly thought of one of the Shakespearean speeches he had learnt years ago for his O level GCE English Literature. He had passed but only just and the speeches he had learnt parrot fashion were of no use in the exam. But they had lived with him and he could still rattle them off whenever the opportunity arose. The one that came to mind now was by Julius Caesar, saying 'Yond Cassius has a lean and hungry look', which seemed to fit the poor stray pretty well. The name Cassius stuck in Ben's head and the dog now had an identity for him. However, he soon had other things on his mind and he was planning which visits to make with Susie that day as he turned into the office car park. Susie had read the four files he had left her with the previous day and was keen to be out visiting. Ben explained that most of her work would be with mentally handicapped people whose condition was unlikely to change very much but that the patients she would be visiting with him would usually be people with a mental illness. Work with the mentally handicapped would mainly be helping them and their families to cope with the requirements of dealing with a lifelong problem. Whereas the mentally ill client's condition was often subject to mood swings and irrational behaviour and nowadays was mainly controlled by medication. He went on to give his usual explanation of the difference between psychosis and neurosis and she seemed to grasp the difference. Ben finished up by saying that, 'Of course what I have told you is an oversimplification as there are lots of overlaps between the various conditions; it is a useful starting point but you must always remember that each client is unique. Let's go and see a couple of my clients and you will see what I mean.'

The first place he took Susie was to 28 Peasedale Avenue, the home of Ruth Andrews and her children, and he could see signs of improvement the moment he walked up the path. It was clear of the ancient dog turds that had previously made it so hazardous. The flag of surrender, namely Mr Andrew's old underpants, no longer hung from the top of the privet hedge and all signs of plastic daffodils decapitated and otherwise appeared to have been consigned to the dustbin. The grass was still badly in need of cutting and the hedges likewise, but a lot had changed in a short time. The changes continued to happen as the door was answered by Ruth, who looked positively wholesome. She was dressed in a colourful jumper and skirt and her hair was brushed and free from nicotine staining. She welcomed them into the living room still furnished with the same battered old furniture but everything clean and tidy and clear of clutter. The biggest change was the absence of the rank smell which had dominated the house previously. It was replaced by the much more pleasant smell of furniture polish.

Ben was keen to learn about Ruth's return to her Catholic faith but he didn't have to ask as Ruth couldn't wait to tell him all about it. She was bordering on elation as she described the whole new experience that was Father MacGinty. 'He's simply lovely and really understands people and is nothing like the old tartars I have dealt with in the past. The girls and I went to midnight mass at Christmas for the first time for years and it was very special and made our Christmas. Unfortunately, my lad Brian wouldn't come but that is what he is like at present, all he wants to do is go out with his mates and I never know what he is up to. I think he must miss his dad but you wouldn't think so if you saw them together. His dad called in on Christmas Day and brought little gifts for us all. It wasn't much but at least he made an effort and he even brought a potted rose for me, which was a first as he had never bought me flowers before.'

Susie dutifully admired the rather sad looking plant which was sitting on top of the television and Ben wondered if this was the first small step towards reconciliation. He would keep his ears open next time he was in Joe's as the grape vine usually predicted the next session of musical beds. He asked how the children had reacted to their father's Christmas visit and Ruth thought about it before answering.

'Katie seemed reserved and never moved far from my side. I guess she was anxious that I might get upset or angry. Angie, my middle one, was all over him like a rash which surprised me as she has never really commented on him leaving. Brian was just awful and wouldn't have anything to do with his father other than telling him 'to sod off as you don't live here any more.' When his dad tried to talk to him he just rushed out of the room and out of the house, slamming the front door in anger. He was gone for hours and I was really worried that he might do something stupid but he just came back during the evening and watched television as if nothing had happened.'

Ben moved back in his chair and left it to Susie to continue to talk to Ruth and get to know her. He concluded that it was never going to be an easy life for Ruth but she seemed well on the way to getting her life back into some sort of normality. He thought that the time was near for him to move things on but he said nothing at this stage as he needed to do some ground work before putting his plan forward. They called back at the office, which was only a couple of minutes away, and stopped for an early lunch and to use the toilets before setting off to see Hanca Parsons. He stopped the car a little way away from her home to remind Susie of Hanca's past and her particularly odd lifestyle. Susie seemed intrigued but even so was more than a little surprised by the location of the house and the wildness of the garden surrounding it. Hanca had made no effort to clear the brambles in the front garden and they had to be carefully negotiated to avoid their vicious thorns.

At the top of the first flight of steps Ben pointed out an old white enamel bread bin partially buried in the earth and explained that that was Hanca's post box for mail and the free newspapers. 'Few people get beyond this point and you will soon see why.' The brambles became denser and more intrusive and soon caused Susie to regret wearing a skirt and stockings. The converted barn appeared out of the undergrowth and looked oddly charming with a couple of climbing roses starting to clothe the front wall set in small little neat beds carved out of the jungle. The solid iron front door with its padlock fastening was as ugly as ever but Ben reminded Susie that it was Hanca's choice to prevent any other 'firework incidents'.

He led them around to the back of the building to discover Hanca part way up the garden tearing ivy and weeds from the walls of some sort of outhouse that appeared to have been lost in the undergrowth for years. The Hanca that walked down to meet them was far removed from the smart lady Ben had returned from Cerne Abbas. Her hair was uncombed and the grey was rapidly replacing the brown that had been coloured by the hairdresser. She was dressed in a sort of all-over boiler suit that did nothing for her appearance but was a sensible defence to the brambles. She shyly shook hands with them both and he noticed that her hand had the texture of sandpaper and her nails were cracked and uneven. But she seemed in good spirits and enjoyed showing them a strip of cleared ground the full width of the garden, which she assured them was only the start of her producing her own food.

'Come and see what I have discovered,' she said as she led them to the old wall she had been working on when they had arrived. 'It's a pair of old pig sties that were probably built here in war time when farmers often kept a secret pig or two for their own use. I believe it was common practice but these must have been abandoned once the war was over as it can't have been very convenient once the need for secrecy was over. The more I see of them the better they become and I am going to use them as a wood store and one day I would like to keep chickens.'

They all headed back into the house and Hanca shyly showed Susie over the house whilst Ben made himself useful by putting the kettle on. The two of them seemed to be finding plenty to chat about but it was very much a question of Susie asking questions and Hanca making short replies. Ben was happy to confirm in his mind his decision to let Susie take over much of the visiting and support with Hanca. Meanwhile, he wandered back into the garden and made his way right up to the top hedges which made up the top boundary of the property. He had never been that far up the garden before as the brambles and nettles had made it impossible but there was now a rough pathway through that Hanca had obviously put a lot of machete action into achieving. A high mound of chopped brambles and other debris was stacked in a heap waiting to be burned and a large circle of damp grey ash witnessed a number of past bonfires. Ben was surprised to spot a small wooden gate in amongst the hedge and exploring further discovered the gate opened on to an old farm track overgrown but still passable judging by the amount of junk that had been dumped all along its edge. Much of it looked to be old farm equipment that was no longer needed but there was also evidence of more recent fly tipping almost certainly by tenants from the estate. This was something that would need to be kept an eye on as it could easily get out of hand. But for the time being Ben just closed the gate and made his way back down the garden.

The tea served by Hanca was not easy to drink as it was made with condensed milk which gave it an unusual taste. He was pleased to note that Susie drained her cup without comment as she continued to chat to Hanca whilst he wandered outside to surreptitiously donate his to the brambles. They spent longer with Hanna than Ben had anticipated and as a consequence he decided to leave his other planned visits with Susie until another day. He had been intending introducing her to the Farthings and the Sullivans but neither visit could be rushed and he was already intending to visit the Sullivans with Paul the following day when they were reviewing the tenants at Chelsea House. He explained this to Susie and asked her to write up her observations about the two visits they had made.

'Don't bother to mention the tea.'

Susie just laughed and pulled a face.

Chapter 26

A Strange Coincidence

The journey into the office was enhanced by a radio programme all about the footballer Stanley Matthews. Ben had heard of him throughout his life as his dad had been a supporter of Stoke City where he had been born and lived in his early days. Stanley Mathews was one of the few things that Ben's dad raved about. They were of similar age and it was clear that Mr Newman senior identified with him and had followed his career avidly. His career was amazing and to Mr Newman's credit he had continued to remain loyal even after Stanley Mathews left Stoke City to join Blackpool in 1947. Not that Ben could ever remember his dad going to a match but he had listened to him reading of their exploits from the Saturday football paper for what seemed like forever. One of his happiest memories of his dad was to do with the FA Cup final at Wembley in 1953. Ben's mum had been trying to persuade her husband to rent a television ready to see the coronation of Princess Elizabeth on 2 June but he had been resisting all overtures and then suddenly capitulated. Ben soon realised that it was a fortunate coincidence that the Blackpool–Bolton cup final was going to be televised for the first time on the 2 May just a month before the coronation. But he made no comment and both of his parents were able to have their own special memories they could cherish. The match proved to be very special and Stanley Matthews was the finest player on the pitch that day. As a consequence, the match was always known as 'the Mathews final', which Ben had always thought was a bit tough on Stan Mortensen, who had scored a hat trick, an achievement never done before or since in a cup final. The 4–3 win was an all-time high for Ben's dad but there were two more special events to come. Stanley Mathews returned to Stoke City to see out his career in 1961 and 'the wizard of the dribble' was knighted whilst still playing top-class football at the age of forty-nine. His mum had rung him to report that his dad had come home drunk that night after celebrating with his railway colleagues in the local pub appropriately named the Railway Arms. As his dad was normally almost tea total Ben guessed it hadn't taken too many pints to make him squiffy and he was pleased for him as he didn't seem to have much joy in his life. The account of Sir Stanley Matthews life and achievements was fascinating and Ben parked up just short of the office to listen to it all before making his way on to the office.

Everything in the office seemed in order and after the usual visit from Alice he collected the post from Mrs Freeman and returned to read it through in his office which still smelt sweetly from the pot of hyacinths. After a while Susie called into him and gave him her reports of their previous day's visits. By the sheer volume of paper it appeared she had done a thorough job and he guessed most of it must have been done by her at home the previous night.

He deliberately set the reports to one side and said, 'Thank you, Susie, I will read them through later.' Leaving her with the impression that this was the normal level of response expected. In reality he was pleased with what he had seen of her work but it was important that she shouldn't be overconfident as that could lead to trouble as he knew only too well from his own experience. He ran through the details of the tenants at Chelsea House and having put them in order decided to use the 'on-call bag' to carry them. As he removed all the mental health admission forms and other paraphernalia to make room for the papers the Christmas card that Katie had sent him dropped on to the desk. He recalled that he had meant to put it in the memory box but couldn't resist going to show it to Susie before safely tucking it away with his other special bits and pieces.

Paul and Ben met up at Chelsea House at ten-thirty as arranged and starting with the ground floor steadily made their way up the block from flat to flat. Most of the visits were straightforward and were merely a matter of recording what each tenant planned to do if there was a power cut. The Knowles seemed unworried, stating quite clearly that they would simply walk around to family who lived only a couple of streets away and who were keen campers and so had all the necessary kit on hand. The blind man Bert Tranter would need help to be evacuated as the stairs were beyond his physical ability and the same went for Louise Eglestone in her wheelchair. Paul advised them both that his men would come and take them to a temporary place of safety if the need arose, and Louise joked that she hoped they would be hunky firemen.

It was midday by the time they got to the Sullivans on the top floor and before knocking Ben reminded Paul to be prepared for a shock when he met Rosie Sullivan. However, it was Ben who received the biggest shock when he went to introduce Paul to Frank and he was amazed when the two men hugged.

'Hello, Skipper, great to see you,' were Paul's opening words. 'I didn't realise we were coming to see you, it's a lovely surprise.' He went on to explain to Ben that Frank Sullivan had been the leading fireman when he had first joined the fire brigade. 'He taught me everything I know and there has never been a better teacher.'

Rosie was without a fag and made sure they all knew it. Paul and Frank obviously had loads to talk about and Ben took over the role of fag supplier from Frank, leaving the two of them time to talk over old times. Rosie didn't seem to mind changing her supplier just so long as the cigarettes kept on coming. Five cigarettes later they got down to sorting out a plan with Frank and it was decided that Paul would loan the Sullivans emergency equipment for heating, lighting and cooking to save the need for them to be evacuated. This equipment was intended for major emergencies and was not normally issued to the general public because of safety reasons but with Frank's experience Paul was happy to make an exception. When they came away from the Sullivans and all the way down in the lift Paul was completely silent. When they got to the cars Paul suddenly said, 'That was a shock, I think I need a drink. Do you fancy a pub lunch, Ben?'

In no time at all they arrived in convoy at the busy car park of the Highfield Tavern, the larger of the two pubs on the estate. As ever the place was heaving with lunchtime drinkers and the noise made conversation impossible. Paul headed straight for a flight of stairs, which led to a small dining room which was all but deserted. A smart young woman with pink hair led them to a corner seat and promptly produced a menu and even a short wine list. Ben couldn't help but smile as he had been in the pub several times before but didn't even know the dining room existed. Paul explained that the landlord's wife was keen to upgrade the place and had recently persuaded her husband to expand to provide a proper meal service.

'In fact, it is quite busy in the evening and I have brought my wife here several times but the usual clientele prefer a liquid lunch so it has yet to take off during the day.'

They each ordered a beer and the steak and kidney pie which arrived with commendable speed, steaming hot and smelling great. Their conversation was limited as they fed the inner man but once the food was devoured with complete pleasure they both sat back with a second half pint and Paul filled Ben in on Frank's story.

'I was just nineteen when I joined the brigade and I was posted to the old sub-station on the other side of the canal. The gaffer, everyone called him Skipper, was the watch leader and he was respected by everyone. He really knew his stuff and he ran a tight ship and he took me under his wing from day one. We all spent hours and hours in each other's company and we did everything as a team. The best part was meal times when we took it in turns to do the cooking. It was mainly fry-ups but when it was Skipper's turn Rosie used to come in with enormous cottage pies that were to die for. She was a lovely lady, very pretty and really good fun. All the lads fancied her but she was strictly off limits and was clearly devoted to Skipper. She would stay and eat with us and always insisted that the pie dishes were properly washed up before she took them back home. It was so sad to see her now and how she has changed, but Skipper seems as devoted as ever.'

Ben confirmed that Frank looked after his wife with admirable care and explained that her fixation with smoking was a major problem which was complicated by trying to cope with her diabetes.

'I had no idea that he had been in the fire service, he never mentioned it. I had kind of assumed that he had always been a school caretaker, which I knew he had done for years. He must have been still a young man when he left the fire service, I suppose it was something to do with his gamey leg. I know he wears leg irons but again I assumed that that was probably the result of him suffering with polio as a child, I have seen such cases a couple of times before.'

Paul shook his head and said, 'It wasn't polio, nothing like that, but it did mean he had to take early retirement from the brigade. I had been in the job for about two years, that must have been about twenty years ago. We got a shout early one morning to say a lorry had smashed into one of the terraced houses down towards the canal. When we got there the damned fool driver was trying to reverse his lorry out of the front of the house and the whole place was shaking. Skipper dragged the driver out of his cab and pulled him a safe distance away. At that point a distraught woman in her night clothes came up to us screaming that her baby was in the little bedroom immediately above where the lorry had ploughed into the house. I don't think I have ever seen anyone move so fast as Skipper that day. He grabbed a ladder and climbed on to the lorry and was up the ladder and through the broken window in a flash. Within seconds he was handing a small toddler to one of the team and was just climbing out again when the whole front of the building collapsed taking the skipper with it. We dug him out of the rubble but he was in one hell of a state and spent the best part of three months in hospital. His leg was smashed into pieces and numerous operations were needed to pin it back together. He eventually returned home and learnt to walk again but needed callipers to make anything like normal walking possible. There was never any possibility of him returning to active service and after a year on sick leave he was awarded a small pension and went with Rosie to Buckingham Palace where the king awarded him the King's Fire Service Medal for Bravery. There was a big splash in the local papers at the time but life moves on and Skipper moved off our radar. There is no doubt that he is a hero and it breaks my heart to see his situation now. He deserves so much more.'

Ben listened to the story and was stunned as Frank had never mentioned anything about being a fireman and had only ever known of him as an ex-school caretaker. He realised that he was once again guilty of assuming he knew the full story, but where clients were concerned that was rarely the case. They finished their drinks and went their separate ways; Ben to fill Oliver in on the plans for the tenants at Chelsea House and Paul to reminisce with his work mates about an old friend suffering hard times.

Friday did not start well as Jack had woken up in the early hours being violently sick and had managed to be sick on both his bed and Nick's, the bedroom floor and along the landing on route to the bathroom. Once the worst was over all he wanted to do was go back to sleep so Sandy and Ben settled the two boys back into their own double bed before stripping the boys' beds and doing general mopping up. The rest of the night was spent with Sandy wrapped in a blanket on the living room sofa and Ben stretched out between the two armchairs pushed together. Neither got much sleep but the boys slept like babies and seemed completely well in the morning. Sandy got the washing machine going whilst Ben made the breakfast. The boys went off to school with Ben as usual who was sporting a king-sized headache and felt grumpy and sorry for himself. As he passed Boxer Mark Two's field he noticed that the old gate had been flattened and someone had parked huge earth moving equipment in the horse's place. He registered the fact but his head was pounding so much he did not attempt to question what was happening.

When he got to the office he retired to his own office as soon as possible and once Alice had delivered his morning tea he firmly shut the door, which was a sure sign that he did not wish to be disturbed. He knew he would have to be on top form for Prof's clinic in the afternoon so he dug a couple of paracetamols from the first-aid kit which was kept in his filing cabinet and swallowed them down with his tea. He sat back in his chair and put his feet up on the upturned wastepaper basket and closed his eyes just for a moment to ease his head. He was asleep in a trice. He woke with a start as someone knocked on his door and just managed to sit up straight as Susie poked her head around the door. She apologised for interrupting him but it was quite clear that she realised he had been asleep but was too tactful to make any comment.

All she wanted to know was if her reports of their joint visits had been satisfactory and he realised that this was important to her and that she had put a lot of effort into them. As he had yet to read them he covered by saying he was about to make an urgent phone call but that he would call her in later in the morning. When he read the reports he felt that they were pretty thorough and she had taken in quite a bit of useful information about the clients and their circumstances. In places the language she used was a little colourful, particularly when she described Hanca's garden as 'a disaster area' and her furnishings as 'drab and basic'. The reports seemed rather long winded and didn't really show much insight into the way Hanca chose to live her life or the progress she had already made.

However, Ben suspected that he was being rather picky and felt now was not the time to be critical. Instead he talked to Susie about the importance of not recording things on file that were unnecessarily judgemental or prejudiced and told her of a file that had been passed to him when a client had moved to his area during his earlier role as the resettlement officer. She had been a young married woman with three children under four years whose husband had been posted abroad with his army unit. The previous worker had described her as hopeless and living in squalor but Ben had quickly realised that she could have been suffering an undiagnosed puerperal depression following the birth of her third child. She had moved from her former home in Sunderland to be nearer to her husband who had been based in the West Country and found herself living in a substandard basement flat in Exworth miles away from her friends and family. When her husband was later transferred to Germany she was quite alone and Ben felt it was no wonder she was overwhelmed trying very hard to meet the needs of her young family.

Being fairly new to the job he had rung the previous worker, a Ms Agnes Smyth who worked in the Housing Department and asked why she felt the client warranted her recorded views. The only comment she could make was there were always mountains of ironing waiting to be done and there were toys everywhere. Ben bit his tongue and did not state the obvious that perhaps she should try bringing up three young children in a rundown flat. He had rung off in disgust but had learnt an important lesson that when you write something on a file it is there for ever and you never know who might read it in the future.

He told Susie that he had worked closely with Paulette, the young woman concerned, for several months getting her and her family resettled but she had begun to get too close and dependent. He had then referred the young woman and her children to a colleague in the children's department who was skilled at helping young families. What he didn't tell Susie was that he had carefully removed the offending reports from the file and shredded them before passing the file on. Unorthodox but effective intervention! He moved the conversation on by saying that he had been considering producing a file front sheet for long-term clients which could be updated as circumstances changed.

'Would you like to try and produce such a form that we could all look at and modify if necessary? No rush, but it would be very helpful.' Susie went away with food for thought and probably wishing she hadn't asked him about the reports. Ben closed his eyes but remained awake and his headache slowly eased.

The clinic went on in exactly the same way as the first week. Wendy was on reception duty and gave him a welcoming smile before continuing to shuffle the piles of files for the various clinics. He joined Raj and the prof and helped himself to a cup of coffee as indicated by the prof who pointed in the direction of the flask. The work was divided up and he went to read through the brief note sent in by the GP of the first client he would be seeing. A pattern emerged throughout the afternoon with all the six clients he interviewed suffering from a neurosis rather than psychosis. The most common problems presented were various degrees of depression with a couple of anxiety states thrown in for good measure. It was clear that the family practitioners were mainly seeking advice about appropriate medication and relied upon the prof to advise accordingly. By the time he finished with his last client he was tired but content that he was up to the job and he set off for home pleased that the following day was Saturday and he could spend time with Sandy and the boys.

Chapter 27

A Brief Lull Before the Storm

The weekend was largely uneventful with the family trapped indoors for the most part as storm after storm swept the town. The boys got thoroughly bored and they even showed only a passing interest in the untidy pile of comics which they had pored over since Christmas. Finally, in desperation Sandy and Ben decided to take them to a matinee at the local cinema. The film being shown was *Father Goose* starring Cary Grant, Trevor Howard and Leslie Caron; neither of them had ever heard of it but they thought it sounded like a comedy suitable for the boys. It wasn't. In fact it was a rather stupid romance which left the boys even more bored, its only saving grace being it was less than two hours long. Fortunately the supporting programme was a short cartoon and an elderly cowboy film, which managed to save the outing to some extent, and a trip to Harry Ramsden for tea did the rest. The Newmans walked back to the car a much happier group and the boys pretended to shoot everything they passed on the way home. Sunday was no more interesting and everyone was pretty fed up by bedtime. It seemed strange to Ben to be looking forward to going back to work and even mentioned the fact to Sandy who confirmed she felt the same.

Ben dropped the boys off at school in good time the next day as for once they were co-operative about getting ready. His journey onwards to the office passed with him being largely unaware of its passing until he slowed to a stop by the old horse's former home. It now consisted of huge mountains of mud which seemed to have been located haphazardly across the whole field. Men and machines had clearly been very busy over the weekend but it was impossible to guess to what purpose. The hedges and old fences had disappeared and the whole site was a mass of soggy mud. The earth moving equipment had been parked up in a row just off the road awaiting a further assault on the field. At that point Robbie's massive lorry came storming down the hill on his way to work and he gave Ben a blast on his horn and a wave but didn't stop. Any further enlightenment would have to wait for another day and Ben drove on to work. As he drew near to the office he saw Ernest sweeping the gutters nearby and was surprised to see 'Cassius' the stray dog stretched out on the roadside just a few feet away from him. As always he acknowledged Ernest by giving a toot on his horn and his mind went on to the planned visit to Foxie and Elsie, which was his priority for the day.

As soon as he got to his desk he rang Andrew Unwin at headquarters who confirmed that the funeral would be done by the Co-operative funeral service under contract to the local authority. 'Just let me know when poor old Foxie passes away and I will sort out the rest. I will see you at the crematorium on the day and you never know, you might even find time to show me the delights of Joe's café afterwards.'

Ben rang off with a laugh and called Susie into his room. He explained to her that when they visited the Farthings he wanted her to spend some time with Penny as she would probably have to sit with her at the house on the day of the funeral. 'It won't be easy as she is quite unique, but don't be afraid of her, she doesn't have an ounce of malice in her.'

Elsie looked washed out and exhausted when they arrived as between the needs of Foxie and Penny she was on the go all day and much of the night. She insisted on making a cup of tea and Susie stepped in and gave her a hand before taking a cup up to Penny, leaving Elsie to talk to Ben.

Elsie sat down with a sigh and told him that Foxie was barely conscious these days but with Mary's help she was determined to care for him until the end. Ben was able to reassure Elsie that the funeral plans were all taken care of and said that Foxie's friend Robbie Scadding was going to try and sort out a memorial for Foxie. Elsie smiled at this point and said that Robbie and his wife Patricia had already been in to see her and were going to sort out something using the family handcart but she wasn't sure what.

'Ernest pushed the cart down to the Scadding's yard over the weekend so we will have to see what happens. Ernest has been very strong for me and sits for hours with Foxie of an evening, I really don't know what I would have done without him.'

It wasn't long before Elsie was back on her feet pouring a cup of lukewarm tea into a feeding cup and invited Ben to go up with her with the tea and to check on Foxie. The smell of death and decay was in the room, the curtains were pulled across and Foxie was little more than a small heap in the bed. Up close he appeared to be awake and Ben helped Elsie to sit him up to drink his tea. He was shocked by how light Foxie was and the arm he held to lift him felt like a thin and twisted bone devoid of flesh and muscle. Foxie seemed unaware of Ben's presence and after a couple of slurps from the feeding cup sank down into his bedding and his eyes closed. Elsie pointed to the door and the two of them crept back out of the room. Ben was left certain of two things, death would be a mercy for both Foxie and Elsie, and Robbie had better hurry with the memorial as it was going to be needed very soon. The journey back to the office was a silent affair with both Ben and Susie dealing with their own thoughts and emotions. When they arrived back they went straight into Ben's office and for a few moments just sat there quietly until the mood was broken by the inevitable arrival of Alice with a couple of teas. Susie needed to share her thoughts about Penny but for once the words seemed reluctant to come.

'I have never seen anyone like her. She must have been a pretty child and she is still only a young woman but she is just grotesque and seems to be away with the fairies. Any attempt to converse with her proves to be pointless and all she seems able to say is silly little comments about her name and old bikes. I tried to talk to her about her family but she just giggled and went on playing with her dolls. I don't know how Mrs Farthing copes with her as she is only about half Penny's size and seems to have to do all the personal care of her. I am sorry, Ben, but all I can say about her is that she is the first person I have ever met who simply appears to be mad and I wish I could give you a better opinion.'

Ben found it impossible to argue with Susie's assessment and told her to write up the visit as he knew from experience the act of writing something down could often make it easier to deal with. When he went into the general office Mrs Freeman and Phil had their heads together in deep conversation which stopped instantly upon his arrival. He was aware of the instant silence but put it down to 'woman's talk' which he wouldn't have wished to be a party to in any case. He took the opportunity to suggest to Phil that she might assist Susie with 'babysitting' Penny when the funeral was taking place, which he indicated would be sooner rather than later. Phil had met Penny on a number of occasions and knew that it might well take two of them to cope so was quite prepared to help out. Ben quickly went through the post with Mrs Freeman before leaving the two of them to resume their tête-à-tête. He spontaneously decided to call in on Robbie Scadding to update him on the Foxie situation but decided to call in at Joe's first to top up his sugar load. On this occasion he chose to drive there rather than walk so he could go straight on to Robbie's afterwards. As he drove around the grass square on route to the café he spotted Ernest sat on his road sweeper cart apparently sharing his lunch with the stray dog Cassius, who was sat a few feet away deftly catching what Ernest threw to him. They looked contented and he refrained from using his car horn and left them in peace.

Joe came out from the kitchen when he saw Ben arrive and sat with him for a few moments to ask about Foxie whilst Mavis brought them over coffees and a doughnut in anticipation of his usual order. Joe was saddened by the news but went on to say that Ernest called into the café most days for a breakfast and he always updated him.

'But it isn't very easy to understand what he is saying at times. For instance, he has started to buy extra sausages which he takes away in a bag and as far as I can make out they are for a friend.'

Ben quickly put two and two together and told Joe about seeing Ernest feeding the stray dog Cassius. The dog had often been discussed by Joe's customers and most people seemed sympathetic to the poor animal's abandonment by the travellers, although one or two thought he looked dangerous.

'I think that could be a friendship made in heaven as they are both gentle giants and both need a friend badly. Thanks for telling me about that I will make sure that I put aside any waste meat for Ernest to give him. I heard you call him Cassius and I guess that he has been named after Cassius Clay, the new world champion heavyweight boxer, who the whole world seems to be talking about.'

Ben refrained from explaining to Joe about his Shakespeare experience at school and in any case thought Joe's conclusion was a lot more logical. Meanwhile his mind had gone off on a tangent and he wondered where Cassius was kept at night as Elsie had made no mention of him. He determined to enquire further at the earliest opportunity. He had his suspicions. At that juncture Beefy Baker the bread man came through the café door full of his usual bluster and sat straight down with Joe and Ben and went into one of his frequent 'humorous rants'.

'So what are you two up to putting the world to right, I suppose?'

For a couple of seconds neither of them responded and then Joe explained that they had been discussing Ernest and his befriending of the stray dog Cassius, named after the world champion Cassius Clay. Almost instantaneously Beefy was ready with one of his quick responses: 'That's an appropriate name for the dog. He's the champ with a chump for a friend.'

He smirked and started to laugh but realised that his comment was not seen as funny by either of them. To his credit he reacted quickly and apologised at once and said that his mouth sometimes moved before his brain was in gear. He moved away to join the customers in the middle room and talked to the men at the middle table about Ernest and the dog, omitting any attempts at humour. They had all seen the dog limping about the estate and were generally pleased that someone was trying to care for it. The name Cassius was conveniently dropped and from that point onwards it was called 'The Champ', a name which Ernest was later happy to accept. It wasn't quite the end of the incident as after Ben had left to go and visit Robbie, Beefy went around the café with a hat collecting for a collar for Ernest's dog. Everyone must have chipped in as Joe was able to present Ernest a couple of days later with a smart new leather dog collar complete with a name disc engraved with 'The Champ' and a proper dog licence as proof of Ernest's ownership. Ernest couldn't have been more proud.

As before, Ben parked his car on the road outside the Scadding's yard and walked in once again to be greeted by the snarling dog pulling on the very end of its chain in an attempt to get at this intruder. Ben circumnavigated it and stopped long enough to talk quietly to the animal, which seemed to confuse it into silence. There was no sign of anyone working and he mounted the stairs to the upper cabin and was about to knock when the door swung open. A cheery Robbie welcomed him in and explained that he had seen him arrive through the window, his attention having been attracted by the barking of the dog. Both desks were covered with piles of papers and Patricia was recording details in a large ledger.

She looked harassed with her hair pinned back with a bulldog clip and a smudge of ink down the side of her nose. Ben apologised for interrupting them when they were obviously busy but they both rushed to reassure him that they were due a break.

'We have been at it since eight this morning trying to get on top of the paperwork ready for the accountant but it just seems to go on and on.'

Patricia stood up and stretched with a sigh and removed the bulldog clip from her head, letting her hair fall back to encircle her face. Ben couldn't help but admire her, thinking she must have been a real beauty as a young girl. Robbie seemed to read his mind and put his arm around her with a laugh and then gave her an affectionate pat on the bum. Patricia took this with good grace then moved away to put the kettle on and unpack a stack of sandwiches wrapped in greaseproof paper. In no time at all they were sat in a huddle with hot drinks and chicken sandwiches with Ben being encouraged to tuck in. The sandwiches were delicious and for the next few minutes they all did little other than eat. When they sat back to finish their drinks, which Patricia quickly topped up, Robbie asked Ben about Foxie and Elsie and seemed to be expecting the gloomy news.

'Well, you will be pleased to know that Tony has almost finished upgrading their old hand cart as a memorial to Foxie. I think he is doing a grand job but come and see for yourself.' He was up and away in a flash and Ben followed some yards behind him, taken by surprise by Robbie's turn of speed. They headed away up the yard and into a lean too where Tony was busy at work, paintbrush in hand. The cart was a revelation it looked spectacular. It was painted in the familiar 'Scadding green' with large lettering painted in black down one side. On closer examination the lettering was the word Foxie and had been constructed from bits of scrap metal welded together. The main body of the cart was almost completely full and Tony told Ben that he had first lined it with galvanised sheets to stop it rotting. In the middle of the cart was a large lorry tyre, which had also been painted green, after being turned inside out to form a planter now filled with soil. The planter was surrounded by concrete, into which had been set several of Foxie's collection of pottery which gave the whole thing a splash of colour. The effect was truly amazing and was a brilliant memorial for Foxie and his life as a totter.

'When Elsie sees it she will be thrilled, it's a great idea and you couldn't have done it better, Tony. It will look terrific in their garden and Elsie will be able to bury Foxie's ashes in the planter.' The men stood and chatted for a few moments whilst Ben told them about the funeral arrangements. Robbie and Patricia both wanted to attend to support Elsie and Ernest and it was decided that Tony would deliver the hand cart whilst they were all at the crematorium so the family would have a good thing to come home to. Ben explained that he would be taking Elsie to the crematorium the day after the funeral to collect Foxie's ashes and that he was hoping to arrange a short service when she put them in the planter. Patricia had walked up to join them by now and suggested that it would look great if the planter was filled with potted plants at the same time. She was keen to sort out the flowers, which Ben thought was a fine idea. Before leaving he tried to draw information from Robbie about what was happening in the old horse field but as before he just tapped the side of his nose and said, 'All in good time.'

On the way out he passed the Alsatian, who let out a couple of half-hearted growls but made no attempt to approach. Ben went straight off to see his friend the Catholic minister Patrick MacGinty in the hope that he would agree to officiate at a short service for Foxie. Patrick came up trumps by listening to the story from Ben and immediately agreeing to help out when required. Ben noticed he didn't even ask if Foxie was Catholic, C of E or even atheist, he just agreed on humanitarian grounds. He was reassured that his friend was a true man of the cloth and Ben set off for the office confident that the plans were coming together nicely.

Chapter 28

Two Men Passing

The month of January slowly rumbled on with the whole team doing relatively straightforward visits to clients on their caseloads. Susie had visited Hanca a couple of times and seemed to have realised that Hanca's idea of a good life was vastly different to her own. Ben made a point of reading through Susie's reports and could see a theme emerging that she was convinced that Hanca was lonely. He made a note to discuss this at their next supervision session, which was in the diary for the following week. Meanwhile he took her to meet Frank and Rosie Scadding as he could see that they were both steadily deteriorating and might need more intervention in the near future. Ben had already decided to put Rosie's name on the waiting list for the local elderly persons home Walberton House, which specialised in care for people with dementia. It had only been built a couple of years before and was state of the art but it was almost always full with a lengthy waiting list of potential residents. Whenever a vacancy arose a conference was called and there would be several social workers attending to put their clients forward. About a year ago Ben had achieved his one and only admission and it had been unusual and caused quite a stir at the time.

Nathan Henry Everly had been a member of the Salvation Army throughout his adult life rising to the rank of captain and had been well respected by everyone, both clients and colleagues alike. As he reached his sixties he began to be forgetful and he resented anybody drawing attention to it. His personality changed with him becoming increasingly moody and unpredictable. Finally the powers that be in the movement were forced to give him early retirement and he lost his way of life and his home as he had been resident in a small flat at the Salvation Army centre for over ten years following the death of his wife. His son and daughter in law took him in and he continued to deteriorate. He came to the notice of Ben when he was asked to visit the daughter in law who appeared to her GP to be very depressed and possibly suicidal.

Ann Everly was about forty and could still have been classed as attractive if it wasn't for the strain registered by every detail of her face. It took a while for her to start talking but once started it flowed freely. She explained that her father in law had come to live with them and she had always respected him as he was a god-fearing man who had done tremendous work in his role as a captain in the Salvation Army. However, as his dementia had worsened he had become increasingly disinhibited and had begun to make sexual advances towards her whenever they were alone in the house. She had tried to avoid him as much as possible but he had taken every opportunity to put his hand up her skirt or to grope her breasts. She had tried to discuss it with her husband but he seemed content to play it down and now she felt unsafe in her own home and had taken to taking strong sleeping pills at night in an attempt to switch her head off and get some sleep. She seemed at her wits end and confessed to Ben that she had been saving sleeping tablets for weeks in case it all became too much. When Ben met her father in law he appeared to be just a harmless confused old man and it wasn't difficult to understand how out of character his behaviour had become.

Ben called back that evening to discuss the situation with Ann and her husband Eric and the discussion which followed was frank and to the point. Eric was clearly torn between his loyalty to his father and his love for his wife. He admitted that their relationship had become very strained since his dad had moved in and reluctantly agreed that Ben should try and arrange some care for his father. Ben had called into Walberton House on the way home that evening and managed to talk to Wynne Baxter, the matron of the home, about the current vacancy situation. Wynne was the sort of person who took everything in her stride and she was immediately sensitive to the family's problem. Fortunately, there was a vacancy which was due to be allocated the following Monday and she added Mr Everly's name to the list of potential residents. On the Monday the meeting room at Walberton House was packed with Dr Froomeshall, the psycho geriatrician, taking the chair. Each of the social workers from across the county talked about their client's needs and Ben was in pole position because he had been the last to add his client's name to the waiting list. When he explained about the captain's sexual advances to his daughter in law there were sniggers from several of the other social workers. At this juncture Wynne Baxter came in very strongly.

'There is nothing funny about this situation. This man's personality has been radically changed by his illness and he is in danger of destroying his family, which I am sure is the last thing he would have wanted. What do you want to achieve, Ben?'

Ben answered simply by saying that ideally he would like to stop Mrs Everly from committing suicide. The room settled down and Dr Froomeshall ran through the pros and cons for each of the potential clients and to Ben's delight selected Captain Everly as having the most need. The following day Captain Everly was admitted to Walberton House by Ann and Eric in their car and both later told Ben that they had been impressed by the high standards of the home and the atmosphere created by the staff. Unfortunately, there was a sting in the tail of the story and it was to do with Dilys, the longest serving resident of the home. Dilys was everyone's favourite. She wandered around the home from morning to night chatting away to herself or to anyone she came across in her travels. Her sole aim in life was to please and she treated everyone with warmth and affection. On the third day of Mr Everly's admission Dilys wandered into his room and he assaulted her sexually and attempted to have intercourse with her. Staff were able to step in fairly quickly but there could be no doubt that Dilys had received a nasty shock. When Wynne Baxter sat her down in the office to talk about it Dilys's reaction was something of a surprise. She told Wynne that she didn't really mind what Mr Everly had done but, 'I don't want any more babies.'

Wynne hastily reassured her that she would not be pregnant and the incident went down in the annals of running a dementia unit. Mr Everly was put on close watch and his medication altered. The staff became skilful at avoiding his advances and three months later he developed pneumonia and died. At the time Ben saw the entry of his death in the hatches, matches and dispatches in the local paper and the entry listed Ann and Eric as the next of kin. He was satisfied that the saga had a happy ending and he now needed to do the ground work in case Rosie needed care at some time.

When he got back to the office he was once again conscious that a conversation, this time between Alice and Mrs Freeman, stopped abruptly as he entered the kitchen. His suspicions were aroused once again and he decided that the rest of the team were ganging up and that he needed to get to the bottom of it. He gave it some thought and decided it was almost certainly to do with Ernest, who came into the office most days and that it was possibly to do with the rechristened dog 'The Champ'. He was sure if he went for the weakest link, namely Alice, he would get the information out of her but she could become very upset in the process and it wasn't worth the risk. He decided instead to go for the strongest member, with whom he had an established bond, and rang through to Mrs Freeman to come to his office with her shorthand note book. When she arrived she took the initiative without being asked and said that she had been waiting the opportunity to put him in the picture.

'As you have probably guessed it is to do with Ernest and his dog. Come on, I will show you.'

She led Ben out into the yard and over to the old bike shed where they put the refuse sacks ready for collection and where Ernest now stored his road sweeper's cart overnight. Right at the back almost hidden by the accumulation of bags there was a large old galvanised water tank turned on its side facing towards the back fence. On close examination it was seen to contain an old blanket folded several times to form a cosy floor and perched on top of the water tank were two old tin plates, one full of water and the other licked clean of food. The Champ's new home must have seemed a real luxury after his former existence with the travellers and Ben's only comment was 'Very cosy, but why here?'

Mrs Freeman went back with Ben into his office and went into a lengthy explanation.

'We are all very fond of Ernest who doesn't have much joy in his life, and he needs The Champ with a passion. With all that is going on in the Farthing household he didn't feel able to take the dog home with him as it appears Penny is terrified of dogs and in the past has become hysterical when she has come across one. Elsie has more than enough to do caring for Foxie and Penny and Ernest was desperate to provide a temporary place to keep his dog. I'm afraid we all talked about it and decided it would not cause any problem out in the shed and it would possibly act as a deterrent to any further acts of vandalism in the yard overnight.'

Ben had to smile at that point as he was impressed by that as a line of argument, which he wouldn't hesitate to use if there was ever any comeback from headquarters. Mrs Freeman ploughed on with a slight note of pleading in her voice.

'We all agreed and we have each of us contributed to making it happen. I provided the blanket, Alice the plates, Phil brought in a grooming brush left over from her pony ownership as a young girl and Susie brings in meat scraps and bones from her husband's butcher shop most days. The dog has never had it so good and is beginning to look a picture, what with all the love and attention Ernest gives him. Sorry we did it behind your back, but to be truthful we thought it would be easier for you to agree if it was a fait accompli.'

Good thinking, thought Ben, but he simply nodded and said that he would let it run for a while but would leave his final decision for the time being. After all, he was the team leader and he had to be careful to resist any attempt at a takeover by the petticoat mafia.

As the month of January passed Ben called in most days on the Farthing family and as each day passed Foxie spent less and less time conscious and Elsie looked more and more drained. On the Sunday morning of 24 January Ben went off as usual to Ma Driscoll's to collect the Sunday paper. He would sometimes walk the short distance there and back but it was pouring with rain and the temperature was not much above freezing so he decided to use the car. It was almost automatic these days for him to switch on the radio and his ears pricked up as there was a special news report being broadcast. Sir Winston Churchill had died at 8.35 am from a stroke. Ben pulled up and just sat there and listened and felt a shudder of sorrow pass through him.

Although he had only been a small boy during the war he had been brought up knowing that Churchill had been a great statesman and had been a major factor in saving the country from the Nazis. He had heard recordings of several of his wartime speeches and had felt the influence that they had had over the whole country at a time of immense danger. The loss struck home with Ben as it must have done all across the country and he was not surprised to find Ma Driscoll 'shedding a tear' when he arrived at the shop. When he got home he told Sandy, who was suitably upset and also attempted to tell the boys. Their reaction was almost non-existent and they were quickly side tracked by the current hit parade being read through on the radio and the announcement that 'Down Town' by Petula Clark was at number one left them unimpressed. The rest of the day was uneventful and there seemed to be an air of gloom over them all and it was almost as if they were just going through the motions of a weekend away from school and work. In the early evening there was a call on the phone and Sandy answered it in anticipation that it would be her mother to talk about the death. It wasn't her mum but it was someone wanting to talk about a death. It was Mary Harris ringing to tell Ben that Foxie had died earlier in the day and Mary had been there with Elsie and Ernest at his bedside when he slipped peacefully away. Penny had been conspicuous by her absence, preferring to remain in her room playing with her dolls. Mary had gone into her bedroom to tell her of her dad's death but there had been no reaction and it had seemed doubtful that she had taken it in. Mary was going back to check on Elsie as she had just virtually collapsed in a heap and Dr Eddoll had attended and prescribed a small supply of a strong sleeping draft and also signed the death certificate. Ben agreed to ring the emergency number for the Co-operative funeral service and arrange for Foxie's body to be removed to their chapel of rest.

Mary arranged to meet with him at the Farthing's home in a couple of hours to prepare the necessary plan of action and to give as much support as possible to Elsie and her family. Elsie was fast asleep on the sofa when they arrived and Ernest was pacing the floor unable to settle. The Co-operative funeral staff arrived shortly afterwards and quietly and efficiently removed Foxie's body in a simple black van with 'private ambulance' printed along the side with several neighbours witnessing the passing. Elsie was just about awake to see Foxie go but retired to her bed once Mary had stripped it and replaced it with clean bedding. She was asleep in no time and left Ernest still pacing the floor and Penny demanding food and a drink.

Between them Mary and Ben saw to her needs including getting her on to the commode, which was no mean feat. It took the combined strength of them both to get her out of bed and Ben found the whole experience quite disgusting as everything touched seemed to be just like an enormous jelly and her body odour made one want to puke. How Elsie coped was beyond imagination and it was completely clear that the status quo could not be allowed to continue, but now was not the time to deal with it. They got her back into bed and Mary agreed to stay overnight and Ben took Ernest out for a walk to give him a chance to come to terms with his change of status and the loss of the guiding force throughout his life. Ben deliberately headed back towards the office and as if by magic The Champ appeared at the car park entrance and greeted Ernest warmly. Ernest settled himself on his road sweeper's bin and fed the dog biscuits that he produced from his coat pocket with practised ease. Ben hung back and left them to it as the dog was doing more to calm Ernest than Ben could ever achieve. He had time to see the dog up close and realised that his suggestion of Cassius as a suitable name would now have proved to be a misnomer. There was nothing of the 'lean and hungry look' about him now, his coat was shiny and he had filled out to be a very handsome beast but still had something of the appearance of a lion about him. Ben started to slowly walk back leaving Ernest to settle the dog down for the night in private. Now was not the time to discuss his temporary home.

The following day Ben got into the office early and he noticed that Ernest's sweeper bin had already departed, presumably along with The Champ. Alice had not arrived so Ben let himself in and busied himself by putting the kettle and heating on. The office had begun to revert to a musty smell as the fading hyacinths lost their perfume but Ben barely noticed. A rather breathless Alice turned up at that point and rushed into the kitchen to resume her usual duties. Ben beat a hasty retreat to his office and sat watching the clock tick around to nine when he would be able to ring Andrew Unwin at headquarters to advise him of Foxie's death.

Once that task had been performed he just sat at his desk and waited for Andrew to phone back with the date and time allocated for Foxie at the crematorium. As he just sat and thought his mind went over the lives of the two men who had died at the same time. They were clearly poles apart in so many ways. Churchill had packed so much important happenings into his ninety years and was rightly admired all over the world for the great statesman he had been and his leadership for the country throughout the war. Foxie by comparison appeared to have spent his relatively short life ducking and diving and scraping a living. His death would mainly pass unnoticed and yet Ben admitted to himself that he had admiration for them both probably in equal measure.

Churchill had used his privilege and power for the general good whereas Foxie had overcome his disadvantaged start to use what strengths and skills he had to provide for his wife and his two stepchildren. Both were worthy of respect and Ben determined to do whatever he could to help the Farthings but was fearful it would all fall apart without Foxie's determined input. The phone rang at this point and the time of contemplation was over as he wrote down the information from Andrew. The slot at the crematorium was set for 8 am on Friday, 29 January and Ben busied himself ringing around to advise everyone he could think of who might be interested in attending.

Susie was sat at her desk writing up her notes and responded quickly when Ben asked her to come and sit with Penny for a short time when he took Elsie to register the death. 'If the need arises don't attempt to get Penny on to the commode by yourself she is far too heavy for you. Just give her the bedpan and let her get on with it I am sure that is what Elsie has been doing with her for ages. I'll be as quick as I can.' On the way to the Farthing's house he filled Susie in on the arrangements for Friday and arranged for Susie to stay with Penny during the funeral, apologising that it would mean a very early start for her. Elsie opened the door to them and returned to sit by the fire, which Ernest had banked up before leaving for work. It was now little more than a small pile of embers and Ben put one good-sized log on to keep it in as he was sure Elsie would need warming up after the formalities to come at the registry office. Armed with the death certificate, Elsie and Ben arrived at the registry office, which was a surprisingly brightly lit welcoming sort of place with a large vase of fresh flowers on the counter and a bell to ring for attention. After minimal delay they were joined by a smartly dressed middle-aged lady who welcomed them with a smile and invited them into her rather cosy office. She introduced herself as Mrs Atwell the registrar and when Ben introduced Elsie and himself she seemed to immediately grasp the nature of their relationship.

She couldn't have been nicer and slowly and skilfully led Elsie through the paperwork. Ben's only previous experience of dealing with a registrar had been when he had registered the boys' birth. That had been a much more formal affair conducted by a rather pompous male registrar of advanced years wearing a shiny suit and 'a couldn't care less' attitude. Mrs Atwell was a big improvement and it was easy to imagine her officiating at weddings and her effect on Elsie was noticeable and not a tear was shed. When they got home Ben ran through the funeral arrangements with Elsie and Ernest, who had called back home to check on his mum. As Ben and Susie left they noticed that Ernest's sweeping bin was being closely guarded by The Champ and he permitted them both to give him a pat, which was progress indeed.

In the car Susie suddenly said, 'I really can't work Penny out. She seems in a world of her own with no interest in anything around her and then she suddenly says something which leaves you wondering if there isn't more to her than meets the eye.' Ben remained quiet and let Susie slowly explain. 'As usual I tried to talk to her but she remained unresponsive, apparently focusing all her attention on her wretched dolls. Then quite suddenly she went off on one of her daft little songs but it was a different one this time and seemed to be very topical as it went like this. "Orange and Lemons says the bells of St Clements now there are only three farthings says the bells of St Martins." Then she would break out in a shrill giggle before repeating the song over and over again. So she is aware of Foxie's death but appears to have no unhappiness about it and it is almost as if she is pleased to have Elsie's undivided attention.'

Ben agreed that Penny was almost impossible to understand as she had been diagnosed as mentally handicapped as a small child and had always been treated as such and yet she presented as possibly psychotic. She could benefit by a fresh investigation and assessment but it was often difficult to get this done as clients like her tended to fall between the psychiatric services and the services for the mentally handicapped. He decided that he would chat to the prof about her if the opportunity arose at his clinic on Friday. As it happened the timing would later prove to be spot on.

After dropping Susie back at the office Ben headed down the hill to Scaddings' yard parking outside as always. Robbie and Patricia were both in the office with Robbie doing some serious business on the phone and Patricia standing by to provide him with any details he might need. Ben couldn't help but hear bits of the conversation and couldn't fail to be impressed with the amounts of money being discussed. It was in the thousands. Finally Robbie put the phone down and punched the air before grabbing Patricia and dancing her around the room. She appeared to enjoy every moment and kissed his cheek before pushing away and lighting the gas under the kettle. Robbie sat down with Ben and explained that he had just completed a deal to provide scrap metal to one of the large steel mills in South Wales.

'It's a contract I have been after for months and it puts our little company up there with the big boys and this is a cause for a celebration. Dig out the whisky, Patsie.'

Patricia was keen to hear all about the arrangements for Foxie's funeral and seemed to fully understand that it would be a simple affair and that it was taking place at an ungodly hour. Ben confirmed that he would be picking up Ernest and Elsie early on Friday morning to go to the crematorium and Robbie and Patricia immediately volunteered to take Mary in their car. Neither of them could think of anyone else likely to want to attend but they all agreed that they would make the planting of Foxie's ashes in the memorial cart as special as possible on the Saturday. Ben went straight on to finalise arrangements with Mary but she was still in bed asleep as she had not had a proper night sleep for weeks. Jessie made a note of the arranged details to pass on to Mary and told him she would be closing the shop for a couple of hours on the Saturday and would be at Elsie's armed with a good supply of cake and sherry.

Friday came and as predicted by Andrew it was a dark and dismal start with the rain coming down in sheets. Ernest was dressed in his 'best suit', which didn't fit him too well and which had probably been one of the gleanings from a former totting round. Elsie was appropriately dressed in a long black dress and a short black winter coat; again neither fitted too well and Ben presumed that they were on loan from Mary. Elsie was carrying a small bunch of carnations, which she placed on the top of Foxie's coffin when they arrived at the crematorium. Otherwise, both Elsie and Edward remained impassive and almost detached throughout the short service, but both jumped visibly when the coffin started to drop down into the floor. Ben arranged to meet up with Andrew back at the office and then loaded Ernest and Elsie back in the old Cortina, leaving Andrew to tie up the loose ends with the funeral service, having arranged to pick up the ashes next morning. When they got back to Elsie's they discovered that Tony Scadding had delivered the cart in their absence and had placed it in their front garden. It looked spectacular and was already drawing attention from passers-by. Both Elsie and Ernest were overwhelmed and the tears flowed freely and it was all Ben could do not to join in.

He settled them down and recovered Susie and Phil from their Penny-sitting duties before returning to base to link up with Andrew. They didn't hang about and within minutes were sat in Joe's enjoying coffee whilst Ben watched Andrew see off a breakfast special and a couple of doughnuts. Somehow Ben wasn't hungry but Andrew's obvious pleasure made the trip well worthwhile. Ben went straight from Joe's to see the minister Patrick MacGinty and they sat down together to set out a short order of service for the internment of the ashes the following day. They agreed that a few prayers, a short eulogy and a couple of verses of 'All Things Bright and Beautiful', which Elsie had told Ben was the only hymn known to Foxie, would seem to be just about right. Ben returned to link up with Mrs Freeman to get her busy on the duplicator to produce some service sheets ready for the next day.

By missing out on lunch Ben was able to get to the prof's clinic in good time and as the first two patients didn't attend he grabbed the opportunity to talk to the prof about the Farthing family. The prof sat back in his chair, clamped his unlit pipe in his mouth and gave Ben his full concentration. As Ben had anticipated the prof grasped the situation with apparent ease and also seemed to understand how much he had invested in time and effort to help the Farthings survive with all their limitations.

'Let them go on as best they can for as long as possible, but the young lady Penny will need professional intervention at some point. I know that is never easy to achieve when there is a combination of mental handicap and mental illness and sometimes patients get lost between the two services. However, should the need arise in an emergency I will ask Raj to get involved and we could take her in for a period of assessment.

I suspect your problem will be getting the mother to agree. She sounds very over protective.'

Ben couldn't have asked for more and went through the rest of the clinic hungry but happy that he could see a way ahead for the Farthings.

Chapter 29

A Day of Mourning

As Ben set off for the crematorium the weather decided to relent and a rare dry day welcomed him, and he even had to pull the visor down in his car to cope with the glare of winter sunshine. He wound his window down and turned the radio on to hear all about the massive state funeral that would be taking place a few days later in London. It was to be the first state funeral to be held in the country for a politician in a century. Many thousands would be lining the streets and dignitaries from around the world would be attending, including the royal family. The coffin was to be carried on a horse drawn gun carriage to St Paul's Cathedral from Westminster Hall where his body had laid in state for three days. After the service it would be transported by water along the River Thames to Waterloo Station and then onwards by rail to its final resting place. In the afternoon Sir Winston Churchill would be buried at St Martin's churchyard at Bladon, which was the resting place of his ancestors and his brother. It was going to be the largest state funeral ever and was most fitting for the great statesman that Churchill undoubtedly was, the saviour of the country just twenty years before.

But Ben couldn't help but compare the great plans for Churchill to their plans for Foxie. A Pauper's funeral, a cardboard box for his ashes and burial in an ex-totter's hand cart! Ben clicked the radio off on arrival at the crematorium and went in to collect Foxie's remains, returning to the car to place the simple square cardboard box in the passenger-side foot well for safety. The simple ceremony in the Farthing front garden proved to be truly memorable. Patrick led the service with warmth and respect and his eulogy made much of Foxie's hard work and devotion to his family. Ernest placed his father's ashes, still in the box, deep in the tyre planter and Tony Scadding topped the earth over it from a pre-prepared sack of compost.

The final touch was five or six pots of daffodils, in full bloom, which Patricia produced from the boot of her car which filled the planter to the top with a huge splash of yellow in contrast to the green of the cart. Quite a crowd of spectators had gathered by this time and some of them joined in with the singing of Foxie's favourite hymn. Patrick led the singing on a guitar and 'All Things Bright and Beautiful' couldn't have sounded any more appropriate. Everyone loved the whole simple ceremony and Tony received loads of praise for his job well done and he was even rewarded with a shy kiss from Elsie. They all moved back into the house where Jessie was ready to hand out much appreciated tea and cake. Penny didn't make an appearance throughout the whole procedure and Ben noticed the first thing Elsie did when she got in doors was to slip away upstairs with a huge chunk of cake, which was big enough to test the gastric juices of a healthy teenager. He felt sure that Penny would cope with it but it was clear that Elsie was unable to control her need to pander to her daughter's compulsive eating. It was going to be an issue to be faced at some point but for now he made no comment.

Chapter 30

Falling Apart

The following couple of weeks by comparison seemed to return to normal with everyday problems at home and at work arising and being dealt with in a straightforward and uncomplicated way. Two days of intermittent snow managed to briefly cause the usual travel havoc and a brief period of snow play for the boys before it all turned into a slushy mess. Ernest came into the office most days to report how his mum was doing and these days he was always accompanied by The Champ. Both of them were well received by the team, with Ernest being warmed up with tea and sympathy by Alice in the kitchen and The Champ seeking out titbits from the ladies as he wandered from office to office. Ben tried to keep a low profile as he didn't really want to make it too obvious that he accepted the dog being kept in the bike sheds overnight, but he also had a stash of biscuits in his desk drawer which he doled out secretly.

On the third week Ernest suddenly made an appearance at Ben's door in a disturbed state. It was not easy to discover what the problem was as the combination of his anxiety level and his guttural speech made most of what he said largely not understandable. He seemed to be saying something about his mum being unwell and that he was having to do more and more for his sister. Ben agreed to visit later in the morning, which calmed Ernest somewhat and he set off with The Champ to get on with his road sweeping. Before visiting Ben decided to call in the health centre to link up with Mary to see if she was aware of any problem with Elsie. He was in luck as Mary was just about to go out on her home visits and agreed to do a joint visit with Ben to the Farthings home. They went off in convoy and parked up half in and half out of the piled slush at the side of the road and slipped and slid their way down the path to the front door, which was partially opened. They knocked a couple of times then let themselves in in answer to a distant voice telling them to do so.

Elsie was in bed and looked really unwell but when asked what the problem was just shook her head and looked pointedly at Ben. He didn't react but Mary got the message straight away and pushed him towards the bedroom door and suggested he should go and make some tea. It dawned on him that this was to be woman's talk and he was in the way, and he swiftly retreated, grateful that he had linked up with Mary to make the visit. He waited awhile and then made some tea before knocking on Elsie's door and passing the drink to Mary, who took it and re-closed the door without a word. He then went on to Penny's room, where she was sat up in bed surrounded by her dolls and she was wearing a lopsided long blonde wig which was badly in need of a wash. The smell in the room was unpleasant to say the least and it was clear that the commode had not been emptied in a long time.

Penny looked like some gigantic Buddha dressed in a thin short cotton nightie with ever expanding layers of fat emanating from her neck in roll after roll of bulbous flesh. She was truly grotesque and he realised that she had piled on an immense amount of weight since he had last seen her a few months ago. It was little surprise that she spent all her time in bed as it would be all but impossible for her to move without help. His sympathy for Elsie and what she had to contend with made him determined to take action as soon as possible but he would need Elsie's consent to involve Dr Rani, as suggested by the prof. Meanwhile, Penny took the cup of tea from Ben without comment or apparent surprise that he had turned up in her bedroom and it was drained in seconds. At this point she started to sing her most recent jingle about the orange and lemons and there only being three farthings, followed by a rather hysterical giggle. After three renditions in quick succession Ben left her to it and went downstairs to wait for Mary.

When she came downstairs Mary looked very anxious and told him that they needed to talk urgently and suggested they returned to the health centre at once. The convoy returned and Ben was taken into the staff office whilst Mary explained her concern. Elsie had shared with Mary that for several weeks she had been having almost continual periods. She had at first thought it might be 'the change' but it had steadily got worse and in recent weeks she had been taking some of the morphine prescribed for Foxie to help cope with the pain. The morphine had now run out and with Foxie gone she had no way of obtaining more. The pain was with her most of the time and she was very frightened. But even now her main concern was what would happen to Penny if she was unable to carry on. 'It sounds pretty ominous, Ben, and she needs investigation urgently.'

Ben explained about the possibility of getting Penny admitted for assessment and Mary went off to get Dr Eddoll to join in the discussion. Between the three of them they decided to try and proceed straight away and Ben rang Dr Rani whilst Dr Eddoll rang the general hospital for an immediate investigation for Elsie. The whole plan proceeded like a military operation and by the end of the day Penny and her tribe of dolls were resident at St Margaret's and Elsie was an inpatient at the general. Penny had put up no resistance to being taken to hospital but neither did she offer any assistance. She simply went limp and a dead weight. It took the combined efforts of the two ambulance men, Dr Rani and Ben to get her out of bed and strapped into a wheeled chair and the trip downstairs was a dangerous affair. By the time they got to the front door the parked ambulance had drawn a group of watchers, who were rewarded with a full frontal of Penny when the blanket she was draped in fell open. A fresh story to be told around the estate, which would no doubt be exaggerated in the telling, but Ben couldn't think how it was possible to exaggerate Penny. It had been agreed that the ambulance would take both Penny and Elsie to their different hospitals at the same time and Elsie was loaded aboard on a stretcher in a much more dignified way. They went off together holding hands and Ben set off to drive around the estate to look for Ernest.

Poor old Ernest didn't know what had hit him but Ben took a long time explaining why it had happened and he seemed to understand the seriousness of his mum's condition. Ernest was clearly feeling very mixed about it all but seemed relieved that he had not been left to try and cope with Penny and he was happy that his mum was being looked after. When Ernest left Ben's office he took The Champ home with him rather than leaving him in the car park as usual. The dog's temporary lodgings were over for the time being and Ernest had a much-needed housemate. He was also accompanied by Alice, whose long dormant maternal urges rose to the occasion and she fussed over him and took responsibility for ensuring he was able to cope at home alone.

The verdict came through ten days later and it was the worst possible news. Elsie had inoperable ovarian cancer and her prognosis was dire. She took the news stoically and confessed to Ben that her main concern was what would happen to Penny. She seemed confident that Ernest would cope alone, especially with the help of all his friends at Ben's office, but Penny was a different matter altogether. Ben reassured her that she would be taken care of and after a dose of morphine Elsie seemed at peace and fell into a deep sleep. As the days passed she stopped eating but remained positive, stating that she couldn't wait to see Foxie again. She was transferred to a local hospice where she slipped away two weeks later with Ernest holding her hand and The Champ sitting at his feet. Ernest was adamant that he didn't want 'a pauper's funeral' for his mum and Ben helped him to arrange a very simple ceremony with the Co-op where their director showed great understanding and did it at cost. It would still take Ernest two years to pay off the debt bit by bit but it was what he wanted to do. With the help of Tony, the box of Elsie's ashes was buried along with Foxie's by Ernest and the daffodils, now little more than fading foliage, were removed from their pots and planted straight into the planter where they should come up year after year. Ernest called into the office most days to see Ben and he regularly brought in any post that had arrived for Ben to sort out with him. As the days went by it became apparent that the main object of his visits gradually moved from Ben to Alice, who seemed to have no problem understanding Ernest's guttural speech. Alice and Ernest became close friends over the following weeks and they made an odd-looking couple, the one tall and matchstick thin Alice in her mid-fifties and the gentle giant that was Ernest a good thirty years younger. They could be seen out walking around Highfield most evenings with The Champ limping along with them and could easily have become the butt of the local youth, but with The Champ there no one dared. In fact it quickly became clear that Ernest had become just another Highfield character along with the likes of Beefy Baker, Hayley Mills and the other regular customers at Joe's. Ernest's life had changed beyond all recognition but his new life had some real compensations. The three of them had never really had a close friend before and now they were a contented trio; Alice, Ernest and The Champ against the world and Ben wished them well. Tony Scadding had reacted quickly to Elsie's death and he constructed her name in scrap metal and fixed it to the opposite side of the handcart and the Farthings memorial was then complete. It remained a local attraction and it was quite commonplace to see people walking down their street and stopping to admire it. Ernest was very proud of it and cleaned it down most weekends in the same way as the few car owners on the estate tended to fuss over their vehicles.

Ben went in to see Penny at St Margaret's a little while after Elsie's death and found her sat at her bedside in a single room with her dolls spread out on the bed before her. She was dressed in rather drab clothes which just about fitted her but there was no sign of the ancient blonde wig. Instead she had had her own hair cut in a short neat style which was a distinct improvement and made her look more her actual age. It was impossible to tell if Penny had taken in the news of her mum's death and Ben figured she would need time before she came up with a fresh jingle to reflect the change. He was able to have a chat to the sister in charge of the ward who reported that Penny had settled in without apparent difficulty other than her compulsive need to eat. Her mobility was slowly improving and the sister suspected that Penny's real incentive to be more active was to be able to reach the kitchen at the other end of the ward.

Meanwhile, the main focus of their work was to control her eating and to get her weight down well below the twenty-one stone she had been on admission. Long-term plans were still to be finalised but the sister shared with Ben her own opinion that with her multiple problems Penny was very likely to spend the rest of her life in one institution or another. The sister told him that Ernest had been in to see Penny on one occasion and had stayed with her a little while, but there appeared to have been no attempt at conversation between them. When he left the nursing staff had found a post office book in the name of Elsie Farthing left on Penny's bedside cabinet. It was ages old and very creased but it still contained over a hundred pounds, which had not been added to for a long while. It was now in the hands of the hospital administrator, who was attempting to get it changed into Penny's name. Ben nodded but made no further comment as he figured that the last thing he needed was to get involved in the complicated bureaucratic actions that would undoubtedly be required to change ownership of the family jewels. He suspected that the handing on of the post office book was an indication that Ernest was washing his hands of his sister. Despite being twins they had never been close with Ernest having to work hard from an early age and Penny disappearing into a world all her own and expecting to be waited on hand and foot.

Chapter 31

Springtime

Early in March, Ben happened to drive past his dad's allotment and on impulse stopped to eat his packed lunch with him. His dad was sat on his usual bag of compost just about to pour himself a drink from his flask, and without asking poured a second cup which he passed to Ben. Ben collected the folding chair from the shed and sat down next to his dad with scarcely a word passing between them. On his part Ben opened the Tupperware container that Sandy had used for his lunch when she had prepared it the night before and offered a sandwich to his dad. It reminded him of the picnics they had shared when he had accompanied his dad to the allotment as a child and he felt very relaxed and content. His dad asked him what he had been up to and he outlined the story of the Farthing family, which his dad listened to without interruption.

He then responded by saying, 'January and February are always a bad time for deaths and it doesn't matter who you are it affects all sorts rich or poor alike. Off the cuff I can think of three famous people who died last month, all of whom were important characters in the world. We lost that special ballad singer Nat King Cole with lung cancer in the middle of the month, he was only forty-five. He had a voice like honey and when we were courting, Mum and I used to love to listen to his wonderful songs like "When I Fall in Love" and "Unforgettable". Then in the same week that famous American activist Malcom X was assassinated when preaching peaceful reform. He was the voice of reason in a hostile world and I am convinced he could have achieved so much if he had not been cut down. Then again within less than a week we lost Stan Laurel, who had been one half of the partnership that was Laurel and Hardy. Together they made over a hundred short films and they toured in many countries bringing their slapstick humour to so many people. I loved them as a small boy and I think I can even remember you watching them with Mum and me when they appeared on "This Is Your Life".'

In fact, Ben had no recall of watching the programme but had no desire to spoil his dad's memories so just nodded his agreement. He had been surprised at the lengthy speech from his dad and whilst they shared the lunch he remained silent in the hope that his dad would continue in the same vein. However, after a long pause his dad reverted to his usual contribution by naming the times and destinations of the trains that passed before them. After an acceptable pause, Ben packed up and headed back to work, leaving his dad to his train watching and his contemplations.

For some reason the traffic going back to the office was unusually slow and he began to be concerned as he needed to be in the office for 1 pm as he was on call then and overnight until 9 am the following day. The reason for the delays became clear when he got just past the Scaddings yard, as there were temporary traffic lights in operation limiting the traffic to one lane. Unfortunately, they were set so badly that they allowed only enough time for about two cars to get through before changing. The problem was added to by some idiot deciding to jump the lights, only to come face to face with a huge lorry loaded with soil coming down the hill. It was no contest and the angry car driver had to reverse back into a road blocked by waiting cars and he ended up stuck sideways on the grass verge.

Eventually it all sorted itself out but Ben's time keeping was shot to hell and it was well after 1 pm when he got back. As always, the ever-faithful Mrs Freeman had covered for him but had missed her bus as a consequence, which meant she was unable to get home to get her husband Steve's lunch. There had been a couple of calls from other social workers about potential problems and a young person with Down's syndrome had wandered off from the adult training centre and had not been seen for several hours. She had been reported as missing to the police and there was nothing requiring Ben's urgent intervention. Meanwhile, Mrs Freeman rang Steve to tell him it would have to be bread and cheese for lunch but sweetened the pill by saying it would be steak for dinner, which was his favourite. She set off to do the necessary shopping and Ben told her to take her time and thanked her once again for covering for him. Armed with a mug of tea from Alice he sat back in his seat and allowed his thoughts to wander. He had been surprised by the intimacy of his talk to his dad and realised that neither of them had been very good at just talking together over the years. It came as a bit of a revelation to gain insight into the way his dad viewed the world and he determined to make a greater effort to communicate.

His thoughts moved on to the traffic problems he'd encountered on the hill to Highfield and he had glimpsed several huge lorries being loaded in Boxer Mark Two's old field and pulling out, leaving a trail of mud on the road. Men with shovels and brushes had been doing their best to keep the road clear, but they had seemed to be losing the battle. Ben's curiosity was sharpened, and he decided a visit to Robbie's yard was a priority. The telephone remained remarkably quiet and he picked up the handset a couple of times just to check the phone was working before settling down to read through the small pile of reports from Susie of her recent visits. Most of them were routine visits that she had made to the small group of long-term clients that he and Phil had selected for her. They were straightforward and rather repetitious but that was only to be expected and he was able to skim through them quickly before counter signing them and putting them in the outbox for filing. Two reports required more attention as they were about two of the more intensive cases that Ben had introduced Susie to but with which he retained an active involvement. The first was Hanca Parsons, who from the dates on the report had been visited by Susie several times a week over the past month. Reading between the lines it appeared that Susie had decided that Hanca needed some comfort in her life and she had decided to change things by developing Hanca's feminine side. There were several references to prettier clothes, hair styling and even the introduction of soft furnishings; not surprisingly all had been resisted by Hanca and Ben made a note in his diary to discuss the issue with Susie at their next supervision session. There was no doubting Susie's good intentions and she had proved to be the caring, mature colleague that the team had hoped for, but she still had a lot to learn about her role in a social work agency and it was Ben's responsibility to help her without appearing too critical.

The telephone rang at this juncture and it was the desk sergeant at the central police station saying that they had picked up a handicapped young woman, lost and crying, wandering in the shopping centre, 'And she looks like one of yours.' Ben didn't comment on what the sergeant meant by that and it was a simple act for him to ring the adult training centre and arrange for a relieved member of staff to pick up the wanderer. Fortunately, no harm done but it could have been a different story if some good Samaritan hadn't taken time out of their busy day to rescue the young woman in distress and to take her to the police station. Someone at the training centre would undoubtedly be in for 'a bollocking' but Ben had his sympathies for the staff who had large groups to manage in a rambling old building which had no real security.

Alice must have been listening for the phone to ring off and had concluded that now was an opportune time to provide another tea and hopefully to have a bit of a chat with Ben. The tea was gratefully received but the chat resisted by Ben pretending to make another call. The speaking clock dutifully answered and Alice was once again fooled into giving up any hope of time with him. He had used the same ploy several times and felt just a bit guilty about it, but not enough to stop him using the time to save wasting time from time to time.

Ben returned to the reports and carefully read through Susie's accounts of her visits to Rosie and Frank Sullivan. He was very aware that their situation was steadily becoming more difficult as Rosie deteriorated and it became harder for Frank to persuade her to do her diabetic monitoring and accept her essential injections of insulin. To add to the problem Frank was suffering with heart problems and Susie reported that he was definitely slowing up and appeared to be in pain, although he denied this. Day-to-day life was becoming more difficult and he had gratefully accepted Susie's offer to do his big shop each week, but the flat was beginning to look rather scruffy and dirty and Rosie appeared less tidy with her clothes often stained and unwashed. Susie had tentatively suggested that they might benefit from Rosie having a short period of respite care but Frank had rejected the suggestion and had become quite angry.

Fortunately, the threatened power cuts which had already happened up and down the country had not affected Exworth very much and Highfield not at all. So all the planning for Chelsea House had been unnecessary and the replacement generator had now been fitted and was up and running. However, one good thing had resulted from the visits made by Paul Humphries and Ben to the Sullivans; Paul was now visiting them regularly and had arranged for the fire service welfare officer to take an interest. Susie reported that Frank got a lot from these visits and he had even started to recount to her stories from his fire service days. Seeing as he had never mentioned his fire service to Ben this seemed to be a positive step forward. However, Susie could see a deterioration in their circumstances, particularly as Frank had to resort more and more to feeding Rosie's compulsion for cigarettes in an attempt to cope with her behaviour and to gain her cooperation with her diabetic testing and injections.

She had noticed that he had started to restrict what he bought to the basics when she did his weekly shopping for them and he had stopped visiting the pub on the days Rosie attended day care at the old people's home. Ben hadn't spoken to the staff at Elmore House for a while and rang straight away to find out how Rosie was when she spent the day with them. The manager, George Dangerfield, welcomed Ben's call and confirmed that Rosie was steadily deteriorating and that her personal hygiene was noticeably a lot worse. 'There's no doubt that Frank is struggling to cope. He gets very breathless and has slowed down a lot. But he remains devoted to Rosie and always turns up promptly at five to pick her up although he can hardly get in and out of the car. It can't be long before the situation becomes untenable but we would obviously like to go on helping as long as it's needed; Frank deserves all the support we can give him.'

Ben and George continued to chew over the situation and between them agreed that Rosie and Frank would both benefit if the day care was increased by an additional day early in the week if Frank would accept it. When the call ended Ben wandered along the corridor and called into Susie's office to discuss the proposal and to suggest a joint visit in the next few days. The rain was teeming down and the car park was a mass of large puddles. Ben was content to be stuck in the office on call and he noticed that neither Phil nor Susie were in any rush to head off visiting and appeared to be in close discussion about the clients they shared. He felt in the way and wandered back to see Mrs Freeman in the general office for a chat but she too seemed happily involved with her typing up of reports.

With a sigh he headed back to the kitchen to resolve his guilt at his earlier avoidance of a bowel conversation with Alice. To his surprise Alice didn't mention her bowels and their intricacies once but talked enthusiastically about Ernest and how well they were getting on. There was no hint of romance, thank god, but her time in the social work office had rubbed off on her and she mentioned a couple of areas of concern she had for him. Ben was impressed with her caring and her understanding of the situation that Ernest now found himself in and reflected that it wasn't that dissimilar to what Alice had faced when she came out of her institution. He had spent hours and hours helping her to adjust and realised that he needed to give Ernest a lot more attention for a while at least, but saw Alice as a practical ally in the task.

The rest of the afternoon passed without any emergency calls and he set off in good time to get home through the continued deluge. The hill down to town from Highfield was a sea of mud from the earth works and the men in yellow jackets had given up all hope of keeping the roads clear of mud. By the time he got home the old Cortina looked like it had been through a swamp and he had to resort to a bucket of warm water and a squirt or two of washing-up liquid to clear the windows ready for the probability of night time call outs. It was a quiet night, which was just as well as the rain never stopped.

Chapter 32

A Strange Sort of Day

Friday was more of the same and the boys were decked out in their wet weather gear right down to Wellington boots. The family set off early so Ben could run Sandy the short distance to Ma's to avoid her having to work all day in wet clothes. It was a little bit out of the way of the school run and involved Ben having to take a roundabout route down small streets which were not part of the normal trip to school. He turned a sharp left and was confronted by flash flooding several feet deep in a dip in the road and someone had managed to break down in the middle of it, blocking the route to the school which was situated in the distance apparently clear of the water. Unfortunately, several cars had followed Ben into the road and he was left with no way forward or back as all traffic ground to a halt.

There was no alternative other than walking the boys the rest of the way. They were fine with their Wellington boots but Ben resorted to rolling up his trousers and walked the boys through the flooding still wearing his shoes and socks, which immediately became waterlogged. The boys thought it was a hoot but Ben was less than happy and once back in the car proceeded with a complicated manoeuvre to get back up the street by mounting the pavement in order to pass a couple of abandoned cars. He had to return home to change his shoes and socks and swap his crumpled trousers for the pair from his best and only suit. He needed to look respectable as he had the prof's clinic in the afternoon. By now he was hopelessly late and rang the office to say he was making a visit on the way in then made himself a coffee and helped himself to another bowl of cereal. He decided to call in on Robbie to see if he could discover any more about the mysterious goings on in Boxer Mark Two's field.

As he was no longer in a rush he turned on the radio and listened to the local news and just caught the tail end of a report of a collapsed sewer down by the canal. They moved on to review the local sports activities for the weekend and he didn't get the full story of the sewer incident until an hour or so later on his car radio after he had visited Robbie. The rain had reduced to a drizzle by the time he pulled up in his usual place just outside the big green gates and he was welcomed by some half-hearted barking from the depths of the dog kennel. The yard was unusually quiet with no one in sight and no sound of heavy machinery ripping into metal.

As he mounted the now familiar stairs to the upper porta cabin the door was flung open by a smiling Robbie. 'Saw you coming, I am on watch today and I have been expecting you.'

He welcomed Ben in and Patricia greeted him warmly and went over to put the kettle on. Ben looked around and there was no sign of the mounds of paper they had been working on last time he visited. In fact, the *Mirror* newspaper was opened to the racing page on Robbie's desk and Patricia's was almost entirely covered by a pile of knitting which she had just put down to make the tea. The Scaddings were not being overstretched today. 'I wondered how long it would be before curiosity got the better of you about the old field, but if I put you in the picture you must promise to keep it to yourself as my plan is at a very tricky stage and I am currently seeking planning permission.'

Ben couldn't help but feel pleased that Robbie was prepared to take him into his confidence and readily agreed to Robbie's proviso. He noticed that Robbie kept glancing out of the window and it all seemed a bit clandestine, but Robbie noticed his concern and went on to explain that Tony was away on a course so there was no one to look after the yard. 'I usually leave all the day-to-day buying and selling to Tony but I am on duty today. We need to keep our eyes peeled in this business as not surprisingly some of our customers are less than strictly honest and scrap yards are generally seen as fair game.' The three of them sat around on the comfortable chairs with Robbie sitting in the armchair facing out of the window looking out over the yard and Ben and Patricia taking the sofa. This meant that the two of them were in close proximity and Ben could smell Patricia's perfume, which was slightly musky and very provocative. She seemed totally unaware of her effect on him and he moved slightly further away for fear of his body responding in an embarrassing way.

Robbie swung back from the window and moved forward in his chair with a look of serious concentration on his face. 'It all started when Tony was just a nipper. He wasn't a bit like our Annie, who loved school and never had her head out of a book. He was as bright as a button mind, but was simply bored by school and was always mad keen on engines and that sort of thing and loved to come to the yard with me where he could tinker to his heart content. Then when he was about seven or eight he started to travel along with me at weekends when I went around the country collecting loads of scrap metal. On this one particular Saturday we had to go down to Bristol and we spotted an advert for a speedway meeting of the Bristol Bulldogs and on impulse I parked up and we went to see the meet. Well that was it, we were hooked, we simply loved everything about it. The noise, the speed, the crowd screaming and shouting and each race was over so fast in no more than a minute and even the hotdogs tasted special. We started to follow the Bulldogs whenever they were racing at home and tried to go to away meets too when they were not too far away. It was a special time for us both, but unfortunately the Bulldogs folded in 1960 when their stadium was sold for development. It was about that time that Tony came across my old Vincent stuck away in the back of a shed and almost buried under scrap. It really caught his attention and we dragged it out together with the intention of trying to get it going. My involvement didn't last long, however, as Tony was determined to strip it right down and to do the job properly right from the start. Well that was never my style so I left him to it. As you know he produced a master class in bike restoration and I learnt just how capable our son was. So as the time passed Tony and I often talked about doing a project together and that is how our current plan developed up until today when the beginnings are already in progress, as you know.'

At that point there was sudden loud impatient hooting from the yard and Robbie hurried off to deal with the huge scrap lorry that had arrived in the yard unnoticed whilst he had been telling his tale. Patricia brought out the biscuit tin and then confided in Ben.

'You know, Ben, this project is really important to Robbie. He has been pretty bored with the scrap business of late and desperately needed a new challenge. Don't get me wrong, we have built up a good business over the years but the kids are older now and independent and most of our old customers who were all real characters have either retired or passed on. Our eldest, Annie, went to Edinburgh University to study languages and got a first-class degree. Of course, we were so proud of her and Robbie was over the moon. I don't know if you realise it but Robbie can barely read or write but he is as sharp as a pin with numbers and has a first-class business brain. I guess he would have been recognised as dyslexic nowadays but in our school days he was just thought to be dim and was left very much to his own devices. He couldn't get out of school quick enough but I have been so proud of him how he has encouraged the kids. Annie is married now and is a deputy head at a school in Scotland so we don't see a lot of her. I can't wait to have grandchildren but I think it will be a long wait. Meanwhile, Robbie and Tony have always been very close but truth to tell Tony can run the day-to-day business and Robbie often finds himself at a loose end. But since they have started on this new project together Robbie is much more his old self and is full of enthusiasm. It's a chancy idea but that seems to add to Robbie's determination to make it work. I'll leave him to tell you about it but please try to be encouraging, he values your opinion.'

Patricia came to a halt and Ben was left even more curious. They both sat back and devoured a couple of biscuits each, which was how Robbie found them when he reappeared a few minutes later. He was totally unaware of their shared conversation and quickly took up where he had left off. He went over to his desk and came back to the coffee table with a rolled-up plan which he unrolled with a flourish and the mystery was made immediately apparent by the large-printed title at the top of a detailed drawing: 'Exworth Speedway Track'. Ben hadn't known what to expect but suddenly all the earthworks made a lot of sense and all he could think to say at first was, 'Well I'll be buggered,' much to the delight of Robbie and Patricia. Robbie could see that Ben was impressed and took considerable pleasure in discussing his plans for the project. The more Ben heard and the more he thought about it the more he was convinced that Robbie and Tony were on to a winner.

Robbie explained that as well as building a track for a professional speedway he also intended to have an inner track complete with jumps and bumps for a cycle speedway which would provide a sporting interest for the youth of Highfield who were bereft of anything to get involved in that didn't involve vandalism. He had approached the local constable Roger Richards, who was very supportive and had agreed to help run the cycling racing and was already trying to source some old bikes from the police lost property office that could be cannibalised to become track bikes. The plans were to be discussed at the next planning meeting and Robbie had been careful to get Councillor Rudge on board and had the weight of Alderman Herbert Anstey, the chairman of Exworth Football Team as a powerful ally as well.

There would of course be all sorts of reactions to the proposal once it became common knowledge as any sort of change was inevitably met with disapproval by some people, but Ben could see that there were answers for all the obvious contentious issues. The discussion between them went back and forth, with Robbie having to cut off several times to serve buyers and sellers. Patricia filled in the gaps by telling Ben that Tony was away for two weeks spending time on a crash course learning the tricks of speedway riding with a professional team, the Swindon Robins.

'The team is run by an old mate of Robbie's from way back who has been very supportive and has had Tony staying with his family. By all reports Tony is loving it and is reported to be a natural. Knowing him he will soak it all up and give it his all as he does with anything that catches his imagination.'

When Robbie returned he was rubbing his hands together as he had just sold a lot of spare parts, which meant good money in the speedway fund. Patricia gave him a peck and busied herself by laying out a pile of delicious ham sandwiches with a tasty mustard dressing and insisted that Ben join them in their lunch. As they ate Ben took on the role of devil's advocate and raised several potential objections that might be raised. The isolated location away from any housing meant that there should be no problem with the noise entailed in bikes roaring around a track at maximum revs, or the crowd noise of the supporting masses. Parking was to be taken care of by the provision of a car park at the bottom layer of the development. No alcohol would be permitted on the site and stewards were going to be recruited to enforce the rule and to deal with any difficult behaviour. Ben could have happily spent the whole day discussing Robbie and Tony's dream but when he glanced at his watch it was already after midday and he had to beat a hasty retreat to at least make a token appearance at the office before attending the prof's clinic. Things back at base had ticked happily on without him and the only thing he needed to act on was a request from Oliver Manning the district housing manager for a call back. Ben tried at once but Oliver was out of his office, probably at lunch, so Ben arranged for Mrs Freeman to ring back later in the day and give his apologies and to say that he would ring him on Monday morning. Then he headed off down the hill to Exworth and the general hospital. He slowed as he passed the old horse field where the earth moving equipment was working flat out. He screwed up his eyes and imagined what the mounds of earth would look like as a stadium but it just seemed to be a sea of mud, which didn't stop him wishing it well with all his heart.

Chapter 33

Lots to Learn

Ben got to the hospital in good time but found that someone else had discovered the secret parking place that he thought of as his own. This meant driving around in circles for several minutes before finally in desperation parking in the multi-storey car park next door to the hospital which would inevitably cost him an arm and a leg. By the time he arrived in the clinic the various banks of chairs were already filling up and Wendy the receptionist was moving files around at a rate of knots. The prof and Raj were already dividing the work up and Ben briefly described his parking problem. They seemed to accept his excuse, recognising that he did not have their privilege of reserved parking spaces, and he was directed to help himself to coffee.

The afternoon went much the same as normal but Ben noted that for the second week running one of the clients he interviewed was open about his homosexuality and moreover seemed devoid of any symptoms of neurosis or psychosis. At the end of the clinic Ben raised the issue with the prof and asked why they had been referred and what they hoped to achieve by attending. 'Well you know, Ben, homosexual activity is still against the law and anyone practicing it is wide open to abuse, blackmail or severe intimidation by some law enforcers. At times the law can be a real ass, take the old law about suicide for example. At one time the punishment for attempting suicide was the death penalty. Now if that's not nonsense I don't know what is! Of course it can only be a matter of time before sexual activity between two consenting adults is no longer illegal but for the time being many people live their lives in the shadows with genuine fear that their secret will be discovered and they could end up in jail. Of course, we occasionally get a referral from a GP, usually one near retirement, who seems to think that homosexuality is a mental illness which can be treated and cured. Fortunately, that attitude is increasingly rare and most people attending these days are people who have a court case pending. They seem to be regularly advised by their solicitors that attendance at a psychiatric clinic can put them in a better light with the court and I guess it might be working as it is rare for such offenders to get more than a fine or caution. It doesn't take up too much of our time and if it helps society to become more accepting of human idiosyncrasies that's fine by me.'

Ben went home thinking about what the prof had said and once again realising what a good human being the prof was and how his own mind was being broadened by his contact with him.

Sandy was in the kitchen preparing tea and was singing out loud 'Ticket to Ride' the most recent song recorded by the Beatles which they had performed on 'Top of the Pops' earlier in the week. Ben crept up behind her and put his hands around her and cupped her breasts. She jumped a bit but then relaxed into the embrace and leant back against him. She made no attempt to push him off and turned slowly around and kissed him warmly.

'I've had another letter from Camila in Jamaica and she is hoping to come over with the girls in the summer.'

The correspondence between Camila and Sandy had developed to a letter every couple of weeks and they never failed to lift Sandy's spirits. Ben welcomed the effect it had on Sandy and the boys had benefited too by starting to take an interest in Dave's family. Camila always used colourful stamps on the envelopes of her letters and Sandy had carefully saved them. They included all sorts of subjects from Miss World to Scouting but mainly beautiful nature subjects such as butterflies, flowers and birds.

Ben had told Mrs Freeman about the stamps and had asked her to save any pretty stamps that arrived on the post at the office so that Sandy could send them to Camila for Elsa and Gloria to collect.

'Do you mean like these?' she had said and then as if by magic she produced a large envelope full to bursting with British stamps of all description from the drawer of her desk. 'I used to collect them for the boys when they were young and somehow couldn't stop even though they lost interest years ago.'

She pushed them across the desk and all Ben could think to say was, 'Brilliant. You're just brilliant.'

The boys were attracted to the highly coloured stamps from Jamaica and Sandy decided that she would encourage them to start a stamp collection, which had been all the rage when she had been a kid. It seemed to have dropped from grace with kids these days, which was a bit sad particularly when stamps were becoming more and more diverse and interesting in more recent times. Sandy shook a few of the stamps out of Mrs Freeman's envelope and Ben and Sandy pored over them together and were impressed by the various subjects represented. As tea was almost ready the stamps were put away for another day but they reminded Ben that he had once collected and that there could just be an old stamp book in the loft with the other remnants of his childhood. For what seemed like years, every time his mum visited she brought yet another collection of stuff he had abandoned when he went to university. Most of it was rubbish and was promptly put in the bin once his mum had gone back home. However, Ben had always cherished his books and any that arrived via mum were boxed up and joined the growing pile of boxes in the loft. Once there they had never reappeared as it took a testing act of gymnastic skill to mount to the very top of the step ladder and pull himself up through the small hatch and into the attic.

He mentioned the possibility of a long-lost stamp album to Sandy and the die was cast; he was committed to an assault on the loft at some point over the weekend with Sandy holding the step ladder. A favourite tea and good programmes on television brought the week to an end and all thoughts of the 'planned hazardous activity' facing him slipped from Ben's mind. Once the boys were bathed and settled for the night Sandy and Ben sat back on the sofa nursing a couple of beers, switched off the television and got down to the serious business of planning Jack's birthday, which was just twelve days away on Wednesday, 12 May. They had discussed it before and had decided that it was time to come up with a new plan for his party. In the last couple of years since he had started school it had been a case of inviting his whole class to a bun feast at the local community centre and to have a hired entertainer to do a show for the kids before organising silly games involving a lot of running around.

The first year's entertainer had been Chirpy the clown, who managed to frighten several of the children and even made a couple of the girls cry. Last year it had been the Great Ricardo, a magician and fire eater who proved to be a far from great magician but a highly combustive fire eater, as he managed to set the fire sprinklers off when blowing a stream of fire from his mouth. That really went down well with the kids, who all managed to get soaked before the caretaker had arrived to turn them off. It had taken Ben and Sandy several hours to mop up but Jack and Nick enjoyed hero's status at school for a while on the strength of it. However, things had moved on during the past year and both boys now had particular friends and there were some classmates who were no longer in favour. Inevitably these included all the girls in their classes who were now classified as soppy and therefore no longer de rigueur.

After much discussion both boys had been permitted to invite four boys each to an adventure evening, details secret until the day, and the invites sent out stressed the need to wear old, warm clothes. The plan that emerged relied very heavily on the input of Robbie and Patricia and had come about at their suggestion. Ben had been talking to them about Jack's birthday and his need to come up with something different. Robbie and Patricia had looked at each other in a rather conspiratorial way and both nodded at the same time. 'How's this for an idea?' Robbie said. 'We were planning a trip to a Swindon on Wednesday to deliver a bike to Tony that he has been working on in the yard for months. He has been picked to ride in a trials meet in the evening and will be riding for the Swindon Robins against the Coventry Bees. It's not a full league match but it should be exciting with plenty of thrills and spills. Why don't you bring a group of kids along?'

The plan just grew and grew from there with Robbie offering to kit out one of his huge lorries with old car seats tied down on each side of the lorry bed and more seats across the back of the cabin.

'This reminds me of numerous trips to scout camps with Tony's patrol when he was keen in his early teens. I even stayed to help on one occasion but only the once as all that dib dibbing and dob dobbing was not for me and I really don't have the legs for shorts. I limited my involvement to transport provider after that until Tony got bored with scouts and discovered his passion for mechanics and girls.'

Patricia soon got into the spirit of the plan and declared that it would be just like old times when their own children were small and the family went out on adventures with a gang of their school friends. She suggested that Ben should ask Sandy to give her a ring so they could sort out the catering together. A series of protracted phone calls had taken place between Sandy and Patricia over the next few days and Ben happily dropped out of involvement in the catering arrangements. However, he did note that Sandy had begun to use the name Patsie rather than the more formal name Patricia that he still used for Robbie's wife. What with that and his failure to use Mrs Freeman's Christian name, Vivian, he was left wondering if it wasn't about time that he reviewed his contact with people who he considered to be friends.

On Saturday morning the family went to do their usual 'big shop' at the Co-op. As previously agreed Ben parked up in the store car park but went off by himself to do other chores whilst Sandy and the boys went to get the food stuff with the promise of ninety-nines from the ice cream van once the work had been done. Ben's chores were straight forward and involved a trip to the toy shop to pick up a Scalextric for Jack's birthday and then a trip to the patisserie to collect his birthday cake in the shape of a motorbike. By the time everyone was back at the car both were safely stowed in the boot and covered by the travelling rug. Ben was sat in the car innocently reading the paper and the boys went along with the pretence but he suspected that his play acting was not fooling them for a moment.

Sunday started with the bedroom windows rattling alarmingly in what felt like gale force winds and the rain was coming down so heavily that Ben could barely see the houses opposite when he pulled back the bedroom curtains. The plan agreed the previous evening by Sandy and Ben, when they finally got two overexcited little boys settled, had been to take them for a drive to the seaside to let off some steam. That now had to go by the board because of the weather and there had never been a plan B. Once breakfast was over, which had been far from relaxed as both boys seemed determined to outdo each other in mischief, Sandy reminded Ben that he still needed to seek out the possible stamp album from the loft. His wobbly trip up the step ladder to open the loft hatch intrigued the boys, who had never realised that there was a whole unexplored territory above their heads.

With Sandy holding on to the stepladder with grime determination Ben put each of the boys in turn on his shoulders and mounted the first few steps until they could just see inside undiscovered attic. The dark and dingy space failed to impress them and they quickly tired of the exploration idea and went off downstairs to create minor mayhem elsewhere. Armed with a torch, Ben climbed up once more and with surprising ease located what he was looking for. His job was made simple as with unusual efficiency he had written 'BOOKS' in large letters along the side of the box. The actual recovery of the box proved more difficult as it only just fitted through the hatch and it weighed a ton. The dismount was less than elegant as he came down all of a rush with the box balanced on his head and ended up in a heap on the floor. Sandy tried hard not to laugh but ended up rushing off to the loo almost wetting herself with the effort of trying to keep a straight face. Feeling rather battered, Ben rescued the box and carried it into their bedroom to explore the contents. On the top layer of the box were four old Lion annuals, which Ben remembered immediately as they had been a major part of his reading as a young lad. He passed these straight over to Sandy for her to take down to the boys in the hope of distracting them from whatever they were up to, which appeared to be no good judging from the bangs and crashes coming from below.

Immediately below the Lion annuals was a neat pile of Famous Five Adventure books which Ben laid out on the bed in a neat row by date of publication. Once again recollections came flooding back and he realised that this box held all sorts of memories from his early childhood. The boys had gone quiet downstairs so it appeared that the Lion annuals were working. Sandy was in the kitchen doing the preparations for lunch and judging by yet another rendition of a Beatles medley was happy in her work. The rain continued to pour down and Ben, finding himself with time on his hands, lay down on the bed and explored the contents of the box and his mind further. From the variation in the state of wear and tear of the Famous Five books it was apparent that the early ones had been cherished and read repeatedly whilst the later ones looked to have been untouched. He remembered that for eight years he had received a new one each year as a Christmas present from Aunt Ivy in North Wales. She had been married to his dad's eldest brother, George, who had returned from the war in a terrible state and who had died almost twenty years ago. Ben couldn't remember having met either Uncle George or Aunt Ivy but without fail she had sent him a new Famous Five novel every year and Ben had always sent her a note each time thanking her for the gift and they just kept on coming year on year. The books were published for twenty-two consecutive years but Aunt Ivy didn't last the time and after sending eight books died and went on her own special adventure.

Ben could remember reading the first book *The Famous Five on a Treasure Island,* probably the first book he had read voluntarily for pleasure. He could recall reading it over and over again and the pleasure he felt when the next one arrived the following Christmas. However, it quickly became apparent that each book followed predictable lines with the same four youngsters and Timmy the dog getting into unlikely situations and triumphing against the odds. After three or four books the remainder remained largely unread but Ben was still compelled to write a grateful letter each year to Aunt Ivy. Had Aunt Ivy lived he suspected he would still have been receiving them when he left home for university. He re-read the first few pages of the first book and was amazed just how simplistic and dated it was. He put them all aside and decided not to try them out on the boys, who were still hooked on Biggles for bedtime reading and it seemed unlikely that they would find the activities of the five and their regular consumption of lashings of ginger beer at all exciting.

The next book out of the box really got his mind working. He thought back to his time as an eleven-year-old when he had bucked the trend at his local primary school by passing the 'eleven plus' and had gained a place at the Exworth Grammar School. His parents were inordinately proud of him and his mother had used all the Co-op dividend she had quietly but hopefully put to one side in order to kit him out with the full uniform and sports kit required. So Ben had found himself at the age of eleven going from being one of the brightest boys in his school year to just one of the herd overnight. It had been quite a shock. To add to the shock he had found himself largely being taught by a series of elderly masters who were mostly going through the motions whilst awaiting their retirement. But there were exceptions and he had been very fortunate with his first form master who also taught him English.

Mr Colston was himself nearing retirement and presented as a figure of fun. He had a huge walrus moustache and was completely bald, hence his nickname 'Ego'. He taught all the usual boring stuff like punctuation and clause analysis but his real passion was reading and he did everything in his power to get the pupils reading for pleasure. He encouraged the class to join the local library and put part of each lesson aside for individual boys to read sections from books of their choice. He gave out shortlists of suggestions of good books and Ben got to realise he knew what he was talking about and George Orwell's *1984* and *Animal Farm* really caught his imagination. When it came to his turn to read he had borrowed *The Day of the Triffids* by John Wyndham, which was well received by the class and it was that book that Ben held in his hand now. Unfortunately, it had been too well received by someone in the school class and it went missing from his desk. As classes moved rooms lesson by lesson it was impossible to even guess who had lifted it. The outcome had been that Ben had to tell the library that it had been lost and it had cost him most of his pocket money for weeks to pay for its replacement. It mysteriously reappeared back in his desk several weeks later but was in a pretty battered condition and the book now showed all the appearances of a hard life. Ben put it to one side to try and read again as he couldn't remember ever having finished reading it. A couple of years ago he had seen the film of the story but it had failed to arise any of the terror that his mind had imagined when originally reading the book.

Books had never featured very much in the Newman household but his father had recognised Ben's interest and sought to encourage it by buying Readers Digest condensed books at regular intervals. Ben had devoured them and they became the basis of his reading for several years and he noticed that on occasions he saw his dad reading them himself but the rest of the family largely ignored them. The next layer of the box once again brought happy memories and consisted of about ten Giles annual cartoon books. Ben had first come across them when he had been dragged along to a church jumble sale by his mother. She had been focusing on the second-hand clothes, which had always been a reliable and cheap source of clothing for her and the family but were of no interest to him and he had wandered over to the bric-a-brac stall, which was loaded down with all sorts of odds and ends. He had flipped idly through a stack of cartoon books and became intrigued by the quality of the drawing and the amount of humour the cartoonist had managed to pack into each page. Coming from a *Daily Mirror* family Ben had no previous knowledge of

Giles work, which had been appearing in the *Daily Express* for years, but he was immediately drawn to it and borrowed enough from his mum to buy all the cartoon books on offer. When he was bored in lessons at school he had a tendency to decorate the covers of his exercise books with his efforts of depicting the cartoon characters of Andy Capp and his wife Florrie. Then the second-hand cartoon books increased his potential subjects by providing him with the new challenge of the whole Giles family. They were much more sophisticated drawings and Ben remembered that his early efforts had been pretty poor. However, after a while he could manage a passable Grandma Giles, who had a look rather like a prickly cactus, and his Aunt Vera, long lean and sniffling, was spot on even if he did say so himself. His ambition at that time had been to achieve an accurate copy of Chalkie, the Giles kid's school teacher who had a passing resemblance to 'Ego', to whom Ben would have liked to have given a drawing of the fearsome Chalkie as a joke. Unfortunately, Chalkie had proved to be beyond Ben's limited ability and the gift was never made, which with the hindsight of years was probably just as well as it might have been misinterpreted.

The box was emptying rapidly and there was still no sign of the elusive stamp album. The next little pile of books to come out was very familiar to Ben and he was pleased to rediscover them as they reminded him so much of his life as a small child in the Newman household. There always seemed to be a pot of tea on the table and anyone knocking at the door was welcomed with the offer of a cup of tea and it had seemed to Ben that the offer was usually well received. His mother had insisted that 'Brook Bond Tea' was the only acceptable cup and had been convinced that loose tea would never be supplanted by the insidious arrival of tea bags from America. Brook Bond packets also had the bonus of a dividend stamp on the side which could be collected and exchanged for cash once the card you stuck them on was full. Simple pleasures, but his mother loved getting something for nothing and she was an even bigger fan when Brook Bond started to put a card, a bit like cigarette cards, into each packet of tea. The original cards were highly coloured sets of such subjects as wild flowers and birds. However, there was no way of knowing which of the forty-eight cards in each set was contained in each individual packet of tea until it was opened.

At first the likelihood of getting a full set seemed almost impossible but the tea company quickly recognised this and introduced advertising boards with numbered slots where customers could exchange unwanted cards for ones they were still seeking. The local corner shop instilled one of the boards and Mr Monk, the owner, said it had drawn a lot of local housewives into the shop. Ben's mum was in her element and made repeated visits, building up six or seven complete sets over the following months, all of which she carefully stuck into the special albums she sent for from Brook Bond headquarters. At the time Ben had shown only a cursory interest, but as he examined the albums now he really admired them and the work and effort that his mum had put in to collecting them. They deserved a better fate than a box in the attic but there was nowhere safer from the inevitable rough handling if the boys got their hands on them. For the time being they would be going back in the box. The apparent last thing to come out of the box was a large scrap album about which Ben had no immediate recall but as he lifted it out he discovered the brown stamp album with a steam train on the cover that he immediately recognised. He opened it up and read Benjamin 'Newman aged 7 years' scrawled in spidery writing on the inside cover. The album had very few stamps in it, with only the Great Britain page having more than one or two and they were mainly repeat definitives, many of which were damaged. Out of curiosity he turned to the Jamaica page, which was a clear sheet which would present the boys and Sandy with a fresh place to start. At the back of the album there was a flap with a cover which contained packets of stamp hinges and a small plastic magnifying glass. He hoped that the boys would show more interest than he had but then he hadn't had a Sandy to encourage him.

As Ben started to repack the box he lifted up the scrap book and a shower of colourful cheese labels fell out all around him. He vaguely remembered when there had been a brief craze amongst his school friends for starting to collect things with each child trying to outdo the others. The most popular had been match box labels, cigarette packets and the different tissue papers that came wrapped around fresh fruit. Ben had spotted an advert for 'worldwide cheese labels' in a copy of his Lion comic and he had used money from his piggy bank to send for them. They took a while to arrive by post and had come back as four large sheets of paper covered with prints of colourful cheese labels, many sporting images of cows, milk maids and the like. He had got as far as carefully cutting them out but by that time the craze had been abandoned and the kids had moved on to yo-yos, conkers, marbles, hula hoops or whatever had been the next craze in the endless chain of childhood must-haves.

Ben gathered all the labels together and returned them to the scrapbook and put it, together with the stamp album to take down stairs for the boy's attention. *The Day of the Triffids* went on his bedside cabinet and the rest was returned to the box, which he precariously returned to the attic. The morning had just flown by and he got downstairs just in time for Sandy to serve up the lunch of ham, eggs and chips. Ben had to smile to himself, thinking just how shocked his mother would be if she knew what was being served for a Sunday lunch. A full roast dinner was all that was acceptable in his parent's home but this Newman family were more than satisfied with what was on offer and clear plates all round showed how much it was enjoyed. The pudding was slices of Arctic roll with hot custard with the boys fighting over the skin from the top of the custard. Whilst Sandy cleared the table Ben produced the stamp album and scrapbook and as he had predicted to himself Jack chose the stamp album and Nick went for the colourful cheese labels. The afternoon proceeded with Sandy and Jack soaking off the used stamps from Jamaica and carefully laying them face down on sheets of newspaper on the kitchen table to dry. Meanwhile Ben and Nick mixed up a paper paste from flour and water and moved on to the floor of the lounge with the scrapbook and labels laid out on the coffee table between them. There followed a rare period of peace and harmony in the Newman household before the boys grew bored of the tasks and left Sandy and Ben to finish up their activities. Fortunately, the newly acquired Lion annuals held the boys attention until children's television started and the day went better than anticipated. The boys were allowed to stay up for 'Sunday Night at the London Palladium' and were asleep almost before their heads hit their pillows. By mutual agreement Sandy and Ben had an early night!

Chapter 34

Lots Happening

After the torrential rain of the weekend Monday started with gorgeous sunshine and the trip to Highfield was accompanied by the roads, pavements and surrounding earth steaming as the sun evaporated the rain-soaked ground. For once Ben avoided listening to the news in the car, preferring to switch to a pop music programme which he sang along to. With the car windows open and a warm breeze passing through he realised that he was in good spirits, which was a rare feeling for a Monday morning. Despite the weather the weekend had been a good couple of days, largely spent at home but generally quite productive and harmonious. Sandy and Ben had enjoyed each other's company and the boys had tuned into the atmosphere. The future speedway track was really beginning to take shape with the three distinct layers of the site largely in place and most of the earth moving equipment had moved on to other sites and other projects. As he pulled into the office carpark he just caught sight of Ernest in the distance, with The Champ limping along behind, going about his daily business with the brush and shovel.

Alice must have seen him pull up and was already coming along the corridor with his morning tea. The first slurp was cooler than his normal mug of tea and he suspected that the pot had been made a while and already enjoyed by Alice and Ernest. Their friendship was developing nicely and they clearly both benefited from having someone to fuss over. Ernest called into the office almost every day, often bringing in post he had received for Ben to sort out for him. On Ernest's behalf Ben had arranged for about two thirds of Ernest's pay to be paid directly into a bank account by his employer. The rest was paid to him in cash in a brown envelope and was his 'spends', of which he was immensely proud. He was learning to manage his money on essential supplies for The Champ and himself and it was a rare occurrence for him to go hungry by a Thursday. His main problem was he couldn't read or write so responding to post was beyond him. Ben had taught him to write his name, which he did with great care on the cheques Ben filled out for him and together they got by. Ernest's account was supervised by Mrs Freeman to avoid anyone thinking Ernest was being ripped off by Ben, as it was easy to attract suspicious accusations when dealing with other people's affairs. On the days he had no post he went straight to the kitchen for a natter with Alice and he sometimes had to be rooted out to go off and earn his keep, particularly when it was pouring with rain. The Champ seemed to enjoy his visits to the office and always made a circuit of each of the offices in the hope of some titbit or other and he usually scored before ending up with his head in Alice's lap munching on a proffered biscuit.

Mrs Freeman had left a note on Ben's desk reminding him that he had promised to return Oliver's call and he rang as soon as he had sat down. The conversation started with the usual pleasantries but Ben could sense that Oliver was worried about something so he cut to the chase. 'What can I do for you on this bright sunny day? Not a problem with Hanca, I hope, as she seems to be a real success story.'

'No, Hanca is fine, but we do have a problem with another of your clients. I am afraid it's Ernest Farthing.'

Ben listened carefully as Oliver explained that Ernest had never had a tenancy in his name and he was currently still in his parents' former home, which was a three-bedroom house which he was in no way qualified to have. In fact he was officially a squatter, which the council couldn't allow to continue and Oliver had been instructed to apply to the court to have him evicted. Ben was horrified, as Ernest had suffered so much in the past and this had been exacerbated more recently by his parents' deaths and his sister's hospitalisation. He had come through it all surprising well, having a job and friends in The Champ and Alice, but losing his home would be a body blow from which he would be unlikely to recover. Ben understood that Oliver had been given an order and that he would have to follow it through.

They talked back and forth and between them hatched a possible plan of action but it depended entirely on gaining the cooperation of Alderman Anstey, the chairman of the District Housing Committee. Oliver could not have made such an approach without causing major waves for himself within his department as the order to seek eviction had come from Oliver's boss. He had already stuck his neck out by putting Ben in the picture of what was happening. However, he agreed to drag his heels with the paperwork necessary for the eviction to give Ben a chance of influencing the decision to evict. Ben settled back in his chair and thought through how he could best approach Alderman Anstey and then picked up the phone and quickly found himself talking directly to the man himself at his business premises. There was no time for second thoughts and he started to broadly outline the problem. He was quickly brought to a halt by the alderman, who said he couldn't talk then as he had an office full of people, but he would call into Ben's office at 2 pm that afternoon for a few minutes on his way to headquarters.

The phone went dead. Ben didn't know what to think as in his experience it was unprecedented for a councillor to visit at the request of an officer, all he hoped was that he could take advantage of the situation for Ernest's benefit. He primed the staff to expect the visit and a hurried check of the premises made sure everything was in order to receive the visitation.

Alderman Anstey strode into the office promptly at 2 pm and Mrs Freeman escorted him straight down to Ben's office where he shook hands with Ben warmly and sat down, crossing one leg over the other apparently very relaxed. No sooner than he had settled he was confronted by the ever-bizarre looking Alice in her multiple layers of dowdy clothes topping off her ancient clumpy boots. Ben realised that she must have overheard him telling Mrs Freeman that they were expecting a special visitor and she was determined to do her bit to make him welcomed. She presented him with a mug of tea in her own special coronation mug and a plate of biscuits before curtsying awkwardly and going out backwards. Ben didn't know whether to laugh or cry but the alderman seemed completely unphased. They both just about managed to stifle their giggles and Alderman Anstey commented that he now knew what it was like to be royalty.

Recognising that Alderman Anstey had limited time Ben dived straight in by saying that he felt committed to trying to help Ernest in much the same way as the alderman had felt about Hanca Parsons. He ploughed straight on and the alderman listened intently as he drank his tea and cleared the plate of biscuits. Ben briefly told Ernest's story from the time his parents ran away from the institution in Cardiff and gained 'their freedom' by getting married. He finished up with the important fact that Ernest, despite all his mental limitations, had gained employment and had successfully supported his ailing parents and his very dependent sister. He had lost them all and was now about to lose his home even though he had no rent arrears and the place was kept clean and tidy. The room went quiet for a couple of moments then the alderman spoke up.

'I can see your point, Ben, and I agree that the man deserves a chance but there is no way he can stay in a three-bedroom house. We are crying out for them for families. I think you and Oliver Manning should get your heads together and see what you can come up with; after all you did pretty well last time. I will ensure a stop is put on the eviction proceedings for the time being and wait to hear from you.'

Then he was on his feet and gone to get on with the rest of his busy schedule. Ben felt exhausted but elated and very grateful that he had a lifeline for Ernest.

The date of the speedway meet in Swindon fell on a Wednesday, which was Jack's actual birthday, 12 May, and it was a very excited group of boys who clambered aboard the lorry after school that day. To add to the excitement they were greeted by a large Black man who heaved them aboard one by one. Ben had invited Dave along and he had rearranged his shifts in order to come much to the delight of Jack, Nick and Sandy. They set off in high spirits with Robbie driving the lorry and Tony beside him in the cabin navigating. Patricia and Sandy followed closely behind the lorry in the Scadding's Mercedes and could be seen chatting away like two old friends. Ben and Dave sat each side of the tailboard surrounded by small boys and with Tony's brand-new motor bike securely tied down the middle of the lorry on its way for its first taste of action in anger. The lorry rang out with a lengthy rendering of ten green bottles until the boys tired of it and it petered out, to be followed by a series of very weak knock-knock jokes with each boy trying to outdo the others. As it turned out the boys were not the only ones to have a surprise that evening as at about five o'clock Robbie suddenly took a sharp right turn down a rough farm track and pulled up by a large sign for 'Horseworld'.

The ladies quickly took control and spread several blankets on the wide grass verge and in no time at all set out a formidable picnic tea. The boys set into the food with a gusto and Robbie and Ben each grabbed a few sandwiches and a couple of apples before setting off along the path in search of their old friend Solomon, alias Boxer Mark Two. There were groups of horses in paddocks to the left and right as far as the eye could see, all contentedly grazing on the lush green grass of well-managed fields. It was several minutes before they spotted their quarry but he had already seen them coming and came wandering over with his familiar gait to make their re-acquaintance. He looked quite splendid. His coat had been regularly groomed, his mane and tail had been neatly trimmed and his white socks brushed to perfection. Both of the men couldn't be more delighted and fed him their apples which encouraged the other old horses in the paddock to come over to investigate, and they were rewarded with carrots from Robbie's jacket pockets. Dave and the boys joined up with Robbie and Ben, keen to know what they were up to and Robbie promised to tell them all about this special horse once they were back at the lorry. Meanwhile, with a little encouragement, the boys each held out the remains of their apples for the horses to eat off the flat of their hands. One little boy was reluctant to get involved as he was obviously intimidated by the sheer size of the horses. This was Simon, who was well known to Ben as a timid child who found it difficult to act spontaneously. He had started school the same day as Nick and they had sat together from day one. They were an unlikely combination but had remained firm friends in spite of being like chalk and cheese. Simon was the only child of elderly parents and always appeared clean and tidy with impeccable manners. He was a very able student and regularly came top of his class in maths and reading tests and just to add to his difference he played the violin to a grade three standard. Ben and Sandy felt him to be a good influence on Nick and the two boys seemed to rub along well together, but they did wonder if Simon's parents were as enamoured by the friendship. This was the first time Simon had done anything social with the Newmans and it was noticeable that Nick had never been invited to their house.

Ben quickly picked the boy up and gave him a carrot to feed to Solomon and by supporting his arm, reached forward for the horse to take it from him. The deed done, Simon happily returned to his normal place of getting lost in the group of boys, who were now sat on the grass surrounding Robbie. He had called the boys to order and they became quiet and appeared to give him their full attention. 'The horse we visited today is a very special one who I have been privileged to know about for many years. His name is Solomon, which means the wise one and everyone who has worked with him over the years has always said it was a most appropriate name. During the war he was born on a farm in South Wales that bred ponies to work in the coal mines and that was where he would have spent his days had he not grown into a really big horse that was too big to go down the mines. The farmer had no use for him and sent him to a horse sale where old and decrepit horses were sent and were usually bought for slaughter for the pet food market. But Solomon was lucky as there was a buyer from the army there looking for horses to act as transport and hauliers to help on the battlefields of Europe in the final days of the fighting. Solomon was able to go where motor transport couldn't and spent his days bringing wounded from the battle fields to the military hospitals set up away from the front lines. He seemed to know instinctively when to go slow and carefully when he had a badly injured soldier aboard but always returned to the front quickly to continue his rescue missions time after time.'

By this time Ben was amazed that Robbie knew so much about Solomon's history, but he then spotted the twinkle in Robbie's eye and realised that he was making it up as he went along in order to entertain the boys. Shades of *Black Beauty*, he thought but he said nothing as Robbie went on through the story of Solomon. 'His next owner, once the army had finished up with him, was a travelling gypsy and horse trader, a good judge of horse flesh who regularly bought horses cheaply and brought them on to sell at a profit. Tom King, the gypsy, used Solomon to pull his tented wagon around the West Country for the rest of that summer before selling him on to a distant cousin who organised the donkey rides on the beach at Weston-Super-Mare.

'Solomon spent that winter out in the fields on a farm whilst his new owner spent his time converting a cart into a model fire engine complete with steering wheel and a large brass bell which could be clanged by the children riding in the cart. Many horses would have been frightened by the bell but after Solomon's experience of the sounds of war he just took it in his stride and spent several summers taking kids for rides on Weston sands and enjoying the attention they gave him. I guess he would still be pulling that cart, but it wasn't to be, as the Weston Council decided that it was too dangerous as the beach attracted more and more tourists. The fire engine was scrapped and the horse was sold once more to end his working days living in a converted garage and pulling a rag and bone cart around the streets of Exworth. The final ignominy was when, after a lifetime of service, the horse was replaced by an electric milk float, but at least we can all see that there is a happy end to his life story. At the age of well over twenty, a good age for a horse, he has been found a lovely home with good food and caring staff and will spend the rest of his days with his friends in the comfort and peace he deserves. So I say three cheers for Solomon, hip hip.'

They all cheered at a volume only achieved by small boys and loud enough to cause a minor stampede in the nearest couple of paddocks before clambering back on the lorry and heading for Swindon. From listening to the conversations going on between the boys it was clear that they were convinced by the story of the old horse's life. One or two even recalled having visited the donkeys on the beach at Weston.

The arrival at the Swindon Speedway track was in complete contrast to their visit to the peace and quiet of Horseworld. The Tannoy system was blasting out 'The Leader of the Pack' by the Shangri-Las at full volume, complete with its backing of the high revving motorbike. It was quite deafening but seemed to increase the excitement of the crowds pouring into the stadium and the group of boys just looked on in wonderment. Robbie was directed over to a small enclosure right by the start and finish line and each of the boys in turn were lifted down from the lorry and sat astride Tony's sparkling new bike with his helmet perched on their head. Patricia had brought along one of the new-fangled Polaroid cameras and each child would later receive their own photo as a souvenir of their visit. They settled themselves on the tiered wooden benches and Tony took over the role of raconteur from Robbie and gave the boys a short talk about the speedway and how it worked. He explained that there were four riders in each team and that they would all ride against each of the opposition during the event. There were always four riders in each race, two from each team, and they always went anti-clockwise for four laps. The races were started off with the four riders spaced out across the track watching a sort of traffic light at the side of the track. When they changed from red to green the starting tapes went up automatically and the bikes roared away.

'It is very important to get a fast start and to try and be at the front at the first corner. Once you are behind it is very hard to overtake. To add to the difficulty the bikes have no brakes and only one gear so it is flat out all the way. The whole four laps of each race will only take about a minute and there are often lots of speedy thrills and spills.'

The floodlights came on at that point and Tony hurriedly pushed his precious bike over to the pits where other bikes were starting up for last minute tuning.

The boys settled on the benches and seemed to be mesmerised by the cacophony of noise from the sound system, the massive tractor circling the track towing a huge rake to level the cinders, the roar of the revving bikes and the shouts and chants from the swelling crowds supporting their chosen team. The whole evening went in a blur and the boys were full of questions mainly about which one was Tony and how his team were doing. At the halfway point there was a short break to let the crowds top up their drinks and to get something to eat from the mobile canteen. The sound system once again blared out 'The Leader of the Pack' but when it finished the commentator came on with what he called a special announcement.

'Swindon Robins are pleased to welcome a group of young fans from Exworth. They are here today to celebrate the birthday of Jack Newman, who is eight today. I understand that Exworth is shortly hoping to open their own speedway track and we wish them well and look forward to competing with them in the future.'

Jack coloured up with embarrassment but was grinning all over his face. With perfect timing Sandy produced a chocolate cake in the shape of a motor bike with eight candles on it flickering in the evening wind. Jack blew them out with ease and their little group started to sing happy birthday, which was quickly taken up by the crowd around them. By the time the song was finished the whole stadium was singing.

To the delight of them all and particularly Robbie and Patricia, Tony had managed two seconds in his first three races. In his first ride he had been hopelessly left at the start and there was no way he was ever going to catch up. Tony had learnt quickly and didn't make the same mistake again and was narrowly beaten into second place in his next two races by much more experienced riders. His final ride was in the last race of the day and the teams were level pegging. The race started with him trailing in third place and it looked all over as the two riders in front battled for all they were worth. The front two were side by side and doing everything possible to get the advantage, then it was all over in a flash as they overdid it at the final corner and collided with the tyre barrier and ended up in a heap. Tony slid through on the inside and claimed first place for the Robins. The result had a large element of luck but his efforts made a major contribution to the single point win for the Swindon Robins, a very satisfying first competition for him. It was an excited but tired group of boys who made their way back to the lorry at the end of the event to be welcomed by Sandy and Patricia handing out hotdogs and hot Bovril they had previously ordered from the mobile canteen. Once settled back in their seats the ladies used the picnic blankets to cover them up warmly as it was after 10 pm and getting cold. The boys slept their way home and were dropped off one by one and each was given a gift bag containing a poster of the Swindon Robins' first team in action, an Airfix kit of a motorbike and their own photo of themselves on Tony's bike. As Dave handed Simon down to his waiting dad he was amused to hear him tell his dad it was great. 'and I fed a horse'. No mention of the Swindon Robins, for Simon the high spot had been feeding Solomon a carrot.

Dave stayed the night on the sofa and was up and away on the pink peril at some on unearthly hour. The Newmans slept in.

Chapter 35

Busy Times All Round

On the Thursday morning, as he was running late, Ben decided to ring Oliver from home to arrange to see him in his office at 10 am. He dropped the boys off at school and went in with them to apologise that they were late. The receptionist Mrs Forester quickly reassured him that no one would be surprised, as the buzz around the school was all about the previous evening's adventure. Oliver, as ever, was welcoming and quickly rustled up a very superior cup of coffee from the percolator bubbling away in the corner of his office. As he passed the steaming mug to Ben he said, 'My little treat to myself, which just about makes working here bearable as the stuff they serve up in the canteen is absolute rubbish.'

The smell was tempting and the taste really good, which made Ben sing it's praises in the hope of a second cup later. They got down to business straight away and were in total agreement about what would meet Ernest's needs and at the same time enable the council to offer the Farthing's house to a family on the waiting list. There were really only two types of suitable properties available, high-rise flats and maisonettes. They quickly agreed that the multi-storied flats were not an option as they had a strict no pet rule and there was no way that Ernest would be parted from The Champ even if it meant him becoming homeless. 'That leaves us with maisonettes and there are usually a few available; give me twenty-four hours and I should be able to let you know where we stand.' Ben was back in his car after just a few minutes, having agreed to call back the following morning. No time for a top-up of coffee but there was always tomorrow to look forward to.

Mrs Freeman had guessed where he had been and in her usual efficient way had dealt with the post and taken a few messages for him. Susie called out hello as he passed her door but as yet there was no sign of Phil. She seemed to be dropping back into her old habits of coming in late each day and Ben realised it was time he got her back up to scratch with her time keeping. When she did eventually arrive later on it was immediately apparent that she was in a foul mood and with some relief Ben put off the time keeping issue for another day. A few minutes later Susie knocked on his door and came in with a pile of her reports for him to read through. She sat down with obvious relief and Ben realised that she was getting away from Phil who must have been difficult to share an office with when she was in her current mood.

Ben opened the subject as tactfully as he could by asking, 'How are you two getting on sharing an office?'

Susie took a deep breath and then it all came tumbling out. 'Usually we get on just fine and she has been very helpful to me, but the last couple of weeks she has been like a bear with a sore head. I don't seem to be able to say anything right and I have been trying to keep out of her way. I know what it's about but can't do anything about it, but hopefully it will soon be over.' She went on to explain, 'Phil's partner Lizzie, who as you know is a teacher, is in France with a group of school children who were on an exchange visit to Lyons for a month. Poor old Phil misses her terribly and her drinking has been a bit out of control in the evening when she is home alone and it has been taking a toll on her for the past three weeks. Still, Lizzie is back next week and Phil should be a lot happier.'

Ben thanked Susie for putting him in the picture and felt rather ashamed that he had not realised what was going on. He felt that he rubbed along reasonably with Phil but it was clear that he was not her confidant. He decided that he needed to put in more effort but that now was not the right time to start and picked up the top report to read through.

He was pleased that it was an update on Frank and Rosie Sullivan as he was keen to know how they were doing and he was conscious that he had not visited them for some time. Susie had been visiting regularly and helped Frank to cope with the day-to-day caring of Rosie, but the situation was becoming more difficult as there was a marked deterioration in Frank's health. She had tried to encourage him to visit Dr Eddoll, his GP, but he had resisted all such suggestions. Susie had also noted that he was continuing to have difficulty with getting Rosie's cooperation to do the glucose testing and insulin injections for her diabetes. The insulin bottle, syringes, sterilising kit and testing strips were still lined up in their usual place along the top of the television but Susie suspected their use was more than a bit hit or miss judging by the contents of the insulin bottle.

When he finished the report he put it to one side and suggested that they should do a joint visit next time, which Susie seemed relieved about. She said that she had planned to visit the Sullivans the following Wednesday and Ben put it in his diary, which was conveniently blank for that day. He was about to move on to the next report when Susie interjected. 'There's something else I think I ought to make you aware of, which I didn't put in the report as I thought it better not to. When I got out of the lift at Chelsea House yesterday there was a great pile of cardboard boxes stacked outside the Sullivan's front door. I suppose I shouldn't have but as the top box was already opened I nosed inside and the box was full of cartons of 200 cigarettes and all were marked up for export only. There must have been several thousand cigarettes in all and even at Rosie's rate of consumption there was enough there to last her for months. My first thought was that they must have been smuggled but I couldn't imagine how they ended up in the corridor of the top floor of Chelsea House. When Frank answered the door he picked up on my curiosity and laughed as he led me back into the flat. The air in the flat was thick with smoke as Rosie was busy consuming her latest fag as if her life depended on it and the ash trays were overflowing and her dress was covered in ash. Frank sank down in his chair with the familiar clank of his leg irons and filled me in on the mystery. He explained that it had come about as a direct result of your visit with Paul, his old fireman friend a few weeks before.

'You probably remember the recent flooding down by the canal caused by the collapsed old sewer. Lots of basements were flooded with foul water and so were several of the canal-side warehouses. One of those was being used as storage for rolling tobacco and cigarettes ready to be supplied to duty free shops at several local airfields such as Cardiff, Bristol and Exeter. Apparently, the warehouse was inundated with about a foot of the stinking water which thoroughly soaked the bottom layer of boxes but the boxes stacked higher up had remained undamaged. After much discussion the tobacco company came to an agreement with their insurance company about compensation for their damaged stock and the agreement involved sending the whole ground-floor stock to landfill. A local company, Howard Haulage, got the contract to transport the cigarettes and tobacco to a little-known refuse site in an old quarry not far from where I live at Little Poppy Field and it was apparently done with complete secrecy in the dead of night. Certainly I have not heard any gossip about it in the village and have seen no evidence of black market cigarettes for sale.

'As you probably know quite a few firemen take on second jobs to help with their finances and it just so happens that a couple of the local firemen are part-time drivers at Howard Haulage. Frank and Rosie's surprise present literally fell off the back of a lorry aided and abetted by a couple of firemen trying to help. Frank assured me that there had been tight security on the lorries, including security tags on the rear doors but fireman are resourceful blokes and Frank had asked no questions. He accepted their offer and I can confirm it has proved to be a real life changer for the Sullivans. The shopping lists Frank has given me the last two weeks have included all sorts of goodies like vegetables, fruit, meat, fish and replacement cleaning materials that they haven't been able to afford for ages when Frank's priority has had to be cigarettes to make controlling Rosie a possibility. I didn't include any of this in my report in case it fell into the wrong hands and brought trouble on the people involved. I know it is technically stealing but the cigarettes were only going to be destroyed and Frank and Rosie need all the help they can get.'

Susie came to a rather breathless halt and nervously looked Ben in the eyes. He paused for thought for a little while and then broke into a grin and reassured Susie that he would have done the same and he didn't think acting as the police was any part of their job. 'Some things are better not written down.' And they moved on to the next report.

The rest of the reports held no surprises and they ran through them quickly and as they came to a halt Susie just sat still, making no attempt to move on. She obviously had something else on her mind but was unsure of mentioning it. Ben used the technique he often used with reticent clients and remained silent. She sighed and it finally came out in a rush.

'Please don't think I am complaining, because, I am not but I am worried about Ernest's dog The Champ, I have noticed that he has started to smell quite badly, have you noticed?'

Ben had to admit that he hadn't but he was aware that his sense of smell was never very acute and he had had a bit of a cold recently. However, he did say that he had noticed that recently the dog was largely walking on three legs avoiding putting his injured foot to the floor.

'That's just it,' Susie continued, 'I am pretty sure that the foot is infected but he won't let me anywhere near it even when I try to bribe him with his favourite meat titbits. He just grabs the food and backs off growling, which is not at all like him. I think he needs a visit to a vet to have it properly examined but I don't really know the best way of arranging it for Ernest.' They talked it through for a while and Ben had a moment of inspiration when he remembered that the People's Dispensary for Sick Animals set up a mobile surgery every Saturday morning in the car park of the Anchor Pub on the high street in town. He knew that their service was basically free of charge, with pet owners making a voluntary payment when they were able. This seemed an ideal solution but he had to reluctantly declare to Susie, 'in strictest confidence please', that it would be impossible for him to get involved on the coming Saturday as he knew Sandy had plans for that day as it was his birthday.

He explained that as his birthday came just four days after his son Jack's they usually celebrated it in a very simple way such as a meal out or a trip to the pictures. However, Sandy had been a bit overwhelmed with the trip to the Beatles which Ben had arranged for her birthday and was determined to do something special for him. 'I have been instructed to leave the day free and Sandy has made it clear there is a three-line whip.'

Susie smiled and didn't hesitate. 'Happy birthday for Saturday but there is no problem, I am quite happy to take him and I think I should invite Alice along to keep Ernest company.'

Susie went off to ring the PDSA and book an appointment and then headed for the kitchen to chat to Alice. By good fortune Ernest was in the kitchen having a cup of tea after popping in to use the loo. There was no sign of The Champ and Ernest explained the dog had been a bit off colour recently and had been reluctant to leave his basket that morning. Ernest had let him out for a sniff around the garden as usual whilst he got washed and dressed but the dog had quickly returned to his basket and for the first time in memory Ernest had gone to work alone. Both Ernest and Alice were very concerned and it was the perfect opportunity for

Susie to quickly explain about the free veterinary service and although full of anxiety the pair of them agreed for a visit with Susie on Saturday. Susie went back to put to put Ben in the picture and he congratulated her and in his head gave her a gold star like the ones he had coveted but rarely achieved whilst in primary school.

He finished up his paperwork and got away in good time and with light traffic arrived home quite early. He was barely through the front door when the boys leap on him demanding that he should help them set up the Scalextric that Jack had been given for his birthday. Sandy had very sensibly stopped the boys from opening the large box it had come in, knowing full well that it wouldn't have survived the boys' rush to get at the contents. The box was carefully unpacked on the kitchen table and put aside ready to be repacked latter. There were two stylish racing cars, one red and one blue, which fortunately fitted in with the colours of the Liverpool and Everton football teams which were the teams superficially being supported by the boys as they were both currently flying high in the first division. Jack was the red of Liverpool and Nick the blue of Everton, but in reality that was about the total of the boy's knowledge of the professional game.

After Ben had read the instructions they immediately hit a snag as the track when fitted together overlapped the table at both ends and the track sagged alarmingly, resulting in a very uneven ride for the two cars. It didn't take too long for Ben to decide to decant the whole set on to the floor in the living room, which was a distinct improvement but rather cramped and awkward for the boys to get in to control the cars. By the time the tea was on the table the boys were beginning to lose interest and Ben reluctantly returned the whole system to its box. It was Sandy who saved the day by suggesting that the boys should take the toy with them when they went to stay at Ben's parents where they were going for a sleepover on Saturday night. It was the first Ben had heard of the planned trip, but guessing it was part of Sandy's plans for his birthday he kept his counsel. The boys were enthusiastic when it was pointed out to them that there was plenty of room in their grandparent's conservatory and it would also be good to have something different to play with rather than the same old box of battered toys which was produced for them to play with each time they visited and which held no surprises.

Friday morning was typically spring like with the warm sun making the use of the sun visor a necessity as he drove up the hill to Highfield. A team of workmen were busy unloading a mountain of metal barriers from an articulated lorry and stacking them along the new tarmac road, which rose up to the top of proposed speedway site. The whole project seemed to be going on at a pace and the site was crisscrossed with trenches being dug ready to receive power and water supplies. Ben didn't like to think what it was costing Robbie and Patricia and he smiled to himself to think it was all based on funding from the earnings of totting. He drove on to the office as usual and spent the best part of an hour going through the post and catching up on his reports with Mrs Freeman. She had heard from both Alice and Susie about the planned trip to the PDSA with The Champ on the following day and confirmed that she had been worried about the dog's smell recently.

Once the decks were clear Ben headed over to see Oliver arriving in time to receive a freshly brewed coffee. Oliver produced a collection of three possible maisonettes and after a general chitchat as they enjoyed the brew set off in Ben's car to view the available properties.

Either of the first two they visited could have met Ernest's needs and were like so many similar properties Ben had visited over the years on the estate. Inevitably they were on the upper floor as the ground-floor flats were always reserved for less mobile tenants, many of whom were in wheelchairs. Oliver sat and instructed Ben on which way to go as they cut across the estate and headed for the third and final possible place and they eventually turned into a street that Ben was particularly familiar with, having walked along it numerous times. This was Dangerfield Avenue and Alice lived in number 44. Before he could say anything to Oliver he was instructed to pull up right outside Alice's flat and Oliver pointed to a maisonette just three doors down on the opposite side of the road. This had to be the best solution and after a cursory check of the property the decision was made; Ernest would be offered a transfer to 71 Dangerfield Avenue. It was agreed that the offer would be made by post in the certain knowledge that Ernest always brought his mail to Ben to be dealt with. It was agreed that Ernest should remain ignorant of Ben's involvement in the offer, leaving him free to aid Ernest in his acceptance and understanding of the proposed move.

It felt like a weight off Ben's shoulders and subject to Councillor Anstey's support all he needed to do now was to wait for Oliver to write to Ernest with the proposal. Ben used the next couple of hours making two routine visits before heading off in good time to the general hospital and the prof's psychiatric clinic. Sandy had made him up a box of sandwiches for his lunch and he contentedly ate them as drove along listening to pop music on the radio. His secret parking place was unoccupied and he arrived at the prof's office just as one of the hospital catering staff was dropping off the two large thermoses.

'Great timing, Ben, just in time to act as mother,' was how the prof welcomed him with a grin and Dr Raj waved from across the room where he was immersed in a deep armchair finishing off a pork pie for his lunch. Ben was quite happy to oblige and after passing the coffee around sat between the two of them. The conversation flowed quite easily and the prof even asked about the Swindon trip on Jack's birthday. Ben couldn't remember having previously mentioning it but was impressed that a busy man like the prof would remember about something as mundane as a child's birthday party. After a few minutes the prof signalled it was time to get on with work by pulling the pile of case notes towards him. He consulted his list and divided the files between them but finished up by making an unusual little speech.

'I have had a call from an old friend and colleague who I have known for years and he has asked me to see one of his patients to give him a second opinion. I think that this will prove to be of interest to you both and I would like you to both sit in on the interview.'

Dr Raj looked at Ben as if to say 'do you know anything about this?' and Ben just made a slight shake of his head.

The prof continued with a serious expression. 'I have had his name added to the end of the clinic so let's get together then. For now, gentlemen, our customers await.'

The afternoon went slowly for Ben as two of the five patients allocated to him failed to show, leaving him at a bit of a loose end. He wandered out to reception to have a chat with the ever-busy receptionist Wendy who was more receptive than usual. She kept waving her hand across her forehead as if to put her fringe in order but it came across as an unnecessary act. It took him only a couple of seconds to realise that the purpose of the action was to draw attention to the small diamond ring on her engagement finger and he promptly admired it. Wendy was delighted and went into a long tale of how her boyfriend, Roger, had got down on his knee in front of the whole pub and asked her to marry him.

'Oh it was ever so romantic.' She went on in great length about the plans for her wedding the following spring and Ben was relieved when Wendy was called away to answer the telephone. Before beating a hasty retreat he reached over and read through Wendy's copy of the prof's clinic list and there on the bottom was pencilled in Randolph Hemmingway. Posh name for a mystery man, but it meant nothing to Ben.

The clinic finally came to an end and the three of them gathered in the prof's office with the prof stating that he would control the interview and that Dr Raj and Ben were to act strictly as observers. The prof pressed the button to light up the 'enter' sign outside the office door and Mr Hemmingway appeared. At first sight it was clear that he was nothing like his namesake Ernest. He was middle-aged, a little over five feet tall, balding, and wore National Health Service wire-framed glasses. He was clean shaven and had a pinkish tinge to his face, which looked like that of a prepubescent child who had not yet seen the need to use a razor. He was dressed in a two-piece grey flannel suit over a patterned jumper, a white shirt with a buttoned-down collar, stripped tie with matching hanky, almost certainly a strip of folded material attached to a piece of cardboard peeping out of his top jacket pocket. Scuffed black lace-up shoes completed his outfit. All together he appeared to be devoid of any characteristics which would make him stand out; in fact he could be described as Mr Anonymous. The prof asked him about his family details and it turned out that he lived with his elderly mother on the Landings Estate and worked in the Exworth central library. He spoke in a high-pitched rather squeaky voice but in a flat monotone way, showing neither emotion nor anxiety. It wasn't until the prof asked him about the reason for his visit to the clinic that he really became animated. The change was instant and he sat bolt upright and announced anxiously but with more than a hint of pride that he was a sex manic. The prof showed no surprise and simply asked him to elaborate, which he did with apparent delight. He went on to explain that he saw all sorts of people, animals and inanimate objects as sexually attractive and that if it had an orifice to be penetrated he felt the urge to oblige.

'It doesn't matter where I am, the urges are with me all the time and it has got me in difficult situations time after time. Why it was only last week that I had to go to casualty to get Mum's vacuum hose removed from a delicate part of my anatomy.'

Mr Hemmingway had all the appearances of wanting to go into more detail of his activities and was becoming ever more excited at having a 'safe audience' to relay his exploits to. Prof finally had heard enough and sat back in his chair, slid his glasses down his nose and looking over the top of them said, 'Well, Mr Hemmingway, from all your wealth of experience what do you think is best?'

Mr H gave it some careful consideration before announcing, 'Well I have to admit that a woman is best, but a mule comes a close second!'

Everyone in the room erupted with laughter, including Mr Hemingway, and the interview came to a natural end.

Rather surprisingly, the prof offered to see Mr Hemingway again at the day hospital for counselling and Mr Hemingway seemed very pleased to agree. Once the patient had left the prof confided that his doctor friend had explained that Mr H was impotent, having the rare condition of undeveloped testicles. The condition was incurable and all his exploits were fantasies.

'The poor man has never come to terms with his condition and he is effectively a eunuch. He desperately needs to be heard and his frustrations listened to but he has had no one to tell.'

The prof had seen him as a favour to his friend who was genuinely concerned that Mr Hemingway might be suicidal. The prof had involved Dr Raj and Ben as it was an unusual referral to the clinic and he had thought it would be a learning experience for them. He admitted to himself that he had enjoyed seeing Dr Raj's and Ben's faces as the interview unfolded and he hadn't anticipated that it would end up with them all laughing together.

'Not very professional, I am afraid, but hey, we all need light relief from time to time and I will do my best to help him come to terms with his condition. Time to go home then, gentlemen, see you next week, Ben.'

Ben grinned all the way home at the thought of the little man mounting a mule. He said out loud to himself, 'He is such a little chap he would have needed a step ladder!'

Chapter 36

Many Happy Returns

Ben woke up with a start as two solid lumps landed heavily on him in the bed. The boy's birthday greetings were forceful but well intentioned and came complete with homemade cards and roughly wrapped parcels. Sandy was nowhere to be seen and he guessed she had slipped out of bed without waking him to make the coffee, which he could already smell from the kitchen. The boys' visit was rapidly turning into a rough and tumble when she appeared in the doorway with two steaming mugs of coffee. She quickly took control and the boys briefly settled down, one each side of Ben whilst he opened his gifts and praised their cards. It was clear that it all had been prepared very recently as the theme running through them all was speedway and they had only been introduced to that four days before.

Ben guessed that Sandy had had a hand in the presents, which were a Swindon Robin's scarf and a mug with a picture on it featuring an action shot of bikes in a race. But there was no doubt that the cards were all the boys' own work and he was impressed with the amount of care they had taken and made a point of praising them and gave them each a big hug. Never ones for cuddling too long, the boys galloped off downstairs to find some mischief to get into. Sandy slipped off her dressing gown and took the boys' place in bed with Ben. They sat side by side enjoying their coffee and cuddled together for warmth and comfort.

She said, 'Happy birthday, love, I am going to give you a special day,' and as she said it she gave a throaty giggle and ran her hand briefly down Ben's body. She laughed at his body's immediate reaction but he was too slow in grabbing her and she popped back out of bed saying, 'All in good time, my boy, all in good time.'

Ben lay back with a smile in the realisation that Sandy had every intention of repaying him for their Beatles day, but in her own inimitable fashion.

In the past his birthday had always been a low-key event usually involving a meal out or a trip to the cinema. His present had always been clothing and a traditional packet of Peter Stuyvesant cigarettes. That tradition had begun whilst they were at university and had started when they saw a really cool advert for the cigarettes at a cinema. The adverts were always fronted by a tall slim rugged cowboy who carried a paper pack of Peter Stuyvesant in his shirt pocket. In the adverts there was inevitably a group of attractive girls swooning over the cowboy as he casually took the packet out and shook a single cigarette straight between his lips. The underlying message was simple: 'be cool and smoke Peter Stuyvesant and you get the best-looking girls'. Ben quickly found out it didn't work for him and that the packet quickly became crumpled and the cigarettes mashed. But it had been an in-joke between them ever since on his birthday, but not this year as he had given up smoking.

By the time Ben had managed to finally rouse himself from his bed, had his shower and got dressed Sandy had the boys ready for their sleepover at Gran Newman's. The boys were excited and keen to get there but this was mainly because they were going to set up the Scalextric rather than any pleasure in seeing their grandparents. Ben's mother welcomed the boys warmly but they quickly removed themselves from her embrace and headed for the conservatory whilst she led Ben into the kitchen. They were soon sat clutching a couple of mugs of tea when Ben's mother let out a long sigh and looked rather sorry for herself. Ben couldn't help but pick up on her mood and asked her if she was all right. She gave him a weak smile and said she was feeling a bit down as it was a year ago this month that Martha had died so suddenly. For the life of him Ben couldn't think who she was talking about and he was pretty sure that there were no neighbours or friends of that name that he knew of. She went on to describe the terrible shock it had been when Martha had collapsed and died in the local pub but it was still ringing no bells with him. Finally he asked which pub it had been and was more than a little surprised when his mother replied

"The Rovers Return, of course."

Then it all fell into place that she was talking about a character, Martha Longhurst, who had been one of the major characters in the soap 'Coronation Street' along with the forceful Enid Sharples and the more gentle Minnie Caldwell. He had forgotten how much his mum lived her life vicariously through watching several of the soaps with a passion that was largely absent in the rest of her day-to-day life. He remembered the time around when he had just started university when he had received a letter from his mother that he could swear was stained with actual tear drops. She had been listening to her daily dose of 'The Archers' on the radio and Grace Archer had just died in a fire at her stables when she was trying to rescue her horse Midnight. His mother was clearly devastated but she wasn't alone, as middle-aged ladies all across the country had gone into mourning. Ben let her ramble on and thought about his parents' relationship, which he had realised years ago was a life shared but only half-heartedly and with a marked absence of joy. His mum had her soaps, her church and her bingo and his dad had his allotment, his train watching and his sport, but although they had rubbed along for years it was without any shared interests; very sad but he suspected not uncommon. After he had said goodbye to the boys, who were still preoccupied with setting up the track, he headed for home but on impulse took a deviation to drop in on his father at the allotment.

As he went in through the five-barred gate he could see several people working away on their various plots but there was no sign of activity on his dad's plot. He went down the grassy path leading to his dad's shed with confidence as the flag was flying on his neighbour's flagpole and it was flying at half-mast. He guessed his dad was in company with his former railway colleague, probably mourning the demise of their beloved railway station, and there was a long blast from a passing railway train as if in sympathetic support. As he approached the rear of the shed he could hear a protracted conversation going on together with the sound of liquid being poured into a bucket. It sounded as if tea was on the way but he was wrong in all his expectations. On stepping off the path on to the seating area in front of the shed he was met by his dad coming out of the shed zipping up his fly. His dad was totally unfazed by the interruption and went over and emptied the bucket on to the compost heap with the words, 'Urine is the beat activator for making good compost that there is, and it's free.'

Well, thought Ben, *you live and learn!* His dad then reached back into the shed and produced a small portable radio which was playing a live commentary of the Lord's test match. This shed was clearly his home from home and he put a chair out for Ben, lit his pipe and sat down on his bum-shaped bag of compost with a contented sigh. Ben explained that he had just dropped the boys off and had popped in to thank him for the birthday present his mum had given him from them both. The look of surprise, hastily covered up, was a sure sign that his dad knew nothing about it so Ben opened his jacket to display the new sweater that he had put on at once to please his mum. Any further embarrassment was avoided by the arrival of his dad's allotment neighbour, the old station master Arnold Farmer, armed with an empty mug obviously intending to share some time with Mr Newman senior. Ben offered him his chair, shook hands and left them to their railway reminiscences. As he got to the gate there was another mournful blast from a passing train as another driver reacted to the flag flying at half-mast.

As Ben pulled up at home he saw that his usual parking place right outside his house was taken up by a familiar Mercedes. He could smell Patricia's exotic perfume long before he joined her in the kitchen. Sandy and Patricia were sat each side of the kitchen table, each clutching a mug of coffee and in deep girly chat. Patricia jumped straight up and came around to Ben to land a warm kiss on his cheek, filling his nostrils with her heady perfume and causing him to blush like a schoolboy.

'Happy birthday, my love,' she said and returned to her place at the table with Sandy grinning at his discomfort. He started to reply with, 'Thanks, Patricia, very kind of you,' only to be interrupted by her saying, 'For goodness sake call me Patsie, Patricia sounds so formal. I know I am nearly old enough to be your mother but I am Patsie to all my friends and that certainly includes you.'

Ben smiled to himself, looking Patsie up and down and mentally comparing her to his own mother who he had just visited. He tried to imagine his mum dressed as Patsie was, knee-length boots below a denim mini skirt topped off with a flamboyant silky blouse displaying a generous amount of cleavage. He suspected it would not be a pretty sight and momentarily felt disloyal, but his eye then fell on a long flat chromed gadget which ran down the length of the kitchen table and he rapidly changed the subject by asking about it. Patsie laughed and said that she was always attracted to new gadgets and this was her latest, an electric plate warmer for keeping food warm. 'I brought it over for Sandy to see.'

Ben glanced around the kitchen and saw that there was a total absence of food but said nothing as he suspected his birthday treat would therefore involve a meal out. He went back into the living room, leaving the girls to their conversation whilst he stretched out on the sofa in front of the television and watched the update of the day's football fixtures. Patsie left soon after, pausing only to lean over and give him another kiss on the cheek, which because of his prone position involved an interesting view down her blouse front. Her accompanying smile made it quite clear she was aware of his enjoyment and she swept out of the front door with a swing of her hips. Sandy watching from the kitchen doorway felt a hint of jealousy but said nothing, returning to the stove to heat up some soup for lunch. The afternoon was a non-event. The house was very quiet with the boys being away and Sandy seemed content to get on with some housework and to tackle the mountain of ironing that always seemed to be building up. She made no mention of any plans to celebrate his birthday and Ben was determined not to pry. The obvious elephant in the room was not mentioned by either of them and the first football results were coming through when the doorbell rang.

Ben wasn't surprised when he opened the door to a smiling Dave, as he had heard the familiar buzz of pink peril as it had pulled up outside. Dave gave him a bear hug and produced a large bottle of the dreaded Jamaican rum from his rucksack.

'Happy birthday, mister, here's a drop of medicine to help you cope with your advanced years,' and Dave passed the bottle to Ben, only for him to have it grabbed by Sandy, who stated firmly that it was not time for medicine just yet and offered coffee instead. The two men settled back on the sofa to watch the football results whilst they chatted over the season so far for Dave's local football team. Coffee duly arrived with a bowl of crisps and another of peanuts which the men tucked into, but there was still a total absence of other food being prepared. Just after 6 pm the bell went again and Ben opened the door to the diminutive figure of Ma Driscoll dressed in her best full-length fur coat and carrying an armful of different shaped parcels. Ben welcomed her in and went to help her with the parcels and to remove her coat. Both offers were rather forcefully rejected and she headed to the relative security of the kitchen, leaving him none the wiser.

If Dave knew what was going on he was not saying anything and just gave a rather gormless shrug in answer to Ben's enquiries. Working on the basis that anything going to happen was beyond his control he joined Dave on the sofa and changed sides on the television to watch 'Juke Box Jury' with them, joining in by voting hit or miss to each new record introduced by David Jacobs. The evening stretched on and it was almost seven-thirty when the bell went for a third and final time and Sandy hurried to open the door to Patsie, Roddie and Tony, all of them loaded down with carrier bags, and as ever Patsie's entrance involved a distinctive smell. This time it wasn't her perfume but the welcomed smell of mouth-watering food. All three of them headed to the kitchen with Patsie pausing long enough to give Ben yet another birthday kiss. With gastric juices responding to the delicious smells Ben and Dave were told to wait to be called but within moments Ben was being directed to the seat at the head of the table. The full length of the hot plate was loaded down with dish after dish of strange looking aromatic food which was unlike anything Ben had ever had before. Ma was at the far end of the table and made a deep bow to each of the others in turn. As she made each bow she said, 'Ning hao, haun ning,' and after a couple of these greetings everybody in turn made an effort to mimic the words. Ma explained that what they had just said was hello and welcome in Chinese. At this point Ma swept off her precious fur coat to reveal a most gorgeous scarlet kimono decorated with massive gold-thread embroidered chrysanthemums on the front and then she did a twirl, paused and spread her arms to display on her back a ferocious dragon also picked out in gold thread. The whole effect was a work of art and they all broke out into spontaneous clapping, much to Ma's obvious delight. She went on to explain that she had spent the first twelve years of her life with her parents in Singapore where her father had been working in the colonial service.

'I didn't learn much Chinese as I went to a special English school, but we did have Chinese servants and I was close to one in particular, Mi Ling, who was our cook. I spent hours with her in the kitchen and she taught me all about Chinese food and it has been a favourite type of cooking for me ever since. So tonight, you are going to have an authentic Chinese meal and to eat it you will each have your own chopsticks.'

She produced a stack of chopsticks, enough for a great game of pooh sticks, from a deep pocket in her kimono and passed them around the table. She then proceeded to describe the various dishes laid out on the hot plate leaving everyone totally confused by the various chow mein, stir fried and chop suey dishes many with vegetables that Ben had never heard of. He commented that he had never heard of eating such things as bamboo slices, water chestnuts or beansprouts and the only time he had ever eaten rice had been his mum's rice pudding and it had looked nothing like the rice dishes in front of them. There were serving spoons provided with each dish and Ma demonstrated how one mixed up a choice from any of the tin foil containers that the food had come in into individual warm basins. She then lifted her basin to her mouth and with neat shovelling motions of her chopsticks moved the food into her mouth without spilling any.

'Or if you want to you can use your chopsticks like this to pick up individual bits,' which she demonstrated with a deftness born of long practice. Everybody helped themselves from the containers and experimented cautiously with the variety of sauces which had been provided, each in its own little pot. So far so good, but within moments the table was littered with dropped food as the group made a pig's ear of transferring food from their bowls to their mouths. Sandy soon took pity on them and passed spoons around as a working alternative to the chop sticks. The food was delicious and everyone became more and more adventurous, trying things which they were barely able to identify. The ladies persevered much longer than the men with the chopsticks but before long they too had given up in the cause of getting a fair share of the feast. Ma carried on alone, enjoying her expertise with the chop sticks being admired by the rest of the group. Ben listened with interest when Patsie explained that she and Robbie had been invited to attend the grand opening of the first Chinese restaurant in town called 'The Oriental Palace' about a month before.

'We thought the food was delicious and were chuffed to learn it was possible to order takeaway from anything on the menu. I happened to mention it to Sandy and your birthday experience just fell into place. It was made complete when Sandy told Ma about it and she told us of her early experience in Singapore.'

Dave then produced several large bottles of Coca-Cola from his haversack and took the top off of the rum bottle. 'Who's for rum and coke then?'

He passed glasses of coke around closely followed by the rum bottle, from which some topped up their drinks. Patsie and Tony declined as they were driving and Dave, who was also driving, said 'just the one' and was surprisingly careful with his top up. The rest poured more generously and Robbie in particular had a heavy hand. The hot plate did its stuff and the food remained hot and tempting with everyone returning time and again for further helpings. The conversation flowed back and forth when eventually Tony announced that he had a further drive for the Swindon Robins on the following day. This led on to Ben asking how the Scadding's Speedway track development was proceeding by saying, 'So how are the Exworth Totters getting on?'

The air was suddenly electric, with the whole Scadding Family reacting with pleasure. Robbie quickly interjected with, 'Ben, my boy, you are a bloody genius, we have been trying for weeks to come up with a unique name for our team and you have got it in one.'

From the expressions on everyone's face it was clear that the new team had been christened. The conversation went on and before long they were trying to come up with suggestions for a name for the local cycle racing club who were hoping to share the facilities. Finally, it was Tony who came up with 'The Highfield Scrappers' and it was agreed that it was just the right description for the lads from the estate and Robbie said he would suggest the name to Roger Richards, the local bobby organising the enterprise as soon as possible.

'In fact I have an interview programmed for next week with the local sports reporter who wants to do an update report on the speedway development. With any luck we may even get a mention in the nationals and our catchy title might just swing it for us. It's cost a small fortune so far and the sooner we get the crowds in the sooner we can start recouping our expenditure. So every bit of advertising is going to help and I am hoping that between Patsie and myself we can get a regular mention in the press.'

The eating and drinking went on for ages and Sandy produced hot banana and pineapple fritters dripping in syrup from the oven where they had been keeping warm. Finally, everyone came to a halt and retired to the living room to recover from the blow out. The atmosphere was terrific and Ben sat back in his armchair and looked around the gathering. There was no doubt that they were a mixed group of people but the most amazing thing he realised was that neither Sandy nor he had known any of his guests at the time of his last birthday a year ago. It had certainly been a productive year as far as new friends were concerned and he felt very lucky to have made such good friends in such a short time. It was Ma who came up with the suggestion of playing a game that was from her own childhood, which she described as a bit silly but good fun. The combination of good food, good company and quite a lot of consumed rum meant that the group were up for anything and Ma went over to a corner with a pad of paper, which she wrote on and then folded up as individual sheets.

'Now this is a simply game, all you have to do is act out what is written on the piece of paper that you choose and the rest of us have to try and guess what you are imitating; I will start to demonstrate.'

The pieces of paper were placed in a paper bag and given a good shake before she pulled one out and read it to herself. She then proceeded to waddle around the room, arms flapping at her side and her chin pointed upwards and moving from side to side. It was a very reasonable interpretation of a penguin and was recognised as such in seconds, much to Ma's pleasure. Next to perform was Tony, who bounced around the room thumping his chest. The room were convinced that he was a gorilla but Ma refused that suggestion as she knew what she had written on the slips. The jumping around and chest thumping continued but although various monkeys were offered as suggestions all were declined by Ma. Finally they gave up and Tony told them that he was a silverback which was greeted by a groan all round, Ma just laughed.

At this juncture Robbie went off to the loo and Ma grabbed the opportunity to set him up. With a twinkle in her eye she explained what they should do and the plan was in place by the time Robbie re-joined the group. The next one to go was Ben, who was soon down on all fours slowly crawling around the room extending his neck as far as possible before quickly withdrawing it into his shoulders. Ben's tortoise impersonation was closely folded by Dave's hedgehog which involved him rolling into a ball and staying like it until someone guessed what he was. It came to Robbie's turn and he proceeded to stomp heavy footed around the room with one arm stretched out in front of him which he swayed from side to side, clearly acting out an elephant. A giraffe, an orang-utan, a cow and so on with ever more unlikely animals being suggested, much to Robbie's increasing frustration. He stomped even more heavily and added loud trumpeting to his performance, with only even more ridiculous suggestions coming from his audience who by this time were struggling to contain their laughter. Then the penny dropped for Robbie who said, 'You buggers are having me on.'

The game came to an end with Sandy curling up in front of the fire pretending to clean herself like a cat and Patsie being a chicken clucking away and even appearing to lay a real egg which she had smuggled in from the kitchen.

Around ten o'clock Dave said that he was sorry but he would have to be leaving quite soon as he had to start work at six on the following day. Both Tony and Ma added that they would also have to leave shortly, one to get ready to go to Swindon for the Sunday speedway and the other to be open for the Sunday papers, which was always a busy time. Patsie and Sandy went into the kitchen and there was soon the smell of coffee brewing. Patsie reappeared with a tray of mugs and a coffee pot of real coffee perked in yet another of her kitchen gadgets saying, 'This is the real thing, none of your instant Nescafé here.'

She was joined by Sandy carrying a mouth-watering chocolate cake complete with lighted candles and she added, 'This is the real thing too, none of your shop-bought rubbish, this a handmade Ma Driscoll special reputed throughout the civilised world.'

Ma's smile said it all.

Over coffee and chocolate cake the chat continued and Ma was telling everybody how much she had enjoyed Christmas Day with Sandy and the family. Sandy suddenly stood up and said, 'Talking of Christmas reminds me I have got another surprise for you, Ben, it's in the bedroom.'

This resulted in rather ribald laughter all round and wolf whistles from Dave. Sandy took their reaction calmly and continued, 'All right you lot I didn't mean that,' then added, 'but you never know your luck, it is your birthday after all.'

She skipped out of the room with a toss of her head and left her audience more than a bit nonplussed. A few moments later she reappeared, carrying a large flat rectangular parcel covered in thick brown paper and tied up securely with string. She put it down carefully on the coffee table and apologised that it was rather coated in dust.

'It's been hidden under our bed for weeks and I am not the most thorough of cleaners, but I knew neither Ben nor the boys would spot it there.'

She hovered behind Ben waiting to see his reaction and as he had everyone's full attention he deliberately took his time undoing the string even pausing to roll it up once he had removed it. Finally, he pulled back the paper and after a rather stunned silence simply said, 'Wow that's just exquisite, thanks, love, I love it.'

The parcel contained a large oak picture frame containing the Victorian jigsaw puzzle of the twelve days of Christmas that Ma had given them back in December. It had obviously been framed by a professional and the result was something unique and truly special. Ma cried real tears with delight and Ben felt that he could easily have joined her, but instead got up to Sandy and kissed her passionately and then reached out and hugged Ma. The party finished on a high note.

Dave was the first to leave and they could hear the buzz on the pink peril all the way down the road and away into the distance. Tony and Ma followed close on his heels and they all came out to see them off. Ma stood outside staring at Tony's shining bike and said rather pensively, 'I have always had a secret ambition to have a ride on a motorbike but my parents always forbid me saying it was dangerous and unladylike, but it has always looked such fun.'

Without any hesitation Tony popped his helmet on Ma's head and said, 'No time like the present, girl,' and kicked the bike into life.

With surprising agility for a lady in her eighties Ma clambered aboard and wrapped her arms firmly around Tony, who nodded his head and revved up the engine. With maximum noise but at an appropriate speed the pair drove down the road with Ma's fur coat blowing out behind her, exposing a flash of scarlet from her kimono. The amazing old woman even managed a wave as they passed under the streetlight and turned the corner at the end of the road, giving just a hint of gold dragon's tail as they turned. The remaining four of them just burst out laughing and Patsie said that she would have loved to have got that filmed with her cine camera.

Patsie wanted to help Sandy to clear up but was told firmly that it could wait until the morning with hugs all round and the by-now usual flirtatious kiss for Ben from Patsie before she got into the driving seat of the Mercedes. Sandy presented Patsie with a good-sized hunk of the chocolate cake safely contained in one of her best Tupperware boxes and Roddie sat in and appeared to drop off to sleep before she had even turned on the ignition. Strong stuff that Jamaican rum. Someone was going to have a sore head in the morning. Ben and Sandy went back inside and started to make a cursory start at tidying up by getting all the waste food in a carrier bag, which was taken straight out to the dustbin. Sandy pushed Ben towards the stairs saying that she would just stack the plates and would follow him up to bed. Within a couple of minutes he had cleaned his teeth, had a swift wash and had undressed for bed, wearing just a tee shirt as usual. He lay back and thought through his birthday and was very content that it had been a total surprise and very special.

Sandy seemed to spend forever in the bathroom and he could feel his eyes closing and began to switch off ready for sleep when Sandy sprang into the room singing 'No, No Regrets' in a sexy French accent. Her hair was tied back in two bunches and she was uncharacteristically wearing a lot of makeup. She had her usual housecoat on but she slipped it slowly off her shoulders and let it fall to the floor.

'Hello, Monsieur Ben, I am Bridget, your playmate, come to play with you.'

Ben immediately realised that she was still playing the acting game and this time she was being Brigitte Bardot, who had long been his fantasy woman. To add to the attraction she was wearing the Anne Summer's underwear that had been languishing at the back of her underwear drawer for months; all thoughts he had had of sleep had disappeared and he reached out for her with a growl. Sandy threw herself down on the bed and still with the same French accent said, 'Come on, big boy, help yourself.'

Ben needed no second bidding and the boisterous and noisy sex which followed was reminiscent of their student days. It was great to be able to be uninhibited with the boys being away and fortunately they knew that Mr and Mrs Reed, the elderly couple living next door, were both deaf as posts. After all that food and especially the rum it was no marathon, but as sprints go it was up there with the best of them.

Chapter 37

The Storm After the Lull

With the boys still at their gran's Ben and Sandy were able to get up in a much more leisurely way than usual and both of them were still in their dressing gowns for most of the morning. After a late fried breakfast and yet more coffee made in Patsie's percolator they reluctantly cleaned it along with the food warmer and packed them both up ready to return to her. They then turned their attention to the dirty dishes and the kitchen was soon looking straight before they went upstairs again to get themselves washed and dressed. That would normally only take a few minutes but they were both still in a playful mood and the horseplay that followed had inevitable consequences.

What passed for Sunday lunch was simply bread and cheese, which avoided making a proper family Sunday lunch as they were confident that Gran Newman would have fed the boys a full roast. They went to collect the boys in the afternoon and were greeted by two very hyperactive young boys. Sandy was sure that they had been thoroughly spoilt and strongly suspected that their sugar intake from sweets, cakes, biscuits and fizzy drinks had been way up, but she made no comment. As usual Ben's dad was 'down the allotment' and Sandy was sorry to have missed him as she had always been fond of him and was secretly sympathetic about his life with his wife.

As they pulled away from the house Ben suggested that they could call in at the allotment as it would give the boys the chance to run off some steam. The suggestion was welcomed all round and they turned left at the end of the road rather than the normal way home to the right. The boys had their usual swing on the gate before running down the path to their grandad's hut and were soon arming themselves with bean sticks before setting off on their adventures. As Ben and Sandy arrived at the hut they were greeted with the familiar shout from Ben's dad of, 'Keep to the paths.' He was clearly pleased to see Sandy, who had never been to the allotment before and made a fuss of her as he pulled out the spare chair and turned off the cricket that he had been listening to on the radio. Ben was left standing so he just leant against the shed and looked out for trains. The flag was flying at full mast and before long there was a brief toot from a distant passing train and Sandy received the full story of the old station closed by the evil Beeching. Ben's dad was quickly on his high horse and the statistics of the infamous Beeching 1963 report rolled readily off his tongue.

'He recommended the closure of over 2000 stations and 5000 miles of railway line. In that one report he brought about the closure of 55% of stations and 30% of route miles. Our lovely little station was one of those closed and it has now been demolished and wiped off the map. Hours of work we put into it and we won the best-kept branch line station on no less than seven times. Now it's all gone and the world is a worse place without it.' Sandy realised that her father in law was near to tears and she put her arm around him and remained quiet. The boys came galloping back at that point and Mr Newman senior covered up his distress by saying he had something to show them and led them part way down the allotment.

He showed the boys several rows of growing carrots which he said needed thinning out and helped them to pull out little bunches, leaving a single carrot every couple of inches along the first row. Most of the carrots that were thinned were very underdeveloped and he put these to one side and selected a handful of the larger specimens. He then led the boys up to the stand pipe and washed them off before returning to the shed. Once he had returned to his compost seat he dug his pruning knife out of his pocket and topped and tailed the washed carrots. These were passed around and once tasted were voted a hit by them all and the boys amazingly ate raw vegetables by choice for the first time ever.

Now fully back in control of his emotions he started to point out various features of the allotments to Sandy. In particular he pointed out two elderly ladies who were busying themselves on the allotment below his.

'They are sisters who worked together as teachers in London for years before retiring and coming to live in Exworth to be near to their elderly mother, who is well into her nineties. They had always planned to retire to the country to grow their own food and keep a few animals but had to put their plans on hold in order to care for their mother. So they have taken two allotments next door to each other and are using them to develop their skills. The two Miss Hiscocks, Doris and Connie, were seen as something of a joke at first as nobody gave them any chance of getting on top of their plots, which hadn't been worked properly for years and were in a terrible state. But they proved everyone wrong and gradually earned the respect of their fellow plot holders by virtue of their determination and hard work. Then they decided to start keeping chickens despite everyone telling them that they would quickly be targeted by one of the several foxes that inhabited the allotments.'

Sandy pricked up her ears upon hearing the word chickens as she had always had a secret ambition to keep hens but had never had the chance. Mr Newman continued, 'They did their homework and constructed a sturdy fox-proof pen with the side fences buried a couple of feet into the ground and surrounded by large stones to prevent burrowing. The result has been frustrated foxes and contented chickens so much so that I had two eggs with double yolks in the last box of eggs that I bought, which is a sure sign of happy hens.'

He could see Sandy's interest and reached into the shed and produced a couple of empty egg cartons, which he passed over to Sandy and told her that the Miss Hiscocks loved nothing more than talking about their chickens and were always keen to sell a few eggs. Of course the boys wanted to go as well and he directed the boys to collect up the remaining carrot thinnings and to take them to feed to the chickens. When they arrived at the gate to the chicken pen both of the Miss Hiscocks were inside, each holding a chicken to which they seemed to be talking warmly. The ladies appeared to be of similar age, both wore their hair up in a tight bun, and were both wearing much darned sweaters over long tweed skirts and heavy walking boots. They looked nothing like any teachers Sandy had ever known but when they saw the boys they promptly went into full teacher mode. They invited them into the pen and introduced them to the two hens they were holding.

'This is Henrietta, one of our oldest chickens which we have had since she was a small chick, and I am afraid to say she is a bit of a favourite. She likes nothing better than a bit of a cuddle and having the top of her head and neck rubbed. Here, try for yourself.'

Without any further hesitation she pressed the hen into Sandy's arms and turned her attention to the boys. By this time they were surrounded by other chickens all showing interest in the carrots the boys had brought with them and with the Miss Hiscock's permission they distributed them to the flapping throng. They all looked remarkably similar with the exception of a strutting white cockerel, which was making sure that he was getting the bulk of the goodies.

'That's Spike and he can be a bit of a bully if he doesn't get his own way but the girls all seem to love him and he has fathered several clutches of chicks. Come and see the latest ones.'

The two ladies led the boys over to a small shed and opened the door to show a small group of chicks cuddled together under a paraffin stove hanging from the roof. The boys were enchanted and even more so when they were encouraged to hold one each for a few moments. Meanwhile, Sandy was still holding Henrietta, who seemed very content having her head rubbed. Sandy told the ladies how she had always dreamed of keeping chickens ever since she had gone on a farm holiday as a young child.

'This has been a real treat for me being able to hold one for the first time and we would love to buy some eggs if you have any to spare.'

The chicks were returned to their friends and the shed door closed up tight to keep in the warmth before they proceeded to the rear of the hen house to see what they could find. A long flap was opened up to expose a row of nesting boxes, several of which contained eggs. The boys were each allowed to choose two eggs and their names were written on them in felt pen by one of the two ladies. The other took the boxes Sandy had brought with her and filled them with a further eight eggs. Money changed hands and the boys set off to show their grandfather their spoils. The two Miss Hiscocks called after them an instruction to make sure they washed their hands under the standpipe, a case of once a teacher always a teacher.

To Sandy's surprise Ben was thinning out the next row of carrots under his father's direction and passing them to his dad who was gathering up a bundle of the largest of them. To her certain knowledge, Ben had never shown any interest in gardening, so this was proving to be a day of new experiences for the whole family. Mr Newman senior passed the bunch of carrots over to Sandy in the manner of giving a bunch of flowers and she kissed him on the cheek before heading back up the path for the boys to have their predictable swing on the gate.

Just before they got home they called in on Ma Driscoll to collect a paper and check she was all right after her excitement of the previous day and she seemed just fine. She immediately produced two large lucky bags from beneath the counter, which she had filled up with the boy's favourite penny sweets. She wisely passed these to Sandy, who thanked her and said she would dole them out over several days. Tea that day was a forgone conclusion. Boiled eggs with soldiers and small but sweet raw carrot sticks. There were no double yokes but the yokes were a rich yellow and tasted so much better than the shop-bought ones. Not quite the Newmans becoming hunters and gatherers, but a start in the right direction and it felt good.

Monday was wet and windy and the windscreen wipers had to work flat out to barely cope with the downpour. The office carpark was awash and the short trip from the car to the doorway left Ben dripping wet and his shoes, which were inclined to leak, meant he would have wet socks for most of the day. He headed for the toilet and grabbed a handful of paper towels, which he used to make a rather ineffectual mop up. Returning to his office he had no sooner sat at his desk than he received a visitor.

It wasn't the usual Alice bearing a cup of tea but quite the most mournful looking visitor he had received in yonks. He wasn't sure a dog could be described as mournful but The Champ fitted the description to perfection. His head was down and he was encumbered with a large lampshade shaped collar which was obviously designed to prevent him chewing at his injured foot. If he hadn't looked so sad Ben would have been tempted to laugh and the bandaged foot only added to the overall comic effect as it was wrapped in what looked like part of a Tesco carrier bag and was tied in place with red ribbon. Ben reached for the biscuit tin and The Champ responded instinctively by thumping his tail several times on the floor and gobbled down the offered biscuit before resuming his mournful appearance. Never one to miss a trick, thought Ben who gave him a second biscuit as a reward for his acting ability. Alice arrived with his regular cup of tea and sat herself across from Ben and proceeded to make a fuss of The Champ.

'Who's a big brave boy then?' she said as if talking to a small child and she cuddled The Champ's head on her lap and fed him the couple of biscuits which would normally accompany Ben's cuppa. She then went into a long and detailed account of the visit to the PDSA on the previous Saturday, stressing how brave the dog had been and how kind Susie had been throughout. Never one to use one word when three would do she rambled on, stopping from time to time to praise The Champ. Ben quickly got the gist of the story but let her carry on as the subject was a big improvement over her usual diatribe about her bowels. She explained that the vet had told them to keep the foot dry, hence the Tesco bag, and they had been given some antiseptic spray to be used at morning and night. They had a follow-up visit programmed for a couple of weeks' time and meanwhile The Champ was spending each day with Alice whilst Ernest was at work. The telephone ringing rescued Ben and Alice and The Champ headed off to the kitchen, content in each other's company. Susie popped her head around the door a few minutes later and sat in the seat vacated by Alice and repeated much of what Ben had been told earlier but in a much more concise form.

Following an x-ray it had been discovered that The Champ had 'a foreign body' deeply imbedded in his paw and the vet had said that the dog must have been in severe pain as the site was infected. The Champ was given a local injection and the vet had cut into the paw to remove the object and clean out the wound. He then showed them the evil-looking bit of rusty barbed wire he had removed and said that with good care The Champ should be back on four legs quite quickly.

'Poor old Ernest and Alice were both terrified and sat and held hands throughout the procedure. I was so glad I was there and really felt we were achieving something really good. It also made me think how funny life can be at times. There was Ernest in his twenties labelled subnormal along with Alice in her fifties with a long history of mental illness, both doing their best to care for The Champ. Three waifs and strays coming together to make up a strange but meaningful family group. It was lovely and I felt very privileged to be able to help them along. If you don't mind

I would like to see the job through with them when they go for the follow-up visit to the vet.'

Ben was happy to oblige, thinking once again what an asset to the team Susie was proving to be. Ernest called in to check on The Champ several times during the day each time putting him on his lead and taking him for a brief walk about the car park 'to do his business'. Any business done was promptly cleared up by Ernest with his shovel and cart whilst Alice rubbed The Champ dry with a warm towel she had prepared in the oven. Ernest's final act after every visit was to give The Champ a sausage from the bag donated by Joe to aid the dog's convalescence. Ernest proudly announced that everyone he met on the estate wanted to know how The Champ was doing and he told Ben that he reckoned that the dog really was The Champ of Highfield. Meanwhile the office ran as normal with everyone pausing from time to time to make a fuss of the dog; he lapped it up. Ben even noticed Phil showing an interest which would never have happened in the past when she had tended to keep herself to herself at best and could be downright surly at worse. Phil seemed a much happier lady of late, long may it last.

Later in the morning Oliver rang to confirm that the letter about Ernest's proposed move was going in the post that day and to warn Ben to be ready for Ernest to bring in for him to deal with. Ben was a bit apprehensive that it wasn't the best of times for Ernest to cope with another problem but realised that Oliver had gone out on a limb to try and help Ernest. Ben just thanked Oliver for all his help and prayed to himself that things would go well. Every day that week Ernest called in several times a day to see to the dog, but the only post he brought in was an odd bill and the usual junk and did not include the anticipated letter. Wednesday afternoon was the time of the planned joint visit to the Sullivans and Ben focused his mind on the job in hand. The lift to the top floor of Chelsea House rattled and groaned as if it was all too much effort but got them safely to their destination. The pile of boxes Susie had told him about was still outside the front door and Ben lifted the flaps of the top box to uncover an almost empty box of packs of export cigarettes.

'That was full when I last visited,' Susie said, 'so it looks as if Rosie has really stepped up her consumption,' and she rang the front door bell.

It seemed a long time before Frank's distinctive footsteps and the related clanking of his callipers could be heard coming to the door. Susie had forewarned Ben that Frank had been unwell of late but the gaunt figure that opened the door still came as a shock. Frank's unwashed hair was badly in need of a cut and the skin on his face seemed almost translucent, apart from heavy black lines around his eyes. Ben followed him into the flat and watched as he held the walls and furniture to maintain his balance as he found his way back to his armchair. He sank into the chair with a deep sigh as Ben struggled to cope with the overpowering smell of stale tobacco. Looking around, Ben could see that the whole place was grubby and uncared for and he moved his attention to Rosie, who was sat in a corner consuming the latest in a long line of 'fags', but she made no reaction to their arrival. He had seen her looking worse but remembered that she had spent a day at the residential home Elmore House on the Monday so would have come back with her hair done and having been given a bath. The care staff would have made sure she had come home in fresh clothes rescued from their bountiful supply of deceased resident's donations. From her appearance Ben suspected she had not changed any clothes since and had slept in what she had on, which was crumpled and liberally covered in ash.

Frank and Ben just looked at each other with both realising that things had got out of hand. Frank seemed to be struggling for breath and from time to time rubbed his arm and his chest in what appeared to be unconscious reactions to pain. Susie automatically went into the kitchen to make a cup of tea and Ben could hear her washing dishes and generally tidying up. He felt sure that Frank would formerly have objected to someone taking over his duties but he was now past caring and just said to Ben that she was a little gem. Whilst they drank their tea Susie sat down by Frank and together they drew up a shopping list with Susie going in and out of the kitchen to check the contents of cupboards with a familiarity born of practice. Frank showed signs of breathlessness and Ben resisted any further discussion to give him the chance to catch his breath. The silence was broken by Rosie having repeated bouts of hacking coughing, which came as no surprise as she was now in control of the cigarettes and lighting one off another in chain-smoking fashion. Susie went off to do the shopping, giving Ben the chance to have a head to head with Frank who surprised them both by breaking down in tears and repeating over and over that he was sorry but it was all beyond him.

Ben put his arm around Frank's shoulders and gently held him and allowed him to take his time to recover his control. Slowly he told Ben that he had been struggling to do his best for Rosie for months but his own health had been deteriorating and he had been avoiding seeing his doctor for fear that he and Rosie would be separated forever.

'We have been married for over forty years and she has always been my best friend. She has been getting more difficult to manage and letting her have control of her cigarettes is the last straw as she is smoking almost nonstop ever since Paul and his mates gave us the free ones. The reality is that it has all become too much and I can only just find the energy to ensure she maintains her diabetic medication and testing.'

At this point he nodded towards the old television set which was covered in diabetic paraphernalia including a couple of bottles of insulin.

'It's essential that she has her regular tests and injections but it is now a real struggle to get her cooperation and it leaves me exhausted. If it wasn't for the two days she spends at Elmore House I think we would have gone under months ago, but just lately I have found that all I do when she is there is sit in my chair and doze. The flat has really gone down and I am doing the minimum of cleaning, washing and cooking whilst I have previously taken a pride in my housekeeping skills. I am worried that Rosie is no longer being cared for as she should be and just listen to her coughing, that really can't be right.'

Rosie continued to cough and to spit repeatedly into a handkerchief but neither stopped her compulsive smoking. Ben was worried about both of them and encouraged Frank to agree to him talking to their general practitioner Dr Eddoll. Frank was clearly anxious about this but agreed that he could see no alternative. When Susie had returned with the shopping Ben left her to sit with Rosie and Frank and headed off to the health centre in the hope of catching up with the doctor. Luck was on Ben's side and he arrived there just as Dr Eddoll was pulling out of the car park and he managed to wave him down. The doctor busied himself by clearing a pile of case notes from the front passenger seat and gestured Ben to sit in.

Ben and Dr Eddoll were old friends and had always worked well together so it was easy for Ben to share his concern for the Sullivans. Dr Eddoll agreed to add them to his list for an afternoon home visit and Ben headed back to Chelsea House to let Frank know.

It wasn't until the next day that Ben learnt of the outcome of the visit and it was startling news; Rosie had been rushed into the general hospital the previous night, seriously ill with pneumonia. Dr Eddoll had left a message for Ben to ring him as soon as possible and he did so straight away. Dr Eddoll thanked Ben for his intervention the previous day, saying it was a touch and go situation and that the prognosis was gloomy at best.

'She is a very sick lady whose condition has been complicated by her smoking, but I think we should use her time in hospital to get Frank seen by a heart specialist. I am afraid that he appears to be suffering from heart failure and could be in need of an urgent heart procedure. I have spoken to an old friend who is a consultant heart surgeon at the general who can see him in his clinic tomorrow if you can get him there.'

Ben assured him that one way or another he would get there and they rang off, leaving Ben with having to explain to the prof that he wouldn't be able to attend his clinic as planned. The prof was not available but the response he got from Mrs Hemsworth, the prof's secretary, was surprisingly warm and helpful. She listened carefully to what Ben had to say and said she would let the prof know as soon as possible and added that she was sure the prof would understand that it was an emergency. Ben went down the corridor to catch up with Susie to tell her of the developments and they went off together to check on Frank, knowing he would be frantic with worry.

They were soon ringing the front doorbell of the flat at Chelsea House anticipating a delay before it was answered but after several further long rings on the bell followed by heavy knocking there was still no reply. Susie dug into her handbag and produced a door key, explaining that Frank had given it to her weeks before so she could let herself in in an emergency. Once the door was open Ben told Susie to wait outside until he had checked that all was okay, imagining the worse possible scenario. The smell of cigarette smoke had reduced noticeably in the living room as all the windows were wide open but there was no sign of Frank. The bathroom was also unoccupied but the bedroom door was shut tight. Ben took a deep breath and pushed the door open to discover a humped figure buried beneath a tangled mangle of bedclothes and an old overcoat. Ben's worse fears were resolved immediately by the deep snores coming from the bed.

He noticed a bottle of tablets on the bedside table and with renewed anxiety picked it up and read the label. He recognised them as a strong sleeping tablet that several of his clients had been prescribed in the past; the name on the label was Mrs Rose Sullivan. When he removed the top he found that the bottle was almost full so he knew that there weren't enough missing to cause any damage. Frank slept on. Susie arrived at the bedroom door looking desperately worried and Ben shooed her out to the living room and reassured her that there was nothing to worry about. After a brief discussion they decided to slip away and leave Frank to get his rest and to come back later in the morning, leaving Frank unaware of their concern.

Sod's law being what it was, Ben returned to the office to find a small pile of letters and junk mail addressed to Ernest sitting on his desk. He shuffled through them and the letter from the Housing Department was amongst them. Ernest was out around the estate but would be sure to be in later as The Champ was in residence and was now sat in front of Ben doing his best to look pathetic. Ernest would need care and time, which Ben didn't have to offer that day so he put the letters in his drawer, fed The Champ a biscuit and went to ask Mrs Freeman to arrange for him to see Ernest on the coming Monday. By the time they returned to Frank's he was up and dressed but appeared to have made no effort to get himself anything to eat or drink, preferring just to sit in his armchair. Susie didn't need to be asked and was soon busying herself in the kitchen whilst Ben talked about what Dr Eddoll had arranged for that afternoon. Frank took it on the chin but was clearly ambivalent about seeing a specialist. However, when Ben told him that he would be able to visit Rose when they were at the general the decision was made and with good timing Susie presented him with a couple of bacon butties and a mug of tea. He ate the lot with obvious satisfaction and Ben could feel his stomach rumbling. Promising to be back to pick Frank up at two o'clock the following day, Ben dropped Susie back at the office and headed for the sanctuary of Joe's, where he remained for a lot longer than was strictly necessary.

The trip to the hospital with Frank was very like his usual Friday trip even down to being able to park in his special secret parking space. That was just as well as it meant that Frank didn't have too far to walk but the effort left him struggling for breath. The heart clinic was in the same block of examination rooms as the prof's clinic and Wendy the receptionist looked confused as he signed Frank in. They had no sooner settled themselves down on the appropriate set of chairs than Frank was summoned into an alcove by one of the nurses to have his weight and height recorded and his blood pressure taken. He was then sent off to the gents armed with a specimen bottle and took so long to return that Ben only narrowly resisted going to check on him.

The wait for the consultant took the best part of an hour and Frank was beginning to get very agitated and eventually asked Ben to go in with him when he was called. Doctor Stevens appeared to have more than a hint of James Robinson Justice, the comedy actor who recently played a doctor in the British comedy film *Doctor in Distress*. He was a large man, sporting a bushy beard and had a rather regal appearance, but that was where the likeness stopped. He had none of the bluster of his actor lookalike and his voice was soft and sympathetic more like that of Kenneth Moore to keep the analogy going, thought Ben.

He did his best to put Frank at his ease as he made a careful physical examination and asked the sort of questions that build up a picture without causing undue anxiety. Ben was impressed as he recognised the professionalism of the man who genuinely seemed to want to help Frank. When the examination was over Dr Stevens sat back at his desk and took his time reading through a lengthy letter from Dr Eddoll. He then concentrated on putting Frank in the picture as truthfully and as clearly as possible. He considered that Frank needed an urgent heart bypass and he could arrange for his admission in the next few days. He said that he knew that Frank was the carer of his wife and he understood that as she was an inpatient herself it would seem opportune to go ahead as soon as possible. Frank just nodded his head in agreement and asked no questions when given the opportunity to do so. Dr Stevens came around his desk and shook hands with Frank, reassuring him that he would be looking after him personally. Ben and Frank walked slowly over to the main hospital building and took the lift up to the geriatric ward on the seventh floor. Frank had gone very quiet partly because he was fighting to get his breath but also to control his concern about what he may find when he got to Rosie. The ward sister directed them to one of the beds towards the middle of the ward and they were both struggling to recognise Rosie.

She was propped up in the bed and had an oxygen mask on her face. The skin on her face was grey, her eyes were closed and she looked more dead than alive. Frank pulled up a chair, grasped her hand and gently pushed back her hair behind her ears so that he could see her face more clearly. He called her name softly but she remained silent and was apparently in a deep sleep. Ben went off to see the sister to explain who he was and to try and get her opinion of Rosie's prognosis.

He received the standard reply, 'She is doing as well as could be expected,' but with a little pressing got a more accurate report. Rosie had proved to be a very difficult patient to contain and on arrival had spent her time approaching staff and other patients alike with her all too familiar demands of, 'Got a fag?' She had had to be controlled by being heavily sedated and had spent the last twenty-four hours in a state of being largely unconscious.

'It's not ideal but this is a ward of very sick ladies and at least we know where she is and we can administer her treatment via a drip. There's a long way to go. She is quite weak and her lungs are damaged by her smoking but you can be sure that we will be doing everything we can to get her through this. Meanwhile, please tell her husband that he can come and see her whenever he can.'

Ben relayed the message to Frank and told him about the sedative and he nodded his head in acceptance of the problem facing the nursing staff. Ben hung around for the best part of an hour but when he suggested that they should be leaving soon Frank said quite firmly that he would stay as long as possible as he was sure Rosie would be very frightened if she woke up in a strange place. He assured Ben that he had the money for a taxi home later on and Ben reluctantly left after explaining what was happening to the ward sister. Before leaving he did something he had never done with a client before, leaving Frank his home telephone number to use if the need arose.

Ben had a slow frustrating journey home with traffic jams the whole way and gloomy thoughts for company. He tried the radio but the pop music on offer seemed inappropriate and did nothing to raise his spirits. He switched it off, using the silence to think over his realisation that Frank and Rosie's time together was in jeopardy. On his arrival at home he was greeted by the sound of Sandy singing in the kitchen as she prepared the tea. The boys were watching Crackerjack on the television and managed only cursory waves by way of greeting. Ben always tried not to bring his work home with him and managed to attempt a happy smile as he joined Sandy in the kitchen, deciding not to mention the possibility of Frank ringing until later in the evening. Sandy pointed to an open letter and a small pile of colourful stamps on the kitchen table and he understood that a fresh letter from Camilla had had its usual effect of cheering Sandy up. He pushed his gloomy thoughts into the recesses of his mind, and determined to have a good weekend reached for the letter.

Chapter 38

The Axe Man Cometh

The weekend proved to be a relaxed and enjoyable time for the Newman family. For a start there was no call from Frank and Ben's anxiety withdrew to the recesses of his mind. The beginnings of summer came with a vengeance and the boys spent most of the day riding up and down the street on their scooters joining in noisy play with several other local kids. Sandy set herself up on a deck chair in the garden with her skirt pulled up over her thighs and her blouse tucked into her bra. They had talked the previous evening about the possibility of having a family holiday later in the year and Sandy was determined to get herself a tan in preparation. Friends had recently had a week at Butlins and had raved about it upon their return. They had loaned Sandy a copy of their week's programme of activities and there seemed loads to do whatever the weather, and best of all it was cheap. Ben thought Sandy looked very desirable but resisted his urge to get involved and got on the phone to Butlins headquarters and ordered a booking form. Unusually for him, as he rarely walked anywhere, he decided to wander down to Ma Driscoll's to get a paper and found himself stopping to chat to various neighbours en route. The sun seemed to have brought out a sunny disposition in everyone he met and he bought a bag of sherbet lemons at Ma's for the boys to share with their friends.

A rather pink Sandy, clothes adjusted, was busy putting together a snack lunch, which they ate on their laps with the boys gulping it down, keen to get back to their mates. The rest of the day ambled along with everyone enjoying the sense of freedom. Sunday came with the same sunny face and the family went out in the car for a ride around, ending up with a picnic on the River Wye. They had discovered the picnic spot the previous year when the boys had had a terrific time getting thoroughly wet playing in the shallows. This visit was more of the same, except Sandy had packed their swimming trunks so the boys could get fully immersed. All in all it was a lovely day and there was an added bonus when they spotted a flash of blue and saw a kingfisher going about his hunting. Ben had not forgotten that Frank might ring and on returning home went straight to the answer phone and was relieved that there had been no callers. Monday morning proved to be another warm and sunny day and Ben drove to work with the windows down and the radio pumping out music from the hit parade. He was still singing along as he pulled into the office car park and he remembered to secure the car against any unwanted interest from the Highfield youth before going in to see Mrs Freeman in her office.

The post had all been opened for him and duly stamped with the day's date, but it was all routine stuff that mainly required no action. Mrs Freeman advised Ben that she had arranged for Ernest to come and see him in his lunch hour as Ben had asked and wished him well with what she knew could be a difficult interview. Ben went down the corridor and into his office where he was greeted by Alice with tea and biscuits and The Champ complete with protective collar and Tesco footwear. Both looked fit and well and The Champ appeared to have got used to the indignity of his post-operation trappings and had lost his mournful look.

Alice went into detail about The Champ's progress but quickly got on to the matter of Ernest coming in for an interview and assured Ben that she would be available if required. It was abundantly clear that she was full of curiosity about the reason for the visit and would have loved to learn more but Ben made no comment. He sat back in his chair and drank his tea whilst feeding bits of biscuit to The Champ. Alice eventually took the hint and wandered off back to the kitchen with The Champ following close on her heels as he had finished all the biscuits. Ben then rang the geriatric ward at the general to enquire into Rosie's condition and was fortunate enough to get in touch with the ward sister he had met on Friday. She was very guarded in her comments and explained that Rosie's condition was not responding to the antibiotics she was on at present.

'I am quite expecting that the consultant will change her medication when he does his ward round later this morning, but she remains a very poorly lady. Her husband has refused to leave her side and he has been with us all over the weekend and we eventually made up a bed in a side room for him as he was out on his feet. Please keep that to yourself as there would be hell to pay if the managers learnt that we had accommodated a man on a lady's ward. Still, we were all very impressed with his devotion and what the managers don't see they don't need to worry about. We finally persuaded him to go home for a break this morning but I am sure he will be back again this evening.'

Ben thanked the sister for her kindness to Frank and said that he would ensure that he receive every support from his team with getting in to see Rosie. His next call was to the local fire station where he hoped to catch up with Paul. The person answering the phone explained that Paul was supervising a training exercise rescuing a body from the top of their tower, which was assumed to be on fire so they were all dressed in full safety gear. Ben left a message asking Paul to ring him back and simply said it was about the Sullivans. Whilst he was waiting for the call back he took the small stack of letters that Ernest had left with him and quickly went through them binning the junk mail and was left with just two to deal with. The first was a straightforward electricity bill, which he dealt with at once by making out a cheque from Ernest's bank book ready for him to sign. The other was the Housing Department letter, which was short and to the point and included the offer for Ernest to call into their office to borrow the key to view the flat at 71 Dangerfield Avenue.

Ernest arrived punctually for his meeting with Ben in an anxious state and before even sitting down asked if he had done something wrong. Ben quickly reassured him that he had done nothing wrong but that he had a serious matter to discuss. Ernest looked terrified and as if by magic Alice appeared at his side. Her presence seemed to reassure him and Ben told them both to sit down and listen carefully as he was going to read out an important letter from the Housing Department. He read the letter through slowly and then explained the reasoning behind it, stressing that the new tenancy would be in Ernest's own name rather than that of his parents.

Alice grasped the significance of the address of the maisonette and happily declared that they would be neighbours. Ernest remained quiet and Ben thought he was going to be difficult but that was far from the truth. He was just weighing up the situation in his own mind and that was inevitably a slow process. However, bit by bit he began to list the positives of such a move. It would be good to live nearer Alice – she smiled and nodded her head in encouragement – it would be cheaper than his current house and it only had one bedroom. He continued to think out loud and explained that with only one bedroom there was no way that Penny could ever be returned for him to look after.

'Just as well really as she hates dogs and I would never part with The Champ.'

It really couldn't have gone better and the two of them rushed straight off to the Housing Department with The Champ limping along behind them beginning to tentatively put his injured foot down from time to time to collect the keys to look at the offered rehousing. Ben breathed a deep sigh of relief and went off to make himself a cup of tea as for once he had been forgotten by Alice. He no sooner got back to his office than Mrs Freeman put through a call from headquarters and Ben was relieved to learn that it was his special Christmas time friend, Pam Townsend, to whom he always enjoyed speaking. He had had infrequent contact with her since Christmas but had contacted her as recently as a couple of weeks before when he had to place an urgent request for section 25 mental health admission forms in readiness for a weekend emergency duty session. Normally Mrs Freeman made such orders but Ben had been stuck in the office on duty and bored so he had taken the opportunity to have a friendly and rather flirtatious chat with Pam, who had been very receptive. Unfortunately, there was nothing informal in her approach today and she came across as genuinely concerned.

'I am sorry Ben but I have bad news for you. I have just spotted an entry in the office diary by the side of Gordon Wood's name, it looks like he is planning to make a surprise check on you and your office next Monday morning. As you know he has got it in for you after what happened at the Christmas party and he really hated the idea of you being well in with people in power. Creepy is simply a pig and would enjoy making your life a hell, so please be on your guard and don't give him any openings to cause trouble.'

Ben listened to the concern in her voice and thanked her warmly for the warning and the opportunity to have a few days to prepare. He managed to come up with something vaguely saucy to make her laugh and they parted on their usual good terms with Pam promising to let Ben know if she learnt of any change in Creepy's plans. Ben sat and contemplated the situation and decided that the best course of defence would be attack. It was clear that Creepy was a bully who liked to use his little bit of power and his influence with the manager Eric Sully to increase his ego and make up for his short stature and unfortunate appearance. Ben valued his remoteness from headquarters and it had been pure bad luck that the bizarre sequence of 'important people' seeking him out in quick succession at the damned office party had caused him to be vulnerable. However, he knew that his strength was based in the support of the team and he went and asked Mrs Freeman to ask everybody to a special team meeting later in the week.

He wandered around the offices trying to look at everything with a critical eye as he imagined Creepy would behave on his visit. The most obvious weakness would be the presence of Alice in the office, which Creepy was bound to pick up on, but the problem was how to keep her out of the way on Monday without causing her distress. With amazing timing Alice, Ernest and The Champ returned soon afterwards and seemed very excited about the potential move. The flat suited Ernest's needs very well but there was a problem about where to locate the hand cart memorial to Foxie and Elsie as Ernest's new flat opened straight on to the pavement with no front garden. Alice, however, had at once volunteered the use of her front lawn as a resting place for the hand cart and pointed out that Ernest would be able to see it from his front windows. But they were both worried about whether the council would agree. The germ of an idea came into Ben's mind and he said he would try to clear it with the Housing Department and the trio went off down the corridor to the kitchen bubbling with excitement.

Before Ben had a chance to try and ring Oliver at the Housing Department, Mrs Freeman popped her head around his door and said that Paul had returned Ben's call but had said that he was going to be tied up all morning on the training exercise but was on a tea break for a few minutes and would be around if Ben rang him back quickly. He got straight on with it and was soon talking to a rather distracted Paul who could be heard giving out instructions to his men. 'Sorry, Ben, but I can give you only a couple of minutes. What can I do for you?'

Ben quickly filled him in on the situation with Frank and Rosie and Paul immediately offered to visit Frank and to take him in for a visit to Rosie later in the day.

'I will let you know how things are, Ben. Meanwhile, can you get a message to Frank to say I will be in later?' Ben confirmed that he could and Paul brought the call to a hasty conclusion. Ben went down the corridor to Susie's room and asked her to let Frank know and she headed straight off. Before there were any further interruptions Ben rang Oliver and invited him to lunch at Joe's, explaining that they needed a chat and it would be nice to mix business with pleasure. Oliver didn't hesitate and within half an hour they were both tucking into a full English breakfast and mugs of steaming coffee. By now Ben and Oliver were good friends and trusted confidants and Ben was quite happy to talk frankly about his problems with Creepy. Oliver's reaction to that name was full of understanding and it was no coincidence that his reaction was identical to Pam's: 'He's a right little shit!'

Ben explained that with Pam's advance warning he had a few days to ensure that his house was in order but he had the problem of Alice. Oliver had seen Alice in the office once or twice and had assumed she was a client calling to see one of the social workers, but he knew no more than that. Ben filled him in on Alice's background and explained how much her place at the office meant to her and how he needed to keep her out of sight for Creepy's visit. 'I am sure that he would make a big issue of a client having the free run of our offices and the repercussions he could cause could have disastrous results for me and for Alice too. The last thing I want to do is upset Alice but unless I can find a way of keeping her out of the office on Monday the visit will be doomed. Now I must confess that I have a solution but it will require your assistance.'

He went on to explain that Ernest liked the flat but it had no garden and there was the problem of relocating the handcart memorial. He told Oliver about Alice's offer to have the memorial on her front lawn if that was acceptable to the Housing Department. Oliver responded without any hesitation with, 'I can't see any problem with that as long as Alice agrees; we have got tenants with all sorts of things stored in their gardens, but I don't see how that helps with your problem with Creepy.'

Ben continued, 'Well as long as the cart presents no problem, I am sure Ernest will happily accept the housing transfer. What I want to ask you is to see if you could hurry the paperwork through so he can get access to the flat before next Monday when Creepy is planning his visit.'

Oliver looked suitably puzzled as he couldn't see any relationship between the two things and said so. Ben nodded his head and went on to explain that if possible he would like to give Alice 'the day off' on Monday to give Ernest's flat a thorough clean in preparation for his move later in the week.

'She knows it has been empty since the former tenant went into an old people's home a couple of months ago and I will explain to her that there will never be a better opportunity to get the place clean and tidy. It's the sort of job Alice loves doing and I am sure she will jump at the chance to do it for Ernest and The Champ. Thereby killing two birds with one stone, and Alice need never know.'

Oliver couldn't help laughing and said that he thought Ben was a crafty old bugger but readily agreed to get the necessary wheels in motion. After a second cup of coffee paid for by Ben they drove back to Oliver's office in the old Cortina and Oliver popped in before returning to drop the keys to 71 Dangerfield Avenue into Ben's hand. The trio were all in the kitchen awaiting news about Ben's visit to the Housing Department, and Ben was delighted with their response when he told them that the move was on and could take place the following week. He went on to ask how Ernest intended to organise the movement of his stuff as the handcart was no longer a working possibility. Ernest was able to explain that he hoped he might be able to pay for the use of one of the cleansing department's lorries but was nervous of approaching anyone in management about the possibility. He looked at Ben with a look not dissimilar to that employed by The Champ when he was playing 'the hard done by' in an attempt to wheedle a biscuit. Ben readily capitulated and sent Ernest back to his street cleaning with the promise that he would see what he could do.

Once back in his office he closed his door away from Alice's innate curiosity and rang his contact in the cleansing department Sam Paterson. Sam was his usual cheerful self and immediately asked Ben who he was trying to get a job for this time. Before Ben had a chance to reply, Sam went on to say if the person Ben was seeking a job for was anything like Ernest and young Nobby he would be glad to have them as they had both proved to be reliable hard workers who gave him no grief. Ben was pleased to hear that his recommendations had worked out well and made a mental note of Sam's comments in case he needed to seek work for another client in the future. He went on to tell Sam all about the developments in Ernest's home circumstances and to ask outright if it were possible to get some help with his move.

'He is moving from his parents three-bedroom house to a small one-bedroom flat, so quite a lot of his furniture will need to be dumped and it would be a real help if the bits he wants to keep could be dropped off at his new home on the way to the tip.'

Ben explained that Ernest had offered to pay for the service but Sam's reaction was to say 'We look after our own, but it never hurts to slip the driver and his mate a quid or two.'

Sam was insistent that anything Ernest wanted to keep would have to be clearly marked as once it was at the tip there was no way of recovering it as everything there got smashed and buried. The removal was agreed for Wednesday of the following week, which fitted in nicely with Ben's plans for Alice when Creepy came to call. He linked up with Susie back at the office and it was agreed that on the Tuesday she would help Ernest to sort through his things and to label what was to be dropped off at Dangerfield Avenue.

The team 'council of war' took place on Thursday and Ben was completely honest with the whole team about why it was so important to be on top form. Both Phil and Mrs Freeman had had dealings with Gordon Wood in the past and fully understood why he was nicknamed Creepy. He was an unknown quantity to Susie but she was left in no doubt by the rest of them that he was 'an evil little bastard', in the words used by Phil to describe him.

'When I was working from headquarters he never missed an opportunity to make some lewd comment about my sexuality, but he always ensured that he was never overheard. I could have willingly wrung his neck but decided he was beneath my contempt and managed never to react, which really seemed to get beneath his skin.'

Ben picked up on this at once and it was agreed that if Creepy spoke to Phil there would always be one of the rest of them in ear shot. Bit by bit the defence plan was formed and each of them went about their allotted tasks in preparation. First thing the following day Paul rang to tell Ben that Frank Sullivan had been given an early slot for his heart surgery and was going into the heart ward at the general hospital the following day.

'I have put our fire service welfare officer on to the job of helping Frank and like me he knows Frank from years ago. It is all happening quickly but none too soon as far as I can see, as Frank's breathing is very laboured and he presents as exhausted. Still, Harry, the welfare officer, has got it covered and I have asked him to keep you advised of developments.'

Ben thanked Paul for his support of Frank and Rosie and called in to tell Susie about the planned admission and she went straight off to visit Frank to help him prepare.

Ben and Susie linked up with Ernest and Alice on Friday morning and carefully went through the plans for Ernest's move the following week. Ben explained to Alice that the Housing Department had said that she couldn't go in to clean the flat until Monday and that it would need to be done in one day.

'Do you think you could manage that, Alice, if I give you the day off?'

Her eager response was entirely as he had predicted. The rest of the plans were agreed and Ernest seemed quite happy to provide a tenner to his colleagues from the cleansing department at the time of the move. Ben handed the keys to the new flat over to Alice and reminded her once again that she must not go in to do the cleaning until first thing on Monday. Ben set off to attend the prof's clinic, happy in his mind that he had done as much preparation for Creepy's visit as he could. The die was cast, let battle commence.

Chapter 39

The Duel

The weekend passed painfully slowly, with Ben unable to settle to anything and having a strong tendency to be short tempered with the boys. Sandy was at her supportive best as she fully understood how anxious he was about Creepy's visit. She did her best to keep the peace and made a special effort to prepare his clothes for the Monday, even down to polishing his shoes to a high shine. After a couple of nights of disturbed sleep Monday morning finally arrived, and when the alarm went off at seven o'clock he dragged himself out of bed straight away. Sandy had arranged with Ma to go in later than usual so she could take on the responsibility of getting the boys to school on time. She insisted that Ben should have some breakfast before he set off but he struggled to manage a cup of coffee, some toast and jam.

After a wet and windy journey Ben pulled up in the car park well before eight-thirty in very good time to open the office for the normal starting time of nine o'clock. A highly polished Morris Minor Countryman now covered in splashes of mud from the car park was parked up in the far corner of the car park. *That will teach you to come to Highfield,* thought Ben as he deliberately ignored it and fumbled in his pocket for his office keys to let himself in quickly, slamming the door behind him. The ball was now in Creepy's court and Ben waited in anticipation of the opening action. He didn't have to wait long as within a short space of time there was someone pounding at the door. In the certain knowledge that Creepy was getting wet he slowly counted to fifty before carefully opening the door just as Creepy had his hand raised for further knocking.

'Hello, can I help you? I am afraid we don't open until nine,' and he pointed to the list of opening times on the notice board by the side of the front door.

'Let me in, you idiot, I am getting soaked,' was Creepy's demanding reply, and he attempted to push past Ben, who held his ground.

'Sorry, we are not open yet, but the office will be up and running by nine and I will be happy to speak to you then.'

'Look, you idiot, don't you know who I am?'

Before he could say any more Ben interjected by saying that he had no idea who he was.

'I am Gordon Wood from headquarters, and I have come to inspect your office, now for god's sake let me in.'

Ben held his ground, and as he was a good foot taller than Creepy they were at an impasse.

'Sorry, but I am not expecting anyone from headquarters and I don't know you, so I must ask to see your identification card.'

Ben thought Creepy would burst but he snarled and went back to his car to find his identification card, which he thrust into Ben's hand on his return. Ben pretended to study it carefully, managing to control a laugh as the photo on the card was a dead ringer for the evil goblin that had been on the front cover of the children's fable book that his mother had read to him as a child. All it needed was a toadstool for Creepy to sit on, and Ben was sure that it must have really irked Creepy to have to let Ben see it. With a bright smile and a thank you he stepped aside to let the thoroughly wet Creepy into the porch and led him down to his office, with the aside that he was sure that he would agree it was important to be sure about visitors. Round one to Ben, but there was still a long way to go and he had to be sure not to get over confident.

Once Creepy was settled Ben explained that he would just get set up for the day before going to turn the central heating on to help Creepy dry off. He unlocked his filing cabinet and put his in-tray, which contained several carefully selected files, on his desk. He knew that Creepy wouldn't be able to resist having a nose at them whilst he was out of the office and he had made sure that they were up to date and contained nothing controversial.

Taking his time, he wandered off and checked that all the team were in situ and gave them each the thumbs up before going to the kitchen to switch on the boiler. By the time he got back to his office, Creepy was sat back in his chair with his hands in his lap, but Ben noticed that there was a different file on the top of his tray. Neither Creepy nor Ben made any comment and Ben just let Creepy make the next call and the silence between them went on a while before Creepy was the first one to crack.

'We at headquarters like to check our little outposts like yours from time to time just to see that things are going along properly.'

Ben enquired if anyone at headquarters had any particular concerns about the way the Highfield office was running and reluctantly Creepy said that it seemed okay. No mention was made of his Christmas party 'friends in high places' and Ben didn't push it.

'Well I suggest that I give you a tour of the office and introduce you to the rest of the team and that you then wander around as you wish and ask any of us anything you want to know. Meanwhile, we will go about our business as normal as we are always busy.'

As if to prove the point Ben's phone rang and he picked it up to be greeted by Paul Humphries, the leading fireman. The basis of the conversation was to advise Ben that Frank Sullivan had collapsed on his way to visiting Rosie with Harry Jones, the fire service welfare officer, over the weekend and had ended up being admitted to the heart ward at the general hospital as an emergency. Paul went on to say that Frank's condition had been stabilised but he was going to have an operation later in the day. Paul didn't know how Rosie was fairing and Ben said he would contact the geriatric ward to let them know about Frank and to check on Rosie's condition.

'We'll keep in touch, Paul, thanks for all your help with the Sullivans,' and he rang off with none of the usual friendly banter. Creepy immediately wanted to know why Ben was working with the fire service and Ben explained about the earlier concerns about power cuts. Creepy quickly lost interest when he realised that there was no criticism to be made of the relationship and got to his feet ready for the grand tour. Ben took the opportunity to make the point that it was essential for all the various professionals on the estate to have a good close working relationship. Creepy just grunted.

Ben started with the kitchen, the loos and the interview rooms before taking Creepy in to see Phil and Susie. He made a point of formally introducing Phyllis Jenkins as a very experienced and valued member of the team and Creepy appeared both stunned and embarrassed as he had clearly forgotten about his input in her transfer to Highfield.

Phil took the initiative and said, 'Hello Gordon, long time no see.'

Creepy managed to splutter hello and immediately turned towards Susie and asked in a rather creepy way, 'And who is this young lady?' Ben stepped in and introduced Susie by saying

'This is our latest recruit, Mrs Susan Fraser, who joined us under the social work assistant scheme. She is proving to be an excellent recruit and a good example of the value of the social work assistant development.'

Creepy shook hands with Susie for rather longer than necessary but she gave him a forbidding look and he withdrew his hand. Ben and Creepy moved on down the corridor and went to meet Mrs Freeman in the general office.

'This is Mrs Vivian Freeman, my longest serving colleague, and we have worked together from day one. She will be able to fill you in on the day-to-day running of the office, so please fill free to ask her anything you want to know. I suggest you start off with Mrs Freeman whilst I get on with my day. Come and see me as and when you want to.'

Creepy didn't seem very happy to be told what to do but as it was the obvious way to proceed sat himself down and Ben left them to it.

Ben went straight back to react to Paul's telephone message by ringing the geriatric ward at the general and was fortunate enough to get through to his normal contact, Sister Franklin.

'I was expecting a call from you, Mr Newman, as I have already linked up with a friend of mine who works on the heart ward and have been keeping myself informed about what has been happening with Frank Sullivan. The last I heard was about an hour ago, Frank had a bypass earlier today and is now back in recovery. It seems to have gone well but unfortunately the same cannot be said of Rosie, who is steadily deteriorating, and she is effectively in a coma most of the time. I am sorry to say that it is only a matter of time and it is to be hoped that Frank will soon be well enough to spend a little more time with her.'

Ben thanked Sister Franklin for her help and said he would pass the information on to Paul and the fire service welfare officer. He did so straight away, having first ensured that his door was shut so he couldn't be overheard by Creepy. He started off by apologising to Paul about being a bit remote when he called earlier and explained about the visitation from headquarters. Paul was duly sympathetic, having been on the receiving end of similar visits himself in the past.

'That's a real bugger, as they are never happy unless they can find some fault or other. Good luck and thanks for the update. I will get our welfare officer to step up his support for Frank, who will be devastated when Rosie dies. He is having a tough time of it and deserves better, but I am sure we will all do what we can to help.'

Ben responded by saying that he would keep Susie on the case as she really seemed to have a good relationship with Frank and finished up by saying that they must have a trip to Joe's soon. Paul laughed and said, 'That would be good but not too often or I won't be able to run up and down the ladders to set an example to my watch.'

Whilst Creepy was involved with Mrs Freeman, Ben took the opportunity to update Susie on the situation with the Sullivans and to ask her to link up with Harry, the fire service welfare officer, to ensure that Frank got every support in the next few difficult days. Creepy reappeared in Ben's office about an hour later sporting a cup of coffee and looking smug. Ben waited for the onslaught but when it came it was all pretty low-key stuff. He wanted to inspect the accident report book and seemed surprised when Ben produced one from his filing cabinet. It only contained two incidents, neither of which were serious nor could have been prevented. One was a small child who got her finger squashed in a closing door and the other was when a visitor slipped and fell in the car park. Both incidents were fully documented, including a recorded follow-up check on any damage done.

Creepy seemed satisfied but rather disappointed that he couldn't find fault. Ben had been confident of the outcome as he had only created the book the week before and the incidents were pure fabrication. Mrs Freeman had had a chat with a friend in headquarters and had been able to warn Ben of the need for such a record. The staff sickness record, leave record chart and property maintenance record were demanded and all met muster, to Creepy's obvious displeasure.

Those few days advance warning from Pam Townsend had made all the difference but Ben's advance preparations were rapidly running out when miraculously assistance came from a most unlikely source. Mrs Freeman rang Ben to say a client had come in to see him, a Mr Ernest

Farthing! Creepy immediate sought to regain control by announcing that he would sit in on the interview, as 'I would like to see you in action. I will go on down to the interview room and let you go and collect the client.'

He didn't attempt to ask any information about Mr Farthing and Ben didn't attempt to offer any, but thought that it could get interesting. Creepy turned left to the interview room and Ben turned right towards the general office and was not surprised to be passed by The Champ on his way to the kitchen to look for Alice and her ready supply of biscuits. Ernest was his normal self, except he was a bit more excited than usual because of his planned move. As a consequence, his speech was more difficult to interpret and both Ben and Mrs Freeman found it harder than usual to understand him. However, as he was clutching a few letters Ben guessed that this was one of his regular visits to get help with his mail. Ben told him to follow him down to the interview room and arrived just in time to see The Champs rear quarters entering the room in front of him. Creepy had made the classic mistake of taking the chair furthest in and thereby making any attempt at escape impossible. Ben arrived just in time to see The Champ firmly push his nose into Creepy's crotch, which produced a high-pitched squeak from Creepy as he attempted to force his body back in his chair. The Champ sat down right in front of Creepy, just inches from his lap, in anticipation of some sort of tit bit and Creepy's hands went to his crotch in defence of his vital organs.

Without comment Ben stood back to allow the huge bulk of Ernest to enter the room and the urgent squeak was repeated and Creepy noticeably blanched. Ernest sat down next to Creepy and Ben continued to introduce them without reacting in any way to Creepy's discomfort. He took the post from Ernest's hand and said, 'I will leave you to get acquainted whilst I go and sort this stuff out for you, Mr Farthing. Perhaps you would like to tell Mr Wood all about your new home.'

He was out of the room in a flash, giving Creepy no opportunity to protest and could hear Ernest starting a long dialogue in his deep guttural incomprehensible worst voice. Ben felt sure that Creepy was fully occupied for a while and leisurely went through Ernest's post, which was all rubbish and confined to the bin. He joined Mrs Freeman and grabbed a quick coffee whilst she assured him that her session with Creepy had gone off without a hitch.

'But he tried very hard to dig some dirt on you. He really has it in for you and got a bit upset when I offered no criticism.'

Ben returned to rescue Creepy eventually and found him still cowering in his corner with The Champ poised a few inches from his nether regions and Ernest still pontificating about his move. With practised efficiently he encouraged both Ernest and The Champ to go on their way, leaving a shaking little figure curled up in the corner.

Creepy slowly recovered his composure and eventually said he had better ring his office to check everything was okay. He made the call from the general office well within Mrs Freeman's hearing and had a loud protracted conversation about a serious problem that urgently needed his special skills to resolve. He quickly made his excuses to Ben and Mrs Freeman and headed straight for his car. Mrs Freeman assured Ben that the call to headquarters had been cut off at the very beginning and that the urgent summons for him to return had been solely of Creepy's making!

Ben went to see him off the premises, only to witness the lanky figure of Alice in all her glory, complete with a bucket and mop hurrying cross the car park towards the office. One sight of her was enough for Creepy, who practically ran over to his car and accelerated away, not even bothering to drive around the deep muddy puddles which added to the disreputable state of his little motor. He must have concluded that Highfield was made up of weird people, whilst Ben said out loud to himself, 'What a wanker.'

He welcomed Alice back into the fold and told her to put the kettle on and he would be right back. He made a quick trip to Joe's for doughnuts all round and the victorious Highfield team gathered together in the kitchen to celebrate mission accomplished. The toast was 'Pam Townsend, our secret weapon'. Everyone was keen to give their impression of how it went and poor old Alice just had no idea what everyone was talking about and soon chose to go off around the offices to do her normal office cleaning routine. When the gathering broke up Mrs Freeman asked to have a private word with Ben and followed him back to his office. She was keen to tell him about something that had come up during her session with Creepy.

'He wanted to examine the petty cash book and cross questioned me on every single item, but fortunately couldn't find anything wrong. But he did raise one issue which I had no knowledge of by asking where the entries were for the cleaner's wages. Thinking on my feet I told him we were in the process of recruiting a new cleaner but had to be very careful because of the confidential nature of our work. This seemed to satisfy him and he went on to the next thing, but I wondered where he was coming from in respect to us being able to employ a cleaner. With your permission, I suggest that I have a word with my contact in the headquarters finance office and explore it further.'

Ben was stunned and realised that by allowing Alice to act as an unpaid dogsbody he had missed a trick all this time and he readily agreed for Mrs Freeman to explore it further. The outcome was a win-win situation all round as Mrs Freeman discovered that an office of their size was entitled to five hours a week of cleaning time. That did not amount to a fortune but it did mean that a delighted Alice would now receive some payment for her labours and it solved Ben's problem of ever having to explain why Alice had a key to the premises. Creepy's visit had resulted in an unforeseen benefit which would undoubtedly have upset him had he known, but some things are best left unsaid.

Chapter 40

Hectic Times

On Tuesday, a sense of calm settled on the Highfield office with the main happening being Ernest's planned move to his own maisonette on the next day. In the late afternoon Susie and Alice joined Ernest at his old family home and ensured that there were clear stickers on all the things he wanted to take with him in readiness for the onslaught by his refuse men helpers the following day. Ernest, unlike his dad, Foxie, was not a hoarder and the things he had decided to take with him were surprisingly limited. He was insistent that he wanted to keep his single bed, which was sensible considering who had occupied the two double beds left in the house. He wanted to take the cooker that had been his mum's pride and joy along with a good supply of pots and pans, crockery and cutlery. A couple of armchairs and a table and chairs completed his furnishings and he chose to keep just one of Foxie's collection of damaged bric-a-brac. It was of no surprise to anyone that he had chosen to keep a plaster statue of an Alsatian with a boy standing beside it.

Like all the other bits and pieces it was a dustbin find but the fact it had a bit of leg missing seemed appropriate somehow. Susie added an iron and ironing board and a broom to the pile to go and Ernest was ready. The three of them and The Champ drove around to 71 Dangerfield Avenue, where Alice was keen to show off her cleaning of the previous day. The flat sparkled and smelt of the heavy scent of pine cleaner. There were curtains up to the windows, lino on all the floors and even a reasonable stair carpet, all of which had been left by the previous tenant. Susie was effusive in her praise of Alice's efforts and Alice seemed to glow with pleasure. Susie left the three of them sat on the floor making plans for the following day whilst she set off for home and a quiet tea with John during which she would as usual tell him all about the day's events in Highfield. He always seemed interested but in truth he was mainly happy that Susie had found a role that she found fulfilling now the boys were away at university.

The morning of Ernest's move had arrived and Alice had rushed off 'to supervise' once she had made the compulsory cup of tea for each of the team. The move went off without a hitch and Alice came back to the office at lunch time and virtually insisted that Ben should come and inspect the flat. Everything was in place, including Ernest sitting in one of the armchairs and The Champ curled up in the other. Ben couldn't help thinking back to just about a year before when Elsie had proudly shown him over their new council house. A lot had happened to Ernest since but he seemed very happy with where he had ended up. It was Alice who gave Ben the grand tour and Ernest seemed content to let her get on with it. The Champ decided that the move to show Ben the kitchen meant the possibility of treats and he jumped out of his chair to join them. He didn't go unrewarded.

After the tour Ben joined Ernest in the lounge and just managed to claim the second armchair, leaving The Champ to give him a dirty look and go and curl up on Ernest's feet. Ernest was clearly already at home and told Ben that the only thing left to do was to move the hand cart to Alice's garden, which he intended to do that afternoon.

The afternoon passed with Ben stuck in the office as he was again on call for emergency mental health calls. One advantage of Creepy's visit was that it had made him get up to date with his paperwork so he cleared up the odd bits and pieces outstanding and picked up the phone to check on the Sullivans' condition. Sister Franklin was not on duty but her replacement, Sister O'Malley, had been made aware of Ben's involvement and was content to put him in the picture. Rosie was hanging on but as before was barely conscious. Meanwhile Frank spent more time with her on the geriatric ward than he spent on the heart ward where he was recovering from his operation.

'He sits with her for hours just holding her hand and talking to her about their life together. He is a real sweetie but I dread to think what he will be like when she passes away. Thanks for your interest. I think he will need a lot of help from you when the time comes.'

Promising to keep in touch, Ben rang off and immediately rang Paul Humphries to update him on the situation. As it happened Paul had visited Frank the previous day and confided in Ben that Frank had asked him to be the executor to his will. 'It seems to me that he is planning for his own death but then with a serious heart condition I suppose it is as well to be prepared. Frank always was well organised and of course I agreed to act as executor for him.'

With that sobering thought the conversation came to an end, with none of the pleasantries they would normally have enjoyed. Ben sat back and thought it through and determined to visit Frank as soon as he was able. From the point of being on call, the phone kept satisfyingly silent and after a while Ben picked it up again and rang his 'stationery friend' Pam Townsend. She received his call in good humour and delighted in telling Ben all about Creepy's return to his office after the visit to Highfield.

'He rushed back into the building looking like thunder and went straight into his office and slammed the door. He stayed there all afternoon and was still there when I went home.'

Ben explained how the visit had gone and Pam was in peals of laughter as he told her about the effect Ernest and The Champ had had on Creepy. He then told her that the visit had been cut short because of an urgent call from headquarters, which she confirmed was pure fantasy and one of Creepy's tricks when things got too tough for him. The conversation went on for a while and finished up with Pam saying with a giggle that she would see him at Christmas. Something for him to look forward to!

No sooner had he put the phone down than his door literally burst open to present an apparently panic-stricken Ernest in a state of high dudgeon. He started to talk at high speed but was so upset that Ben could make little of what he was trying to say. It appeared to be something to do with the handcart and it was clear he wanted Ben to go with him. The complication was that Ben was on call for mental health emergencies, and problems with a hand cart didn't really match the criteria! But what the hell, it was only a couple of minutes to Ernest's new home and he was sure that Phil could be expected to hold the fort, as he had covered for her on numerous occasions. The deal was settled with Ben assuring Phil and Mrs Freeman that he wouldn't be long and Ben, Ernest and The Champ clambered into the Cortina and sped off.

The problem was all too obvious when they pulled up at Alice's garden. The handcart was in the garden okay but Ben could see it was in a sorry state. It was tilted at a crazy angle, balanced on one wheel with the other wheel almost lying flat on the ground. The shafts of the hand cart were right across the garden path, meaning the only way of entering the garden was by clambering over the two foot brick wall which fronted the garden. It was this wall that they had all overlooked when planning Ernest's move and which had been the cause of the catastrophe they were now faced with. As Ben surveyed the damage Beefy Baker, the local bread delivery man, got out of his van parked opposite and came over talk to him. He explained that when he had been delivering along the road he had come across Ernest trying to lift the cart over the wall single handed.

Always one to enjoy a weightlifting challenge Biffy had offered to help and had quickly recruited the local window cleaner and his mate who were working nearby to assist. Between them they had managed to lift one side of the cart over the wall but in order to finish the task they had to negotiate stepping over the wall themselves. Unfortunately, the window cleaner had caught his foot on the wall and the steady movement of the cart had suddenly advanced at pace as he had fallen to one side. The resulting crash of the cart was followed by an enormous crack from underneath and the heap before them was the consequence. The window cleaner and his mate had made a hasty retreat but Biffy to his credit had remained to see what might be done to sort things out. One thing was clear, the cart had made its last journey on its own two wheels but it would still have to be moved to allow the flat occupiers to get into their homes. Ben thought fast and decided it was time to call on the skills of Tony Scadding and told Ernest to stay with the cart whilst he got help. He thanked Biffy for his input and sent him on his way to finish his bread deliveries.

Ben parked in his usual place outside the Scadding's yard and was welcomed by little more than a throaty growl from the Alsatian, who didn't even bother to raise himself from his prone position in the sun. Tony was busy swinging cars around with his crane like some giant game of conkers but this time under the direction of a short, bald middle-aged man Ben had never seen before. With the current wreck safely deposited on the top of a stack Tony swung athletically down from the crane cab and came over to greet Ben. The man followed him across and Ben noticed he walked with a pronounced limp. Tony introduced him as,

'Frudo, an important addition to our team.' Ben swiftly filled Tony in on the problem with the hand cart that he had worked so hard to fix up and got exactly the reaction he had hoped for.

'Leave it to us, Frudo and I will sort it out.'

Ben went on to explain that he was on emergency duty cover and should be back at the office to deal with any problems and Tony waved him back towards the yard entrance. The Alsatian did nothing more than open one eye before returning to his sunbathing. Having called in on Ernest on his way back to the office to tell him Tony would be along shortly Ben went back to the office to take over from a relieved Phil, who went straight off on her visits to avoid any further requests to stand in.

As it happened she had no need to worry: the phone didn't ring for the remainder of the afternoon. Ben left a little earlier than usual so he could stop on the way home to check on developments at Alice's. He arrived just in time to see Tony and Frudo loading a large trolley jack back on to their lorry. The hand cart was now positioned in just the right spot on the lawn and was back on an even keel. Tony explained that the hand cart had a broken axle and was only being held in place by a couple on stacks of concrete blocks underneath the two bits of the axle.

'It's completely secure but the only way it could be moved in the future would be by breaking it up so I guess it is now in its permanent resting place.'

Ernest seemed delighted with the result and Alice was enjoying herself by telling the small gathering of watchers all about the cart and its significance. Ben thanked Tony and his mate for rescuing a difficult situation and went on home ready for his tea and hopefully a quiet duty session.

Sandy had a favourite tea all ready but that was as good as it got as the phone rang several times during the evening and resulted in similar visits to each of the two major psychiatric hospitals in Exworth with requests from consultants to convert the status of two separate patients from informal status to compulsory status under section 30 of the Mental Health Act. It was unusual for this to happen out of office hours and twice on the same night was probably unique. That it was happening at all reflected the level of concern for the patients involved but the mental health of both of them had deteriorated and they were now considered to be active suicide risks.

The first patient had been brought into St Margaret's by her husband the previous day as a voluntary patient but had become very aggressive and unpredictable. St Margaret's was situated alongside a busy motorway and a staff member going home from work had spotted the lady concerned attempting to throw herself off a motorway bridge on to the busy road below. A tragedy had been narrowly avoided and it was only with extreme difficulty that the staff member had been able to hold on to her until other staff members came along. The job for Ben that night was relatively straightforward and the section was made in conjunction with Dr Rani, his friend and colleague from the prof's clinic.

The second referral was an elderly man who had been a long-term patient on one of the back

wards at the Chalfont Clinic for years with a schizophrenic condition which was normally reasonably well controlled. However, over the past few hours he had suddenly developed an acute manic state and become completely unapproachable, self-harming and overtly violent. Staff strongly suspected that there was some physical reason for his rapid deterioration and their concern was that this needed urgent investigation as it could potentially be life threatening. They needed to get him sedated but this would inevitably involve a 'hands-on' situation which could have dangerous consequences for the patient or staff. The need for urgent action was obvious to Ben but the consultant on call was notorious for being reluctant to attend emergency situations out of normal hours. He would always try to postpone any action until 'a more civilised hour' and the ward staff had so far failed to get him to come in and see the patient.

It was three in the morning when Ben telephoned him and the telephone kept on ringing for several minutes. Finally, a very disgruntled doctor answered and the conversation that followed was far from friendly but Ben held his ground in spite of being threatened with a formal complaint to the medical officer of health about his attitude. Eventually the doctor capitulated and appeared on the ward dressed in an overcoat over stripy pyjamas. He barely looked at the patient and hurriedly signed the necessary forms with Ben looking over his shoulder to check they were filled in properly. The smell of drink on the doctor was very apparent and

Ben made it obvious that he had picked up the smell and made a point of asking the charge nurse whether the patient had been drinking. He was assured that there had been no alcohol on the ward and Ben turned back to the doctor, who blushed and headed off back to his car. If there was any justice in the world he would get stopped by the police on the way home. That never happened, but two other things did. There was never any complaint made to Ben's boss and unfortunately the male patient died three days later from an acute brain condition, encephalitis. It was five-thirty before Ben climbed into bed and he slept soundly until well after ten in the morning.

Chapter 41

And So It Goes On

When Ben eventually crawled out of bed he felt really rough. His head was throbbing, his mouth tasted foul and he needed to rapidly head off to the toilet as his bladder thought it was bursting. A shower and the vigorous use of his toothbrush improved things a little and he made it safely to the kitchen to get a coffee. Sandy had left all the makings of a breakfast out for him and a note from her was propped against the Nescafé jar. She had seen the boys off to school and had also rang Mrs Freeman to tell her that he had been out most of the night and would be late in as he needed to try and catch up on his sleep. Sometimes he was very aware how lucky he was to have Sandy as his wife. After a second cup of coffee and a dish of Sugar Puffs he started to feel better and eventually turned up at work around midday.

Mrs Freeman had held the fort well and the only thing outstanding was an unusual request from Phil to have some time with Ben. This was very unlike Phil, who usually wanted to 'do her own thing' without any intervention from him, so the likely scenario was that there was a hefty problem coming his way. However, she had booked herself out on visits for the rest of the day and Ben assumed she would be starting with a liquid lunch somewhere to fortify her for the visits ahead. He asked Mrs Freeman to put a session in the diary for the following morning and to let Phil know when she rang in as she did most afternoons to check everything was okay back at base. Mrs Freeman was anxious to get away to give her husband Steve his lunch and Ben found himself alone in the office, which was blessedly quiet. He sat down in Alice's comfy old armchair in the kitchen and gently nodded off. A few minutes later he was awoken by The Champ poking his cold nose into his hand and by the time Ernest and Alice had caught up with the dog he had managed to appear wide awake and he was making a fuss of The Champ.

Alice and Ernest were very excited with the new living arrangements and Alice was full of making plans for sharing meals, walking the dog together and them watching her television of an evening. They were very happy about the way The Champ had taken to living in Dangerfield Avenue and he was already moving freely between the two maisonettes. Initially this caused a strong reaction from Alice's cat Benny, who took advantage of the hand cart and withdrew to the high ground on top of it in preparation to defend his territory. The Champ just treated him with disdain, having no truck with cat and dog fights, preferring to concentrate on the serious business of locating Alice's biscuit tin. Benny settled down to claim the inner part of the old lorry tyre planter as her special place and from day one could regularly be seen taking the sun from her elevated viewpoint. In no time at all, they all settled down to their new way of living and Foxie and Elsie were rarely alone in their unique memorial, hopefully content to share the space with Benny.

During the afternoon Ben rang the geriatric ward as he did most days to get an update on the Sullivans. Sister Franklin always seemed to be able to find time to talk to Ben and told him that many of her patients had little or no contact from their family or friends.

'It's really sad that Rosie is so poorly that she seems unaware of Frank's regular visits, not that that deters him, and he still spends most of each day with her. In fact I think he is probably deliberately slowing up his recovery from his operation in case he is discharged and has to return home without Rosie.'

Ben arranged with Sister Franklin for him to make a visit to the ward to see them both the following week and still feeling jaded from his duty time activities, cleared his desk and headed for an hour of comfort in Joe's back room. Mavis provided him with coffee and Joe sensing Ben's condition sent her in with a bacon sandwich which Ben hadn't ordered. The fire was little more than a few embers but it completed the atmosphere of peace and quiet that caused Ben to put his feet up on the settee and sigh with contentment. It was a much happier man who arrived back at the Newman home that evening and once the boys were settled in bed Sandy and Ben sat at the kitchen table and filled in the forms for their Butlins holiday.

This was a new experience for the family as there had never been enough money previously to afford a holiday, but the prices of the all-in holidays at Butlins were so reasonable that it was only a little more than their normal weekly budget at home. Even so the prices shot up in school holiday time so they had decided to book for the third week in July, which was a week before the schools broke up. That was still about eight weeks away and they decided not to tell the boys about it as they would be sure to get overexcited. The next family event to be planned was Nick's birthday towards the end of June and after the success of Horseworld and the speedway for Jack's birthday it would have to be something different. But that was planning for another day and they cuddled up on the sofa and watched a dreadful old film which they had seen before, but they were too lazy to get up and either switch off or change channels.

The following day was another bright and sunny one with just a hint of a breeze to make the trip to the office pleasurable. There seemed to be any number of young girls in miniskirts swishing their way along, getting admiring glances from every male who passed and more than a few ribald comments, usually from white van men. Ben kept his comments to himself but nevertheless enjoyed the view and made grateful thanks to Mary Quant for her liberating clothes designs.

As he did from time to time Ben stopped at the site of the future speedway track to see how it was going on. The carpark was laid in gravel and a lengthy solid corrugated iron fence ran almost the whole of the width of the site and had been painted in the inevitable vivid green that was the Scadding trademark. Robbie had once confided to Ben that he had a whole lockup full of the stuff that he had taken as payment for a debt owed to him by a firm which had gone bankrupt. A tarmac road had been laid up the right-hand side of the site which disappeared behind the green fence at the top. Nothing much else could be seen from where Ben had pulled up but it was clear that the project was coming along at a pace and Ben determined to call in and see Robbie very soon to catch up on the progress. He arrived in the office in good time and to his surprise Phil was already in. However, the meeting had been set for ten o'clock by Mrs Freeman to take account of Phil's usual arrival time. Ben suspected that her prompt arrival reflected the seriousness of her concern but used the next hour to clear the post, enjoy his tea and biscuits supplied by Alice and to prepare himself for what was likely to be a tricky problem. Certainly, the way Phil came into the office was very determined and after sitting across from Ben presented him with a sheet of paper which he could see contained a list of a dozen or so names, most of which were familiar to him.

'It's like this, Ben, Susie and I have been talking about our clients and in no time at all we came up with those names, all of whom share the same problem. They are all isolated in their own homes with no friends of their own and no social groups to belong to. What they desperately need is a group or club pitched at their level where they can socialise safely and pleasurably. Susie and I would love to set up such a group and we think we have found just the place for it.'

Ben could barely control his surprise, as this was totally unexpected and his immediate reaction was that this was a very positive suggestion. However, he knew that Phil was a shrewd operator and that there was probably going to be a sting in the tail so he simply said, 'Go on.'

Phil continued, 'The solution to finding somewhere suitable came to us as the result of Creepy's visit. As you know he poked his nose into every nook and cranny desperately trying to find something at fault but we had all bases covered. However, he took no interest in the rest of the building, which has been empty since the planning department left well over a year ago. It seemed to Susie and me that the premises have simply been forgotten about so it could be going begging and it could be put to good use by us as a day unit for some of our clients.'

Ben sat back in his chair just a little amazed by how much of a pleading look had come on to Phil's face. This was clearly important to her and the last thing he wanted to do was dampen enthusiasm in the team. It was in fact over two years since his former colleague in the planning department had dropped the keys to the rest of the building on his desk. At the time Ben had just slipped them into his desk drawer and he had thought little about them ever since. His immediate reaction was sympathetic to Phil's suggestion but realised that there were all sorts of potential complications to be considered. After a few minutes thought he fumbled in his desk drawer and came up with the keys.

'I am not promising anything but we might as well go and look if it could meet your needs.' As they went back down the corridor they were joined by Susie and Mrs Freeman, both eager to see what might be available. It looked like the female mafia was back in operation and that he would have to tread carefully if he wasn't going to end up in the mire. The entrance to the building was at the far end away from the office main entrance and was situated around a corner tucked in out of sight. The door lock was stiff from not being used and the double doors creaked from want of oil, but they opened to reveal a long room which seemed gloomy and full of abandoned junk. Fortunately, the electricity was still connected and the use of a small bank of light switches improved things by lighting up the whole room with a series of fluorescent lights running the full length of the room. It was bigger than Ben had anticipated and there were two further doors at the far end of it, which proved to be a small but usable kitchen and an old-fashioned but functional toilet and wash basin. The whole place was grubby and had obviously been well used but neglected before being abandoned and the amount of rubbish would require a couple of skips to dispose of it. But there was no sign of water penetration, the electric and water were still connected and the central heating system appeared to run off the same system as the main office next door. In fact the place really had potential and anything needing doing could hopefully be done on a shoestring. Ben left the women mulling over what might be achieved and departed back to mind the fort, saying that they should all give it some thought over the weekend and then have a brainstorming session in the following week.

Ben found that he was quite excited about the prospect of increasing the services that they could offer but was concerned about how to proceed. He tidied his papers away and made a start on the packed lunch that Sandy had prepared for him. She knew that Fridays were often a rush for him because half the day was committed to working with the prof at his clinic. Normally Ben would be running late and would have to resort to eating his sandwiches driving along, which on occasion had proved to be a messy business. But today he was in good time and used his lunch break to mull over the issues involved in converting the empty building to a functioning part-time day centre. He made a few rough notes, which he stored away in his briefcase ready to be reconsidered at home over the weekend.

The prof's clinic ran as normal but not for the first time Ben noted that there was an emergency appointment added on to the end of the clinic. Strangely Ben had observed that the emergency appointments were almost exclusively for young women and he had noticed that the prof had always insisted on dealing with them personally. Ben had said nothing about this before but couldn't help imagining all sorts of scenarios. Finally, he drummed up the courage to raise his observations with Dr Rani, who was happy to put Ben straight.

'It's nothing unprofessional, quite the reverse. Those poor ladies are seeking medical support to have a legal abortion on the grounds that to have the baby would result in serious mental distress. As you may know the prof is a staunch Roman Catholic and abortion is against his religious beliefs, but as a psychiatrist he has a duty to decide on the best interests of the clients. I know he agonises over each lady but insists that no one else in his team should have to be involved in making such an important decision. It all added up even more to commanding my admiration of the man. He really is something special and I am sure he puts the needs of the clients before his own religious doctrine.'

Ben felt very humbled that he could have ever doubted the prof's motivation and thanked Dr Rani for putting him straight. The rest of the afternoon went through without incident and Ben was pleased at its passing.

Chapter 42

The Time for Making Plans

Nick's seventh birthday was just three weeks away and both Ben and Sandy were wracking their brains to come up with something original to do for his party. They had made the task more difficult than in past years by making each of the other family birthdays this year something special. Sandy had had her Beatles weekend, Jack had visited Horseworld and speedway and Ben had had his Chinese experience. Coming up with something different for Nick was proving difficult and the two of them were beginning to panic. Sandy had cleverly arranged for the boys to have a sleep over at Ben's parent's house leaving them a few hours together to come up with a solution. The boys were excited by the idea of being spoilt by their grandmother, particularly as she had promised to take them to the summer fair which was held each year at their school, Ashley Park Primary School. They had been there every year ever since Jack had started at the school and had always enjoyed the entertainment going on at previous fairs, plus lots of sweets and cakes stalls and always a mammoth jumble stall with loads of toys and general junk.

Ben took the boys over to their gran's during the Saturday morning and gave them both a bag of mixed change for them to spend at the fair. No doubt Gran would be adding to their cash before setting off to the school after lunch. As usual Ben's dad was 'down the allotment' and as before Ben dropped in to see him on the way home. There were signs of activity on many of the surrounding plots including the Miss Hiscocks who were busy cleaning out their hen house. By comparison nothing seemed to be happening on his dad's land but that proved to be an inaccurate conclusion. His dad was the picture of contentment as he sat outside his hut using his pruning knife to top and tail a sizeable bag of gooseberries which he had freshly picked that morning. His radio was tuned in to cricket, his pipe was clenched between his teeth and the remains of a bottle of beer was at his side. What more could a man want?

He welcomed Ben without fuss, found him a seat and passed over a very worn old kitchen knife with the warning that it was very sharp. The next few minutes were spent by them sharing the task of top and tailing, which was yet another new gardening experience for Ben. As usual his dad kept up a running commentary about the trains that passed and when the gooseberries had been finished he reached back into the hut and produced a newspaper which he passed to Ben.

'This is the current copy of the Railway digest, which as you know I get every month from the railwayman's union. I like to try and keep in touch with developments but mainly I just like to read the obituaries to see who I have outlived. Have a look at the front-page article, which I think is very special.'

The front page was dominated by a large photo of a huge steam train in full steam pulling a long train of ancient-looking carriages up a steep incline, leaving a great trail of black smoke.

'I bet you have never seen that engine before, Ben, in fact I have only seen it twice myself. That's the Flying Scotsman number 60103 and it's generally agreed to be the most famous engine in the world. It has built back in 1923 for the LNER and was the first steam train to achieve 100 miles an hour. It ran the long-distance service from London to Edinburgh for almost forty years but was with withdrawn from service in 1963 and was due to be scrapped. Fortunately, it was saved by a preservation society whose supporters even included the prime minister at the time, Harold Wilson. Some enthusiasts claim that another famous locomotive, the Mallard, is even more important because it later set a new world speed record at over 120 miles per hour. It was certainly a handsome engine in bright-blue livery and with an unusual wedge shape streamlining but most of the old railwaymen agree that the Flying Scotsman was the greatest. In many ways it equates to the famous runner Roger Bannister, who was the first to run a sub-four-minute mile, others have run faster since but he was the one who passed the landmark.'

Once again Ben found himself surprised by his father's obvious passion as he spoke about his beloved railway and he remained quiet in the hope that he would continue. He didn't have to wait long.

'It's truly amazing but British Rail have agreed that the preservation society can use their mainline rail system to run a whole series of short excursions criss-crossing the country designed to enable as many people as possible to experience riding on a world-famous steam train. Apparently, they are starting in Scotland and finishing in Cornwall and the average trip will be about thirty miles. I guess it won't be cheap but the society have done wonders to keep the engine running and it is going to take a small fortune to keep it up it scratch so they need all the money they can get. I'm really excited and planning to take a trip on it with my old Blandford Street Station mate Arnold, and you can bet that we will be flying a flag on the flagpole over on Arnold's plot that day!'

As his dad was chatting to him Ben was reading through the front-page article, which listed the dates and places that the train would be visiting on its grand tour. One date leapt out at him, Saturday, 25 June, which just happened to be Nick's birthday! Perhaps this could be the special event they were looking for which could be the beginnings of a birthday surprise.

Ben kept his thoughts to himself but asked his dad if he could borrow the paper to show Sandy. His dad seemed pleasantly surprised that he was taking an interest as they had rarely talked about the railway before but was happy to loan the paper. He assured Ben that there was no hurry to return it as he knew that Arnold had a copy and in any case his friend was the one making all the arrangements for their trip going on the stages from London to Gloucester. He went on to explain that they were planning to travel up to London on the 9.38 am diesel from Exworth on the Friday to see the sights to include a few 'watering holes' before staying the night in an hotel. They would be joining the Flying Scotsman mid-morning at Paddington the next day and staying on board for two stages of the trip, getting off at Gloucester, ending their adventure with a short hop on a local train back to Exworth. The conversation moved on with his father taking Ben on a tour of his plot, offering various vegetables for him to take home to Sandy. Ben readily accepted everything offered which included rhubarb, which none of Ben's family liked. But he knew it wouldn't go to waste as Ma Driscoll would appreciate it as it was one of her favourites.

Before heading off for home he wandered down to the two Miss Hiscocks to admire their brood and to buy a dozen eggs. They invited him to come and see how the young chicks they had hatched had developed and to Ben's amateur eyes they seemed almost full grown. The two ladies asked after Sandy and the boys and Ben was impressed that they had remembered the boys' names after meeting them briefly only once. They made sure that Jack and Nick both had their names written on two of the eggs they provided, telling Ben to be sure to tell the boys that their favourite hen Henrietta had laid them especially for them. With a carrier bag full of goodies Ben went back to his car, pausing only to enjoy a childish swing on the gate as it slammed shut.

He went home and found Sandy stretched out on the sofa, coffee cup by her side watching some mushy old pre-war film on the television. She swung her feet around on to the floor and went to stand up, but Ben waved for her to remain seated and went into the kitchen to make himself a coffee. He collected Sandy's mug en route and as it was stone cold presumed that she would like a top-up. With the coffee made and armed with an unopened packet of Jaffa Cakes he plonked himself down by Sandy and watched the truly terrible film to its bitter end. Inevitably it ended with someone dying and with Sandy in tears but as she got up to turn off the set she declared that she had really enjoyed that. Sometimes Ben concluded that he would never understand women. Sandy was keen to know if the boys were okay and received Ben's allotment gatherings with the comment, 'Great that's tea sorted.'

He then showed her his dad's railway paper without any comment, which she looked puzzled about until she got to the bit about the dates of the trips and smiled in recognition of the 25 June. 'It's a thought, a real thought and would be something unique for the boys to do. However, before we get carried away let's ring up the booking office for more details.'

After a quick lunch of cheese sandwiches the afternoon was spent seeking out details and fitting together a comprehensive plan. Bit by bit the whole thing came together and by the time Sandy was cooking an omelette and chips for tea as Ben watched the football results they had a workable birthday surprise for Nick. During the afternoon Sandy had rung Patsie and Ben had rung Dave and both had been happy to be involved in the excursion. All in all it was going to prove to be quite costly but should prove worth it as it could possibly even top the success of Jack's party in school bragging rights. They agreed that Sandy would draw the whole plan together in the next few days but that they would give no hint yet to the boys until it was firmed up and invitations could be sent out. The rest of the evening was spent in watching rather boring programmes, starting with the 'Dick Van Dyke Show', which tended to have similar plots week after week but was easy to watch. However, from Ben's point of view its main attraction was the bubbly Mary Tyler Moore, who he had always found to be a rather sexy lady but he had never declared that fact to Sandy. He reasoned that after all, some things are best left unsaid.

They then went on to watch the beginnings of an edition of 'Hogan's Heroes' but the story line was once again very predictable and typical of American comedies and by 8.30 pm they had turned off the television and were soon cuddling up in bed preferring to take full advantage of the boys' absence. They could hear their elderly next-door neighbours Mr and Mrs Reed's television on full volume, which on this occasion was not needed as sound proofing. There was no desire for any histrionics tonight, which turned out to be just a coming together of two compatible people in full agreement on how to proceed.

Sandy had agreed to work on the Sunday morning to allow Ma Driscoll to attend mass at her church so she had set off early armed with the rhubarb Ben had brought home from his dad's allotment. Ben found himself alone and fancy-free and able to indulge himself with breakfast. He wandered down to the kitchen, dressed just in his pants, and got himself a couple of boiled eggs with soldiers, a dish of the boys' Coco Pops and a large black coffee. He set it all out on a tray and added a notepad and pen to the collection and returned contentedly to bed.

Once he had finished eating he turned his mind to the possibility of using the spare office space productively and without ruffling any feathers. He started by writing down a few basic rules that would need to be followed. There should be no way that the day centre could be allowed to interfere with the day-to-day provision of service by the team to the Highfield area. Its use would be restricted to a few hours one day a week. It could not be allowed to cause any additional expenditure to the department. It should have a low profile and the restricted membership would be selected by the team members. Ideally the club should have a small steering committee led by Phil and include an independent honorary treasurer to deal with all income and expenditure. The project would need to be developed in stages, the first being to upgrade the premises to an acceptable level. All sorts of other ideas were going through Ben's mind but he had already told himself that it was essential to get the ground rules established before getting bogged down with details. Undoubtedly the project could result in serious aggro from headquarters, however, 'nothing ventured, nothing gained', but he knew it could come back to bite him. All in all, the weekend had been pretty productive and by way of celebration he took Sandy down the pub for a roast dinner before going to pick up the boys.

Chapter 43

Sad Times

Monday started like any other working day with Sandy getting everybody up in good time and the boys checked to see they had washed behind their ears and had their school bags ready. With a hurried peck on Ben's cheek and a pat on the head for each of the boys she shot out of the front door still finishing a piece of marmalade on toast. Ben had time to sit at the table with the boys to tuck into the bowls of cereal that Sandy had prepared for them. The boys had their favourite, Coco Pops, which Sandy tried to avoid giving to them whenever possible because of the high sugar content. Ben always tried to support Sandy about this but secretly thought they were delicious and when he could get away it, as he had done the day before, he treated himself. The trip to school went without any hold up and he had enough time in hand to be able to pull up at the speedway track to check on progress. From the road everything looked almost complete. There was the top of a crane appearing from behind the vivid green fence but it was impossible to see what was happening. The fence itself was in the process of having Exworth Totters Speedway painted along the side in six-foot-tall letters. The fact that the painters had only got as far as Exworth Tot meant it looked more than a little incongruous. A large notice board had been constructed at the entrance off the road up to the track and there were several notices attached. Ben's curiosity got the better of him and he climbed out of the car to get a closer look. The board included all sorts of instructions for the various construction workers but also a colourful poster advising that the grand opening of the speedway track would be with a guest speedway event, with representation from eight different clubs, all invited to compete for a silver trophy. This was to be followed by a firework display and barbeque with music provided by the well-known local rock group 'Vic and the Senators' all to take place on bonfire night, the 5 November. It was apparent that Roddie and Tony's plans were proceeding at a pace and Ben determined to call in and see them as soon as possible to learn more.

The first thing Ben did once he was settled at his desk was to ring the general hospital for news of the Sullivans. Sister Franklin was pleased to hear from him as their circumstances had changed and Frank was due to be discharged from the heart ward later in the day

'He is sure to make his way back to Rosie's side at the earliest opportunity but I am afraid there is no way we can let him stay here on the ward after normal visiting time. Obviously he can come in to spend time with her each day and I am afraid that Rosie is very near the end. The trouble is he is still quite unsteady on his feet and he will need help with getting in and out for visiting.' It was agreed that Ben would try and sort something out to help and as soon as he rang off he rang Paul to see what could be done.

It was quickly agreed that Paul and Harry, his welfare colleague, would cover the weekdays, leaving Ben and Susie to do the weekends. Ben agreed to pick up Frank and get him home that evening, which would enable him to let Frank know what had been arranged. Meanwhile he asked Susie to do a shop for Frank so he had the basic supplies of bread, milk and the like for when he arrived home after his hospital stay.

The whole team squeezed into Ben's office just before lunch to share their thoughts about setting up a small social day club in the empty office space. The meeting went surprisingly well with the whole group accepting Ben's general suggestions about how it should be established and run. Phil was enthusiastic about being identified as the leader and coordinator of the project and Susie offered to do an initial cleaning of the premises with the proposed involvement of the ever-willing Alice. Mrs Freeman made a cautious suggestion that her husband, Steve, might be prepared to act as an independent treasurer.

'As you know he can't really get out very much and he is very bored much of the time. He always asks about things going on in the office and over the weekend I told him of our plans for the club and he was very interested. I could ferry things back and forth when necessary and I am sure he would prove to be a real asset.'

Everyone thought it was a great idea and Mrs Freeman said she would discuss it with him over lunch and let Phil know his reaction. On Ben's suggestion it was agreed that he should approach his rotary contacts Albert and Sam Watts to see if they would be willing to give the place 'a lick of paint'. The meeting broke up after only a half an hour with each of them going about their normal business but clear about their individual courses of action. Ben tried to ring Albert and Sam Watts but got Albert's wife instead, who turned out to be very chatty and with whom it was more than a bit difficult to get a word in edgeways. Ben suspected that she might be at least a contributing factor to Albert being so keen to get out and about with his cousin Sam doing little jobs as charity work. She finally got around to helpfully advising Ben that the two men could usually be found having a pint or two at the Highfield Tavern most lunchtimes and Ben was eventually able to bring the call to an end. After what had felt to be a diatribe he considered that he deserved a pint himself and abandoned his planned lunch at Joe's and headed straight off to the pub.

Sure enough Sam and Albert were there sharing their usual pies and pints whilst enjoying a competitive game of dominoes. Ben waved over to them on his way to the bar and gestured with his hand asking if they wanted a top-up. Their immediate grins and nodding of their heads left him in no doubt of their answer. He joined them at their table and handed out the drinks before taking a long draught himself. The dominoes were abandoned and he quickly had their full attention as he explained about the day club and how he would be grateful of their help. Their enthusiasm was immediate and they said they had been looking for a project they could get their teeth into for some time. Ben explained about the need to keep a low profile and the fact anything they did would have to be self-funding, as he couldn't ask the department for finance as that would at best involve all sorts of red tape and at worst could be the end of the project before it had got off the ground. The two of them seemed totally unworried about the restrictions and Albert finished his drink and stood up, saying, 'Well you best let the dog see the rabbit, there's no time like the present.'

The old Cortina and the Watts's van went straight back to the office in convoy where Ben was pleased to find Phil doing dictation with Mrs Freeman. He introduced Albert and Sam to the others and explained that the project had been Phil's suggestion and that she would be acting as leader of a selected steering committee. Ben recovered the keys from his desk drawer and, along with Phil, took the two Watts along 'to see the rabbit', as Albert had put it. Once inside, the men wandered this way and that immersed with the task in hand and Sam already had his notebook out and was taking notes. Meanwhile, Albert was running his tape measure over everything with Phil helping out by holding one end of the tape. Ben felt rather superfluous and was happy to leave them all to it, parting with an invite for them to come back to his office when they were ready. Over an hour later the three of them, looking suitably grubby from rummaging around in the accumulated dirt of the long neglected premises, joined Ben and he went off to arrange with Alice for some tea. As ever she was delighted to be of use and was already getting out the best biscuits, which she usually tended to reserve for The Champ. On the way back he invited Mrs Freeman and Susie to join the gathering, which rapidly took on the appearance of a game of sardines as they all squashed up in his office.

Albert spoke first on behalf of himself and his cousin and seemed to be very positive and keen to get into the project. 'We are both agreed that there is no reason why it shouldn't be a goer. Mind you it will cost a few pounds for materials, but it is a sound property, with all the services in situ, it needs quite a bit of decorating and a tweak here and there but we can see no reason why it couldn't be up and running in no time.'

This was music to the team's ears but Albert hadn't finished yet and continued. 'Now we understand that there is no money in the kitty and no possibility of the council picking up the tab. Well you couldn't have timed this better as we have a committee meeting of our rotary branch this Friday coming and I reckon they would be happy to make a charitable donation for your project. I am sure they will be sympathetic, particularly after the recent talk you made, Ben, to the group.'

This really was good news but Ben felt he had to stress the point that this was going to be an unofficial club run by a voluntary steering group and no arrangements had yet been made about controlling the finances. Mrs Freeman spoke up at this point and explained that her husband Steve had offered to act as honorary treasurer and she briefly told Albert and Sam about Steve's background and his medical condition.

'If you agree I will tell Steve to arrange a bank account in the club's name and he can operate it from our home. All we need then is to decide a name for the club, but I guess that can wait for another day, all in good time.' It was left that the group would get together again on the following Monday, by which time Albert and Sam would be able to report back from the rotary meeting and the ladies would have been able to make a start on cleaning up the premises. It was also agreed that Steve Freeman should link up with his bank manager and get the wheels in motion to set up a bank account for the club. Ben closed the meeting by asking everyone to give some thought for a name for the club that was distinctive but suitably anonymous.

Ben had already left a message for Sandy on their answer phone to explain that he would be late home because of having to pick up Frank from the hospital and had suggested that the family should go on with tea without him. He thought that he might just pick up fish and chips for himself and Frank, which would allow him the chance to have a long-relaxed talk with Frank to check on how he was coping. There was still a couple of hours before he was expected on the ward so he got Mrs Freeman to make a list of who would be taking Frank in to see Rosie over the next week or two. Paul and Henry were going to cover the weekdays and Ben was down for Saturdays and Susie was doing Sundays. Once Mrs Freeman had typed the list Ben slipped it into his pocket to give to Frank and left with the idea of calling in on Robbie and Patsie to catch up with the development of the speedway.

As usual he was made to feel welcomed by everyone with the exception of the Alsatian, who for some reason was back to his belligerent worst. Tony was busy dropping cars into an enormous crusher which turned family saloons into square lumps of metal that were then being stacked on to a huge lorry, presumably for onwards transit to Robbie's recently acquired contract with the smelting works at Port Talbot. Frudo was once again directing operations and it was him who approached the dog waving a big stick as he approached it; the dog retreated and reduced his volume to a face saving growl. Ben wandered over to where the two men were working and thanked them both for sorting out Ernest's problem with the handcart. They were obviously very busy doing a job that required their full concentration so he didn't hang about and quickly returned back to the stairs up to the site office.

Robbie was stretched out on the sofa almost half asleep whilst Patsie was busy shuffling papers and making entries in a leather-bound ledger. They both looked pleased to see him and on this occasion it was Robbie who filled the kettle and lit the Calor gas. 'To what do we owe this pleasure then, Ben? Not that we don't like to see you anytime.'

Ben explained that he had wanted to thank Tony and Frudo for their help with Ernest's problem, but his main reason for his visit was to catch up on the speedway development. 'Well I guess you have seen our poster giving a date for opening. We thought a bonfire night display should pull in the punters and with a bit of luck still leave us enough time to get everything organised. Mind you, it is going to be a bit tight so keep your fingers crossed for us. Most of the groundwork is on target and we have begun to recruit staff so we can train them up ready for the opening. Patsie has found us a caterer with a super modern refreshment van and we have agreed a contract with him to share the profits fifty-fifty. I see that you have already met Frudo and there is quite a story to be told about him. He was introduced to me by my old mate at the Swindon Robins Speedway Club. His full name is Joshef Frudonski and he originates from Poland where he is well known as an international champion speedway star. He knows speedway inside out and would still be riding now if he hadn't had a very serious accident which left him lame and unable to bend his right leg. After some treatment in Poland he came over to this country to get specialist treatment in a London orthopaedic hospital and took a liking to life over here. Once the treatment had finished he sold up everything he had in Poland and brought his family over to join him. It was a brave thing to do as he knew nobody over here, had no job, and had a wife and two young children to support. However, he is the sort of man who can turn his hand to anything and quickly got himself a job in a car factory in Swindon where one of his fellow workers who is a speedway fan recognised his name.

'The rest, as they say, is history and his co-worker put him in touch with the Swindon manager who in turn got in touch with me. I am delighted to say Frudo now works for me in the yard but is also the new manager of Exworth Totters. He is a great bloke and has already proved invaluable with all the experience he has of the speedway game. We are getting very excited as the track has now been laid out and I have negotiated a contract with the local coke company to take fifty lorry loads of their waste ash over the next two weeks to lay out as the racing surface. The beauty of the deal is that they are actually paying me to take it as they have to normally pay to have it taken away to landfill. So in no time at all we will be giving trials to possible riders who can then be trained up under Frudo's and Tony's guidance. How's that for a story, Ben? I feel that the gods are looking favourably on us.'

Patsie put her paperwork away and finished making the tea before joining Robbie and Ben on the sofa. It was a tight squeeze and as usual Ben found her perfume intoxicating, particularly as she was pressed up against his side. With a smile she said, 'Well, Ben, you have heard our news, so how are things with you and your family. I have spoken to Sandy a couple of times recently and I am really looking forward to being involved with Nick's birthday trip. If it's even half as good as Jack's then it should be great. It was good fun being with the group of boys. They were certainly a lively group. But what about you, Ben, what's new with you?'

That was how Ben soon came to be telling them all about the secret plans for the empty part of his office. As ever they were full of encouragement and could immediately see the potential value of the scheme for some of the more disadvantaged people of Highfield. Robbie jumped in at that point with 'I reckon I might be able to help you a bit with that. Come and have a look of what is tucked away in one of the lockups.'

Robbie reached over the desk and sorted through a pile of keys before coming away with an ordinary Yale key with lockup five printed on an attached label. The two of them set off downstairs, leaving Patsie with the task of washing out the cups. The up and over door of garage number five screeched in protest as Robbie lifted it and it proved to be full to bursting with stack after stack of green metal chairs. They were in various stages of disrepair but were all identical. Robbie explained that they had come out of an old army barracks that had closed many years ago and he had bought them on impulse at auction as they were going for next to nothing.

'I always figured that I could strip off the old canvas seats and backs and turn the metal frames into scrap, but just never got around to it. I reckon if you pick through them you should be able to make a good twenty or more reasonable ones. If they are of any use to you feel free to help yourself, and I am sure Tony and Frudo would be happy to help you pick them over.'

Ben said that he thought it was a generous and useful offer and that he would tell Phil about it as he had put her in charge of the project so he could keep a low profile. The afternoon had flown by and after a quick look at his watch he explained that he needed to pick up a client from the general.

The journey to the hospital was not easy as he had to compete with the rush of people going home from work, but fortunately his secret parking place was vacant. Sister Franklin had gone off work by the time he arrived on the ward but Sister O'Malley was on duty and Ben tried hard to conceal his surprise and embarrassment at his own reaction as he had never met her before and he had assumed from her name that she would be of Irish descent. In fact, she was Black and obviously of West Indian heritage. She demonstrated something Ben had experienced frequently before with all sorts of people when they discovered that they were talking to a social worker, a keenness to talk about their lives. She saw through his cover up in an instance and simply said, 'I was born in Ireland after my parents came over to Ireland from Jamaica to work in a TB sanatorium near Dublin. I went to school there and later trained as a nurse in Belfast. I met my husband when he was on the ward where I was working and with his gift of the Blarney Stone he swept me off my feet and we were married within six months. Sean is a trained architect but found it hard to get a regular job in Ireland but applied for and got a job with the council here in Exworth. We moved here four years ago and are glad that we did as we are very happy here. Mind you, it has not always been easy as some people don't like mixed marriages, but we know that we are a good example, showing that mixed marriages can work out well.'

Ben found her open reaction completely charming and listened with interest as he warmed to her, concluding that her patients were lucky to be in her care.

'Well that's quite enough of me. I am sure you want to hear about Rosie. I am afraid the news is not encouraging she is simply slipping away and it is more likely to be a matter of hours rather than days before she passes away.'

Sister O'Malley went on to report that Frank seemed resigned to the inevitable but remained determined to see Rosie through her last days.

Ben went off to the side room where Frank was sat holding Rosie's hand, and he nodded to Ben in welcome. He looked terribly drawn and exhausted but reached across and kissed Rosie on the forehead before getting up ready to leave with Ben. He attempted to pick up the small suitcase of things he was taking home with him and swayed unsteadily on his feet. Ben took the case from him and offered Frank his arm as he seemed incapable of walking far unaided. Together they slowly shuffled their way off the ward and made their weary way back to the old Cortina. By the time they reached the flat Frank was literally exhausted and declared that he didn't want anything to eat or drink, preferring to stretch out on the bed. Ben showed him the list of people who would be taking him in to see Rosie and left the list by the kettle in the kitchen as Frank was beyond taking it in. Frank was already asleep. Ben covered him with a blanket and tiptoed away.

As he travelled down in the groaning lift he wondered if he would be taking Frank to see Rosie as planned on Saturday. His strong suspicion was that he thought it unlikely and so it was to later prove. To try and cheer himself up he switched the car radio on in time to hear most of the new Rolling Stone record 'I Can't Get No Satisfaction' which the DJ reported had just given them their first number one in America. The world goes on, with some on the way up, whilst others are going down. On that philosophical thought he pulled up at the chip shop for sausage and chips, which he ate off his lap as he drove home.

Chapter 44

A Fitting End

The boys were just going to bed when he got home and he called in on them and finished off reading the current bedtime Biggles story 'Biggles Flies Again'. Earlier in the year Ben had trailed around the local second-hand bookshops and acquired half a dozen Biggles books that he could remember enjoying as a young boy. They were now lined up on the boys' bookshelf and as he had just finished the second one, pulled down 'Biggles in France' to be started next. Ben had been surprised how boring the stories were but the boys lapped them up and he secretly hoped the boys would soon be able to read the books for themselves so he could move on to something more exciting.

Sandy had finished the tidying up and had prepared the boys' packed lunches for the following day by the time Ben joined her on the sofa. She had made them both a hot chocolate and was curled up relaxing but had not switched on the television, which she would normally have done. She asked him about his day and listened with half an ear as he told her about Frank and Rosie. She had known them from the time they had been caretakers at the local primary school and she was saddened to hear that Rosie was failing fast. However, it soon became clear that she had other things on her mind and Ben sat back to listen. She wanted to share with him how her plans for Nick's birthday were coming together and she was clearly very excited. She virtually had it all organised, which was just as well as there were only three weeks to the 25th. It was to start with Sandy and Patsie each driving their own cars around to pick up four boys each and rendezvousing at Exworth Railway Station for ten-thirty to catch a local train to Bristol Temple Meads. There they would link up with the Flying Scotsman to go on a short excursion to Weston-Super-Mare travelling in a compartment that Sandy had already booked for their exclusive use. Meanwhile, Sandy and Patsie would have driven the two cars to meet them off the train at Weston and drive them to the large outdoor pool on the seafront. The plan was to let the boys play in the water, under the supervision of Dave and Ben, before all tucking into a picnic lunch provided by the ladies. The afternoon would then be taken up with a walk along the seafront to the pier and the chance to enjoy the amusements and rides at the end of the pier. Tea was to be a bag of chips each eaten out of the paper on the beach before the drive home in the cars. To Ben's ears it sounded terrific and he secretly prayed for fine weather whilst praising Sandy for putting such an interesting day together.

The next two days settled down to be uncomplicated and routine, with the team all doing their own thing visiting clients who were on their everyday case lists. Susie made one of her regular visits to Hanca Parsons and reported to Ben that she was doing well and that she had an idea for improving Hanca's lot. It was unfortunate that Ben's phone went just as she was talking to him. The call was a protracted one and Susie went on her way before giving him any idea of her proposal. It had been a bit of a throwaway comment and Ben thought no more of it, which was later to prove to be unfortunate.

On the Tuesday evening Sandy and Ben told the boys about their plans for Nick's birthday and asked them each to name three children who they would like to invite. After some determination the same group of boys who had enjoyed Jack's birthday were decided upon and that suited Sandy and Ben well, as they agreed that it was 'better the little devils you know' when you are going on uncharted territory. That evening Sandy sat down with Nick to make a start with the invitations, which emphasised that the boys would need their swimming togs as supervised water play was intended as part of the activities.

The Wednesday followed a similar pattern and Ben managed to link up with Phil to tell her about Robbie's offer of the stacking chairs. At her suggestion they went along to the vacant building to check what if anything could be salvaged from the abandoned furniture. There wasn't much of any use in the main room apart from three rather tatty tables that they agreed could be put together in a line down the room to provide a useful work bench and could double as a dining table. The chairs that remained were only fit for firewood but there was also a large built-in dresser with plenty of shelving, drawers and cupboards, which when emptied of their rubbish would provide useful storage. The kitchen came complete with an electric cooker, a Belfast sink and a vintage refrigerator that was smelly and yet to be tested.

Overall they agreed that it wasn't a bad haul but there was no doubt that Robbie's chairs would be well received. They agreed that when Susie and Alice were doing the tidy up it would be helpful to ask Ernest to work with them by removing the unwanted bits and pieces and get them stacked in the car park ready for removal. Phil said she would have a word with Susie and let her know what needed to stay and what needed to go. Meanwhile, Ben said he would link up with Sam Paterson, his contact in the cleansing department, to get the rubbish removed in due course. Things seemed to be going well and they both looked forward to their next meeting with Albert and Sam to see if there was any money available to help make things happen.

First thing Thursday morning Sister Franklin rang to tell Ben that Rosie had died at 3.50 am. Frank had remained at her bedside throughout the night and was with her at the end. Sister Franklin reported that it had been a peaceful passing and that Paul had just arrived to take Frank home. Ben thanked her for all the care she had shown to the Sullivans and said he would visit Frank later in the day but would leave it for a little while as he felt sure that Frank would be exhausted and in need of sleep. He went down the corridor to tell Susie the news and they agreed to make a joint visit after lunch. Ben collected the keys for Frank's flat from Susie in anticipation of having to make frequent visits to support Frank in the days to come. Paul rang Ben later in the morning to ensure that he knew of Rosie's death and to let him know that Frank was 'out on his feet' and had gone straight to bed. Ben explained that he was intending to visit Frank later in the day with Susie and that they would ensure that he had enough to eat in the flat. They agreed to keep in touch and after sharing the sorrow they both felt for Frank the call was terminated. Ben went to Joe's for an early lunch and a quiet think in the back room.

Three or four hours later Ben and Susie knocked on Frank's door and let themselves in with the keys Frank had recently given to Susie. Frank was sat in his usual chair, immobile and apparently in a stunned silence. Ben pulled up a chair beside him and talked to him in a gentle voice, asking Frank about the last night he had had with Rosie and saying how comforting it must have been for her having him there. Frank remained silent for some time but eventually a couple of tears ran down his face and he was soon weeping profusely. Susie went and made some tea, which she laced from a brandy bottle she recovered from the side board. Frank drank it down automatically but it seemed to help to get him started talking about his life with Rosie. Once started, he needed no prompting from Ben and the words tumbled out in quick succession. Susie left them to it and busied herself tidying the kitchen and emptying the numerous overflowing ash trays that still littered the place. That task completed, she checked what provisions were needed, then in a way obviously borne from previous experience collected some money from a jug on the windowsill and went off to do a food shop at Tesco.

She returned about an hour later with several bags of groceries and put them all away before putting the receipt and change back in the jug. Frank was still talking but there were signs that he was slowing up and Ben was grateful when Susie persuaded Frank to let her cook him an omelette. He ate the lot and had a further cup of brandy-laced tea before starting to nod off in his chair. Satisfied that they had done all that could be done for the time being they left him to his memories and dreams and went back to the office. Susie agreed to check in on him the following day and recovered the keys from Ben.

First thing on Friday Susie made the visit to Frank and reported back to Ben that he appeared to have spent the night in his armchair. He hadn't had much to say but had shuffled into the bathroom to have a wash and shave whilst Susie cooked him a fried breakfast. Once again he ate the lot and even followed up with cheese on toast, which he assured Susie had been one of Rosie's favourites. Frank told Susie that he was expecting a visit from Paul on the following day and assured her that he had everything he needed for the weekend. It was left that Susie would call in during the following week and on balance Susie felt that Frank was better than expected. Ben was able to get on with a couple of routine visits in the morning and then went off in a leisurely fashion to the afternoon at the prof's clinic and when parked had his sandwiches whilst reading an old copy of the *Daily Mirror* which he had picked up at Joe's earlier in the week. As usual he started with the strip cartoons, as he had always done when he lived at home and had used to dip into his dad's daily newspaper. Sadly, the humour in his 'old friends' Andy

Capp and Wellington seemed very old hat and he browsed on through the paper in a rather disinterested way. Suddenly a headline caught his eye and that did make him laugh, as it seemed so bizarre. Harold Wilson the prime minister had awarded the Beatles MBEs for their service to music. Although Ben thought the Beatles were great the idea of them receiving awards for doing what they enjoyed and what was earning them a fortune just seemed totally ridiculous. It never ceased to amaze him what politicians would do to gain a few votes.

Ben joined the prof and Raj for coffee as usual and they had a general chitchat. For no particular reason Ben enquired about how Penny Farthing was doing and was told that she had been transferred from St Margaret's to part of the St Benedict's campus 'Elm House'. Dr Rani had been involved with the transfer and explained the thinking behind the move. After a period of assessment the decision had been made that her primary problem was sub-normality, and her move to Elm House had been arranged. Her mental state was largely unchanged but the period of hospitalisation in St Margaret's had brought about a reduction in her weight of several stones and had got her up and moving about. Elm House was a large old country house which offered long-term care to mentally handicapped women, most of whom had spent many years in institutions. Penny had apparently settled in well but continued with her obsession for Barbie dolls in preference to relating to the other women in the home. As far as Dr Rani knew Ernest had had no contact with his sister, which came as no surprise to Ben as he knew they had never been close.

The afternoon clinic went as normal and Ben's last interview was over by 4.30 pm, meaning he was able to go home early for once. On impulse he bought a bunch of flowers for Sandy from the flower seller at the entrance to the hospital, which reflected how he felt to have the working week over with. The hug he received from Sandy when he presented the flowers to her confirmed that it was something he ought to try and do more often.

Saturday was taken up with household chores in the morning and a trip to the local recreation ground where the boys played on the equipment and hide and seek with a group of friends from school. Sandy was soon having a good old gossip with some of the mothers she knew from the school run and Ben wandered over to watch the football for want of something better to do. Luckily, he came across Dave, sitting on an upturned bucket watching his team St Margaret's getting thrashed.

Ben pulled up a spare bucket and took the opportunity to catch up on Dave's news before filling him in on the plans for Nick's party. Their conversation came to an abrupt halt when Dave was called away to administer his magic sponge, which coincided with a sudden downpour of rain causing the Newman family to run for the cover of the old Cortina. Sunday was taken up with an invite to Ben's parents for lunch to celebrate his mum's birthday. The full roast dinner was quite something and was followed by gooseberry crumble with Dad proudly pointing out that all the vegetables and gooseberries came off his allotment. Once the meal was over he was anxious to get back to the allotment and Ben and the boys opted to join him, leaving the ladies to do the washing up. The look Sandy gave Ben made him reflect that more flowers might be a good idea sooner rather than later.

On arriving at the allotment, Ben's dad armed the boys with bean sticks before sending them off on their adventures with the usual warning to stay on the paths. He settled himself on the bag of compost and indicated for Ben to sort out a chair from the shed. He clearly didn't intend to get on with any work but clicked on the portable radio and reached under a pile of old sacks and produced a couple of cans of beer. Predictably the radio was tuned into the test match with England playing against New Zealand and he began to run through the team for Ben. He focused mainly on Freddie Truman, who he described as the finest fast bowler of the age and he was genuinely upset that this match was to be Freddie's last test.

"It would be great if he went out on a high but whatever happens he will be a real loss to the game."

The two men sat mainly in silence and enjoyed their beer, with Ben's dad identifying every train that passed more from habit than anything else. Ben guessed that his dad did this even when he was alone but thought it probably helped to keep his mind ticking over and dementia at bay. Ben told him about the planned trip on the Flying Scotsman for Nick's birthday and his dad simply said, 'The boys will love it and won't ever forget the experience, there is nothing quite like it nowadays with the boring diesels instead of the special old days of steam.'

The cricket commentary rumbled on with England batting and nothing much happening. The combination of warm sun, a full lunch, the beer and the monotonous commentary had a soporific effect on Ben and he soon nodded off. When he came awake with a start he was being confronted by the two boys demanding to be taken to see the Miss Hiscocks's chickens. The two elderly spinsters were both down on their hands and knees weeding between row after row of crops. When they saw the two boys coming towards them they sprang up with a natural grace which belied their years. There was a new clutch of chicks for the boys to admire and they were each allowed to hold one of the young chickens that were the ones they had seen on their last visit. The boys seemed enraptured and soon became quite confident and competent at handling them. Ben once again bought a dozen eggs and two were adorned with smiley faces and the names of Jack and Nick. With some difficulty Ben managed to drag the boys away but they spent some little time arguing about what they should name 'their chickens'.

When the Newman family arrived home the boys plonked themselves down in front of the television ready for their daily helping of children's television. Sandy headed for the kitchen to sort out the vegetables given by dad and the eggs bought by Ben. Two things were already decided by her: it would be boiled eggs for tea and Ma Driscoll would be receiving a fresh supply of rhubarb. Ben sat in his armchair in preparation for another nap but he was quickly distracted by a light flashing on the answer phone. It was a short message but a puzzling one and he played it through several times to be sure of it. The big surprise was that it was from Frank Sullivan and it took Ben a moment to remember that he had given Frank his home telephone number several weeks before. The message simply said could Ben please call in to see him on Monday morning and that on no account should he send Susie. Ben couldn't begin to guess what it was all about and it played on his mind all evening and well into the night. After a very restless night which inevitably caused Sandy to have a disturbed night as well she eventually pushed him out of bed at six in the morning. She said that she would walk the boys to school and would get in to Ma Driscoll's later than usual, 'Just get on and check on Frank as soon as you can, that's the only way you will have any peace.'

Ben made himself some breakfast and took a cup of tea up to Sandy but she was already in a deep sleep and he left the drink on her bedside cabinet just to show willing. It was a little before seven when he left for work and it was barely light. The streetlights were still on but there was no traffic to speak of and he pulled into the car park almost two hours earlier than usual and almost ran a surprised Ernest down. Ernest was just picking up his dust cart and was keen to show Ben the pile of old furniture and rubbish that he had removed from the future club premises over the weekend. It was a whole heap of stuff but unfortunately he had stacked it against the building and Ben considered it lucky that the youth of the area hadn't spotted it. It was just asking for some would-be arsonist to put a match to it; which could have resulted in the whole building going up in flames. Ben got Ernest busy moving the heap well away from the building, patted The Champ on the head and went into the office to collect Frank's keys from Susie's desk. He waited long enough to write himself a note to remind him to ring his contact, Sam Patterson, later in the day to get the rubbish removed from the car park as soon as possible. Having found a biscuit for The Champ, who had followed him into the office, he locked the office up, praised Ernest, who had made inroads into moving the heap away from the building, and headed off to Frank's.

The lift made its full repertoire of grinding noises and the stack of superfluous boxes of cigarettes remained outside the front door. Out of courtesy Ben tapped lightly on the door but was not surprised to get no reply as it was still early to be receiving visitors so he tried the door, which was unlocked. It looked as though Frank was anticipating the visit and Ben let himself in, calling out Frank's name as he walked down the hall to the living room. Frank was fully dressed sitting in his usual armchair but was both immobile and silent. He appeared to be very peaceful but there was no doubt he was also very dead. Ben did not panic as there was nothing to be frightened about and he tentatively checked for any signs of a pulse. There was none, just cold flesh and a rigidity to the body which was in an advanced stage of rigor mortis. Ben had never dealt with finding someone dead before but as an avid reader of detective novels he understood that the correct procedure was to advise the police. He reached for the telephone then stopped in his tracks as he realised that there was an added problem; namely the boxes of cigarettes outside the front door. It wouldn't require much thought by the police to link the cigarettes to the recent flooding of the warehouse. It would then be a simple case of following up with the haulage company and onward to the part-time fireman drivers. Their act of kindness for an old colleague could easily result in them losing their jobs and facing criminal charges. Ben didn't hesitate but phoned Paul rather than the police and shared the problem with him. After a brief discussion they agreed that Ben would delay ringing the police for thirty minutes to give Paul a chance to sort things out.

Ben sat in the other armchair opposite Frank and found himself liberally covered in a coating of ash that had been spilled by Rosie's smoking over the years. He gazed around the room and noticed for the first time an envelope on the small table at the side of Frank. He reached for it and discovered that it was in fact addressed to him as 'Confidential for the attention of Ben Newman only'. With a shaky hand he ripped the envelope open and read the handwritten letter it contained with a sinking heart.

Dear Ben,

I want to thank you and Susie for all the help and support you have given to Rosie and me over the past few months. As you know it has been a particularly difficult time for me having to watch my precious Rosie slowly deteriorate day by day. It is a blessing that she is finally at peace but I miss her every minute of every day. Sorry that I have left you to sort things out but I know you will do your best for us. Paul knows all about my wishes for the funeral arrangements and what I want done with my belongings. I believe it is quite proper that Rosie and I will pass on together. God bless you both.

Your friend, Frank.

It was immediately clear to Ben that Frank had decided to end his life but there was no sign of blood or agony. Ben remembered the bottle of Rosie's sleeping tablets, which had been kept on her bedside cabinet and reluctantly went into the bedroom to check. An almost full bottle was still there. Then he remembered her diabetic medication and paraphernalia that was always kept on top the television so returned to living room. It all seemed to be there; the urine testing kit, a couple of huge syringes and a full bottle of insulin were all lined up.

Then Ben recalled that there had always been two bottles of insulin in place, one in use and one in reserve, but there was no sign of a part-used one. Of course, Frank might have just confined the old bottle to the refuse chute but in his heart Ben didn't believe that. He had a few moments to consider what to do but there was never really any doubt in his mind. He slipped Frank's letter into his pocket and decided to say nothing to anyone. Ben sat back heavily in Rosie's chair, which caused a small cloud of cigarette ash to rise all around him and just for a moment thought he heard Frank laugh, but realised it was just air passing out of the body. Several minutes later there was a knock on the door and by the time he answered there was no one there but the boxes had gone and he could hear the rattle of the lift descending. It was now a quarter-past nine and Ben decided that that would be a plausible time for him to get things moving as if he had only just discovered Frank's body. He rang Roger Richards the local constable and was welcomed with, 'You have just caught me. I have been up seeing the kids in at the secondary school as there has been some bullying going on and I thought a police presence might help. What can I do for you today, Ben?'

Ben got his message across in a couple of brief sentences and Roger's reaction was immediate, saying for Ben to hang on in the flat and he would be with him directly. In less than ten minutes Roger arrived and after a brief check on Frank asked Ben to fill him in on the background. Ben told him about Rosie's recent death and about Frank's very recent major heart operation. Roger asked about Frank's general practitioner and Ben was able to tell him that it was the Dr Eddoll and Dr Smyth's practice and that he knew they had both been involved in recent months. Roger took over and prepared to do what was necessary, having dealt with sudden deaths several times before. It was arranged that Ben would call into the police station later in the day to make a formal statement and without a backward glance he headed back to the office.

Susie was in her room and Ben asked her to come to his office where he told her of Frank's death. He made no mention of the letter or of his suspicions but was able to quite truthfully tell her that Frank looked very peaceful. The shock hit Susie with some force but she managed to hold back the tears until she reached the privacy of the ladies' loo. Ben went along the corridor to update Mrs Freeman, who had never met either of the Sullivans but knew all about them from the reports she had typed up over the months. She headed off to comfort Susie and Ben went back to his office and closed the door firmly. He sat at his desk before pulling the letter from his pocket and reading the words all over again. It almost seemed unreal but after a couple of minutes he put the letter back in its envelope and sealed it with tape. It was added to his memory box, which was returned to the back of his bottom desk drawer and buried under a pile of miscellaneous papers. He then spotted the note he had written to himself, reminding him to ring Sam Patterson about the rubbish in the car park.

Sam was full of the joys of spring and went straight into a joke that was doing the rounds of the dustbin men. Ben went along with it as positively as he could. After all, life had to go on and there was no reason to spoil Sam's day. Sam as ever came up trumps and agreed to arrange for the rubbish to be removed the next day. As he came off the phone Mrs Freeman popped her head around the door and said that Susie was holding up okay and reminded Ben that there was a three o'clock planning meeting about the club after lunch. 'Now get yourself off to Joe's for a lunch break. You have had quite a day.'

Not for the first time Ben thought that Mr Freeman was a lucky man.

Chapter 45

Double Date with Destiny

Sam and Albert turned up in good time for the three o'clock meeting and from the grins on their faces it was quite clear that they were the bearers of good news. But they were immediately aware of the air of gloom in the office and Ben had to give them an outline of the day's events so far. They were extremely sympathetic and volunteered to put the meeting off for another day, but the whole team were for going on with the planning.

Both Phil and Susie had told Ben how much effort Alice had put into getting the place clean and he felt it was quite appropriate to invite her to join in on the planning meeting. The whole group, with the exception of Mrs Freeman, who stayed behind to man the office, went along the car park to the side entrance and Alice's, Susie's and Phil's efforts had transformed the rooms. They were still well used and in need of decoration but the vision of what they could be like was most encouraging. Sam and Albert were more than pleased and quickly enjoyed telling the team about the outcome of their approach to the rotary for assistance. The most important thing was that they had been offered a donation of £250 to get the club up and running. It seemed like a fortune and the men were confident that that amount of money would more than cover the materials required.

Albert had done some preliminary costing and he was confident that the club would be starting with a small but significant bank balance. The discussion then went on to consider which day of the week would be most convenient to hold the club and for no obvious reason they decided on Thursdays. The ladies were keen to discuss colour schemes with Sam and Albert; Ben was happy to leave them to it but before he withdrew he raised the thorny question of a name for the club which needed to be decided urgently so that Steve Freeman could open a bank account for the club. It was resolved almost at once by Alice, of all people, who out of nowhere said why not call it the Thursday Club. It was perfect, not labelling in any way and suitably anonymous. Once this was agreed Ben excused himself and left them discussing colour schemes whilst he went off to update Mrs Freeman and to ask her to get her husband to open a bank account in the name of the Thursday Club.

Returning to his desk he just sat there and worried. He made a couple of attempts to sort out some files but he couldn't concentrate as his mind kept on returning to what was happening at Chelsea House. He had heard nothing from Constable Richards and knew that he was going to have to make an official statement later in the afternoon. He knew that there were things he could say and in fact probably should say but he had been entrusted by Frank to do his best to sort things out and that is what he hoped to achieve. He reached into his bottom drawer and recovered Frank's letter, which he slit open and read through yet again, even though he could remember it verbatim. The knock at the door made him jump guiltily and he hurriedly pushed the letter into the drawer and slammed it shut. He was relieved when it was only Albert at the door who asked if he could have a word in private. Once he was sat down he presented as being rather embarrassed and Ben did his best to put him at ease by saying how grateful he was for all his and Sam's efforts. Albert took a deep breath and came straight to the point.

'It's a bit sensitive, but as you know we did some decorating for your client Desmond Davis a few months back and he has come on in leaps and bounds ever since and is now a good friend and also a member of rotary. And there lies the problem, as Desmond just loves coming on decorating jobs with Sam and me but the reality is he is a lousy painter and decorator. We always have to go back over his work to sort it out and on a big job like the club it will slow us down something awful. What we really need is something for him to do which is helpful but not under our feet all the time.'

Ben was quick to sympathise with Albert saying that he knew just how skilled their work was and his own attempts at DIY in the past left a lot to be desired. 'Leave me with it, Albert, I will come up with something.'

The call from PC Richards finally came at a little after four and it was a relaxed affair with him introducing himself as Richard and calling Ben by his Christian name. He had contacted Dr Smyth, who had attended the flat and signed the death certificate listing the cause of death as heart failure. Frank's body was now at the Co-op mortuary and Paul was dealing with all the necessary arrangements from here on. Ben agreed to call in on the police station on his way home and with a sigh of relief resealed Frank's letter in the envelope and returned it to his memory box. His subsequent statement outlined the circumstance of Ben finding Frank dead but omitted Frank's phone call, the letter, the missing insulin and Ben's suspicions. Richard never mentioned anything about cigarettes and neither did Ben. By the time he got home he had had enough but Sandy immediately wanted to know what had happened when he had visited Frank. He told the tale, leaving out his suspicions. Sandy wrapped her arms around him and cuddled him to her. It was a lovely warm feeling and he felt like crying but the boys were right there and that would never do. They found it off-putting when Ben and Sandy showed any physical behaviour to each other and to see their dad cry would be a total antipathy for them. The evening passed pretty well with the family sharing their weekly dose of 'Top of the Pops' and Sandy offering Ben more intense comfort once the boys were safely tucked up in bed. After the previous disturbed night Ben went out like a light and had a dreamless sleep throughout the night.

The rest of the week passed without further incident at work and on the home front the main occupation was putting the plans for Nick's birthday into motion. The Saturday proved to be a typical high summer day, much to Sandy and Ben's relief. Dave buzzed up on the pink peril in time to join the family for breakfast and moments later there came the purr of Patsie's Mercedes. The boys were beside themselves with excitement and couldn't sit still and Dave eventually took them out into the street for a kick-around whilst the others enjoyed the opportunity for an adult chat and a coffee. Soon after 9 am Patsie and Sandy set off in the Mercedes with Nick to collect his three friends and Dave, Ben and Jack followed suit in the long-suffering Cortina to collect his three guests. The two groups linked up at Exworth Station in good time to catch the local diesel to Bristol Temple Meads with Sandy taking over the Cortina and leading Patsie's Mercedes off in tandem to Weston-Super-Mare.

The majority of the boys had never been on a train before and they were determined to enjoy the experience with the high spot being going along the corridor to use the toilet. Once the first boy had returned from his trip full of pride at having peed standing up as the train vibrated along they all had to have a try. The view out of the window proved a poor substitute for this newfound adventure and Ben and Dave had eventually to call a halt to toilet visits as some were on their second or third visit. Ben was pleased to note that Nick's very shy friend Simon did join in the activity but made no comment about the experience so it was probable that he just needed to go! Within in a few minutes of getting the boys settled down the train pulled into platform one at Temple Meads. Across the tracks platforms three and four were heaving with people, most of whom were carrying cameras. The boys quickly picked up on the fact that something unusual was happening and were anxious to get involved.

Ben and Dave sorted the boys into their two groups and stressed the need for them to keep together or they could get lost in the crowd. They headed off to the underpass, reappearing on platform four with Ben leading the way to the far end of the station. The boys gathered around and Ben explained about the very famous Flying Scotsman, the first steam train to top 100 miles an hour, and the fact it was due to arrive at any moment. As if by magic the huge steaming monster rushed in to the far end of the platform in a cacophony of noise and came to a halt just a few yards away from them with a long blast of its whistle. The boys couldn't fail to be impressed and Dave produced Patsie's Polaroid camera from his knapsack and snapped each of the boys in turn posing by the engine's brass nameplate with clouds of steam surrounding them. The train driver leaning out of his cab chatted to them and when he discovered it was Nick's birthday treat he let him climb aboard and put his own driver's cap on Nick's head to have his photo taken. The grin on Nick's face said it all and by now the engine was being photographed from all angles by a sea of enthusiasts so Ben and Dave gathered the boys up and went off in search of compartment 7C, which was reserved for them for the trip to Weston.

There were no further trips to the toilets as there was no corridor on the train but the boys were content to spend the trip waving to the many people on the track side at every turn! They had never felt so important or popular and didn't seem to comprehend that it was the train not them getting the adulation! The station at Weston-Super-Mare was much smaller then Bristol Temple Meads and had none of the grandeur that Isambard Kingdom Brunel had lavished upon the Bristol station, but if anything it was even more crowded with train enthusiasts.

Much to the initial embarrassment of the boys, Ben insisted that they form a line behind the tall distinctive figure of Dave and then they did a sort of conga through the crowd and out of the station. By the time they successfully linked up with Sandy and Patsie in the station carpark they had got themselves into the spirit of the dance and were kicking their legs in all directions and singing the conga tune. They piled into the backs of the two cars and in no time at all were deposited outside the massive art deco Weston Swimming Pool, which was impressive with its spectacular high diving boards. The ladies went to park the cars further along the seafront before returning carrying the essential supplies for lunch. The whole group set up camp beneath a large ornamental statue of a pineapple, which was clearly visible from all parts of the pool. Much to the boys disappointment the pool was temporarily closed off with a sign advertising a high diving display by the Great Britain Olympic diving team to start at 1 pm. The boys were allowed to wander around and explore for a few minutes whilst the ladies set out the lunch, but their explorations were kept to a minimum as the lure of food proved the more popular. They all sat around eating food off their laps and were entertained by a spectacular demonstration of graceful and intricate diving from terrifying heights.

By the time the exhibition was over the food was all but gone and the boys were anxious to get into the pool, which was now open for use. With a nod from Ben, the boys did a rapid and uninhibited strip tease tossing their clothes into untidy heaps before jumping into the pool under the watchful eye of Dave. The exception was inevitably Simon, who shyly changed under his towel and folded his clothes neatly before going over to steps to lower himself rather gingerly into the water. Ben followed him to the pool side, apprehensive in case he got into difficulties, but he didn't need to worry. Simon simply pushed himself off from the wall and proceeded to set off with a stylish breast stroke. Ben went back to the ladies and told them that once again Simon had not failed to surprise and they agreed that whenever he did anything he always did it well.

After a while the boys came back to base after succeeding in getting Dave thoroughly soaked. They all looked a bit blue about the gills and were shivering with cold and had their teeth chattering as they quarrelled over which towel belonged to whom. Simon wandered up at this point and recovered his towel from beneath his neat pile of clothes and fully finished dressing before the rest had sorted out their belongings. Patsie pulled a couple of flasks of hot chocolate from the picnic baskets and the boys sat around clutching cardboard cups of chocolate in cupped hands. Peace reigned with just the odd claim that somebody was wearing the wrong clothes but Sandy sorted it out as best she could.

The group packed everything up and left the pool, turning to the left to walk along the front to the pier. On the way they packed all their swimming things and the food baskets into the boots of the cars, which were parked quite near to the pier entrance. The boys seemed intrigued by the idea of walking on a wooden pathway over the sea, but their interest was soon taken up with the joys of the amusement hall at the pier head. Ben and Dave divided them up into twos with Dave taking Nick and Ben taking Simon. They headed straight for the dodgems and Ben paid the proprietor for the use of five cars for two sessions and the boys were let loose. All hell broke out as each pair tried to bash the others as heavily as possible. The exception was Simon, who set out to drive around and around with minimal contact with anyone else. His driving put Ben in mind of an old woman so much so that he quite expected Simon to start giving hand signals at any moment. Unfortunately, the other boys spotted Simon's exploits and ganged up to attack him from all directions, making the last few minutes of Simon's turn at driving a painful experience for them both.

At the end of the session all the drivers changed places with their passengers and Ben determined to wreak revenge for Simon. Dave had seen what the boys had been up to and gave Ben the thumbs up and the two of them set about delivering knock out blows to the opposition. Ben noticed that Simon was holding on for grim death but amusingly had a huge grin on his face and was egging him on to inflict maximum collateral damage. Everyone came off laughing and Patsie showed them a whole heap of photos that she had taken of them in action. From their facial expressions it was very clear that a good time was had by all. Sandy and Patsie grouped the boys around them and gave each of them a small cash bag of loose change for them to go and play the slots. They needed no second bidding and were straight off but Simon seemed reluctant to go and Ben asked him if there was a problem. Simon had his serious face on and suddenly produced a couple of carrots from his trouser pocket. He went on to remind Ben that when they had gone to Horseworld for Jack's birthday party he had met the old horse Solomon and he had fed him carrots.

'Well Mr Scadding told us that Solomon had worked on Weston beach pulling a cart for children to ride on. When I knew we were coming down here I brought some treats with me in case there was another old horse working on the beach. Do you think we could go and try? I would much prefer to do that rather than play on the machines.'

Patsie had overheard the conversation and took hold of Simon's hand and they set off down the pier, calling over her shoulder that she would meet them by the pier entrance in a few minutes. Most of the boys lost their money quickly and the adults gathered them up and after a quick headcount set off back down the pier with the boys surprised that they were no longer walking over water and Ben explained that Weston's water appeared to go out miles when the tide was out, leaving acres of black mud in its place.

Patsie and Simon were sat on the sea wall waiting for them and were both smiling contentedly. The ladies casually asked if anyone would like some chips and got an immediate positive response from the group including Ben and Dave. Sandy suggested that the boys should make a visit to the gents as they would be settling off for home once they had eaten their chips. By the time they had wandered to the toilet and had returned to sit along the wall the ladies had returned with pack after pack of chips each wrapped in a cone of newspaper. As anticipated everyone agreed they tasted great! Whilst they were eating Patsie told Ben and Sandy about Simon's visit to look for a horse on the beach. There had been no horses but there had been a group of donkeys taking children for rides along the beach. They were just setting out from beside a large horse box leaving behind an old man sat on the tail board and a lone donkey tethered beside him. Simon shyly went to speak to the man and was soon sat beside him on the tail board. Patsie left them to it but remained within earshot and listened with interest as the two of them chatted easily together in spite of being at least two generations apart. Simon told the old man about his visit to Horseworld and his meeting up with Solomon. The old man told Simon that he had been working on the beach for over thirty years and could remember the days when they had given cart rides but confirmed it had been stopped years ago.

'I still work with my donkeys but leave all the walking up and down to my son and his lads these days as I am getting old now, just like this old lady over here.'

He had then led Simon over to the tethered donkey and explained that it was his oldest donkey and it was too arthritic now to give any rides.

'But she been a great little mare and I have had several healthy foals from her over the years. She should really be spending the rest of her days eating good grass and resting. But she would miss the trips to the beach so us pair of old codgers come along for the ride and keep each other company.'

Simon's carrots had been well received and the old man shook Simon's hand as a fellow animal lover.

The trip home was uneventful with only a couple of hold-ups for traffic jams en route. Each boy was dropped off at his home and left with a photo of themselves next to the Flying Scotsman and one of them at the wheel of a dodgem, and for good measure a stick of Weston rock. Simon had an additional photo of him feeding his carrots to a pretty little donkey with the name 'Bunty' painted on its harness, not quite what he had planned but an acceptable substitute. The day had been a roaring success and Ben made a point of praising the team for all their help. The news of the trip raced around the school after the weekend and Nick and Jack's bragging rights went up another notch.

Chapter 46

A Time for Mourning and Celebration

Ben felt mixed emotions as he sat at his desk on the following Monday. He was still on a bit of a high as the birthday trip had been so enjoyable, but the circumstances of Frank's death still played on his mind. He couldn't help but feel that Frank and Rosie had been so devoted to each other that neither of them would have felt complete without the company of their partner. But his suspicion that Frank may have committed suicide remained with him and his decision to keep the information to himself weighed heavily upon him. He told himself repeatedly that he was only carrying out Frank's wishes and he re-read the letter several times to confirm this view. He knew that it felt like he was being dishonest and he had rarely been one to be unorthodox. There was of course a part of him that worried about being found out and the disgrace his deceit could cause him and his family. He consoled himself that once the funeral had taken place he would be able to draw a veil over the whole sad business and Frank's reputation would remain untarnished.

As if he was reading his mind Paul rang Ben later in the morning to tell him about the funeral arrangements. Everything was in hand and a double cremation had been booked for the following Monday. Paul went on to tell Ben to get a copy of the evening paper on the way home as he had arranged for Frank's death to be publicised. Ben's nerves remained on edge as he knew they would be for the next full week and he worried about what the news report might contain. He needn't have worried; the report was a masterclass of positive reporting and there was no suggestion that the death was anything other than natural causes.

'Death of a Highfield Hero' was the eye-catching headline which dominated the front page. It told the story of a brave fireman who had rescued a small child from a collapsing building in the nick of time and with no thought of his own safety. The paper went on to tell how the child had been saved unharmed but that Frank Sullivan, the fireman concerned, had been severely injured when the building collapsed on him. It went on to say that he had been awarded the prestigious award of the King's Medal for Gallantry and there was an accompanying large picture of a young Frank and Rosie, with Buckingham Palace in the background, holding the medal and smiling into the camera. It was a charming and completely appropriate report and just ended by saying that Frank and his wife Rosie had both passed away within a few days of each other and that their joint funeral was to be held the following Monday at Ensley Crematorium.

It was difficult for Ben to concentrate on anything during the rest of the week as he kept on thinking that his withholding of information would be discovered and he would have to face the consequences. He decided to keep his head down as far as possible and spent so much time in Joe's back room that Joe finally confronted him and asked if he was okay. Just for a moment Ben was tempted to spill the beans but decided that it would be unfair to lumber Joe with his concerns and just said that he was feeling a bit under the weather. His next cup of coffee delivered by Mavis was generously laced with whisky, which had been Joe's old mum's cure all. The days dragged by and even Ben's session at the prof's clinic on the Friday, which he generally enjoyed, failed to do much to raise his morale. He was the duty social worker on Saturday and each time the phone rang he answered it with trepidation, fearing that it might be some difficult official questioning. At one point when the telephone rang he was never more pleased to hear his mother in law on the phone and passed the phone across to Sandy with none of his usual signals to keep the conversation short.

Monday arrived at last and Ben went off to work as usual but was dressed in a suit and wearing a black tie in anticipation of the funeral timed for eleven that morning. Susie had arranged to take the morning off as she was intending to attend the funeral straight from home with her husband, John. Mrs Freeman and Phil were holding the fort, leaving Ben free to pick up Sandy from Ma Driscoll's on the way to the crematorium. At least it wasn't raining, unlike his last two visits to the crematorium, once for the pauper's funeral for Foxie Farthing and later the funeral for Foxie's wife, Elsie. Both had been grim affairs and he hoped that the Sullivan's funeral would be a more satisfactory occasion.

On arrival at the cemetery the difference was immediately apparent as there were cars randomly parked the whole length of the drive. The chapel was crowded with extra seating being hurriedly put in place by a harassed caretaker. The main body of people were firemen, many of them in full dress uniform which at another time and place would have satisfied the fantasies of many a woman. There was an air of relaxed behaviour, with a babble of many quiet conversations rising and falling punctuating the classical organ music which resonated around the chapel. On the dot of eleven the undertaker appeared with his top hat under his arm and the room went quiet. The vicar and the two coffins paraded down the aisle to the front of the chapel. One was placed on the usual raised platform and the other on two trestles alongside. The coffins were smothered in colourful wreaths and bouquets of flowers and were carried by two ranks of fire brigade officers each led by two older members who would have been of Frank's vintage. From his vantage point near the back of the chapel Ben surreptitiously looked around the congregation and found that he recognised quite a lot of them. Just in front of him was Sister Franklin from the geriatric ward at the general, where Rosie had spent her last days. Ben guessed that she must have to deal with death on a regular basis and that there was no way that she could or would want to attend all of their funerals. But today was as much about Frank as it was about Rosie and Sister Franklin had been astonished by Frank's devotion to his wife; no doubt she was here out of respect for them both.

Across the aisle he picked out the head of Ashley Park Primary School where Frank and Rosie had worked as caretakers and just in front of him was George Dangerfield the manager of Elmore House, where Rosie had been so well supported with day care. All these people were busy professionals but each had been touched enough by the Sullivans to want to find time to come and pay their respects to them both. Ben could feel himself welling up but managed to control his tears by listening hard to the words from the vicar.

The service proceeded along the usual lines and Paul went forward to the pulpit to deliver a moving eulogy about Frank and Rosie's life together. He finished by retelling about the fateful day over twenty years before when Frank had risked his life in a heroic act to save the life of a small child. He continued by pointing out that the child had been saved unharmed but that Frank had been permanently handicapped and his life had changed dramatically as a consequence. At this juncture he held up Frank's King's Gallantry medal, which he said was destined to be placed in the Fire Service Museum in London in a place of honour.

The chapel remained in respectful silence as Paul resumed his seat and the vicar asked if anyone else would like to say a few words. A pretty young woman in an advanced state of pregnancy went forward and eased her awkward state up into the pulpit.

'My name is Peggy Harrison and I am the little girl whose life was saved by Mr Sullivan's bravery. I don't remember anything from the day in question but my mum has described the event to me many many times over the years. I always meant to seek him out to say thank you but somehow life goes on and I never made the time to find him to thank him. Now it is too late I regret it, so I have to do the best I can. As you can see my baby is due in the next few days and without Mr Sullivan's intervention all those years ago I would never have been a wife or a mother. My husband Martin and I were surprised to read in the newspaper about the death of the "Highfield Hero". I realised at once that it was my Highfield Hero and welcome the opportunity to be here to say thank you and goodbye. We have been told that our baby is a boy and we have decided to call him Frank so that Frank Sullivan's memory will live on.'

As Peggy carefully stepped down from the pulpit there was scarcely a dry eye in the place. Then a smattering of clapping started which was taken up by the whole congregation and it swelled into a burst of applause which echoed around the chapel for what seemed like an age. The vicar began to show signs of being a little edgy and went on to the next stage of the ceremony by quickly announcing the hymn 'Love Divine' – 'The first and last verses only.'

It was clear to everyone that the Sullivans' funeral was running over its allotted time and people could be heard gathering outside for the next cremation in the nonstop business of funerals. The organ burst into life, playing the introduction to the hymn at a volume intended to support the level of hymn singing normally associated with such ceremonies. On this occasion the organ music was all but drowned out by the lusty singing of the fine group of men and women. The hymn resonated around the chapel, leaving everyone present in a state of high emotion. The committal followed with first one coffin and then the other disappearing into the vault below as the Sullivan's went on their last journey together. After a final prayer the vicar shook hands with everyone as they filtered out of the side entrance, but there were no family members to be offered condolences.

On a small table by the exit there was an open basket with a notice asking for donations to a dementia charity in the memory of Frank and Rosie. By the time that Ben and Sandy reached the basket it contained a pile of money, almost all bank notes of various denominations. They made their contribution to the basket and went out into the memorial garden to join up with the throng of mourners gathered there.

Almost everybody seemed to be lighting cigarettes and Ben felt a pang of nicotine deprivation for the first time in weeks.

Paul had arranged a buffet lunch at the Highfield Tavern, which had been Frank's pub of choice on the days that Rosie had been receiving day care. The crowd thinned out rapidly and after a brief chat to Susie to arrange to meet up at the pub Sandy and Ben joined the cavalcade heading in the general direction of Highfield. By the time they arrived the place was heaving with people all helping themselves from the long tables of food and attempting to get served at the bar. Remembering his last visit to the tavern, Ben led the way up the stairs into the restaurant above and hit the jackpot. The same waitress who had served Ben before showed them to a prime site at a table by the window and invited them to help themselves from the delicious looking buffet set up along the far wall.

Very few people had yet discovered the joys on offer in the upstairs rooms and the waitress was on hand to serve them with drinks. Sandy was the first to speak and said she could murder a coffee and the others all agreed with her. Ben introduced Sandy to Susie and John and Susie in turn introduced John. John proved to be nothing like Ben's imagined idea of Susie's husband, who he had thought would be tall and debonair and a match for Susie's bubbly personality. In reality he was short, a good ten years older than Susie and could only be described as looking ordinary and nondescript. As they ate, the conversations naturally split with the ladies talking together, leaving the men to their own devices. John quickly told Ben how delighted he was with Susie having a full-time job.

'She has always been a bundle of energy and found herself at a loose end with the boys away at university. Of course she has been a big help to me over the years building up the business but now I have had to cut back to only running our shop in Little Poppy Field on a day-to-day basis, there really wasn't enough for her to do. She has been much happier since she started working for you and comes home each day full of it.'

Ben's mind started to wander as John was talking and in his mind's eye he saw this short, red-faced, stout man dressed in a straw boater and white apron just like the image of Mr Brown the butcher in the pack of happy families he sometimes played with the boys. He was tailor made for the part and Ben found himself warming to John.

Their conversation moved on from Susie and they were soon discussing football and the chances of England doing well for once in the world cup, which was starting a few months away and would be taking place on home soil. The upstairs of the pub suddenly began to fill up as the food downstairs ran out and somebody directed the hoards to the fresh supply in the restaurant. The crowd noise was soon at a level to make normal conversation impossible and they mutually agreed to cut their losses and head for home. Ben waved across at Paul and gave the thumbs up and made the gesture of a telephone call later and Paul nodded his agreement. Sister Franklin must have seen Ben's wave and had twiddled her fingers in response from her situation of being surrounded by hunky fire men. She seemed to be enjoying the attention.

Susie and John offered to drop Sandy off at Ma Driscoll's, leaving Ben free to get back to the office. Within minutes he found himself sat at his desk carefully cutting out the newspaper report on the Highfield Hero. This was folded together with Frank's letter and added to the memory box. For the first time in a couple of weeks Ben felt relaxed and secure and was left in no doubt that his lack of action had been fully justified.

Chapter 47

Moving On

With just two weeks to wait for the planned holiday to Butlin's at Minehead the Newman family were getting very excited and were in full planning mode. The old Cortina had been coughing and spluttering of late and Ben was concerned that it might not be up to the round trip. He had never had the car serviced despite his total dependence upon it for his job, day in and day out, and to be fair it had never let him down apart from the odd flat battery and a couple of punctures. His tyres had been replaced at considerable cost when the car had failed its last MOT but he decided that a complete service was long overdue and would put his mind at rest for the longish trip. It meant being without a car for a weekend when it was being checked over by a mechanic friend of Tony Scadding who did 'foreigners for cash' at his garage at home but normally worked for the local Ford Agency. Tony assured Ben that he had known the guy for ages and that he regularly bought spares from the Scaddings' second-hand stock.

'He even looks after our mum's Mercedes and that's her pride and joy, so I am sure your old banger will be in safe hands.'

The boys got pretty bored over the weekend and to complicate matters the weather decided to change overnight from gorgeous sunshine to pouring rain and high winds. Any sort of outside activity was out of the question and with the holiday in sight the boys were at their argumentative worse. Finally, Sandy lost her rag with them with a force that frightened them into passivity but it clearly wasn't going to last long and Ben had to step into the breach. Without the use of a car the options were quite limited and the best he could come up with was a bus ride to the local flea pit and the possibility of a visit to Harry Ramsden's to follow. A quick look in the *Journal*, which was the local freebie newspaper, confirmed that the film on show was suitable for children even if it held no appeal for Sandy or Ben. The film was *Those Magnificent Men in their Flying Machines* and the title told virtually the whole convoluted story about an international air race across the English Channel. There were all sorts of underhand activities and numerous crashes which wrote off planes but from which the intrepid pilots stepped largely unscathed. It was the sort of film which, had it been on television, Ben would have switched off. However, the boys loved it and were genuinely amused by the various mishaps, meanwhile Sandy and Ben cuddled up and dozed. The film went on and on and in fact was so long that there was an interlude halfway through for the cinema to cash in on selling ice creams and to show the trailers of films to be shown in the near future. Both functions cost Ben money as he had to buy ice creams all round and one of the trailers was for the Beatles new film *Help* which was coming out on 29 July. It was sure to be popular and the whole Newman family, as massive Beatles fans, wanted to be amongst the first to see it. Ben slipped out to the reception area and booked and paid for four tickets for the weekend after they were due back from Butlins. This trip out was proving to be expensive and the fish and chip supper they all enjoyed after the second half of the film just about cleaned Ben out of cash. On the plus side it was a happy family that went home with no bickering and even the rain had stopped.

Sandy and Ben had a little conflab as they were coming too in bed the next morning and they struck a deal. Sandy agreed to take control of the boys in the morning as long as Ben took over after lunch. It was too good an offer to turn down as half a day of trying to keep two over excited boys as calm as possible was much better than a full day. Sandy got straight out of bed and after a quick shower shouted up the stairs that she was just popping down the road to get the Sunday paper from Ma Driscoll's. Ben turned over and by some miracle the boys remained quiet and the Newman household enjoyed a few minutes of peace. Sandy was soon back and brought the paper up to Ben along with a coffee and toast; no doubt she would get her pound of flesh later but Ben reasoned it was worth it. The house erupted soon after and Ben slipped out of bed and closed the bedroom door to maintain his solitude. When Ben finally got out of bed around midday he discovered the boys sat reading comics on their beds with the debris of a small parcel of sweets on the floor beside them. He wasn't sure if this had been part of Sandy's plan or an act of generosity on Ma's part but he sensibly asked no questions. The kitchen table was covered with newspaper, which was liberally covered by soaked-off stamps from several weeks of Camilla's letters. It was easy to tell which had been done by Jack and which by Sandy but they were all now dry enough for her to collect them up into an old chocolate box ready for sorting at a later date. Ben made them both another coffee and put his arms around her and kissed her tenderly. The act was well received and progressed a little further in a familiar and satisfactory fashion. So far Sunday was proving much better than Saturday.

They determined that lunch would be one of the boy's favourites, beans on toast, and Sandy finished clearing the table whilst Ben got busy with the toaster and can opener. The telephone went when they were all sat around the kitchen table and Ben swallowed his last mouthful before going into the living room to answer it. It was Tony's mechanic friend ringing to say the car was ready for collection and that there was twenty-eight pounds to pay. Ben arranged to collect it that afternoon and went back to discuss finances with Sandy. Ben's wallet was all but empty from the trip out the previous day and the agreement with the mechanic had been a cash one with no receipts given, so his cheque book was useless. However, Ben had been paid his monthly salary a week before and, as they always did, Sandy and Ben had drawn cash to be put in weekly envelopes of fifteen pounds for housekeeping. Two of these would have to be dipped into and Sandy reached for the biscuit barrel that she used for a cash box. The conversation moved on to discuss finances in general and it was clear that they were going to be tight this month. On the bright side the holiday was already paid for and all the food and entertainment was included in the cost. Petrol for the journey and a few ice creams for the boys and even a drink or two for themselves wouldn't break the bank. Also it was more than likely that the two grans would donate a few pounds 'spends' for the boys. So it might have to be 'bread and dripping' when they got home from Minehead, but they decided to worry about that when the time came.

With a bit of nagging from Sandy the boys reluctantly cleared the table and wiped up whilst Ben did the washing up. Sandy obviously felt that she had fulfilled her part of the bargain and pointedly retired to the sofa and stretched out with the Sunday paper. The mechanic's home was a good half mile away and the boys and Ben set off on foot during a brief break in the rain. The boys were still full of energy and amused themselves on the walk by seeing which of them could fart the loudest. With the assistance of the baked bean lunch both were very proficient and it was fortunate that being a Sunday there were few people about to hear them. The car was sitting on the road outside the mechanic's house and he was already busy under another car on wheel axles in his garage. The boys were intrigued when he shot out from beneath the car on a trolley and sprang upright, wiping his hands on a filthy old rag.

The money was exchanged for car keys and the mechanic's closing comment was music to Ben's ears. 'She's good for another fifty thousand miles, she's a good old bus.' As he got into the car Ben noticed that the bodywork was liberally splattered with grubby finger marks and on impulse decided to give 'the old bus' a treat by a visit to the car wash. This was one of the boys' favourite adventures and it never failed to please them. On the way home Ben was impressed with the change in the old Cortina. Everything seemed tighter and more responsive and the first time he had had to brake sharply it was reminiscent of the emergency stop he had done in his driving test. He might be broke but he was content that it had been money well spent and once again he had reason to be grateful to Tony for his advice. The rest of Sunday passed in a series of petty quarrels between the boys and both Sandy and him enjoyed a celebration beer once the boys were safely tucked up. Once in bed it took him a while to drop off, which is always annoying when your bedfellow is snoring soundly. In an attempt to drop off he let his mind wander to the things he needed to sort out in the week ahead to leave the place sorted so he could go on holiday with a clear conscience. Out of nowhere he remembered that he had promised to sort out a task for Desmond Davis in order to leave the way clear to let the professionals get on with decorating the club rooms. He suddenly had the inkling of an idea and his last thought as he fell asleep was that he would call in on the Scaddings on his way into work the following day.

Chapter 48

Time for a Much-needed Break

As he had planned in bed the night before, Ben called in at the Scaddings' yard on the way into work. The dog was alert and very vocal but went quiet when he was shouted at by Tony, who was in the process of starting up the big machines before beginning a day of swinging cars around and crushing them to square lumps of metal. Ben thanked Tony for his introduction to the mechanic and was pleased to report that it would be some time yet before Tony got to crush it. Predictably, Robbie was coming to terms with another day of labour by being sat at his desk with a coffee reading the paper. He hastened to point out that he was checking the current commodity prices as he had a stockpile of lead, copper and zinc to dispose of when the market price was right. Ben was once again aware that Robbie may have only had a very basic education but he could more than hold his own in the business world.

Not wanting to waste Robbie's time Ben came straight to the point with every confidence that Robbie could be trusted not to talk out of turn. He had already shared his plans for the office space and he now told him about his need to find a useful occupation for Desmond Davis, which would enable his professional builders, Albert and Sam, to get on with upgrading the building without hindrance.

'Don't get me wrong, Desmond is a lovely man and very well-meaning but he is not very good with a paint brush. He is okay on small jobs but is very slow and Albert and Sam find they have to go over his efforts more often than not. What I would like to do is to take him away from the office and set him to work on those old chairs you have offered. I think he would be no trouble and could be helpful to you by recovering the metal from the chairs you don't want so you could add them to your heap of scrap.'

Robbie recovered the garage key from the key board and chucked it over to Ben.

'That is fine by me, just make sure that Tony and Frudo know about him. I wouldn't like them to set the dog on him.'

Fortunately, Ben could tell by the smile on Robbie's face that he was only joking and they parted company with Robbie returning to his paper and Ben setting off to persuade Desmond of the importance of getting the chairs sorted. By the time Ben arrived at the office both Susie and Phil had been in and had already gone out visiting. Mrs Freeman had the post ready for Ben and there was nothing else to report, but she did mention that Susie had seemed quite excited and had gone off to see Hanca Parsons in good spirits. It was unusual for Mrs Freeman to make any personal comment about one of the team but she did say that she was impressed with how well Susie had coped with Frank's death. Ben knew how upset he had felt and Susie had worked a lot with Rosie and Frank in the past few months so he readily agreed with Mrs Freeman. In the absence of anything more pressing he wandered along the car park to the future club room and found the beginnings of a major improvement in the accommodation. Albert and Sam had a radio going full blast and were busy with rollers and paint transforming the main room into a light and airy space. Desmond was giving the old tables a fresh coat of gloss yellow paint and even Ben could see that the effect was less than professional with runs in the paint all over the place. Ben called the men together and shared his problem of converting a pile of old stacking chairs into usable furniture for the Thursday Club.

Albert saw through Ben's proposition straight away but retained his thoughtful expression before coming to the conclusion that it might well be something that Desmond could tackle. Desmond looked less than confident but Ben moved swiftly on to explain that the iron frames needed sanding down and then given a coat of some bright coloured gloss paint. The canvas seats and backs needed sorting through and then the best used on the prepared frames using the existing nuts and bolts. Sam got in on the act to say that he was sure they had some red paint back at their base which had been left over from a job they had done for the play equipment of a local toddlers' group. Ben said he would take Desmond to see the chairs the following day and Albert and Sam agreed to get all the fixings up together. To be fair, Desmond's feet never touched the ground, as he was well and truly railroaded.

So far so good, Ben was more than a bit smug as he left to go to his office, particularly as he received a thumbs up from Albert, who was out of sight of Desmond. Another problem nearly solved and his wind-down week to the holiday had started well. That all changed in a flash as he was met at the general office by a distraught Susie who was shaking like a leaf and crying profusely. Mrs Freeman had her in her arms trying to comfort her but she was sobbing and out of control with tears and snot running down her face. She kept repeating over and over again, 'I have done something terrible, I have pushed Hanca over the edge and I really don't know why.'

It was several minutes before Susie was under control enough to begin to make any sort of sense and even then it was hard to work out what she was trying to describe. After a couple of false starts she suddenly jumped to her feet and headed out of the main door of the office. For a moment Ben was concerned that she might be going to drive off, which would have been very dangerous in her present state, so he followed close on her heels. In fact, once she had unlocked her car she didn't attempt to get behind the wheel but simply opened one of the rear doors and recovered a cardboard box which she brought back with her into the general office. Neither Ben nor Mrs Freeman had any idea of what to expect but could hear rather plaintive noises coming from within.

When Susie lifted the flaps a little head popped up and Susie lifted out the most adorable little Persian kitten it was possible to imagine. It was impossible to imagine how such a beautiful creature could have been the cause of such distress for Susie. She cuddled the animal to her and told the others her tale of woe. She explained that she had a widow friend called Helen Hancock who ran a small knitting shop just a few houses down from their butcher's shop in Little Poppy Field.

'She's had a hard life and is very independent. Her husband died very young and they never had any children so she chose to perform the role of babysitter for all and sundry in the village. She manages to scrape a living with her wool shop but it is no mean feat. We have been friends for years ever since she babysat the boys when they were small and they really love her and always pop around to see her when they are home from university. Well, when they visited at Easter, they came home with the description of a delightful litter of kittens that Helen's cat Sadie had produced. So I suddenly had, what I thought was a bright idea that Hanca would like to have a cat as a companion and so I called in to see Helen to place an order for this little chap.'

The kitten remained snuggling into Susie's chest totally unaware that he was the subject of the conversation. 'I thought it would be a way of killing two birds with one stone, as it meant Helen could make a little money and Hanca would be less lonely, but it all went horribly wrong. Hanca took one look at the kitten and reacted really badly. She pushed it back in the box and hurried me out of the door repeatedly saying, "Cat will kill, cat will kill." I have no idea what she meant, perhaps it is something to do with witchcraft. All I know is she was very distressed and couldn't get me out of there quick enough. I meant it as a kindness but think I may have caused her some sort of mental breakdown.'

Ben reassured her that there was probably a simple explanation and immediately ruled out any suggestion that witchcraft might be involved. He remembered what had happened to Hanca in the past when she had been thought to be a witch and was amazed that Susie had even thought it possible. The whole thing certainly sounded bizarre, then Hanca was different to most people and presented as both a bit odd and eccentric, however, Ben had never considered her to be mentally ill. He had the utmost respect for her and her chosen lifestyle and decided to set straight off to try and sort out the confusion.

Hanca was in the garden when he arrived and was quick to say that she had been expecting him. 'I'm sorry, I realise that I must have frightened Susie and I didn't get any chance to explain. I'm sure she meant well and it was a pretty little kitten but it could have ended in disaster.'

Ben obviously looked puzzled, Hanca took the initiative and caught hold of Ben's arm in an uncharacteristically familiar way and led him into her kitchen. She took him over to the window overlooking the garden and told him to keep very still and very quiet. 'Watch the wall at the back of the old pigsties and you should then understand the problem.'

Hanca then went to her pantry and took an already opened tin from the meat safe and went back into the garden. She removed something from the tin and put it on the wall before joining Ben back in the kitchen. She whispered, 'Now, we watch and wait.'

Nothing happened for several minutes and Ben began to wonder if Hanca had after all blown some sort of fuse. Then a large black shape appeared on the wall and crawled stealthily towards Hanca's contribution. It was the largest cat Ben had ever seen but was nothing like a domestic cat. At some time it had really been in the wars with a mangled left ear, the appearance of being blind in one eye and a broken tail, which dragged along the floor. But for all its injuries it had a full glossy coat which shone with good health.

'This is my friend, I call him Cat and he was already living in the garden when I moved in. He is a wild or feral cat and is used to finding his food where he can. No animal is safe from his hunting skills. Susie's little kitten would have gone the way of every other animal who has dared to enter Cat's territory. Now I feed him pilchards three times a day and as you can see he is looking in good health on his new diet. One day, I hope he will let me stroke him but that is still a long way off. Meanwhile, I enjoy feeding him and watching him and knowing he is there.'

Ben remembered a conversation he had had with Jessie at the Landings shop a few months before when she had mentioned that Hanca's weekly shopping always included a lot of tinned pilchards; so that was another mystery solved. Cat devoured the fish in a leisurely fashion finishing by briefly cleaning himself before returning along the wall and dropping out of sight.

'I have made a sort of bed for him in one of the old pigsties that I use for storing my wood and we seem to muddle along quite well, but there is certainly no space for another kitten.'

Ben thanked Hanca for the explanation and promised to explain the situation to Susie when he got back to the office. On the way down Hanca's path, Ben, out of habit more than anything, lifted the lid of the old enamel bread bin that Hanca used to receive her mail. It was more than half full and he made a note to mention this to Susie as Hanca tended to ignore the contents except when she needed wastepaper to light her wood burner. By the time Ben arrived back at the office Susie had got herself back under control but she still looked very worried. Ben recounted the story as quickly as possible to put her out of her misery and she even managed a small laugh of relief.

However, Ben had already decided to use the situation as a learning exercise for Susie as he realised that he should have given Susie more direction from the start. The last thing he wanted to do was to restrict her natural ability to relate to clients and her common-sense approach had largely proved successful so far. But she needed to be made more aware of her role as a professional social worker representing the Health Department and it was his job to help her. He sat down opposite her and started by again reassuring her that no lasting damage had been done this time but went on to state quite categorically that she had fallen down on one of the most basic rules that they should work by. He avoided telling her what he meant, preferring to let Susie reach the conclusion by herself if possible. She gave it careful thought and then said, 'I made a mistake getting the kitten.'

Ben nodded his head but pressed her further for a fuller reason but she was floundering and he had to help her out.

'We have to realise that a couple of the basic rules of social work are that we need to always start where the client is and not where we would like them to be. Also, clients are entitled to self-determination. We can advise but we normally can't decide things for them. Of course there are exceptions when dealing with mentally ill persons who may need our intervention if they become a danger to themselves or other people. This is a rare occurrence and your mistake was that you thought you knew what Hanca needed and went ahead without sounding her out. I am sure your intentions were honourable, but we must remember we are not dealing with our clients in the same way as we might act towards a friend. It is fine for us to encourage, enable, even attempt to persuade but it is their life and we must always try to respect that.'

Susie seemed to accept the criticism in a thoughtful way and agreed that she still had a lot to learn about social work in the community. 'I have tried to look for books in our local library without success they just have nothing on the subject other than a few copies of legislation and the like.'

Ben finished the session by agreeing to look amongst his books at home to see what he could find. He knew he still had all the books he had used back in the days when he was studying for his own qualification the only problem was they were stored in the attic. It would involve another act of gymnastics on his part to recover them but it was great that they would be useful once again.

The rest of the afternoon was taken up with Ben trying to clear his in-tray of the accumulated paperwork much of which was weeks out of date. This exercise always had a cathartic effect on him as it allowed him to shred the majority of it and start afresh. Susie came back into his office as she left for home to say she was going to keep the kitten herself to remind her of her mistake. She had decided to call it 'Misty', which was as near as she could get to 'Mistake' without having to offer an explanation of its name to anyone else. But she would remember. They laughed together and parted friends as well as colleagues.

Chapter 49

Can't Wait to Get Away

Ben left home that morning with his mind set on tying up ends and not starting on anything new that might need his ongoing attention. With just four days to the long-awaited holiday it should be achievable but would require more than a little luck and perhaps Phil having to step up to the crease.

His primary concern was that he had swapped his emergency duty day for the following week with a colleague from the central office which left him doing two duty days in the next four days. This had the advantage that it involved him being stuck in the office for two afternoons awaiting the dreaded phone referrals but it could all go horribly wrong all too easily. Emergency duty was very unpredictable it could be a doddle and often was but it could also be a nightmare that left one exhausted the next day. Two sessions in three days was asking for trouble but needs must when you want to go on holiday.

When Ben arrived at the office, he briefly linked up with Mrs Freeman before walking around to the future premises of the Thursday Club. The two cousins, Albert and Sam, were already busy covering the prepared walls with a sort of creamy magnolia emulsion. The radio was tuned into a humorous panel show where four well-known comedians tried to outdo each other by their quick-witted comments on the subjects suggested by the question master. It was one of Ben's favourite programmes but he usually had to wait for the repeat on a Saturday when it often coincided with his family having lunch. He was tempted to sit a while and enjoy the treat but Desmond was perched in an awkward manner on one of the old tables swinging his legs and looking apprehensive. He had made his preparations for his allocated task and appeared to be taking his job very seriously. He was wearing a spotless pair of overalls, the trousers even had a crease in them, shiny metal-toed work boots and an improbable baseball cap.

By comparison, the two professionals working busily with their paint rollers looked a proper couple of scruffs. They were decked in string vests and paint-splattered dungarees which showed the evidence of numerous paint jobs in the past. Despite being in his sixties Desmond had the appearance of being a new apprentice armed with a smart little toolbox and a workman's satchel over his shoulder. Before they left, Sam presented Desmond with a pot of bright red gloss paint, a pack of sandpaper and a couple of paint brushes wrapped in a clean piece of old towelling. The cousins returned to their painting, Ben and Desmond got into the car for the short journey to Scadding's yard. Ben parked up as usual just outside the gates to the yard and as usual their approach through the gates was greeted by angry barking. Ben turned towards Desmond to let him know that the dog was safely restrained but was amazed to see Desmond walk straight up to the dog showing no sign of fear and in fact reassuring the dog that all was well.

'Hello, old fellow, you're a good old boy, nobody's going to hurt you.'

Then he reached into his satchel and produced a sandwich wrapped in greaseproof paper which he had obviously prepared for his lunch. This he fed to the dog, which had stopped barking and was now wagging his tail furiously as he let Desmond ruffle his ears.

Desmond couldn't have made a more dramatic entrance if he had tried and it hadn't gone unnoticed as Robbie came trotting down the stairs and joined them in the yard. 'How did you manage that? Most people run a mile.'

Desmond quietly explained that during in the war he had been a security officer at the top secret base Bletchley Park. 'It played a very important part in our being able to win the war and the work done there on learning the secrets of the German Enigma Code machine made a tremendous difference. Of course it was all very hush-hush and we all had to sign the official secrets act. The security service always worked with German Shepherds and they are almost always friendly if treated right. The secret is to not show any fear and to make sure they know their place in the pecking order, but once established they are all heart. I just loved working with them.'

Ben was amazed as he had no idea about Desmond's earlier life and he immediately recalled how he had discovered about Frank Sullivan, the 'Highfield Hero', months after he had started working with Frank and Rosie. He realised that there would always be things about his clients of which he would be unaware, but he recognised that he did tend to focus on the here and now and that he ought perhaps to spend more time listening and exploring what made his clients tick. The three of them walked up the yard with Desmond chatting away with Robbie about his wartime experiences and Robbie pointing out the all-important loo and the small kitchen where he could make a brew. They passed Tony and Frudo, busy as ever on their mammoth machines, and both gave a wave. Ben passed the key for the garage back to Robbie and left them to it as he climbed the stairs to give his regards to Patsie. He was rewarded with a peck on the cheek, an intake of her heady perfume and a steaming hot cup of coffee.

Patsie was keen to hear about the preparations for the Thursday club and also told Ben about the current stage of the speedway development. It sounded very promising but there was still a lot to be sorted out if they were to be ready to open by November the fifth and she reported that Robbie was working very long hours trying to keep all his balls in the air. Ben waited long enough for Robbie to reappear in the porta cabin before thanking him for his help and making himself scarce so as not to inconvenience the Scaddings anymore. The old Cortina was facing away from his office and on the spur of the moment Ben decided to drop in on Jessie at the Landings as it had been several weeks since he last called on her.

As ever she made him very welcome and between customers wanted to hear all his news. He told her about the planned holiday at Butlins and also about the progress of the Thursday Club. She immediately offered her help if he needed anything and she was already familiar with the voluntary work done by the two cousins.

'They have done a lot of little jobs for some of the older people in the prefabs and they are particularly good at fixing handrails and laying wheelchair ramps for people as they lose their mobility. I am sure they will be much in evidence when we start getting the Landings ready for the Battle of Britain celebrations in September. The conversation went back and forth and in no time at all an hour had elapsed.'

On the way back to his office Ben decided that he might as well be hung for a sheep as a lamb and headed past the turning to the office and straight on to Joe's for an early lunch. The busy lunch period was still a little way off and Joe was able to join Ben in one of the cubicles to enjoy a coffee break before the rush started. Mavis looked the same as always. She was perched on her stool behind the counter smiling to herself and to the room in general. Ben decided to grab the opportunity to tell Joe about the plans for the Thursday club. His relationship with Joe was so strong that he felt able to explain to Joe that he was planning to use the empty office space without seeking permission to avoid getting tied down in all the usual red tape. As they both knew, Joe was no lover of bureaucracy and he quickly caught on to Ben's thinking. Ben pressed ahead by explaining the thinking behind the club and explained that there were several mentally handicapped people living on the estate who were stuck at home with no friends of their own and no sort of social activity to look forward to.

In no time at all Joe was on Ben's wavelength and said, 'You are thinking that my Mavis would enjoy that sort of thing and I must say I have often wished she could have a friend or two of her own. I don't think she is lonely as she meets loads of people every day but it is not like having proper friends. As you know I love her dearly but there are times when I wish I could have a few hours to myself.'

Ben was impressed that Joe had felt able to admit his own need for the occasional break from having Mavis's company the whole time. Joe was obviously enthusiastic, offering to help in any way he could and suggested that he could sort out some spare catering equipment which might be useful. Ben explained that he had put Phil in charge of getting the club off the ground and agreed that he would bring her around to meet him when he returned from Butlins.

The midday rush started and Mavis began to get flustered and Joe hurried over to get involved. Ben slipped out of the café and sat in his car for a few moments and thought over his morning's activities. Not hard work by any stretch of the imagination but really quite productive and he headed back to the office in good time to man the emergency duty rota. Mrs Freeman was alone in the office and had her coat on ready to go off to get her husband's lunch. She had taken a message from one of the other offices about a domestic that was occurring in a family where both parents had a history of mental illness and both had several admissions to psychiatric hospitals in the past. Ben had had previous contact with the Crawford family and knew that their situation blew hot and cold at regular intervals. However, it was always helpful to be updated on potential problems and Mrs Freeman had attached the new message to the existing file from the records system. Ben put it to one side to read through later and took the small pile of incoming post all opened and dated by Mrs Freeman in her usual efficient way and again put them to one side to read through at his leisure. However, Mrs Freeman recovered the top letter and proceeded to do a little dance on the spot, much to Ben's surprise, but he soon saw why.

It was a letter from the chairman of the local rotary and pinned to it was a cheque for £250! Such a generous donation was more than they could have ever anticipated; the Thursday Club was up and running. Mrs Freeman took the cheque straight home to Steve so that he could now open the club's own bank account and she also agreed to write a letter for Steve to sign in his role as treasurer, thanking the rotary for their generous support. It was not often that Ben had the office to himself, which he relished as the opportunity to shut his eyes for a while and relax. Normally he would have been anticipating a cup of tea from Alice the moment his bum landed on his office chair. However, he was already awash with coffee from his morning activities so that was no loss and there was the advantage of no risk of a conversation with Alice about the functions of her bowels. In fact now he thought of it Alice hadn't raised the subject for ages. He had been vaguely aware of subtle changes in her which had started as her friendship with Ernest had developed but he had thought nothing of it as Alice was simply a part of the team and did her own thing without making waves. His mind moved on, his eyes closed and he leant back in his chair and dozed off.

He came to in response to a loud cough from just outside his office door and Phil appeared a moment after with a grin all over her face. She plonked herself down in the visitors' chair and it was pretty obvious by her 'relaxed manner' that she had enjoyed a liquid lunch. Ben was on his feet and heading for the kitchen before she had time to speak and was back with a black coffee for her and a tea for himself in minutes. Phil accepted the coffee and the unspoken reprimand in the spirit they were offered and Ben filled her in on the developments with the Thursday Club that had happened that morning. He told her about Desmond starting on the chairs, and about Joe's offer of catering equipment and his agreement that Mavis should join. He went on to explain to Phil that he had told Joe that she was in charge of the club and that he would introduce her to Joe so that she could decide what catering equipment would be acceptable. He didn't want to step on her toes but he also had every intention of ensuring that she didn't gain access to his secret haven in Joe's third room.

Finally he passed the letter from the rotary over to Phil and her eyes nearly popped out of her head. She rather clumsily reached across the desk and gave Ben a peck on the cheek which was the first physical contact that had ever happened between them during the whole time they had worked together. It was questionable which of them was the more surprised but Ben was pleased as it showed how much Phil cared about the success of their project. Mrs Freeman arrived just too late to have seen the kiss, which perhaps was just as well and she told them that she had already taken Steve down to the Lloyds Bank on the high street and they had banked the cheque.

'He should get a paying in book and a cheque book in the next few days and I will type the thank you letter for him to sign this afternoon. He is really excited to be doing something useful and if it is okay by you, I have said I will bring him in on Saturday to see the premises and to meet Alfred and Sam.'

Ben and Phil readily agreed and Ben was pleased to note that Steve was prepared to let people see his disability, which was a major step forward for him.

The sound of Alice arriving in a rush came from the hallway and the meeting broke up with the ladies going about their business and Ben returning to his contemplation as he waited for the telephone to ring to summon him to action. It remained silent the whole afternoon! After waiting for a while, he went and told Mrs Freeman that he was just going next door to check things with Sam and Alfred. The place was really beginning to look the business. They had polished the cement floor to a high shine. In the large room, the woodwork, the radiators and the built-in dresser were almost all painted in white gloss and one wall had been covered with cork tiles which they thought would be useful as a large notice board. The magnolia emulsion was awaiting a final coat on the rest of the walls and the ceiling, which they assured Ben would only take a day or two at the most. Leaving just the kitchen and toilet to be upgraded. Ben thanked the two men for all their work and of course for the donation they had arranged from the rotary. He explained that Steve Freeman had already set up a bank account for the club and that he should be able to pay them for their expenditure on materials within a few days. He left it that they would leave any receipts that they had, together with an invoice for out-of-pocket expenses, with Mrs Freeman who would act as go-between to Steve on their behalf.

With perfect timing Alice appeared with tea and biscuits for the workers and they pulled her leg a bit about her culinary skills, which caused her to blush with pleasure. She even managed to give them a saucy reply which showed Ben just how far Alice had come in the recent past. When he returned to the office he went and sat down with Mrs Freeman and shared his view about Alice's progress with her and she readily agreed.

'I think Alice's life has improved dramatically over the last few months. She has now got Ernest to care for and they have become almost inseparable, and of course they both share looking after The Champ. I think the fact she now has a paid job has helped her to be more confident and has meant she has a little money that she can afford to spend on herself. I don't suppose you know but she has discovered the delights of Woolworths and goes there regularly. Most of what she buys is cheap jewellery, like the big spider broach she is wearing today, but she also takes notice what Susie wears and sometimes saves up for something more expensive. Have you noticed that her old clumpy boots have been replaced by Dr Scholl wooden-soled shoes just like Susie wears, and the balaclava has been replaced with a colourful head scarf. Alice has taken to wearing it tied up as a sort of turban like women used to wear in the factories during the war. It really doesn't look too bad from the front but she a lot of straggly grey, rather coarse hair hanging down at the back and it looks like she has never seen the inside of a hairdresser's shop. Mind you she still tends to clump about but her overall appearance is generally a lot less bizarre and I know that Susie is working on getting her to agree to have her hair styled. Look a bit more closely next time you see her, Ben, and you will see she is really looking quite pretty with a sort of elfin face, but her clothes still need a lot of work.

'It is fortunate that you were out of the office at the prof's clinic last Friday as she turned up here wearing what the girl in Woolworths had told her was the height of fashion. She had exchanged the long brown socks she habitually wore for fluorescent green socks of the sort much fancied by the Teddy boys. She really looked dreadful. Fortunately, Susie was on hand to take her shopping for a few pairs of pop socks. I know that Susie is slowly trying to influence Alice towards the world of Marks and Spencer and more attractive normal clothes befitting Alice's age. Keep your eyes peeled, Ben, I suspect you haven't seen anything yet, as Alice is slowly catching up to life in the nineteen sixties!'

With Mrs Freeman's words ringing in his ears, he made his way back to his office with the realisation that he hadn't even noticed the changes in Alice's dress sense so far and felt guilty that he had been so unobservant. The rest of the week slipped by with the two duty periods being largely uneventful and the prof's clinic presented no surprises. He took the opportunity to observe Alice more closely when she brought his tea in and his conclusion was that Susie was doing a good job and that he would leave her to it.

Chapter 50

In Holiday Mode

Ben and Sandy had planned to set off to Minehead early on the Saturday in the hope of avoiding the worst of the holiday traffic, but the dreaded A38 was solid with cars heading south. In places they just crawled along and in others they came to a complete halt. Various entrepreneurial youngsters were going from car to car carrying trays of things for sale, looking a lot like ice cream sellers from a local cinema. Ben declined all such produce until they were delayed at the village of Puriton, where he just couldn't resist the offer of a large punnet of Cheddar strawberries for five shillings. They tasted delicious and the atmosphere in the car went up a notch. It finally took the best part of three hours to travel the eighty miles before they were able to turn right on to the A39 for the final part of their journey. The boys were becoming fractious and Sandy was in urgent need of the loo so Ben pulled into the first transport café they came to.

The place was heaving with lorry drivers consuming mountainous fry-ups and Ben ordered a couple whilst Sandy found the toilet and came back moaning about the fact there was no toilet paper. The four of them each had a fork and together tackled the mounds of food before them, but even though they had only two meals between them they had to admit defeat, unlike the other customers, some of whom even went back for seconds.

They finally turned on to the front at Minehead Bay and with the long sweep of the beach on their left and a variety of seaside amusements on their right they drove along to the enormous tent-like building that was the gateway to Butlin's Minehead. They had all looked through the brochures but they had in no way prepared them for the sheer scale of the place. Once they had parked up they were welcomed in at reception by a friendly redcoat who presented them with a programme of events, a dining room pass for second sitting and the key for chalet F11, which was to be their home for the week. In no time at all they were aboard a sort of land train and were chugging around the complex along with their luggage trying to take in all the sights to be seen at every turn. Everything looked fresh and new and there were people of all ages roaming around the complex. It was a whole new world and the Newman family were hooked right from the start.

Chalet 11 was towards the middle of the terrace of wooden single storied brightly painted huts that made up row F.

The accommodation was basic and not much more than glorified camping but it was clean and functional. There was a small double bed for Ben and Sandy and the boys had bunk beds which were the same set up as they had at home. All bedding was provided and the brochure advised that there was a chalet maid service for bed-making and general cleaning. A small table and four chairs together with a plywood wardrobe completed the contents. Sandy discovered that the shower block and toilets were situated just two doors down, which proved to be both very convenient, and much to her surprise immaculately clean. It was far from luxury living but, for what they were paying, more than lived up to expectations and with all the activities available to them they didn't plan on spending much time in F11.

The family used the time up to teatime to explore what the site had to offer and they were spoilt for choice with things they wanted to try. They were stopped outside one of the activity centres by a guy dressed as a pirate, complete with a stuffed parrot on his shoulder brandishing a deadly-looking wooden cutlass. He told them that he was looking for recruits for his band of fearsome pirates and he thought that Jack and Nick looked suitably bloodthirsty. He reached into his swag bag and produced two black eye patches and a couple of plastic swords to seal the deal and his crew had gained two enthusiastic new members. He explained to Sandy that the 'Buccaneers' club met each morning in the Regency Ballroom at 10 am and generally got up to organised mischief in and around the complex for a couple of hours in the morning and again in the afternoon.

'It means mums and dads get a break from the kids in the knowledge that they are well supervised and I can honestly say we haven't lost one yet. Mind you, any insubordination and they get to walk the plank.'

After the trip around everywhere they joined the queue for high tea at the main dining room, which no doubt would be crammed to capacity once the school holidays had started, but was not much more than half full, confirming the wisdom of their decision to take the boys out of school a week early. They were met at their table by a pretty young girl called Helena who was to be their waitress for the week and the boys developed an immediate rapport with her when she slipped them a few sweets. The menu offered few alternatives and Ben and Sandy quickly learnt to follow Helena's recommendations as she had insider's information, as far as the food went, because her boyfriend Ian was one of the chefs. During the meal one of the camp redcoats explained over the microphone that the whole camp was divided into three 'houses' named after famous sea captains and all the various competitions during the week involved gaining points for your house. The Newmans had been allocated Nelson House at reception and were advised that they should wear yellow sashes when taking part in any of the games or competitions.

There followed a series of practice cheers led by the redcoat with each of the houses trying to outdo the others. Bedlam resulted, which was to set the pattern for much of the activities of the week, clearly Butlin's was not the place for anyone who wanted peace and quiet. Ben noticed that quite a few of the older holiday-makers sported numerous metal badges in their lapels, which they seemed to wear with almost military pride. When he asked about them he learnt that each badge represented a holiday somewhere in the Butlins empire and many seemed proud that they were already planning their next Butlins holiday.

Over tea Ben and Sandy consulted the programme of events and decided that a trip to the camp cinema to see the James Bond film *Thunderball* would be a good way to finish the day. The film was great, but by the time they had got back to F11 the whole family were ready for bed. A quick trip to the washrooms to clean teeth and use the loo was followed by the whole family settling into their beds. The dreams were a mixture of planned activities, but the awakening was a rude one, as the wireless speaker set up by the ceiling burst into life at 7.30 am with 'Zip–A-Dee-Doo-Dah' played at full volume. A full day of fun was on the cards and there was no chance of lying in at Butlins.

The pattern of the holiday was set from day one which was greatly helped by the sun deciding to shine the whole week through. The family established a base in one corner by the pool, where they gathered together each mealtime for the short walk to the dining hall. The boys simply disappeared for the rest of the day with an occasional glimpse of them in a gang of kids chasing some poor redcoat in fancy dress like a pack of hounds after a fox. The redcoat invariably ended up being made to walk the plank along the spring board and into the pool.

Meanwhile, Sandy and Ben smothered themselves in Amber Solaire and built up a tan. Ben had always fancied growing a beard so abandoned his razor for the duration of the holiday and the result of his efforts were visible by the end of the week, but only just. The boys burned up energy with their daytime activities, whilst the adults were quite the reverse having spent their days in enjoyable idleness. A solution to the problem was at hand, when Helena offered to baby sit the boys if Sandy and Ben wanted to go out during the evening. With the range of entertainment and activities available it was a no brainer and a deal involving an acceptable amount of cash and their agreement that Helena's boyfriend Ian could keep her company. The week just flew by with the boys generally running wild and Sandy and Ben enjoying each other, having a bop most nights in the Hawaiian Ballroom to the sounds of Bill Cleaver and the Swordsmen. The family tended not to take part in the various races and competitions that took place throughout the day but Sandy did put Ben's name down for the knobbly knee competition. He felt like killing her but tried to take it in good part and was unsure whether to be pleased or sorry when he came third, winning five points for Nelson House.

The Friday evening show was presented by the redcoats, most of whom had some talent for dance, singing or comedy that would hold them in good stead for their hoped-for future in entertainment. One of the traditions of Butlins was to top the bill on the last night with a mystery well-known person. The staff usually got to know who was expected but it was a job-risking thing if you let any camper know in advance. Helena went as far as to say with a knowing wink that the boys would enjoy the show and so the Newman family went en mass.

The theatre was packed and the show was really good but there is only so much singing and dancing that little boys can take. The boys were beginning to get restless and Sandy was considering cutting the evening short when the special top of the bill was announced. It was none other than Norman Wisdom and the theatre erupted as the diminutive figure in the tight suit and cap ambled on to the stage, tripped and fell flat on his face. The boys couldn't believe their eyes, as they had seen him in several films and on the television and he was one of their favourite performers. He did a whole hour of brilliant entertainment involving slapstick, pathos and playing a whole series of musical instruments including the bagpipes and using an ordinary watering can to function as a trumpet. He finished his act with a couple of his hit parade number ones which left the audience shouting for more. He obliged with an encore of 'Don't laugh at me cause I'm a fool' and received a standing ovation for a performance that was really memorable.

They had to vacate the chalet by 10 am on the final day and breakfast was the last meal that they had provided for them as part of the package. Helena made sure that they had plenty of everything to eat and drink and she received a sizeable tip from Ben for all the help she had given to them over the week. Both boys were sad to say goodbye to her but Ben and Sandy realised that she would soon be transferring her attention to the next family occupying F11. The weather continued to be sunny with a gentle breeze off the sea and they decided to prolong the holiday for as long as possible and spent the best part of the day by the pool whilst the boys messed about in the water and enjoyed the largely unoccupied slides and other play equipment. Lunch was takeaway fish and chips from the camp chip shop and it was after 5 pm by the time they drove away from the camp.

Ben was prepared for a nightmare journey home but the heavy traffic kept moving steadily and the rest of the family dozed off right up to the time they pulled up outside their home. There was a small stack of mail, mainly junk mail and a couple of bills, waiting behind the front door and a couple of messages on the answer phone. Nothing to cause concern and the best thing was a message from Ben's mum inviting them to Sunday lunch the following day. That proved to be a bit of a life saver as there was not much food in the house and Sandy popped around to Ma Driscoll's to get the basics in prior to doing a Tesco shop on the Sunday morning.

Chapter 51

Strange Happenings

The weather took a change for the worse on Sunday and the Newman family arrived at Ben's parents through the drizzle but looking suitably brown from their week in the sun and with Ben's facial hair just about recognisable as a beard. Predictably, his mother made no comment and concentrated her efforts on making a fuss of the boys. His dad raised his eyes from the Sunday paper and took a long look over the top of his reading glasses and with difficulty avoided a snigger. The dinner was all but ready and the family were encouraged to sit straight up to the table whilst Ben's mum dished out the food. Sandy offered to help but her mother in law wouldn't hear of it and got deserved praise for a delicious meal of roast beef, Yorkshire pudding, scrunchy roast potatoes and a range of other vegetables which Ben's dad proudly pointed out were all home grown. Ben had always loved his mum's traditional Sunday lunch but had been careful to tactfully avoided making any comparisons between his mum's cooking and Sandy's. However, his mum's gravy was something else and Sandy was the first to admit that hers came nowhere near.

During the meal the discussion was all about Butlins and the Newman family were unanimous in their praise of 'their best holiday ever'. Ben did notice that his dad seemed a bit down but didn't worry too much about it as he was generally quite a quiet man. After rice pudding with generous quantities of strawberry jam the adults were content to sit and enjoy a cup of tea whilst the boys went into the conservatory to set up their Scalextric. By the time the women had finished doing the washing up, after Ben's half-hearted offer to help had been turned down, the rain had stopped and Sandy set off in the car to do a big shop at Tesco.

Ben's dad suggested that Ben and he should take a stroll down to his allotment to collect some fresh vegetables for them to take home with them. They were soon in the now familiar location sat in front of the hut watching the trains go by.

Out of nowhere, Ben's dad suddenly started talking about how shocked he had been earlier in the day to hear the news of Fred's death, particularly as it sounded like murder. For the life of him Ben had no idea what his dad was talking about but remained silent in the hope that it would all become clear.

'I don't know if you remember, Ben, as you were only quite young at the time, but we sat and listened to a recording of the fight when he won the World Light Heavy Weight Championship back in July 1948. It was an amazing achievement, as the fight took place in America and Freddie was very much the underdog and it was unheard of for a British fighter to win such an important fight on American soil.'

Ben realised that his dad was talking about Freddie Mills, a very popular British boxer and a particular favourite of his dad, who was a keen follower of all sports but football and boxing in particular. In reality, Ben didn't really agree with boxing but he did recall listening to the fight and being amazed how excited his dad had been with the result. His dad went on to say that the morning news had been all about Freddie Mills being found shot through the eye in his car, a silver Citroen DS 19, parked behind the night club he owned in Soho. His dad was clearly very upset by the news and went into great detail about Freddie and all his achievements.

As it happened Ben was able to make some contribution to the story as he had been briefly involved with a client who claimed to know Freddie personally. He had met Alec Murphy, known as Spud, in the police cells at the central police station one evening when he was on emergency mental health duty. Spud, the only name he would answer to, had been arrested having apparently attempted to set fire to his ex-wife's house. He was a shambles of a man, stinking of drink and presenting as actively hallucinating. The police didn't want to take any legal action against him and readily accepted the offer by the duty psychiatrist of a bed for him on the alcoholic unit at the St Margaret's Hospital. Both the station sergeant and Ben were surprised at the offer but Ben learnt later that the duty doctor was writing a thesis on alcoholism and its relationship to psychotic illness. The result was that Ben took Spud to the hospital in his car and throughout the journey all evidence of hallucinations disappeared and Spud went into a long diatribe about his life story.

The major part of the story was about his life as a fighter in a travelling boxing booth when he had to take on all comers, having as many as ten fights in an evening. His claim to fame was that for a time the famous Freddie Mills was one of the same troop of travelling boxers.

'I fought exhibition bouts against him on a regular basis so I can rightfully claim that I fought the world champion many times, and there aren't many who can say that!'

Ben suspected that the story was largely made up but had probably got Spud a fair few free drinks over the years. As it was it passed the journey in an amiable fashion and gave Ben an interesting titbit to share with his dad. He immediately confirmed that he had seen about Freddie Mill's career in boxing, when he had been the subject of 'This is Your Life', and he had indeed started out in a travelling boxing booth, so Spud's story may well have been true, but Freddie and Spud's lives had clearly taken very different paths. A rare point of contact between father and son came to an end as Arnold, his dad's railway friend, arrived on his allotment two plots over and waved across. His dad wandered straight over clutching a couple of bottles of beer and after a brief discussion a Union Jack was hoisted to half-mast on their flagpole and they stood to attention and raised their beer in a toast. Ben remained seated in his chair and watched the two men with half an eye. It was clear to him that this place for his dad was the equivalent of Joe's to him, a haven to escape to when the need arose. The vegetables were collected, including enough rhubarb to keep Ma Driscoll occupied for a week, and they returned home in comfortable companionship.

The following day, as Ben got ready for work, he agonised about whether to retain his attempt at growing a beard. It was obviously a project in the making but he came down on the side of giving it a bit longer to develop as he had no plans for further time off in the foreseeable future and he had already invested ten days in its growth so far.

As it happened he needn't have worried about the reaction of the ladies at the office as he had already been upstaged by Alice. The hair sticking out of the back of her turban was bright orange! Mrs Freeman explained to Ben that Alice had been listening in to a conversation between her and

Susie a few days before when they had been discussing how they used dye to colour their hair. The new 'fashion-conscious' Alice had decided to give it a try and had bought an auburn rinse to use over the week end. What she hadn't realised was that the rinse needed to be washed out after ten minutes and she left it in for several hours and had ended up with a head topped like a Jaffa orange. Hence Ben's attempt at a beard paled into insignificance and the women of the office were focused on how to repair the damage for Alice. Predictably, it was Susie who came up with the solution, when she arranged for Alice to visit her own hairdresser friend back in Little Poppy Field and almost frog-marched a nervous Alice out to her car. Mrs Freeman was impressed with Susie's power of persuasion; as she knew Alice had never been into a hairdressing salon before and had always cut her own hair, which Ben thought probably explained her addiction to balaclavas!

Phil arrived soon after nine, which was early for her as she was not usually a morning person and tended to avoid human contact until she had topped up her caffeine levels. But today was an exception and she came straight to Ben's office positively bursting with enthusiasm. She wanted to tell him all about the way the Thursday Club was progressing and Ben was delighted to see how important the project was to her. He realised that Phil must have been very frustrated with the way her career had gone so far and was grateful that he had decided to make her responsible for the formation of the Thursday Club from day one. He responded by asking her to show him how things were coming on and she happily led him around to the entrance. The large room was completely redecorated and was a transformation.

It was bright and airy and the cork wall covering was enhanced with colourful pictures of animals and the inevitable Beatles poster. A row of smartly red painted chairs, that Desmond had recycled from Robbie's, were lined along the wall with others placed strategically around the three tables that were lined up down the middle of the room. Desmond had done a pretty good job on the colourful chairs and they were complimented by the garish striped oil cloth that covered the tables. Phil made a point of drawing Ben's attention to the bright yellow curtains at each window that Susie had made and the overall effect was flamboyant and bright. As Ben was admiring the room there was a sudden rush of banging from the kitchen and he walked across to explore the source. Albert and Sam were surrounded by tools and were busy plumbing in an electric hot water urn above the Belfast sink. The room was also freshly decorated and colourful, wall tiles provided a splashback along the back of the kitchen units, which were covered with boxes of kitchen pots and pans and stacks of crockery.

Ben was amazed at the progress that had been made during the week that he had been away and was quick to praise the men for all their efforts. Phil explained that she had already linked up with Joe, who had happily donated all the kitchen equipment, including the major contribution of the hot water urn. It had done valiant service in Joe's café for several years but had recently been replaced with an elaborate espresso machine, Joe had assured Phil that it had years of life still in it. 'He was really most generous and about the only thing he couldn't help us with was cutlery as he explained he has difficulty keeping up with the speed at which it gets nicked.'

The only place left for Ben to inspect was the toilet, which had been painted and thoroughly cleaned but was otherwise unchanged, apart from a new simple door lock which Sam assured Ben could be unlocked with a special key from the outside should the need arise.

It seemed to Ben that Phil and the helpers had thought of everything and he felt proud of their efforts and success.

'I think you are quite right, Phil. We are almost ready to start, but please let's remember to keep a low profile as we mustn't rustle any feathers in high places.'

Phil was keen to start the club up as soon as possible and it was agreed that the team would get together the following day to decide who should be invited to be the founder members.

Ben's intention was that he would spend the whole day in the office catching up on paperwork and easing himself back into work mode. However, after an hour or two he began to feel stir crazy and he decided to treat himself to lunch at Joe's. The café was showing all the signs of having been very busy as there were dirty dishes in several of the booths and also on the main table and the counter. Mavis was steadily collecting them up and carrying them through to the kitchen ready for a mammoth washing-up session later. Ben gave her a helping hand and Joe smiled his thanks and, as if by magic, produced a bacon butty which he brought out to Ben for his lunch. The café was having one of its rare quiet moments and Joe gratefully sat down with Ben for a brief respite from his labours. Mavis was quick to come over with two black coffees for them, knowing full well the way they preferred it. Joe looked on with pride and thanked her warmly.

'You know, Ben, she is a real joy to me. We have never had a cross word but I do worry about what will happen to her in years to come. I have been giving a lot of thought about your suggestion that she should come to the club you are starting and I agree it would be good for her to have friends of her own. It would be a good start for her to have a day off each week and we will have to see what develops.'

Ben spontaneously shook Joe's hand and the deal was settled.

He went on to thank Joe for his generous support by providing so much kitchen equipment and Joe laughed out loud. 'I have been in catering for years and stuff needs replacing quite regularly, but I tend to be a bit of a hoarder and I am reluctant to throw anything away when it has still got some life in it. Phil and you have actually done me a favour as I never seem to have enough room for all the café provisions.'

They went on to chat about how the project was going and Joe suddenly said that he would have to get someone to help on the days when Mavis was at the club.

'In fact. I have been thinking about recruiting some help for quite a while, as we are very busy and it is a lot for Mavis and me to do by ourselves. It's funny though, in all my years of working I have never had to recruit staff. I started off working with my mum at first, then it was me and my wife and since her death it has always been just me and Mavis. We do need help but it would have to be someone who recognised Mavis's special needs but also respected her special qualities. It is difficult to know where to start. Have you any ideas, Ben?'

At this juncture Ben had one of his off-the-wall ideas and replied, 'Leave it with me, I just might know the very person. I will come back to you in a day or two.'

The lunchtime rush started with a vengeance and Joe returned to his cooking whilst Ben enjoyed a top-up of his coffee as he finished up his now rather cold bacon sandwich before heading through the door and back to the office. Everyone was out except Mrs Freeman and she was sat with her top coat on ready to rush off at the earliest opportunity to get Steve his lunch. She quickly told Ben that Jessie from the Landings was trying to contact him and that she had seemed quite anxious. She also reported that Alice was next door in the club room, cleaning it for the umpteenth time; which was very much a labour of love for her. Once Mrs Freeman had gone off to catch her bus, Ben settled down to think about the best way of approaching his idea for Joe's helper. It was several weeks since he had last visited Ruth Andrews and at that time she had seemed much more in control of her life. She had become an intricate part of the Highfield Catholic community and seemed to have grown in stature as a result.

The headmaster at Katie's school had recently told Ben that she continued to make good progress and no longer came to school looking as if she had the weight of the world on her shoulders. Ben knew that there was no likelihood of Mr Andrews returning to live with his wife and family and that he made only limited and irregular payments towards their income. Mrs Freeman had looked much more up together but it was pretty obvious that money was a real problem for her and there was never anything over for her once the kid's needs had been met. Ben resolved to give it a go and metaphorically crossed his fingers that he was making a good decision. He quickly finished catching up on his paperwork and worked his way through the never-ending paper edicts from headquarters, most of which had no relevance or interest for him and went straight into the shredder. When she returned from lunch, Mrs Freeman enquired what Jessie had been worried about and Ben reached for the telephone as he confessed he had forgotten to make the call.

Chapter 52

Back with a Vengeance

Jessie picked up the phone on the second ring and sounded relieved when Ben identified himself. She quickly explained that she had a complicated problem which she felt would need his professional intervention.

'It is too difficult to discuss over the phone and in any case a bus load of customers have just arrived all wanting serving before the bus left. Ideally I would like Mary to be here when we talk and I wondered if you could possibly call in after work when she will be here.'

It all sounded very mysterious and very unusual as he had never been asked for help by Jessie or Mary before so he readily agreed to call in later.

'Thanks ever so. You are a saint, come in for tea with us, we are having chicken curry.'

The line went dead before he had time to react but as Ben loved a curry he wasn't about to argue. He picked up the phone again and rang Ma Driscoll's shop, which was the first time he had ever rung Sandy at work. She immediately thought that there must be a problem with one of the boys and Ben quickly explained about Jessie's invite. Sandy was equally intrigued and sounded more than a little envious of the promised curry.

'Thanks for letting me know. You can tell me about it later. Don't forget a doggie bag for me!'

As she rang off Ben could hear voices in the background and it was obvious that the shop was busy. He eased back in his chair and rested his eyes, thinking it was great to have nothing much to do whilst the rest of the world was busy, busy, busy. His siesta couldn't last too long and after few minutes he pushed himself to his feet and set off on foot to see Ruth Andrews. The walk was only a few hundred yards and by the time he arrived at the house he was sufficiently awake for the task ahead. The outside signs were promising as the garden was very tidy and the windows shone in the sunlight. When Ruth opened the door she looked as good as he had ever seen her. Her natural smile was that of someone who was genuinely pleased to see him and the kitchen she led him to smelt deliciously of baking. They were soon sat each side of the kitchen table clutching mugs of tea and eating 'what Katie calls "Mummy's little cakes".'

Ruth was happy to tell Ben all about the ups and downs of her life and as she talked he noted that although her clothes were far from new they were clean and pressed and all signs of nicotine stains were absent from her hands, face and hair. Ben thought she looked wholesome and a million miles away from how she had presented when he had first met her just about twelve months before. Predictably, she was full of praise for the priest, Patrick McGinty, who she described as a saint and she was particularly happy that Katie was always keen to accompany her to services at the church. She was very proud of how Katie was getting on at school and was happy to report that she had discovered that she had a good singing voice and was now in the choirs both at her school and at the church. She went on to tell Ben that her older daughter Angie was growing up fast and had a Saturday job at Woolworths.

'She has a regular boyfriend now called Clive and seems to spend most of her evenings at his house in Ensley and does seem to be a lot easier to live with. My boy Brian has had his moments and even had a spell in a detention centre after being charged with burglary, but he is home again now and the detention centre experience certainly frightened him a lot; he is now being supervised by a probation officer who he seems to quite like. He has been encouraged to join up with the bike racing group being organised by the local bobby and he is busy building himself a bike from bits he has collected together. He still has a temper on him at times but there are some positive signs that he is getting over his dad leaving. His dad calls in from time to time to see the kids but never thinks to offer any financial help. The tart he moved in with is now looking very pregnant and with him having a new family to support there is no way I am going to get any help from him. I guess I will just have to struggle on as best I can.'

It presented Ben with the perfect opportunity to tell Ruth about Joe looking for a helper and Ruth's reaction was just what he had expected; she immediately expressed her concern that she had never had a paid job and wouldn't know where to start. They talked it over and went round and round with Ruth expressing her doubts and Ben continuing to try and reassure her. Ben finally won the day with Ruth agreeing to come and meet Joe during the morning of the following day.

It was well after three by the time Ben got back to the office and he was met by a terrific surprise. The transformation in Alice was almost beyond belief. The turban had gone the way of the balaclava and her head was now covered in a neat, auburn bobbed hair style reminiscent of that favoured by the sixties icon Mary Quant. The style framed her elfin face and although she was no swan; she was far from being an ugly duckling. Alice was barely able to contain her delight and kept admiring her reflection in the mirror of a small powder compact that Susie had loaned her. Susie's hairdresser had performed a minor miracle and Susie confided to Ben that she had every intention of helping Alice to continue to make her transformation. 'Just watch this space, Ben, you will be amazed what I can achieve with a little help from Marks and Spencer.'

A very happy Alice positively skipped off to the kitchen to catch up on her tea-making duties which she extended on this occasion to include Albert and Sam next door. She was blushing upon her return and it seemed that her new appearance had not gone unnoticed. Ben fiddled about in the office for a little while longer before returning to Joe's to tell him about what he had arranged with Ruth for the following day. Joe reacted well to Ben's suggestion and asked a few straightforward questions about Ruth's circumstances without attempting to pry into the reason that Ben was in contact with her. He repeated several times that he had confidence in Ben's judgement and it was soon agreed that they should meet up in the morning at about 10.30 when things in the café were usually relatively quiet. For once Ben didn't stay for a coffee as he explained to Joe that he had an invitation to dinner with some good friends. Errands all complete, he arrived at Jessie's well before Mary's arrival home and Jessie left him sitting comfortably on the settee nursing a cup of tea and a slice of chocolate cake watching the early evening news. Peace reigned and Ben relaxed.

Chapter 53

A Lot Going On

It was a good half hour before a rather breathless Mary put in an appearance and after the briefest of hellos she dashed off to the kitchen. Jessie was still busy in the shop but had done all the preparation for the curry and Mary just naturally took over the actual cooking. After the sounds of pots and pans being brought into action, Mary popped her head around the living room door and invited Ben to join her for a chat in the kitchen whilst she got on with the cooking.

'We normally don't get down to eating our evening meal much before seven when Jessie has served the last customer and even then there are often later callers for the odd pint of milk and the like. Make yourself useful, lay the table, the knives and forks are in that drawer and the condiments are in the cupboard above. I met Alfred and Sam earlier today and they told me you are hoping to start the club next week.' Mary charged straight on with Ben unable to get a word in edgeways. 'Now I have got a couple of neighbours who are just the sort of people the club is designed to help. I don't think you know them but I do know that Phil is aware of the family. The family are the Watsons and they live in the compound just a little way up from the entry to the Landings, do you know where I mean?'

Ben had to admit that he had no idea, but when Mary described the location further he did recall an enclosed yard: he had never given it any real thought and certainly had no idea that anyone lived in what he had assumed was just another industrial yard.

'The Watson family have run a travelling fair for generations and usually spend eight months of the year moving around from place to place all over the southwest. Then the whole Watson family over winter in the yard up the road and spend the time there renovating the various rides and stalls. George Watson inherited the fair from his father and the main workers have always been members of the Watson clan with groups of casual labourers recruited as they moved about. George's dad was a good man who ran a safe fairground and he stood for no nonsense. George has always been fiercely loyal to his dad and resisted all attempts by his own sons to update the fairground rides and attractions and the fair had become a bit tame for today's tastes. But then George suddenly died of lung cancer last Christmas. He was only in his early sixties, and his three sons inherited the complete fairground. They have wasted no time in abandoning the old and taking up the new. George's wife, Gabriel, and two of her daughters, Faith and Charity, are no longer required on the fair's travels as the hoopla stall and shooting range that they always ran are no longer part of the son's new image for the fair. As a consequence the three of them are now living full time in a static caravan in the compound, which must feel like being in a prison.

'George would have never allowed it but his sons are cut from a different cloth and it is the two girls Faith and Charity that I hope you can help. Their mum, Gabriel, calls in most days for supplies and she usually settles herself down in the seats at the far end of the bus and enjoys a coffee and a chat with a few other older ladies who use the bus as a meeting place. The girls have come with her once or twice but unfortunately they present as quite odd and the other ladies largely ignore them. The two girls are in their thirties and both have the classic symptoms of untreated congenital microcephaly, you know, poor slow growth, rather swollen eyes, weak muscle toning and marked mental retardation. In years gone by it used to be a relatively common condition but nowadays it is picked up at birth by a simple blood test as part of the new born screening programme. Unfortunately, Gabriel spent most of her pregnancies travelling with her husband and had no prenatal care with the first girl, Faith, and by the time it was diagnosed the damage was already done. Gabriel just took it in her stride and was pregnant again within a few months but this time was different as she made sure her whole pregnancy was monitored by the local health visitor. When Hope, her second daughter, was born she was "the perfect baby" and has grown up to be a vivacious and lovely person. She's married now with kids of her own and does what she can for her mum and her sisters but her husband runs his own transport business and Hope has a very full life.

'Gabriel had been convinced that lightning never strikes the same place twice and reverted to her relaxed manner when she again became pregnant and the result was Charity, an almost identical copy of her sister Faith. They are cheerful little souls who cause no bother but they are both severely disabled and will never be able to live independently. They spend their whole time together "chirruping away" in high squeaky voices and had really enjoyed running their own hoopla stall, which they had done for years every spring and summer. Their winters were spent back at the static caravan when they occupied their time making plaster models and then painting them ready to be used as prizes on their stall.

'Their whole way of life changed when their brothers decided to modernise the fair and now they just sit around and get very bored with nothing to do. Their mother has got herself involved with various activities in the community and has been an invaluable help on the planning committee for the Battle of Britain celebrations in September. But poor old Faith and Charity have been left high and dry and I think your new club might be able to give them a much-needed lift.'

Ben listened with interest as he had read about the condition whilst on a residential placement on his training course but he had never come across anyone living in the community with it. He explained that actually Phil was running the club and would have the final word, but he promised to discuss it with her at the planning meeting the following day. Mary just nodded and got up to finish preparing the dinner, which smelt delicious and reminded Ben that he hadn't had anything much to eat during the day.

With perfect timing, coming from loads of practice, Jessie joined them in the kitchen just as Mary was dishing out the steaming chicken curry accompanied by hunks of bread ripped off from a French stick and a selection of colourful dips.

'The dips are all homemade by Mary and she can be a little heavy handed with the spices so proceed with caution,' Jessie warned.

His first taste confirmed her description. The whole meal was like nothing Ben had ever had before and it was a new experience that he really enjoyed, with the added bonus of the dips effectively clearing his sinuses. They all came back for seconds and one or two of the dips were completely consumed leaving just one bright red one largely untouched. Mary cleared the plates and placed a dish of fruit in the middle of the table.

'Just to clear your palate whilst I put the coffee on.'

Once the percolator was bubbling nicely they returned to the lounge and settled themselves all down on the comfy three-piece suite satiated and ready to share their concerns.

'Well as you know, Ben, there is no such thing as a free lunch and we do have need of your professional involvement in a tricky situation that has developed here on the Landings.'

That was how Jessie started the ball rolling. However, the story that followed proceeded with contributions from both Jessie and Mary and seemed to pass seamlessly between them like a well-rehearsed double act. They wanted to tell Ben about one of their neighbours, Daniel Collins; who appeared to be urgently in need of help. In order to help him fully understand they were determined to take the story way back to their primary school days. Ben realised that it was going to be a protracted tale but he was nicely full, sitting comfortably with two dear friends and was in no hurry to be anywhere else. Jessie started the story by explaining that before the war the Collins family had lived just around the corner from her dad's shop down near the canal and she had known them all her life.

'Horace and Anne were a lovely couple who were always prepared to assist if anyone in their tight community was in difficulties. Horace was a rarity amongst the people living in the area. For a start he was a white-collar worker and to add to this difference was a Methodist lay minister. The couple held religious meetings in their home and Anne spent a lot of her time visiting the elderly and sick living around them. They were generally liked and respected but perhaps inevitably they tended to be kept at arm's length and not totally accepted as just one of the neighbours. They had three sons, Joseph, Abraham and the youngest Daniel, who is the one we are concerned about now.'

Mary and Jessie went on to describe the three boys who had all gone to the same primary school as they had attended. They told of three exceptionally bright boys who consistently stood out academically as being well ahead of the rest of their fellow pupils. Added to scholastic ability, their good manners and smart clothes meant that they really didn't quite fit in and this resulted in them having no close friends other than their own brothers. They weren't bullied or anything like that but were simply ignored by the other pupils who got on with general mischief in the normal way. All three boys in turn moved on to Ensley Grammar School as they reached the age of eleven but this meant that the youngest, Daniel, spent a lonely two years before it was his turn to move on.

'I remember him as a sad, introverted little boy during this time but fortunately the head master was bilingual, as he had a French mother, and he took him under his wing and gave him French lessons to keep him motivated. Daniel welcomed the challenge and seemed to absorb the language like a sponge and I learnt later that he passed his school certificate in French at the tender age of twelve.'

All three boys worked hard at grammar school and were quickly identified as potential university candidates and were tutored accordingly. They studied whilst others played and they watched whilst others fought out their battles on the rugby field. But for all their pacifism the older two were amongst the first to be called up to be part of the war effort. Daniel remained at the grammar school for a further year, during which he concentrated on becoming fluent in both French and German and then he disappeared with no explanation forthcoming for the neighbours from his parents or teachers. Rumours flourished amongst the people of the Cuttings and the consensus of opinion was that Daniel had been whisked away to London where his language skills could be used to good effect.

Any questions to Horace and Anne about their son's wellbeing were always responded to politely but offered no actual information. It was clear to everyone that Anne was immensely proud of her boys and Horace always included a special prayer for them at his Methodist meetings. Jessie picked up the story and became a little distressed and Mary reached for her hand which was the first time Ben had ever witnessed any physical intimacy between them.

'Then came the fateful evening of Sunday first of March 1942, which is a date I will never forget. It was about eight pm and I was at home with my dad doing some stacking up of the shelves in the shop. We had had a number of air raids targeting the warehouses on the canal and it was no great surprise when the siren went off. Whenever this happened we would hurry down to the air raid shelter in the nearby park and sit the raid out, often singing along with Mr Hoskins who invariably brought his precious accordion along with him. We were heavily into "Roll Out the Barrel" when a distant thump was heard quickly followed by a series of enormous bangs which got nearer and nearer. Suddenly, the whole shelter shook, making clouds of accumulated dirt, which turned the air in the shelter into a dense choking fog. When we eventually emerged the scene was one of utter chaos. Our shop and most of the house had suffered a direct hit and had been reduced to rubble. Most of the other houses in the street had lost tiles, windows and In some cases doors, but the Collins house had been wiped off the face of the earth. There was no trace of Mr and Mrs Collins and the only blessing was that if the raid had been thirty minutes earlier there would have been a full congregation of Methodists at prayer in their home. I will never forget the sounds and sights of that night and still suffer the occasional nightmare over twenty years later.'

Jessie paused and dabbed her eyes whilst Mary continued the tale. 'In the months that followed news filtered back that the two older boys were both prisoners of war. At least they were alive but there was no news of Daniel. At the end of the war Joseph reappeared back at the site of the former family home, which was now just a massive hole in the ground. The local bobby on his nightly beat discovered him sitting on a pile of debris looking utterly lost and sobbing uncontrollably. Despite them having grown up and gone to school together the constable hardly recognised him. He was barely able to stand, as he had an old shrapnel wound in his leg that had never been properly treated, he was very thin, emaciated and his hair had gone grey. After an operation to remove shrapnel from his leg and a lengthy period of recuperation he was allocated one of the new prefabs on the Landings Estate and the community rallied around to make it habitable.

'Soon after news came through that Abraham had not survived and was reported to have been killed a couple of years before whilst trying to escape from his prison camp. Joseph seemed to be doomed to face life alone as there was still no news of Daniel. Then one day he turned up at the prefab as suddenly as he had originally disappeared and there was no explanation offered. He was in much better physical condition than his brother, who was left permanently handicapped as a result of his injuries and the subsequent surgery. Joseph could still walk without too much difficulty although it was very apparent from his lopsided gait that it involved a fair amount of pain. His main problem was and still is that he can't remain seated for very long before the pain becomes unbearable. Meanwhile it quickly became clear that Daniel had come back with a marked mental disorder that meant he fluctuated between deep depression with overt symptoms of paranoia and hyper-manic behaviour with periods when he often appeared to be hallucinating.'

When she paused for breath Jessie swiftly stepped in to resume the dialogue and Mary busied herself topping up the coffee cups. 'The Landings community tried to be supportive but the two brothers made it clear that they preferred to keep themselves to themselves. Joseph found a job as a porter at the local fruit market and spent long days trundling stacks of fruit and vegetables from the market to the buyers' vehicles. It was distressing to see him as he walked past by the shop on the way home from work. He could barely manage to put one foot in front of the other and we knew that he still had to contend with his brother's problems when he got home. At that time we saw very little of Daniel but from time to time he would set off from home, but his paranoia caused him to make repeated changes of direction and he never got off the estate before arriving back at his starting point. Joseph continued to reject all offers of help and I am sorry to say people started to label them as "the odd couple". Unbeknown to anyone, Joseph had confided in their long-term family practitioner, dear old Dr Forester, who had known the family and their history from way back. It appears that between them they hatched a plan which involved him prescribing medication in Joseph's name for him to administer to Daniel in his food without his knowledge. Unorthodox to say the least but over time it had a huge impact. Joseph regularly dropped a shopping list through my door on his way to work and Daniel started to call in during the afternoons to collect their groceries. Over time he began to be much more approachable and although he could never be described as chatty his behaviour in no way warranted the description as odd. A few weeks later it was Joseph who suddenly started to collect their order on his way home from work.'

Mary stepped in that point as Jessie went off to respond to a ring at their bell. 'It was about this time that I had to take a couple of days off work to help Jessie in the shop as she had an upset tummy. Joseph looked exhausted when he called in but at the same time seemed elated about something. Ever the nosey one, I encouraged him to sit down for a while and offered him a cup of tea. Much to my surprise, he accepted and we had a good old chat. He told me, "in confidence as you are a nurse", all about how Dr Forester and he had brought about the change in Daniel. His euphoric state had been enhanced by the fact that Daniel had been offered a job at Exworth Council. He suspected that it was a post that few people would have wanted as it involved shuffling endless bits of paper into a meticulous filing system deep in the bowels of headquarters. It involved little contact with other staff which suited Daniel just fine and his mood had remained stable for several weeks. In fact, when Joseph had left the shop to prepare their tea he seemed full of optimism. The two brothers have rumbled along together with only minor hiccups ever since and have remained fiercely independent. Their prefab in Spitfire Close had always been neat and tidy, in keeping with the rest of the estate, but was unusual as the front garden had been completely paved over. This was partly to accommodate a government-issued invalid carriage used daily by Joseph but also reflected their lack of interest in gardening. Of course they have no need to grow fruit or vegetables as Joseph's gleanings from the market provide them with a healthy diet. They certainly have no interest in anything considered by them to be feminine and to them the idea of growing flowers fell well into that category. So over the years the Collins boys ceased to be of special interest and they became just another part of the Landings community.

'Daniel's latent ability was soon recognised by the powers that be at headquarters and he was promoted to become the official county archivist, meaning the boys were financially secure.'

Jessie re-joined them at this point and Mary, somewhat reluctantly, allowed her to take up the story. Ben realised that the ladies were coming to the meaty part of the story and switched his mind into overdrive.

'Without warning their world suddenly collapsed just two weeks ago. A stack of crates of apples fell on to Joseph when he knocked into them with his trolley and he suffered a compound fracture to his good leg. Despite his initial refusal to be hospitalised, when the head consultant told him that without specialist treatment he could lose the leg he agreed to be admitted to the orthopaedic hospital out at Bevington. Without Joseph being around to look after Daniel the outcome was inevitable, but the speed in which it has happened has been truly alarming. Joseph had rung Mary from the hospital and asked her to keep an eye on Daniel and to make sure that he had enough food supplies in the house. Mary had called around with a box of food straight away and after repeated knocking a rather wild-eyed Daniel came to the door and took the box from her without saying a word. That was the last time anyone had seen Daniel and he had not responded when Mary had knocked the door any day since. He has simply cut himself off from the outside world and after what happened in the night the whole estate is now buzzing about it. Come on, let us show you what has happened.'

Mary led the three of them out of the prefab and turned sharp left along The Runway. The first cul-de-sac they came to was Spitfire Close and as they turned the corner the cause for concern was all too obvious. The end white-painted prefab now had the addition of the word BASTARDS roughly painted in three foot-letters right across the front of it. Ben held back whilst Mary tried knocking one more time. As before, there was no reply but from where he was standing Ben saw a flicker of movement of the nets in one of the rooms so at least they knew that Daniel was in the prefab and was alive. By the time they had returned to Jessie and Mary's home Ben was already forming a plan for action. The known history linked to the current situation really meant there was only one course of appropriate action and it was up to him to arrange it. There needed to be a full domiciliary assessment involving Daniel's GP Dr Forester, a psychiatrist and Ben, but it was evident that Daniel would not be cooperating. The joint visit would be relatively straightforward to arrange but there was the question of gaining access to the premises. Ben borrowed Jessie's phone and rang Bevington Hospital to arrange a visit to see Joseph the following day.

It was almost nine o'clock by the time he got home and the boys were in bed, but judging from the volume of noise coming from their room they were still very much awake. Despite feeling tired he let out a sigh and went straight up to read the final chapter of the current Biggles book that had been their bedtime story for the past couple of weeks. Once finished he added it to the others on their bookshelf in the hope that the boys would get around to reading them for themselves in due course as Ben had done when he was about their age. When Ben had last gone into the attic, amongst the books he had recovered had been *1984* by George Orwell, which had been part of his school's English Literature O level syllabus. At the time he had thought the boys might sometime like to read it but on the spur of the moment he plucked it out of the bookshelf and took it into his own bedroom, lay on the bed and began to read it. When Sandy came up to see where he was a few minutes later she found him fast asleep. She pulled the door to and left him to it.

Chapter 54

The Invisible Man

The next morning Ben was woken up by a shaft of bright sunlight shining directly upon him as Sandy threw back the curtains. She was up, dressed, and busy putting her face on in the dressing table mirror when Ben rolled over to look at the bedside clock. It showed a little after six. He was about to make some comment about it being the middle of the night when he remembered that the boys had just started their long summer holiday from school. This had been the first holiday that Sandy had been working long hours at Ma Driscoll's and the boys' day care was very dependent upon them spending the three days she had to work at their gran's. This in turn relied upon Ben getting the boys up and fed before dropping them off at his mum's and then going on to work himself. It sounded simple but Ben knew the boys now considered themselves to be on holiday and getting them going in the morning was not going to be easy.

The next six weeks were going to be tough but 'needs must' and the facts of the matter were that the Newman household was far from flush for cash and their two incomes were essential. Ben heard the front door shut and would have dearly loved to settle back down for a bit more shut eye but he knew that could prove disastrous. Instead, he plumped up the pillows and stacked them up to provide a comfortable seat whilst he let his mind wander over their financial situation. On balance they were now earning enough to get by but what with increased mortgage rates and the boys growing out of their clothes before they were worn out there was little left over for luxuries. Ben's major concern of late was the possibility that he might have to replace his car when it was next due for an MOT. In his mind he had always thought of the old Cortina as 'Sheba number two' which was a follow on of what he had called the super motorbike that had been his pride and joy in his teens. He had bought his first motorbike at seventeen, which had been a little Francis Barnet which he had predictably called 'Fanny'. It was a poor buy. It was an underpowered two-stroke which was a pig to start as it was forever oiling up its spark plug. By doing two paper rounds six days a week he had managed to save up the deposit for a very swish Triumph which he had named 'Sheba' after the queen of the same name. Unfortunately, when the time came for him to go to university he had no way of keeping up the payments and the bike had been returned to the shop he had bought it from. When he had later purchased the old Cortina he had considered calling it 'Sheba mark two' but the name did not fit comfortably on the rusty rather battered car that had already had a hard life. So he had always referred to it as simply 'the old Cortina'.

However, as he lay there he thought back to the book he had been reading the evening before and he recalled that something he had read had struck a chord with him and he reached for *Animal Farm*. It came back to him almost at once, the faithful old work horse in the story which was ever reliable was called Boxer. This was too much of a coincidence to be ignored. After all, there had already been two boxers in his life. Both had been horses so why not something with horsepower being named Boxer the third? After his initial idea he reluctantly decided that that was a step too far but he still felt strongly that 'the old Cortina' had proved to be very reliable and was deserving of a name. Having given the concept further thought he decided to use the initials for Boxer the third, BTT, which he quickly converted to the way it sounded, 'Beatie'. Then and there 'the old Cortina' acquired the name Beatie and Ben smiled at the solution he had come up with. Decision made, he went off to have his shower and dress before shaking the boys into action and going off to prepare breakfast.

The boys eventually put in an appearance and immediately started to quarrel about whose turn it was to choose which cereal to have. The trouble was Sandy always bought variety packs of cereals, which were targeted by Kellogg's to satisfy the sugary desires of children. There were eight individual little boxes in each variety pack and for three mornings there was no problem as there were two the same of Frosties, Coco Pops and Rice Krispies, so there was no need to argue. However, on the fourth morning there were always two different boxes left and today it was Corn Flakes and the dreaded All Bran, which both boys disliked with a vengeance. If Sandy had been on breakfast duty she would have known whose turn it was to choose but Ben had no idea. Instead he took immediate action and mixed the two remaining packs in the boy's dishes, which effectively stopped them arguing but made them gang up to complain in unison. They were still sulking when Ben delivered them at his mum's front door but he felt sure she would sort them out in her usual effective way: sweets.

When Ben arrived at work he quickly explained to Mrs Freeman about his need to visit Joseph Collins on ward nine at Bevington Orthopaedic Hospital and without even sitting down headed back out to Beatie. Alice was left in the corridor holding his usual morning cup of tea with her mouth open ready to say something but he was gone too quickly. She realised that there would be no discussion of her bowels that day unless she could get the attention of Mrs Freeman, and she made for the general office in a vague hope.

Bevington Hospital must have been a grand house in its day but it would have needed a small army of servants to run it as such. It had long since developed a utilitarian appearance as it had moved on to be used for a variety of purposes over the recent decades when it had been a school, an elderly persons home and a military hospital during the Second World War. Subsequently it had emerged in more recent times as a centre of excellence for orthopaedics with a particular emphasis on treating people with spinal injuries. The ground floor was inhabited by a group of young men in wheelchairs enjoying causing good-natured mayhem for the nursing staff, who seemed to be enjoying the chaos every bit as much as their patients. Ben was directed to Ward 9, which turned out to be a small room on the second floor occupied by four patients all apparently bed bound. It wasn't very hard to guess which one was Joseph as he was the emaciated person ensnared in a complex structure of pulleys, ropes and bandages. In any case there was no need to guess as he was waving frantically to get Ben's attention and to point him to a chair already drawn tightly up to his bedside. Ben went to shake his hand and Joseph clutched it tightly as if his life depended on it. Tears began to trickle down Joseph's cheeks and it was several seconds before he got himself under control and was able to speak.

'I am so pleased you have come, I have been so worried. I just knew Daniel was in difficulties. I started off ringing every day whenever they brought the telephone trolley around and at first he would do little more than grunt before putting the phone down on me. But for over a week now the phone has been continually engaged and it is pretty clear that he has left it off the hook. I have been frantic imagining all sorts of scenarios, as without his medication Daniel becomes very paranoid and it is impossible to reason with him. I was so desperate that I even considered discharging myself but as you can see they have got me well tied down here. Have you seen him? Is he okay?'

Ben spent the next half hour explaining about the current situation and the requirements for an assessment section, which he explained would be the likely outcome. Joseph listened carefully, asking pertinent questions from time to time.

'I understand what you are saying and I realise it's for his own good, but please be sure to treat him kindly. He really is a lovely man and I am sure he will be very frightened.'

With that Joseph passed the key to their prefab over to Ben in order that they could get in without having to be heavy handed. On the return journey to the office Ben thought over the obvious devotion Joseph had for his brother and how he had cared for him every day by concealing medication in his food. There would be no end to it, as it was a job for life, but then Ben remembered the loss of their parents and their other sibling during the war and it became clear why Daniel was so precious to the damaged little man Ben had just left.

Ben called in at Dr Forrester surgery on the way back to the office and managed to slip in to see him between waiting patients. He quickly explained about his visit to Joseph and that they now had the means of getting in. Dr Forrester suggested a joint visit the following afternoon at about 2 pm when he would have some time between surgeries and Ben left him to get on with the aches and pains queuing up to see him in the waiting room. The next stop for Ben was at Jessie's so he could put her and Mary in the picture. She had little to report as there had been no additions to the daubing and no sign of Daniel. Mary had called at the prefab the previous evening and the result of her knocking several times was a string of abuse from behind the door. Apparently Mary had been very surprised that Daniel knew such filthy language and there had even been some words Mary hadn't recognised.

'And that's saying something, as she has heard most things working at Highfield!'

Ben smiled and nodded his agreement and the two of them got down to planning the following day's event. They obviously wanted it to be as unobtrusive as possible but that would be well-nigh impossible in a close-knit community like the Landings.

Ben went to use Jessie's phone in their living room and was lucky to get straight through to Dr Rani, the prof's senior registrar who was always keen to get experience of work in the community. Ben knew full well that the fee paid for domiciliary assessments would always be an added incentive but Dr Rani had three small children so he understood only too well the need to earn a little extra. He always felt it was a bit unfair that the social worker involved in such assessments received no fee but they didn't and that was that. After telling the tale to Dr Rani they agreed to meet up at 2 pm the next day at Jessie's and to walk to the prefab rather than all pull up at the cul-de-sac in cars. No doubt they would be spotted, but at least they would have tried to protect Daniel's privacy.

On arrival back at the office he tidied up the plans by confirming the time and meeting place with Dr Forrester and also had a word with Roger Richards, the local police constable. He was already aware of the unusual happenings at the Landings and readily agreed to be 'on patrol' nearby when the planned visit was due to take place in case the outcome proved unpredictable.

The following day the two doctors met up with Ben at Jessie's and after a brief discussion the three of them walked along to Spitfire Close. They passed PC Richards parked up at the kerb side just before the street entrance. They didn't acknowledge him in the hope that the neighbours would be unaware of what was taking place but Ben could feel several sets of eyes from behind twitching curtains as they approached the prefab with the unfortunate decoration. They knocked the door several times without response of any sort and Ben inserted the key into the lock and pushed the door open. He called out as he entered but the only sound was the buzzing of numerous bluebottles and flies. The stench of rotting food filled the atmosphere and together they moved from room to room but there was no sign of anybody now being there. The whole place was chaotic with mounds of apparently untouched vegetables providing a luxurious meal for the swarm of flies, which reacted by seeming to fill the air in protest to the interruption. On closer examination it became obvious that the flies had been active for some time and their offspring in the form of maggots were already present in large numbers.

The rest of the kitchen table was covered with opened tins of soup, baked beans and the like, several still containing spoons where the contents appeared to have been consumed straight from the tins. The three men searched all the potential hiding places but Daniel was nowhere to be found. The lavatory in the bathroom had clearly not been flushed for days and Ben instinctively pulled the chain of the flush in an attempt to clear the accumulated waste. He had to do it two further times before leaving the prefab to make it reasonably sanitary. Ben tried the back door and found it to be unlocked and went out to see if Daniel was hiding there. The back garden consisted of a small area of grass, badly in need of cutting but otherwise quite barren, and there was a gate out to a lane at the far boundary. When Ben wandered to the gate he discovered that the lane ran parallel to The Runway for the full length of the Landings but there was no one in sight in either direction.

The three of them held a quick discussion and concluded that he must have slipped out of the back door and with some relief they vacated the prefab to regroup at Jessie's. Ben stopped on the way to tell PC Richards what they had found and he confirmed that he had not seen Daniel coming out of the close, so the mystery deepened. The police man started his car up and headed back to Highfield where he had other fish to fry, leaving the three of them without backup.

As they were already gathered together they decided to wait for a while and then try again, meanwhile Jessie made them welcome with her usual hospitality. They were quite relaxed in each other's company as they knew each other well from their various roles in the community mental services and had quite often worked together with the same clients. Dr Rani and Ben's roles were obvious, but Dr Forester, as a general practitioner who had run a single-handed practice based in his large Victorian home in Ensley for over thirty years, could have been expected to be less involved. In fact, in addition to being a general practitioner he had also been the chief police surgeon for Exworth for a good many years. This meant that he was frequently involved in assessing people who were being held in the cells for various reasons. His most common task was to test the alcohol level of suspected drunk drivers but there were also all sorts of 'odd people' who presented in need of psychiatric help. Both Ben and Dr Rani had linked up with Dr Forrester at many late-night sessions in police stations and had worked well together in the past.

Whilst waiting for their return trip to Spitfire Close their conversation predictably turned to past shared experiences and after a while Dr Forrester moved the conversation on to one of his current problems.

'I have got this guy who has come to the notice of the police several times in the past few weeks and he really is an odd ball. I won't say any more now as I have referred him to the prof's clinic, so you will be meeting him shortly, but I look forward to your opinion of how best to deal with him. He goes by the name of Austin Spencer-Hamilton and he appears to be some sort of addict, but he is nothing like any addict I have ever met before.'

Ben's ears pricked up at the mention of drug addiction as he had only the week before been reading in a social work journal about the epidemic of addiction currently sweeping America. The article had hypothesised that it was only a matter of time before there would be similar problems in Great Britain. Ben had to admit to himself that his experience of drug addiction was very limited, in fact he had just one family on his caseload where drug misuse was a feature.

Norman Ainsley had first met Carol McBain whilst they were both on a drug rehabilitation programme having both been referred there from the courts. Carol was in her mid-forties and had spent large parts of her adult life in various hippy communes and along the way had produced a son called Dale who had been found to be addicted to heroin at birth. He was now sixteen years and had been completely clean from drugs from a small child but was an odd little lad as he had suffered some brain damage that had restricted his development both mentally and physically. However, the two of them had somehow managed to stay together but from a very young age Dale had at times been his mother's carer when she had relapsed into her addiction. At the time of her most recent court appearance for repeated shop lifting the magistrates had made it clear that she had to cooperate with a drug rehabilitation programme or accept that she would go to prison with Dale going into care. She chose the offered programme and was currently free of heroin surviving on methadone prescribed by her general practitioner. Carol and Dale had been allocated a flat in Highfield and Ben had worked with them from day one of their arrival. There had been several ups and downs over the months but Dale and his mum managed to hold the situation together and then there was suddenly a 'cuckoo in the nest'. Carol had recognised Norman Ainsley about a year ago when they both just happened to be in a café at the same time. They got chatting and Norman had admitted to her that he was using again, living in night shelters or on the streets and surviving on benefits or by begging. In no time at all he had become a member of Carol's household and poor little Dale found himself relegated to the position of 'also ran'. Norman was some twenty years younger than Carol but within weeks Carol found herself to be pregnant and she professed to be delighted. She was also determined that she would not be repeating giving birth to a drug-damaged baby. A few weeks ago she had given birth to a premature but healthy little girl who they called Norma after her father, who appeared to take no interest in her care.

As the baby had been premature she had remained in the maternity hospital for an extra couple of weeks, during which time the ward staff became aware of Carol's drug history. This caused them to be concerned for Norma's safety and their concern heightened when they observed Norman's obvious drugged state when he visited one day with Carol. During the baby's second week in hospital Carol had appeared with a black eye, which she explained by saying she had walked into a door. The ward sister shared her concern with the hospital almoner who in turn made a referral to the Child Care Department. Ben had attended the subsequent case conference and a childcare officer had been appointed to work with the family, with Ben continuing to focus largely on working with Dale.

After thirty minutes or so they again went back to Spitfire Close and repeated the process of looking for Daniel, only this time Ben went in the back door to prevent any possibility of Daniel slipping out that way. Nothing appeared to have changed in the prefab and as before there was no sign of him. They returned to Jessie's but on this occasion Ben located the backdoor key in its obvious hiding place on top of the door frame and secured the back door, taking the key with him. The three of them put their heads together and agreed to make an early morning visit the following day. Ben once again borrowed Jessie's phone and rang Bevington Hospital and arranged for the charge nurse to update Joseph. The best part of the afternoon had gone with little achieved and Ben decided to call it a day and went off to collect the boys from his mum. On the way over to her home he became conscious that his car was finding it increasingly difficult to maintain its speed on hills. He found himself speaking out loud to the car in an attempt to encourage it to struggle on. Surprisingly it seemed to work but he was all too aware that it was only a temporary reprieve and that it wouldn't be too long before Beatie joined her friends in Scadding's yard.

Chapter 55

Daring Deed and a Mystery Resolved

As Ben was finishing work early because he hadn't been able to locate Daniel, he didn't really want to arrive at his mum's too soon as it would interfere with his mum's plans for the boys' tea. If he collected them he would have to buy them the usual fish and chip supper, as he had to take care of the boys because it was Sandy's night for night school. Tuesday night's treat tended to make a sizeable hole in his 'pocket money'. With time on his hands he decided to call in on his dad at the allotment. As he expected, his dad and his old mate Arnold were perched in front of the shed putting the world to rights. They were in deep conversation and appeared to be discussing something of great importance and they also seemed almost anxious to include Ben in their considerations.

'Hi Ben, you might just prove to be the man we need because we are talking football and it is not something we normally talk about very much. Arnold has come up with a proposal which could prove very profitable but it is a long shot, a very long shot indeed. You probably don't know that Arnold likes to have the occasional flutter on the horses and even manages to win a few pounds from time to time. He always puts his bets on in the corner betting shop, just down from where he lives, and a couple of days ago went to place his bets and spotted a large notice which he could hardly believe. The sign was offering odds of a hundred to one on England winning the 1966 World Cup and we have been talking about little else since.'

Arnold took up the story from that point, whilst Ben's dad went into the shed and came out with three bottles of light ale. 'I have never heard of anything like those odds and I would really hate to miss out on the opportunity of making a killing with the bookmakers for what would be a relatively small outlay. So your dad and I have been doing some research and we have tried to look at all the pros and cons. It's not easy, as there are all sorts of ramifications that need to be considered, not least being England's past history of never having won the World Cup Competition. We have gone round and around in circles and I think we are near to a conclusion, but it would be interesting to get the opinion of a third person.'

Ben reached for a beer, made himself comfortable and listened with interest at their thoughts on the situation. Ben was careful not to express his surprise that his dad was even considering having a gamble. He had never been one to waste his brass and Ben was sure his mum would have a blue fit if she knew what he was thinking about. Ben's dad took up the story saying that he would outline the cons and would leave Arnold to point out the positives.

'The obvious problem is that England has never done well on the world stage and their recent international results seem to suggest that they haven't improved very much. When you look at the quality of the opposition they will be facing, teams such as Argentina, Brazil and Germany, the task would appear to be well-nigh impossible. I suspect that we might just as well pour our money down the drain.'

Arnold was becoming quite restless at this point and it was pretty obvious that he wanted to get on to the positives. He was clearly much more of a gambler than Ben's dad and Ben suspected that Arnold had already decided to make the bet with or without his dad's participation.

'The first thing to remember is that the competition is taking place in this country so we have home advantage. In addition we have some very strong players on all parts of the field. Men such as Bobby Charlton, who have got a shot like a rocket. Then of course we have one of the most prolific goal scorers in the world in Jimmy Greaves who can make a goal out of thin air. Add into the mix the finest goalkeeper in the world in Gordon Banks and we have both ends of the field taken care of. For a mid-field general and team captain we have Bobby Moore, who despite his young age commands the respect of the whole football fraternity with his style and control. But none of that is the most important consideration. My main reason for suggesting it is a worthwhile investment is that I believe England has got a priceless asset in our manager Alf Ramsey.

'I knew he was considered to be good by what I have read in the press over the years but when I researched his background down at the central library I was truly amazed by what he has achieved. He is still a young man, in his mid-forties, but he commands a lot of respect, insisting that he has total control over any team he manages. That is in direct contrast to the last England manager, Walter Winterbottom, who had his teams selected for him by a committee of the FA and we all know about the problems with committee decisions, always watered down by compromise.'

At this stage Arnold reached for his wallet and produced a carefully folded piece of paper which he flattened out on his knee. 'Just listen to this for a history: Alf played for England thirty-two times as a defender between 1948 and 1953 and captained the team on three occasions earning him the nickname of "the general" He retired from playing at thirty-five and took on the job of manager at Ipswich, who were in the third division at that time. Now listen carefully to the next bit as it is truly impressive.

'Between 1956 and 1962 Ipswich moved up from the third division to the first division and ended up as Champions of England in 1962, all achieved under Alf Ramsey's control. A unique achievement, so who's to say he can't do the same for England in the world cup? He certainly thinks he can and has openly predicted that England will win. I rest my case!'

After a longish silence Ben's dad and Arnold started to discuss how much they should bet and the decision to go ahead had been made without Ben expressing an opinion. They settled on each betting ten pounds, which would mean winning a thousand pounds each if their gamble paid off. A fortune in anyone's eyes and in Ben's mind could mean replacing 'Beatie' with the brand-new Cortina he had coveted in the showroom of the Ford dealership he had eyed up when last in town. The price ticket had been £650, which was way out of his reach, but £10 was a very different matter.

As if he was reading Ben's mind, Arnold turned to him and said, 'Well, young Benjamin, my lad, do you want to come in on this project?'

Now Ben had been put on the spot and he was very tempted, but £10 was what he usually allowed himself for a week's spending money and he had to buy his petrol, coffee and doughnuts out of that! But for some time when he undressed at night he had been putting his odd change into a demijohn left over from his student days of home brew and usually drinking it within days. It hadn't tasted very good and he had never taken it up again since he had married. In its current use it did offer him a limited source of income if he offered up the ten-pound note currently safely tucked in his wallet. Like his dad, he had never been a gambler, but if it was good enough for his dad, he decided it was good enough for him. With exaggerated aplomb, he reached for his wallet and handed over the ten-pound note.

Later, when Ben's dad, Frank got in the car for the short drive to his house for Ben to pick up the kids, he simply said, 'We won't tell the ladies,' to which Ben readily agreed. It felt good to have a shared secret with his dad and it somehow reinforced the closeness he had been feeling with him in recent months. The next time he saw his dad he was given a betting slip confirming the bet. This was carefully filed in Ben's memory box back in the office for safe keeping. Arnold later told them that the bookmaker had subsequently removed the poster offering the huge odds, much to the dismay of several other punters who had left it too late to take advantage.

The following morning Ben made an early start, leaving Sandy with the task of bussing the boys to their holiday day care at Ben's mum. Ben rarely talked about his work at home as he was conscious that Sandy found it all worrying. There had been the occasional call to his home when he had been on emergency duty when Sandy had to take the call because he was already out on another case. It had always made her anxious in case she missed something important. However, the evening before he had explained to her why he had to make an early start and she had been intrigued to find out what was going on. She readily agreed to sort out the boys for him even though it meant she would have to make two bus journeys there and back before she started her own job. Normally, she would have objected in very strong terms and Ben rewarded her cooperation by taking her a cup of tea in bed before he left. A rare occurrence indeed.

The traffic was very light and Ben made good time despite the fact the rain was pouring down and quickly forming small flash floods where drains were blocked by accumulated litter and the first leaves of the approaching autumn. He was the first to arrive at Jessie's, a good ten minutes before the planned 7.30 am arrival. Predictably, she was up and dressed and perched on her stool behind the counter with the coffee percolator already singing a comforting song. By the time Ben had greeted her she was pouring him a great-smelling black coffee with extra sugar that she thought might be necessary to give him energy for the task ahead. Within minutes, a couple of cars could be heard pulling up outside and Jessie was again pouring coffee when the two doctors mounted the steps and came into the coach. The three of them withdrew to the seats down the far end to enjoy their coffee and to finalise their plan of attack. As before they walked along to Spitfire Close in the vain hope that the neighbours might be unaware of their presence. But old people tend to get up early and the net curtains moved prefab by prefab as they progressed up to their target.

Loud knocking on the door brought no reply, which came as no surprise, and Ben used the key to gain entry. Calling as they went, they moved from room to room and everything seemed the same as the day before except the flies seemed to have increased in number. Ben left the two doctors searching out possible hiding places and went back into the bathroom. The evidence of the toilet having been used since he had flushed it the previous day confirmed that Daniel was here somewhere, but that was the only definite sign of him. Ben surmised that Daniel had given up using the flush to avoid any possibility of someone hearing it and therefore realising that he was at home. They congregated back in the living room and discussed in normal tones what would be their next course of action. Ben was amused to see that Dr Forester had washed out a milk bottle and was now busy watering the collection of cacti which were along the window ledge and a tatty rubber plant in the corner that looked more dead than alive. He had been unaffected by the chaos all around him but was instinctively moved to try and save the lives of living plants in distress.

The three of them held a debate and reached the conclusion that they would have to try again another day and made a noisy return to the front door, where they slammed the door firmly. But as previously agreed they remained on the inside and quietly returned to the living room where they chose to sit on the arms of the three-piece suite rather than risk the piles of junk which occupied the proper seats. The atmosphere was increasingly unpleasant and the urge to cough difficult to control, but they maintained their silent wait.

They had previously agreed to give it fifteen minutes and after five were all checking their watches. The time dragged on and they were beginning to think that they were wasting their time when there was a faint scratching noise from the main bedroom The three of them crept towards the noise and arrived at the bedroom door in time to see the door of the airing cupboard swing open. The space within was almost entirely filled by a large hot water boiler which was covered by a chunky padded jacket that appeared to fill the space. As they watched further sounds occurred and a panel dropped down on top of the boiler from the ceiling of the airing cupboard. As they watched a pair of feet in grubby khaki socks appeared followed by a pair of rather fat legs contained in grey flannel trousers. The feet came to rest on top of the boiler, paused and then the rest of Daniel appeared as he slid down to the floor. It was a very tight fit and the delicate manoeuvre was accompanied by a string of grunts and groans. With his feet now firmly on the floor Daniel turned into the room and froze in shock to find he had company. His face registered a look of abject terror and he stumbled over to sit on the bed. He looked a mess; his hair was all over the place and his growth of beard was equal to Ben's recent efforts but was uncombed and untrimmed. His clothes were dirty and smelly and it was very apparent that he had not changed in days.

Ben sat beside him but Daniel made no further reaction to any of them being there, he just sat with his hands in his lap and stared at the floor. They did their utmost to let him know why they were there and Ben made a point of trying to reassure him that his brother Joseph was making good progress in hospital, Daniel remained mute and made no reaction of any sort to all the attempts to explain their concern for him. It was clear to all of them that he needed a period of psychiatric assessment and treatment at St Margaret's and Ben went back into the lounge and put the phone back on its cradle. He quickly rang the ambulance control and requested an ambulance for a compulsory admission to hospital and as usual was given priority status.

With an estimated time of arrival of ten minutes Ben had just enough time to complete the necessary section forms and fee forms with the two doctors. Daniel shuffled out to the ambulance with an ambulance man each side of him looking like the defeated man he undoubtedly was. As compulsory admissions go it was very straightforward with nothing much for the neighbours to chew over. Ben went and collected his car from outside Jessie's just in time to fall into convoy with the ambulance on its way to male admissions. Ben was able to ring Joseph at Bevington from the ward and after a bit of persuasion got a nurse to take the telephone trolley to Joseph's bedside so he could talk to him directly. The level of Joseph's concern was very apparent from his voice and Ben took several minutes reassuring him that Daniel was safe and in good hands. The conversation ended with Ben agreeing to call out to see Joseph the following week when he should know more about Daniel's condition and treatment.

Chapter 56

Plans Come to Fruition

It was a little after eleven when Ben got away from St Margaret's and he drove straight back to Jessie's to update her and to thank her for her help over the past couple of days. As he drove along he mulled over the best way of clearing up the mess back at Spitfire Close as it would need sorting before the brothers' eventual return home. The shop in the coach was unusually full of customers all wanting to give their version of what they thought had taken place that morning,

Jessie was busy serving them and trying to take the steam out of the often total misinterpretations of what had happened and when she saw Ben she surreptitiously gestured for him to go straight on into her lounge. Within a few minutes Jessie had cleared the shop and had closed up with a sign on the door 'back in 15 minutes'. When she came through she was carrying two mugs and with her usual efficiency produced a tin of homemade biscuits, which Ben was happy to dive into as he had only had a piece of toast for breakfast and that had been hours ago.

Jessie just waved away Ben's thanks and got straight into the business of how the brother's prefab could be returned to normal. Ben explained that he was going to see Joseph the following week and he would have to get his agreement before allowing anyone in to clean up. Meanwhile, he had decided to ask his rotary friends Albert and Sam Watts if they would tackle the task of painting out the offensive graffiti from the front of the prefab. He was pretty sure that the council would have got around to cleaning it up at some time but he knew that they always had a long waiting list of maintenance jobs and that the prefab refurbishment would not have been given high priority.

However, Ben was hopeful that he would be able to persuade his contact in the Housing Department to supply the paint as it would be one less job for the council to do. Jessie then stepped in and offered to get the ladies on her committee for the Battle of Britain celebration to sort out the inside of the prefab if Joseph agreed. 'They are a great bunch of ladies who are all dead keen to get on with something, but it is too early to put our plans into action as it is still four weeks away. But it would be good to get the place tidied up before we are overrun with people on the fifteenth of September. They are all doers rather than just talkers and with Mary and me at the helm I reckon that we could get the place straight in a couple of days.'

Ben had discovered over time that if you wanted an important job done well, get a busy person to do it, and Jessie and Mary certainly met that criteria. He smiled his thanks and said he would suggest her offer to Joseph when he saw him at Bevington. He then set off to the office but made a diversion en route when his stomach told him it was time for lunch at Joe's.

Chapter 57

The Thursday Club

The first thing Ben saw as he opened the door of Joe's was the familiar figure of Ruth Andrews behind the counter working alongside Mavis. As usual, at this time of day, there was a queue of people waiting to be served and there was a fair amount of back chat being directed at Ruth by the men at the counter. As Ben held back to watch he could see that Ruth seemed to be taking it all in her stride and she appeared to be a natural in the job. It must have been a huge change for Ruth to have men showing her attention, even if it was only the friendly banter that went with the job. She dealt with it in an easy detached manner and moved on to deal with next customer. Meanwhile, Mavis was enjoying telling Ruth how to do things, which Ruth seemed to be accepting with good grace even if the advice on how to pour coffee was repeated each time it was ordered.

Ben looked across at Joe in the kitchen, who immediately gave him a fulsome 'thumbs up' indicating that Ruth was proving to be a success. She certainly looked the part, dressed in a white blouse, grey knee-length skirt and with her hair pinned back with a large tortoiseshell comb. Ben admitted to himself that she looked more attractive than he had ever seen her and most importantly seemed to be enjoying her newfound status. She greeted Ben with a warm smile and listened yet again to Mavis's coffee-making instructions whilst writing his order for a bacon sandwich and adding it to the small stack awaiting Joe's attention. This meant that Joe no longer had to remember Mavis's verbal orders which must have proved a real help at busy times. Mavis insisted on serving Ben his coffee and later his sandwich in the third room where Ben enjoyed a few moments to himself.

Unfortunately, he couldn't take too long over it as he knew the team would be waiting for him back at base, ready to decide the founder members for the Thursday Club. They got together around the colourful table in the main club room and after a brief chat about nothing in particular Phil opened the file in front of her and took control. It quickly emerged that the majority of the members were easily chosen. Phil started the discussion by laying down the ground rules that they should restrict the initial membership to ten and that the main intention of the club was to provide a social activity to clients who were generally isolated by virtue of their mental health. Alice and Ernest were the first two names on the list as they had both worked hard to get the rooms ready and would be of general help right from the start. Ben made the point that they needed to ensure that Ernest only attended in his lunch hour as he needed to be seen to be continuing to do his job as a road sweeper to the high standard he had already achieved.

After them it was a forgone conclusion that The Champ would also be welcomed as a sort of honorary member, but he was not included in the head count. Ben then told the others about arranging for Mavis to attend by killing two birds with one stone and fixing Ruth up with the job at Joe's. He then went on to suggest considering Peggy Knowles, the young woman with Down's syndrome, who lives with her mother Agnes on the ground floor of the Chelsea House flats.

'As you know that is just across the way from Joe's and yet Mavis and Peggy have never met. I suspect that the two of them could form a friendship at the club, which could possibly blossom into much more. I certainly think it is worth a try so I would like her to be invited. Mind you, her mother Agnes will take some persuading as she tends to have Peggy at her beck and call, but I am happy to give it a go.'

With no more ado Phil added both Mavis and Peggy to the list. Ben sat back in his chair and Phil stepped into the silence by proposing Faith and Charity Watson, the fairground women that Mary had reminded her about. Phil had known them for years and had always found them to be living a full and active life as an integral part of the travelling fairground. So much so that she had discontinued visiting a couple of years before and had been unaware of their change in circumstances now that their brothers ran the business.

Following Mary's comments she had called in to see them and found them spending all their time stuck in their caravan surrounded by the ten foot high fence which enclosed the site. Of course they had each other for company but their only stimulation was the television, which was switched on from morning to night.

'When I visited they were sat looking at an interlude of a potter's wheel going round and round, it was doing my head in after the first minute.'

Their names were added to the list, six down four to go. Susie quickly spoke up as Phil was adding the names of Faith and Charity to the list and said that she too had a couple of names she would like to propose.

'I know that you will be familiar with the men I would like to suggest but they are quite without friends of their own age and ability. They are not unlike Mavis and Peggy as I suspect they could form a friendship given time and the opportunity.'

Ben permitted himself a little smile in admiration of the way Susie had used his suggestion to help make her case.

'As you know Tim Hutchinson is a resident in The Cedars elderly persons' home despite the fact he is only in his mid-forties. He was born to his mother Maudie when she was well into the change and he has never moved far from her side since. The bond between them is very strong and when Maudie became too frail to remain at home the department agreed to keep them together by admitting them both to Cedar House. It was very unorthodox and was well intentioned I am sure, but it has left poor Tim surrounded by old people who largely sleep all day and tend to treat him like a family pet. He is always smartly dressed, looking rather like a little old man and is polite in the extreme, but has missed out badly on anything hinting of fun.

'Unfortunately, Maudie is now bed bound and probably not long for this world and Tim will need to be moved somewhere more appropriate to his age and needs. But he has never been out from his mother's apron strings and I think we could help to bring him out of his shell and more ready to face a major change in his circumstances.'

Both Phil and Ben were familiar with Maudie and Tim and their situation and were in complete agreement with Susie's recommendation that Tim's name should be added to the list. Before Susie could come up with her other suggestion Phil took over the meeting again in a rather severe manner and spoke up very slowly and thoughtfully.

'I can't help feeling that we have tended to be over cautious in our selections as all of them should be able to come together without difficulty.

I know we want to start the club off in a positive manner but I feel that we could be missing a trick here. There are, I am sure, other clients who are more problematical who could benefit from being members of a professionally run therapeutic group. There are three further places left and what I would like to suggest is that each of us comes up with a name of one of our clients who they think might benefit but who could involve us thinking a bit outside of the box.'

The tone of the meeting seemed to change to become much more formal and the room went silent for several moments as they all thought over what Phil had proposed. Ben knew she was right and, in his head, agreed that they should use this unique opportunity to do something more demanding, but he was also aware that the whole scheme could blow up in his face if it went haywire.

After a while, he said simply, 'I see where you are coming from, Phil, and I will of course try to support you as far as possible. Do you have anyone in mind?'

Phil being Phil had done her planning and immediately volunteered. 'The person I would like to attend is someone who I believe to be neither mentally ill nor mentally handicapped, although he has been labelled as one or the other by the authorities over many years. I have known Stanley Wiltshire and his mother Beatrice for several years ever since he moved back to live with her about three years ago. The file that came with him from the hospital where he had lived for almost thirty years made a very sad read. He had been placed at Hortham Hospital in Gloucester soon after it had been opened at a time when the new hospital had a shortage of the patients which it needed to justify its existence. As a consequence patients were shipped in from all over the country, which effectively isolated them from their homes and families. Out of sight and out of mind in most cases and in Stanley's case the round trip of sixty odd miles was virtually impossible for anyone without transport. He was only five years old when he was admitted and must have been a very frightened little boy. To her credit, his mother had maintained regular letters had never failed to send him a card and a gift for his birthday and at Christmas. But that was all she could manage as she had remarried when Stanley had been a baby and her new husband had rejected Stanley and refused to have any contact. From the reports on his file it seemed that Stanley and his stepfather had never bonded and appeared to be in competition for Beatrice's attention. Stanley was described as being a very wild child who was out of control, frequently stealing food and refusing to obey any attempts to control his behaviour. His stepfather's reaction had been to resort to using his army belt for corporal punishment, which just had the effect of increasing Stanley's "disturbed behaviour".

'As a small child he had been slow to thrive, had never talked and appeared to live in a world of his own. Some doctor at the time gave him the diagnosis of being mentally subnormal and he had been classified as uneducable. At least partially to ensure his safety from his stepfather's ideas about childcare his mother accepted residential care for him and he ended up in Hortham Hospital in Gloucester. He remained there for almost thirty years and would probably still be there if his stepfather hadn't conveniently got himself knifed in a drunken fight outside some pub or other.

'Once Beatrice had buried her husband she immediately increased her contact with Stanley and started to visit him at the hospital on a regular basis, a trip which involved two buses and a train trip both ways. Reading through Stanley's hospital file there was a whole series of reported incidents over the years when he lost control and became aggressive. By the time he was in his mid-twenties the authorities had at long last recognised that he was profoundly deaf, which went a long way to explaining his frustrations, but he already had the label of mentally subnormal and no action was taken to explore helping him with his deafness. Inevitably he became institutionalised with no one ever questioning the need for him to remain in the hospital. His behaviour had improved by the time he was in his late twenties and he had for several years since held a privileged position working alongside the cooks in the kitchens. From the brief annual reports on his file it was clear that Stanley enjoyed his work and Phil guessed that access to food had remained an important consideration for Stanley throughout his life.

'After several visits Beatrice decided that she would like to have her son home for a short holiday but the board of governors were resistant to the suggestion. They were concerned about his reputation for outbursts of aggressive behaviour and at that time it was almost unheard of for long-term patients to be allowed back into the community. I was asked for a home circumstance report by the hospital and was allowed access to Stanley's hospital file. When I read it I was struck by the fact that Stanley had never made any sort of attack on other people; his acts of aggression were always directed towards smashing windows or furniture. I formed the opinion that his problem of not having speech and being totally deaf left him with no alternative way to express his frustrations. After talking to Beatrice at some length I also visited Stanley, who seemed elated at the idea of visiting his mother. Whilst at the hospital, I took the opportunity of speaking with the staff who dealt with Stanley day after day. The ward staff and cooking staff, when pressed, agreed that Stanley was really a "bit of a pussy cat" who tended to keep himself to himself but never caused any concern. In my report to the governors I stated that I thought it was safe to allow Stanley to have a holiday at his mother's and much against their better judgement they agreed, making it quite clear that if it went wrong it was on my head!'

By this time Phil had the full attention of both Ben and Susie, neither of whom had ever heard her speak of the Wiltshires, before and Ben was once again aware of how much Phil tended to work in isolation.

'I visited the Wiltshires several times during the holiday and it soon became clear to me that there was more to Stanley than met the eye and that he was far from being subnormal. He delighted in going shopping for his mum and was just setting of to do some local shopping when I arrived at their house. At the time I was a smoker and I had run out of fags so took advantage of the opportunity and gave him a note and some money to get me some cigarettes. He looked at the note and immediately covered one eye and put his other hand into the front of his jacket. My note read "20 Nelsons", which was the brand I used to smoke and Stanley had read it, understood it and reacted to show me that he understood. This was not the actions of someone who was subnormal and who had never received even a basic education. His face broke into a massive grin and he went off to do his errands laughing out loud as he hurried on his way. His mother confirmed that she wanted her son back and explained that her husband had been a control freak who she should have parted from years ago but she had little money of her own and nowhere to go. His death had been a shock but also a relief and she felt she was now free to offer Stanley a home. My report back to the hospital governors suggested that Stanley should be discharged to his mother's care but the board of governors were still unconvinced.

'Fortunately, an unusual compromise was accepted by them but only by the decision going all the way up to the medical officer of health, Doctor Wynne-Jones, who came up with a clever solution. He proposed that Stanley could be accepted under the guardianship of the local authority, thereby absolving Hortham of any untoward consequences from his return home. I vaguely knew that this was possible under the mental health act but had never seen it used before or since. So I have been acting as Stanley's guardian ever since on behalf of the department. I am convinced that we could help Stanley to improve both his reading and his communication skills. At the moment he relies upon lip reading to know what is going on and has developed a sort of play acting of his own invention to try and get his thoughts across but he is often difficult to understand. I think we could get him some lessons in sign language at the club and both Susie and I would like to learn it too. I have a friend who is prepared to come along as a volunteer to try and teach him and who knows, we may even end up being able to get him involved with the deaf society who meet regularly in St Peter's church hall in Ensley.'

Ben was impressed by Phil's dedication and well thought out plan and said so in an enthusiastic way. Phil blushed, which was quite unlike her and Stanley's name was added to the list. Susie stepped in to pick up the discussion and admitted that she had two other potential club members in mind but wasn't sure if either were suitable.

'My immediate thoughts when we decided the criteria for membership would be trying to provide social interests for people who are isolated because of their mental health condition, which made me think of Hanca Parsons. She is undoubtedly isolated, in fact I suspect that she must be one of the most isolated clients that we have. However, on reflection I think she is a special case as she has deliberately chosen her rather unique lifestyle in her remote home. For that reason I feel we should respect her wishes and if you agree, Ben, I will not be putting her name forward.'

Ben nodded and Susie continued. 'My other person, Sidney Sellers, is perhaps a bit concerning as he comes with the additional problem that he suffers with Grand Mal Epilepsy as well as being mentally handicapped. Over the years his family have become very overprotective, as in the past they found that he often seemed to suffer a fit when having any change in his day-to-day routine. He is a pleasant enough young man but is reported to become verbally aggressive when he has a fit and unfortunately usually loses control of his bladder when fitting. The result is that his elderly parents have dedicated their lives to playing it safe and Sidney's days are spent doing jigsaws, watching television and playing his records in his bedroom. In reality his epilepsy is largely under control, involving regular medication with anti-convulsant drugs to suppress his abnormal electrical activity. I think he would benefit from getting out from time to time and the club would seem to be a safe environment for him to widen his horizons a bit. However, I must admit to having some concerns as I have never had to deal with someone having a fit and I would need to have help at first. Also I am a bit worried how seeing someone have a fit might alarm the other members.'

Both Phil and Ben had visited Sidney and his family from time to time and agreed with Susie's assessment of his situation. Both had previous experience of coping with people having an epileptic fit and were confident that with their help Susie would soon learn the simple rules about helping the person through the fit. On balance they both felt it would be a chancy but appropriate risk, Phil in particular felt it was unlikely that Sidney's parents would agree. Susie, however, was reasonably confident and knowing her dogged determination Ben suspected that she would gain their cooperation. Sidney was pencilled in as the ninth recruit. This just left one more member to select and following Phil's suggestion that they should look at selecting a few more complex clients Ben went right off-piste.

'I think you both know something about the couple of drug addicts that I visit on a regular basis, where there is concern about the care the two of them provide their children. Carol McBain the mother is in her forties and until a couple of years ago I had no real concern with the care she provided for her son Dale who attended the junior training centre regularly and they felt that he was reasonably happy. There was the odd concern when his hygiene was a bit suspect and his clothes needed replacing but she always reacted when I brought it to her attention. I was able to get an occasional grant from a charity or the National Assistance and by and large things went on fairly well. Then she met up with another drug user, Norman Ainsley, who is twenty years younger than her and they have since become an item with him moving in to live with Carol and Dale. She seems to be besotted with him and poor old Dale is now largely left to try to care for himself. He has now stopped attending the training centre and seems to be treated by a dogsbody by Carol and Norman. To add to the problems Carol has recently had a baby and the "family" are now being supervised by the children department who are concerned about the couple's history of drug use and their ability to care for the baby. I have agreed to continue to try and help Dale but Norman is very uncooperative. I frequently find it hard to get beyond the doorstep and I strongly suspect that Norman is actively using again and has possibly encouraged Carol to participate too. I think it would be good if we could offer Dale some support and gain his confidence to share any concerns he may have. Dale is only just sixteen years old so would be the youngest by a long way, but I am sure he would benefit and would welcome a bit of care and attention. His home situation is very unstable and could disintegrate at any time and his attendance at the club could possibly provide me with an early warning that things were about to collapse.'

It didn't take much further discussion before Dale was accepted and the founder members of the Thursday Club were agreed upon. The meeting broke up soon, after with each of them setting off individually to begin to recruit their recommended members. Ben headed straight back to Joe's and found the place empty of customers other than a couple of elderly ladies each with an old mongrel dog, which they had been taking for an afternoon constitutional. The dogs were now both fast asleep and the women seemed to be enjoying a good old gossip over a couple of mugs, which had long been drained of their final dregs of tea. Ben could see Joe and Ruth through the ever-open door of the kitchen and they were side by side doing the washing and wiping up that remained from a busy day in the café. They had their backs to him and hadn't heard him come in as any noise he may have made would have been drowned out by the peals of laughter coming from the third room, the one marked private. His curiosity got the better of him and he went over to the door and gently pushed it open.

The activity underway was clearly most enjoyable for the participants and Ben had the greatest difficulty in not joining in their merriment. Katie

Andrews was swivelling her body with practised ease to demonstrate her skill with the hula-hoop. Mavis was attempting to copy her by shaking her rotund hips whilst firmly holding the hula-hoop she was using quite stationary by one hand. Needless to say the moment she let it go it fell straight down on to the floor and the two young girls convulsed with laughter. Ben slid the door shut but was impressed by the obvious harmony of the situation he had just witnessed. He returned to the main room and was spotted by Joe, who gestured for him to sit down and came out with a tray of teas for Ben, Ruth and himself and had also brought extra mugs for the two old ladies, who accepted without surprise and Ben guessed it wasn't the first time Joe had treated them to a freebee. Ben quickly advised Joe of his idea of linking up Mavis with Peggy Knowles and suggested that they might be allowed to walk to the club together, giving them both some greater independence. Joe had some reservations but Ruth offered to walk with them both ways for the first couple of times and Joe gratefully accepted.

Now all Ben had to do was to convince Agnes Knowles that her daughter should be allowed to attend and even more difficult that she should be allowed to walk there and back with Mavis. It was still only four o'clock so Ben drank the tea, and thanking Joe and Ruth for their cooperation went straight over to Chelsea House. The door to the flat was answered by Peggy, who recognised Ben straight away and invited him in and led him into the living room. Agnes was sat in an armchair partially covered by a blanket despite the flat being heated like a sauna. She went straight into full moan mode telling Ben about all her aches and pains that made her life so difficult.

'If it weren't for our Peggy I am sure I would have to be in a home by now. She does things for me all the time and between her and the home help we struggle on pretty well but it doesn't get any easier. It is ages since I have been outside the front door and Peggy does all the shopping these days. Of course the rest of my family call in from time to time but they are all working so are busy with their jobs and their own children. Still, having Peggy is a blessing. Put the kettle on, there's a good girl.'

Peggy went straight off and could be heard filling the kettle and sorting out the cups. Ben took advantage of Agnes taking a breath and dived straight in.

'Obviously, I think it is great that Peggy is such a help but I am a bit concerned that she doesn't seem to have any friends of her own. This is often the case for people with a mental handicap, particularly it they live with their parents and never go anywhere to socialise. Peggy is a pleasant young woman who could benefit from having friends of her own age and of similar ability and that is precisely why I have called in today to see you both.'

Ben went on to explain about the club and also about Mavis, who could attend with her if she wished. Agnes looked about to raise all sorts of objections but Peggy brought a tray of tea in at that juncture and Agnes remained quiet for the time being. Ben turned his attention to Peggy and chatted generally about any hobbies she may have, what music she liked and what she liked doing most. It was no surprise to him that what she enjoyed most was doing the shopping and the opportunity to meet people and chat. By the time he had left the flat it had been agreed, albeit reluctantly by Agnes, that Peggy would give the club a try and would be picked up on route by Ruth and Mavis the following Thursday.

That left only Dale McBain to be recruited by Ben but he had already decided to leave that to the last moment to try and avoid Norman putting his oar in. He went straight back to the office to try and sort out the problem of the graffiti at Spitfire Close. His run of good luck continued and he got an immediate reply when he rang Albert Watts on his home telephone number. Albert was already aware of the problem at Spitfire Close and listened with interest as Ben filled him in on the situation. It turned out that Jessie and her committee had already lined Albert and Sam up to help with the preparations for the celebrations and Albert was sure that they would be able to sort out the problem given the necessary paint.

'Leave that to me, Albert, I have got an idea about that and will get back to you once I have cleared it with Joseph. As ever thanks for all your sterling work it really makes a difference for our clients.'

The final phone call of the day was to Fred Harris the foreman at the buildings and maintenance department of the district council. Ben didn't hold out much hope of a reply as he knew that the council men tended to finish on time and that had passed ten minutes ago.

He liked Fred and had loads of dealings with him in the past and always found him to be down to earth and reasonable to deal with. He wouldn't go so far as to describe him as a friend but he suspected he could become one given the opportunity. He had heard on the grapevine that Fred had had a bit of a breakdown when his marriage broke down a few months ago but he knew that he was now back at work and apparently on the mend. The phone rang on for ages and Ben was just about to hang up and wait for another day when the phone was picked up and in a rather weary voice came the reply.

'Hello, can I help you? Fred Harris speaking.' Ben greeted him warmly and on impulse he told Fred that he had something to chat to him about and suggested that they should meet for a pint at the local pub, the Highfield Tavern. Fred response was almost instantaneous.

'That sounds like a great idea but not at the Highfield Tavern as all my workmen tend to gather there after work and I have seen all I want to of them for today. I usually call into the Wellington at Ensley for a jar or two most evenings, would that suit you?' They agreed to meet up around six-thirty which gave Ben just enough time to ring Sandy to say he would be delayed.

It didn't take Ben long once he arrived at the pub to realise that Fred was a regular customer and as such was greeted with considerable attention from the shapely barmaid, which included a rather deliberate view down the front of her quite amazing cleavage. Ben got the beer in and they moved across to a corner table with Fred calling back over his shoulder.

'I'll have the usual in about thirty minutes, Gloria.' She giggled a response and Ben was left wondering, with his mind boggling. Fred left Ben to wonder for a couple of minutes before explaining that he regularly called into the pub on the way home from work and usually had the special from the menu for his tea.

'I don't even look any more what is on the menu and enjoy having a surprise for tea most days. The food is invariably good, much better than anything my ex-wife ever cooked, and you must admit that Gloria has a couple of points that are outstanding.'

Ben could only nod his agreement and was happy that Fred seemed over his emotional difficulties. They made the sort of small talk that men are generally comfortable with before Ben got down to the business he had wanted to discuss. Fred signalled to Gloria for another pint but Ben declined when offered as he still had to drive home and didn't want to risk his licence. Fred listened attentively to the problem of the graffiti and how it had come about, but before he had an opportunity to respond, Ben went on to explain about Albert and Sam his volunteers and the need for him to provide them with the necessary paint. 'I have to be a bit careful, Ben, as I mustn't be seen to be using non-union manpower or I will have a strike on my hands in no time. Mind you, if your men don't do the job it will come back on the council to sort it out and that could end up being on the waiting list for months.'

Nothing more was said and after a few more minutes Ben got up to leave and Fred said rather cryptically, 'I'll walk with you to your car as there are often unsavoury characters hanging about and I am not sure that I locked my van.'

The car park had only about half a dozen cars in it and there was not a person in sight. Fred's van was parked almost next to the old Cortina and when he checked the rear door it swung freely open to display a van packed with decorating materials. He reached into the van and removed two large tins of masonry paint, which he passed over to Ben with no further comment.

'Thanks, Fred. I owe you one, these will do the job nicely.'

They shook hands and Fred headed back to the pub for his evening meal and a bit of flirtation with Gloria. Ben headed home for tea with Sandy and the boys happy with a successful day's work and satisfied that his relationship with Fred had progressed.

Chapter 58

Getting In order for the Festivities

Ben had arranged to visit Joseph at Bevington Hospital at about 10 am on the following day and had decided that it wasn't worth battling through the morning traffic only to have to return the same way almost at once to get to Bevington some thirty miles away. The day was dry but there was a distinct chill in the air when he attempted to sit in his garden with his morning coffee. He looked about and realised that the small flower beds and rather battered apple tree had a very neglected look about them and had all the scars of the boys' uncaring play. Sandy started out each spring with ideas for growing their own vegetables but it never came to much and they were always grateful for his dad's regular offerings from his allotment. It proved too cold to hang about outside and he returned to the warmth of the wood burner before setting off in 'Beatie'.

The worst of the morning traffic was over but the old Cortina was sluggish and reluctant to break the speed limit. Ben reached for the radio and flipped through the channels in the hope of finding something worth listening to to take his mind off the odd noises coming from the engine. The familiar voice of Roy Plomley of Desert Island Discs fame came through on the home service and he was introducing a reprise of one of his programmes that had first been played on 12 November 1956. Normally, Ben would have gone on flipping channels as when he had chanced to hear Desert Island Discs previously he had found it to be rather mushy and lacking in depth. However, he was delayed in changing channels by a build-up of traffic which demanded his full attention and before he had the opportunity to change, Roy Plomley had already introduced his castaway as Donald Campbell. Ben was hooked and all thoughts of changing channels disappeared as who could fail to be interested in a man who had broken both the world land speed record and the world water speed record in the same year? The journey proceeded at a steady pace with the bulk of the traffic going in the opposite direction taking people to their work in Exworth. The programme was easy to listen to and informative as Roy took Donald through his early history when his father Malcolm had broken the world land speed record nine times and the world water speed record four times between 1924 and 1935. These adventures were all funded by family money earned by their chain of grocery shops.

Malcolm was clearly a hard act to follow, but Donald had taken up the cudgel with considerable success in his boat and car both call 'Bluebird' out of respect for his father, who had called all his record breaking boats and cars the same two words 'Blue Bird'. As one might expect, Donald's choice of music for the programme was largely classical but he then made the surprising selection of Doris Day singing 'Tea for Two'. All in all, Ben really enjoyed the programme but still hadn't changed his personal opinion that Roy Plomley should have been called Roy Plumy as he had such a posh voice. He was also at a loss why so many 'castaways' chose the works of Shakespeare as their author of choice. His own experience of Shakespeare was limited to studying *Julius Caesar* at school for O level English Literature and he had found it less than interesting. Ben did, however, recall one good thing that had come out of his brush with The Bard when the school had taken his class for a very rare trip out to see a professional performance of the play. The play had been as boring as the book but Ben had found himself sitting next to a very pretty girl with beautiful dark brown eyes who attended the local high school. He discovered her name to be Bunty and they managed to surreptitiously hold each other's hand throughout the play under the unsuspecting eyes of the teachers in the row behind them. Ben never saw Bunty again but the memory of their clandestine meeting still brought a smile to his lips. He thought that his own choice of reading would be something like Agatha Christie, who always managed to come up with a twist in the tail of her stories.

But his mind moved on to an adventure story he had just read, having picked it up second hand at Jessie's shop. It was *The Golden Keel* by Desmond Bagley, who Ben had never heard of before, but who had written a classic adventure story that had really held his attention.

The programme had finished and Ben was still mulling over his possible choices of music and reading when he pulled into the car park at Bevington. He happily retained some of the more unusual bits of information he had heard on the programme to be regurgitated when he had his next session with his dad at the allotment.

As before the reception area of the hospital was a bustling mass of young men in wheelchairs charging around involved in a complex game trying to get a beach ball into a waste paper bin. The whole scene was one of frantic activity and much shouting, heavily laced with familiar swear words. A small Asian nurse was trying to control the activity to prevent unwanted injuries but the young patients largely ignored his intervention. They threw themselves into the activity with obvious pleasure and no real concern for their own safety or that of their opponents and Ben guessed that it was a way of dealing with the frustration of being wheelchair bound. He tiptoed around the perimeter of the hall and headed for Joseph's ward.

Nothing much had changed from his last visit. The same four men were occupying the same four beds with each contained within their individual apparatus. The television was on quietly in the corner but no one was taking any notice of it or of each other. The contrast between the hive of activity of the reception area and the total lack of stimulation of this ward was marked and Ben wondered how these guys dealt with their boredom. Joseph had obviously been looking out for his visit and waved Ben across the room with a broad welcoming smile. He was keen to learn of his brother's situation and Ben filled him in on the situation so far. He was able to reassure Joseph that Daniel was in good hands and explained that he was in the care of Dr Rani, who Ben could check with every Friday when they worked together at the prof's clinic. He also mentioned his close friend Dave, who worked as a charge nurse on the admission ward and with whom Ben was in regular contact. Joseph seemed reassured by this but became more serious when Ben went on to discuss the current situation with the prefab at Spitfire Close.

Ben moved swiftly on to explain the arrangements he had made for the graffiti to be removed and Joseph was pleased to accept the volunteers, Albert and Sam's offer of help. With some trepidation Ben went on to explain about the situation within the prefab and the need for it to be sorted out as a matter of urgency. He explained that Jessie and her team of helpers had offered to tidy things up and Joseph's immediate reaction was one of embarrassment and a flat rejection of the ladies seeing his home in such a dirty and unsanitary condition. Ben gave him time to think the situation over and then gently kept plugging away at the sense of his suggested solution. Finally, Joseph agreed that Jessie and Mary had been good friends and neighbours to him and his brother over many years and they both understood his complications with maintaining Daniel's mental health at a functioning level. He finally agreed that they could be given a house key but insisted that he should be allowed to make a donation to the Battle of Britain celebration fund by way of thanks. Ben recognised Joseph's need to retain some control, however limited by his hospitalisation, and they shook hands on the deal.

A nurse pushing a tea trolley came into the ward at that juncture and the men in each bed came to life in anticipation of something breaking their monotony of immobility. This was clearly a daily trigger for conversation and back chat was soon happening on all sides. Then the nurse produced, as if by magic, a chocolate cake complete with candles from beneath a clean white tea towel and used his cigarette lighter to light it up. This was taken over to Ted in the corner bed, who seemed both surprised and moved that his birthday had been remembered. After a somewhat ragged version of 'Happy Birthday' each of the other men produced small gifts of chocolate, tobacco or shaving soap which they had all bought secretly from the WVS shopping trolley which came around weekly. The cake was devoured by the patients and the nurse and Ben as a visitor were included in the ritual.

After the pleasure of the brief interruption to yet another long boring day the men went back to their solitary ways of coping, but Ben was pleased to note that Joseph seemed in better spirits.

'By the way, Ben, I have had one bit of good news from my union rep at the fruit market when he visited me over the weekend. My employer, Olivers, have promised to keep my job open for me and are going to keep paying me full wages for at least six months. I have spoken to the doctor and he has assured me that I should be back on my feet well before that. In fact he said that the bones were healing well and he hoped they would be able to get me out of bed in a week or two. That's not all, Arthur Rupp my union rep is attempting to get me compensation for an industrial injury from the firm's insurance scheme. It's not sorted yet but he seems pretty confident and thinks it could be a nice little earner. So I have been lying here dreaming about how I might be able to get rid of my old disability carriage, which is only for a single person, breaks down frequently and has, a couple of times, let me down when I am on the way to the fruit market at 5.30 am leaving me high and dry. If I get a reasonable payment I would really like to buy an adapted Mini, then I would be able to take Daniel out to places in his time off.'

Ben was delighted that Joseph was expressing some optimism about the future and felt admiration for his tenacity against all odds. When Ben left he promised to visit Joseph the following week and offered to bring him in some clothes as Joseph had told him that the nursing staff had had to cut off the clothes he had been wearing at the time of his accident in order to get to his injuries. Joseph quickly gave him a list of what he needed and once again thinking of his brother asked if he could also be sent in a change of clothes. Ben said he would sort it and left feeling content that the meeting had been an all-round success. The reception area was free of frantic wheelchair operators and he guessed they had run out of steam and were resting before their next assault on their imposed limitations.

The journey back to the office went with Ben in automatic mode, with Beatie's odd noises largely drowned out by a pop music programme being presented by a very straight-laced announcer talking in the typical BBC manner. Ben's mind quickly began to wander as he much preferred the more flamboyant style he had been brought up on in his early teens listening beneath his bedclothes to Radio Luxembourg on his homemade crystal set. He later moved on to listening to a vintage Phillips valve radio which he had been given by his grandmother as a memento of his grandfather after he had died and with whom he had regularly spent Saturday afternoons listening to the football. Ben really loved that old set and still had it stored away in a cardboard box in the attic.

When he had gone to university the same grandmother had treated him to a small portable radio to take with him to Bristol. That had been a constant companion ever since and had more recently allowed him to listen to the Pirate Radio station on the ship Caroline that was moored just outside the UK territorial waters. Ben had been addicted to it from day one in 1964 when Simon Dee made the first transmission. The whole team of DJs, of which Tony Blackburn was his firm favourite, presented a relaxed modern show that made the BBC presentation seem totally dated.

As he drove along he let his thoughts wander to what his choices would be in the unlikely event of ever being invited to go on 'Desert Island Discs'. His choice of a luxury item was easy it would have to be his portable radio and a good supply of batteries. Donald Cameron had chosen mainly classical records but Ben's knowledge of classical music was very sparse and his choices of records would inevitably mainly include a number of Beatles songs. It was hard to choose which ones, as he liked them all, and he decided not to overstretch his brain at this point. He felt he ought to come up with something a bit more highbrow to complete his music and after due consideration managed to dig up a possible couple of 'probables', both of which he had been introduced to at school.

The first was the Hallelujah Chorus from Handel's Messiah, which had been the grand finale of a concert he had taken part in during his relatively short membership of his school choir. He still occasionally broke into a series of hallelujahs when the mood took him and Sandy and the boys never failed to react with mock horror. The rendering was always done at full volume with loads of passion, which was what his schoolteacher had demanded as essential to the piece. Fortunately for all concerned, Ben's total recall was restricted to a series of ten hallelujahs closely followed by 'For the Lord God omnipotent reigneth' and then a few more hallelujahs before shuddering to a halt.

The other possibility had also been part of a music lesson at school when his teacher had played a series of records which parodied various things in life. The 'Coronation Scot' had been named after a particular steam train that ran from London to Scotland which had been inaugurated in 1937 to mark King George VI's coronation. It was a very catchy tune and sounded just like a train trip, but more importantly from Ben's point of view it was also the theme tune to 'Paul Temple', the weekly detective story on the radio that Ben's whole family had always made a point of listening to. That just left him with deciding what books to take and that proved no problem as he quickly settled for the James Bond books by Ian

Fleming. He knew there were about a dozen in the series and he had read most of them in his late teens but was confident that they could bear a second reading. After a pleasant, relaxed journey Ben was soon pulling up in the bus parking space outside Jessie's. He knew that the next bus wasn't due for a good half hour and he didn't intend to hang about.

With only just over two weeks to go to the Battle of Britain event he was somewhat reluctant to add to Jessie's load by letting her loose at Spitfire Close. But she had been quick to offer her help to the brothers and as they say, never look a gift horse in the mouth. He went straight into the shop and as expected found her in the seating area at the rear of the coach surrounded by her band of willing helpers. The table in front of them were littered with piles of paper which they were all studying with great concentration. When she spotted him Jessie went around the group introducing them to him in turn by name. Most of the names went over Ben's head but he did make a special note of Gabriel Watson, who was the mother of Faith and Charity, shortly to be two of the Thursday club's founder members. She was the sort of woman who would have stood out in any crowd. Her iron grey hair was unusually long and was drawn back in a bunch which went down nearly to her waist. Her face was lined and her skin was tanned but her outstanding feature was the deepest brown eyes Ben had ever seen. They seemed to almost penetrate your very being, but it was in no way threatening, quite the reverse. They seemed to envelope you like a comfortable blanket. It was with some difficulty that Ben managed to break eye contact when Jessie asked how it had gone with Joseph. Ben told her of Joseph's grateful acceptance of her offer of help and passed over the prefab key and the cheque that Joseph had insisted on donating to the celebration fund.

Ben went on to confirm that he had obtained the necessary paint for the graffiti cover up. 'I just have to see Sam and Albert to give them the paint but I haven't been able to catch up with them yet.'

Gabriel spoke up then and told him that the two cousins were at that very moment down in her yard doing some painting as part of the festival preparations. Her voice matched her presence and Ben was convinced that Gabriel had more than a hint of Romany blood in her background and he was prepared to bet that somewhere along the line she was related to the equivalent of 'Romany Royalty'. He set off in his car just a hundred yards up the road and pulled up on the gravel drive leading to the yard. The massive double doors were firmly closed but there was a small pedestrian door set in the right-hand one which was a little ajar. The yard that confronted him was mind blowing with several monster lorries parked in three columns, all of which were attached to equally large trailers. The trailers were each fully loaded with strange-shaped loads all covered in tarpaulins, many of which were emblazoned with colourful sign writing identifying them as being 'Watson's Travelling Extravaganza'. Ben squeezed his way through the narrow gap between the nearest lorries and eventually emerged into a square yard with Dutch barns to the left and right and a very large static caravan at the far end. One of the barns was filled with tightly packed touring caravans which Ben guessed were used when the whole shebang was on the road. The other Dutch barn contained stacks of garishly painted components that made up the various sideshows that were part and parcel of a traditional travelling fair.

Albert and Sam were hard at it giving the faded paintwork a fresh look and they explained to Ben that most of the stuff they were working on had been in moth balls since the sons had taken over running the business. They were making light work of their painting, using several paint rollers, one for each colour in use. Sam came back to Ben's car with him to collect the paint and seemed confident that they would complete the prefab in good time for the festivities. With his tasks for the two Collins brothers complete for the time being, he really only had one thing that needed doing fairly urgently but he was happy that it could wait until after he had stopped for lunch at Joe's.

Ruth was working away behind the counter and gave him a warm smile and had all the appearances of being completely at home in her new position. Mavis was still telling her how to use the coffee machine each time a cup was ordered, but Ruth just let it go over her head whilst Ben couldn't help but notice that her hair had recently been cut and styled by a professional hairdresser. It was good to see her spending a bit of her hard-earned cash on herself. The place was full of customers and noise and Ben was pleased to escape to the sanctuary of the back room with its sofa and smouldering fire.

After a restful lunch in his haven Ben drove straight around to visit Dale McBain and his mother Carol to invite Dale to come to the Thursday Club on the opening day the following week. Norman was stretched out on their old settee apparently dead to the world. There was a strong smell of cannabis which Ben had become familiar with since Norman had moved into the McBain household. Both Dale and his mum seemed pleased to see Ben and readily accepted that he should try the club out. In some ways it helped that Norman was a non-participant in the discussion as he was generally very unpleasant and always attempted to control Carol and criticise Dale.

The baby was happily sucking a dummy in a carry cot on the floor and looked bonny and clean when Carol took her out to proudly show her off to Ben. Dale chatted away to her in baby talk and made her giggle by tickling her tummy. Carol confided to Ben that life could be difficult with Norman.

'At the moment he seems to be able to survive with just a bit of weed and his methadone. I have managed to stay completely clean ever since I fell pregnant and like they say, I take one day at a time.'

Ben congratulated her on what was a terrific achievement considering how many years she had been addicted and they agreed that Dale would benefit from having social activities of his own. In order to ensure that Norman didn't interfere with the plan Ben agreed to collect Dale for the first meeting and to see how it went from there.

Ben finally made a first appearance of the day at the office a little after three and as ever Mrs Freeman had everything under control. The only thing that was in any way urgent was something that Susie wanted to discuss with him, but she had given up waiting and was out doing visits. She had left a note for him on his desk saying she would be back about four so he settled down to make a start on his paperwork. Just after four o'clock Ben heard the familiar clip clop of Susie's high heels as she hurried along the corridor to his office. She seemed slightly flushed and he guessed she had been hurrying to keep to her written time of arrival. She came in with a smile and sat in the chair opposite Ben with a sigh. However, before she could get started on the concern that she wanted to discuss, Alice arrived with a mug of tea for her and asked Ben if he would like one. Unusually for him he declined, preferring to get on with the business in hand and Alice left without comment.

Susie pushed an important-looking envelope across the desk to him and after having a slurp of tea went on to explain. She told Ben that on several visits to see Hanca she had been forgetful about checking the 'bread bin post box' for mail as she had made her way up the winding steps up to her house. However, when she had visited Hanca that morning she had lifted the lid of the old bread bin and found a whole mishmash of mainly junk mail and free newspapers, which she carried up to the house to go through with Hanca. Most of the pile went straight into an old beer crate, where Hanca kept her fire lighting materials for her wood burner, but amongst the debris were a couple of electric bills and the important-looking envelope now on his desk in front of Ben.

The letter was addressed to Hanca Parsons nee Kowalska and when Ben removed the enclosed letter he immediately realised that it was written in a foreign language which he thought might be German but that was pure guess work on his part. The lengthy letter was on headed note paper which read 'Erbe Jager Verbunden' which took him no further forward. Susie confirmed that it was indeed German and Hanca had been able to confirm that from her school days basic learning. But she was Polish by birth and had only very limited understanding of German and was unable to make any sense of the letter. Susie had said she would try to get it translated and had come to Ben to see if he had any idea how it might be achieved. After the briefest of thoughts he told Susie that he did not have the knowledge to help directly but announced, 'I can't be of any help but I think I know a man who can.'

He picked up the phone and within a few moments he was sharing the problem with Mr Hamilton the headmaster at the local junior school who, as always, reacted positively. He was able to tell them that one of his staff, Mr Ericson, was married to a German lady who he felt sure would relish helping with a mystery. In no time at all it was arranged that Susie would drop the letter straight around to Mr Hamilton and she set off in a rush without even finishing her tea. All in all a satisfactory day and Ben headed for home in a good sense of humour. On the spur of the moment he decided to call in to see Robbie and Patsie, who he had not seen for some time as he was keen to learn about the progress with their speedway project.

As usual, he parked outside and walked into the scrapyard expecting the usual hive of activity but the whole yard was silent with no sign of anyone. Surprisingly, even the dog was absent and Ben's approach to the office went unheralded. He was just about to mount the stairs when the office door opened and a smartly dressed older man came hurrying down the steps. He was almost upon Ben before either of them saw the other and even then it took a few seconds before they recognised each other and they then spontaneously broke into a welcome and a firm handshake which could easily have become a hug. There before Ben was Desmond Davies, who now presented a vastly different persona from the deeply depressed man Ben had admitted to St Margaret's only a few months before. He had an obvious sense of purpose and quickly explained to Ben that he was on a mission and was running late. With that he let himself into the old army jeep that Robbie used as a run around and drove off at speed in a cloud of dust.

Wondering what he had just witnessed, Ben mounted the steps and let himself into the office where he received the usual warm welcome from Patsie, who was soon pouring him a hot drink from a large thermos flask almost before he had stepped inside the door. To Ben's surprise the cup was full of a delicious-smelling vegetable soup which Patsie assured him was her homemade speciality. It turned out to be really special and had a distinctive different taste, which he suspected involved the addition of alcohol, but he wasn't complaining and finished it with pleasure.

Robbie was sat at his desk watching Ben over his reading spectacles and enjoying Ben's obvious enjoyment of his welcoming drink. 'By the way, Ben, I want you to know that I owe you one for introducing me to Desmond. As you know, he came originally to sort out those old chairs for your club. He went far beyond just doing your chairs and ended up clearing the lot out with all the others stripped down and on the scrap pile, leaving me with an empty garage ready for my next bulk buy of something or other.'

He went on to explain. 'Patsie and I have been under increasing pressure in recent weeks what with getting the speedway up and running and having to constantly produce enormous amounts of scrap for our major contract with the Port Talbot steelworks. Tony and Frudo are spending less and less time in the yard as they are working hard trying to build and train a team of riders ready for the opening in November. It's not easy for them, as even though there is a bit of raw talent about, they are generally nowhere near the level of professional riders. Unfortunately, we can't match the wages of the existing clubs and Frudo is having to seek high and low amongst his contacts trying to recruit riders who are coming to the end of their careers but who could give us a season or two and could help bring the youngsters along.

'I am having to spend a lot more time in the yard on the heavy machines producing the scrap we urgently need. Not that I mind. I quite enjoy it as it is quite nice to do a heavy day's work but it does mean that Patsie is left doing all the office work by herself. Just to add to the problems we discovered that materials and tools were going missing from the speedway works and on a couple of occasions I asked your friend Desmond to supervise the delivery of some materials to the site, which he handled very well, and I began to find more and more ways in which he could help us.

'Finally, it all fell into place and I have now employed him as site manager with his own office at the speedway track. Part of the deal is that he will take over the care and control of our guard dog, Fang, and together they make a formidable team. He keeps me fully informed each day, handles all the deliveries and queries and generally makes my life a lot easier. So as I said, you did me a favour when you introduced Desmond to me.'

Ben was pleased that there had been such a good outcome for all concerned and simply said, 'It was all the result of your kindness offering us the chairs in the first place, so you owe me nothing. You got your just deserves and Desmond has started a new chapter in his life so it is very satisfactory all round.'

As Ben drove home that evening he mused over how sometimes things work out well all by themselves, but he would never have guessed that Desmond would end up with a new full-time job which suited him so well.

Friday morning saw Ben working in the office doing the post and his dictation with Mrs Freeman. As always, she took an interest in how their regular clients were doing and she showed real pleasure that Desmond Davies was once again functioning satisfactorily. Ben realised that she lived with the fear of losing her husband whilst he was still a relatively young man, but from the little she said recently about his condition it seemed that he was in a lengthy period of remission.

Ben had arranged to have a supervision session with Susie at eleven o'clock and used the time before her arrival to read through her most recent stack of reports. Overall, he was impressed with her insight, energy and willingness to accept guidance and after a little thought decided that the time was right to begin to explore with her the possibility of her taking professional training. He was aware of the recently established training courses called 'CQSW' that were particularly designed to give usually older unqualified social workers an opportunity to gain a professional qualification. Many local authorities, Exworth included, had a scheme where they continued to pay the worker's salary whilst they were training in return for an agreement that the worker return to work for the sponsoring authority for at least two years.

The nearest courses were in Exeter, Bristol and Cardiff, all of which would mean staying away from home during the week, so it was a big commitment for a married woman like Susie. Ben was also aware that there were several other unqualified social workers employed by the county who possibly would want to take advantage of the secondment scheme. A place on a course was not automatic and would depend on the applicant having a successful interview by the course staff.

In his own mind Ben felt that in a year or two Susie would be a strong applicant but she really needed to register her interest as soon as possible in order to be in the running. Susie, as usual, arrived bright and chirpy for her supervision session and Ben raised a few routine issues arising from her reports. The session went well and after about thirty minutes he raised the issue of Susie possibly going on for professional training. Her reaction was pure Susie, a mixture of surprise, pleasure that Ben had confidence in her and anxiety that she wasn't academic enough to cope with the theoretical work which would be required. Ben explained that the CQSW courses were specifically designed for experienced, more mature workers who didn't have the academic background for university training. He also told her about the secondment scheme and what would be required of her if she received such sponsorship.

'Thanks, Ben, for your suggestion, I am really chuffed that you think I could do the course and become a fully qualified social worker. To be honest with you I really enjoy what I am doing and I have never really given any serious thought beyond my social work assistant role. You have given me food for thought and I need to think it over and talk to my husband, John, as it has implications for him as well. I'll think about it and come back to you but thanks for your interest and encouragement.'

It was a very thoughtful and somewhat less chirpy Susie who left his office and Ben decided to say no more and await Susie's eventual reaction.

A quick lunch at Joe's followed and he arrived at the prof's clinic in good time having claimed his special parking place. When he got into the reception area he borrowed the receptionist client list for the afternoon in the expectation of seeing Dr Forester's mysterious referral somewhere on it. But there were no double-barrelled names and the only late addition was a lady in her thirties who Ben suspected would be one of the prof's difficult abortion candidates. As ever, Ben felt sorry for the lady and for the prof, who had to make a difficult decision; it was not something he would ever wish to have to do.

The clinic proceeded at the normal rate and halfway through Ben took the opportunity of asking Raj about Daniel Collin's progress. It seemed things were going along as anticipated, with Daniel cooperating up to a point by taking his medication under supervision. He was still virtually mute and remained rather aloof from the other patients and the staff. There was an exception, however, and conveniently it was Ben's old friend Dave. Raj thought this might be because Dave was black and would never therefore be suspected by Daniel of being a member of the dreaded Gestapo, who Raj believed to be the basis of Daniel's paranoia.

Ben later queried the prof about the whereabouts of Dr Forester's mysterious referral and was told that the prof and his old friend Dr Forester had already got their heads together and hatched a 'treatment plan', which would be something for them all to look forward to at next week's clinic. None the wiser, Ben finished his interviews and headed for home, leaving the prof with his last client for the day.

Chapter 59

All Sorts Happening

The weekend was the beginning of a minor heatwave and the boys were content to spend their time playing with their friends in the street. The current craze was marbles and both Jack and Nick had a good collection, which they kept in cloth bags made for them by Sandy at her night school class. Ben had added to their collection with some ball bearings that he had acquired from Tony at the scrap yard. They rapidly became the marble of choice amongst the boy's friends; as the fact they were heavy seemed to make them more accurate. The boy's cloth bags became ever more full, so much so that they even returned some to their opponents in order to extend the number of games they could play. With the boys happily occupied Ben turned to Sandy to ask what they should do together but was quite hastily put off by her claiming that she was busy, although there was no sign of action. The phone went soon after and Sandy beat Ben to it and pushed him into the kitchen so she could take the call in private.

Inevitably Ben's curiosity was aroused but when he later enquired he was fobbed off with 'nothing important'. It didn't help matters that there were a couple more mysterious phone calls on the Saturday, both with no explanation offered. Finally, as Sandy was preparing the evening meal the phone rang yet again and Ben was quick off the mark. A somewhat familiar female voice asked to speak to Sandy but rang off when he asked who was calling and the mystery deepened. But at least it was a female voice, which removed any suspicions of 'funny business' he had begun to have.

The following morning was a bit of a repeat with two additional telephone calls fielded by Sandy, again without any explanation to Ben, who suspected that she was enjoying his frustration. The family went to have tea with Ben's parents in the afternoon and Ben and the boys made a trip to Roger's allotment whilst Sandy got her head together with

Ben's mum, who seemed to be anticipating a discussion. They returned home with a healthy load of vegetables and fresh eggs and a mysterious bundle in brown paper tied up with string which Sandy kept hold of. The evening was pleasant enough with an evening of television, which included their favourite, 'Sunday Night at the London Palladium'. Ben was feeling rather left out about what was going on but had given up trying to get answers and had decided to wait and see what happened. They went to bed quite early with Sandy feigning sleep the moment her head hit the pillow whilst Ben just couldn't get comfortable. The night involved him making several rather unproductive trips to the loo.

The boy's summer break from school was now over and Ben was once again charged with running the boys to school on his way to work. Sandy had been up at six and away to Ma's so there was no opportunity for him to try and find out more about the mysterious telephone calls. As he drove up the hill to Highfield he tried to recall the voice on the phone which had seemed so familiar. The answer was there in the back of his mind but try as he might he couldn't call it to mind. Then as he was passing the gateway to the Scadding's yard the solution to the mystery jumped into his mind, The mystery caller had been Patsie, which made complete sense as it clearly meant that she and Sandy were up to something. He still had no idea what was going on but was satisfied that anything those two were up to would be something nice and he was content to wait and see what developed. He relaxed back in the driving seat a little, eased his foot off the accelerator just a fraction and concentrated on enjoying the pop music on the radio and the warm sunshine through his windscreen.

It was a contented Ben who took his place in his office and Monday turned out to be a very straightforward day with nothing of particular note happening. When the family got together for tea they all seemed to have had a pleasant and uneventful day too and the principal subject of conversation was their individual reaction to Sandy's choice of menu: kippers. This was a rare choice in the Newman household and was down to a new door-to-door wet fish service that a neighbour had recommended to Sandy. Three out of four of them declared the kippers a hit but Nick was put off by the bones that needed to be picked clean and rejected his out of hand and settled for Marmite on toast. The rejected fish was shared between Jack and Ben, who both ended up making a kipper sandwich by putting the fleshy fish between two rounds of bread and butter. Fortunately, the pudding of tinned peach slices and the cream from the top of the milk was acceptable to them all and the boys went off to see what they could find on the television, leaving Ben and Sandy to clear up and to have a quiet cup of tea. Sandy passed the post over for Ben to deal with in the knowledge that it was junk mail and a couple of bills. As he flipped through the small stack he pulled out a single colourful sheet advertising the forthcoming Battle of Britain event at the Landings. Sandy had already seen a copy, as one had been delivered to Ma's shop earlier in the day by a couple of Girl Guides who told her that they were being delivered to every house in Exworth by the combined efforts of the local Guides, Scouts and the Boys Brigade.

Sandy said that the girls had been very enthusiastic, not least because they would be taking part in a grand parade but they were also going to be allowed to boost their funds by running a soft drinks and cake stall on the day. The circular stressed that it was free entry to the event, open to everybody, with all sorts of attractions commemorating the time in early 1940 when the people of our country had had to stand up and be counted. It finished up by asking as many people as possible to come dressed in an outfit appropriate to the war time. With a laugh Ben registered his concern about what to wear, 'As I was only about one at the time, where will I get a baby grow to fit me now?'

Sandy smiled at his attempt at humour and reassured him that he should do the same as always and leave the planning to her. The mystery of the secret phone calls became clear and he wisely said no more and opened the bills to check how long and loud he needed to moan about them.

Judging by the cars in the car park it appeared that both Susie and Phil were in the office ahead of Ben when he arrived the following day after dropping the boys off at school. But as he walked the length of the corridor he found no one in any of the rooms. Even Mrs Freeman and Alice were conspicuous by their absence. He got as far as the kitchen and filled the kettle to make the cup of tea normally provided by Alice and then had to hurry back to the general office to answer the ringing of a persistent telephone call. Fortunately, it wasn't some irate councillor or a client in difficulty but it was Mr Hamilton, the local headmaster, who had rung to say he now had a translation of Hanca's 'important letter' and he added that it made very interesting reading. He would say no more as he had to rush off to take school assembly but invited Ben and Susie to come into the school at lunch time the following day to meet Harry, the teacher whose wife had helped by doing the translation. Mr Hamilton finished up by saying, 'I will just mention that Harry and his wife both enjoy a good bottle of red wine, hint hint!' and he was laughing as he put the phone down. Ben was very grateful for the help given so readily by Mark Hamilton and his staff and that had the effect of reducing his anger at finding the office open and unmanned.

He perched himself down at Mrs Freeman's desk and occupied himself by opening the post and entering it up in the post book. Normally, Mrs Freeman would have this all done ready for Ben's attention and it suddenly dawned on him that there was no sign of her coat on the coat hook on the back of the door where she usually hung it. Once again his thoughts were interrupted by the phone ringing and the voice on the other end was in fact a rather anxious sounding Mrs Freeman. She explained that her husband Steve had had a fall in the bedroom when making his rather shaky way back from the toilet and it had taken her almost thirty minutes to get him back in bed. She was most apologetic but went on to explain she was awaiting a visit from her GP to have him checked over and would get into the office as soon as possible. Ben reassured her that everything was under control and that she should take however long she needed.

It became much clearer how the office had been left so vulnerable and whilst it was understandable, it did throw up an area of concern about the volume of staff who might be drawn into next door once the club was up and running. This was something he obviously had to sort out with Phil and Susie as a matter of urgency.

Ben remained in the general office until Phil returned a few minutes later and he called her in as she passed the door. She was more excited than he had ever seen her and was full of their plans for the following Thursday. Ben let her have her say, not wanting to dampen her enthusiasm in any way, and heard that everything was in its place and Susie was at that moment planning the activities for the first meeting. It was apparent to Ben that Susie was going to have a big input into the week-by-week running of the club and Phil seemed very happy to let her take a lead. This included her taking responsibility for providing the means for lunch by mainly providing things such as sausages, burgers or chops at cost price from her husband's shop. She would also supervise the cooking by different club members each week as part of their development. Phil suggested to Ben that club members should be asked to pay subs of a shilling each week to assist with club funds remaining in the black and after consideration he agreed that should be about right.

He briefly interrupted Phil's flow to tell her to ensure that all expenditure had to be covered by receipts, including the charge for the meat from Susie's husband, John, the receipts and income from subs to be passed each week to the treasurer via Mrs Freeman. Phil readily agreed with him and looked around to confirm this with Mrs Freeman and noticed her absence for the first time. She looked puzzled and Ben explained about Steve's fall and Mrs Freeman having to wait at home for the visit from their family doctor. He continued, 'I was very concerned to find the office wide open and completely unmanned when I arrived this morning, which meant anyone could have come in and helped themselves from our records or anything. It could have resulted in all sorts of consequences. We were lucky this time but we must ensure it never happens again. It does, however, throw up a potential area of concern about the amount of professional time we are committing to the new club. After all, the membership is largely made up of long-term clients who are presenting no complex problems and I am not sure that we can commit two thirds of our social work staff for most of Thursday each week. I think we need to get our heads together and look at rationing our input and possibly recruiting volunteers to help.'

Phil's mood deflated instantaneously as she interpreted Ben's comments as criticism of her but to her credit she gave it some thought before she responded.

'I quite understand what you are saying and I agree that Susie and I will have to box and cox once we have got things up and running. But I think we had both better be fully involved for the first couple of weeks so we can iron out any teething problems. On the question of involving volunteers I agree that the right sort could be a real asset but to be honest I can't think of anyone offhand but Susie might have some ideas and

I will talk to her about it.' Ben saw that sort of reasoned reply was a very positive response and demonstrated that Phil was much more of a team player these days. Ben agreed with her suggestions and the time for recriminations regarding the office being left unmanned slipped away.

By the time Mrs Freeman arrived an hour or so later Ben had cleared his in-tray and prepared his notes ready to dictate his reports up to date in due course. Mrs Freeman was quite flustered and grunted a relieved sigh when she sat down at her desk. Having first found out from her that Steve was none the worse for his fall Ben went along to the kitchen and made her a strong sweet cup of tea. She made a bit of a grimace when she first sipped it as she didn't normally take sugar but she understood the sentiment and continued to take little occasional sips. She was pleased to be rescued by the telephone ringing and Ben left her to it when she gesticulated that the call was for her.

He returned to his office and gave some thought to what he should do to use up what was left of the day and it didn't take too long for him to decide to take a quick early lunch and to then take over from Mrs Freeman so she could go back home to sort out her husband. Mrs Freeman's smile of gratitude showed how much she appreciated Ben's proposal. He went straight off to Joe's and noticed in passing that her tea mug was still almost full. Oh well, the thought was there. En route to Joe's he briefly popped into the club room and told Susie he would like to see her after lunch. She immediately looked worried, obviously feeling she must have done something wrong and Ben hastily reassured her that there was nothing to worry about.

He really enjoyed his lunch of a full breakfast, which included fried bread. That was something Sandy had strictly banned from the Newman household, which therefore added to Ben's satisfaction at having a naughty and rather idle day. Ruth was busy dealing with a queue of noisy customers when he arrived and looked every bit as if she had been doing the job for years. Once again there was a lot of back chat being directed at her but Ben was pleased to note that its content was pretty restrained. He strongly suspected that the presence of Mavis alongside her was a major factor in this as no one would want to face Joe's wrath if he heard anything untoward being said near her. Mavis welcomed Ben with a massive smile and loudly declared that she was looking forward to their date on Thursday. Naturally that attracted some slightly ribald reactions from the queue. Ben and Joe chose to ignore them.

Susie appeared at his office door before he had even had an opportunity to sit down. She still had a worried look and Ben hastened to reassure her that there was nothing wrong and explained that he wanted to arrange for her to do some joint visits with him the following day.

'As you know we have a rule that if we are going to deal with an empty property when the owners are away, which usually means that they are in hospital, then we must always go in with a second person. Well tomorrow I have to go in to the Collins brothers' prefab to pick up some clothes for them both and I need you to come along. As I am sure you have heard, the place was left in a real mess, so I also want to check how it is coming along.'

Susie's anxiety disappeared and she said that she had heard something about it, but this would be the first time she had any involvement where there had been a compulsory admission. Ben recovered Daniel's file from his cabinet and passed it over for her to read up. She got up as if to leave but Ben interjected, 'Oh, by the way we are also going to see Mr Hamilton tomorrow lunchtime as he has had the letter translated and he said it is very interesting so we will have to wait and see as I know no more.'

A much 'happier bunny' went off with a positive hop of excitement in her exit.

Ben and Susie arrived at the office at much the same time the following morning and both Alice and Mrs Freemen were already in situ. Phil's car was also in the car park and Ben guessed she was in the club room just making final preparations for the club's low-key opening the following day. Ben arranged with Susie that they would start off at 9.30 am and she hurried off to link up with Phil whilst he sorted out the post and let Mrs Freeman know the plans for the day. She quickly reassured Ben that Steve had fully recovered from his fall and that he was looking forward to becoming involved remotely with the running of the club.

The two of them set off on time and arrived at Jessie's just a few minutes later. Jessie was busy as usual but handed over the keys to the prefab with the cryptic comment that everything was in apple pie order and ready for inspection.

They drove the short way to Spitfire Close as there was no longer any need for secrecy and they had to pick up the clothes for the brothers. As Ben drove around the corner the impact of Albert's and Sam's efforts was immediate. The brother's prefab positively shone. Sometime later Ben learnt from the men that it had taken three coats of paint to fully obliterate Daniel's handy work, but when Ben praised them for their work he was pleased to see that they were justly proud of the job they had done. The improvements achieved in just a few days were matched by what he found as he let Susie into the prefab. The only sound was the steady tick of the grandfather clock in the hall. The previous buzzing of flies was no longer present and the overpowering stagnant stink of decaying food was replaced by the combined smells of disinfectant and pine furniture polish. They wandered from room to room and Ben left Susie with the task of preparing a couple of small suitcases of clean clothes for the two brothers.

It was simply amazing what Jessie and her ladies had achieved. All the dirty clothes and bedding had been laundered, pressed and put away. The beds had been made up with clean bedding in readiness for the brothers' eventual return. Ben moved on to the kitchen to discover that every surface and cupboard had been thoroughly cleaned and the cooker almost looked as if it had never been used. He wandered over to the window that appeared to have been cleaned inside and out and glanced up the garden and couldn't help saying 'bloody hell.'

What had previously been like a hayfield was now a neatly trimmed lawn and he was still admiring it when Susie reappeared, clutching two small bags of clothes, each neatly labelled with the name of a brother. She was keen to see where Daniel had hidden and Ben led her back into the main bedroom and opened the airing cupboard door. The hatch to the roof space was still open and Susie reacted instantly. Before Ben realised what was happening, she pulled a chair over to the cupboard, kicked off her shoes and hitched her skirt up above her knees. 'Hang on to the chair, Ben, I really must see this.'

In no time at all she had climbed on the chair, which wobbled alarmingly before Ben grabbed it. With commendable agility she clambered on top of the boiler, which presented Ben with a prolonged view of stocking tops, suspender belt and a quite lovely pert bottom clothed in sensible

Airtex knickers. She disappeared from view leaving a surprised Ben, who found the whole sequence both charming and memorable but made no comment.

'It's a very small space with no room to move around. Poor old Daniel must have felt very claustrophobic but there is something up here which I think you will want to see. I will try and pass it down to you.'

There followed the sound of something being dragged along accompanied by a few grunts from Susie before a wooden box appeared at the opening. By standing on the chair Ben was able to take the box from her and his first impression was that it was an old portable wind-up gramophone. He clambered down from his unsteady perch and placed the box on the bed.

When he opened it he immediately realised that the contents were in no way designed for entertainment; they were deadly serious. The box contained a vintage two-way Morse code transmitter. This confirmed the local community's generally held belief of how Daniel had been employed during the war and fully explained the look of abject terror on the face of Daniel when they had discovered him. When Ben looked closer at the contents of the box he noticed a drawer set in the base of the box. He couldn't resist exploring further and was shattered to discover that it contained a wartime pistol wrapped in a rather oily piece of rag. With shaking hands Ben broke the gun open and discovered it contained one round of what appeared to be live ammunition. The obvious conclusion was that the gun was intended to be used by the operator on themselves if he or she had been about to be discovered by the enemy. Ben felt a shiver of fear go down his spine and for a moment he had difficulty in catching his breath. It didn't bear thinking about how Daniel's admission might have gone so horribly wrong with the possibility of their intervention resulting in his death or even the death of one of the three of them who were just trying to do their job.

Instinctively Ben pocketed the live round, rewrapped the gun and replaced it in the box. He then passed the closed box back to Susie and asked her to put it back where she found it. He made no mention of what it had contained when she scrambled back down and she didn't ask. She quickly adjusted her skirt, picked up her shoes and headed to the toilet to clean herself up and to straighten her hair style, which had become rather lopsided during her activities. The bullet later found its way to the security of Ben's memory box, not needed.

They secured the house and returned to the car and drove around the Landings' central lengthy strip of grass before pulling up briefly opposite Jessie's shop. When Ben called in to congratulate Jessie and her ladies on their fantastic efforts, the place was buzzing with activity. He surprised himself by calling for quiet and was amazed that his request was reacted to and the place almost instantly went silent. He made a quick off the cuff speech, praising the way the community had stepped in to help resolve one of their neighbour's problems. He ended by saying, 'You should be very proud of yourselves, it would be a much better world if every community cared so much for each other.'

With a round of applause ringing in his ears Ben made a rapid retreat and hoped it wasn't too obvious that he was quite emotional.

The trip to Bevington was all the more enjoyable having Susie and her bubbly personality for company. When they entered into the main hall, there was the familiar rowdy beach ball and bashing game in full flow, but the individual participants each came to a full stop as they caught sight of Susie's presence. Just like bees around a honeypot she was swiftly surrounded by a traffic jam of wheelchair-bound young men all eager for a little female attention. It clearly didn't seem to worry them that Susie was probably the same age as their mothers; she was there in person and their imaginations did the rest. Susie took it all in good heart and gave them all a cheeky wave as Ben rescued her and got them safely into the lift to the second floor. Her impact continued when they went into Joseph's ward and the stupor that was present when they entered quickly evaporated as all four residents sat up and took notice.

Ben was delighted to see that Joseph was sat at his bedside fully liberated from the harness that had previously restrained him. He even attempted to stand up to politely welcome his guests, but the grimace of pain that flicked across his face showed them all that he still had some way to go in his recovery. Ben pulled up a chair and introduced Susie whilst she put the case of Joseph's clothes down on the bed and started to unpack it and put the things away in his locker under Joseph's direction. Once it was all tidied away she moved around the room, taking time to talk to each of the other patients in turn. When Ben related the details of the visit to Sandy that evening he suggested that a dose of Susie each day would have a better effect on the patient's wellbeing than much of their regular treatments.

Ben was happy to tell Joseph about the transformation to the prefab but made no mention of the discovery that they had made in the loft. Joseph was anxious to know about Daniel and how he was coping with being in St Margaret's and Ben was able to reassure him that he had been cooperating and was once again taking his regular medication with there being signs of it beginning to have a positive effect. Joseph seemed very pleased that Daniel was back on his medication and seemed confident that he would be back home with his brother in the not-too-distant future. He was keen to hear all about the preparations for the Battle of Britain celebrations, but admitted that it was probably a good thing that Daniel wouldn't be around for them.

'I know he had a tough time during the war and he was only a young man when he was whisked away for some sort of specialist war work. He has never talked about his experiences but for years after he came home he suffered with terrible nightmares and woke up screaming night after night. Even as a small boy he found it difficult to mix with people outside our immediate family and the loss of Mum and Dad and our other brother left him with only me for company. Still, we rub along quite well and I am hoping that if I get some compensation for my accident we will be able to plan some trips out together.'

Before Ben left the ward he passed over a carrier bag full of mail that he had picked up from the prefab with the comment, 'Here is just a little homework for you to deal with.'

When he opened the top drawer of Joseph's locker to store it away he noticed a well-thumbed copy of a brochure advertising Mini cars. A bright red one with white flashings had been circled and that was obviously Joseph's plan for any compensation he might get. Ben sincerely hoped he would have his wish, as he had had more than his share of bad luck in his life so far. Joseph produced a letter from his dressing gown pocket and asked Ben to give it to Daniel when he visited him later in the day. When Susie and Ben stepped out of the lift back on the ground floor they were immediately surrounded by a cavalcade of wheelchairs, which provided them with a good-natured procession of mobile outriders all the way back to the old Cortina. Susie went along with the fun and gave a series of regal waves as Ben pulled away.

'That was quite something, wasn't it, Ben? But I could weep for those young men who have been cut down with all their lives before them. I can't help thinking of my two boys away at university and thank god that we have been so lucky.'

Of course Ben's two boys were much younger but he shared Susie's sentiments and they both remained silent for most of their return to Highfield, lost in their own thoughts. Ben decided to take a shortcut in an attempt to avoid the several lots of road works they had encountered on their way down to Bevington. Unfortunately, as he drove around a blind turning he was confronted by a large herd of cows ambling back to their grazing field having, he presumed, just been milked at the nearby farm. There was nothing he could do about it so he switched the engine off and tried to remain calm. After several glances at his watch he broke the silence.

'I'm afraid that we had better change our plans and put off our visit to St Margaret's until this afternoon. We need to get to see Mr Hamilton to find out about Hanca's letter and he has only got about half an hour during which he can see us.'

The last of the cows eventually went through the open gate and Ben returned the cowman's friendly wave with as much good grace as he could muster. He accelerated away with the old car spluttering in protest.

As they finally pulled up at the school gates they discovered that they were hard on the heels of a tall, rather elegant lady who was very steadily getting out of a rather swish classic bright-blue convertible beetle car. When she turned around it was immediately apparent why she was moving with so much care as she was very obviously in a fairly advanced stage of pregnancy. As the three of them walked across the playground together Susie and the other lady quite naturally got into a discussion on the joys and trials of having babies. Ben sped up and moved ahead in preference to getting involved in the conversation and they were joined at the school entrance by the familiar figure of the headmaster Mark Hamilton. He was accompanied by a tall rather geeky skinny man who was clean shaven but sported a small ponytail secured by a rubber band. He looked every inch a teacher but his reaction came as a surprise.

He broke into a grin and kissed the woman rather passionately on the lips. Mr Hamilton quickly explained that they were a married couple and added in a false whisper that they hadn't been married very long. That caused smiles all round and everyone introduced themselves in a relaxed way.

Eva Ericson spoke really good English but her heavy Teutonic accent left one in no doubt about her German origins. She explained that she was also a teacher but was currently bored at home on maternity leave. 'It was a bit of a treat to feel useful translating your letter and really turned out to be one of the most exciting things I have done in ages.'

She produced a handwritten copy of her translation which Ben and Susie eagerly read through together. The crux of the letter explained that the company which had written to Hanca was an international company which specialised in locating the heirs of unclaimed inheritances worldwide. The letter went on to explain that they did everything necessary to locate and link the heirs with the unclaimed estate for a set fee of 30% of the monetary value of every satisfactory conclusion. If the claim failed then it was guaranteed that there would be no fee. All the company needed to act for Hanca was proof of her identity. The letter finished by giving the address and telephone number of their office in London and the assurance that staff there would be prepared to proceed with the application if Hanca got in touch.

After a few seconds silence, whilst they took it all in, everyone seemed to start talking at once. They went round and round in circles but were all agreed that it was a very exciting prospect. Initially they thought that 30% seemed like a big chunk of any claim but after thought realised that without the company's efforts there was no way Hanca would have ever been linked with her inheritance. Mr Hamilton also pointed out that the company must have concluded that there was sufficient money involved to make their efforts viable. 'It looks to me as if Hanca is in for a nice little windfall but I guess it will all depend on her being able to prove her identity.'

Some of the euphoria evaporated a little and Susie declared her intention to tell Hanca all about it as soon as possible if not sooner. Ben simply said that they would talk over the next step later in the day and went on to thank Eva and her husband Harry for all their help and promised to let them know how it turned out. Right on time Susie then produced two bottles of wine from her sizeable handbag and passed them to Eva with the comment, 'For you to wet the baby's head.'

Mr Hamilton nodded his approval and the group broke up in high spirits.

When they got back to the office Ben showed Mrs Freeman the letter and asked her to make a couple of copies of the translation and then headed off to Joe's for a snack before getting on with the rest of his day. Suitably refreshed he returned back to the office and recovered the translation and the copies from Mrs Freeman and made his way to his desk where he swiftly placed one of the copies in his memory box and the other on Hanca's file. He locked the box back in the bottom drawer of his desk and considered how rare it was to add two things to the box in as many days. In a way there was a tenuous link between the two things; one being a bullet from the Second World War and the other being a letter from the country which had previously been the enemy.

Susie arrived at his office soon after, complete with a mug of tea in the absence of Alice, who Susie told him was busy next door giving the whole place yet another total clean. Susie was obviously keen to get round to Hanca's to tell her about her good fortune and Ben felt the need to caution her to tread lightly as it was uncertain how Hanca might react. However, on balance he felt it was appropriate to let Susie make the visit and decided that he would make the trip to see Daniel at St Margaret's by himself and said that they should meet up back at the office later in the afternoon to update each other. Susie collected the original letter and Eva's translation to show to Hanca and went off in a lightly disguised excited state and Ben picked up the phone to ring Dave at St Margaret's to arrange to meet him there later in the afternoon.

As arranged they got together over a cup of tea in the staff canteen at the hospital and as ever they fell into a comfortable chat about how they were and primarily about their families. The really big news was all about Dave, Camila and the girls, Elsa and Gloria. Ben was delighted to learn that they were all going to be living in England, hopefully by Christmas if Dave could find a house within his price range to buy in Exworth. Ben gave Dave a spontaneous hug which he rather regretted as it was a bit like going into a clinch with a healthy gorilla and they both ended up laughing. Ben declared that he was going to enjoy telling his family the good news that evening. The news of Daniel's progress was also good but Dave said that there was still some way to go.

'He is still very suspicious and generally uncommunicative with most people, but does seem to be more trusting with me and also with Doc Rani. Raj thinks that his original breakdown was probably as a result of his war experience but Daniel is still very unforthcoming on the subject. We suspect that his acceptance of us is simply down to the colour of our skins. As you know, there would never have been any possibility of there being any Black men in Hitler's Gestapo.'

Ben swore Dave to secrecy before sharing the information about the transmitter they had found in the loft with him as it clearly helped to support Dr Rani's theory about the origins of Daniel's paranoia. Dave fully understood the reason to protect Daniel's secret and Ben resisted the urge to say anything about the gun or the round he had removed from it. It was decided that Ben would not attempt any approach to Daniel and he passed the case of clothes and Joseph's letter over to Dave for him to deliver. The two friends parted soon after with the agreement that they should meet for a pint before too long. Ben clicked the radio on in the car and drove the short journey back to the office with musical accompaniment and pleasant thoughts at being able to surprise Sandy about Dave's family coming to live nearby.

Chapter 60

The First Day of the Club

En route to the office, Ben called into Jessie's to let her know about the Collin brothers' progress and to drop the prefab keys in to her. Joseph had agreed that it would be sensible to leave the keys with Jessie in case anyone needed to gain access to read metres or for any other day-to-day reason. Jessie, as ever, was only too happy to be helpful by keeping an eye on the premises for the brothers and agreed to pick up any post and to let Ben know if it appeared to be anything important. Content that all the ends were tied up nicely he drove back to the office and was barely through the front door before Susie was in his face. She immediately started to recount her meeting with Hanca and Ben registered his surrender by lifting his hands up in submission. Susie got the message and followed him down to his office.

She again told Ben about Hanca's reaction to the letter, which was primarily one of considerable surprise as she had always believed that all her family had been killed in the Holocaust. She didn't show any great interest in the fact that she could be getting a large amount of money but was anxious to find out more about any relatives that there might be still alive in Poland.

Susie went on, 'The good news is that she has got good documentation to prove her identity. When I asked her about it she went to a drawer and took out a piece of oilcloth that had been stitched up to form a body belt. When she unwrapped it, she produced her original Polish birth certificate, which was rather tatty but still intact. She also had her handwritten marriage certificate written in French by the priest who had married her and her husband Terry back in 1945. Believe it or not, she even had several of her old school reports and a couple of special birthday cards which her mum had sent to her all those years ago. The whole thing was obviously very precious to her as it was all she had of her early history and I think we both shed a tear or two as she showed me through it all. Just imagine she must have had this simple homemade oilcloth body belt strapped around her throughout her lengthy trek to her new life with Terry in England.'

Susie had left it that she would get in touch with the London office of Heir Hunters and find out how Hanca should proceed to register her right to the inheritance. When Susie finally came to a stop, Ben allowed a pause before carefully stressing that this could prove to be the start of a long, drawn out and possibly complicated process. Taking into consideration Susie's commitment to the start of the Thursday Club, the following day, he said that he thought it best to leave taking any action until after the weekend. Rather reluctantly Susie admitted the sense in the suggestion and they agreed that she should make the phone call on Monday with Ben listening in on an extension.

The early part of the evening was taken up with the boys watching yet another episode of 'Dr Who' versus his deadly enemy the Daleks. When 'Dr Who' had first been broadcast the boys had both been genuinely frightened and spent much of the show out of sight behind the sofa. But once Ben had pointed out that anyone could easily get away from a Dalek by the simple act of going up stairs, as being on wheels they could not follow, the boys seemed to lose their fears. The programme was now a firm favourite with them but Ben was bored by it and had always considered the casting of the old actor William Hartnell in the role of the Doctor as a hopeless piece of miscasting. When he had thought about it in the first place he realised that Hartnell looked a lot like his old headmaster at grammar school, who in Ben's opinion had been a pompous prat who lauded it over the place but was in fact a waste of space. He could never have been seen as a hero, which clearly coloured Ben's enjoyment of the programme. Fortunately, the local freebie newspaper was always delivered on a Wednesday so he was able to catch up on the local news without any distraction by the television.

The first day of the Thursday Club proved to be dull and overcast but at least it was dry so the new members would be able to walk in without getting wet. Phil, Susie and Alice were all in the club room well before 10 am, when it was due to start and had also been joined by The Champ, who seemed well aware that something interesting was afoot. Before Ben went to pick up Dale McBain he called in to check everything was ready and was surprised that several of the members had already arrived. They were sat around the table chatting away like old friends and enjoying tea and Jaffa Cakes distributed by Alice. When he got to Dale's house Carol and Dale were waiting at the gate and there was no sign of Norman Ainsley. Unfortunately, Carol was sporting a black eye which was only partially disguised by makeup, but she made no mention of it and neither did Ben as he decided that his priority was to get Dale along to the club. By the time they got there the group were all busily decorating drinking mugs which they had each chosen from the miscellaneous boxful that Joe had generously donated.

Ben was interested to notice that all the boys were sat at one end of the table and all the girls at the other, but he was sure that Phil or Susie would soon get them mixing. He was also pleased to see that Stanley Wiltshire, Phil's client who was profoundly deaf, took the initiative and made a place for Dale at the table. Once Dale was settled Ben went back to his office and rang his colleague in the children's department to let her know about Carol's black eye. She was grateful for the information and said that she would visit the home later in the day and would also check that the baby was fit and well. She was not altogether surprised by the development as she felt that Carol and Norman's relationship was wearing thin, largely because of Norman continuing to use a variety of drugs and his attempts to get Carol back using. The good news was that Carol had so far resisted and seemed determined to remain clean to be a good mother for baby Norma.

Ben resisted the urge to check how things were going at the club and busied himself by clearing paperwork and fielding phone calls. The time slipped by until Mrs Freeman popped her head around his door to say she was off to get Steve's lunch. Suddenly Ben was on his own and he realised that he hadn't brought sandwiches and he was feeling decidedly peckish. The problem was resolved almost immediately by Alice appearing with a tray containing a knife and fork, a plate of two piping hot hotdogs and a portion of fried onions with a generous dollop of tomato sauce on the side. He noted that the accompanying mug of tea had his name neatly painted on the side, which he presumed made him an honorary member of the club. Alice put the tray down on his desk and produced a rather crumpled paper napkin from her skirt pocket, which she placed by the tray and then stood back and waited. Ben thanked her as a matter of course but she still waited. For a moment he thought she was expecting a tip but then he realised that she was waiting for him to pay for his lunch like everybody else. The agreed price of a shilling was passed over and Alice went on her way leaving Ben to eat in peace. The meal was very good and the sausages were exceptional, confirming that Susie's husband John really knew his stuff.

Once Mrs Freeman had returned Ben washed his mug and plate up to show willing before returning them to the club room. Ernest was just coming away to get on with his street cleaning and The Champ was just a step or two behind him. The dog must have worked out that there were no more sausages to be had and he was keen to get back on his beat with his master.

'That was good grub, we both enjoyed it,' was Ernest's rather cryptic comment and Ben confirmed his agreement by nodding his head. The whole group were sat around the table as he entered the main room and they were no longer conforming to sitting in segregated groups. They all seemed to be concentrating on pieces of paper covered with a series of different pictures. Susie was sitting at the head of the table turning over cards from a pack in front of her and calling out various letters of the alphabet as they appeared. He quickly realised that this was a form of bingo, but not like any sort he had ever seen before. Phil gestured for him to follow her into the kitchen where she explained that the game had been designed by Susie when she had run the Brownie pack and she had found that a little girl in the pack with Down's could keep up with the rest and handle it.

'When she calls out a letter she also calls out something beginning with that letter, which corresponds with a picture on some of the papers. Susie called out reasonably slowly at first but they all seem to be on top of it and concentrating hard on trying to get their hands on the prize, which today is a bar of chocolate. The first to get every square on their paper covered will be the winner.'

A loud guttural shout from the main room by Mavis, 'Got it,' was greeted by several groans from the others, who all thought they had been in with a chance. Ben left them to it, after telling Phil that he would come back to pick up Dale and walk him home at 4 pm.

The afternoon was mainly a waste of time for Ben, but he thought that he had better remain in the office to deal with anything that might arise. In reality the only call of any significance came when it was almost time to collect Dale. It was from his colleague in the children's department who had just checked up on Carol and Norma. She reported that Norma was fine, happy and lively with no sign of any injury when the childcare officer had insisted on seeing her undressed. The only visible problem was a small area of nappy rash, which Carol had been treating with a zinc cream prescribed by their family doctor. Carol's black eye was a different matter, however, as she had immediately admitted that it had happened during an argument about money with Norman. He had been occupying his usual position stretched out on the sofa when Carol had been talking to the social worker but he made no comment to anything that was being said.

Carol claimed that it was the only time he had ever hit her and stressed that he was now on a final warning. 'If he ever raises his hand to either me or the kids ever again I have told him he will be out on his ear. This is my home, rented in my name, and he is no more than a lodger. I don't have to put up with any sort of violence. I had enough of it from my dad when I was a kid, so he knows where he stands, any problem he will be homeless.'

Norman had remained silent. Ben told Beth Evans the social worker that he would shortly be walking Dale home from the club and he undertook to try and find what Dale thought about the situation at home. When Ben went back in to the club room the members were beginning to leave and there were lots of 'see you next weeks' going on. Things looked promising and Ben suggested that Phil and Susie should review the day with him when he returned from seeing Dale home. Dale was all smiles and had clearly enjoyed the day and seemed quite happy to talk about his home situation when Ben raised the subject as they chatted. Apart from saying that Norman was lazy and expected to be waited on, his only other comment was that he could be very miserable at times when he ran out of weed. Dale's face lit up when he talked about his little sister and he openly admitted that he was very proud of how his mother had been staying clear of drugs for so long.

'She's a different person these days and I am a lot happier myself these days. Mind you, it would be no loss if mum kicked Norman out any day soon, but he is Norma's dad so I suppose he has some rights.'

Ben thought to himself that this young man had had a lot to put up with, but it's not all bad, as Dale was welcomed by a hug from his mum when she came to the door to let him in.

By the time Ben got back to the office everyone except Alice was sat around in the kitchen discussing how they felt the day had gone. Apparently, Alice had insisted that she should get straight on with tidying the club premises and the others had left her happily singing to herself as she got busy with the cleaning. The general conclusion from Phil and Susie was that the day had gone well with everyone seeming to fit in together.

There had been something of an incident when Sidney had suddenly collapsed on the floor and had a full-blown epileptic fit. By the time Phil and Susie got to him he was already being cared for very efficiently by Stanley, who knew just what needed doing. He had loosened Sidney's collar, cushioned his head with a pillow from the sofa and had put the handle of a spoon between his teeth in his mouth to stop him biting his tongue. The fit had run its course and Sidney was soon able to sit up but was a bit confused for a while. Unfortunately, he had wet himself during the fit but was able to point to his duffle bag in which his mother had put clean trousers and pants just in case. Stanley led Sidney into the toilet and helped him get changed and by the time they reappeared the bingo was underway again as if nothing had happened. Phil could only surmise that Stanley had been used to dealing with epilepsy during his many years at Hortham hospital and his experience was now proving to be very helpful. Several things came up in the conversation which followed and they agreed that they had done enough for today but it would be useful to discuss their ideas further at another time.

Susie had taken the idea of volunteers on board and had a couple of her friends in mind who might be interested in helping. For now, they all agreed it had been a good start and Ben suggested that they should all meet up again after the weekend to bring their thoughts to the table. Mrs Freeman collected the subs, receipts and register from Phil to pass on to

Steve that evening for him to deal with in his role of treasurer. The group called it a day and the Highfield office was locked for the night.

No sooner had Ben walked through his front door than the boys came rushing over to him and he was only too aware that such an enthusiastic welcome meant they wanted something. He realised what they were after with the first word they uttered, 'conkers'. Ben knew exactly what that meant, as it had been an important part of his own childhood and he remembered it with great affection. It was the time once a year when all other crazes were abandoned in favour for the joy of collecting the shiny brown nuts of the horse chestnut trees and preparing them to do battle with other kid's favourite nuts. In Ben's day there had only be one place to seek them out and that was his local park St Austin's, which had a couple of massive horse chestnut trees. They were far too tall to climb so they were annually assaulted by hordes of small boys hurling pieces of wood up into them in an attempt to knock down the best conkers. It was an assault which came with the risk of a clip around the ear from the resident park keeper. Fortunately, in Ben's time their 'parkie' was disabled, having lost a leg during the war which had been replaced by a wooden peg leg that slowed him down considerably! Inevitably someone would spot him coming and would shout out that Long John was coming and they would all make a hasty retreat with their treasure.

After a couple of years 'Long John' got the upper hand by getting himself a brutish looking husky dog and Ben had outgrown his interest in conkers.

He knew that times had moved on and the days of each park having its own park keeper were long gone. They had been replaced by a couple of ex-coppers who patrolled all the parks in Exworth randomly. They had been equipped with Velocette 149cc motorbikes, which were commonly used by a lot of police forces. The motorbikes weren't very fast but had the unique quality of being very quiet so you simply didn't hear them coming before they were right alongside you. The rather funny-looking motorbikes were universally nicknamed as 'Noddy bikes'. Until quite recently, Ben had always assumed that they had gained this description from their toy like qualities, which wouldn't have been out of place in the books written by Enid Blyton about Noddy and Big Ears and their adventures in Toyland. He had since seen an article about the bikes in a classic motor magazine and now knew that the connection to Enid Blyton's character Noddy was only part of the story. It turned out that when the bikes had been initially issued to serving policemen they were under an instruction to salute any senior police officer they might pass. This had resulted in several minor accidents and a compromise had been agreed that instead of saluting the rider should nod their head as they passed. Hence the connection to Noddy was quickly adopted. The instruction to nod was soon rescinded but the nickname had stuck ever since.

Ben didn't want to expose Nick and Jack to any difficulty but was happy that they should enjoy participating in the tradition of playing conkers. He talked to Sandy about it and they decided that if the weather was good at the weekend they would make a day of it and go for a drive to the New Forest to see the ponies and to try and stock up on conkers.

Chapter 61

All About Ash

The evening news on Thursday forecast a couple of days of rain followed by a dry and sunny Sunday, so the conker trip was delayed until Sunday. This clashed with a planned meeting Sandy had already arranged to meet up with Patsie to sort out the costumes for the Battle of Britain event, so she opted out, leaving the conker outing as a male-only trip which was an unusual happening in the Newman household. In order to be included in the project Sandy undertook to sort out some string for the conkers and to do any baking of the conkers required to toughen them up.

The boys were surprisingly excited by the plan and co-operated with getting ready for going to school, obviously keen to boast of their conker hunt to all their schoolfriends. Once he had dropped the boys off Ben drove steadily through the torrential rain to Highfield with the majority of traffic on the opposite side of the road. The car park was already beginning to flood and Ben's leaking shoes meant he would probably have damp feet for much of the day. As usual, the only person in so far was Alice and in the privacy of his own office Ben slipped off his wet socks and put them on the radiator to dry. When Alice brought his tea in she immediately spotted the socks and she whipped them away, saying that she would sort them out. Before he had a chance to argue, she was halfway down the corridor on her way to her domain in the kitchen.

The others arrived in quick succession and the day proceeded like most others except Ben remained at his desk with his bare feet safely out of sight. He only had two things that he felt he really had to do that morning and the first was to let Beth Evans, the childcare officer, know how Dale had responded when asked about Norman Ainsley. The resulting joint decision was that they would both keep a watching brief and would be sure to let each other know of any developments or concerns. Once Ben had put the phone down he reached for a handwritten note about an elderly lady who Dr Smyth had asked him to check on. Mrs Upson had been on Dr Smyth's list since she had moved to the area a couple of years before but the first time he had met her was just a day or two ago when she attended his surgery with a chesty cough.

'I checked her over and she seemed relatively fit for her age but she was quite grubby and smelly and seemed to be very suspicious. I prescribed some antibiotics but suspect she won't take them judging by her reaction to me. I would be grateful if you could visit her to see if she is coping okay.'

Ben recovered his socks from the oven in the kitchen where Alice had chosen to dry them and they were a joy to put on his feet, which were still suffering from the cold of their earlier soaking.

The rain had slackened but there were puddles everywhere, which he attempted to avoid by resorting to a meandering route on tiptoe out to his car. The right foot remained dry but his left one quickly became soggy, which he supposed was a bit of an improvement. The short drive to Mrs Upson's maisonette in Marlborough Terrace was over in a matter of minutes and his arrival coincided with a resurgence of the deluge. Ben decided that there was no rush and parked up and remained in the car and listened to the news on the radio. The main subject under discussion was the series of serious weather incidents which seemed to be occurring around the globe. The two most recent ones had happened during the past two days. Louisiana in New Orleans had been devastated by Hurricane Betsy, the previous day with winds of 145 MPH killing seventy-six and causing $1.42 billion of damage. Whilst in the early hours of this morning on the other side of the world in Japan, Typhoon Shirley had killed sixty-seven and left thousands homeless.

Ben reached forward and switched off the radio and felt a proper wimp that he was allowing a bit of rain to stop him working when people elsewhere were coping with life-threatening weather. He turned his collar up and stepped out of the car, only to put his right foot straight in a stream of rainwater running along the gutter. With both feet now soaking wet again he headed down the path of 87a Marlborough Terrace. He knocked a couple of times and the window immediately above the door was pushed up and a grey-haired old lady popped her head out. 'What do you want?' Ben was not surprised to hear a voice from above as this was a fairly usual reaction from upstairs maisonette tenants who didn't want a trip up and down their stairs.

Ben explained that he had been asked to visit by Dr Smyth to see if he could be of any help.

'Wait a minute, I've got something for you.' Her head disappeared from the window and Ben took a step or two back in anticipation of having to catch a key to let himself in. However, that was not on offer and Mrs Upson reappeared with a chamber pot in her hands, which she attempted to empty over Ben. 'Bugger off,' was the accompanying message and the window slammed down with a crash. Had Ben not made the steps back he would have been covered from head to foot but as it was it was only his trouser legs that caught the worst of the discharge. The strong smell of ammonia left no doubt about what the pot had contained. Ben didn't hesitate to obey. He 'buggered off' as directed and headed straight home to get cleaned up ready for the prof's clinic.

The rain continued to fall with a vengeance and he risked winding down all the car windows just a fraction in an attempt to rid himself of the toxic pong. The first thing he did once he arrived home was to slip off his urine-soaked trousers and risked a quick trip out into the garden to hang them on the line. As far as he could see there were no witnesses. He then headed for the bathroom and stripped right off and had his second shower of the day using one of Sandy's perfumed shampoos to eradicate any lingering odour. The top half of his clothes were still good to go but he had to rummage in the wardrobe to replace the rest. Clean pants and socks were no problem and his suit trousers would suffice until his work trousers had been dry cleaned down at the local launderette. The main problem was with what to replace his leaky shoes as he discovered when he looked at the motley collection in the bottom of the wardrobe it was a straight choice between a pair of winkle pickers from his teenage years which hadn't seen the light of day for years, a pair of plimsolls or a pair of brown brogues. The brogues had been a present from his mum, who had spotted them in a jumble sale she was helping with at her local church. They were a good make, Clarks, and were well-made shoes, but not really to Ben's taste and in any case proved to be a couple of sizes too large. As a consequence he had never worn them but, as it was a case of Hobson's choice, they were going to get a first time airing that afternoon.

He made himself a quick sandwich and a coffee, which he consumed as he stuffed the toes of the brogues with screwed-up newspaper in an attempt to make them fit better.

When Ben had parked up at the hospital he took his time going to the clinic as he was unusually early, so he shuffled around the hospital shop looking at what was on offer. Nothing really took his fancy but on impulse he bought a bunch of carnations for Sandy and some chocolate for the boys. The reception area was beginning to fill up when he arrived and Ben risked the wrath of a rather flustered Wendy by briefly commandeering her copy of the list of clients for that afternoon. A man with a double-barrelled name was the last name on the list and Ben felt pretty sure that there was every likelihood that this would prove to be Dr Forester's anticipated patient. As usual Ben joined the prof and Raj Rani for a milky coffee whilst they decided who would be seen by whom. The prof confirmed that the last client on the list, Austin Spencer- Hamilton, was indeed the person referred by Dr Forester and went on to tell Raj and Ben that they should 'watch and learn' as he thought it very likely that he would be using a treatment plan rarely seen these days. He went on to say that he had had several telephone discussions with Dr Forester, who had been happy with the plan he was probably going to propose. 'So Ben, I want you to take a social history for me as usual and I would like you both to sit in when I see him later this afternoon.'

The prof explained no further and Ben suspected he was enjoying being mysterious.

At different times during the afternoon both Raj and the prof asked why he was limping but Ben pretended to have stubbed his toe to conceal his embarrassment about the 'potty incident'. The clinic proceeded like many others and Ben gave Mr Spencer-Hamilton no further thought until towards the end of the clinic when the volume of noise coming from the reception area suddenly increased in intensity indicating that Mr Spencer-Hamilton had arrived. When Ben called him in a few minutes later he burst into the room, like some ham actor performing the classic dame in a grotesque pantomime. As he came through the door he announced in a shrill voice, 'Well hello, I'm Austin Spencer-Hamilton.' As he mentioned each of his three names he paused for a second or two and raised a finger in the air as if writing an imaginary full stop. 'But you must call me ASH, everybody does,' and he accompanied this statement with exaggerated circular motions of his arms as if including the whole world.

The reason for the increased volume in the reception area was all too apparent as ASH clearly intended to be central stage and to make his presence felt. His handshake was spongy and did nothing to enhance his presentation and he moved the client's chair nearer to the desk and then made great play of crossing one leg over the other as he settled back in the chair. He tugged at his trousers to straighten the sharp creases stitched into each leg and made great play at fluttering his eyelashes at Ben.

As this performance was progressing Ben tried to take in the aberration before him. He was about thirty years old, five foot tall and almost the same width, giving him the appearance of a large rubber ball. He was dressed head to foot in a green tweed three-piece suit that fitted him tightly and strained to contain his rotund figure. It had clearly been made to measure and would have certainly been expensive, but it was hard to imagine anyone else who would have wanted one like it. It was topped with a pink shirt open at the neck, which was decorated with a bright yellow cravat held in place by a large diamante brooch in the shape of a spider. If the brooch had been real diamonds it would have been worth a small fortune but it looked what it was a bit of costume jewellery there for effect only. It was easy to see that all of this was part of a persona that ASH wished to present. Such avant-garde clothing might well have gone unnoticed on Carnaby Street in London but here in Exworth it was guaranteed to attract attention.

Ben's mind immediately moved on to the thought that ASH was the splitting image of Gerald Campion, the middle-aged actor who had played the role of Billy Bunter, the silly fat boy of Greyfriars School, on the television. Ben's parents had bought their first television in 1953 so that his mum could watch the queen's coronation and his dad could be one up on the neighbours and see the FA Cup final live. It was of course a black and white set with a minute screen, but at the time Ben had thought it revolutionary and had watched whenever his parents allowed. In practice his viewing had been almost exclusively children's television and the antics of the stupid, greedy Bunter had been an all too often contribution to the service. At the time there had been only the one channel, so on the basis that something was better than nothing, Ben watched numerous rather repetitive storylines. The arrival of ITV two years later offered a welcomed alternative viewing and even the novelty of advertisements seemed preferable to the frequent interludes that were a regular part of BBC viewing.

Gerald Campion and Bunter eventually drifted off the screen and Ben had assumed that he had either retired or perhaps had even died. He had therefore been very surprised to spot Campion playing a bit part in the film *Those Magnificent Men in their Flying Machines* that he had taken the boys to see just a few weeks before. He had looked much the same as when he had played the role of Bunter all those years before.

Now Ben was confronted by this guy ASH, who was the double of Campion, with the same slicked-down hair, the matching round head with little beady eyes and the pink face appearing to be as smooth as a proverbial baby's bum. The likeness was so strong that Ben wouldn't have been surprised if ASH had broken out in a series of Yarooooghs, which had been Bunter's catchphrase, but it didn't happen. As ASH crossed and re-crossed his legs attempting to straighten the creases in his trousers, Ben's attention was drawn to ASH's feet. For a start they were tiny, to the point of looking incapable of supporting his bulk. But the most startling feature was his shoes which were shiny black patent leather sandals with ankle straps sporting diamante spider buckles. The only time Ben had ever seen men wearing patent leather shoes was when he had occasionally watched 'Come Dancing' on the television. The pair that ASH was wearing bore no resemblance to the elegant footwear of the ballroom dancers and Ben immediately suspected that they had actually been designed to be worn by a woman. He suddenly felt a whole lot better about the oversized brogues which he had safely hidden under the desk.

Ben realised that he had been staring at this apparition and he blinked and pulled himself together. He managed a smile as he said, 'Hello, I am Ben Newman, the social worker attached to the professor's team. My role is to take a social history from you to relay to the professor before you go in to see him.'

The usual way the interviews proceeded from this point was that Ben would ask a series of questions and would record the patient's answers to build up a comprehensive history. But that wasn't going to happen this time, as clearly nothing went normally with this guy, as he dived into a lengthy detailed tale with a practised ease borne from regular telling. His favourite subject was very obviously himself and Ben found it difficult to keep up with the amount of information being offered and he finally resorted to recording single words here and there as an aid memoir. ASH started by explaining that his childhood home had been a large Victorian house situated in the depths of Surrey called Winford Grange. It had been in their family for generations but now that servants were a thing of the past it was just about maintained by a couple of local villagers who came in to do the cleaning and the garden. It was a rambling old building with a lot of rooms that were mainly never used.

'You will probably remember Pa, who was a cabinet minister in the Tory government when Alec Douglas-Home was prime minister a year or two ago.'

Ben didn't respond but recalled that the Tories had lost control to Labour in the subsequent election and that Douglas-Home's time in office had largely been a non-event.

ASH continued, 'Of course, Pa was made a Lord in the New Year's Honours for his service to the country and he now spends most days in the House of Lords. He tends to spend most of his nights living in his bachelor flat in London so that he is near to the Houses of Parliament where he works. Ma has a suite of rooms on the ground floor of Winford Grange where she eats, sleeps and holds her bridge sessions. She is an international bridge player of some renown and often plays with famous players such as the Egyptian actor Omar Sharif. From an early age I was taught that her space was only to be entered by invitation and those were few and far between. Meanwhile, I was brought up on the first floor by a series of nannies who rarely lasted long, as I adopted all sorts of acting up in the hope of getting my parents attention. My two brothers are years older than me and they have always done their own things, which didn't involve little brother. I can remember being dreadfully lonely and spending many nights crying to myself in bed. Eventually I was ready to start school and Pa arranged for me to attend a local private school, which lasted no time at all. After being rejected by a further three such schools, I had attracted the label "disturbed" and Pa arranged for me to have home tutoring. Mr Power, my so-called tutor, was particularly keen on discipline to the extent that today it would have gained him recognition as a paedophile and would have certainly ended his career as a teacher and possibly even resulted in his imprisonment. Pa returned to the house for a few days over one Easter and took me swimming in a nearby pool. He noticed bruising on my back and got the information out of me, despite my fear of what punishment I would later receive from Mr Power. But there was no later as my father kicked him out as soon as we got home, but never reported him to the police as he preferred to avoid any adverse publicity.

'This left Pa with the problem of what to do about my education and his solution brought me even more agony; he sent me to boarding school at the tender age of seven. There followed two years of misery for me as I started and was excluded from three different public schools. The consensus of opinion was that I was mentally unstable, which was contributed to by determined outlandish behaviour by me, including not eating and threatening to self -harm. Of course I never did more than the odd scratch on my arms but there was enough blood to make the schools give up on me as a lost cause. From my point of view it worked better than I could have possibly hoped for as Father's next plan was to appoint a live-in housekeeper whose almost exclusive job was to look after me.'

ASH's whole manner lightened at this junction of the diatribe, his eyes sparkled and a natural smile came to his lips. For the first time since he had come into the room Ben felt he was seeing a genuine reaction rather than the controlled delivery that had characterised his presentation so far.

'This was when Nanny Harris came into my life and I loved her from day one. She was in her fifties, a bit taller than me but a proper mother figure who seemed to understand me like no one had ever done before or since. We lived together for the next eight years and I can honestly say it was the happiest time in my whole life. I attended the local secondary school and then the comprehensive school and no longer felt the need to act up in order to survive. Mind you, things were still not easy for me as I have never seemed able to make friends, but Nanny gave me support in all things and we had loads of adventures at weekends and in holidays. Sport and physical education caused real problems for me and I began to get mysterious chest infections and stomach problems whenever those activities were about to happen. Nanny Harris understood my difficulties and wrote note after note asking for me to be excused from such physical activities. Finally, the school gave in to her pressure and I was allowed to spend those periods in private study in the school library. For the first time I started to take an interest in reading and Nanny was always ready to suggest book titles and subjects for me to explore. I regularly secretly borrowed books from school which Nanny and I would read together of an evening. I still used to get fairly regular chesty coughs and queasy tummies but Nanny was a strong believer in the healing power of Collis Browne, an over-the-counter medication available from the chemists. She would produce the brown bottle of thick syrupy liquid, which didn't taste too good but was always followed by a piece of delicious Turkish delight from Nanny's personal supply. I loved seeing that bottle come out and treated myself to the odd secret slurp from time to time.

'Nanny planned regular trips to wonderful great houses and gardens run by the National Trust and to art galleries all over the place. We often travelled by train on these adventures and spent hours just talking about what we had seen or were going to see. I suppose it would have seemed a bit odd to some people, a young teenager and a middle-aged woman enjoying the same pastimes, but we did and I remember feeling genuinely happy for much of that time.'

The smile slowly disappeared from ASH's face to be replaced by a deep frown and a distinct pout of his mouth.

'I didn't do very well in my O levels, passing just one in English Literature, which was mainly as the result of the many hours I had spent in the school library. My father insisted that I should stay on an extra year in the hope of improving my qualifications and I managed just two more O levels in art and history. Nanny was pleased at my relative success but Pa was much less so, however, he somehow managed to get me a job as a clerk with one of his many business contacts. I hated the job, which involved endless filing and making the tea for all and sundry. Predictably, history was repeated and I was soon given the sack and I was told that I just didn't fit in and that there had been numerous complaints about my attitude. I just couldn't wait to get back to Nanny Harris and to take up where I had left off, I have never seen Pa so angry but he decided to leave me to Nanny's fair hands and we had a whale of a time on adventure after adventure. Then just when life was so good disaster struck, I was called up to do National Service.'

From the look on his face Ben could see that this had indeed been a disaster as far as ASH was concerned. Ben could feel some sympathy for him as he had always considered himself lucky that he had never been called up himself as he had just been a few weeks too young to qualify when National Service had been phased out. He knew for certain that his life would have been very different if he had had to waste his time doing square bashing for eighteen months.

With a deep sigh, ASH continued with his tale. 'It was horrible, truly horrible. I was sharing a dormitory with a whole bunch of uncouth yobs who liked nothing better than having a go at me. I spent my days trying to keep out of their way but I was hopeless at all the tasks we were set and everyone hated me because my shortcomings caused them all to get extra duties. I spent my nights in genuine fear as some of the more despicable recruits did all sorts of abusive things to me. I cried myself to sleep every night and after the six weeks of basic training I was summoned to the medical officer for an assessment of my suitability for the army. I was formally discharged as mentally and physically unfit a week later. I couldn't wait to hand in my gear and walk out of that terrible place. I had the greatest difficulty in not breaking out in song as I mounted the train for home and back to Nanny Harris and my normal life. When I got home I went straight to her rooms and my life hit an all-time low: the rooms were devoid of all her things. I found an envelope on the mantel piece addressed to me along with a bottle of Collis Browne and a full box of Turkish delight.'

At this juncture ASH produced his wallet from his inside pocket and took out a carefully folded piece of paper which he passed over to Ben with a shaky hand. Ben opened the paper up carefully, as it was obviously precious to ASH, and he read the short handwritten note.

My Dear Ash,

Now that you have gone off to do your National Service there is no longer any reason for me to stay here. Your father has kindly agreed that I should take retirement and he has been very generous to me. I am going to live with my eldest sister, who is quite frail now and could do with my help. I will always remember our time together with great fondness. Be a good boy as you make your way in life and make me proud of you.

Your good friend,

Nanny Harris

Ben read the note to himself and looked up sympathetically at ASH, whose lower lip was quivering as he remembered the contents of the letter that he must have read over and over again, and still struggled to contain his sense of loss. Ben folded the note and passed it back to ASH, who carefully returned it to his wallet before continuing. 'As you can see there is no address on the letter and I had no idea where her sister was living. I remembered her once mentioning a visit to relatives on the Isle of Wight and I went there repeatedly in the hope of finding her, but I was wasting my time as I didn't even know the name of her sister.

'At the time I collapsed in a heap on her bed and for the first time I devoured the whole bottle of Collis Browne in one sitting. I passed out but when I came around I somehow felt more at ease as if the familiar taste of her "special medicine" brought us nearer for a while. That weekend Pa summoned the whole family to a council of war. My brothers, Harvey and Maurice, were there along with Pa, but Ma was predictably absent as she had an important bridge match to play in Edinburgh. It came as no surprise to me as she has never made me feel important to her.

'It quickly became clear that there was only one subject up for discussion: me. It also was very apparent that the other three had already decided what action was required and their attitude to me was "take it or go without". As it happened, I found their proposal acceptable as they were offering me a sort of pension, until such times as I was in the position of being able to support myself. The offer was conditional upon me doing nothing to cause them any embarrassment in the localities where they lived and worked. Basically, this means the whole of Surrey, Sussex and the Home Counties. However, this leaves me with plenty of other parts of Great Britain which I can explore and even though my behaviour does cause a bit of a stir from time to time it has never impinged too much on my family.

'I have now spent the past ten or so years staying in reasonable hotels and visiting various grand houses and art galleries just like I did with Nanny Harris. I still miss her of course and always think I might just bump into her on one of my visits. When it gets too lonely I resort to treating myself to a bottle of her special medication, which usually causes a brief incident when I consume it all at once. Quite often somebody rings my parents to let them know what happened but they never react other than to keep on making the regular payments into my bank account. And there you have the story of ASH.'

He finally went quiet and sat back in his chair to draw breath whilst managing to look self-satisfied. Ben briefly thanked him and asked him to return to the reception area and wait for a call to see the prof.

As the clinic was coming to an end the three of them got together in the prof's office and Ben ran through the social history as usual. But unusually the prof then went on to ask Ben what he had made of their last remaining client of the day, who was now sitting in splendid isolation in an empty reception area.

After a few moments' thought Ben replied, 'On the one hand he is just like a young kid who has never grown up, he is both childish and attention seeking. However, I strongly suspect that this is an adopted manner as it serves his aims very well. He seems to live the life of Riley, doing exactly what he wants at his parents' and brothers' expense. He keeps the money coming in by using his regular minor brushes with the health services and police, making sure one way or another that his activities are reported back to his family. His beloved Nanny Harris started him off on Collis Browne and he has adapted its use to enable him to blackmail his way to constant funding. He lives in reasonable comfort in small hotels and spends his days looking at places of interest all the time projecting this strange persona which seems guaranteed to attract attention wherever he goes. He is now in his thirties and I can't see him ever changing. When he outstays his welcome by causing too many problems in chemist shops, wherever he happens to be, he simply up stakes and heads to pastures new. He doesn't seem to be mentally ill to me but I do think he has a strange personality, which has probably been at least partially caused by his disjointed upbringing.'

The prof nodded thoughtfully then said, 'Okay, let's have him in and see where we go.' The interview that followed was surprisingly short, with ASH being given little opportunity to demonstrate any of his usual dramatic presentation. Whenever he started to attempt to go into too much detail the prof simply interrupted him by say that Mr Newman had already informed him about that and ASH was soon floundering. Finally, the prof asked one fundamental question of ASH, and that was what did he hope to achieve by coming to the clinic that afternoon? ASH spluttered for a bit before saying that he was worried about his misuse of Collis Browne and would like help with stopping it. The prof quickly responded by saying that he would try to help with that and told ASH to make a further appointment in a month's time. The ASH that walked out of the clinic was a lot more downbeat than the one who had arrived earlier.

Meanwhile, neither Raj nor Ben were any clearer about the prof's mysterious treatment plan. The prof made no attempt to put them in the picture, simply picked up the phone and rang a number which he knew by heart. The mystery deepened when all the prof said when the call was answered was, 'It's fine by me, all systems go.' Then he hung up and burst out laughing, clearly amused by his colleague's confusion. 'Okay, I'll put you out of your misery and explain what is going to happen. As you know Dr Forrester and myself have been friends for years and what you won't be aware of is that my wife and I regularly go out with him and his wife Millie for a meal or to see a show. It usually ends up with the ladies gossiping and us blokes enjoying a few drinks, chatting about sport or putting the world to rights. We rarely touch on work issues, which is why I was surprised when he suddenly started to tell me about a repeated problem he was having with an odd man who had recently moved into the area. As you know Ian Forrester has been a senior police surgeon for many years and part of his role is to check on the poison registers held by Exworth's chemist shops. Basically, this means that he has to make regular but random visits to check that the poisons in their stock agree with the entries in their poison registers. He has been doing this for at least twenty years and is well known and well respected by all the chemist owners and managers. Inevitably these visits involve some time talking with the staff and for the past couple of months he has been hearing stories about a weird chap who causes concern by drinking whole bottles of Collis Browne and then passing out dramatically. Last week, the man did his thing in Boots and a passing policeman took him to a place of safety, namely the local nick, on a section 136 as he thought he might be mentally ill in a public place. Ian Forrester was called in to assess him and could find no sign of psychosis or neurosis and came to the conclusion that ASH was one of life's oddities. He had done nothing wrong which he could be charged with but Doc Forrester felt he should do something to protect the people of Exworth from this regular nuisance behaviour, which was causing a lot of distress.

'When we were chatting in the pub, after seeing a show, he shared with me an idea for a possible way of resolving the problem but he wanted confirmation of his assessment of ASH before putting it into practice. Apparently, ASH was more than happy to attend the clinic today as it would show his parents that he was trying to sort out his problems and presumably help keep his bank balance healthy. I have just rung Ian and told him it was safe to put his plan into operation. From tomorrow there will be no Collis Browne on sale anywhere in Exworth all the chemists will clear their shelves of it and will be displaying a sign to say "temporarily out of stock". The beauty of the plan is that we are genuinely helping ASH to stop using it, which is what he claimed to want. In reality, I strongly suspect that Exworth will shortly be shot of him and he will resume his nonsense elsewhere.'

A couple of weeks later Ben tried to contact ASH at his last known address to confirm the new clinic appointment and was advised by the hotel manager that ASH had vacated his room and left leaving no forwarding address.

Chapter 62

Clobber and Conkers

Ben found himself breaking out into a spontaneous grin as he made his way through the evening traffic on his way home. He had had no inkling about what Doc Forrester and the prof had hatched up to deal with the nuisance that was ASH but he was impressed that they had quietly gained the cooperation of all the chemists to achieve their objective. He had to admit that he would never have thought of the plan himself and he concluded that they were a couple of wily old practitioners who could teach him a thing or two about dealing with people.

The moment his key was in the front door it swung open and Sandy appeared in the doorway looking extremely cross, Ben quickly gave her the flowers he had bought for her at the hospital shop earlier but this did little to reduce her mood and she frog-marched him into the kitchen. The trousers he had left on the washing line were now laid out on newspaper on the kitchen table. Sandy started straight into an angry dialogue about arriving home to be accosted by the old lady from next door, complaining how shocked she had been to look out of her back bedroom window to have seen Ben running around the garden in his underpants earlier in the day.

'Then I discovered these hanging on the line and frankly they stink. Now I understand that old men tend to leak a little but you aren't even thirty yet so what is your excuse?'

When Ben explained about the chamber pot incident Sandy quickly calmed down but she then caught sight of his footwear and with some extreme difficulty just about managed to contain her mirth.

'So what happened to your proper work shoes? Why are you wearing those monstrosities? They clearly don't fit properly.'

Ben told her about his usual work shoes leaking and how his feet had got soaked.

'These were the only alternative pair I have got and I had to stuff them with newspaper to try and make them wearable. I'll tell you this they are bloody uncomfortable and on balance I prefer wet feet.'

Sandy put her arms around him and said, 'You are an idiot. I am not having any husband of mine going to work in that state looking like a tramp.'

She went straight over to the kitchen cabinet and reached down the vintage teapot which had once been her gran's from the top shelf from which she produced a small sheaf of bank notes.

'I have been saving this to buy you a birthday present but you better have it now so you can go into town tomorrow and get yourself some new shoes and a second pair of work trousers. Meanwhile I will take this smelly pair to have them properly dry cleaned.'

She then folded up the trousers and put them in a carrier bag which she dumped under the stairs ready for the trip to the launderette the next day. Ben grabbed hold of Sandy and gave her a prolonged kiss and Sandy responded warmly with the words, 'Happy birthday, love, just a bit early.'

After tea the whole family sat and watched the weather forecast in order to plan when would be the best time to go on their conker hunt. It didn't take much planning as Saturday was predicted to be yet more heavy rain and wind but Sunday sounded much more promising. Ben was delighted to take off the cumbersome brogues and contentedly spent the rest of the evening in his stocking feet leaving his old work shoes to dry in front of the fire. The boys were allowed to have the chocolate that he had bought for them whilst they too sat in the warmth of the fire and watched their usual Friday night television. Ben gave Sandy a hand to wash up the tea things before making a fresh pot of tea for them to share whilst they firmed up their plans for the weekend.

Sandy was already committed to working on both Saturday and Sunday mornings at the shop so Ben should have been looking after the boys then. They both agreed that it would be difficult to do the clothes shopping he needed to do if he had to drag the boys along. A quick telephone call to Ben's mother, Anthea, resolved the problem for the Saturday shopping trip as she readily agreed that the boys could spend the day with her. That meant that Ben was doing the shopping alone, about which Sandy expressed some concern. Over the years clothes shopping had become her sole prerogative, which suited Ben well, as he detested traipsing around the shops and having to try things on. However, tomorrow he was going to hit the town and was going to spend her hard-earned savings so she wanted to be sure he spent his time and her money wisely. She told him he should focus all his attention on a visit to the large C&A store that had recently opened on the high street.

'They have a huge stock and their prices are very reasonable so you should have more than enough money.'

A brief chat to the boys confirmed that they were quite happy to spend the best part of Saturday playing with their Scalextric on Gran's conservatory floor. So the plans for Saturday were all set and Sunday's possible conker hunt was in the lap of the god's and what the weather turned out to be.

Next morning Sandy slipped out of bed as the first daylight appeared between the gap in the bedroom curtains and Ben remained half asleep but could still interpret her movement around the house: her usual brief visit to the loo followed up the flushing of the toilet and the creak of the stairs as she went to the kitchen, the short rush of water as she filled the kettle with the gap between filling and boiling being taken up with the washing machine being loaded and the motor started. Ben loved this sort of familiar start to the day and couldn't help but feel fortunate to be the one snuggled down in bed in a contented stupor. Minutes later Sandy put a gorgeous smelling mug of coffee on his bedside cabinet and went off to have her shower. The sound of torrential rain splattered against the bedroom window and it looked as if Sandy would be having more than one shower to contend with. She came back into the bedroom wrapped in a bath towel vigorously rubbing her hair dry with a hand towel. Ben moved up in the bed and started on his coffee whilst enjoying watching Sandy dress. He never got bored of this part of the day. There was a brief break in the downpour but the wind was still rattling the windows when Sandy set off for work, hoping to avoid a soaking. She went armed with an umbrella but she kept it unopened as it would struggle to survive if opened in the mini gale that she had to force herself through.

Ben turned over and enjoyed having the bed to himself, choosing to ignore the sounds of battle resounding from the boys' bedroom. Breakfast came late even for a Saturday and involved the usual quarrel as to which of the boys got the Coco Pops. It was settled democratically by playing stone, paper, scissors with Jack winning two to one. Nick had to settle for the Sugar Puffs but got first choice of which piece of toast to have from the rather burnt offerings from their dad. It was almost midday by the time Ben dropped them off at their gran's and he then went on his reluctant shopping trip starting with a swift pint at a convenient pub. He left his car in the pub carpark and walked down a handy lane, out on to the high street. Boots, the main chemist shop in Exworth, was a matter of four shops down the road and on impulse and from curiosity he decided to check if the plan for ASH was already underway. Sure enough part of the shelf for cough and cold medicines was empty except for a printed notice saying that Collis Browne was temporarily out of stock. Round one to Doc Forrester and the prof; Now it was just a case of waiting to see if the prof's predicted result came to pass. Despite the torrential rain there were still loads of people about and they all seemed to be heading in the same direction, directly to the large corner shop, namely the recently opened C&A. It was the sort of shop that Ben would normally avoid like the plague and when he entered the whole place seemed to be heaving with people, almost exclusively women of all ages. Many of them seemed to have lost their natural inhibitions and were openly removing their top clothing to try on the apparent endless supply of colourful cheap clothing on offer. Fortunately, the men's department was located in a far corner which Ben made straight for whilst trying not to focus on the distractions going on all around him. It took no time at all for him to realise how right Sandy had been about the reasonable prices of the goods on offer. Admittedly the range of goods was quite limited but he had no problem finding a couple of pairs of trousers suitable for work and a pair of black slip-ons to his taste. He tried the shoes on to check they fitted but not the trousers as he was more inhibited than some of the other customers. Within a few minutes Ben was in his favourite omelette bar having ordered his food and started on his black coffee with four sugars.

He passed the time by adding up the change in his pocket from the money given to him by Sandy. She would even be paying for his lunch and he was so pleased with his morning's shopping that he decided to pick her up from work to save her getting another soaking. As Ben returned up the lane to pick up his car he passed a lockup garage with a swinging boot sign that squeaked loudly as it swung back and forth in the wind. Despite the pouring rain, the double doors were fastened wide open and the dingy space inside had all the appearances of being a cobbler's workshop from a Victorian age. The figure sat on a high stool, hammer in hand and several nails held between his teeth stopped what he was doing and looked up and somehow managed to mumble a sort of greeting from between his clenched teeth. Ben had never realised that this cobbler's workshop existed, although it was now painfully obvious that both the workshop and the cobbler had been there for many years.

The old man spat the nails out into his hand and invited Ben to come in and seemed keen to have a chat. In no time at all, Ben was getting another life story to listen to and he learnt that Josiah the cobbler had been mending shoes for well over fifty years. He was now well into his eighties but still chose to come into work a couple of days a week 'just to keep my eye in.' It seemed to Ben that this contact was far too opportune to miss and he slipped his leaky shoes off for Josiah to examine. By the time Ben was on his way to the car he was wearing his new shoes leaving his old ones with the cobbler to try and make them watertight. The price quoted seemed reasonable but in fact wasn't much less than the cost of the new pair he had just bought from C&A. However, Ben had been impressed by Josiah and admired a man of eighty preferring to still go into work rather than slowly vegetating at home, so he was pleased to be able to encourage him to continue to feel useful.

The rain storms continued with a vengeance and had the effect of reducing the numbers of cars on the road so the journey to Ma's shop was achieved in record time. Sandy was busy serving customers and didn't notice Ben's arrival. Ma was sat on her usual high stool in contented inactivity and spotted him immediately, lifted the flap in the countertop and waved him through to the back room. She seemed delighted to see Ben, who was a rare visitor to the shop, and reacted as if he were a VIP visitor. The sofa was cleared of debris, cushions plumped up and Ben was encouraged to stretch out whilst Ma put the kettle on and produced a cake tin enclosing a rich homemade fruit cake. Even Harry, Ma's ancient dog, was keen on getting in on the act and managed to clamber on the sofa along with Ben, half burying him and breathing smelly dog breath into Ben's face. The two of them sorted themselves out into some sort of order once Ma had put a cup of tea and a generous slice of cake on the side table. She was then content to leave the two of them to get along and returned to her former position alongside Sandy behind the counter. Ben drank the tea and Harry ate most of the cake before the two of them settled back for a doze. They were both fast asleep when Sandy popped her head around the door and she left them to it and returned to finish the rest of her shift in the shop.

It was still bucketing down when they left Ma's and Sandy was grateful for the lift and keen to know how Ben's shopping trip had gone. He told her all the details and she was pleased at what he had achieved with his birthday money. She was also intrigued about how quickly the prof's plan had started and also confirmed that she had no recall of Josiah the cobbler. She did question, however, when Ben would get his repaired shoes back as there was clearly no fixed opening times at Josiah's, but said she would try each time she went shopping until she was successful. Sandy was keen to meet the character who had made such an impression on Ben.

When they arrived to pick up the boys the door was opened by Ben's dad, Roger, which was a very rare event as he would usually be 'down the allotment'. Ben guessed that it was simply too wet but his dad said, 'There is England playing a friendly on the box and they have just started the second half; it's one all at present but I think we are getting on top.'

Sandy pecked him on the cheek and headed to the kitchen where Anthea could be heard working with pots and pans. Meanwhile Ben joined his dad on the sofa saying, 'Well let's see how our big investment is doing.'

His dad gave him a knowing wink and put his finger to his lips as a reminder of the need to keep their bets a secret. It was years since Ben and his dad had watched a football together and they quickly got into it together, commenting freely as the match progressed. England managed a further two goals to end up winning three–one. It was far from a spectacular event and the opposition was one of the emerging African nations, who were excellent athletes but not so hot on team play. England's performance could at best be described as solid, with one or two players showing their extra class. Ben and his dad concluded that there were a few positive signs for them to have a modicum of hope that their money was not going to disappear in the preliminary rounds of the World Cup. The ladies managed to time their arrival and took over the television in time to watch the evening news, leaving the men to sort the boys out ready to head off home. Ben and his dad wandered out into the greenhouse so that Roger could pick some tomatoes for Sandy to take home and Ben couldn't help but admire the neat lawn and colourful flowerbeds leading down to a rustic bench set below a flourishing old apple tree. The tree still retained much of this year's crop and Ben helped himself before sitting on the seat to enjoy the peace and tranquillity of a proper gardener's garden. He reflected on his own garden at home, which was a scrappy affair with an ancient apple tree that never bore fruit. He knew that by nature he was no gardener and was grateful that having two active little boys was the perfect excuse for inactivity, but that didn't stop him admiring his father's handiwork and he thought, *who knows what might happen with me once the boys have grown.*

He started to tell his dad about the conker hunt planned for the following day but Roger had already heard about it from the boys. 'Did I ever tell you, Ben, that I was the local conker champion when I was a boy, and I intend to teach the boys all my old tricks.'

This was the first time Ben could remember his dad ever mentioning an interest in playing conkers but then to be truthful they had never communicated very much about anything when he was small. He felt mixed emotions about all the wasted years when they could have shared all sorts of things. On reflection he realised that his mum had always been the dominant one during his developing years, as in common with most of her neighbours and friends as she had never worked so was always home for Ben and his sister. By and large men worked long hours and spent their leisure hours down the pub or watching sport. Ben's mum had controlled the purse strings, with his dad being given a sort of pocket money from the wage packet he passed over to her each week. To his credit, he didn't join the pub brigade, preferring to spend his leisure time 'down the allotment' or watching amateur sport down the local recreation ground. Unfortunately, Ben had never shown any interest in either activity and it was only in the past year that the two of them had started to find any common ground.

When it was time for them to get ready to set off for home Ben's dad suddenly suggested that they should all come around for a Sunday lunch on their way back from the conker hunt in the New Forest. Such an invitation was quite a common one and was certainly not one to be turned down but it had always been Ben's mum's suggestion before and both Ben and Sandy looked to her for confirmation that the invitation had her approval. To her credit there was only the smallest hint of surprise which flickered across her face before she enthused about them coming. As they went out in the rain and hurried to the car Roger's passing shot to the boys was, 'I'll show you how it's done to be a champion conker player, there will be no holding you.' Ben was amazed at his dad's unexpected enthusiasm for conkers but looked forward to one of his mum's special meals, including the best roast potatoes imaginable. He had tactfully never mentioned it to Sandy that her roasted spuds fell someway short of his mum's.

The relentless storm blew itself out at some point during the night and the sun was bright and high in the sky, leaving beams of sunlight reflecting on the remaining puddles and the various hews of green in all the verges on their trip to the forest. Sandy had set off for work much earlier in the morning leaving Ben with the task of entertaining the boys and they were to say the least rather over excited. They could barely sit still in the back of the car and were soon niggling at each other as to which of them was going to get the biggest conker. Ben tried to let them get on with it and attempted to remember the route he had planned using the ancient AA book which he had found in the old Cortina when he had first bought it. After several unplanned detours the countryside suddenly changed to dense forests and after a couple of miles the previously light traffic built up to a slow-moving column for no apparent reason.

The cars inched forward, with loads of stopping and starting until they took a sharp turning to the right which bordered a flat open area of grassland. Several cars had pulled up and stopped on the grass whilst others still inched forward with the occupants rubbernecking at a small herd of ponies which included two very cute young foals. The ponies were busy scrounging titbits for the car drivers and passengers and seemed completely unafraid of the cars and unaware of the danger they were potentially in. After the boys' recent experience of feeding the horses at Horseworld they quite naturally wanted to get hands on with these pretty little ponies. They groaned at their dad when he refused to stop and instead picked up speed once he was past the animals.

A little while after, there was a sign directing the way to a picnic area well back from the road which turned out to be fenced and equipped with cattle grids at its entrance. Once parked and without a pony in sight Ben carefully explained about the danger involved by attracting the ponies to the road. The animals roamed free and there were a lot hurt or even killed when they wandered on to the road, particularly at night. The boys appeared to understand and they climbed out of the car and set out their picnic that Sandy had prepared for them on a vacant picnic table under the branches of an ancient oak tree. There were several other families doing the same and once the boys had devoured their lunch they began to make tentative contact with other children, one of whom produced a ball. In no time at all an improvised kick-around was underway and all thoughts of conker hunting were temporarily put on hold. Ben sat back, content to enjoy the sun and a second cup of tea. Bit by bit the individual families gathered their things together and went on their way. The collection of kids was down to the last six when the ball owner together with his ball headed off with his parents. Ben and the boys finished up the remnants of their picnic and armed with their now empty carrier bags finally set off on their conker hunt.

Ben was conscious that the afternoon was slipping away and that it was more than his life was worth to get the boys back late for his mum's Sunday roast, but he soon realised that he didn't need to worry as almost immediately they reached a whole group of horse chestnut trees. What is more, the ground was literally covered with conkers and all the boys had to do was pick them up. A bit of Ben missed the satisfaction of flinging bits of wood up into the tree branches in an attempt to knock down the shiny brown treasure. This was all too easy and lacked the risk of things dropping on your head. Not that the boys minded at all and were now rapidly filling their carrier bags until they were bulging. With carrier bags and pockets now full they were anxious to get back to their grandfather to show off their plunder.

For the second day running the front door was answered by Roger would was suitably impressed by both the volume and the quality of the conkers and hurried them all out into his garden shed. This was a rare privilege, as this was very much Roger's special place and was normally padlocked. The inside of the shed was set out as a proper little workshop with rows of tidy tools, jars of nails and screws and a full-size workbench complete with vice and a collection of power points. Ben noticed that many of the tools bore the engraving of GWR and it was impossible to miss the station sign for Blandford Street Station that was mounted down the full depth of the shed. There was an electric drill stand set up on the bench and it had been equipped with a homemade wooden jig which Roger demonstrated could neatly contain an individual conker.

'This is my special hole maker for preparing conkers for competition and I would like you boys to try it out.'

He placed the first conker in the jig and showed the boys how to turn the drill on and how to pull the handle down once their hands were well away from the action. The boys were intrigued and under Roger's supervision the shed was soon a hive of conker production. Ben slipped away to enjoy a few minutes solitude with the Sunday newspaper and was soon catching up on the weekend's sport and enjoying a close study of the latest antics of the Giles family. When Ben had been small his dad had always taken the *News of the World* but his mum had never approved of it because of its concentration on 'sex, sleaze and smut' and once Ben and his sister had started to take an interest it had rapidly been replaced by the *Sunday Express*. It remained a sore point with his dad, who called it a Tory rag, but the sport was okay and Ben had quickly grown to love the brilliant artwork and humour of the very talented resident cartoonist Carl Giles.

As always Ben started to read the paper from the back to the front with his priority being to read about the most recent Manchester United result. A satisfying two-one win against Liverpool on this occasion. If asked, Ben would always claim to be a Manchester United supporter but had never actually seen a single live match of theirs. The basis of his support went back to the tragic day in February 1958 when twenty-three people including eight of their first team died in an air crash in Munich when returning from an European cup match against Red Star Belgrade.

That horrifying event had had a real impact on Ben at the time, coming as it did soon after the death of Eddie Evans, who had been a special mate in senior school. Eddie had everything that Ben could have wished for, being brilliant academically and also a talented sportsman representing the school and the county at both football and cricket. Yet despite their obvious differences Ben and Eddie had been close friends throughout their school days. Eddie had gone to university a year early when he achieved first-class A level grades whereas Ben had stayed on a further year to get his necessary qualifications.

Inevitably the two of them went their separate ways and the next thing Ben learnt about Eddie was when he had read in the paper that he had been killed in a climbing accident in Scotland. At the time it hit Ben for six and it took weeks for him to come to terms with it. Somehow, Ben had linked the two tragic events together in his mind and he now never read anything about Manchester United without also thinking about Eddie. In particular, he had always followed the recovery of two specific men who were both been severely injured in the crash but managed to fight back and recover to become synonymous with Manchester's rise back to the top of the England game. Matt Busby and Bobbie Charlton would always be true giants of men in Ben's eyes and Eddie would always be a much loved and missed dear friend.

By the time that Sandy had finished her shift at the shop and had walked to meet up with the family, she discovered Ben stretched out on the sofa dead to the world. The newspaper he had been reading had slipped down on to the floor and had spread itself out into an untidy mess. She picked it up and put it back in order but decided to leave Ben in peace and headed to the kitchen to make herself useful to her mother in law. Ben's peace didn't last long as he was soon joined by the boys, each swinging a collection of conkers all attached to lengths of pink laces. He couldn't imagine where the laces had come from but they appeared to be very strong and well up to the task that they were being used for. The boys moved on to the kitchen to show the women what they had achieved and then headed straight back into the garden to get the promised coaching from their grandfather. Sandy shortly joined Ben on the sofa, having been ejected from the kitchen with Ben's mum firmly saying that everything was well under control. Ben said nothing but felt it was probably a missed opportunity for Sandy to learn his mum's secret of the perfect roast potato!

The two of them talked over the events of the day and in passing Ben asked Sandy if she knew where the pink laces had originally come from. 'I don't think you could have guessed in a month of Sundays and I had no idea until Anthea put me in the picture just now in the kitchen. It is quite a story and goes back years and is really all to do with women's vanity. For centuries women have worn various types of corsets as under garments in an attempt to adjust their natural shape so that they could wear clothes that were fashionable at the time. One of the most common forms of corset was developed in this country and is called the Spirella corset, in many ways it is an interesting concept. It has always been advertised in both the local and national press as "a trim, knowledgeable and smart corset designed to keep tummies flat". But it has never been available in any shops and could only be bought by having it fitted in the privacy of one's own home by a Spirella qualified fitter. Thus each corset was unique, especially made to fit one particular lady, and owning such underwear became a must for the more wealthy middle-class ladies. Then your mum had gone on to explain to me that the introduction of largely working-class women doing war work meant that some of them had surplus cash for the first time in their life, but there was nothing in the shops for them to aspire to and for a while owning a Spirella corset became a much desired purchase.

'Apparently many women soon found them to be instruments of torture and your mum found that they began to turn up regularly at the various jumble sales she helps with. Nobody wanted them as they really only fitted one person, being as they were always made to measure. They regularly ended up with the pile of unwanted stuff at the end of the sale that the rag man then bought up for a few shillings. Your mum hated the waste and began to save the laces from the corsets, which she thought would be useful for your dad to use to tie up his bean sticks on the allotment. Your dad rejected them out of hand and now they are being put to use by the boys, who have got no idea of their origins.'

They agreed that it was unlikely that any other kids would have any more knowledge either and it would be best to refrain from making any comment. The whole family enjoyed a super meal with potatoes so delicious that even Sandy drew attention to them.

'I really must get you to show me how you do them, Mum.'

Ben managed to hold his tongue but did make a firm nod of agreement.

Chapter 63

Still No Time to Be Bored

Sandy didn't have to work on the Monday, which meant that she could help to get the boys off to school. They were at their most cooperative as they were unusually keen to get to school to show off their conker trove. Ideally they would have liked to show their friends just how many first-class conkers they had collected and it took a lot of insistence from Sandy and backup from Ben to limit them to taking just two conkers each.

It was another fine day so Sandy and the boys walked, leaving Ben to arrive at the Highfield office earlier than usual. Alice was already on duty in the kitchen, but she wasn't alone and it was Susie who brought Ben his tea. She could hardly contain herself and dived straight in to ask if he had decided how they should progress with the Hanca situation. Ben played for time by agreeing that Susie could ring the heir company to clarify how they would want the matter handled and to report back to him. Meanwhile, Ben anticipated that the company would want to meet with Hanca face to face, which would necessitate a trip to their London office. There was no doubt in his mind that Hanca would find it impossible to make such a trip without Susie acting as escort and that was the problem he was now struggling with.

Ben was completely confident about Susie undertaking the contact with Heir Hunters but his real concern was how to fund the trip for the two of them to London and also the possible need for an overnight stay. The potential cost involved was way beyond Ben's spending authority and would normally involve seeking a committee agreement. That in turn would require the staff at headquarters being consulted, which would mean the involvement of 'the diabolical duo' namely Eric Sully and Creepy, his little henchman. Such an approach would be guaranteed to be turned down with every likelihood that Ben would be sanctioned for getting the department involved with someone who had never actually been diagnosed as either mentally ill or mentally handicapped.

The last thing Ben and his team needed right now, particularly with their use of the empty office space to start up a mini day club, was to attract the attention of Creepy. There had to be another way, but the only idea Ben had come up with was potentially dynamite. Soon after Susie came back into his office having had a telephone conversation with the Heir Hunters office and she confirmed that a trip to London was the only way forward. Once again Ben asked Susie to leave it with him and firmly shut his door after she had rather reluctantly left.

With some trepidation, he picked up the phone and rang Alderman Herbert Anstey at his engineering company headquarters. After brief conversations with their telephonist and Mr Anstey's secretary Ben found himself talking to the main man. He took a deep breath and simply said that he would welcome the opportunity to discuss a problem concerning Hanca. The alderman's response was just what Ben had hoped it would be and he was invited to meet Mr Anstey in his office anytime that morning up until twelve, after which time he was committed to council business. The timing couldn't be more perfect as Ben was due to be on emergency cover from 1 pm so that would fit in nicely. Having advised Mrs Freeman that he would be back by one, he dashed off in his car leaving Susie frustrated by his apparent lack of action about Hanca and her windfall.'

Exworth Engineering Company was an enormous complex of buildings, many appearing to date back to the Victorian age. The whole site was surrounded by a high barbed wire topped fence and the entrance was controlled by a uniformed security officer who occupied a smart little hut with a glass-fronted sliding window. Ben had parked on the street a few yards past the entrance and walked back and tapped on the window. It promptly slid open and Ben was greeted civilly but rather formally and with just a hint of suspicion. However, as soon as Ben explained that he had been invited to attend by the chairman, the security guard checked his clipboard and came straight out of his cubicle and directed him. The main office was of relatively modern design and was surrounded with colourful flowerbeds, in contrast to the rest of the functional site. The next hurdle for Ben to confront was a smartly dressed receptionist who had obviously already consulted her clipboard and personally led Ben down a long, carpeted corridor ending at a panelled door with 'Chairman' printed in gold leaf across its central panel. The receptionist knocked at the door and gestured for Ben to enter but he had still not yet reached Mr Anstey. Instead he was greeted by Ms Poperwell, who explained that she was Mr Anstey's secretary and that Ben would have to wait a few minutes as her boss was currently in a meeting.

The seat offered to Ben was deep and comfortable and he was relaxed enough to enjoy watching Ms Poperwell and her great legs going about their duties. She broke off from what she was doing to offer Ben coffee, which she produced as if by magic from a percolator bubbling away behind a screen. Ben thought he could get used to this treatment but he knew in reality he would have to be grateful for being looked after by Alice, who sadly fell a long way short of the attractive Ms Poperwell on many levels. After a quarter of an hour the chairman's door suddenly opened and a good dozen suited men came out. They all carried identical thick brown folders and their faces all showed that it had not been a comfortable meeting. One or two nodded to Ms Poperwell, but there was no conversation between them and they all gave the impression that they couldn't get away quick enough. Ben guessed that the meeting had been a difficult one and he became even more anxious about how Alderman Anstey might react to his visit. The phone on Ms Poperwell's desk bleeped and she picked up her dictation pad, checked her hair in a mirror attached to the side of her filing cabinet then hurried into her boss's office quietly closing the door behind her. Ben waited for what seemed like an age but was actually just a few minutes. The wait had a detrimental effect on his increasingly factious nerves and it took all his control to avoid making a swift exit, but he knew that that was out of the question.

When Ms Poperwell reappeared she was carrying a similar brown folder to the ones the other people had been carrying and Ben was able to make out the label 'Financial Targets'. She walked over to Ben and seemed to understand his apprehension as she smiled and simply said, 'He can see you now,' and she gave Ben the lightest of pats on his arm as encouragement. Ben took a deep breath and followed her over to the chairman's door and stepped into the inner sanctum.

The room was not what he had expected. There was none of the opulence he had anticipated; this was a functional space with a long table surrounded by identical chairs which almost filled the room. At the far end was a fireplace with a flickering fake gas fire making a rather feeble attempt to soften the ambiance and there were a couple of armchairs set one each side of the fire. Mr Anstey was sat in one and he waved Ben over to sit in the other. He reached over and shook Ben by the hand before getting straight on with the matter in hand.

'It's good to see you, Ben, but I hope you are not having a serious problem with Hanca. I have seen her a couple of times and she seems to be happy and doing well in her own little world.'

Ben started by saying that there wasn't a major problem with Hanca and in fact it was quite the reverse. 'I am sorry, sir, but what I want to talk to you about is rather sensitive and I must ask you to treat this conversation as confidential. Hanca is not aware that I have come to see you and neither does anyone in my department have any idea of this discussion.'

Mr Anstey nodded and said, 'I understand what you are saying, so go on and I will stop you if I think we are getting into dangerous waters.'

Ben told him all about the approach from Heir Hunters and the need for Hanca to be escorted by Susie to the meeting in London. 'I think that sounds really good and I am delighted that Hanca should have some good fortune as she has certainly had a tough life, but I don't see the problem, Ben.'

Ben went on to explain that the problem was simply how to fund the trip; what with transport costs, food and drink and even the possible need for an overnight stay in London. 'All that will cost a lot more than I have the authority to agree so it would need to be referred up to headquarters and probably on to committee, and there is the rub. I am afraid that I am not flavour of the month with a couple of senior staff there and I think that they might just use this situation as a stick to beat me with. They don't like the autonomy I have working from a small, rather isolated office and I think they are likely to pick up on the fact that Hanca has never actually been diagnosed as mentally ill or mentally handicapped, which is our normal client terms of reference. I am completely satisfied that our work with Hanca is totally justified but what I don't want is for them to have any excuse for interfering in the day-to-day running of my team. I am pleased to have a committed group of colleagues who get on with the job with enthusiasm and I really don't want to rock the boat.

However, I need to source the funding somehow if Hanca is to get access to her inheritance.'

Ben came to a halt and sat back in the chair leaving Mr Anstey apparently deep in thought. Finally, he looked straight at Ben and said, 'I have worked around councillors and officers for years and have seen every sort of petty jealousy imaginable, so I do understand where you are coming from. To be quite frank with you, Ben, many of them wouldn't last five minutes in a commercial setting and I find it hard at times having to put up with their nonsense. I keep my ear to the ground and I only hear good things about the work of you and your team. I am aware that I played no small part in getting you involved with Hanca, who is special to me because of my connection with her husband Terry Parsons.'

At that he reached into his pocket and pulled out a cheque book and promptly made a cheque out for £100.

'I won't make it out to Hanca as I would prefer her not to know it came from me; perhaps I should make it out to your colleague, Susie who is going with her.'

Ben readily agreed and told him Susie's full name, Susan Fraser. They agreed that Susie would get receipts for all expenditure and send them to Mr Anstey in due course, along with any outstanding money. The successful interview was over in about ten minutes and once again Ben admired the dynamism of the man. He stopped on his way out to thank Ms Poperwell and was rewarded with a flashing smile and the comment, 'I am pleased it worked out for you.' She again patted him on the arm as he passed her, which Ben found most acceptable.

He was even left with enough time for a quick lunchtime snack at Joe's before he needed to get back to the office, ready to go on call. He ate his food in the main part of the café and enjoyed the usual banter and was pleased to note that Ruth added her own contribution to the conversation, which seemed to be just fine with Joe.

As soon as Ben was settled back at his office desk he received a visit from Susie who had clearly been waiting to see him. She took the initiative and said that she wanted to inform Ben about a possible volunteer for the Thursday Club.

'I think I have found our first volunteer to help with the club and I think she should prove to be a great asset. Helen Hancock is a very dear friend of mine who lives quite near me in Little Poppy Field. I have known her for years and in fact John and I bought our shop and home from her when we first moved there. Helen is a single lady, who lived with her widowed mother in our place from birth and together they ran the shop as a wool shop and haberdashery all through the war right up until the mid-1950s. Unfortunately, Helen's mum became increasingly frail, which coincided with a falling off of people doing their own knitting and dressmaking. Her mum eventually died, by which time the shop was very run down and the property was in urgent need of a bit of tender loving care. When John and I first saw the place it was in a sorry state and it had been on the market for months. However, we could both see the potential of it and put in an offer matching the price being asked by the estate agent. From day one Helen and I have been close friends and with the money that we paid her she was able to buy a small terraced cottage at the far end of the village. She started to run her front living room as a small haberdashery shop and has built up a thriving knit and natter group which is very popular with the ladies of Little Poppy Field and the surrounding area. She and I have also worked together to run the local Brownie pack, which proved to be very popular to the extent that we regularly had a waiting list of girls wanting to join. Things were ticking along nicely but unbeknown to us the headquarters of guiding have a strict rule that nobody over the age of sixty-five is allowed to be a leader for a Brownie or Girl Guide pack.

'Suddenly, last year I received a letter from headquarters saying that Helen could no longer help. I actually had no idea that she was sixty-five as she has always seemed so active and loaded with energy. I tried to appeal the decision but there was no way they would consider any alternative and she had to discontinue her involvement with the pack. I struggled on for a while in the hope that someone else would step into the breach, but there were no offers of help and once I started my job here I couldn't continue and the pack just folded.

'I suspect that the age restriction was introduced years ago when being sixty-five meant you were in your dotage, but that is not the same today and valuable resources are being wasted. Still, the Brownies' loss can be the Thursday Club's gain and it would be great for me to be working with her again. I have spoken to Phil about Helen and she likes the sound of her and is keen to get her involved. I have asked her to come along on this Thursday and would like you to meet her, to see what you think.'

Ben picked up on Susie's enthusiasm and agreed to call into the club after lunch on Thursday. 'Now, Susie, whilst I have got you here I have something for you to see,' and with no further discussion passed Mr Anstey's cheque across the desk to her.

Susie looked at it and then looked up at Ben and said, 'What on earth is this for? I don't understand.'

Ben laughed and said, 'Sorry Susie, I don't suppose you do, but that cheque is to fund your trip to London with Hanca. Let me explain.'

Ben explained the problem he had been grappling with and why he had had to seek funding from an unusual source. Susie quickly cottoned on to the fact that Ben had been brave in the way he had dealt with his dilemma and rushed around the desk and gave him a smacking kiss on the cheek.

'Do you know something, Ben, you are the best, you really are.'

Blushing madly, she hurriedly returned to her seat. Ben felt more than adequately rewarded for his efforts. They sorted out the need for Susie to keep a record of all expenditure and to get receipts wherever possible and she set off to start Hanca's preparations ready for her great adventure.

The next few minutes passed without interruption and Ben allowed himself to daydream about nothing in particular but finally focusing on the practicalities of being on call. Being on call was generally peaceful but at any time a single telephone call could require you to snap into action to deal with some emergency or other. The duty period ran from 1 pm to 9 am the next day and for all of that twenty-one hour period you had to be available on the end of the phone for any mental health emergencies that might occur anywhere in Exworth. There was no additional payment or time off for being on call or for being called out often for several hours at a time.

It also had implications for Ben and Sandy's family life and this rankled from time to time when it got in the way of something they wanted to do as a family. Ben had considered taking it up with his union rep but he would have needed to get the support of his mental welfare officer colleagues across the department and he had always put it off for another day. He knew at least part of his reluctance to make the effort was the vulnerability he felt about being the only decentralised office. He wasn't proud of the intimidation he felt from 'the diabolical duo' at headquarters but he valued what he had with his team so the unreasonable expectation of the 'on-duty problems' went on the back burner for another day.

Almost as soon as Susie had left his office, Alice appeared with a cup of tea for him and sat herself down in the chair only recently vacated. 'No peace for the wicked' was Ben's automatic reaction as he prepared himself for an update on Alice's bowel movements, but that never happened and instead she chatted away about her excitement about the Battle of Britain celebrations at the end of the week. Ben only listened with half an ear but did take the opportunity to study how she was looking. He had to admit to himself that there had been a real improvement in her general appearance in recent months. Susie's influence regarding her dress sense, together with her encouraging Alice to have her hair done regularly had radically improved the way she looked but there was much more to the transformation than just clothes and hair. Alice just seemed more 'normal' and aware of the world around her and it would be unlikely that a stranger would have any inclination of her problematical past. She went on to share her ideas for wartime costumes for herself, Ernest and of course The Champ. Ben tried to think when he had last been subjected to a bowel conversation by Alice and realised that it was weeks ago. Her current obsession was the much healthier one of her growing friendship with Ernest and the dog and Ben suspected that this was probably the first real friendship Alice had ever had. Together the three of them made an unusual family group but he had no doubt it was of real benefit to them all.

Once Ben had finished his tea he returned the empty cup to her and Alice went on her way, leaving him to get on with his work.

The telephone remained comfortingly silent and Ben was preparing to head for home when the next call came in. He anticipated that it was likely to be a colleague ringing to give him some information about a potential overnight problem and he opened his notepad in readiness for note taking. The caller was Beth Evans, the childcare officer who worked with Carol McBain, and it had nothing to do with Ben being on call. It was, however, to share some news with him about developments that had taken place over the weekend in the McBain household.

The situation with the family was always likely to be of concern because of the history of drug use by Carol and her partner Norman Ainsley. Since the birth of baby Norma, Carol had managed to stay drug free, but Norman had continued to use and had tried repeatedly to get Carol back using. Ben was therefore fearing the worse, but the news Beth had to share with him was totally unexpected. Carol had kicked Norman out over the weekend and arranged for the council to change the house locks. Beth explained to Ben that on the previous Saturday Carol had had her child benefit stolen from her handbag by what was obviously 'an inside job'. The money had been earmarked for nappies and milk powder for the baby and Carol was forced to borrow from a sympathetic neighbour to cope over the weekend.

Of course, Norman had denied any involvement in the theft but it was clear to Carol that he had been able to buy a new supply of cannabis; the remnants of which she found hidden away under the sofa cushions. The last straw, as far as Carol was concerned, was when Norman suggested that Dale must have been the thief. She was furious and physically threw Norman out, closely followed by his few possessions. Earlier in the day, Beth had been able to arrange an emergency cash payment for Carol so she could repay her neighbour and stock up on the required baby things. Ben and Beth were both happy with the development but agreed that they should intensify their support for the family as Carol would find being a single parent demanding. When he put the phone down, Ben allowed himself a most unprofessional dance of glee around his office.

Once again he started to pack ready to head off home when the phone rang just as he was walking out of the door. He hesitated for a second or two, deciding whether to ignore it or not, but put his professional behaviour back in place and picked up the receiver. The caller was someone who was always welcome and Ben returned to his seat in anticipation of an enjoyable long catch up with Dave, his former student from St Margaret's Hospital. Ben and Dave had hit it off from day one and although they only met up occasionally they quickly fell into an easy banter. Dave was bubbling over with pleasure and couldn't wait to share his news with Ben. Everything in his life was falling into place. Now that he was fully qualified, the hospital management had confirmed his promotion to charge nurse, which meant a really good pay rise. Having spent the past three years living in the shared accommodation provided by the hospital for their nursing staff he was anxious to get his own place. He had considered renting but decided that he should go the whole hog and buy a place. This was a huge step for him but he had, that day, signed the contract to buy a small terraced house using all his savings as a deposit and getting a mortgage from the building society. Dave couldn't keep the excitement out of his voice as he went on to explain that the house was structurally sound but had had nothing done inside for years.

'But I am sure that I can get it updated over time and the good news is that it is only about three streets from where you live so I am now in the process of making the arrangements for Carmen and the girls to come over to live here and I hope that I will have my family back together by Christmas!'

Ben was delighted and said so in no uncertain terms. 'When you get the keys, I would love to see it and I know Sandy will be over the moon to be living so near Carmen and the girls.'

Meanwhile, Ben was already thinking how he could best help to get Dave's new home fit for his family to move into. Ben's decorating skills were pretty limited but he did know people such as Albert and Sam Watts, the decorating duo he had met at rotary. Then there was also the local furniture auction, where reasonable furniture could often be bought for very little money. Ben had to rein his thoughts in, as the practicalities were for another day, and he listened as Dave repeated himself over and over again as if he could scarcely believe all his dreams and plans were coming to fruition.

As Dave finally came to a halt he added a little postscript by way of information for Ben. 'We will be working together in the near future as the prof's project has been allocated a house in Ensley for us to use as a minimal support group for the remaining six people in the original group. The prof is really chuffed, as this means the experiment to get a group of long-term inpatients back in the community has worked, despite a lot of cynicism from all sorts of quarters. I reckon that over time most of the long-term hospitals will close and the future for the service is going to be community care, which means you are going to be busy, Ben my man.'

The journey home was a nightmare as Ben hit the worst of the worst of the evening traffic. He had intended to be there, ready to receive messages by five-thirty at the latest and it was a full hour later that he arrived. Fortunately, there had been no callers but that didn't mean he wasn't in demand, as both of the boys wanted his immediate attention. They started straight into a long moan about how unfair it was and Ben was left none the wiser about what they were going on about. By way of explaining both boys presented him with identical official looking envelopes addressed to 'Dear parent'. The contents were self explanatory.

Dear parent,

We are once again at the time of the year when children collect conkers and use them in competition with other children. I am sure we are all familiar with it and will have taken part in such games when we were children. I and my governors have, however, decided that no conkers are going to be permitted on the school premises. This is mainly on the grounds of health and safety but also to avoid additional litter, which is already a constant problem. I have today confiscated all the conkers that children have brought in with them and these will be available until the end of the week in the school office for parents to collect if they so wish.

Thank you for your cooperation with this.

Mr A Steadman

Headmaster

Ben's immediate reaction to yet another example of the nanny state was that he thought that the ban on conkers was a bit over the top, but didn't mention that to the boys. Instead, he tried to explain the thinking behind the decision but the boys were not so easily satisfied. Ben quickly came to the conclusion that the fact of the matter was that the boys had wanted to show off their 'superior conkers' to their friends in the playground. In order to pacify them, he agreed that they could take some of their conker reserves out into the street for half an hour to show the other kids. This was a rare privilege to play out when they had school the next day and they moved swiftly in case Ben changed his mind. The house regained its peace and Sandy called from the kitchen that tea would be on the table in five minutes. As usual when he was on call, Sandy produced a cold meal as she could never be sure when he would be home to eat. Early on there had been several dinners which had become inedible by her trying to keep them warm in the oven, but that was a thing of the past. Salads was now the order of the day, Ben's favourite being tinned salmon and his least favourite being Spam, which always reminded him of school dinners. Today it was corned beef, which he always enjoyed, and Sandy came to join him at the table and they talked over their days activities. Sandy had already eaten with the boys but occasionally pinched an odd bit of tomato off Ben's plate in contented familiarity.

She was thrilled to hear the news of Carman and the girls but as usual wanted more information about the plans than Ben knew to offer. They agreed that it was time to invite Dave over for a meal so she could find out all the nitty gritty. Once Ben had finished eating she cleared the table and got out her writing stuff to let Carman know how much she was looking forward to having her living just up the road. Ben watched the last bit of the news before calling the boys in and getting them ready for bed prior to them cuddling down on the sofa to watch the latest 'Z Cars' episode.

The telephone remained silent and Ben eased himself between the boys and relaxed with only half an eye on the screen as he had no idea what Fancy and the others were up to in their usual all-action activity. The boys, however, were completely into the story and edged forward as a high-speed car chase absorbed their concentration. The phone, which was situated in the living room, chose that moment to burst into life and Ben jerked into action, turning the television right down before picking up the handset. The boys knew better than to complain as that could result in the television being completely turned off. Fortunately, it was only Patsie Scadding ringing for a chat and Sandy had already come straight in from her letter writing in the kitchen, as she could never resist the telephone. Ben returned to the sofa, turning the television back up a little en route so that the boys could enjoy the rest of their programme. He knew that Sandy and Patsie were up to sometime but hearing only half of the conversation meant he was none the wiser. Sandy kept it short, knowing that Ben was on call but the conversation ended with the girls agreeing to meet for lunch the following day. Sandy offered no information to Ben and he knew better than to ask despite itching with curiosity. The programme came to an end and the boys were tucked up in bed by Sandy before Ben stepped in to read them a new bedtime book about Just William and his gang. Ben thought it was rubbish, but the boys seemed to like it and that was all that really mattered.

The rest of the evening passed peacefully with Sandy returning to her letter writing and Ben working his way through the local free paper *The Exworth Echo,* which was largely adverts, which were the life blood of the paper. Ben found it worth the effort as there were often little gems of information about council business and planning applications but sadly there were never any cartoons of note. As the evening progressed he lifted the telephone to check that he still had a connection but it remained quiet and by 11.30 he assumed it was a clear session and joined Sandy in bed. She was already fast asleep and he was relaxed enough to soon join her. Little did he know that within a few hours he was going to have one of the most disturbing experiences of his social work career!

As tended to happen when he was on call he woke in the early hours with the urge to pee. He knew from bitter experience that the need could not be ignored if he was to get any further sleep so he forced himself to move and wandered naked into the bathroom. The cold hit him like a punch and by the time he was passing water he was shivering and rapidly coming out of the remnants of his soporific state. At that precise moment the phone downstairs in the lounge burst into life and continued to ring as Ben desperately tried to stop urinating. It seemed that he was going on for ages and that it was completely beyond his control. He finally dried up enough to start his descent in the pitch dark; succeeding in stubbing his toe on lounge door frame before switching on the light and reaching for the phone.

A quick glance at the clock on the mantlepiece informed him that it was just after 3 am and he groaned to himself knowing calls at 'the witching hour' were invariably bad news. Normally it would be a summons to assess the mental health of some poor soul in a police station, the local casualty unit or on occasion at their own home, mostly on one of the council estates. This time it was different, very different in all sorts of ways. For a start Ben could barely believe his ears when the caller announced himself as Dr Rowan Westbourne, head consultant at St Benedict's Hospital. Ben almost reacted by saying 'pull the other one', as it was well known by everyone in the mental health service that Dr Westbourne never went out into the community. He left all such activities to his minions and reportedly spent all his working days in his palatial office at the hospital, working on a series of books about unusual and rare mental health conditions and syndromes. Nothing had yet been published!

Ben had never had any direct dealings with Dr Westbourne but everything he had heard about him gave the same opinion of him. A pompous self-opinioned prat who was best avoided at all cost. In any case Ben was given no opportunity to say anything as the demanding voice ploughed straight on.

'I am at the Fieldings on Rochester Road, Ensley along with Dr Arnold the family practitioner and I want you here at once as I have a patient who needs a section. It is top priority and I have already booked an ambulance for thirty minutes' time. The patient is a married woman aged thirty called Magdoline Holmes-Penrose.'

And before Ben could ask for any further information the phone went dead, leaving him with no doubt that he had indeed just been issued with an instruction by the notorious Dr Rowan Westbourne, but Ben mused there couldn't be many who could claim that they were stark naked when they first communicated with the legend that was Dr Westbourne, senior consultant.

Ben had a quick wash and brushed his teeth before sitting on his bed and struggling to get his clothes on. Inevitably his movement around the bedroom awoke Sandy, who surfaced enough to mumble asking what was going on. Ben simply said that he had been called out on an emergency and Sandy reacted by wishing him good luck before turning over and falling back to sleep within seconds.

As he was pulling away from home he put his brain in gear to consider what he already knew about what he was going to have to deal with. In fact, he realised that he knew quite a lot about the location of his visit, as he had read about it repeatedly in the local press over the years. The Fieldings was a very select enclave of half a dozen or so modern houses that had been built relatively recently in an attempt to imitate the Tudor classical black and white buildings. Historically, the site had originally been occupied by a very grand seventeenth century house with mixed forest to the rear of it covering a small range of hills. In the front of the house, historically, there had been extensive grass lands which were used for cattle and a very large deer park. The house suffered the same fate as many such houses over the years, it was destroyed by fire in the nineteenth century, by which time large parts of the grasslands associated with the original property had been sold for Victorian house-building. Hence the current area known as Ensley slowly grew street by street to become a popular area of owner-occupied houses built to a high standard. The remains of the derelict house were abandoned and over time the ruins became lost as the ancient forest encroached upon it.

When Ben had been on the first year of his professional training his whole group of students had been set the task of researching the history of the Poor Law implementation in their home areas up and down the country. As a consequence, he had spent much of that Christmas holiday digging his way through a variety of local history books and dusty old committee records from the last century. To his surprise, he found it quite interesting and compiled a very comprehensive report that earned him a rare 'A' from his tutor when he handed it in upon his return to university.

The relevance of him remembering it now, as he drove through the empty streets of Exworth, was that the house he was heading for had been built on the site of Exworth's Victorian workhouse. Legislation in the 1830s had required the local authorities of the time to establish work houses to provide work and shelter for poverty-stricken people. With the usual efficiency of the Victorians, Exworth had replaced the ruins of the seventeenth century house by a functional, three-storey barracks of a building as their provision of a workhouse. There had been no attempt at style or grandeur and photos from the time showed a grim red brick building with few windows occupied by forlorn-looking people all dressed in dark tatty clothing. The grimness of the regime matched the building, with families being split up and everyone being expected to do unpaid work in return for very basic board and food.

The concept of workhouses finally came to an end in the 1930s and the already deteriorating monstrosity was abandoned to its fate and the encroaching forest. The building got a brief reprieve in the early years of the war when it had been 'tarted up' to be used as a military hospital for injured soldiers from the front. However, it proved to be very unsuitable and was once again abandoned after only a couple of years. There followed ten years of slow deterioration and vandalism, when there were plenty of other issues to be sorted out by the council. Oddly enough, there was one further quite extraordinary plan for its use when an Italian immigrant proposed to turn it into an ice cream factory. The local press gave him full publicity and a few months later briefly reported that he had gone bankrupt and was believed to have gone back to Italy to lick his wounds.

In the years that followed, various riffraff broke into the building and caused all sorts of damage. It became a haunt for vagrants, alcoholics and drug users and the people of Ensley suffered peripheral damage which got steadily worse. The local press once again started to take an interest and ran several stories of fires taking place in the building caused by the squatters using the internal woodwork to light fires presumably in an attempt to keep warm or to cook. The crunch came when one such fire destroyed a major part of the roof and the burned bodies of two people were found by the fire service when they attended to put out the blaze.

The people of Ensley had had enough and formed an action group to pressure the council to sort the mess out. Ensley was a solid Conservative area and the council was run by the Conservatives so the Victorian work house site became a red hot political item. There followed months of council debate with no signs of a solution any time soon. The pressure group kept pressing, the local press made it front-page headlines and the Labour members of council took every opportunity to use it to hammer the conservatives for their ineptitude. After years of debate and a prolonged press campaign the council finally came to a conclusion: it would sell the site for housing. Why it had taken so long to make such an obvious decision was never explained and the 'Ensley Mafia' went quiet but kept watching.

With ready cash available, up stepped Douglas Holmes-Penrose, who just happened to be the husband of Magdoline Holmes-Penrose, the patient Ben was on his way to visit. The old Victorian building was demolished without delay and Holmes-Penrose's company, Enterprise Developments, submitted a planning application for the construction of forty-eight houses on the site. The Ensley Mafia swung into action and raised all sorts of objections. It was fair to say that Enterprise Developments had 'a finger in all sorts of pies' involving numerous small businesses that operated in and around Exworth. Many small businessmen had good reason to regret getting involved with Holmes-Penrose and his company as they lost control and found that they were subjected to asset stripping and quite often eventual bankruptcy.

Holmes-Penrose had never been charged with anything illegal but had developed a reputation for being a ruthless entrepreneur. He made regular generous donations to Conservative Party funds, had joined the Freemasons and it was rumoured that he was getting ever nearer to being mentioned in the honours list. He considered himself to be a man of influence and as such thought his proposals for the site would proceed without a hitch. However, he was considered by many to be a bully and was generally disliked. He had considered that planning permission for his proposals would go forward without difficulty but he had grossly underestimated the opposition of the Ensley community and the residents of Rochester Road in particular. Rochester Road was a narrow road which was the only way into the site and was a dead end. The sheer volume of traffic that forty-eight new houses would produce caused his original plans to be rejected.

The next proposals put before the planning committee caused a major hiatus, with reactions from all sorts of people and the local papers had a field day and there was even some interest from one or two of the nationals. The ancient woodland on the hill beyond the site formed a natural barrier between Rochester Road in Ensley and the large recreation field that acted as the hub of all sorts of amateur sport in Exworth. The compact woodland prevented the diverse activities from interfering with each other and the status quo worked to everyone's satisfaction. The exception being Holmes-Penrose, who was now suggesting clearing the woodland and putting in a link road joining Rochester Road across the recreation land and joining up with one of the major roads through Exworth. The reaction was predictable and instantaneous. The Ensley Mafia did not want their peaceful lives disturbed by a through road, with every likelihood of it developing into a rat run. The Naturalists of Exworth insisted that the rare and precious woodland had to be protected at all cost and the recreation field sportsmen did not want the inconvenience of their activities being contaminated by a roadway. The new proposals were also rejected.

At this juncture of his muses, Ben had turned into Rochester Road and the eventual use of the site opened up before him. The final agreed plan was far removed from Holmes-Penrose's original intention, to fill the site with almost fifty little boxes. The site was now taken up with five large, detached houses, each set in its own sizeable garden and surrounded by high fences fronted by double electrically operated gates. The houses were set in an arch with the centre one set furthest back and a little higher than the others. Four of the houses were in darkness but the centre one was lit up like a Christmas tree and the gates were wide open.

Ben drove up the drive and pulled up behind a row of vehicles. As he got out of the car he was met by Sean Summers who he knew quite well from several casual conversations in Joe's from time to time.

'Hi Ben, we have got a real handful here tonight. It's certainly not going to be easy and that bloke inside there isn't going to make it any easier. Come and sit in the cab and I will fill you in on what we have got.' Sean's modern ambulance with its logo SS Private Ambulance Service along the side was the front vehicle on the drive way and Ben climbed aboard and couldn't stop himself complimenting on its quality.

'Yes, it's the newest one in my fleet and just as well, as that bloke inside is a right bloody snob, all he seems to be worried about is his own reputation. Do you know he even asked me to sign a guarantee that I wouldn't speak to the press? I ask you what an idiot, he didn't seem at all worried about the patient, his wife. She is a real cracker by the way and years younger than him but she really seems off her trolley and has done a good job of smashing the place up. Old Dr Arnold is doing his best to calm her down but the husband and Dr Westbourne have left him to it and were enjoying a drop of scotch in another room when I last saw them. This is a one-off for me as most of my work is carrying injured people returning from holidays abroad for insurance companies. I also get to move a lot of dead people around the country often when they have passed away on cruises, but I am a bit out of my depth with this situation so I will be advised by you.'

Sean and his uniformed driver followed Ben through the rather grand front door and were immediately confronted by signs of devastation. It looked like a hurricane had passed along the hallway. Furniture had been overturned, pictures pulled from the walls and their glass smashed and what had once been an enormous glass vase full of roses was now reduced to shards of glass and a mess of broken flowers lying in a pool of water. The three of them tiptoed through the confusion and went to confront their patient who could be heard spouting a jumble of meaningless words in the room at the end of hall.

Whatever Ben had been anticipating it was nothing like the sight that confronted him. His immediate thought was that he could quite see why Sean Summers had described the patient as 'a cracker'. She was like something out of a glossy fashion magazine. For a start she was almost six feet tall, slim with small breasts and a tiny waist and very long legs. Her hair was jet black and cropped close to her head but the most striking thing about her was her outfit. She was dressed in a psychedelic full-body stocking in vivid oranges and yellows which covered her from neck to feet and fitted like a second skin. In her manic state of agitation Ben couldn't help but notice that she appeared to be wearing no underwear as her nipples were clearly visible through the material. Normally, Ben would have found having such a dramatic beauty so nearby titillating but he found himself feeling anxious and uncertain as to how to proceed. Meanwhile, Magdoline paced the floor rambling in some sort of mish-mash language and striking out at any furniture or ornaments that got in her way. Ben had read about people suffering a psychotic episode suddenly starting to 'talk in tongues' and there had been several hypotheses suggested about the origins of this behaviour. He had never seen it in action before and had no idea of the best way to proceed. But as it happened it was Magdoline who took the initiative and her actions took him totally by surprise.

It was as if she had suddenly become aware of his presence in the room and her constant ravings came to an abrupt halt. She moved towards him with slow purposeful strides and stopping just in front of him reached up to run her fingers gently through his beard. He didn't dare to move, not even to flinch but it took considerable effort on his part to appear to remain calm. Then as if having reached a decision Magdoline let out what can only be described as a hoot of joy and fell on her knees before him and exclaimed loudly in perfect English, 'You have come. I hoped and prayed you would and now you are here. You are my saviour.'

Then she wrapped her arms around Ben's legs and pressed her face into his crotch. This was all a bit too much for Ben to cope with without his body reacting in some totally inappropriate way and he hurriedly put his hands under her arms and gently eased her up and led her over to a settee. Fortunately she co-operated easily with all her attention given over to staring straight at Ben with a beaming smile of sheer joy. Old Dr Arnold was the first other person to react and he moved across the room to sit beside her and attempt to get her attention. Whilst she was a little distracted Ben slipped out of the room, having first quickly reassured her that he would be back very soon. Dr Westbourne and Magdoline's husband were sitting at the kitchen breakfast bar sipping glasses of scotch with a half full bottle between them.

Ben opened his briefcase and pulled out the necessary forms for a section 25 assessment order for the two doctors to complete and sign and passed Dr Westbourne his copy to fill in. He huffed and puffed a bit and even asked whether all the paperwork was really necessary as she was going to be admitted to a private clinic where he was a member of the management team. Ben enjoyed being able to remind him that it was a legal requirement if they felt she required a compulsory admission. It became clear just how unfamiliar Dr Westbourne was with the procedure and Ben had to guide him through the completion of the form. Dr Arnold joined them in the kitchen at this point and completed his form with the confidence of a seasoned general practitioner.

Ben managed to get the bones of a social history from Holmes-Penrose but it was a bit like drawing teeth and his replies to Ben's enquiries were almost totally devoid of any feeling or emotion. Ben went back into the other room to find Magdoline still on the settee with Steve on one side and his driver on the other. As soon as she saw him she leapt to his feet and came and stood beside him. The two doctors prepared to leave and Dr Westbourne's closing comment to Holmes-Penrose was very informative: 'See you at the lodge on Friday, Douglas.'

Holmes-Penrose's reply confirmed their link, 'Fine, Rowan, I suggest we meet in the bar for a drink before the meeting starts.'

It suddenly became clear to Ben why Dr Westbourne had turned out to make a domiciliary visit at some ungodly hour. They were both Freemasons and that was enough for Dr Westbourne to change the habit of a lifetime. Unfortunately, that left Ben to wonder about whose best interests were being served by the order being made. From his experience of her behaviour so far he felt that there was every possibility of Magdoline being psychotic but he had to wonder whether Holmes-Penrose's uncaring attitude towards his wife was a major contributing factor. He had advised Ben that Magdoline was in fact his second wife and that they had been together for less than four years. He went on to explain that his first wife of twenty years had committed suicide whilst being treated for severe depression at Barrow Hospital near Bristol. She had simply walked out of the hospital and apparently had walked several miles to the Clifton Suspension Bridge and without hesitation had jumped straight off into the river many feet below. Ben was amazed at the way Holmes-Penrose showed no emotion whilst telling him this and Ben formed the impression that he was a complete and utter cold fish. In reply to Ben's questions he had answered that he met Magdoline within a year of his first wife's death, he said through a dating agency, and they were married soon after meeting.

In reply to further questions from Ben he rather reluctantly went on to explain that Magdoline was an immigrant from Romania and had been working as a hostess in the night clubs around Soho. When they set up home together she had seemed very happy at first and took a lot of interest in running their home. However, she had no contact with her family back in Romania and he had actively resisted her maintaining any contact with her friends in London. She had not fitted in well with the circle of people that Holmes-Penrose sought to develop and he admitted that they rarely went out together. Ben suspected that Magdoline had been viewed as attractive 'arm candy' by her husband and he had lived to regret his decision to remarry.

With the doctors having both left, it was up to Ben to explain to Magdoline what was happening, but it was doubtful whether she had taken in what he had told her. She simply stood beside him and stared into his face with a rather bizarre look of deep satisfaction. Mr Holmes-Penrose resisted Ben's suggestion that he should travel with his wife in the ambulance opting to follow behind in his car. Ben did wonder how much he had had to drink and whether he was safe to drive, but he had enough to worry about with controlling Magdoline's admission without worrying about Holmes-Penrose risking his licence.

The inside of the ambulance was only dimly lit but Magdoline followed Ben in and sat down close to him on the side bench seat without hesitation. Sean sat on her other side and helped her into her safety belt before both Ben and him fixed their belts too. From long experience they both knew how bumpy rides in ambulances could be. Once he had closed the rear doors on them, the driver set off and the journey proceeded at a pace well within the speed limit. Neither Ben nor Sean had ever been to the Windsor Clinic before but were both aware of its reputation as an exclusive sanatorium based in a large country house on the far reaches of Exworth. The atmosphere in the ambulance became quite relaxed but none of them felt any need to converse.

Part way into the journey Magdoline reached across and took Ben's hand in hers and began to run her finger nails gently along his palm. The passage of her nails began to get more firm and suddenly she stuck her nails in with terrific force and the bright red of her nail varnish was joined by Ben's oozing blood. He ripped his hand away and swore loudly, only to be interrupted by Magdoline screaming, 'Where are the scars of the nails? You have no scars on your hands. You can't be Jesus, you must be the devil!'

She jerked herself forward and somehow broke free of the seat belt before diving for the back doors in an attempt to get out. Sean was the nearest to her and managed to drag her back from the door, meanwhile Ben ignored the pain in his hand to release himself and join in the fray. Between the two of them they were able to get her down on the stretcher and lay across her in an undignified heap and just about managed to prevent her from bucking free.

The driver had become aware of the hiatus and had rapidly increased his speed and turned on the blue lights and the siren. The remainder of the journey only took about ten minutes but it seemed a lot longer and the constant whooping of the siren just added to the chaos. Sean shouted through to the driver to kill the siren and in the relative quiet that followed told him to radio back to base to ask the staff member on duty to ring the Windsor to prepare them for a difficult arrival.

To give them their credit, the Windsor Clinic staff were on the ball and there were three uniformed staff waiting on their arrival. The two female nurses and a male nurse took in the situation and sprung into action and within seconds Magdoline was on the receiving end of an injection through her body stocking and into her rump. The wail of anguish from Magdoline told Ben that it was probably Valium, which he had witnessed being used before, and had been informed then that it was painful but effective. Magdoline went quiet, appearing to have fallen asleep and was carried into a small side room on the ambulance stretcher. One of the nurses spotted Ben's injured hand and insisted on sterilising the wound and covering it with neat strapping. Once this had been done and the paperwork duly dealt with Ben went out of the clinic to get a lift back to his car but the ambulance was no longer there. Instead there was Holmes-Penrose pacing up and down and constantly consulting his watch as if he couldn't wait to get away.

'So there you are, you took your time. I sent the ambulance off as I didn't see paying for it to provide you with a taxi service. You can come back with me as I need to have a word anyway.'

Ben felt mentally, physically and emotionally drained and was past worrying about whether Holmes-Penrose was sober enough to be driving. He sat in the front of the top of the range Jaguar and belted up in anticipation of a hairy drive but in fact that never happened as the journey that followed was comfortably within the speed limit. Holmes-Penrose was alert enough to realise that driving around at this time of the night in a fast car would be likely to attract the attention of any patrolling police car and one appeared in the rear-view mirror as if by magic. It followed the Jaguar for a few minutes before turning off to look for prey elsewhere.

Unfortunately, it had the effect of starting Holmes-Penrose talking and once started he droned on and on, basically appearing to attempt to convince Ben of what a brilliant operative he was. Most of it went over Ben's head but he pricked up his ears when Holmes-Penrose started to talk about his development of the old Victorian workhouse site. He claimed that the building of the five detached houses had always been his intention and Ben couldn't resist mentioning the earlier proposals for about fifty smaller homes. Holmes-Penrose seemed amazed that

Ben knew about the history of the site and quickly claimed that the final development had been a major success as once he had sold the other four houses he had acquired his at a 'knocked-down' price. Ben let it pass and closed his eyes and enjoyed the warmth and comfort of a first-class ride. Holmes-Penrose talked on and on but it was all about him and he never once mention any concern for his wife. Ben hypothesised to himself that Magdoline must have seen Holmes-Penrose as a comfortable and secure life far removed from what she had been enduring in the seedy atmosphere of Soho. For his part, Holmes-Penrose probably saw the young attractive woman as an asset in his consistent aim to present as a successful entrepreneur. Sadly, both seemed to have missed out and it was difficult to imagine where their future lay.

When the car stopped they were back at the house and Ben started to get out but Holmes-Penrose told him to wait a while.

'As you know, Ben, I am well known in Exworth and the last thing I want is any bad publicity, so I am relying on you to keep what happened here tonight out of the press.'

At this point he reached into his pocket and attempted to hand Ben some banknotes. Ben was furious and pushed his hand aside quite forcibly. '

I am a professional social worker and confidentiality is my byword, I certainly do not need a bribe to do my job properly. Good night, Mr Holmes-Penrose, I think my work here is finished. Why don't you try and consider how Magdoline is feeling and perhaps you could give her some of your attention, as she is your wife after all.' Ben climbed into his car and drove straight off without a backward glance. 'What an absolute shit,' he muttered to himself well out of the other man's hearing.

It was well after seven when he arrived home and he flopped down on the settee and crashed out. That was where Sandy found him a little while later and she eased his slip-ons off, covered him with a blanket and made sure the boys crept around quietly as they ate their breakfast and set off for school.

Chapter 64

The Start of an Entertaining Week

It was approaching ten in the morning when Ben jerked into consciousness as the post clattered through the letterbox and landed with a thud inside the front door. He had a thumping headache, a cramp in his neck and a rotten taste in his mouth. It took him a few moments to try and work out why he had spent the night fully dressed on the settee and initially his thoughts surrounded the suspicion that he must have had a bust up with Sandy, but then the events of the night came back to him and he confirmed his memory by examining his bandaged hand. He was still far from comfortable about the whole procedure and felt that Magdoline had been the victim of a very calculating husband. He stretched and pushed himself erect and made his way into the kitchen, recognising that he had done the whole process to the best of his ability and that Magdoline should now be receiving good professional help at the clinic. However, it looked pretty clear that her future was at the best uncertain, but it was now out of his hands.

Sandy had left everything ready for his breakfast and had also left a brief note saying she had rung Mrs Freeman to explain that he had been out on call all night and wouldn't be back in the office until after lunch. He smiled a grateful thanks and moved on with his day at a leisurely pace. Around midday Ben was in his car and approaching the hill to Highfield. Sandy had bought him some time and on the spur of the moment he turned off the road and pulled up outside Jessie's shop.

The view up The Runway was truly an amazing sight, with colour everywhere and all sorts of temporary structures seemingly to have been constructed where there had previously only been grass. The whole central island running the length of The Runway had been covered by a series of vintage fairground equipment. There were swing boats, a shooting range, a towering helter-skelter, all sorts of other sideshows and in the far distance, in the front garden of the Tower House old people's home, Ben could just make out a full-sized spectacular carousel complete with numerous golden prancing horses. The whole effect was magical and he couldn't wait to tell Jessie so.

However, when he went into the shop he was surprised to find the small space behind the counter occupied by Mary rather than Jessie. She must have found it a very tight squeeze as she was considerably larger than her soulmate but she welcomed Ben warmly as always and explained that she had taken annual leave to give Jessie a helping hand.

'She is busy from morning to night with the festival arrangements and she and her team of helpers have worked wonders and I am simply keeping our feet on the ground and making sure our normal life is maintained. If you want to have a word with her I think she is having a council of war in the other coach. Do me a favour if you will please, Ben, as I don't find it very easy to extract myself from behind this wretched counter and I need to know what drinks the group want for their elevenses.'

Avoiding making any comment about her problem of being a tight fit, he smiled, gave her a salute and headed next door.

The seating area at the far end of the second coach was occupied by Jessie, Gabriel Watson from the travelling fair, Albert and Sam Watts, the volunteer decorating cousins, and a couple of other ladies who he didn't recognise. They were all armed with clipboards with long lists on them most of which were now crossed through. The planning was obviously at an advanced stage and the meeting looked as if it was about to break up. Ben pretended to be a waiter taking their drinks order and returned to Mary to ask for two lattes, three americanos and a black tea. Once the drinks were ready, with one for him included, he carried the tray back together with a date and walnut cake still warm from the oven for them to share. The meeting had passed the point of any other business and there was general chatting amongst the group who seemed to be very relaxed and friendly in each other's company. It was very apparent that Jessie ran a happy ship.

'If you like, Ben, you can come with me now to see what we have got planned as I am just about to go around to check everything is on target.'

The grand tour followed and Ben couldn't help but be impressed with all that he saw, as it appeared that they had thought of everything. Just outside of Jessie's shop a small group of scouts were busy putting up a bell tent with canvas sheeting, forming a secure enclosure around it. Jessie explained that on the day this was going to be a first-aid tent manned by the local Red Cross. It was also going to double as a lost child centre and would be equipped with a megaphone to summon the families of any such children. The whole length of the central grass land was now completely covered by vintage equipment which had all been loaned by Gabriel Watson and her family. She had been delighted to get it out of moth balls as none of it had been used since her sons had taken over the travelling fair following her husband's death. Albert and Sam had been working on it for weeks and it all looked very attractive with its highly painted panels and refurbished traditional artistry and signage.

Along each side of the pavements were a series of tables and stalls which were so far unused, but Jessie explained that they were intended to be used for all manner of refreshments, craft work, bric-a-brac and information about the work of various voluntary groups such as the British Legion. As they walked along The Runway Jessie came to an abrupt halt on the corner of Spitfire Close and pointed up towards the prefab belonging to the Collins brothers Daniel and Joseph.

'Can you see anything different about their prefab since you were last here, Ben?'

At first glance he could only see the immaculate paintwork and the total absence of graffiti but that was nothing new as it had been like that for weeks. Then he spotted what Jessie was alluding to. In the short drive, by the side of the prefab, the battered old disability vehicle had been replaced by a shiny Mini car in British racing green. Joseph's union rep at the fruit market had succeeded in getting him his insurance pay out and the two brothers now had something very practical to look forward to when they eventually got home. Jessie had heard from Joseph only a couple of days before and told Ben that he was hoping to be discharged home very soon. He was then planning to get his brother home for weekend leave and if all went well to have him back home in time for Christmas. Jessie and Ben talked the situation over and agreed that the Battle of Britain celebrations could have proved difficult for the brothers as neither had good memories of their involvement in the war.

They walked on and at the top end of the road were confronted by the magnificent spectacle of the massive golden carousel which had taken over the Tower House garden.

'It's wonderful isn't it?' said Jessie. 'And we are so lucky to have it here as it is very rare and very valuable. It's Victorian and is still driven by that fantastic steam-driven organ over there. It is the only ride left by their father that Gabriel's sons still use. Gabriel delights in reminding them that it brings in more money than any of their new-fangled rides. It tends to be rented out at huge cost to private functions up and down the country and I understand that it has even been placed at Buckingham Palace and Windsor Castle from time to time. Gabriel had to put her foot down with the boys to get them to bring it here but she reminded them that technically she was the boss.'

Jessie and Ben wandered around the whole site with her giving words of encouragement to all the helpers they passed. 'And now, Ben, what do you think of this?' and she stopped at the entrance of a prefab which had high hedges surrounding it. There, tucked in on the short driveway, was a genuine gypsy caravan, complete with canvas canopy and a flight of steps leading up to a wooden door with an intricate stain glass panel. 'This is Gabriel's pride and joy and will be occupied by the world-renowned fortune teller Madame Zara, alias Gabriel, on Saturday, so why don't you give it a try when you come?'

Ben was confident that he would be giving that a miss but was equally sure that Sandy would be a customer as she was a keen fan of all things to do with fortune telling and horoscopes. By the time he was back in his car he could really feel the excitement brewing. All that was needed was a fine day and it had all the makings of a truly memorable occasion.

When Ben arrived back at office he was a little concerned that the only ones in occupation were Alice, Ernest and The Champ, who were having their lunch in the kitchen. The unmanned offices were potentially vulnerable to an opportunistic thief but Ben was instantly reassured by the immediate arrival of The Champ coming to check on who had arrived. His most suspicious attitude quickly changed to a frantically wagging tail and a brief but warm show of affection before the call of his lunch demanded his return to the kitchen. Alice called out that Phil and Susie were both in the club next door setting up things for the Thursday meeting. Mrs Freeman was no doubt getting her husband's lunch so Ben returned to his office for a few more moments of peace and quiet to ponder further on the events of the night.

No sooner had he sat down than the sound of music started to come in through his partly opened window. The record being played was all too familiar to him and instantly took him back to his student days. He had not been a particularly conscientious student and always seemed to be having to seek time extensions to get his work in. This became an issue in his second year with his tutors threatening all sorts of dire consequences if he failed to conform. Ben was aware that he was at fault but he was easily distracted and all too ready to put off until tomorrow what really should be done today. Fortunately, he was already in a full-blown relationship with Sandy and was also living in the same student house as his friend Andy. The two of them hatched a plan to get Ben up to the mark on his course and still have time for a little fun. Basically, he had to study for three hours on every Tuesday, Wednesday and Thursday nights leaving a long weekend for the more pleasant activities of student life. To sweeten the pie, Andy loaned Ben his redundant old Dansette record player that he had replaced with a fancy state of the art stereo system financed by Andy's absent and somewhat guilty rich father.

The record player came complete with a handful of American long players grabbed at random from Andy's extensive collection. The plan was simple but effective: Ben would shut himself in his room on the specified days and would play background music whilst he worked. His housemates agreed not to approach him when they could hear music coming from his room and Sandy would be the only one allowed to drop in from time to time to provide occasional refreshments. The plan worked and his tutors were suitably impressed at his apparent improvement. The records Andy had loaned were a mixed bunch and included singers familiar to Ben like Elvis, Sinatra and the Everly Brothers. But two artists soon became his favourite musical accompaniment. Nat King Cole and Paul Robeson were both Black Americans and both were mainly performing in the first half of the twentieth century but they were very different artists. Nat King Cole had a voice like honey and sang melodious ballads that surrounded the listener like a comfortable blanket. Ben's all-time favourite was 'Unforgettable' and he had been genuinely sad to hear of Cole's death just a few months ago in February at the age of just forty-six. Paul Robeson, a bass baritone, was still alive and largely sang Black spirituals such as 'Old Man River' in a unique, deep, soul-searching voice. Ben had loved both singers and played their records over and over again. He suspected that his housemates were probably heartedly sick of hearing the same songs but he really didn't care as it worked well for him. Andy, as ever, couldn't resist telling Ben obscure facts about both artists from his encyclopaedic knowledge of all things to do with American pop. He pointed out that Elvis was the only real king of pop and that Nat Cole had only gained the middle name of King from the nursery rhyme 'Old King Cole'. Paul Robeson had been an outspoken activist against racism in America and had bravely even questioned why Black Americans should fight for their country in the Second World War when they were subjected to such racism by white Americans. As a consequence, he had been accused of being a communist, which at the time nearly finished his career as an entertainer.

Ben was quite content to sit at his desk and to sing along to the dulcet tones of Nat King Cole and was pleased to realise that he was still almost word perfect. As he sang along he reached for paper and pen and began an outline of last night's admission in preparation for dictating a report to Mrs Freeman later in the afternoon. Normally, he would do his dictation using only the briefest of factual notes but he wanted to record his concerns about the way Magdoline's husband had controlled the situation the previous night and his apparent lack of concern for her wellbeing. He felt he had to choose his words carefully, just in case there was some sort of problem in the future. As far as he could see the admission had been quite lawful but he was left with a bad taste in his mouth by the way it had been set up.

After a while, the music came to a stop and Ben wandered along to the club room in anticipation of sharing with Susie his enjoyment of Nat King Cole, but to his surprise it was Phil's record that had been playing and it showed a soft side to her that Ben had never seen before. By way of explanation she rather shyly shared that the record was very special to her as it had been the first gift that her partner Lizzie had given her when they had first started courting. Ben realised that this was the first time Phil had shared anything of her home life with him and he enjoyed telling her all about why Nat King Cole was special to him. This brief exchange of intimacy between them seemed to be of satisfaction to them both and Phil hastily moved on to explain that they were planning to end each club meeting with music, which might just become a mini dance session. 'We don't have the funds to buy a player so I am using mine for now. However, we are thinking of trying to collect green shield stamps in the hope of being able to save up for one. Mind you it might take a while.'

She ended with a warm giggle and Ben returned to do his dictation, feeling that there had been something of a breakthrough in his relationship with Phil, but felt it was sad that it had taken the best part of two years to happen!

Mrs Freeman returned from lunch soon after and she came straight down to join Ben in his office, together with the day's post for him to look through and with her shorthand book ready to take dictation. Ben had no reservations about his relationship with her and felt that their shared understanding was the result of many months working in harmony. The post was mainly departmental edicts which rarely effected the workings of their small, isolated office. Still, all needed to be read through in case there was some hidden potential problem before they were either filed away, never to see the light of day again, or were placed at once on the pile of useless paper awaiting shredding by Alice. Today's contribution all went the way of Alice and would at least give her some pleasure, as she had become passionate about shredding.

The dictation took longer than usual as Ben was still suffering from lack of sleep and kept stopping and starting. Mrs Freeman read the signs and once they had finished went off and returned with a black coffee containing a generous amount of sugar. Ben nodded his thanks and was left to cat nap as she closed his door on her way out. Ben recalled that he had recently read that Winston Churchill had cat napped throughout his years as prime minister during the demanding war years. If it was good enough for Churchill then it was good enough for him, and he closed his eyes and lowered his face on to the blotter on his desk top. The coffee went untouched and Ben went to sleep.

Mrs Freeman ensured that none of the others disturbed him and let him be until 4.30 pm when she knocked on his door, waited a while and then let herself in. She thought that Ben looked a bit like he had a hangover but knew full well that that was not the case. She reminded him that it was a Tuesday and that Sandy would want him home on time to take over the care of the boys. Tuesday was her night school class night and she really valued it as it involved meeting with a regular group of friends and a few drinks afterwards in the local pub the King's Arms on the corner at the far end of their road. With only token resistance, Ben allowed himself to be eased off home and drove off rather slower than usual as he felt pretty muzzy headed. When he turned into his home road he was surprised to see a large car parked right outside his house exactly where he would normally park. He pulled up behind it feeling an unreasonable amount of anger at being usurped, but as soon as he recognised the car as Patsie's Mercedes his attitude softened completely.

The boys were just up the road involved with a small group of friends in an intense conker competition. The gutter was liberally scattered with the results of previous battles and Ben couldn't help but feel sorry for the extra work it caused old Joe, their regular road sweeper. There was no sign of the ladies when he went in but he could hear their chatter from upstairs as he walked into the kitchen. He filled the kettle and set it to boil before shouting up to them that he was making a brew.

'Hi love, thanks for a drink, we will be straight down.'

Ben had no sooner settled down on the sofa than there was a loud clattering of feet on the stairs and the apparition of two dowdy factory girls from the war years paraded into the room. Their hair was enclosed in woolly scarves tied up as turbans and their bodies were dressed in layers of baggy grey jumpers and ankle-length skirts which totally camouflaged their normal curves. They did a slow twirl in front of him which revealed the black lines drawn on the back of their legs as a substitute for stockings. Finally, they drew attention to the wartime wooden shoes they were wearing by doing a short-improvised clog dance, which explained the clatter they had caused coming down the stairs. They then posed in front of Ben in a pseudo provocative manner and Sandy asked Ben if he liked their new look.

Ben was genuinely impressed by the effort they had made and gave them three cheers and a resounding clap of approval. Then Patsie piped up, 'Well my boy, you ain't seen nothing yet, Are you ready, Sandy? One two three.' And in perfect unison the two of them turned around, hoisting their skirts above their heads to display a matching pair of knee-length red flannel bloomers and proceeded to provocatively wiggle their bums in the manner of the famous Folies Bergère dancers of Paris.

After a few moments they dropped their skirts back down and Patsie turned and rather teasingly said, 'Just look at his face, Sandy. I think we confused the boy.'

The two of them returned upstairs giggling like a couple of schoolgirls.

The reality for Ben was the experience had all the sexual charm of a performance by the comedy drag artist of the 30s, 40s and 50s Arthur Lucan. He had made a successful career of dressing up as an old Irish washer woman 'Old Mother Riley' of music hall fame and numerous short black and white films. However, Ben had felt genuine embarrassment at the sight of them lifting their skirts as it had immediately reminded him of Susie climbing up into the prefab roof at Spitfire Close. The image of her legs, stocking tops, suspenders and pert round bottom in its pure white knickers was not one he wanted to recall in front of anyone and certainly not Sandy.

Fortunately, the girls had been preoccupied by their display and Ben covered his confusion by going to make the tea. By the time Patsie had set off for home, Sandy was running late and was happy to consume the toast and tea Ben had prepared for her and there was no time for any chatting as she hurried out of the door. Ben heard her call out goodbye to the boys, who in no time at all appeared in the kitchen in the hope of getting their usual Tuesday tea from the chippy up the road. For no particular reason, Ben decided to go one better and the three of them ate high, by a rare visit to Harry Ramsden's. The rest of the evening went in peaceful harmony and all three of them were in their beds by the time Sandy got home from the pub.

She was in good spirits when she appeared in the bedroom and Ben quickly gave up on the book he had been laying there reading. Sandy had clearly enjoyed her evening with her friends and was full of chat all about other members of her class, who Ben didn't know from Adam or more accurately from Eve as it was an all female group. Ben propped himself on the headboard and struggled to give the impression of concentrating on Sandy's gossip. In reality he simply enjoyed watching her undress ready for bed. It was one of his simple pleasures, that he had unfailingly enjoyed very many times over the years.

As her conversation slowly dried up she appeared to become aware of his interest and began to play along with it. She sat on the bed with her breasts exposed by her nightdress buttons being undone and proceeded to brush her hair with long steady strokes. Ben decided that there was only so much a man could take and the consequences were inevitable. After a most satisfactory coming together, they cuddled down satiated but still not quite ready for sleep. Sandy asked Ben what he had thought of Patsie and her costumes as wartime factory girls.

Ben confirmed his previous reaction but did ask where the red flannel bloomers had come from. Sandy laughed and told him that they had come from Ma Driscoll and Ben was more than surprised as she was such a tiny little lady and the bloomers were massive. Sandy went on to explain that they had belonged to Ma's mother, who had had them specially made to wear in winter when she was working in the shop before the war. At that time the only heating in the premises had been a coal fire in the back room and the door to the shop remained fixed back the whole time they were open. Apparently, the first thing Ma had done when she had inherited the shop was to get central heating installed and had it topped up by an electric fire next to her stool at the counter. Thus the bloomers had become redundant and remained so until they had resurfaced to be borrowed for the Battle of Britain costumes. The last thing Sandy said before turning over was that she had arranged for him to call in on his parents on the way home the next day to collect some bits and pieces for the boys and his costumes. Ben felt pretty sleepy and his last thoughts before he dropped off were that he hoped he would remember to call in at his parents the following day.

Chapter 65

The Build-up to the Weekend

The trip to the office on the Wednesday was far from easy. Every traffic light seemed to be against him and for some unknown reason the traffic was even heavier than usual. To add to the confusion, there was a serious water leak on the final approach to Highfield which had caused ever-increasing flooding on the roadway. Some bright spark had contrived to break down in the deepest part of the flood water, effectively reducing the traffic flow to a single lane. From his place in the line of waiting cars Ben was able to witness all sorts of pent-up frustrations displayed by his fellow travellers but against all odds he was able to see the funny side of what was happening all around him. He turned the radio over to a classical music programme and just chilled out. He grinned to himself in recognition that he was still enjoying the aftereffects of his previous night's bedroom gymnastics with Sandy. He arrived at the office some thirty minutes late but in a comfortable unpressurised state. The day turned out to be a very low-key affair with him taking the opportunity to make several routine visits to some of his less demanding clients. There proved to be no nasty surprises and he finished the day back in the office with a lengthy dictation session with Mrs Freeman that brought him bang up to date.

His relaxed mood had stayed with him all day and he set off home in good time, content to virtually allow the old Cortina to set its own pace. The floods had been dealt with and the traffic flowed as normal and he was within spitting distance of home when he remembered his need to call in on his parents. A sharp about turn saved him having to confess he had forgotten and ten minutes later he was parking alongside the allotments where he felt sure he would find his dad. Sure enough he found him 'chewing the fat' with his old railway mate Arnold, on their usual perches outside Roger's shed. The Union Jack was flying from Arnold's flagpole, presumably to mark the forthcoming Battle of Britain celebrations. A chair and a bottle of beer appeared for him as if by magic with scarcely a break in their conversation about boxing, which was one of their favourite subjects.

Roger explained that they were debating who their favourite sportsmen were in each of various sports. They had only just started by selecting their favourite boxers, and they had already produced a shortlist of three but were bent on selecting the top two in each sport. 'So let's have your ideas, Ben, who would you choose from the world of boxing?'

Roger shared his list of potential candidates by starting with Rocky Marciano, who had been the world champion back in the day and had the distinction of being undefeated throughout his career for a total of forty-nine fights. Ben was suitably impressed but it had all happened whilst he a was a small boy so it was of no personal interest to him and he just nodded and waited for his dad to go on. Arnold took over the discussion, with the nomination of Sugar Ray Robinson, another American ex-world champion, this time at middleweight, who once fought ninety-one times consecutively without being beaten. Again, Ben felt out of his depth as it had all happened before his time so once again he remained silent. Arnold passed the discussion back to Roger, whose final name selected was much more familiar to Ben, namely that of Henry Cooper. Now here Ben felt he had something to say, as he had recently watched the fight between him and the rising heavyweight star from America, Cassius Clay.

Clay was an athlete with all sorts of attributes the like of which had never been seen before in the boxing ring. He was only twenty-one, very fast on his feet, looked like a film star and had never been knocked down, but one of his more unusual characteristics was that he was very articulate, which he used to great effect to ridicule his opponents before each of his bouts. In the case of his fight with Cooper he had called him 'a tramp, a bum and a cripple not worth training for'.

The result of this affront against one of Britain's most popular fighters 'Our Henry' was that the Wembley Stadium was sold out to 35,000 spectators for the fight. The fight itself was to live in the memories of all those who witnessed it as it was full of incident. The two of them fought twice and Ben had sat down with his father to watch the recording of the first fight a couple of years ago. Clay had come with a formidable reputation, having won his previous nineteen bouts fifteen by knockouts, in addition he had a twenty pound weight and over a four inch reach advantage over Cooper but his dad had been convinced that Cooper would annihilate 'the young pretender'. The fight had started with Cooper on the attack and the first three rounds were mainly Clay ducking and weaving to stay out of trouble. As the fight progressed Clay began to get a series of blows into Cooper's face and particularly around his eyes, which had always been a particularly vulnerable area for Cooper. He began to bleed excessively from above his eyes and his vision was impaired by the blood running down his face. The fourth round was going Clay's way with him adopting a style that he later described as 'floating like a butterfly and stinging like a bee'. Then suddenly towards the end of the round Cooper caught him with a massive left hook, which lifted Clay off the ground and left him flat on his back on the floor.

The bell saved Clay but he appeared to be badly shaken and his corner worked frantically to bring him around. Some observers claimed that his seconds used smelling salts, which was strictly against the rules. This was never substantiated but what did delay the restart of the fight was damage to one of Clay's gloves which had to be fixed which gave him a few more precious seconds to recover. The fight was stopped in the fifth round with Cooper bleeding profusely from a two-inch cut over his eye. Clay went on to become world heavyweight champion a few months later by spectacularly beating the then champion the formidable Sonny Liston. Ben felt he had made a good case for Clay, now known as Muhammed Ali, because he was following the teachings of Islam, to be added to the list but both Roger and Arnold remained unconvinced. Roger was particularly critical of Clay's verbal attacks on his opponents and this seemed to outweigh any recognition of his obvious exceptional boxing ability. Ben attempted to explain that success at sport at a world-class level was changing and it was no longer just a matter of displaying technical ability. It was now big business. There were huge sums of money involved and the general public demanded entertainment. Clay's overt antics provided this dramatically and his behaviour helped to attract the 'box office' that was the lifeblood of the boxing scene. Ben also pointed out that Clay had retracted his abusive comments about Cooper and when interviewed after the fight went on to praise him and to describe him as the toughest fighter he had ever met.

Roger and Arnold remained unconvinced. Ben resumed his silence and the discussion moved on to consider the most famous footballers. Ben sat back to slurp his beer and let the conversation flow around him. He began to realise that this conversation was a sort of game that the two men must have played repeatedly over the years of their friendship. They seemed to be in total agreement but used it as an opportunity to remind each other of interesting little facts associated with each person they identified. It appeared to be simply a way of having a trip down memory lane for them and the inclusion of him in the discussion was no more than a courtesy on their part. The discussion on the footballers seemed to fully confirm his hypothesis. The speed in which the two friends got to their shortlist of footballers clearly indicated that they were going over familiar territory. Ben could quite understand their first choice, as he was already well aware of Stanley Mathews background and the fact that he was still playing professional football at the ripe old age of fifty. Nevertheless, both men enjoyed sharing their knowledge with him, delighting in throwing odd bits of miscellaneous information into their debate. In a matter of moments he had learnt that Mathews played at outside right, initially for Stoke from 1932 to 1947 and then for Blackpool up until 1962 when he returned to Stoke. During those years he had won fifty-four England caps, the last when he was aged an amazing forty-two years old. He was considered to be the greatest dribbler ever and was knighted when still playing, which was an unique honour. After a while they moved on to their other choices, which were of a similar vintage but only names as far as Ben was concerned. In quick succession he learnt that Nat Lofthouse was a prolific goal scorer for his club team Bolton Wanderers and for England earning the nickname of the Lion of Vienna. He also discovered that Billy Wright had played 105 times for England, but perhaps of more interest was the fact that he had married Joy Beverly of the popular Beverly sisters.

Ben would have liked to suggest the likes of the wonderful Pele or the ever-rising star at Manchester United's George Best but in an attempt to keep within the time period that Roger and Arnold seemed to be working to came up with the name of Danny Blanchflower. He recalled that Blanchflower had been captain of the winning Spurs team that had won the double in 1961, the first time it had been done for sixty years. To add interest to his suggestion he reminded the others that Blanchflower had caused quite a stir when he had declined to take part in the television programme 'This is Your Life' leaving the presenter Eamonn Andrews clutching the famous red book live on television. The whole ethos of the programme was that it should come as a total surprise to the recipient but on this occasion the surprise was on Eamonn who was left with no one to interview. The memory raised a laugh from the two men but no addition to their shortlist and Ben realised that the selection committee was restricted to the two old friends.

The discussion moved away from football and the two men began to consider a shortlist for cricketers, which was a subject that held little interest for Ben. But he then spotted the two Hiscock sisters busy working with their hens on the allotment down from Arnold's and he was pleased to take the opportunity to make a break for it by saying that Sandy had asked him to get some of their free-range eggs.

In no time at all, he had a chicken thrust into his arms and the full attention of the two women. As always their primary interest was news of Nick and Jack and also of Sandy, all of whom they remembered by name. This was somewhat embarrassing to Ben, who remembered that the sister's names were Doris and Connie but not which was which. Fortunately the one sister said, 'I have just got to get this lot back into their house ready for the night so why don't you let Connie show you our latest project.'

He passed the contented chicken he had been smoothing back to Doris and followed Connie down the allotment to what was a large new pen and hen house almost doubling the size of their chicken complex. When Connie carefully opened the outer door of the sizeable hen house they both slipped in quickly to be surrounded by a host of young hens all busily scratching for grain in the sawdust-covered floor, drinking from the upturned water droppers or just siting gently clucking to no one in particular.

'They were all bred here on our allotment and what you are seeing is about sixty Christmas dinners which will be the tenderest meat you will find anywhere. We are already taking orders from people in the know and they will all receive a fully prepared bird ready for the oven.'

Without hesitation, Ben placed an order for one but did wonder how two elderly school teachers could decide to kill and prepare birds that they obviously cared so much about. Just as he was about to explore this further they were interrupted by the loud sound of heavy rain falling on the hen house roof. Stopping just long enough to purchase a dozen eggs he headed back up the path to his dad's shed. Rain had stopped play and the two men had already packed up. They made a hurried retreat to Ben's parked car, leaving the flag to remain in place but now hanging dejectedly wrapped around the flagpole in a soggy tangle.

The journey to Arnold's flat was taken up with the two friends updating Ben on their thoughts about their choice of cricketers. WG Grace going to bat armed with a broomstick, rather than a bat and still managing to score thirty in a charity match was their number one choice. Don Bradman, the Australian known as the Don, scoring 100 in 22 balls and Jack Hobbs, alias the Master, who was the leading run scorer and century maker in first-class cricket were all high on their list. The names just kept on coming and Ben switched off, content to concentrate on his driving through the teeming rain.

After what seemed an age but in reality was only about ten minutes Ben dropped Arnold off at his home and headed for his parent's house. Not a long journey but long enough for his dad to add another name to the list that of Arthur Milton. He emerged as a rather lesser known hero of Roger's but nevertheless one he seemed to particularly favour. He explained to Ben that Milton was one of only a handful of players who had represented England at both football and cricket.

'In those days there was no real big money to be had in either football or cricket and lots of sportsmen played both professionally just to make a reasonable living. Arthur Milton was a West Country man who played cricket for Gloucester in the summer and football for Arsenal in the winter. I met him a couple of times and he was just a lovely man, who had no side to him despite his almost unique claim to fame.'

Ben wasn't sorry to pull up outside his parent's house and to follow his father in. He couldn't remember ever hearing his dad talk so much or with such passion and although he had quite enjoyed the experience he was pleased that his mum called them straight through to the kitchen.

The smell that greeted Ben was all too familiar to him and he immediately recognised the delicious odour of his mum's special beef stew.

'Sit yourself down, Roger, you too, Ben. I have made extra especially as I knew you would be calling in to get the stuff for Saturday. It will be on the table in a minute or two.'

Ben told his mother that he better ring Sandy to let her know he would not be home for tea. However, when he rang, Sandy told him the boys had come home starving and were currently on their second round of boiled eggs with soldiers.

'I thought you and I could have a takeaway so will you please bring something in on your way home.'

Ben's mum, Anthea, had overheard the conversation and sprang into action by telling him, 'Plan B, go and relax for a while in the living room and I will sort something out for you to have with Sandy later.'

Reluctantly, he did as she suggested but his gastric juices were already in full flow and he felt rather cheated. After working her magic in the kitchen and the addition of some spices and curry powder his share of the stew had been converted into a beef curry. Mum had also cooked a portion of rice which together made a good-sized meal for them both. The meal was carefully packed into a couple of sealed Tupperware containers that Anthea said she had received months before as a gift for holding a Tupperware party in her home.

'I knew they would come in useful one day but please don't forget where they live as I would like them back.'

Ben heard his dad push his empty plate to one side and get up from the kitchen table. 'Hang on a minute, Ben, I have something for you.'

He wandered off down the garden to his shed and returned with two wartime gas mask boxes containing some battered and brittle gas masks and a carrier bag containing a variety of miss-shaped bits of metal.

'I thought you and Sandy might be able to make use of these genuine gas masks and I am sure the boys will get some good bragging rights with my shrapnel collection. It really comes home when you think of the damage any one of these bits could have caused and I collected them all from around here when I was doing my air raid warning work.'

It had stopped raining when Ben returned to his car, which was just as well as he was desperately juggling with various oddly shaped parcels as well as the additional contributions from Roger and Anthea. The parcels were wrapped in several layers of newspaper and tied securely with lengths of pink corset laces, a sure sign of Anthea having done the packing. The supper was reheated in the oven and went down a treat with Sandy and Ben. The parcels were put under the stairs to be explored the following night and by the time the boys had settled, all Sandy and Ben wanted to do was to cosy up on the sofa and doze whilst half watching a rather silly and predictable old black and white film.

Chapter 66

A Useful Volunteer Joins the Team

Ben was prepared to have to run the office for the majority of the day, in the knowledge that the Thursday Club would impact on the way the office could be manned. There was the added complication that Phil was the duty social worker for the county from 1 pm through to 9 am the following morning and could be called out on an emergency at any point during that time. Ben didn't mind manning the phone in the afternoon to allow her to get on with the club but he was determined that if any action was required then Phil would have to get on with it. He was only too aware that she didn't like being on call, as the emergencies almost always involved dealing with mental illness rather than her chosen speciality of working with the mentally handicapped. In the past she had called in sick, leaving Ben to step in to do her duty period on a couple of occasions; Ben was determined that that wouldn't happen again.

On the way into work Ben did a couple of routine visits before dropping in on Carol McBain to check that Dale had made his own way to the club as they had previously agreed. Carol appeared to be as well as he had ever seen her and she was in the middle of bathing the baby in the sink in the kitchen. They both seemed in good spirits and Carol explained that using the sink as a bathtub allowed her to utilise the hot water from her emulsion heater, which was a lot cheaper than running a bath upstairs.

'Money is still tight but it is a lot easier with just me and the kids to provide for and the change in Dale since Norman left has been wonderful. He sees himself as the man of the house and he is really helpful with the baby. He hasn't stopped talking about the club and the new friends he has made and he was up and dressed ready to go at seven this morning. I had to give him jobs to do to slow him down, otherwise he would have been there far too early. As it was he left before nine so I guess he will have been the first to arrive.'

The whole time she was talking to Ben she was playing splashing games with the baby, who returned the favour, resulting in water all over the kitchen floor. Nobody seemed to mind and Ben decided to give the childcare officer a call later in the day to describe the scene. After all, we all like to get good news from time to time rather than the doom and gloom which was a social worker's more common lot.

When he arrived at the office he was not surprised to find Mrs Freeman alone and she confirmed that Phil, Susie and Alice were all next door at the club. She didn't seem at all concerned but Ben made a mental note to remind Phil and Susie of the need to ensure that the office was properly manned at all times. Alice was a different matter altogether as she now had a foot in both camps, both as a client and a part-time member of staff as the office cleaner. She still worked many more hours than she was paid for and Ben saw no reason to interfere with her work pattern. By way of thanking Mrs Freeman for her dedication, Ben made the tea and raided the biscuit tin, which was usually controlled by Alice.

They sat one each side of Ben's desk and were comfortable in each other's company as they caught up with the news of each other's family. Mrs Freeman was happy to report that Steve, her husband, was enjoying a period of remission and was looking forward to his role as treasurer of the Thursday Club. '

He still spends long periods at home by himself but I try to leave him little jobs to do to help pass the time and he is keen on the radio. He used to enjoy reading but his vision is not what it was. However, he has now joined an audio tape club which was set up for vision impaired people and that gives him a lot of pleasure.'

Ben updated Mrs Freeman on the current activities of the Newman home and tea finished she got up to leave. No sooner had she left than she returned to say, 'I should have told you the prof's secretary, Mrs Hemsworth, rang first thing and asked to speak to you. I left it that I would get you to ring when you came in. She did say it was nothing very important but I am sorry to say it slipped my mind.'

Ben had found Mrs Hemsworth to be rather fierce at first but as the weeks had passed since he had started to assist at the prof's clinic, she had definitely softened towards him. Having said that, they were still on surname terms only. When Ben rang her she was receptive but there was no hint of chattiness and she was straight down to business.

The prof had asked her to let Ben know that there was one of his current inpatients that he would like to discuss with him at the clinic the following day. He had noted that her home address was on Ben's patch and he thought it likely that Ben would have had some previous knowledge of her. The patient was a lady currently on a section 25 assessment order at St Margaret's; her name was Wendy Tiler and she was in her mid-fifties. Ben wrote the name down on his pad and tried to recall what knowledge if any that he had of her. It was certainly a name that rang bells with him but he couldn't remember why, so he went along to Mrs Freeman to ask her to check the records.

In her usual efficient way she was soon passing a thin file over to him and he sat on her desk to read it through. All it contained was a report from one of his social worker colleagues from the main Exworth office who had dealt with the lady as an emergency whilst on standby. The report explained that the social worker had been called to the house by the local police, who had broken in after a neighbour had reported a strong smell of gas. Mrs Tiler had been found slumped over the kitchen table with all the gas taps and the cooker turned on but unlit. The gas was no longer escaping as the meter had run out of money. After domiciliary visits by the duty psychiatrist and the GP, Mrs Tiler had been admitted to St Margaret's for assessment. When Ben had received the report three weeks before it had all seemed fairly straightforward and he knew the hospital social workers would be dealing with her whilst she was in hospital. They would undoubtedly contact him if there was any need to follow up later on so he had passed the report to Mrs Freeman for filing. In the hope of finding out a little more, Ben rang Roger Richards, the local police constable, to see if he could give him any additional information. Roger was as ever very approachable but admitted to feeling exhausted as he had spent most of the night trying to apprehend a couple of youths who were tearing around the estate on a stolen motorbike.

'I know they are local kids, as they knew every shortcut, alleyway and narrow lane, which they used to great effect to avoid me every time I got near to them in the police car. I did finally recover the motorbike but they were long gone. I have my suspicions who they may have been, but unless they left fingerprints that's all I have got for now. Still, enough of my troubles, Ben, what can I do for you?'

Ben explained about trying to find out a little more about the incident with Wendy Tiler. Roger expressed his surprise that Ben wasn't familiar with Mrs Tiler, who he described as a miserable woman who seemed determined to stir up trouble for everyone who she came across.

'I have received numerous accusations from her about all sorts of people on the estate to say they were involved in criminal activity. Initially, I followed up on her complaints but could never find any evidence to support them and I ended up cautioning her for wasting police time, what I can tell you, Ben, is that I am very doubtful that she actually attempted to gas herself. The gas had run out when we broke in but when I checked the meter there was a neat little pile of shillings stacked on top ready to be used when required. I reckon it was very possibly another example of her making a nuisance of herself. Having said that I am glad she is receiving treatment as her behaviour has always seemed disturbed to me.'

Ben thanked Roger for his background information and left him to follow up on his night time chasing. He sat back in his chair and realised that the story about Mrs Tiler rang very distinct bells with him but it was from early on when he had been working as the resettlement officer during the early days of the estate. Mrs Freeman managed to dig out from the depths of the filing system a tattered old brown file with the name Wendy Tiler written on the top-left side of the cover. It all came flooding back to Ben as he read through the rather scanty series of handwritten notes from his first few months on the Highfield Estate. He immediately recalled the sour-faced old woman who had haunted him from day one and numerous days after. She managed to make complaints about everyone and everything she had dealings with, and Ben, being new to a post that had never been properly defined, had initially felt the need to follow up and investigate each and every one of them. He had soon realised that none of the complaints had any real substance and that Mrs Tiler just delighted in causing trouble for trouble's sake. So he adopted the system, of simply saying to her 'leave it to me' and then took no further action.

The last dozen or so complaints recorded in her notes had the cryptic NFA written beside them. Mrs Tiler must have eventually realised that she was being ignored and had moved on to pastures new. Ben recalled that at the time the first Church of England minister on the estate had been an old boy called Reverend Adamson, who had come out of retirement to take up the task of running the temporary C of E church. It was based in a building that was constructed out of corrugated iron sheeting. It was painted a ghastly brown colour and its impact on Highfield had been slight with both the church and the minister being largely ignored.

Unfortunately, the impact of the community on Reverend Adamson had been much greater and he only lasted about six months before suffering a nervous breakdown. A rumour circulated in Joe's at the time was that the minister had been worn down by some 'old bitch' who had made his life a misery. Thinking about it, Ben now suspected that the infamous Mrs Tiler was a likely candidate for the role of 'old bitch'.

Once he had updated himself about Wendy Tiler, he wandered along to the club room to see how things were progressing. A quick count of heads showed him that everyone except Ernest and the Champ had attended and the whole place was a hive of activity. No doubt Ernest and the dog would arrive in time for their lunch, which Ben could smell being prepared in the kitchen. There was the background sound of softly playing music, which he recognised as being the distinctive harmony of the Everly Brothers. The long central table was where all the activity was happening and a rather diminutive older lady was moving from group to group giving advice and encouragement. There was no sign of either Phil or Susie but they didn't seem to be needed, as the little lady clearly had the situation under control.

Ben waited a while and took the scene in. He presumed that the lady was the new volunteer that Susie had brought along to the group. He remembered that her name was Helen Hancock, that she was a spinster and she ran a small knitting business from her home a few doors away from Susie's home in Little Poppy Field. She appeared to be just as Susie had described her. She was barely five-foot-tall, with grey hair twisted into a plait which she wore wrapped around her head. She was pleasantly plump without being obese and she had a smiley sort of face with tiny little glasses perched up on her forehead. The whole group were involved in doing French knitting with the boys busy hammering nails into cotton reels whilst the girls concentrated on learning the art of manipulating wool around the nails and through the reels to form long cords of wool.

Ben was just about to go over to welcome Helen when Susie suddenly came out of the kitchen, spotted Ben and came hurrying over to make the introductions. Helen's handshake was surprisingly firm but Ben was careful about how hard he squeezed as it felt tiny, just like a child's. The other instant thing he noted was her eyes, which were a combination of powder blue with a distinct grey fleck and there was an obvious twinkle to them. It gave her the appearance of someone with a warm sense of humour. First impressions were that it looked like Susie's recommendation could prove to be a real gem. After a few pleasantries they left Helen to it and joined Phil in the kitchen. It was warm and steamy in there and Phil had her hands in water, busy scrubbing large potatoes with what appeared to be a nail brush.

Lunch for the day was going to be baked potatoes filled with mashed corned beef and onions with a rice pudding with jam to follow. Good wholesome food but probably not to Ben's taste, and in any case, he had already decided to give it a miss so he could have a break from the office and spend an hour or so at Joe's. This would have the advantage of making his point to Phil and Susie that they couldn't both spend all of Thursdays at the club: the office still needed to be manned.

Joe's was the same as ever, the all-day breakfast including black pudding and three mugs of coffee was very much to Ben's taste, even if it was probably a lot less healthy than what had been on offer at the Thursday club. Ruth Andrews was in sole control at the counter and it seemed likely that it was a relief for her to have a break from Mavis's constant instructions. She appeared to be receiving more backchat than usual in the absence of Mavis but she remained unphased and carried on serving. With Mavis being absent, Ruth also had to go out from behind her counter to clear the tables but Ben saw none of the customers behaving improperly towards her, as might have been anticipated. These days Ruth looked most attractive but Joe kept a proprietary eye on her through his kitchen hatch. Ben as always got a friendly smile from her in recognition of their history together.

When he arrived back at the office a little after 2 pm he found everything under control and Susie and Mrs Freeman chatting in the main office. Presumably, Phil had pulled rank and had allocated office cover to Susie and it was quite clear where Susie would prefer to be. However, as Ben had put Phil in charge of setting up the Thursday Club he did not feel the need to intervene; but it was something he would need to keep his eye on as time went on. Susie followed Ben down to his office and began to praise how easily Helen the volunteer had settled in.

'It was her idea to get them going on French knitting and she brought all the wool and other bits and pieces in with her. They all seem to enjoy doing it and she has provided each of them with the necessary kit to do it at home if they want to. You never know, it might just end up being the latest craze for the kids on the estate. I think she is going to be a real asset to the club and the members certainly seem to have accepted her.'

Ben listened and nodded in agreement, as usual impressed by Susie's enthusiasm, and she went on to tell him all about the arrangements for her and Hanca to go to London for their appointment with *Heir Hunters* on the following Monday. She had arranged for Hanca to have her hair done and her nails tidied up and the outfit she had worn when she returned home from her stay at Cerne Abbas had been resurrected and dry cleaned. Hanca was going to look her best for what could just turn out to be the most important day of her life. Ben once again thanked Susie for all her efforts on Hanca's behalf and sent her back to the club, accepting he would hold the fort for the rest of the afternoon. It was a particularly quiet afternoon and he went home on time for a pleasant family evening. He told Sandy about the French knitting, which she remembered from her childhood, and she told Ben that the boys might enjoy trying it. He doubted it somehow but agreed to ask Helen for a couple of kits, on condition that he wasn't actually involved in trying get the boys interested. The deal was agreed.

The family had a quick tea of beans on toast and once the meal things had been cleared away they all sat around the table and sorted out their costumes ready for the celebrations on Saturday. Sandy had it all worked out, and as she had the boys' attention she started with them. She had been to the library and had brought home a book all about the evacuation of children from the cities during the war. There were lots of photos of small children all being herded on to trains with their mothers remaining on the platform trying hard not to break down in tears at their parting. The boys had learnt a little of this at school but the enormity of the disruption of lives didn't seem to have made any impact on them and Sandy could see no value in elaborating. They did like her plans for their costumes, which simply involved wearing old clothes, having untidy hair and rather dirty faces. A couple of Grandad Roger's old caps and a large label giving their name, age and home address completed their outfits.

Sandy pointed out the gas mask boxes worn by each child and explained that she and their dad would be making them each one that night. It was the first time Ben had heard of it but he made no comment. With both of the boys' apparent satisfaction with their costumes Sandy also mentioned that in the pictures several of the kids were clutching dolls or teddies and would the boys perhaps like to carry a favourite toy? The boys were in harmony with each other and declared 'not a chance'.

Sandy didn't push it and moved on to outline Ben's outfit, which had largely come from his dad, Roger. He had been a firewatcher throughout the war and had fortunately hung on to his gear down in his garden shed. So Ben was kitted out with the official fire watcher's helmet, a first-aid kit, a whistle on a short chain, a small haversack complete with thermos flask and a long brass stirrup pump that was currently used to spray Roger's roses. A thick wool scarf and fingerless woollen gloves together with a battered gas mask box made up the ensemble. All Ben needed to add was his own heavy overcoat, which would have been essential for anyone on duty throughout the night in all winds and weathers. Sandy explained to Ben that when she had unpacked the parcel from Roger she had attempted to take the gas masks out of their boxes and the brittle plastic had started to disintegrate in her hands. She suggested that they ought to sit down later to make replacement boxes rather than damage the original ones further.

It was well after nine before they managed to finally settle the boys and when Ben came downstairs from them for the final time Sandy was already busy on the kitchen table. She had a small stack of cardboard boxes which had previously contained the strong smelling Gitanes cigarettes that Ma Driscoll stocked especially for Tony Scadding. This collection must have represented several months of Tony's cigarette consumption but Ma was well known as a hoarder and this time it had proved useful. The boxes didn't take long to convert. Simple string straps were attached and the vivid blue and white boxes were then given a coat of brown poster paint and 'hey presto', there were four acceptable gas mask boxes ready for the big day. Once they were dry, Ben added a surprise in each of the boys' boxes by inserting a collection of genuine shrapnel and a couple of actual fins from a war time incendiary bomb that his dad had collected whilst on duty as a fire watcher. He was confident that the bits and pieces would be sure to appeal to the boys.

By the time Sandy had tidied all the costumes away and had laid up the table for the next day's breakfast Ben had already undressed and was cuddled up in bed. He had no recall of her joining him but felt her comforting warmth against him later in the night when he awoke with the usual need for his nocturnal trip to the loo. He managed to achieve this without waking her and the next thing that happened was when the alarm went off to get the family moving the following morning.

Chapter 67

An Unusual and Rather Worrying Proposal

Friday at the office started in a relaxed way. Ben had asked Mrs Freeman to set up a meeting for all the team over coffee at 10 am. The primary reason was to review how the Thursday Club had gone and to let all the members of the team, including Alice, have the opportunity to have their say. They gathered in the general office to allow Mrs Freeman to be present, to hear about any suggestions being made so that she could relay them to her husband, Steve, for his comments on any financial implications that there might be. Ideally, Ben would have liked to involve Steve more, as the club was having to be run on a shoe string and finances were going to be critical, but with Steve's physical limitations that was unlikely to ever be possible.

Phil chaired the meeting and reported that the opening two club sessions had run well with full attendance and obvious enthusiasm. Alice nodded her head vigorously at this point but retained a helpful silence, which came as bit of a surprise to Ben. Both Susie and Phil were full of praise for Helen, the new volunteer, and the way she had been able to relate so seamlessly to the club members. Phil reported that Helen had offered to loan a knitting machine to the club and to provide free wool from her collection of odd balls of leftover wool in her shop. Both Phil and Susie approved of the idea and were sure that the machine could be set up to knit simple squares for blankets or scarves ready for winter. With an eye to business, Mrs Freeman suggested that they could knit some scarves in the vivid green of the new speedway team, which they could perhaps sell to raise funds for the Thursday Club.

Ben simply said, 'Let's not run before we can walk, but let the ideas keep on coming as it is important that the club keeps on developing.'

Somehow or other the conversation got on to the possibility of saving green shield stamps to enable the club to buy its own record player. As if by magic, Mrs Freeman produced a green shield stamp catalogue from her desk drawer, which just happened to be turned down to the page for electrical gadgets. Ben was seeing a fresh side to Mrs Freeman that he had previously been unaware of and he saw that her commitment to the club and of course to her husband's involvement was going to be most helpful.

She went on. 'A Dansette record player, like yours, Phil, can be had for fifty books and as each book contains 1280 stamps we only need to collect a mere 64,000 stamps, which is a whole lot of stamps, but I have an idea about that. By involving one of our members, and with her dad's approval, we could put a collection box for green shield stamps in at Joe's. Of course we would have to word a sign carefully so we don't get too much publicity about the club's location, but with Mavis on the job of drumming up support I reckon it could just work.'

Ben agreed to give the idea some thought and to discuss it with Joe before taking any action. The meeting broke up soon after and the team all went about their business. Ben cleared his desk and went off to Joe's for an early lunch as he wanted to meet up with the prof early to allow plenty of time to discuss Wendy Tiler before the clinic started. His plans were nearly thwarted when the old Cortina repeatedly spluttered and stalled en route to Joe's and he decided to cut his losses and headed straight to the clinic.

He managed to limp along slowly to the hospital, at the cost of missing out on lunch, and even so the prof was already there when Ben arrived looking very hot and bothered. As ever, the prof was sympathetic as he fully understood that a social worker's pay for someone with a young family did not go far and after pouring Ben out a coffee he even offered him a sandwich from his own lunch box. Ben didn't have to be asked twice and gratefully enjoyed the generously filled ham and mustard sandwich.

As they were munching, the prof raised the question of Wendy Tiler and whether Ben had had any contact with her in the past. Ben recounted his rather difficult dealings with her in his early days working on the Highfield Estate as the resettlement officer. He explained that it was a weird job with no real defined job description other than to try and smooth out any disputes that arose. He reported that Mrs Tiler had proved to be a consistent moaner who had haunted him day after day, with venom about all sorts of people and on all sorts of subjects.

'I soon realised that she was attempting to use me to fire bullets of her making and she seemingly delighted in causing friction and unhappiness. It got so bad that if I saw the sour-faced old woman coming I would lock myself in my hut and simply didn't answer her persistent knocking. I admit to being very naïve at the time. It was after all, my first social work job after qualifying, which I genuinely wanted to do to the best of my ability. However, I adopted a particular system for dealing with Mrs Tiler. I would listen to her, take notes, tell her to leave it to me and then simply do nothing other than file the notes on her file.

'Nothing ever came back to bite me and she eventually gave up on me and moved on to bother the elderly Church of England minister on the estate. I don't think it was a coincidence that he took early retirement on health grounds a few months later; that's the effect she has on people. I have had no direct dealings with her since but from time to time have been aware of her continuing unpleasant behaviour and the effect it has on the people who have the misfortune to cross her path. Then I was advised of the circumstances around her admission to St Margaret's a month or so ago. I have since had a word with PC Richards, our local bobby on the estate who knew her previously and was involved at the time in her admission. He told me that he has received lots of complaints from her and also about her over the months but had never felt the need for any official action. He did comment that he doubted the seriousness of her attempt to gas herself, as she had not topped up the gas meter despite a pile of shillings being readily available on top of the meter.'

The prof stayed quiet throughout Ben's comments but then confirmed that nothing he had reported came as anything of a surprise.

'She is proving to be a real mystery to my staff. She has chosen to be effectively mute, refusing to have any verbal contact with any of the staff, but does leave short vindictive notes around the ward claiming abuse of all sorts by the staff. Other patients have told us that she does speak to them when they are out of earshot of staff but only to stir up trouble just like she did with you. I suspect that she has a long-term depressive condition and that she has a very jaundiced view of the world. None of the medication we have prescribed has had any effect and the staff strongly suspect that she manages to either spit them out or sick them up if she does actually swallow them. It may surprise you Ben, but I am actually thinking of treating her with a brief course of ECT in an attempt to shake up her brain cells and assist her to become a more pleasant and contented human being.'

He paused at this point and looked at Ben, anticipating a reaction. Ben's shocked expression said it all and the prof then went on to ask Ben what experience he had had of electro-convulsive therapy. Ben thought about his answer for a moment before explaining that as a student he had had a residential placement in a hospital in the north of England where there had been a consultant who seemed to prescribe ECT for almost all his inpatients whatever their diagnoses might be.

'The nursing staff seemed hardened to this and quite content to administer the treatment. I witnessed the procedure a number of times and frankly thought it was barbaric. I also witnessed the effect that the treatment had on some of the patients who suffered nausea, confusion, headaches and some loss of memory afterwards. I guess I was not there long enough to see what value there may have been for some patients. However, I came away from there feeling very uneasy about the way that consultant chose to prescribe the wholesale use of ECT.'

The prof remained silent for a little while before removing his glasses and rubbing his hand over his beard as if he was troubled and trying to find the right words to use. It was rare to see him apparently indecisive and when he did speak he appeared to be speaking to Ben as an equal professional.

'I can understand exactly what you feel Ben, there is no doubt that ECT is a very tough treatment and I firmly believe it should not be prescribed liberally. As I am sure you already know, it is done under general anaesthesia and the patient is always given a muscle relaxant to avoid them damaging themselves by their physical reaction to the electric shock, but it does involve passing an electric current through their brain causing a seizure which has a scrambling effect. There can be disturbing aftereffects but I have also seen spectacular results with patients being liberated from their chronic mental ill health conditions and being able to resume a meaningful life outside of the hospital. I strongly suspect that Mrs Tiler may have been suffering a deep depression over many years, which now for the first time has been recognised following her admission. Her total lack of cooperation with treatment of any sort could well result in her further deterioration and her potentially ending her days in some back ward of the hospital. She is still only in her fifties and I believe that with help she should be able to resume a place back in the community. But she has no insight and presents as completely determined not to cooperate with any sort of treatment. In order for me to try and improve her life I need to be able to proceed with treatment without her authority and I therefore need to place her on a treatment order. I would normally at this stage seek a meeting with her nearest relative, in this case her daughter, to involve her in the treatment plan. There is, however, a complication as her daughter lives in Coventry and I understand that she is disabled. What I would like you to do is to visit her in my place, to fully put her in the picture and to seek her agreement for us making the order and proceeding with a course of ECT. I have given this careful thought and am convinced that ECT could have a positive effect on Mrs Tiler's life and I can assure you, Ben, that the use of ECT is not something I prescribe lightly.'

Ben's confidence in the prof's integrity left him in no doubt of his sincerity and he decided that his own reservations about ECT should be put aside. He readily agreed to the prof's request and it was also agreed that Ben would be involved in making the section 26 treatment order when the time came.

The afternoon clinic went along familiar lines and it was only during a break between patients that Ben thought about the practical problems of a trip to Coventry. Then it hit him like a blow, the old Cortina was in a sorry state and would struggle to get him home tonight let alone make a long return trip to Coventry. He had no access to another car other than the unlikely prospect of borrowing one of the council's rather tatty vehicles in the carpool. However, it was common knowledge that access to them was controlled by a carpool manager who had the reputation of doing everything in his power to avoid them going out. More in hope than expectation, Ben used the phone on reception to approach the guardian of the cars. The response was as anticipated, useless, as he was informed that any request had to be in writing and usually took a week before receiving a reply.

'I suggest you use the train, young man,' was the determined reaction and the phone went dead as the guardian hung up on him.

That evening Ben got busy on his phone at home and arranged for the old Cortina to be resuscitated by Tony's friendly mechanic mate, Eric, who had done good work on the car in the past and who importantly charged reasonable rates for his expertise. Eric agreed to try and work more magic on Monday, which was the best offer he would make and Ben accepted that his trip to Coventry would just have to be on public transport. His next phone call was to Mrs Tiler's daughter, Beatrice Phillips, who spoke very quietly, giving the impression of being very shy. Ben explained who he was and that he would like to talk to her about her mother. A long sigh was her immediate reaction followed by a lengthy silence. She then agreed rather half-heartedly that Ben could visit her at her home on Monday morning and once again the phone was hung up on him. His final call of the evening was to the British Rail ticket office to get times of trains on Monday, this was dealt with most efficiently by a young lady who seemed to be pleased to help. Hopefully, that was indicative of what Ben might experience on his unusual trip on public transport in due course. He joined the family in front of the television and chatted away to Sandy about the celebrations the following day. An interesting weekend beckoned.

Chapter 68

A Remembrance to be Remembered

The late evening news had forecast a day of intermittent rain with wintry temperatures but when Sandy pulled the bedroom curtains back the sun simply poured in. For once Ben was pleased that the weathermen were regularly a long way short of perfection in their predictions. He and Sandy had had a bit of a chat when they cuddled together the previous night before going off to sleep. They were looking forward to experiencing an enjoyable day with the boys but agreed that they thought it was also an opportunity to teach the boys about a little of the reality of life during war time. Sandy had invited Patsie to join them for a good breakfast before they all got togged up in their various costumes. Out of curiosity Ben had done a little research into wartime rationing and had been amazed at the restrictions on the amount of several essential supplies that each person was allowed to purchase.

They agreed that they would use the breakfast that morning to try and bring the reality of rationing home to the boys. When Patsie arrived at ten, as arranged she was still dressed in her normal clothes and in no time at all she was playing with the boys, racing their Dinky toys on the living room floor. Sandy had spoken with Patsie on the phone earlier so she was fully prepared for what was to follow. Sandy called from the kitchen that breakfast was ready and they all went to join Ben at the kitchen table. The plate of food each was given consisted of a small slice of a fried egg, a minute bit of bacon, and a bit of cheese about the size of a penny piece. This was accompanied by a half slice of toast with just a scraping of margarine and a cup of very weak tea with just a dash of milk.

The room went very quiet with the three adults simply clearing their plates without any apparent reaction. The boys, however, couldn't contain themselves and demanded to know what was going on. Ben simply explained that today they were all experiencing what people had to cope with during war time and even for a few years after.

'Sweets for example were rationed right up to when I was older than you are now. Times were tough for everyone.'

Sandy topped up everyone's plate generously from the rest of the food she had prepared and concealed in the oven. As they ate, Ben read off the list of each individual's weekly rationing allowances he had researched earlier. 'One egg a week, two ounces of tea and butter, one ounce of cheese, four ounces of bacon and meat to the value of one shilling and two pence. Fortunately there was no rationing for fruit and vegetables but they were often in short supply. In fact people all over the country dug up their lawns and flower beds to grow vegetables. Without this combined effort many people would have starved.'

Both Sandy and Patsie were shocked about the severity of the rationing and the boys couldn't really take it in but Ben noticed that they both ate everything put before them.

As the girls cleared up Ben emptied the bag of shrapnel and fins on to the table and attempted to try and explain how random the whole senseless activity of war really was. By feeling the sharpness of the bits of exploded bombs the boys could begin to understand, but mainly they just seemed to be delighted to be able to handle their grandfather's souvenirs. Not wishing to spoil the enjoyment of the day in any way, the three of them shared the spoils out and put them safely away in the boys' gas mask boxes. The boys resumed their game with their cars and Ben made himself a cup of coffee and retired to the lounge to put his feet up, awaiting further orders from Sandy. The girls had disappeared upstairs to get into their costumes and after what seemed like an age, two wartime factory girls made their grand entrance. The boys were almost totally underwhelmed and after the most cursory of glances returned to playing with their cars under the kitchen table. With a cheeky grin, Patsie couldn't resist giving Ben a quick flash of her bright red bloomers. Ben did his best to remain unaffected but the simple act of her lifting her skirt caused an unwanted response from his body. Patsie knew, but just laughed and the moment passed.

Sandy came into the room at that point loaded down with the outfits for Ben and the boys. Ben put on his heavy old overcoat and added the accessories of the tin helmet with 'Fire Watcher' printed in white across the front, the knapsack complete with its empty thermos and sandwich box, a long faded rather moth-eaten woollen scarf, the genuine wartime whistle on its chain and just to finish off, an old pair of fingerless gloves. Roger had also lent him the essential bit of fire watcher's kit, a long brass stirrup pump. However, by this time he felt so loaded down that he found it hard to imagine how the watchers could have clambered up on roofs and he surreptitiously dropped the pump behind the sofa to be conveniently forgotten.

Finally, the finishing touches were made to the boys' costumes as evacuees. Their hair was messed up, smudges of dirt added to their faces, luggage labels recording their names, ages and addresses tied through the top buttonhole of their jackets and flat caps from their grandfather's collection plonked skew-whiff on their heads. At different times all three adults had slipped each of the boys a few coins to spend on the stalls and rides and these were added to the contents of their gas mask boxes. The party all clambered into Patsie's Mercedes and headed off to the carnival in high spirits.

Everyone seemed to be heading in the same direction and it quickly became apparent that the vast majority of the people they saw had made an effort to dress appropriately to reflect the significance of the day. The majority of the men were dressed in service uniform from one of the three main services. Most of the uniforms were undoubtedly from the war and the fact that they seemed to frequently be on the small size reflected how today's diet had piled on the pounds. However, many wore medals with obvious pride and everyone seemed to have made a proper attempt to make their uniforms as smart as possible. There were fewer women in military uniform but they were joined by land girls, nurses, WVS workers and many factory workers. It looked as if every child they passed was about to be evacuated but without exception they seemed overjoyed at the prospect. As they approached the entrance to The Runway the traffic slowed almost to a halt and the people walking on both sides of the road were able to progress at a more rapid pace. A rather harassed PC Richards supported by a couple of special constables were doing their best to keep the traffic moving, but people were attempting to park in every available space, including pavements and grass verges. Richard popped his head in to speak to Patsie to direct her on up the hill to the Speedway carpark where there were still places available. He moved on to the next car but Patsie disregarded his advice and took a sharp left turn, pulling up outside Scadding's yard. The entrance was blocked off by a red and white barrier and there was a uniformed security guard with a fierce-looking Alsatian on guard duty. The guard's reaction was immediate. With a wave, Desmond Davies raised the barrier and Patsie drove straight in and pulled up less than fifty yards from the action.

Robbie had planned well ahead and they were very grateful but Ben ensured that he didn't get too close to his old adversary, Fang the Alsatian. However, under Desmond's control the dog remained silent and it was probably just Ben's imagination that he thought it had given him the evil eye. With the barrier back in place and Desmond and Fang back on patrol, the group slipped across the road between the crawling traffic and joined the throng pouring into The Runway.

The place was teeming with humanity and the miles of bunting and colourful fairground rides and stalls did much to contribute to the carnival atmosphere. Ben drew the boys to him and laid down a few ground rules before releasing them to explore as they wished. Accepting that they must stay together and return to the steps to Jessie's shop when it was time to go home, the boys dived off and were soon lost amongst the wandering crowd. The ladies were in high spirits and they too were quick to assure Ben that they would stick together and return to the meeting point at the end of the day. They each gave him a rather exaggerated kiss on the cheek before joining the throng, giggling together once again like a couple of schoolgirls.

Ben sat down on the steps and was grateful of a few moments to himself. He reached into his pockets and fumbled around before realising he was instinctively looking for a packet of fags out of historical habit. Of course, he remembered that he no longer smoked and was determined never to start again, but he was equally sure that he would have really enjoyed one right there and then.

Ben quickly realised that he knew more people by sight than he could have imagined. Unfortunately, because everyone was wearing unfamiliar clothes, he frequently failed to realise how he knew them or what their names were. He settled on trying to keep a low profile and resorting to a jolly smile whenever he was recognised. To some extent it worked pretty well but he was aware that all that smiling was not natural for him and would almost certainly result in a proper jaw ache by the end of the day. He decided that he would be an observer rather than a participant. Truth to tell, he was not a lover of fairground rides ever since he had been dragged on to a spinning monster ride by a so-called mate when he was a teenager. The ride was called 'The Rotor' and it spun around at a terrifying rate and everyone on it became stuck to the wall by centrifugal force. Just as it seemed it could get no worse the floor dropped away and everyone was suspended in mid-air revolving like a demented spinning top. He had been violently sick, had lost his bus fare home in the process and managed to avoid funfairs ever since.

The first of the fairground stalls that Ben came across was manned by the familiar faces of the two Watson sisters, Faith and Charity, who were surrounded by loads of kids, all desperate to have a go on their hoopla stall. Ben watched from a distance, interested to see what was attracting the kid's attention. It didn't take too long for him to realise that the girls were giving out prizes to kids irrespective of where their hoopla rings, bought for a few coppers, ended up.

Each and every child came away with a small live goldfish in a sealed plastic bag half filled with water. Ben thought it was likely that most of them would die long before they arrived at their new homes and he guessed that the sewers of Exworth would be transporting a lot of little corpses out to sea later in the evening. The girls had obviously been told to ensure that all the children had to have the joy of winning and they were clearly enjoying obliging. Ben spotted Jack and Nick in the crowd and each had already got their plastic bag clutched in their hands. He quickly linked up with them and persuaded them to put their prizes into his gas mask box for safety. The boys seemed relieved to agree and were soon lost again in the crowd. The noise level just went up and up as more and more people crowded into The Runway. The combination of general conversation, outbursts of laughter and shouts and squeals of delight were mixed up with the rhythmic thump of a distant traditional fairground organ.

Next to the hoopla there was a row of swing boats and Ben immediately spotted Mavis from the café sitting opposite Katie Andrews, who was being jerked soaring up into the air in the catch weight contest resulting from their unfair weight distribution. Their pleasure in each other's company was great to watch and Ben was particularly delighted to see Joe and Ruth Andrews standing behind the safety barriers watching the girls at play. He noticed that they were standing very close and holding hands and decided to move on rather than interrupt their personal time together. He thought it would be a real result if romance was in the offing, but time would tell.

The swing boats were being managed by Hope Watson, Faith and Charity's gorgeous sister, who looked every inch a true Romany beauty but he decided to move on with the intention of coming back later when she was less busy for a chat! Every prefab that Ben passed seemed to have something on offer. Cakes and teas were very popular but there were also toffee apples, homemade sweets, ice cream, candy floss and fresh orange juice, all of which would have been very much sought-after treats during war time. The gates of several of the prefabs had a large printed note attached, alongside a collecting tin for the British Legion. The message was the same on each of them: 'Lady's toilet available please make a donation to the British Legion. Gent's toilets at far end of The Runway.'

As ever Jessie and her team's planning was much in evidence! A large group, almost exclusively of men and boys, was gathered at the barrier of the next attraction. Ben joined them and admired the large multi-coloured Helter-skelter, which now looked quite pristine after the combined efforts of the cousins, Albert and Sam Watts, and their paint brushes. The reason for the gathering of males quickly became apparent when a young girl in a Wren's uniform appeared from the end of the shoot and landed in a heap on the carpet at the end of the ride. She made a valiant effort to protect her modesty by tugging her skirt down as she landed. However, she was too slow to prevent the audience from having a clear view of her lacey pants that were definitely not of military issue. Blushing with embarrassment she dropped her mat on the pile by the ride's entrance and got herself lost in the crowd. The crowd waited in anticipation of the further opportunity for voyeurism and became quite restless when they were confronted by a group of scouts appearing one after the other to end up in a tangle of arms and legs on the mat at the end of the ride. They were clearly enjoying themselves but were not appreciated by the male gathering.

Ben was ready to move on, when he spied an all too familiar flash of red appear from the shoot. First Patsie and then Sandy in close pursuit made their landing with no real attempt to restrict the view of their bloomers. Ben noted, however, that there was an obvious variance in the men's reaction. Many of the younger ones turned away muttering in disappointment, but some of the older ones let out distinct sighs of satisfaction. He could only think that the sight of knee-length red knickers had helped them to recall some wartime dalliance. The girls were just out to enjoy themselves and went straight around for another ride, almost as it they were unaware of the attention they were getting. Ben was sure that was not the case but it was all innocent fun and he left them to it and moved on with his tour around the event.

He arrived next at the entrance to Spitfire Close and for no real reason wandered up to the Collins brothers' prefab. It still appeared to be in perfect condition, sparkling white with no hint of graffiti of any sort. The front garden was full of flowers and the small lawn was neatly trimmed. The signs were that the community was still determined that the two men would have a pleasant home to return to. The one thing that he did note was that there was no sign of the neat little Mini that had recently been parked there and Ben resolved to ask Jessie for an update when they next got together. The central green of The Runway held a whole variety of other attractions, all of which were doing good business. It was all traditional stuff like coconut shies, skittles and a shooting gallery made up of several tin boxes each containing a row of figures ready to be shot down. Like most men, Ben couldn't resist the chance of trying out a gun, and he joined the queue waiting for a turn. He was amused to note that the figures had recently been repainted, admittedly rather amateurly, but it was recognisable that each and every one was now a representation of Adolf Hitler. Ben flattened the lot when it was his turn and turned away with a smug look on his face. There were no prizes on offer but it was prize enough to be confirmed as a crack shot. Anyone watching would have soon come to the conclusion that there were an awful lot of crack shots about.

The top of The Runway was occupied by the fantastic carousel with three ranks of golden horses chasing each other around, each mounted by a rider of all ages from small children in their parents' arms to matronly women in an obvious state of joy and second childhood. The ride was of considerable age but was in tip-top condition and had none of the tatty qualities one would normally expect to find on a modern fairground machine. This ride was real quality and was further enhanced by the huge steam-driven organ parked next to it which provided the ride with power. The music coming from it appeared to be a Strauss waltz but the volume was dominated by the clashing of cymbals and the rat tat tat of drums. There was mechanical movement going on all over the front of the organ and it took a little while to take it all in. A vintage WVS mobile canteen had been set up on the bend of the circuit road and there were semi-circles of folding chairs set up in front of it. All the chairs were facing towards the carousel and organ and they were full of people supping tea and taking in the view. Ben joined them.

The ride was controlled by two rather swarthy middle-aged men who were dressed in the

traditional garb of the historical Romany traveller. They both wore colourful waistcoats complete with heavy-looking silver watch chains. Their corduroy trousers were held up by well-worn broad leather belts fronted by large silver buckles in the shape of horse heads. They both wore silk scarves tied around their necks, one blue, one red, and they had small pork pie hats perched on the back of their heads, both displaying a full head of glossy black locks. These were undoubtedly two of Mrs Watson's sons who had inherited the funfair from their dad and they looked every inch the part of proud owners. They appeared to be a magnet for the ladies of all ages and as Ben watched he could see that they were almost having to fight them off. *Powerful stuff this Romany blood,* he thought, but then he recalled the classic Romany beauty of Hope Watson and felt sympathy for the female customers and their fantasies. After a few minutes, Ben went over to the WVS canteen and bought himself a mug of tea. Their menu boasted traditional wartime fare which on closer examination meant various sandwiches. The range had been deliberately restricted to reflect the rationing of war time and nothing on the menu was of any interest to Ben. Spam, beetroot or pilchard sandwiches did nothing to tempt Ben's taste buds and he rapidly moved on along the road to join the queue at a mobile fish and chip van which was producing the mouth- watering smell of frying.

Sid's Chippy was well known in and around Exworth, where Sid had for many years visited a whole series of surrounding villages each on a regular evening of the week. Tuesday was his evening to visit the village of Little Poppy Field where Susie lived and the following day she was always full of praise for his takeaways. The fish and chips that Ben purchased were piping hot and generously flavoured by salt and vinegar. The whole thing came in a convenient newspaper cone complete with a two-pronged wooden fork to save any customers burning their fingers. Ben sat on a nearby garden wall and enjoyed every mouthful and could totally understand why Susie and her family looked forward to their Tuesday teas. He took his time enjoying the food using his fingers in preference to the little wooden fork and tried to remember when he had last eaten chips with his fingers out of newspaper. He thought it had probably been on the pier at Weston when one of the boys had gone there on a birthday trip. He recalled that that had been a special day, one to be remembered, but suspected that today would prove to be even more memorable.

As he looked around him, he noticed that the gate he was sat next to bore the by-now familiar sign offering female loo facilities. There was a second sign stating simply 'Gents' with an arrow pointing to a group of bushes and trees on the far left of the estate. His first reaction was to laugh to himself that the event planners had concluded that a few bushes were an acceptable provision for male toilets. However, needs must. He screwed up the empty newspaper and popped it into a convenient bin before heading for the bushes. As he got nearer, he realised that there was a sizeable tented structure set up in a clearing in the bushes. The canvas side bore the wording '34th Exworth Scouts, toilet tent' and an additional handwritten sign said 'please make a donation to the British Legion'. There was a bucket set into the ground under the sign with a few coins in it. Ben just hoped that no one would be tempted to use the bucket for a more basic sort of donation. The tent was open to the sky and the urinal was simply a long strip of roof guttering sloping away to the far corner, presumably to soak away outside amongst the trees. There were two small toilet tents pitched by the back wall which probably contained a couple of Elsan toilets. Ben didn't have the need or inclination to confirm that. The whole set-up was pretty basic but it was functional and surprisingly lacking in the unpleasant odder of ammonia often associated with men's loos. As Ben made his way along the other side of The Runway the throbbing beat of the stream organ came to an abrupt halt and after a few seconds of near silence a burst of military-type music burst forth from the direction of the entrance to The Runway. A quick glance at his watch confirmed that it was 3 pm and that was the time for 'the grand parade'.

He cut across the central island and headed for the steps to Jessie's shop. It seemed as if there were literally hundreds of people milling about the entrance and spilling back to fill the roadway up to Highfield. Fortunately, PC Roger Richards and his special constable assistants were holding the traffic back and most of the delayed revellers seemed content to be out of their cars and taking in the chaos. Amongst the people milling about one small lone figure appeared to be the only one attempting to make sense of the proceedings. Jessie, armed with her clipboard, had so far got the Boys Brigade band at the head of the parade and they had moved a short way along the route, making way for others to follow. Bit by bit, Jessie got them in the required order and the Cubs, Brownies, Guides and Scouts all formed up and the procession started on its trip around The Runway. The Boys Brigade band had obviously practised very hard and the combined bugles and drums produced a firm beat which was easy for them to follow. It was perhaps unfortunate that everybody didn't start on the same foot, so it all appeared rather ragged, but it was great to see so many youngsters taking an active part in the commemoration of the wartime event which had happened before any of them had been born.

A new sound erupted from the roadway, which almost drowned out the sound of the band. It was instantly recognisable to Ben and he stood up on the top step of the shop to get a proper view. The unmistakable figure of Tony Scadding dressed in full Arabian costume and mounted on his beloved vintage motorbike crawled along behind the marchers. As he drove, he repeatedly twisted the throttle to produce a series of deep roars from his magnificent machine. The crowd loved it and everyone was left in no doubt that this was his interpretation of Lawrence of Arabia. From Ben's modern history lessons whilst he was at school he was well aware that Lawrence's time in the limelight had been during the

First World War. So this was the wrong war, and Tony was riding a far superior bike to the Brough Superiors that Lawrence had favoured. He had managed to get one special detail right by fixing a swagger stick to his handlebars just as Lawrence had done, but historically he was well off beam. Not that anyone seemed to mind, as he was received by generous applause all along the route. Never one to miss an opportunity, Robbie had arranged for several of the members of the new Speedway team to walk behind Tony, giving out flyers about the plans for the opening day of the Speedway. The team were all dressed in their full bright green racing uniforms and were attracting a lot of attention, particularly amongst the girls. There was a brief lull in the action until a camouflaged jeep swung into The Runway, driven by a uniformed serviceman with a large Alsatian dog at his side with its head sticking out of the passenger window. Standing in the rear of the Jeep was the unmistakable figure of Winston Churchill dressed in his traditional outfit of a boiler suit under a long black overcoat complete with bowler hat, cigar and the two-fingered victory sign.

The whole crowd erupted and Ben just burst out laughing. His friend Robbie certainly did nothing by halves and he had achieved a very passable interpretation of the great man. Robbie spotted Ben on top of the stairs and momentarily reversed the victory salute before resuming his characterisation. What happened next was a spontaneous reaction by the on-lookers, who in no particular order joined the parade behind Robbie's jeep.

It was quite moving to see all the people dressed in a hodgepodge of wartime costumes, both military and civilian, marching proudly to the beat of the Boys Brigade Band. Ben stayed where he was and took in the spectacle. This was people watching on a grand scale and he spotted loads of familiar faces but none more familiar than Alice and Ernest. They had decided to dress as refugees; just two more displaced persons like so many who had been left wandering across Europe seeking a safe haven. Their choice of costume was clever as all they had to do was resurrect their oldest clothes, which in Ernest's case was what he wore to work each day. Alice was dressed in what had been the usual odd collection, which she had worn up until a year ago since when Susie had taken her in hand. The two of them pushed a battered old pram between them, which they had loaded with an old mattress and various pots and pans. Echoes of Ben's first sight of the Farthing family as they had appeared over the brow of the hill on their way to their new home in Highfield a year or two ago. They really looked the part but the whole portrayal was made a lot less convincing by the obviously well-fed dog perched on top of the loaded pram. The Champ looked in magnificent health and had been decked in a special coat made out of a cut-down Union Jack flag. With his glossy mane he really looked quite the best portrayal they were going to get to represent 'a proud British lion'.

More and more people joined the parade, all attempting to march to the beat of the band as it moved along into the far end of The Runway. Ben was mesmerised by the sheer mass of humanity who were content to join in with the patriotic reaction. There was a complete lack of any sort of dissension. Everyone was happy to participate with the mood of the moment.

There was nothing other than grateful admiration for the brave men and women who had defended our country so bravely. His mind went to the words of Winston Churchill in one of his wartime speeches about 'never had so much been owed by so many to so few' and he had to surreptitiously brush a few stray tears from his cheeks. The sound of the band was growing louder indicating that they had turned at the top of The Runway and were on their way back down the other side. The people joining the parade had dribbled to a halt and the final person to join was an elderly man in a wheelchair with an empty trouser leg where his right leg once was, Ben was in two minds about joining in on the end as he had originally planned to do, but that had been before the last recruit, who was such an appropriate reminder of the casualties of war. So Ben stayed on the stairs and as a consequence was probably the first person there to pick up the sound of a distant plane coming from over the town. It made a unique sort of roar, which could only be the sound of the Merlin engine of a Spitfire. Ben was truly amazed at the perfection of the timing of its arrival, and the impact on the parade was immediate. The Band stumbled into silence and the parade seemed to freeze before the participants burst into cheering and began to wave frantically to the pilot, who flew low over The Runway before rising steeply and looping the loop. He made a further pass of The Runway and wagged his wings as he flew over Tower

House and disappeared into the distance. The band struck up again and continued on to the entrance of The Runway before being given the order to stand down.

Everyone headed off in all directions to enjoy the attractions but it was clear that the arrival of the Spitfire was the high spot of the afternoon for the majority of them. None more so than Ben, who had always had a soft spot for the plane as it was the first one he had ever seen as a very small child. He resumed his seat on the steps and was soon confronted by Jessie bustling rapidly up to her prefab.

'I can't stop right now, Ben,' she said, and she hurried past him down her garden path and into her prefab. She returned a few minutes later and joined him on the steps.

'Sorry about that, Ben, but sometimes one just needs one's own bathroom.' He nodded his understanding and began to offer his congratulations for the way she had timed everything with the Spitfire fly past. However, she at once confessed that she had had no part in arranging the fly past and it had come as a complete surprise to her.

The mystery was explained later in the week by a curious reporter from the local paper. A lady called Agnes Crompton was a resident at Tower House and her son Arthur had flown Spitfires during the war. Subsequently, he had become a prosperous businessman up in Sheffield and had bought a redundant Spitfire and had then spent a small fortune having it made fully airworthy. His escape from the pressures of high finance was to take part in vintage air displays up and down the country. He had been on his way to Exeter Airport to meet up with a variety of other planes in readiness for a number of air displays all along the south coast the following day. He had decided 'to wave' to his mum and the timing had been purely coincidental. What wasn't recorded in the paper was that poor old Agnes had been having a nap and missed her son's fly past, emerging just in time to see him disappear into the distance. The manager of Tower House had shared that with Jessie later, but as he said, at least Agnes had her moment of fame with a photo of herself with her son on the front page of the local rag.

Jessie seemed grateful to sit and chat for a while and even put her clipboard down. Ben took the opportunity to ask her about the Collins brothers and the news was all promising. Joseph had been allowed home for the weekend a week or two before to see how he managed and whether any adaptations were needed to the prefab. It went well and all that was required was a handrail to the front door, which was due to be installed the following week. Meanwhile, Joseph had driven himself back to the hospital and was apparently giving his mates there trips out, which seemed to involve dropping in at the village pub. Joseph's popularity had never been so high. He had advised Jessie that Daniel's condition was much better and he was cooperating with the staff and was even taking medication, but as usual reluctantly. Joseph was planning to have his brother home as soon as possible but did say it was a good thing that he would not be around for the wartime celebrations. It might just have started his paranoia off again, and nobody wanted that to happen.

Jessie was far too busy to sit down for long and after a quick consultation of her notes she dashed off with renewed energy. Ben sat for a while longer and heard the old steam organ wheeze back into life as the whole scene returned to its chaotic life. From where he was sat he had a good view of Faith and Charity on their hoopla stall, which seemed to be attracting a lot less attention. He wandered over and could see that there were no more little bags of goldfish. The girls had exhausted the supply and the remaining prizes of plaster cast models and misshapen stuffed toys obviously didn't hold the same appeal. Not that the girls seemed to mind as they were making no effort to draw the punters in and were content to sit on a couple of stools and chirrup away in their usual conversational manner.

Ben didn't interrupt them and moved on in the hope of a chat with the gorgeous Hope, but he was disappointed to find the swing boats were now being managed by a burly looking guy. Ben nodded to him in passing and cut across the grass to continue his tour. The rest was mainly tables with a variety of things for sale such as food, craft work and general bric-a-brac. The only thing to attract Ben's attention was an elderly lady selling slices of bread pudding, which looked just like what his gran had made for him when he had been a small boy. He had no hesitation in buying several slices to share with the family later. He couldn't resist buying an extra slice to eat at once and the taste of the soggy pudding full of dried fruit brought back happy memories of his nan who had been dead for several years.

His tour was nearly complete but there was one more attraction that he had noticed a few days before. On the perimeter of the estate one of the prefabs had a larger square of garden than the other prefabs for some reason. The garden itself was obviously much loved, with a trim hedge along the front of the property and well-tended lawns and flowerbeds leading to a proper vegetable patch just bursting with produce. All in all it was very attractive, but the main attraction today was an immaculate gypsy caravan parked on the lawn. It was a beauty, with meticulous carved woodwork to its body all painted in vivid colours and a green canvas hooped roof. It was the real McCoy, with a heavy-looking wooden chassis and massive wooden wheels. It would certainly require a powerful, heavy horse to move that home around the highways and byways of the English countryside. There was a short flight of polished steps leading to the open doorway but a beaded curtain prevented prying eyes seeing within. There were a number of ordinary dining chairs lined up on the roadside in front of the hedge and about half of them were occupied by women just sat there waiting for something. Just inside the gateway there was a little round bobbing, three-legged gypsy table with a pile of booklets and a large brass hand bell filling its surface. A colourful, ancient painted board was attached to the hedge and declared 'Madame Zara, renowned international fortune teller available for consultations.

As Ben was watching from the roadside it became evident that the proceedings were being controlled by a wizened and rather bent ancient lady dressed in traditional gypsy clothes sat at the table. She was as brown as a berry and as wrinkled as a prune but it was quite clear that she was in charge. She consulted her watch and reached for the bell, which she shook with surprising vigour. As if by magic, the beaded curtain parted and a middle-aged woman dressed as a wartime nurse made her way down from the caravan and went off smiling. The woman sat nearest to the table stood up and passed a pound note over to the elderly bell ringer, who promptly gave her a booklet from the table and directed her to go up the steps and into the caravan. The remaining ladies all moved along one seat and the old gypsy lady beckoned for Ben to come over to her. As he had no intention of having his fortune told he hesitated to respond, but the old lady was having none of it and became so agitated that he felt he had no alternative and so he wandered over.

Much to his surprise she knew his name and addressed him as Mr Newman and explained that she had been told all about him by her granddaughters Faith, Hope and Charity. She made no attempt to persuade him to have his fortune told. Instead she talked to him about the caravan which had been her home for the first thirty years of her life. She presented him with one of the booklets, proudly telling him that she was the author, despite never having had any formal education. It was entitled 'Living in a Vardo', which she explained was the gypsy word for their traditional wagon. She went on to tell him that the ability to read minds had for generations gone down the female side of her family and for many years she had supported her family by using her gift.

'But it is very draining and I am very old, so I leave it to my daughter to carry on the family tradition. She calls herself Madame Zara as a suitably exotic title. Somehow Mrs Gabriel Watson doesn't have the right impact.'

Ben could have gone on chatting to her for ages but her business demands took over and after checking her watch again she reached for her bell and it was time for the next customer.

Ben realised that the day was coming to an end and he had not seen the boys or Sandy and Patsie for ages, so headed back to his perch on the coach steps ready for them to meet up with him. He resumed his seat and began to thumb through the booklet. He found it fascinating as it spelt out in very basic language the trials and tribulations that had been the day-to-day life for travelling Romany families. It must have been far from easy but the travellers were obviously very resourceful and skilled at using the things that nature provided. Ben was even able to confirm something he had read in a storybook that hedgehogs baked in clay were considered to be good eating. All the practical problems of living in a horse drawn caravan were discussed in detail and it was quite evident to him that this booklet was in fact a historical document of a way of life that had all but disappeared.

He was immersed in his reading when he was suddenly joined by the Winston Churchill lookalike, who plonked himself next to him and presented him with a mug of tea. Without speaking a word Robbie reached into his overcoat and produced a hip flask from which he poured a generous quantity of whisky into the two mugs. 'Cheers, my boy, what a great day, but I am really pleased to get rid of that damned cigar. I don't know what the old boy saw in them. Quite frankly its left me feeling quite sick, but this brew should see me right.'

They both drank back the reinforced tea with some satisfaction.

'Now, Ben, when I've got the chance I've a bit of a cheeky proposition to put to you. It's just an idea and I don't want to put you under any obligation but it would be a real help to me.' Ben was intrigued, but having no idea what was coming cautiously replied, 'Fire away then, you know I will help if I can.'

'Well, the fact of the matter is that I am trying to plan a treat for Patsie. As you know we have been working flat out to get the speedway up and running and we haven't had a break of any sorts for ages. Patsie has been really supportive and never complains, but if I am going to do anything it will have to be in the next few weeks before the speedway project gets started. Well, I spotted an advert about the Royal Ballet doing a performance of Tchaikovsky's Swan Lake at the Bristol Hippodrome in mid-October and on the spur of the moment I sent off for and booked two of the best seats in a box there. I am sure she will love it but on reflection I really don't think it is my scene. All those blokes in tights prancing around supporting skinny women in short skirts walking on the tips of their toes. It is a whole load of nonsense as far as I am concerned, and I could either end up laughing or falling asleep and snoring out loud. Then I had what I thought was a brainwave, or at least I think with your help it might prove to be one. I remembered hearing you and Sandy talking about the Beatles trip that you arranged for her birthday last year. I recall that Patsie was very impressed by it, so I suddenly thought why don't we make it a foursome? Patsie and Sandy could go to the ballet and there just happens to be wrestling at the Colston Hall at the same time. I have never been but I have seen it from time to time on the box and it could be a good laugh for you and me. What do you think?'

Ben hadn't been expecting any such suggestion and needed to mull it over before responding. On balance he liked the idea, as it could be just what he needed as a present for Sandy's birthday in November. The girls had really let their hair down today and obviously enjoyed each other's company. However, he wasn't too interested in going to see live wrestling as it seemed to be constantly on the television. To his mind it was obviously mostly play acting, with the familiar old characters the likes of Jackie Pallo, Mick McManus and Giant Haystacks all apparently bashing each other into oblivion week after week. It was clever but was in no way enhanced by the constant jabbering of Kent Walton, the principal wrestling commentator, who seemed to be in a constant state of excitement. The other consideration was the cost involved, as there wasn't a lot of spare cash and the old Cortina could be on its last legs. As Ben was slow to react Robbie pressed on.

'I thought we could all go in the Mercedes and we could book into that posh hotel that you enjoyed so much. I am quite happy to pay for the tickets, so all you would have to find would be the cost of the hotel. What do you think, Ben? Come on, it would be a fun weekend.'

He didn't hesitate any further. This was far too good an offer to resist and he was sure that it would be something which Sandy would really enjoy. He reached across and shook Robbie's hand warmly.

'I think it's a great idea and a very kind offer. Of course I agree, and I think we will be able to kill two birds with one stone and I can give Sandy a special birthday present at the same time.'

The men agreed not to mention anything about the plan to the girls and nearer the date would just say they had a surprise trip out planned. By way of sealing the deal Robbie added another generous glug of whisky to their mugs. Ben had rarely had whisky and was already feeling the effect, but thought what the hell and knocked it back anyway. The sun had dropped and there was now a definite chill in the air, but the warming liquor and the fact both men were wearing overcoats meant that they were comfortable enough. However, the same could not be said of the boys or Sandy and Patsie, who joined up with them complaining that they were cold. Robbie spoke up to say that he had just the cure for that and Ben was immediately concerned that it was going to be whisky all round. However, what actually happened was that Robbie led them all out of The Runway and across the road to the scrapyard. There they were confronted by a roaring fire burning brightly on an old upside-down lorry bonnet in the open space in the middle of the yard. Tony, Desmond Davis and Frudo were busy putting together a semicircle of car seats downwind of the fire. By contrast to the make do and mend, there was a nearby modern gas barbeque already producing the most acceptable smell of frying.

Everyone was satisfied to sit around and eat as well as to share their opinions of the day. In particular, Ben was interested to hear about the girl's visit to the fortune teller. They were both convinced about Madame Zara's ability to foretell the future. She had told Sandy that a dark stranger would be coming into her life shortly and Sandy immediately thought of Camila coming from Jamaica. Madame Zara had also told her that she would be coming into a windfall sometime soon. Sandy could only think that at long last the twenty-one premium bonds her parents had given her for her twenty-first could be coming good. Ben thought of his bet on the world cup but decided to still say nothing of it.

Patsie was perhaps a little less convinced by Madame Zara, who had told her that a new project would work out well, which was good to hear but everyone in the locality knew about the speedway opening soon. Apparently Madame Zara had also told her that she would be having a treat soon but Patsie said simply, 'some hopes'. Ben and Robbie glanced at each other and had similar thoughts that there was perhaps more to Madame Zara and her predictions than either of them had expected. Maybe they were just a pair of old cynics.

As it grew dark the boys snuggled into their mum and fell asleep in the warmth of the dying fire. Patsie ran the family back home and Sandy took the boys straight up to bed whilst Ben made the night time drink. He remembered the two goldfish housed in his gas mask box and with some trepidation pulled the two bags out. Much to his surprise they both seemed fit and well and he had to then find somewhere better to keep them. He dug around in the kitchen cupboards and came across a hideous ornate mixing bowl that a maiden aunt had given them as a wedding present. They had never used it but it would meet the fishes' need until something more permanent could be found. When Sandy came back she seemed suitably impressed at Ben's initiative but simply said, 'I hope there is room for one more,' and produced another bag from her gas mask box and poured another fish in to join the others. The boys had named their fish Spit and Fire and Sandy decided to name hers in a similar vein. Her fish was trailing a long strip of faeces so Ben suggested it looked like a bomber dropping its load. His suggestion of Wellington or Halifax sounded too formal to Sandy and she happily settled for simply 'Bomber'.

The Newman family slept well that night.

Chapter 69

Mission Accomplished

After all the excitement of the previous day Sunday was inevitably an anti-climax and the whole family just drifted through the day with the boys checking on the mixing bowl of goldfish at regular intervals. Both boys claimed to be able to recognise their own fish but Ben couldn't see any difference between any of them now that 'the Bomber' had unloaded his excess baggage. It took some firm intervention from Sandy to stop the boys from feeding the fish almost anything to hand and Ben promised to buy some proper fish food as soon as possible. A trip to the park to get some fresh air was cut quite short as it had turned bitterly cold, and in any case the play equipment was locked up for no apparent reason. Ben suspected that the park attendant, who was an old soldier, was probably suffering for his indulgencies of the previous day when all the pubs they had passed on the way home looked packed to the gunnels. They spent the rest of the day just mooching around but finished on a high by watching 'Sunday Night at the London Palladium' together. The revolving stage brought the programme to an end and Sandy made hot chocolate all round whilst Ben got the boys into bed and read them the next chapter of their current night time story.

It had been a non-eventful day but that in itself was a rare experience and very acceptable in their busy lives. Tomorrow was going to be a whole new experience for Ben as he had never been dependent on public transport to do his job before, but the old Cortina was in urgent need of Tony's mate's magic touch so he had no alternative. Also, it was only the second or third time that he had been involved in a section 26 treatment order and it was such an enormous intervention into someone else's life. It could result in the patient being detained in hospital for up to a year with no rights of appeal for the first six months. Not that Ben had any concern about the prof's sincerity in seeking the order, that went without saying, but the punishment for quite major crimes often involved doing a lot less time.

The day dawned dry and windy and the early morning weather forecast on the radio promised outbreaks of sunshine later. Ben had set the alarm for 6 am, which was just as well as he had found it impossible to sleep soundly and he was feeling muzzy headed and badly in need of a shower. The rest of the family slept on, apparently having had no reaction to the demands of the alarm clock, so Ben was able to have use of the bathroom and then the kitchen without any interference. Toast and tea and a cup for him to take up to Sandy when he went up to get dressed was greeted with a grunt of gratitude before he slipped out of the front door at an unearthly 6.45 am. He unlocked the car and hid the car keys under the passenger car mat ready for Eric to collect later. He patted the car roof with genuine affection and whispered to it, 'Take care, old lass, you have to go on for a little longer yet.'

Fortunately, the street was clear of people so no one overheard the brief but one-sided conversation. As he walked down the street and around the corner Ben tried to remember when he had last caught a bus and decided it was months before. Train journeys were even rarer but he did recall the trip to Weston for one of the boys' birthday treat. He had no knowledge of the times of the buses so had allowed himself plenty of time but was amazed to find a long queue of people waiting at the bus stop for the bus into town. Everyone seemed to be smoking and nobody seemed to be talking, as apparently barely awake they waited in a disorderly queue surrounded by a cloud of tobacco smoke. When the bus arrived the vast majority of passengers headed up the stairs to contribute to the fug created by the smokers already up there having their early morning cough and spit. With some relief Ben passed into the only partially occupied lower floor and claimed a double unoccupied seat ready to enjoy an early morning trip through the town of Exworth. The trip was uneventful and the chirpy banter from the bus conductor was a welcomed alternative to the rest of his morose travelling companions. At each stop more and more people clambered aboard with almost nobody getting off. A large lady with the general appearance of an office cleaner claimed the vacant seat next to Ben and her overall bulk forced him hard up against the window. He was no longer at all comfortable as he attempted to breath in harmony with the rise and falls of her generous mounds.

When the bus pulled into the town centre there was a flood of activity as the passengers from both up and down stairs seemed to stampede off the bus. There were now plenty of seats to be had but Ben's neighbour showed no sign of wanting to move and he didn't have the gall to suggest it. After a few more minutes of minor suffocation the bus pulled up at the train station and Ben attempted to stand up to get out. Fortunately the lady got the message and with much huffing and puffing stepped out into the aisle to let him out. Holding his briefcase in front of himself as a sort of battering ram to fend off the various rotund mounds which still partially blocked his exit, he made his escape. Not a word had passed between them for the whole of their shared journey.

Ben's watch showed 7.35 am and he was due to catch the 8.03 am to Coventry. Having confirmed the time of the train and the platform it would be arriving at, he purchased a *Daily Mail* at the station kiosk and settled down to await the train. He smiled to himself when he thought what Roger, his dad, would have had to say about his choice of reading matter. It would have been rejected out of hand as a Tory rag but this was Ben's day out and he much preferred the *Mail*'s sports journalism over his dad's choice of the *Daily Mirror*. He set about reading from the back page forward as he usually did but found there were too many distractions for him to take very much in. He pulled out a pen and started on the quick crossword, which from time to time in the past he had almost completed. He had long since given up any attempt at doing a cryptic crossword; as far as he was concerned the clues might have just as well have been in Chinese. It was described as the quick crossword but fifteen minutes later he had managed only three clues. He gave up his attempt, put the pen away and folded the paper and put it in his briefcase for later.

As he just sat there his mind went back to an incident about three years ago when the family had hired a caravan at Dawlish Warren for a long weekend break. It was a cheap offer as it was well into October and the weather was inclement and beach activities were simply not possible. The boys had rapidly become bored and you can only make so many jigsaws or play so many games of Ludo or Snakes and Ladders. On one of Sandy's trips to the club house to use 'the facilities' she got into a conversation with a local woman who came in each day to clean the toilets. It seemed both women were starved of conversation and Sandy was away for ages before returning with an idea for a distraction. The woman had told her that the train journey south from Dawlish Warren was all along the coast and was spectacular and her own kids had loved it when they were younger. Sandy had suggested an adventurous trip into the unknown linked with a picnic tea on arrival at 'who knows where'. The whole family were heartedly fed up of being confined in a large tin box, with the beat of rain on the roof a regular feature and worst of all no television. Wrapped up warm against the chill wind and almost constant drizzle the intrepid explorers arrived at the station, which was totally devoid of staff but an exceptionally long train was already drawn up at the side of the platform. The family clambered aboard and sat and waited. They had waited and waited and nothing happened.

Finally, Ben and the whole family got out again and walked back to the tiny ticket office at the far end of the platform. It consisted of a small office and a slightly larger waiting room which had a blazing fire burning away in an old-fashioned coal burning stove. The only occupier was a portly station porter who was making himself some toast using a toasting fork. He was obviously pleased to have some company and was soon involving the boys in the cooking of his tea, which turned out to be Marmite on toast, which was a firm favourite of Jack's but a real no-no as far as Nick was concerned. Ben explained that they had been waiting for ages on the train as they wanted a trip along the coast as a special adventure. The porter just burst out laughing, much to Ben's surprise, but then went on to explain that they had narrowly missed a very eventful happening. It turned out the train they had got on was not an operational one. It was in fact a collection of carriages from the north which were about to be taken nonstop to Penzance, and there would have been no connected communication cord so they would have been trapped until they had reached the end of the journey. Sandy was relieved that the worst had not happened but had inevitably blamed Ben for letting them get on without checking first.

Never one to make the same mistake twice, as the 8.03 am pulled in Ben double-checked with the porter that he was getting on the right train. He was suitably reassured but received a funny look from the railway man, who had given him identical information only a few minutes before. Ben found an empty compartment and took a corner seat, but his peace and quiet was soon interrupted by a group of school kids who clearly met up each day on their way to school. The train was a stopping train and the whole journey was a series of starts and stops as it pulled up at even the smallest of halts. The horseplay of the schoolkids was good natured and Ben was quite sad to see them all pile out after a few minutes. Their replacement in the compartment were two country-looking women who were both armed with rather ancient, battered baskets which appeared to contain a considerable quantity of eggs all packed in transparent egg boxes each containing half a dozen eggs. They spread themselves out on the same side seat as Ben after lining their baskets along the opposite seat. They seemed a jolly couple and dived straight into a conversation with him by explaining that they were both married to farmers and they attended a weekly farmers' market in Coventry where they sold their free-range eggs. They admitted that the weekly trip into town was the high spot of their week, when they used the money they earned from selling their eggs to seek out shopping items not available from their small local village shop. Having declared their mission to Ben they looked at him expectantly, clearly waiting for him to explain why he was going to Coventry.

There was no way that Ben could even begin to explain anything about his mental health visit so he resorted to saying he was going to visit the famous modern cathedral that he had heard so much about. This was in fact true, even if it was not his principal reason for the trip. The women were happy to confirm that it was well worth a visit but then they appeared to lose interest in Ben and started to gossip between themselves about people they both knew. Ben dug his paper out of his briefcase and made a fresh start on the crossword with little success. On arrival at Coventry train station the ladies collected up their baskets and hurried away, obviously anxious to get about their business.

Ben took his time and located a street map of Coventry, which was fixed on the wall of the station just by the main entrance. The sun was doing its best to warm up the day and the gentle breeze was more comfortable than disturbing. The map was a newish electronic one, with a series of individual buttons which could be pressed to highlight the location of a whole list of places in the city. There was a convenient prominent luminated red arrow bearing the wording 'you are here'. The city centre looked to be in easy walking distance and the cathedral was also easily found. The address for Wendy Tiler's daughter was 11 Glebe House, Highfield Road and this proved no harder to find on the map. Ben was able to plan a simple route for him to follow to get to his destination. Originally, he had planned to take a taxi but it was proving to be a nice day and he had plenty of time so he decided to walk and sightsee en route.

In the past he had heard quite a lot about Coventry from his dad and also as a small boy from his dad's older brother Uncle Ted. Edward Newman was a bit of a hero in the eyes of the Newman Clan as he had been a fireman in Exworth throughout the war. In particular, Ben had been told about the extreme bombing which had taken place in Coventry during the early days of the war. Coventry had the reputation throughout the world as a major centre for the production of the quality cars Daimler as well as having large factories producing bicycles. Hitler had obviously recognised that such factories, with all their tooling already in situ, could be easily adapted for the production of weapons of war. As a consequence, he had ordered a massive four-day air attack on the town, which turned large areas of it into a raging inferno. Fire crews from across the country had been drafted in to get the destruction under control. Half the housing stock was destroyed or extensively damaged and well over 500 people were killed with almost twice as many injured. This resulted in Uncle Ted and his team fighting fires almost nonstop for four days and nights. Roger often claimed that it had affected his brother both physically and mentally for the rest of his life and swore that Ted had lost a lot of his previous lust for life. Ted didn't often speak to anyone of that time except to repeat within the family about the losing battle his team had fought trying to save Coventry's medieval cathedral. Once the fire was out all that remained were a few scorched timbers and a couple of outer walls. He would scarcely contain his tears whenever he talked of it and he was particularly sad that St Michael's had the unfortunate distinction of being the only cathedral in the whole country destroyed in the war.

Ben was well aware that a modern cathedral had been started on the same site in the mid-fifties and that the two remaining walls of the original cathedral had been incorporated in the rebuild. He was sure that Uncle Ted would have loved that but he wasn't around to see it. Soon after the end of the war he and his family took up the government's offer of a cheap passage to Australia and had never been back to England since. When Ben knew he was coming to Coventry he determined to visit the cathedral and to buy a guide book to send to his uncle when he sent his usual Christmas card and letter later in the year.

He ambled along his planned route, looking to the left and right at the buildings, and the evidence of the war devastation was all too apparent. The nearer he got to the centre of the city there were less and less signs of any old town buildings. The rebuilding had been built on rigidly straight streets flanked by boring square-shaped fifties-style of buildings, functional but lacking in charm. Just as he was beginning to feel disappointed with his visit Ben entered Broadgate Square and was confronted by a huge bronze statue of the naked Lady Godiva mounted on a magnificent horse. The detailing of her body and long flowing hair together with the precise muscling of the horse demonstrated a sculpture of an expert quality. Ben was very impressed by it and circled it several times admiring it from every angle.

He was just about to move on when he notice a quite a large group of people of all ages gathering on the south side of the square and ever nosey he wandered over to see what it was all about. They appeared to be staring at a modern building situated on the fringes of the square which bore the sign 'The Lady Godiva Newsstand'. It seemed to be a rather odd building with an ordinary modern newsagent on the ground floor, a peculiar galleried area covering the width of the first floor and a large clock above an opaque window on the top floor. As he drew up to the small gathering he became aware of a young man standing on a small stepladder addressing the group about the building in front of them. They were all clearly part of a guided tour and he had arrived just in time to hear the guide say, 'Wait for the first chime of the clock's bell and you will witness all the action.'

The clock's minute hand moved jerkily towards the hour point and then started to chime ten o'clock. On the first strike a door sprung open on the right side of the gallery and a mechanical model of Lady Godiva on her horse travelled slowly across the width of the building and disappeared through a door which shut behind her on the left. As she moved across the gallery the guide called out and drew the attention of the group to the window just below the clock, which dropped open to reveal the grotesque face of a very ugly old man.

Once the procedure had finished the guide explained that according to the legend the old man was called Tom and as a consequence of his voyeurism he had been rendered blind. He went on to say that that was the origin of the commonly known saying of 'peeping tom'. Ben had enjoyed the interlude and kind of wished that he could move off with the group as they followed the guy with the stepladder to pastures new. However, he was conscious that his appointment was in thirty minutes' time, but he did take the time to call into the newsagents to buy a leaflet about the story of the clock. He would enjoy reading it on the train home and after sharing it with Sandy it would very likely end up with his other bits and pieces in his memory box as a memento of the time he was 'sent to Coventry'.

The walk to Glebe House took about twenty minutes and Ben found himself outside a modern multi-story block of flats not dissimilar to those at Highfield. This block, however, had none of the state of neglect of those he was familiar with. The grounds surrounding the property were neatly trimmed lawns, with well cared for flower beds lining the path up to the front door. There was no sign of any graffiti and a lone carrier bag scuttling around in the breeze was the only sign of litter. Ben was fortunate to arrive at the front door just as someone was leaving and he was able to slip straight into the lobby which smelt slightly of disinfectant but surprisingly had a selection of potted plants which looked both healthy and prospering.

The lift arrived swiftly and smoothly and held none of the smell of stale urine that was Ben's normal expectation back at base. Before pressing the button for the fifth floor he examined the information that was displayed on a notice board at the back of the lift and all became clear. Glebe House had a resident caretaker and a resident's house committee, which were advertising a whole series of events to be held in the common room on the ground floor. Such luxuries would be the thing of dreams in the Highfield high-rise flats which provided basic housing and very little else. Ben was suitably impressed by the Coventry style of provision and smiled to himself at the thought that many of the Exworth tenants wouldn't mind being 'sent to Coventry' if it meant this superior quality of housing. The ride up in the lift was smooth and there was no sound of ominous noises, just a low hum of well-maintained machinery. The doors opened and Ben found himself right opposite number eleven and the doorbell responded to his touch by playing a rather tinny rendition of Greensleeves.

When the door was answered it was not, as he had anticipated, by Beatrice Phillips, but by a small man with a full ginger beard who Ben instantly recognised. 'Well I'll be damned, what on earth are you doing here?'

The beard broke into a broad but rather misshapen grin and in an all too familiar voice replied, 'I think I should be asking you that, Ben, I just happen to live here! Still, come on in and meet Beatrice.'

Simon Phillips was an old acquaintance who Ben had chatted to many times at Joe's café. At the time he had been working as a milk delivery man on the Highfield Estate and his last stop each day was at Joe's, where he usually delivered a crate of milk and enjoyed a free coffee for his troubles. He was a lovely man but very shy, preferring to sit in one of the cubicles in the front room rather than join in the cut and thrust of the long table in the main room, but Simon had a problem, as he had been born with a cleft lip which had been repaired by numerous plastic surgery operations over the years. He was left with some noticeable scaring which he had largely disguised by growing a moustache and a large beard. Unfortunately, his speech had also been affected and he was left with a distinct whistle that seemed to randomly sound out when he spoke more than a couple of syllables at a time. He was acutely aware of it and was embarrassed to the extent that he avoided getting involved in the general banter of the tradesmen at Joe's. Not that anyone ever drew attention to it, and even the likes of Beefy Baker, the sharp-witted chief tormentor, had never been known to mention it. Slowly over the months Ben and Simon tended to seek out each other's company and Ben learnt more about Simon's background, and it proved to be a sad tale.

He had been abandoned at birth, being left on the steps of a local church. Normally, such a new-born baby would be placed for adoption very easily as there were always childless couples who for various reasons were unable to conceive naturally, but Simon presented with major problems, as he was unable to feed normally and had initially had to be fed by tube, which was a complicated procedure.

The result was that Simon had spent much of his childhood in a Barnardo's family group home. Other children came and went but Simon needed numerous corrective operations and he just stayed on and on at the home. Fortunately, 'Auntie Iris and Uncle Ian', his house parents, were committed to their job and formed a close bond with Simon and he grew up feeling loved and wanted. Sadly, the family group home was only for young children, but with the help of Barnardo's, Simon obtained a council flat tenancy at the tender age of seventeen. He admitted to feeling lonely at times but still maintained regular contact with his former house parents and seemed to really enjoy being busy on his job as a milk man.

Now he thought of it Ben suddenly realised that it was ages since he last had a chat to Simon at Joe's. He had not given it any thought as they only got together by chance when they happened to be there at the same time. The fact that he turned up in Beatrice's flat in Coventry needed an explanation, but before he could question further he found himself following Simon along the hall and into the living room. A short, nervous-looking lady was perched on the edge of the sofa and Ben could see at once that she seemed on the verge of tears. Two other characteristics were immediately apparent. She was in an advanced stage of pregnancy and she was wearing a heavy-looking built-up boot on her right foot. This visit was proving to be full of surprises and Ben found himself floundering about how to proceed, but Simon quickly stepped up with an explanation.

'This is my wife, Beatrice, and this is our home since we moved here about six months ago. We have settled here and are very happy and as you can see we are expecting our first child in a few weeks. To be quite honest we are both very alarmed by your visit and before you ask, we must tell you that we are determined not to have Beatrice's mother here to live with us. She has caused Beatrice nothing but pain throughout her life and since we got married she has constantly tried to undermine our relationship. We love one another Ben, and before you ask I am telling you right now that old bitch is not coming over our doorstep.'

Beatrice was nodding her head as Simon was talking and she reached out and grasped his hand in a clear sign of her agreement with what he was saying. Ben put his hand up in front of him, as if to fend off the level of hostility his old friend was expressing, and hastened to explain the reason for his visit and to reassure the couple that there was no suggestion that Wendy should come and live with them. He went on to carefully explain that the professor was wanting to try to modify Wendy's mental health by trying electro-convulsive therapy. He explained that she had been admitted on a twenty-eight day assessment order following an incident at her home but that she had made no progress in that time and was now electively mute and refusing to eat or drink for days at a time. Ben explained that ECT was used only rarely these days, as improvements in medications proved them usually to be much more effective and therefore widely used. Sadly, they had not helped in Wendy's case and the staff were suspicious that she had been spitting the tablets out in the toilet as an act of defiance. He didn't pull any punches and explained what was involved in ECT treatment, but added that in some cases the results have proved to be spectacular.

'Why I am here today is to ask for your permission to transfer your mother on to a section 26 treatment order, which would allow the staff to proceed with the treatment without having her permission. As her nearest relative you can agree for us to proceed with the order and with the treatment. This could mean that she could have to stay in hospital for up to a year, all depending how she gets on.'

Ben went on to explain the ramifications of what he was proposing and understandably both Beatrice and Simon looked rather overwhelmed about the whole thing, but at the same time clearly content that she would not be coming back into their lives. At this point Beatrice joined in the conversation and in a soft and rather shaky voice she spoke directly to Ben for the first time.

'Well, that certainly wasn't what we expected. In fact, we had no idea that she was in hospital. The last time we spoke to her was on the phone months ago when I rang to tell her that we were having a baby and her reaction was the last straw as far as I was concerned. I don't think I will ever forget her actual words, which were "Well a gimp like you and a freak like your husband are bound to produce a monster. Go and get an abortion as soon as possible."'

Ben almost fainted at the thought that any mother could be so hurtful about their daughter giving her a grandchild.

Beatrice continued, 'I just couldn't stop crying for days and Simon arranged for me to see a gynaecologist privately to put my mind at rest about the baby. We were given a complete all-clear about my pregnancy and we are really looking forward to the birth of our healthy little boy. We decided there and then that we wanted to be as far away as possible from my mother and we decided that we would both give up our jobs and move right away. Then we had an enormous stroke of good luck when we saw a card on the notice board at the Highfield newsagents from someone in Coventry who wanted to move to Highfield to be near her mother. She turned out to be a nurse who had recently separated from her husband and needed to have help with childcare for her toddler. We rang her and she came down to see us and she was a really nice lady who seemed to be very genuine. She liked our flat in Highfield, which is in easy walking distance of her mum's and wanted to exchange, even though it was smaller than her one in Coventry, so we visited her in Coventry and fell in love with the flat here. We couldn't believe our luck, and the swap went off without a hitch. There was even a super little bonus which I will show you later when we show you around.'

The two of them sat on the sofa with their arms linked, the picture of relief and happiness; all Ben could do was shake his head with shock about what an evil bitch Wendy had proved to be. The atmosphere in the flat had quickly changed to one of convivial friendship and Beatrice struggled to her feet to go off to make some tea. Simon attempted to rise as if to take over but was pushed back down by her with the comment that he should save his strength in readiness for the challenges of bringing up a new baby.

When Beatrice was in the kitchen Simon took the opportunity to fill Ben in on some of the background of the two of them getting together. Beatrice had worked at the big Co-op in Exworth and Simon had worked for the Co-op as a milkman. Each day, after completing his round Simon had to park his milk float in the garage at the back of the store for it to be charged up for the next day's round. The two of them met over their lunchtime sandwiches in the small canteen at the store and the rest was history. They were both lonely and shy and unsure of themselves but slowly their relationship developed and they began to court, much to the intense anger of Wendy, who tried to cause trouble between them by constant criticism and lies. Instead of splitting them up, this had the opposite effect and they decided to get married at the local registry office, with Simon's foster parents Auntie Iris and Uncle Ian acting as witnesses.

That night the newly married couple returned to Wendy's house to collect Beatrice's clothes and a few knickknacks and to inform her that they were now married. Simon went on to say that the shocked look on Wendy's face was well worth the stream of venom that followed.

'We have never seen that evil old crow face to face since and quite honestly I think she deserves everything she has got coming. I hope the treatment is as tough as you say but I don't think any treatment will ever change the way that woman is. Beatrice is a truly lovely person but she has been constantly undermined throughout her life. Her own mother used to refer to her as "the gimp" just because she had the misfortune to be born with one leg shorter than the other. I ask you, how could any mother be so cruel?'

Ben noticed that the whistle was still present in Simon's speech but it in no way detracted from the sincerity of the man.

'I don't know if you are aware, Ben, that Beatrice's father walked away, leaving her to suffer with her mother's constant negativity. She was about ten at the time and the school began to worry about her becoming very withdrawn and generally failing to thrive. The education department were sufficiently concerned to suggest that Beatrice would benefit from residential schooling, to which Wendy readily agreed. Beatrice spent the next six years of her life attending Periton Mead Residential School in Minehead and she describes it as the happiest days of her childhood. She was taken under the wing of the maths teacher, a Miss Morris, who helped her to gain in confidence and to make good academic progress. Miss Morris, predictably nicknamed Minor, was able to offer Beatrice care and understanding and helped her to accept that she was a very special little girl and a person of worth. Several of the children, including Beatrice, spent the long summer holidays at Periton Mead and it was a time of relaxed fun for kids who otherwise would have a tough summer break. Perhaps because she wanted to please Minor, Beatrice developed a real passion for mathematics, which helped her get to get a job as a junior clerk in the accounts department of the Co-op when she left school. Beatrice and Miss Morris still write to each other several times a year and Minor's joyful reaction to our marriage and the news of the baby went a long way to detract from Wendy's hateful reaction.'

Beatrice reappeared from the kitchen with a tray of tea things and a Battenburg cake cut into generous slices. No sooner had she started to hand around the tea when there was a rattle from the door out on to the balcony and a beautiful pure white cat appeared through a cat-flap and came straight over to Ben and quickly made herself comfortable on his lap. She started to paw gently by way of establishing a nest for herself and then curled up purring loudly as Ben smoothed her long soft fur. Simon explained that the cat, who was called Princess, had come with the flat and had proved to be adorable.

'She had belonged to the previous tenant but unfortunately the nurse's mother was asthmatic and allergic to cat hair, but we were only too happy to keep her. She really is the perfect lap cat and tends to join anyone who sits down in the flat. We have since learnt that all white cats with blue eyes are born profoundly deaf, so she would be in danger if she roamed around outside, but seeing as we are on the fifth floor that doesn't apply. Princess is a house cat with a balcony for fresh air and her litter tray and she gives lots of affection in return for her food and drink.'

Ben thought to himself that the cat being handicapped seemed to be a natural fit with the two of them with their own physical disabilities. Of course he kept the thought to himself and relaxed back into the warmth of this loving family home.

The next couple of hours passed with the couple sharing bits and pieces of their lives with Ben whilst unconsciously demonstrating the closeness of their life together. They both admitted that they were sorry to have left jobs in Exworth, with Simon's principal loss being his daily visit to Joe's. So far he hadn't located a similar café in Coventry, but with Beatrice waiting for him at home it was much less of a loss. Beatrice was more definite about her sense of loss having left the Co-op, as her special job there had been very fulfilling. She explained that she had spent her last year there working in the raised cabin up in the ceiling of the store dealing with the flying apparatus that delivered all the payments for goods in canisters run on wires from the various work counters around the store. She proudly told Ben that she had been the youngest person to get the job and she loved the responsibility and the resulting extra pay. She went on to say her mother's comment on hearing of her promotion had been, 'I suppose they wanted to hide you away up there so you didn't frighten the customers, being a gimp.'

Ben didn't know what to say at such cruelty but moved the conversation on, asking all about the flying system and how it worked. He also confessed to having been fascinated by the way the cannisters sped to and fro across the shop ever since he had been in the Co-op numerous times with his mother as a small boy. He explained that his mother had always been a firm fan of the Co-operative movement and had relied upon her earned dividend at Christmas time year on year. Ben had been taught his mum's Co-op number at an early age and still quoted 74338 if he bought from them. He went on to tell the tale of the Co-op handling his grandfather's funeral and how the resulting increase in dividend that year had helped to pay for his new school uniform when he had passed the eleven plus. After a while, the cat slowly stretched to her full length before dropping down from Ben's lap and sedately wandering over to the cat-flap, where she stopped half in and half out. Simon got up quickly with a grin and said 'It's her lunch time and her royal highness is just checking if lunch as arrived yet. I had better feed her, as if I take too long she will start yowling and that can be a truly heart-stopping performance.'

He wandered off to the kitchen and returned with a colourful dish, full of the contents of a tin of salmon topped off with some scrunchie looking biscuits which he carefully mashed together to form one small neat stack.

'She is a terribly fussy eater and always has to go through the process of examining her dish from all angles before attempting to tuck in. Come and watch, it's quite a performance.'

Ben joined Simon at the window as Princess proceeded to circle the bowl two or three times before deigning to start on her meal. Once started there was no stopping her and within minutes the dish was empty and the cat was sat back, busy preening herself. Simon pointed out beyond the balcony and asked, 'So what do you think of our view?'

For the first time, Ben looked into the middle distance and was amazed to see virtually all of what was a quality football ground and stadium. In large letters along the full length of a covered grandstand were the words, 'Coventry City Football Club'.

'You jammy bugger, you can get to see every home match from your own living room and free of charge too. Are you a fan?'

'To be quite honest with you, Ben, I have never been into any sport very much, I have just followed the cricket reports in the paper, but then only test matches more or less. So I wasn't immediately attracted by the view, but in fact it has indirectly had a huge impact on our lives. When we moved up here I obtained a transfer from the Co-op Dairy in Exworth to work as a milkman for the Co-op here in Coventry. They seemed pleased to employ me but it was a big change for us both, as we knew nobody and I had no knowledge of the area at all. But the foreman of the dairy here, a chap called Vic Needham, took me under his wing and showed me the route and introduced me to many of the customers I would be delivering to. Vic is a good twenty years older than me but we hit it off straight away and when we got to the weekend I invited him to come over with his wife for an evening meal. Beatrice was quite nervous about it as Vic was technically my boss and she was frightened that her cooking might not cut the mustard. I had no concerns about that as she is a great cook, but that wretched mother of hers has caused her to lack confidence in herself. As it turned out, she had nothing to worry about as Vic's wife Annie is simply lovely and was soon chatting away in the kitchen with my wife. Meanwhile, Vic had wandered over to the window and suddenly let out an enormous whoop. It turns out that he is an avid Sky Blues supporter and was more than a little impressed by our view of the ground. Well, to cut a long story short we now watch all the home matches together from the balcony and his passion for the team is infectious and I am rapidly getting the bug. I get all the history and updates from Vic and now know that the team have a great manager in Jimmy Hill, and our central forward is a goal machine called George Hudson nicknamed "the Hud".'

Ben noticed that the old familiar whistle in Simon's speech still popped up occasionally but Simon didn't seem aware of it and just ploughed on. He continued, 'Annie often comes over with Vic, and she and Beatrice talk baby plans and discuss how best to make our second bedroom into a nursery fit for our firstborn. Annie is everything that Wendy isn't and Beatrice has formed a firm relationship, and I can honestly say that Vic is the nearest I have ever had to a best friend. We have been really very lucky in our choice of relocation, long may it last.'

The pair of them went on, happily telling Ben what a friendly place Coventry was proving to be and stressed that their neighbours in Glebe House had made them most welcome.

'There aren't many young children living in this block, but even though most of the other residents are over retirement age they are full of life and there is always something going on that we are being invited to. Today we are all meeting for a lunch down in the community room, which is being run by our caretaker and his wife. He is an ex-teacher who spent most of his working life in India working in some of the poorest parts of major cities there. His wife is in fact an Indian lady who is really elegant and always looks immaculately turned out in an apparent endless supply of vividly coloured saris. the other day she held a special session for all the ladies of Glebe House and attempted to teach us all how to dress in a sari. Believe me, it's not easy, but with her help and after a lot of laughter we all managed to begin to master it and I must say I was impressed with my reflection in her bedroom mirror. However, this lunch hour we are going to be sampling a proper Indian lunch full of spices and exotic flavours. Neither Simon nor I have ever tried such food before and I am going equipped with indigestion tablets just in case, but it is all good fun and something different to look forward to.'

The time spent with Simon, Beatrice and Princess too had been very rewarding and with the paperwork completed and safely ensconced in his briefcase, Ben moved to leave. It was well after twelve and he knew that the couple were looking forward to experiencing an Indian lunch with their friends. They walked with him to the lift and after a firm handshake from Simon, accompanied by a nuzzle from Princess, who was in his arms, and best of all a peck on the cheek from Beatrice, Ben stepped into the lift and smoothly left the company of what was clearly a contented couple. The strong smell of the spicy cooking that greeted him in the lobby got him feeling hungry, but he also felt relieved that he didn't have to try such exotic fare. Ben rarely moved away from traditional English; Chinese and Italian from time to time, but that was about his limit.

Chapter 70

A Time for Contemplation

The day had settled down to be one of late summer sunshine, not hot enough to raise a sweat but warm enough to encourage walking. Ben remained determined to visit the cathedral which his Uncle Ted had tried so hard to save. By asking directions as he walked into the town he was able to reach it without difficulty. Everybody in Coventry knew where it was and most were keen to sing its praises. It proved to be quite unique and Ben found it to be rather awe inspiring. He was by no means a religious person and since retiring as a choir boy at the tender age of twelve he had attended a couple of weddings, three christenings and a funeral or two. The cathedral was receiving all sorts of visitors, some choosing to pray and others like him just wanting to look. He didn't stay long as it wasn't a habitat that he would normally attend, but a couple of features struck him in particular and he knew that the sight of them would remain with him for ever.

A huge tapestry of Christ dominated the wall behind the altar and it was truly magnificent, but funnily enough it wasn't the thing that impacted on him the most. That was a large cross constructed from two burned beams from the cathedral that Uncle Ted had tried to save. It made the memory of the horror of the war seem very real and Ben found himself holding back the tears himself when he thought about how senseless the war had been. As planned, he stopped at the souvenir kiosk just outside the main entrance and bought a condensed guide book to send to Uncle Ted in a month or two's time.

The walk back into the centre of town was the exact reverse of his walk to Glebe House and he remained bored by the architecture and the modern, medium sized shops that could be found in almost every town in the country. Then, just by chance, he happened to spot a covered archway that led into a neat little pedestrianised square of cobbled stones divided up by several large urns overflowing with loads of bright red geraniums.

Rather rusty looking Victorian style garden benches were dotted about and the overall effect was charming in direct contrast to the modern design of the rest of the city centre. The square was surrounded by a half dozen small shops that all seemed occupied by individual traders with no apparent influence from any of the large operators that were the usual fare of the day.

This proved to be a rare little bit of the original Coventry that had somehow survived the wartime devastation. Many of the benches were occupied by small groups of young mums with their sleeping babies in pushchairs or one or two discreetly breast feeding whilst continuing with the flow of conversation with their friends. Ben was drawn to it like a magnet and was delighted to find it was everything he had been looking for. The first shop was a sort of second hand or antique shop called All Our Yesterdays and seemed totally packed with all manner of junk. Ben gave it a miss as his home was already fighting a losing battle against being overfilled with his families unnecessary acquisitions.

The next shop, a double fronted one, had a large sign across its full width, Pets Paradise, with hand-painted pictures of various small pets between each letter. The steamy windows were displaying two collections of young animals, one of puppies and the other of kittens. The puppies were scampering around in their pen, playing a game of their own which seemed to involve a lot of mock fighting. The kittens by contrast were curled up in a heap soaking up the late summer sun that was focused on their window. Both windows were attracting a lot of admirers of all ages and the air was full of 'oohs' and 'aahs'. This shop was just what was needed to enable Ben to purchase the fish food that he had promised the boys and he entered and was quickly transported to a very different environment. The walls were covered with all sorts of cages and tanks, all occupied by traditional family pets such as canaries and budgerigars, hamsters and rabbits and an extensive selection of fish, from the humble goldfish to all manner of tropical fish. The hubbub of noise was continuous and everything seemed clean and there was signs of recent feeding and fresh water everywhere. There was a distinct smell but it wasn't unduly unpleasant. Ben enjoyed wandering around but was in no way tempted to take any of the stock home with him.

Basically, his childhood home had never really gone in for pets. The only occasion that his sister had been permitted to have a pet she had chosen to have a tortoise. She had called it Tommy and it was given the free range of the back garden which had solid walls topped with six-foot fences. There was nowhere for it to hide but it still managed to disappear regularly, much to his sister's distress. After regular family search parties they were eventually always able to locate it in some bizarre place or other amongst the shrubbery, but it never stayed in sight for long. Finally, Ben's dad had got fed up of the regular upheavals and resorted to painting Tommy's shell bright yellow with gloss paint so that it would be easily spotted. That winter, Tommy was prepared for hibernation as usual by being put in the garden shed in a box full of straw to keep him comfortable. He was dead when they went to check on him in the spring. Ben suspected that the yellow paint may have been a contributing factor to his premature death, but said nothing to the rest of the family.

Tommy was buried in a shoe box in the garden with 'full military honours' and the incident was put down to experience. But it wasn't quite the end of the story as a week or two later Ben had discovered that an animal, probably a fox, had visited the garden and Tommy had been exhumed and consumed, leaving just his empty yellow shell in the middle of the patio. Ben had done what seemed right to him at the time and covered over the empty grave and had put the shell in a carrier bag before placing it in the neighbour's dustbin. To this day he had never told anybody about it. However, it was fair to say that Ben was not attracted by the idea of having a pet of any sort. He walked straight past the rows of confined animals and made his way directly to the counter at the rear of the shop. Within the shop there was the constant din of chirping birds, the rustling and bustling of the many other residents and the reverberating sound of a telephone going off. Judging by the frequent telephone calls the shop was a very busy place. There were several children and adults of all ages gathered in front of the various displays but it was pretty obvious that most of them were 'sight-seeing' rather than buying. The counter was unmanned when Ben arrived and he was immediately distracted by a large, wrought iron, vintage bird cage taking up a good third of the counter. It was occupied by a very spectacular grey and green parrot that immediately came across the cage towards Ben as if seeking companionship.

Ben was intrigued and moved forward with the intention of stroking the head of the bird when he spotted a large notice attached to the outside of the cage. 'My name is Captain Jeramiah, I am an African Grey Parrot, I am not for sale and I love to bite people. You have been warned!' Ben whipped his hand away in the nick of time with his fingers intact. The parrot bounced up and down as if in frustration and then proceeded to let out a series of bleeps which were the exact sound of a ringing telephone! Before Ben could attempt to seek assistance, he found himself effectively surrounded by what appeared to be a well-practised pincer movement. An elderly couple in their late seventies or early eighties had obviously identified him as a paying customer and introduced themselves as the owners of the shop, which was confirmed by the words Pet's Paradise printed on their baggy t-shirts.

With the best will in the world they could only be described as a very odd looking couple. One was male and the other female and they appeared to be so alike that they were almost certainly twins. One was bald and the other had shoulder-length grey hair, but it was most unfortunate that it was the woman who was practically hairless. They were both almost as fat as they were tall and Ben was left with no room for escape so he began to tell them about the reason for his visit. They were not impressed by the way the Newman family had acquired their fish and stated firmly that most of the fish given out at fairgrounds died within days and ended up being flushed away down numerous toilets. They made their views very clear and were quite adamant that giving away fish in that way was cruelty and should be banned. Ben was very much on the backfoot and couldn't think of anything in his defence before the couple took control. In no time at all they produced a small plastic fish tank, which they then filled with what they felt to be the minimum that the fish would require. A bag of coloured gravel, several strands of pond weed neatly secured into a bunch by a small strip of lead, a box of fish food with the instruction to be used sparingly and a plaster model of a ruined castle 'to give the fish somewhere to hide' were all packed together. Ben felt that he had been mugged but handed over the £5-12d requested and grabbing the neatly packaged bundle hurried from the shop before he was totally bankrupted.

He moved on along the square passing first a rather old-fashioned dress shop with windows full of headless mannequins dressed in tweed-looking outfits in muted tones of green and purple. There was no one in there, nor was there anyone in the next shop, a jewellers, and Ben paused to look at the sparkling objects on offer, then moved right on, amazed by the prices being asked. He turned right heading back towards the archway but the very next service being offered struck a real cord with him as he had only had a couple of slices of Battenburg since he had left home all those hours ago. The café was called the Mad Hatter's Tea Party and was pleasantly presented in black and white.

Ben didn't hesitate and pushed the door open, setting a bell jangling as he entered. One thing was immediately apparent to him: it was not Joe's. There was no familiar smell of fried bacon and coffee, no fug of cigarette smoke, no sound of general chit chat, augmented by outbursts of raucous laughter. The customers were almost exclusively middle-aged and older women! It really wasn't Ben's scene but he was hungry and as they say, 'any port in a storm'. The café went back almost the full depth of the building and the large rectangle space featured randomly placed tables, each set out for up to four people. A smartly dressed middle-aged woman stepped forward to welcome him and directed him to an empty table towards the back of the room. The waitress was dressed in a black long-sleeved dress, over which she wore a spotless white apron decorated with lace frills. She reminded Ben of the 'nippy' waitresses he remembered from the Lyon's corner house he had once visited as a child whilst on a trip to London with his mother. He was left with a menu and settled down in the seat looking towards the front of the shop.

In no particular rush, as his planned train home was not due for another two hours, he did what he often did: he began to people watch. He started by taking in the surroundings, which were clean and tidy but very much from a former age. Each table was dressed with a white linen table cloth, a single flower in small cut-glass vase and was laid with silver cutlery and folded napkins. Most of the decorations, laid out on high shelving around the room, were a mismatch of *Alice in Wonderland* themed china which must have taken the owners years to collect. It was all rather twee but somehow harmonious and certainly seemed to attract a specific type of customer; this wasn't a café, it was a tea room, aimed at attracting gentile ladies, and it was definitely succeeding in attracting their target clientele.

Most of the tables were occupied with small groups of smartly dressed ladies, all of whom were consuming pots of tea and using small forks to daintily devour small cakes selected from the three-tier cake stands placed in the centre of each table. The other customers, with one exception, were all female, the exception being a teenage boy of about fourteen who seemed to be doing his best to hide behind a large aspidistra plant housed in a hideous majolica jardiniere. He was just within Ben's peripheral vision and he noted that the lad visibly jumped each time someone came in and set the shop bell ringing. The signs were all too obvious to Ben, who concluded that the boy was almost certainly bunking off school. The lumpy duffle bag at his feet suggested that it was a sports afternoon that he was avoiding. Surreptitiously studying the lad further he suspected that he was probable one of the small band of unfortunate kids for whom sport was a miserable experience.

He was very overweight and suffered from a bad case of acne and it didn't take much imagination to put him in the group of 'geeks' who nobody wished to have in their team. Ben was sympathetic, but doubted that either his level of anxiety or his acne would be improved by the chocolate eclairs that he was consuming with obvious enjoyment!

Ben's mind went back to his own school experience when, on occasion, in company of his two best friends of the time, namely Hush and Smithy, he too had bunked off games. Once they had realised that no registers were taken at the sports field on the recreation ground bunking off was always an option. In his day the autumn term had been football, which he loved, the spring term had been rugby, which he quite enjoyed, but the summer term had been cricket, which bored him, and the ball was unpleasantly hard too! The attraction for him to bunk off had nothing to do with chocolate eclairs. His pleasures had been a bag of chips, a few fags and possibly a shared bottle of cider. The location for the activity was always the same: the bandstand at the local Victoria park, where there was always an outside chance of meeting up with truants from St

Bernadette's Girl School, which was nearby. The three of them lived in hope but there had been little in the way of success.

Ben was brought back from his reminiscences by the approach of a younger version of the waitress who had shown him to his seat. She was armed with a pad and pencil, ready to take his order and on his enquiry confirmed that she was the daughter of the other waitress. Ben apologised that he had not yet studied the menu and she seemed content to come back later. Ben reflected that all the shops in the square were probably small family-owned businesses, which were becoming rare now a days, more the pity. The menu was rather limited but he managed to cobble together a reasonable choice for himself of homemade mulligatawny soup, followed by scrambled eggs on toast, and if the young man hadn't eaten them all perhaps a chocolate éclair for pudding. Ben would usually order a black coffee but he decided that he would try a pot of tea, as that seemed to be the norm for this establishment.

He sat back and idly started to pick off a few white hairs from his lap which had been left there by his earlier encounter with Princess. A framed vintage sampler hanging on the wall beside him caught his attention and he turned to study it, as it looked interesting. The colours were quite faded but it didn't detract from the intricacies of the work, which was of a very high standard. The carefully sewn name and date across the bottom confirmed its antiquity. It had been created by an eleven old girl, Hannah Peters, in 1872. It was exquisite workmanship and must have taken her many months to complete. The usual alphabet and the numbers one to ten formed the border around an elaborate text. The text had retained enough colours to highlight certain significant words which had been sewn in such a way as to stand out from the rest. Ben surprised himself by remembering the proper name for the technique that Hannah had used to get the raised effect. Sandy had come home from her sewing class a few months before with a small test piece that she had completed that evening. She had explained to him that it was called stump work, which involved stitching over small bits of wood to give the embroidery a raised effect. She had created a small flower with shaped petals and an oval centre, which he had really admired. He had subsequently had it framed as a surprise for her and it now hung on the bathroom wall at home.

He was amazed that an eleven-year-old child had used the technique to highlight the key words on her sampler all that time ago. Hannah would almost certainly have died years ago, but here was her work having a profound effect on him almost a century later. He suspected that it was very unlikely that anything he achieved would be having such an impact in the 2060s, but then he reminded himself that Sandy and he together had created their two sons, and that was their important lasting contribution to the future. The framed sampler smacked of the Victorian age but somehow had caught Ben's attention so much so that he made a note of the wording in the back of his diary to share with Sandy later. *Happiness is not a destination, it's a way of life.*

He sat back and reflected on the statement and it really struck a chord with him. His mind flitted through the various people, places and activities that made up his life. Sandy and the boys, his extended family, his work colleagues and his small but cherished group of friends all contributed to his way of life. He had never really considered it before but the realisation was that Ben Newman was lucky enough to have a very happy life. It even amused him to realise, particularly after the celebrations on Saturday, that he actually enjoyed being part of the community that was the Highfield Estate.

Ben was brought back to the here and now by the arrival of the waitress with his soup. Its aromatic smell was most attractive and it appeared to consist of generous chunks of chicken in a rich spicy sauce. All his muses stopped whilst he concentrated on ripping the accompanying warm bread roll into strips, which he dunked into the sauce and fed by hand straight into his mouth. He could almost feel the disapproval of the ladies all around him at the table manners of this unusual customer, but he couldn't give a damn. He was content with the realisation that he was a happy man, with a happy way of life. Just like Hannah Peters had recorded all those years ago, he knew with certainty that happiness was not a destination, it was indeed a way of life, his life.

Ben finished up his meal, which had proved to be tasty and surprisingly satisfying, and with time on his hands he ordered another pot of tea and a couple of chocolate eclairs. The older of the two waitresses seemed pleased when he complemented her on the food but the look from the young lad on the nearby table was pure hatred. He had obviously overheard the waitress say that Ben was lucky as it was the last two eclairs. Ben nodded to him in a friendly way and the boy coloured up, easily embarrassed and looked away. Ben shrugged and thought no more of it as he sat back to enjoy his gooey treat and let his mind wander were it may.

He had certainly enjoyed the whole experience of his trip to Coventry and it felt like it had been successful. It had also given him the opportunity to contemplate his current lifestyle, which was a rare happening as he usually just spent his time getting on with just living things as they happened. The sampler had impacted on him and he thought over how things had changed since he first stepped foot on the Highfield Estate. He was now confident and comfortable with his role as team leader, he had a small but united and able group of colleagues, a close group of new friends and most of all a loving and happy family. The fact he was a happy man was a no brainer, and he smiled to himself as he poured yet another cup of tea.

THE END